Professor Bill Napier is a Scottish astronomer at Armagh Observatory and an honorary professor at Cardiff University. His two other thrillers, *The Lure* and *Shattered Icon*, are also published by Headline. He lives in Ireland with his wife.

Praise for Bill Napier:

'Pacy and sharp' *FHM* magazine

'A fascinating primer on code-breaking and the importance of calendars in human history'

Irish Independent

'A nail-biting page turner' *Edinburgh Times*

'It's excellent fiction: a way to catch up on some physics and planetology while an entertaining and gripping story unfolds. The story has a gritty authenticity'

New Scientist

Also by Bill Napier

The Lure
Shattered Icon

Nemesis
and
Revelation

Bill Napier

headline

NEMESIS
first published in Great Britain in 1998
by HEADLINE BOOK PUBLISHING

REVELATION
first published in Great Britain in 2000
by HEADLINE BOOK PUBLISHING

First published in this omnibus edition in 2004
by HEADLINE BOOK PUBLISHING

A HEADLINE paperback

10 9 8 7 6 5 4 3 2 1

ISBN 0 7553 2260 6

Printed and bound in Great Britain by
Mackays of Chatham plc, Chatham, Kent

Papers and cover board used by Headline are natural, recyclable
products made from wood grown in sustainable forests. The
manufacturing processes conform to the environmental
regulations of the country of origin.

HEADLINE BOOK PUBLISHING
A division of Hodder Headline
338 Euston Road
LONDON NW1 3BH

www.headline.co.uk
www.hodderheadline.com

Nemesis

NEMESIS

I AMERICAN SHINDIG

II ITALIAN MASQUE

III MEXICAN CARNIVAL

PART ONE

AMERICAN SHINDIG

shindig [?] 1. a dance, party or other affair. 2. shindy, a noisy disturbance; commotion.

THE FIRST DAY

$E = 10^7$ Mt, $I = 45°$, Target=Tertiary Andesite

The meteor comes in high over the Gulf of Mexico, in a blaze of light which darkens the noon sun from the Florida Keys to Jamaica.

Two thousand miles to the north, and ten minutes before he dies, Colonel Peter 'Foggy' Wallis is in his office watching television. The office itself is dark and comfortable, a restful place. It is made of steel. It sits on springs whose coils are made from steel rods three inches in diameter. Steel walkways connect the office to another fourteen similar, self-contained rooms. The entire office complex is contained within a giant cavern hollowed out from a granite mountain. Steel pins up to thirty feet long are driven into the cavern walls, and steel mesh is suspended below the ceiling high overhead, to protect him from dislodged boulders should a hostile giant ever strike the mountain. Access is through steel doors, each weighing twenty-five tons, and along a tunnel fourteen hundred feet long.

The television picture comes from a camera twenty-five thousand miles above the surface of the Earth. It is beamed down into a huge antenna near Alice Springs, relayed across two oceans, cabled a thousand feet into the bowels of the Rock and then up into the colonel's television set for his personal perusal.

The colonel pulls open a Seven-Up and sips at the fizzy lemonade. An oil well is burning in Iran. Its long smoky trail, bright in the infrared, has been longer at every shift for days, and now it has at last reached the northern Himalayas. Otherwise nothing much has changed. He flicks a button and the black night-time Pacific now appears, ringed by lights. To the left, the Sea of Japan glows softly, illuminated from within by the lights of the Japanese shrimp fishermen. Hawaii appears as a central dot. Idly, he flicks a switch and the dot resolves itself into a string of coastal lights dominated by Honolulu on Oahu and Hilo on Big Island.

Suddenly the lights fail; the VDUs dissolve into snow and die. A chorus of surprised profanity begins to emerge from the dark, but almost immediately the lights flicker and come back on, and the screens return to life.

'Now what was that?' Wallis asks nobody in particular. Rapidly, he scans the screens, flicking through the signals from sensors on land, sea, air and space. They reveal nothing: no anomalies, no intrusions. On the other hand, power cuts have never happened before.

'David, check it out.'

While the young major sitting to the left of Wallis speaks into a telephone, Wallis himself taps out a command on the console in front of him. A mass of coloured symbols obscures his god's eye view of the world. He types again, and all but a handful of the symbols vanish.

Over the Barents Sea, just north of Novaya Zemlya, a patrol of ageing Tupolev Blackjack bombers is high over the pack ice and the seals; another three hours on that bearing and they would invade Canadian air space, heading south for the Kansas silos. A flock of MiG 23s is heading out over the sea of Japan: six hours, if only they had the range, and they would reach Hawaii.

Only ten minutes ago a big KH-11 satellite passed over Kirovsk on the Kola peninsula, recording the Badgers, Backfires and MiGs which swarm like bees in and out of the four military air bases surrounding the city; elsewhere inside the mountain, careful men watched their movements; they collated and analysed, using massive computers: alert for the unusual, paranoid towards the unexpected. But the computers detected no strangeness in the patterns, and the careful men relaxed.

For twenty years following the collapse of the Empire, Kirov has been a ghost city. The bees flew to distant Eastern bases, or were executed by order of disarmament treaties. Some of the careful men were reassigned to tinpot dictatorships; most left to take up lucrative jobs with McDonnell Douglas or IBM. They no longer collated and analysed. But then came the food riots; and the Black Sea mutiny, which spread like a plague first to the Pacific Fleet and then to the elite Tamanshaia and Kantcrimov divisions; and the chaotic elections in which Vladimir Zhirinovsky, heavily supported by the Red Army, swept to victory. The man who had publicly threatened to nuke Japan and the United King dom, and whose declared intention was to expand the Russian Empire by force, was in the Kremlin.

And now the Badgers are back in Kola, and the careful men have returned to the mountain.

Stuff like that doesn't bother Wallis in the slightest. It just makes his job more interesting.

He types again. Thirty assorted ships in formation. Slava and nuclear-powered Kirov cruisers, skirting Norway and heading for Scapa Flow.

So what?

A handful of dots appears on the screen, obtained at vast expense from hydrophone arrays sprinkling the seabed along the GIUK Gap, the choke-point bridging Greenland, Iceland and the Orkneys. A couple of ancient Yankees and a Foxtrot are heading out into the North Atlantic. Yesterday, the combat team followed a Typhoon heading north, twenty-four thousand tons of displacement whose signals were soon lost in the clicking of shrimps and the cry of whales.

The hell with it. There are no abnormal movements; the computers are seeing no suspicious patterns. It has been a long shift, and the colonel, five minutes before he dies, leans back in his chair, stretches and yawns.

It strikes ground in the Valley of Morelos, a hundred miles south of Mexico City. It is sparse, hard land, a countryside of dry, stony tracks, overloaded burros, maize fields and giant cacti.

In the time it takes Wallis to yawn the asteroid has vaporised, ploughed to a halt ten miles under the ground and generated a ball of fire five miles wide and a hundred thousand degrees hot. Shock waves carrying four million atmospheres of pressure race outwards from the fireball, ancient granites flow like water.

'Sir, the generator people say it was some sort of ground surge. It seems the national grid got it too.'

'Any reason for it?'

'They're checking it out. There's a big storm complex around Boulder.'

'Okay. You're looking bushed, boy.'

The major grins. 'It's the new baby, sir. She never sleeps.'

'The first sixteen years are the worst,' Wallis says.

In the time it takes to discuss the major's baby the fireball scours out a hole fifty miles wide from the Mexican countryside. The hole is twenty miles deep and a sea of white hot lava pours upwards through the cracked and fissured mantle. Around the rim of the big hole, a ring of mountains builds up from the torrent of rock. Molten mountains are hurtling into the stratosphere, leaving white-hot wakes of expanding air. The blast moves out over the map. Mexico City vanishes, an irrelevant puff of smoke.

The ground waves too race outwards from the hole, leaving a wake of fluidized rubble. The rubble is forming into ripples and the ripples, tumbling rocky breakers reaching five miles into the disturbed sky, roar towards

Panama, Guatemala and the United States.

All the way up the Pacific seaboard the morning mists are rolling in. Foghorns wail round Vancouver island like primeval monsters, a thick white shroud blankets San Francisco and the traffic is snarling up in downtown LA. But now electric currents surge overhead as the fireball pierces the stratosphere, rising back through the hole punched out by the asteroid, and electrons spiral back and forth between the Earth's magnetic poles. Spears and curtains burst into the black Arctic sky and dance a silent, frenzied reel, while the frozen wastelands below reflect the shimmering red and green. Counterflowing currents surge over the Americas; cables melt, telephones die, radios give out with a bang, traffic stops in the streets.

Just over the border from Mexico, early morning shoppers in Tucson, Yuma and San Diego see long black fingers crawling up from the horizon to the south. The fingers reach out for the zenith. And as the shoppers stop to watch, the blue-white fireball too rises over the horizon like a bloated sun, and with it comes the heat. Everything combustible along the line of sight burns; and all living things along the line of sight crisp and shrivel.

And in Wallis's office, apocalypse stirs.

'Sir, we have a system interrupt on OTH,' says the major. 'We're losing Chesapeake and Rockbank.'

'Roger.'

'Hey Colonel, I'm not getting a signal from the DSPs.' This from Lieutenant Winton, the solitary woman on the team.

'Sir, Ace has just bombed out.'

'What the . . .?' Wallis says as the images in front of him dissolve once again into snow.

'Sir. We've lost Alaska, Thule and Fylingdales. Colonel . . . we've lost all coverage on the Northern Approaches.' Wallis goes cold; he feels as if a coffin lid has suddenly opened.

'Okay, soldier, keep calm. Get the general down here. Major, would you get me Offutt? Pino, interrogate REX, get a decision tree on screen Five.' Wallis issues the orders in a level voice.

'Sir, are we under attack?' The nervous question comes from Fanciulli, a tough, grey-haired sergeant to Wallis's right.

'Pino, where are the warheads?'

'Yeah but we got some sort of EMP . . .'

'Nuts; all we got is cable trouble.'

'Negative, sir.' It is Lieutenant Winton again, her small round face unusually pale. 'We have tropospheric forward scattering modes up top, and we've lost on VHF. There's some sort of massive ionospheric disturbance.'

'Sunspots?'

'No way, sir.'

'Colonel we have reduced bandwidth on all—.'

An alarm cuts into the chamber and a light flashes red. Somebody wails. And Pino, his face wax-like, mutters a string of profanities as he types rapidly on a keyboard.

'Colonel, Screen Three.'

Covering the walls of the office are enormous screens. Mostly these show arcane lists of data – coded refuelling points, the tracks of satellites in orbit, numbers of aircraft aloft – but one of them is instantly comprehensible. It is a map of the USA. And on the map, red lights are beginning to wink.

'The General, sir.' Wallis looks up at the glass-fronted observation room. General Cannon has appeared, flanked by a civilian and a second general: Hooper, Chairman of the Joint Chiefs of Staff. Wallis snatches up a telephone, but Cannon, impassive as an Indian chief, ignores the urgent ringing.

One of the screens has changed. There is a blurred, jerky picture. Somebody is pointing a camera from an airplane cockpit. They are flying high over a city and the plane is tilted so that the camera can look down. There are skyscrapers, and long straight roads with cars, and parks. The camera pans and there is an ocean wave. It is almost level with the aircraft, and it covers half the city. Here and there, on the lower slopes of the wave, the tops of the skyscrapers protrude, some of them already slowly tilting over. Wallis stares in utter disbelief. The wave towers high over the remaining buildings; it looks frozen, but white specks are falling off the top and tiny cars are dotted here and there in the broad rising sheet of water. Someone shouts, in a voice edging on panic, *That's San Diego!* Wallis kills the alarm.

The camera points backwards. It is unsteady, like an amateur movie. The ocean stretches into the distance and the wave with it. There is a long smoky contrail and a glimpse of wing, and racing up from behind is a churning black wall as tall as the sky, and then the camera shakes and there is a helmet in close-up, and inside a young black face, eyes staring in fright, is shouting silently, and then the screen goes blank.

The major gabbles into the phone. Fanciulli, tears streaming down his cheeks, points to one of the big screens. New red lights are winking on virtually every second. Winton is saying Sir, why doesn't the General answer. Then.

'Offutt, sir.' Wallis snatches up another telephone, the blue one. But already new messages are flashing; lists of names are tumbling down the screens faster than they can be read. Wallis, his ear still to the telephone, stares at the map of the USA. The red lights, each one a Strategic Air Command base scattered to the winds, have formed a broad front, slowly creeping up from the south.

The decision tree is up. REX is requesting more data.

A voice on the telephone. It speaks in harsh, staccato tones. Wallis forces his attention from the advancing wave and listens. He replies, hearing in astonishment that his own voice is shaking and frightened: 'Sir, I agree a threat assessment conference ... no sir, we lack dual phenomenology ... negative, negative ... not if we go by the book ... we have no evidence of hostile warheads or hostile intent ... agreed ... agreed ... sir, how the fuck would I know? Some sort of blast coming from Mexico ... I urgently advise we do not get Eagle into Kneecap ... repeat do not get the Chief aloft ... no sir, keep the B-2s on the tarmac, their wings would just tear off ... sir?'

The line has gone dead.

There is a stench of fresh vomit. Wallis feels a tug on his sleeve. The major has apparently lost the power of speech; he is staring ahead, as if looking at his own death. Wallis follows the young man's line of vision. The wave of red lights is now passing in a long arc from California through Kansas to Virginia. Its progress is slow but steady over the map. It has almost reached the Rock.

'Sir, we're buttoned up. Hatches closed and filtration on. Sir?'

But Wallis is looking helplessly up at the observation room. The civilian and the generals look stonily down.

Then it reaches them.

Abduction

Buachaille Etive Mor, Glencoe, Scotland. 0630 GMT

Something.

The young man opened his eyes with a start, some dream fading from memory, and stared into the dark. Unaccountably, his heart was thumping in his chest.

At first he could make out only the flap-flap of the canvas inches from his head, and the *Whee!* of the wind around the guy ropes. And then it came again, a distant roar, deep and powerful, coming and going over the noises of the storm. Puzzled, he strained his ears.

Then it dawned.

Avalanche!

He shot out of his sleeping bag and tugged frantically at the rope lacing up the front of the hurricane tent. The knot was an impenetrable tangle and the noise was growing in intensity. Desperately he scrabbled in the dark for a breadknife, found it, cut the rope, hauled back the canvas and pitched head-first into the dark night.

The blizzard hit him with a force which made him gasp.

For a panicky moment he thought to run into the dark but then remembered where he was: on a mountain ridge next to a precipitous drop. And the roar was coming from the gully below.

He dived back to the tent, and felt for the paraffin lamp and a box of matches. The wind blew the match out; and the next and the next. The fourth match worked, and he hooked the glowing lamp up to an aluminium pole. He looked around. Snowflakes like luminous insects were hurtling from the void into a circle of light about ten yards in radius around the tent; he could just make out the edge of the ridge, about twenty yards away.

A cone of bluish-white light rose out of the gully, passing left to right before disappearing from the man's line of vision.

Avalanches don't come with blue lights.

The man's legs were shaking, whether with cold or relief he didn't know. The light cone was drifting up and down in a sweeping pattern, snow hurtling through the beam.

It occurred to him that a man in a Glencoe blizzard, dressed only in boxer shorts, probably had a life expectancy of minutes. Already his back was a mass of sharp, freezing pain. Hastily, he reached in for corduroy trousers and sweater, pulled them on and slipped into climbing boots. He tripped over untied laces, picked himself up and ploughed through deep snow to the edge of the ridge overlooking the Lost Valley. The sweater, he realized, bought him at most another five minutes: the wind was going through it like a chainsaw through butter.

The light cone rose and approached. It was scanning the mountain slopes. Suddenly light flooded the ground around him. An intense spotlight rose into space and approached; the roar became overwhelming; the ground vibrated. Dazzled, the man caught a glimpse of a whirling rotor passing straight overhead. A giant insect, a yellow flying monster of a thing, circled him and then sank towards a sloping patch of snow about thirty yards away. It almost vanished in the blizzard kicked up by its rotors. It tried to settle down, backed off, tried again, but its undercarriage slithered over the snow and the machine slid perilously sideways towards the edge of a precipitous drop. The pilot gave up and rose over the man's head.

A spider emerged in silhouette from the side of the machine, and began to sink down on a swaying thread. It settled on to the knee-deep snow within arm's length of him, resolving itself into a young airman in a khaki-coloured flying suit. 'Flt Lt A.W.L. Manley' was stencilled on his helmet. 'Doctor Webb?'

Webb stared in astonishment, and nodded.

'You're coming upstairs. Quickly, please.'

⏳

St-Pierre de Montrouge, Paris. 0730 Central European Time

Five hundred miles to the southeast, in Paris, the Atlantic storm had softened from the harsh reality of a potentially lethal blizzard to a bitter, wet, gusty wind.

As was his custom, the professor left his apartment at 7.30 a.m. precisely. Dark clouds swirled just above the rooftops, a newspaper streaked along the road and a solitary pigeon was attempting a speed record; but he was well clad in trenchcoat and beret, and as usual he walked the two hundred yards to the Café Pigalle. There he took off his sodden trenchcoat and sat at the marble bar. Without waiting to be asked, Monique served him two strong espresso coffees and a croissant with butter and strawberry jam, which he consumed while watching the early morning Parisians scurrying past.

At eight fifty, as he always did, he set out along the Rue d'Alesia, jumping over the flowing gutters and avoiding the bow waves from passing trucks. He turned off at the church of St-Pierre de Montrouge and headed briskly towards the Sorbonne. He had no reason even to notice the man purchasing cigarettes at the kiosk. The man was squat and bulky, with grey hair close-cropped almost to the scalp. His bull neck was protected from the rain by the pulled-up collar of his sodden jerkin. A policeman stood on the edge of the pavement next to the kiosk, his back to the professor, watching the flow of traffic through the little waterfall pouring from the brim of his sodden cap.

As the professor drew level with the kiosk, the squat man suddenly turned. 'Professor Leclerc?'

Startled, Leclerc looked into the man's eyes, but they showed no expression. 'Who are you?'

From the corner of his eye the professor saw a big Citroën pull up, the rear door open and another man step out: thin, tight-lipped, with eyes set back in his head. Suddenly, and instinctively, the professor was afraid.

'Please come with us, Professor.'

'Why? What is this?'

'I do not know. A matter of national security. Get into the car.'

Thinking assassination, Leclerc turned to run; but powerful arms seized him, held him in a painful neck lock. He wriggled furiously, his beret falling to the ground, but another pair of hands twisted an arm behind his back. Half-choked, he tried to shout but he was pushed into the back seat of the car, one man on either side of him. Leclerc forced his arm free and hammered on the rear window. The policeman turned away a little more, his back squarely to the professor. The driver took off swiftly, cutting into the path of a taxi. The man at the kiosk tidied his newspapers, the Parisians scurried by, and the policeman, water streaming down his shiny cape, tossed the beret into a litter bin while keeping his eye firmly on the glistening rush-hour traffic.

⧗

Baltimore, Maryland. Midnight

The warm ocean which powered the Atlantic storm was also dumping its energy into the far north of the planet; here the air, turned away from the sun, was exposed to interplanetary cold; here, it responded to the Earth's ancient rotation, and circulated anticlockwise around the Arctic Ocean: a huge blizzard howled out over the pack ice and the seals, the killer whales and the sunless wastelands.

The blizzard rampaged over the pole, down through Alaska and the North West Territories, passed over a thousand miles of Baffin Island, and howled through a few Inuit hunting groups who knew it as the Chinook, a hostile force which drove itself up nostrils and winkled out tiny gaps in snow goggles. The blizzard was still a blizzard over Quebec Province and New York State but, far from the oceanic heat engine, it was beginning to die. Even so, swirling along Broadway and Times Square, the dying snowstorm could still send late evening theatre crowds scurrying into warm bars, and traffic cops into a state of sullen paranoia.

Passing over the Great Lakes, the wind went into a rapid decline until, in Baltimore, Maryland and Washington, it finally died, leaving only snowflakes drifting down on sleeping houses: a traditional Christmas, all Bing Crosby, Silent Night, and Christmas trees glittering from a million dark windows.

In at least one Maryland suburban home, however, the night was neither still nor silent, and the owner barely heard the chime of the doorbell above the party hilarity and the raucous dance music. Reluctantly, Hilary Sacheverell detached herself from her white-haired, tall dancing partner, and weaved a path through the party. In the hallway she stepped over a young couple sitting together on the floor, backs to the wall. She opened the door, a smile half-formed on her face in expectation of late arrivals. A gust of freezing night air wafted around her exposed shoulders and she shivered.

Two men, in their thirties, one white, one black. Strangers. Snow sprinkled their heads and dark coats like tinsel decoration. A black Buick Convertible had somehow snaked its way through the Mercs and Dodges which cluttered the driveway. A third man, in the Buick, just discernible through its dark windscreen. The woman was suddenly alert.

'Mrs Sacheverell?' the black man asked.

She nodded uneasily.

'Is your son here?'

'Which one?'

'We're looking for Doctor Herbert Sacheverell, ma'am.'

'Herby is here,' she said. 'Is there a problem?'

'If we could just have a word with him.'

A hardness about the eyes; a professional alertness. Some instinct prevented her from inviting them in from the bitter cold. 'Wait a moment, please.'

It was a full minute before she found a skeletally thin, middle-aged man with thick spectacles and red, spiky hair seated at the kitchen table with the Ellis woman. A near-empty bottle of Jim Beam stood between them. The girl had her elbows on the table and was resting her head in cupped hands, staring into Sacheverell's blue eyes with open admiration. Sacheverell, thus encouraged, was extolling the merits of legalizing cannabis, itemizing the points with the aid of his bony fingers.

'Herby, two men for you,' Mrs Sacheverell said, looking through the Ellis female. 'They look sort of official. Have you been naughty?'

Herby shook his head in bewilderment. He stood up carefully, oriented himself towards the open kitchen door and navigated towards it with exaggerated steadiness.

'Enjoying the party?' Mrs Sacheverell asked.

'Oh yes, Mrs S. Herby is really good to me.'

'Tell me, have you tried anything for that big spot on your chin?' Mrs Sacheverell asked, curling her lips into a smile.

The smile was returned. 'I'm using a cream. It's supposed to be good for wrinkles too – I'll hand it in to you some time.'

'That would be lovely, dear. Do keep drinking.'

A minute later, the doorbell rang again. Herb Sacheverell stood between the two men. He was tight-lipped, and his face was white and strained. 'I'll be gone a few days. Urgent business.'

She glanced in alarm at the men on either side of her son.

'There's something going on here. Who are these people?'

'Mom, it's okay. But one thing. It's important that you tell nobody about this. If anyone asks, friends have turned up and I'm taking a few days' holiday.'

Hilary Sacheverell's suspicion was overlaid by her sense of the practical. 'Let me pack a suitcase for you.'

'There's no time. They'll look after me. Now I have to go.'

Hilary Sacheverell watched the dark Buick snake through the driveway and then, on the road, accelerate swiftly away. She wended a path back to the living room, a smile firmly fixed on her face.

⌛

North Atlantic, 0650 GMT

'You've got the wrong man. I'm not a medical doctor.'

'This isn't a rescue mission. If you're Webb, you're wanted on board.'

'Who are you people?'

'We don't have a lot of time, sir!' the airman shouted.

'The hell with you!' Webb shouted back.

'Sir, I am authorized to use force.'

'Don't try it. On whose authority?'

'We don't have a lot of time, sir.' The airman took a step forward. Webb instinctively turned to run but, looking into the whirling blizzard and the blackness beyond, immediately saw that such an action would be a lethal folly. He raised his hands in an angry gesture of surrender and furrowed his way through the snow back to his tent. The downdraught from the big rotor was threatening to flatten it and the guy ropes were straining at the pegs. Inside, the noise of the flapping canvas was deafening and the paraffin lamp was swaying dangerously. Papers were fluttering around the tent. He gathered them up, grabbed a laptop computer, turned off the lamp and ploughed back towards the lieutenant, tightly gripping papers and computer. The airman pointed towards the white blizzard and the man ran forwards into it; under the big rotor, the downdraught was fierce, and he felt as if he was being freeze-dried. The airman shouted 'Hold on!' and slipped a harness around him. Then Webb's feet were off the ground and he was gripping the papers fiercely as the winch swung and spun them upwards through the gusting wind.

A Christmas tree, tied tightly, and with baubles attached, lay along the length of the machine. Half a dozen sacks with 'Santa' in red letters lay on the floor. Two civilians, men in their fifties, were at the back of the helicopter. They were identically dressed in headphones, grey parkas and bright yellow lifejackets. Webb recognized one of them but couldn't believe his eyes.

The airman pointed and he tottered to the front, flopping down on the chair behind the pilot. The wet sweater felt horrible against his skin.

The pilot turned. He had a red, farm-boy face and seemed even younger than his navigator. His helmet identified him as W.J. Tolman, and 'Bill T.' was printed on the back of his flying suit.

Manley said, 'It's force eight out there, mister; we're not supposed to fly in this. Put on the lifejacket!'

Webb looked out. Daylight was trying to penetrate the gloom. Across the glen, he could just make out sheets of snow marching horizontally against the backdrop of granite mountains. The top of the ridge opposite was hidden in dark, sweeping cloud. He began to feel faint.

The pilot pulled on the collective and the big machine rose sharply upwards. Webb's stomach churned. Tolman looked over his shoulder. 'What gives with this trip? Are you some sort of James Bond?'

The helicopter began to buck violently. Webb looked down and glimpsed his hurricane tent, a tiny black dot against the massive, white top of the Big Herdsman. Then the machine was roaring over the Lost Valley and they were rising bumpily towards the Three Sisters. As it reached the summit it was hit by the unshielded force of the blizzard. It lurched and tilted on its side, throwing Webb against the fuselage. 'Jesus Holy Mary Mother of Christ!' the pilot yelled. Then the helicopter had righted and was thrusting roughly into the wind, its wipers clicking in vain against a wall of white, while another wall, made of granite, skimmed past.

Webb stared out. His faintness had given way to terror. Below, white Highland peaks came and went through dark scudding clouds; and then they were passing along Loch Linnhe and the Sound of Mull; and then they were heading out over an ocean made of white churning milk; and the waves on the milk moved in slow stately progression; and they were bigger than houses.

The pilot turned again. 'I was supposed to meet a nurse tonight,' he said accusingly. 'Knockers like melons and game for anything. James bloody Bond on a secret mission I do not need. By the way, your pals from Smersh are waiting.'

The young man made his way unsteadily to the back of the machine. 'You don't mind if I smoke, Webb?' asked the Astronomer Royal, lighting up a Sherlock Holmes pipe. He was buckled into a seat at a small circular table screwed into the metal floor. There was no telling what lay behind his blue eyes and Webb judged that the man on the chair next to him wasn't an artless rustic either. He collapsed into a seat opposite, buckled in and put on the headphones in front of him.

'This is the fellow,' said the AR.

'Walkinshaw,' the stranger said. He looked like a headmaster, half-moon spectacles mounted on a grey skull-like head. It was a civil servant's handshake: prudent, cautious, economical. The helicopter was into its stride, moving briskly if roughly about five hundred feet above the big waves. The civil servant glanced forward at the airmen; they too were wearing earphones.

'I expect you're wondering what's going on, Webb,' said the Astronomer Royal, unscrewing the lid of a flask.

'The question did flicker across my mind, Sir Bertrand,' said Webb angrily. 'I have, after all, just been kidnapped.'

'Don't exaggerate. The Sea King is transporting us to Skye.'

'Skye?'

'Skye. Where Walkinshaw and I will be dropped off. You, however, will continue on to Iceland.'

'Iceland?'

'Webb, try not to sound like a parrot. I am informed that we have only twenty minutes to brief you. Six of these have already gone.' A match flared and Webb waited while the King's Astronomer got up more smoke. 'Father smoked an ounce a day, lived to ninety. Walkinshaw here is from some God Knows What department of the Foreign Office. Webb, we have a problem.'

'Just a moment, Sir Bertrand. Sorry to interrupt your Christmas vacation, Doctor Webb.' Walkinshaw nodded at the sheets of A4 paper, covered with handwritten mathematical equations, which the man was still unconsciously clutching. 'Although you seem to be on a working holiday.'

'Will someone tell me what is going on here?' Webb said. He was trembling, through a compound of shock, fear, anger and cold. He folded the papers up and slipped them into his back pocket.

'First there are a couple of formalities. Number One.' Walkinshaw leaned forward and passed over a little plastic card. Webb held it towards the nearest window. There was a polaroid photograph of the civil servant, looking like a funeral undertaker, over an illegible signature. Next to the photo was a statement that

W.M. Walkinshaw, Grade Six, whose photograph and signature are adjacent hereto, is employed by His Britannic Majesty's Government in the Foreign and Commonwealth Office, Department of Information Research.

Webb nodded warily and returned the card.

'And Number Two.' The civil servant reached into his briefcase again and handed over a sheet of paper. 'An E.24, quite routine. If you would just sign there.'

The Astronomer Royal unzipped his parka. 'It's hot in here,' he said, holding out a pen. Webb ignored it and read

OFFICIAL SECRETS ACT

To be signed by members of Government Departments on appointment and, where desirable, by non-civil servants on first being given access to Government information.

My attention has been drawn to the provisions of the Official Secrets Act set out on the back of this document and I am fully aware of the serious consequences which may follow any breach of these provisions.

Webb felt the hairs prickling on the back of his head. On the back, he read that if any person having in his possession or control any secret official code word, pass

23

word, sketch, plan, model, article, note, document, or information which relates to or is used in a prohibited place or any thing in such a place, or which has been made or obtained in contravention of this Act, or which has been entrusted in confidence to him by any person holding office under His Majesty or which he obtained or to which he has had access owing to his position as a person who holds or has held a contract made on behalf of His Majesty, or as a person who is or has been employed under a person who holds or has held such an office or contract, communicates . . . or uses . . . or retains . . . or fails to take reasonable care of, or so conducts himself as to endanger the safety of, the sketch, plan, model, article, note, document, secret official code or pass word or information, then that person shall be guilty of misdemeanour.

He handed it back unsigned.

The Astronomer Royal made no attempt to hide his annoyance; his teeth audibly tightened on his pipe. He returned the pen to an inside pocket, and glanced quickly at Walkinshaw. The latter nodded briefly.

Tolman's voice cut sharply into the intercom: 'Do not smoke. Put that pipe out immediately.'

Sir Bertrand continued to puff. Bleak Atlantic light from a window had turned his wrinkled face into a mountainous terrain. The helicopter was filling with blue smoke. He said, speaking carefully: 'The Americans suspect that an asteroid has been clandestinely diverted on to a collision course with their country.'

Webb stared at him, aware of a sudden light-headedness as he struggled to take it in. '*What?* You could be talking a million megatons.'

'Webb, I'm aware that you think I'm just an establishment hack. However even I can multiply a mass by the square of its velocity.' Sir Bertrand pushed a little metal stubber into his pipe. 'The Americans informed their NATO allies late last night – the Eastern bloc partners excepted of course – and the Foreign Office requested my assistance at four o'clock this morning. But as you know asteroids are not my field.'

'An asteroid like that would devastate half the planet. This has to be wrong.'

'If only.'

'Which asteroid?'

'You're missing the point,' said the AR. 'The idea is that you tell us.'

Webb tried to grasp what he had just been told. The AR and the civil servant watched him closely. 'Okay you've scared me. What you're asking is insane. It would be easier to find a needle in a haystack.'

'Nevertheless it must be done and done quickly. The Americans will need to find some way of diverting it.'

'You must have some information about it.'

The AR shook his head. 'None whatsoever. All we can say is that at some unknown future time it will manifest itself over American skies as a meteor of ferocious intensity.'

'An asteroid impact on North America could leave two hundred million dead. Suppose I fail, or make a wrong identification? I can't take responsibility for that.'

'There is nobody else. And I would prefer a more respectful tone.'

Webb felt his mouth beginning to dry up. 'I'm sorry, Sir Bertrand, but the moment I say yes, I'm swallowed up in God knows what. Get someone else.'

The Astronomer Royal's voice dripped with acid. 'I know this will sound absurdly quaint in this day and age, Webb, but there is the small matter of one's obligations to humanity.'

'Hold on a minute. I went to Glen Etive for a reason.' He tapped his back pocket with the papers. 'Listen. I'm on the verge of something. I think I can put some meat into general relativity. You know GR is just a phenomenology, it lacks a basis in physical theory, and that Sakharov conjectured . . .'

The Astronomer Royal's tone was icy. 'You were instructed not to spend time on speculative theoretical exercises.'

'I happen to be on leave, trying to do some real science for a change. You have a problem with an asteroid? Get someone else to look into it.'

The Astronomer Royal took the pipe from his mouth, his face wrinkling with angry disbelief. He made to speak but Walkinshaw quickly raised his hand. 'Please, Bertrand.' The civil servant lowered his head, as if in thought. Then he leaned forward, to be heard above the engine. 'Doctor Webb, I apologize for the melodramatic descent from the skies, but the fact is that we are engaged in a race, with an asteroid, which we must not lose.' The helicopter was tilting and Webb gripped the table. He sensed that his face was grey. 'The Americans are trying to put together a small team to look into this. They have specifically requested a British contribution. We do not know when impact will occur but it must be clear that time is vital. We must get you to New York instantly. As Sir Bertrand says, there is nobody else in this country.'

The AR, at last, poured a black liquid into the plastic lid of the flask. Webb took it and sipped at the warm tea. His stomach was churning and he was beginning to feel nauseous. 'Who diverted the asteroid?'

The civil servant remained silent.

'There's some risk attached to this, right?' Webb peered closely at Walkinshaw, but the man had the eyes of a poker player.

The AR turned to Walkinshaw. 'A wasted journey,' he said contemptuously. 'Turn the Sea King back. I'll get Phippson at UCL.'

'Phippson? That idiot?' Webb said in astonishment.

The AR waited.

'But the man's a total incompetent.'

The AR cleared his throat.

'He couldn't find the full moon on a dark night!'

The AR stubbed the tobacco in his pipe, a smirk playing around his lips.

'Damn you, Sir Bertrand,' Webb said.

Sir Bertrand removed his pipe, exposed his teeth and emitted a series of loud staccato grunts, his shoulders heaving in rhythm. Webb was enveloped by a wave of nicotine-impregnated breath. He gulped the tea and handed the flask lid back to the Astronomer Royal, who was grinning triumphantly.

Walkinshaw's eyes half-closed with relief. 'Very well. The country is grateful etcetera. Now the quickest route from here is the polar one. After this briefing—' Walkinshaw glanced at his watch '—which must end in four minutes, we will be dropped off on a quiet beach near the Cuillins. You will carry straight on to Reykjavik Airport. There you will board a British Airways flight to New York. It's the quickest route we could devise from this Godforsaken land.'

He pulled out a buff envelope from a briefcase. 'Your ticket, some dollars, an American Express number on which you can draw, and a passport.'

'How did you get my photograph?'

'You would be amazed, and at four o'clock this morning. You are Mister Larry Fish, a goldsmith. A precaution in case unfriendly eyes are watching the movements of asteroid people. What do you know about gold, Webb?'

The Sea King was sinking fast, and Webb's stomach rose in his diaphragm.

'Atomic number seventy-nine, isn't it? The least reactive metal but alloys with mercury.'

Walkinshaw assimilated this answer. Then he said in a toneless voice, 'In no circumstances hold any sort of conversation with anyone en route.'

'Unfriendly eyes,' Webb said. He felt almost paralysed with fear. 'So there is some risk attached to this?'

'My goodness no,' said Walkinshaw blandly.

'If there is trouble nevertheless?'

'Never heard of you. You're a crackpot.'

'A popular opinion in some circles anyway,' Webb replied, giving the Astronomer Royal a look. The AR stared unflinchingly back.

The long backbone of the Cuillins was hidden by low, fast cloud sweeping in from the Atlantic. They stepped out into low, fast sleet sweeping in from the Atlantic. Fifty yards away on the black sand, a dark insect was poised to jump. It was bigger than a house. It had mysterious protrusions, and a row of windows along its dark side, and huge twin rotors throwing spirals of water into the wind. The sand under the Sikorsky was rippling and the Sea King was suddenly a child's toy.

Webb stared in alarm at the monstrous thing.

Walkinshaw shouted, 'The Air Force will make sure you catch the plane at Reykjavik. Sign the credit card as Larry Fish. Any expenditures must be accounted for but you shouldn't need it.'

'Then why give me it?'

'A precaution,' was the enigmatic response. 'I am informed that you know the Goddard Institute at Broadway. You are expected there around now. Still, they tell me you can beat the Sun at polar latitudes. Something to do with the Earth turning, but we pay you people to know about things like that, don't we, Bertrand?'

'What about my tent?'

'Webb,' the AR replied with a show of infinite patience, 'Have you quite grasped the situation? The issue here is not your scientific research, nor your evident fear of flying nor the fate of your blasted tent. The issue is the survival of the West. His Majesty's Air Force have laid on travel gear in the Chinook, and His Majesty's Astronomer will personally dismantle your tent and return it to your office.'

'I'll be missed at the Institute,' Webb pleaded.

'The hell you will!' the Astronomer Royal roared. 'Nobody knows what you do in that damned basement all day. Anyway, you sent a note saying you've extended your leave. My secretary does signatures.'

'I'm not getting into that contraption!' Webb finally shouted, but he knew he would.

'Just find the asteroid, Webb,' the Astronomer Royal shouted back. 'And quickly! And keep your mouth shut!'

⧗

The freezing rain drove into the Astronomer Royal's wrinkled face, and he screwed up his eyes as the massive helicopter rose and tilted over the sea. He watched as it dwindled upwards and vanished into the clouds. He puffed reflectively on his pipe, the wind blowing a thin stream of smoke across the beach.

Walkinshaw looked worried. 'Bertrand, are you sure about this? What sort of man spends Christmas alone on a mountain, in a blizzard, calculating?'

'A hermit, of course. Speaking as his Director, he's a nightmare.'

'In what way?'

'He's restless, the very devil to control. Needs a woman if you ask me. He keeps diverting from well-established lines of research into cosmological speculation. There's no funding for stuff like that these days, and anyway nobody quite understands what he's about. However he pursues his ideas with great exuberance and determination.'

'Family?'

'I know little of it except that he comes from a large, poor one with no sort of academic background.'

'Then I understand him,' Walkinshaw declared. 'A large family with little privacy will make him invent his own private space, a world in which he can daydream. Hence the cosmological speculation. And the need to compete with siblings will make him pursue his own ends with determination. Throw in an exceptional intelligence and there you have him.'

A deeply sceptical expression came over the AR's face. 'Very neat, Walkinshaw, wonderfully glib. I don't suppose you're into palmistry as well as amateur psychology?'

'His evident unworldliness has the same source. There is no great ingenuity without an admixture of dementedness. Seneca said that, not me. Still, Bertrand, I'm worried. We need a team player for this one, not some go-it-alone eccentric.'

The Astronomer Royal smiled a thin, sour smile. 'That, I fear, is a problem for our American cousins. After all, they wanted him. Indeed, they were very insistent.'

The Goddard Institute, New York

Outside the warm Kennedy terminal, a gust of icy air hurt Webb's ears, watered his eyes and froze his ankles, and he found that the Royal Air Force had given him a suit transparent to wind. A man with a Cossack hat rode a strange, shaking machine which sucked up dark-streaked snow from the road and sprayed it at him. The morning sky was a menacing, dull grey. He headed for the airport bus but two men, warmly wrapped against the cold, emerged from the background and intercepted him. 'Mister Fish? I am Agent Doyle of the FBI, and this is my colleague Agent O'Halloran. Forgive us if we don't show our badges in a public place. Would you come this way, please?'

Webb settled into the back seat of a nondescript Buick with darkened windows. The car was deliciously warm. Agent O'Halloran took it silently over Brooklyn Bridge towards Central. Patches of crystal blue sky were beginning to show through the cloud. On Broadway, they continued north to the edge of Black Harlem. Good smells drifted from delicatessens and coffee shops. The snow was deep at the side of the road, and the breaths of pedestrians steamed in the bitter cold.

They stopped at the entrance to the Goddard Institute, an anonymous doorway with neither sign nor symbol to proclaim its NASA affiliation. Webb stepped out of the car. Across the street, rap music was blasting out of a stereo from a first-floor window. A phalanx of black children swooped down threateningly, but at the last second split and reconverged past him with marvellous precision. The stereo went off with a swipe, and the skateboarders swept off round the corner, ghettoblasters screeching. The limousine drove off.

'Mister Fish, good morning, we've been expecting you,' the stout, black guard at the desk said cheerfully. 'First floor, elevator's over there.'

On the first floor was a door with a sheet of paper saying 'Do Not Enter' pinned on it. Webb knocked and a key turned. The room was bleak and almost unfurnished, apart from a green baize table strewn with notepads and water carafes. Four people sat around the table. The man who had opened the door, slimly built with close-cropped hair and light blue eyes, shook Webb's hand. 'Welcome to New York, Doctor Webb,' he said. 'Have a seat and we'll get on with it.'

Webb sat down and looked round the table. The smell of cigar smoke hung lightly in the air. Through it Webb thought he detected a sour odour which he could not place. Three of the faces he knew; the others were strangers.

Noordhof's tone was informal but decisive. 'First, gentlemen, a small organizational matter. This is a USAF project and as of now you are under my direction. The Europeans included, by consent of your respective governments. Does anyone object to this?' He looked round the table.

'Okay. Now we're all here, let me make the introductions. Proceeding from my right, we have Herbert Sacheverell, from the Sorel Institute at Harvard.' A man of about forty, his red hair standing vertically on his scalp thin, greasy-skinned and wearing a dirty black headband, nodded at the assembled group. 'Doctor Sacheverell is our top asteroid man.' Jesus, Webb thought, America's answer to Phippson: who put that loud-mouthed clown on the team? Sacheverell's expression returned the compliment.

'Next to him we have Jim McNally, Director of NASA.' McNally, a slim, balding man of about fifty, dressed in a business suit with a slight, up-market shimmer to it, smiled and said Hi.

'The American contingent is completed by Wilhelm Shafer. What can you say about a hippie with one and a half Nobel Prizes?'

There was no need; a huge intelligence clearly lay behind Shafer's restless grey eyes. He was, like McNally, about fifty; he wore a copper-coloured T-shirt decorated with a Buddha, and an elastic band held his long grey hair back in a ponytail. He grinned and nodded towards Leclerc and Webb. For Webb, the presence of the awesome Willy Shafer on the team underlined the gravity of the emergency as much as any lecture by the Astronomer Royal.

'On my left, let me introduce our two European partners. Oliver Webb, still catching his breath, is the British asteroid man. Next to him we have André Leclerc. André knows as much as anyone in the West about the space capabilities of the former Soviet bloc.' A tall, gaunt man, with a red bow tie and a black and white goatee beard, smiled and bowed to the centre of the table.

'And I'm Colonel Mark Noordhof. I know a thing or two about missile defence technology.'

'Who needs the Brits?' Sacheverell asked, staring at Webb with open hostility. 'We have all the know-how we need in the States.'

'In part this is politics,' said Noordhof. 'An attack on America is also an attack on NATO. If we get zapped on Monday the Russians could roll over Europe on Tuesday. But the essence is we need the best for this one.'

Sacheverell continued to glare, his eyes tiny through his thick spectacles. 'Webb is a bad choice.'

Noordhof added: 'And security. Sure we're up to our ears in civilian experts but what if they started dropping out of sight wholesale? We can't treat this like the Manhattan project. So, we're using minimum numbers, drawn from a widely dispersed net. Small is beautiful is what the President wants. Kay, now let's get down to it.'

Noordhof produced a cigar and played with the cellophane wrapping. He continued: 'My brief comes from the President. I have to lead a team which will find the asteroid, estimate where and when it will impact if it does, estimate the impact damage, and determine whether it can be destroyed or diverted. I report directly to the SecDef, Nathan Bellarmine. He in turn informs the President, the DCI and the Joint Chiefs of our progress. The resources of these people are available to us and that's some awesome resources. If you want the Sixth Fleet in Lake Michigan, ask and it shall be given unto thee.'

'Seek and we shall find,' said Shafer. 'I hope.'

'Understand this,' said Noordhof. 'This is not some cosy academic conference. This is a race, and the prize is survival. We have no precedent for this situation, no experience we can call on. We have to make up the rules as we go. Comments, anyone?'

'I'm not long out of bed,' Webb said. 'How do we know that an asteroid has been diverted towards the States?'

'I'll pass on that for now.'

'What are the political implications? Does it connect to the Red Army takeover?' Leclerc asked, speaking good Parisian English.

'That we don't know.'

'We need a handle on the time element,' Sacheverell said. 'It could be hours, weeks, months, years before the asteroid hits.'

A smoke ring emerged from Noordhof's puckered lips. 'We've been given five days to identify the asteroid and formulate an effective deflection strategy. This is Monday morning. Deadline is Friday midnight.'

Sacheverell laughed incredulously. 'In the name of God . . .'

Noordhof continued. 'And I'm authorized to say this. If at the end of five days we have failed to identify the asteroid, the White House will then formulate policy on the assumption that it will never be found before impact. I think it's safe to assume that aforesaid policy will be highly aggressive.'

Shafer said quietly, 'I think the Colonel is telling us that either we find the asteroid by midnight on Friday or the White House will retaliate with a nuclear strike.'

The room went still. Sacheverell paled, McNally flushed purple and Leclerc puffed out his cheeks. Noordhof leaned back and took a leisurely puff, whirls of blue smoke curling upwards. Webb felt suddenly nauseous.

'So we split the effort. Item One. Our masters want to know what will happen if the asteroid hits. Which one of you eggheads wants to take that one?' Noordhof looked round the table.

'I guess I'll look into that,' said Sacheverell. 'Sounds like a big computing job and we have the hardware at the Sorel.'

'Agreed?' Noordhof asked Webb, who nodded. The issue had already been raked over by experts; Sacheverell couldn't do much harm channelled into that one.

'Item Two. Say we detect the asteroid on the way in. What can we do about it?'

'That's a solved problem,' said McNally. 'NASA looked into this on instructions from Congress some years back, when it was all a theoretical exercise. Anything we do will involve getting up there and zapping it.'

'Now hold on, zap it how?' Shafer asked sharply.

'With nukes, of course.' McNally looked bewildered.

'I've seen that stuff, and the Livermore Planet Defense Workshop, and the Air Force 2025 study. Theoretical's the word. What do you think you'll be zapping, Dr McNally, shaving foam or a giant nickel-iron crystal? Hit it with nukes and you might wipe us out with a spray of boulders. We have to divert the thing without busting it up. How do you propose to do that without knowing its internal constitution?'

'It was only a suggestion,' McNally complained.

'Willy, Jim, liaise on the problem of how to handle the asteroid if we do find it. I'll fix access to classified Lawrence Livermore reports as well as the public domain one. That leaves Item Three: where is this thing? Opinions anyone?'

'I can draw up a list of candidates,' Webb said, still feeling queasy, 'And get them checked out. We'll need to use wide-angle telescopes.'

'Like the UK Schmidt?' suggested Sacheverell.

'They've mothballed it. I'm thinking more of supernova patrol telescopes, say a fast Hewitt camera with a CCD. The Australians have one at Coona.'

'Colonel, this is an example of the security you can expect from these guys,' said Sacheverell. 'Time on these machines is more precious than gold. You can't just break into established observing programmes, not without people shouting like hell.'

'Ever heard of service time?'

'Cool it, gentlemen,' said Noordhof. 'Wait until you see what we've laid on.'

Sacheverell said, 'Whatever you've laid on, Colonel, our chances of identifying this rock in five days are practically zero. Especially with Webb guiding the search.'

'Jesus frigging Christ, don't say things like that.' Noordhof stubbed out his cigar agitatedly.

Webb said, 'What especially worries me is that these things are invisible most of the time. It could come at us from sunwards, in which case the first we'll know about it is when it hits.'

Noordhof poured water from a carafe into a tumbler and took a sip, wetting his dry lips. Tense little wrinkles lined his face as he assimilated Webb's information. He said, 'Let's name this beast.'

'I suggest Nemesis,' Sacheverell said. 'After the Greek Goddess of Destruction.' There were nods of assent.

Noordhof said, 'Nemesis. Good name. I have to tell you there is no chance of identifying it by conventional intelligence-gathering techniques. It's down to us.'

'Many orbits will be unreachable by the Russian Fed eration even with their Energia boosters,' said Leclerc. 'Perhaps Doctor Webb and I can co-operate.'

'I have programmes at Oxford which might help,' Webb said.

Noordhof nodded curtly. 'You'll have facilities to FTP them over. Now, gentlemen, we're heading for Arizona. We have a Gulfstream waiting for us at La Guardia. And from now on you free spirits are firmly corralled. No wandering the streets, no phone calls, no e-mails to colleagues. Lest you think this is paranoid, consider this. If the Russian leadership learn that we know about Nemesis, they can anticipate getting nuked in retaliation. So they'll get their strike in first, to minimize damage to themselves.'

Shafer completed the logic: 'Except that, since we know they'll be thinking that way, we'll have to get in first.'

Noordhof nodded again. 'A careless word from anyone here could trigger a nuclear war.'

They stared at each other in fright. At last Webb recognized the sour odour. It was the smell of sweat, induced not by exertion but by fear. The chairs scuffled on the wooden floor as they stood up. 'Strictly,' Webb said, 'Nemesis is the Goddess of Righteous Anger. Have you people upset somebody?'

Southern Arizona

The desert air was cold, the sun was setting, and a bright red Pontiac Firebird, straight out of the nineteen-seventies, was waiting for them. It had fat tyres and a front grille like twin nostrils, and flames extended from the air intakes back along the bonnet and down the sides in a wonderful expression of psychedelic art from the period. The woman leaning on the car was about thirty, small, with shoulder-length, curly, natural blonde hair. She was wearing a slightly old-fashioned dress which didn't disguise the fact of elegant bodywork underneath. She waved cheerfully at them.

Noordhof took the driving seat, Shafer sitting next to him. Webb added his holdall to a pile of luggage in the boot and squeezed into the back beside the blonde. She was diminutive against his strong six foot one frame. Leclerc sat on the other side of her and immediately delved into a sheaf of papers.

'Judy Whaler,' she said, shaking hands. 'So you're our European astronomer.'

'What's your field, Doctor Whaler?'

'I'm a Sandian.'

'Is that a religious cult?'

She smiled tolerantly. 'Sandia National Laboratories. The Advanced Concepts Group. We're supposed to identify threats to national security and propose countermeasures.'

Noordhof said, over his shoulder, 'The rest of the team's

on site.' He eased the car on to the road. Once on Speedway he opened the throttle and they moved throatily north on the broad street, past Mexican restaurants and cheap motels. It took about twenty minutes to cross the city and then they were clear, still heading north, and the grey Catalina Mountains were getting bigger. Paloverde cactus and little creosote bushes started at the roadside and stretched into the far distance. The sky was blue, but streaky clouds were beginning to form around the peaks, and above them was high cirrus. A four-engined jet was drawing a contrail.

In the confined space it soon became clear that Judy enjoyed bathing in cheap perfume. Her thigh was warm against Webb's but he tried not to notice that – after all, she was a colleague. The road began to climb and twist and they passed over narrow bridges straddling deep canyons. Webb's scrotum contracted, as it always did when he faced great heights or imminent danger. It would do a lot of contracting over the next few days.

Half an hour north of the city Shafer fell in impatiently behind a big, gleaming American truck with a vertical exhaust. The corrugated door at the back portrayed a leering, gluttonous child, with a frost-covered head, eating a Monster Headfreeze Bar. The road went steeply up the mountainside and the truck dropped gear noisily with a surge of exhaust smoke, labouring heavily. A second truck appeared on the skyline like a hostile Indian and bore down on them at alarming speed. Noordhof put his foot flat down and they sailed past with ease.

'Six point six litre V8,' Judy said, 'delivering three three five bhp. The suspension's too simple to cope with it.' The truck drivers blasted their air horns but the big Pontiac was already long past. At the top of the hill Noordhof slowed, and turned sharply off on to a stony, unpaved track. In seconds they had lost the highway and were heading steeply upwards, towards high mountains.

Something momentarily glinted silver, on the summit of a high distant peak. The cactus gave way to a scattering of scrub oak and piñon pine.

After some minutes a cluster of timber houses appeared, straight out of the Wild West. A notice said *Piñon Mesa, alt. 5500 ft.* There were no signs of life.

'Survivalist community,' said Noordhof. 'They're armed to the teeth and they don't like us. But you won't be down here.'

The track ended at a wooden barred gate, and Noordhof kept the engine running as Webb fumbled with a padlock, feeling exposed. The buzz of a chainsaw came from the woods beyond, but he saw nothing through the trees. Then the real climb got under way, and the engine started to labour in earnest, and the air got colder, and Judy's thigh got warmer, and the scrub oak gave way to juniper pine, and then the juniper gave way to big, heavy ponderosa. Through the trees Webb caught glimpses of the setting sun to the left, and tiny bugs crawling along a ribbon cutting through the desert. The Firebird's suspension coped well with the potholes, but the heating didn't seem to work.

Higher still, and the branches were covered with thin, freshly fallen snow, and they were following the tracks of some vehicle which had gone before.

They ran into cloud from below, and for the next fifteen minutes were enveloped in a light freezing mist, visibility about fifty yards, as the car continued to toil upwards. Finally the road began to level, the tops of buildings appeared over the trees and then the car was round a last hairpin bend and driving past the buildings into a paved car park at the side. Noordhof turned to them. 'Eagle Peak. I'm told nobody ever comes here in the winter apart from astronomers and the odd black bear. But I still want you people sticking close to the Observatory. No wandering the hills.'

'Why haven't you fenced it off, Colonel?' Shafer asked.

'Just in case some stray backpacker comes by. Guards and fences going up round a civilian building might draw attention. Our best protection is the semblance of normality.'

They climbed out, stiff, breaths misting. The air was fresh and pine-scented. Judy flapped her arms against her sides. To Webb, the combination of hairstyle and dress made her look like a resistance heroine from a World War Two movie. He stretched and walked round to the front, curious to explore his new surroundings. The snow was powdery underfoot and Shafer was having problems assembling a snowball. Noordhof piled their luggage out on to the tarmac.

A small, wiry man, with a neat grey beard, appeared at the front door. 'Doctor Webb,' he said, stretching his hand. 'Heard you in Versailles last year. Delighted to meet you at last. And I've read a fair number of your papers, of course. I feel as if I know you.' So this was Kenneth Kowalski. His Polish origins were obvious in his polite manner and his slightly clipped accent: second-generation American. Webb knew Kowalski's reputation. Amongst observers, he was highly regarded, a careful stargazer who had transformed Eagle Peak from a dilapidated museum piece into a respected scientific tool. It didn't have the world-class clout of Gemini at Cerro Pachon or the huge Keck ten metre on Hawaii; but for rapid sky coverage, which is what the problem called for, it had these monsters licked. 'We must talk about your work on the revised steady state theory after this is over. Of course you're wrong. It's an observed fact that the Universe is different at high redshift.'

Webb returned the grin and bowed. 'All right-thinking people agree with you. So, this is the famous Eagle Peak Observatory?'

'You're just at Base Camp,' Kowalski said. 'The telescopes

are much higher up.' He pointed to a squat grey building fifty yards away, and just visible in the mist. Through its windows Webb could see a small silver cable car. A thin cable stretched up from the roof of the building like a giant metal beanstalk, disappearing into the grey mist overhead. He looked at the tinny death trap apprehensively before realizing that, as a theoretician, he would have no reason to go up in it.

He smiled in relief and said, 'Eagle Peak is a private benefaction?'

'Yes, it was a gift to the nation from the Preston dynasty in the thirties. It was modernized a few years ago with NSF funding. We were swarming with Air Force personnel yesterday, putting in extras for our visitors.'

Leclerc and Whaler joined them, and they made for the building. Sculpted in red sandstone over the outer door was a circularly coiled snake swallowing its own tail: the Pythagorean symbol of perfection and eternity. Inside, separating the atrium from the inner sanctum, was a double swing door made of glass framed in mahogany; each partition had the zodiacal signs engraved on it, six on each, in two columns. Through these doors and into the building proper, the warm air enveloped Webb like a hot bath towel. Kowalski led the way along a corridor lined with framed NASA photographs. Two doors led off to the left, and both were open.

The first of these revealed a large square kitchen with a long, cluttered farmhouse table. Then there was the common room, airy and spacious, with a panoramic window and a view of fog. In this room was a snooker table, and armchairs, and a bookcase full of paperbacks, and a coffee table with magazines and bowls of fresh fruit and sweets. Sacheverell and McNally were head to head in an animated discussion. As Judy passed the open door Sacheverell stopped in mid-conversation, adopted an angelic smile and said 'Well hi there,' and Webb hoped

Nemesis would smash through the roof and turn Sacheverell into a red pulp.

The end of the corridor led into an open, glass-fronted area from which further doors led off. One led back into the common room. Kowalski pointed to a red door opposite it. 'The nerve centre,' he said. 'Later.'

Straight ahead of them was a flight of stairs, covered with a deep-piled blue carpet, so as not to disturb night observers sleeping by day. They went up these and found themselves in a long corridor. 'The four rooms at the end are taken. If you like a desert view, take One or Two. If you like to look at mountains, take Seven or Eight.' The nearest door handle to Webb was attached to Number One and he took it. Leclerc took Number Two, while Judy Whaler presumably liked mountains and headed for Room Eight, directly opposite Webb's.

The room had a log cabin feel to it and smelled of new pinewood although, again, a thick pile carpet covered the floor. A red, bloated sun was beginning to penetrate the fog.

Alone at last, Webb flopped on to the bed and tried to take stock:

(a)   He'd been whisked off a remote Scottish mountain,
(b)   told a tale of imminent Armageddon,
(c)   transported to Iceland in a giant helicopter, in a blizzard,
(d)   been flown over the roof of the world thence down almost to Mexico, and
(e)   he was now on a remote mountain site surrounded by backwoodsmen.
(f)   And he thought,
       I don't need this.

Money, Webb had learned soon after he joined the Institute, drove everything. Science was something you snatched in precious moments in between writing grant applications and publicity handouts. And in between meetings: the management loved meetings. The science, he had also learned, had to be Approved. The streetwise might aspire to soft carpets and executive desks, but the iconoclast stayed in an icy basement. The point of Buachaille Etive Mor had been to escape, get to work on real science. Webb wondered how they had found him, in that remote mountain setting.

What I do need is deep, dreamless, eight hours of sleep. He had a shower, washing away the camping and travel, and wrapped himself in a large white towel. The beautiful, climactic moment came when he approached the bed, weary muscles tingling in anticipation of flopping down on it. He savoured the moment, he flopped, and there was a sharp knock on the door.

Noordhof was in Command Mode. 'The cable car. Five minutes. Observing suits in the dormitory cupboard.'

You're in the army now, Webb thought.

The tiny silver cable car barely took four people and had the feel of something cobbled together by an enthusiast with a Meccano set. Noordhof, Sacheverell and Webb squeezed in, dressed like Eskimos, with Sacheverell taking up three quarters of Webb's bench. A notice said

On no account stand up, change seats, shake the car or lean out of the window. Keep clear of the door handle in transit.

Kowalski marched over to a control panel, pressed a red button and pulled a lever. On the panel, a row of lights flashed on. There was a clash of engaging gears, a loud whining, and a large metal wheel started to turn. He trotted swiftly to the car and climbed in next to Webb, pulling the door shut just as the cable took up the slack and the car started to move. 'It's quite safe,' he said. 'If you work it by yourself just remember to get in quickly.'

From about fifty yards up, the ground faded into the mist and they lost nearly all sense of motion; they were sitting in a gently swaying cable car, immersed in a co-moving grey bubble. After some minutes they cleared the mist. Far above, almost over their heads, was a pinnacle of rock, still in sunlight. On its summit Webb could barely make out a building. Near-vertical rock faces fell away from it in every direction; lines of ice filled the ridges and angles. Webb looked up at the dizzying height and thought *Why not? What more can they throw at me?* Below them, the receding cloud turned out to be fairly localized, and they could see the track they had taken in the Firebird, twisting through the forest. Beyond it, the desert was now dark.

Webb assumed that his hypothetical Meccano enthusiast had known all about wind-pumped resonances, and metal fatigue, and the tensile strength of tired old steel. He was delighted to see that Sacheverell was even more terrified than him. There was sweat on the man's brow and his eyes were staring. He produced a handkerchief and wiped his face with it. Mischievously, Webb turned the screw a little. Trying to sound casual, he asked Kowalski: 'Ever been an accident with this?'

Kowalski looked at him curiously and glanced quickly at Sacheverell. Then he nodded solemnly. 'Once.'

The car began to sway, a long, slow oscillation as the cable vibrated like a bowstring. After some minutes the vibration died and the car's upward climb slowed; the machinery seemed to be struggling. Only a few yards away was an icy, vertical rock face; the car was being hauled almost vertically up its cable. Sacheverell giggled, but it was a bit high-pitched. The car edged up and slotted into a gap in a concrete platform projecting into space. They piled out. There was a gap of nine inches between car and platform, and about three thousand feet of air below the gap.

Eagle Peak was a spacious natural platform, about a hundred yards by eighty. Its perimeter was marked out by a stone wall about four feet high. There were two observatory domes, copper-coloured in the light of the sinking desert sun. One small, no more than fifteen feet in diameter; it was dwarfed by its companion, about a hundred feet across. The air was wonderfully clear, and bitterly cold.

Kowalski took them into the little dome. He picked up a metal handset from mobile steps and pressed a button. The dome was filled with the noise of machinery as the shutter opened. Temporarily Webb had the illusion, familiar to an astronomer, of standing on a rotating platform underneath a static dome. Kowalski rotated the dome until the sinking sun streamed into the open slot. In the centre of the circular building stood a circular metal platform about three feet tall and six wide. The top of the platform was clearly built to rotate, and two stanchions rose from it, supporting between them what looked like a big dustbin about three feet in diameter and six feet long.

'The supernova patrol telescope,' Kowalski said with, Webb thought, a touch of pride. 'With an altazimuth mounting,' he added, mentioning the obvious, 'to save weight. This is a fast survey instrument and it needs to travel light. For supernova searches we're just measuring the apparent magnitudes of galaxies, looking for any change which might indicate a stellar explosion. Speed is the priority and we don't need long exposures.'

Webb asked, 'How faint do you go?'

'Magnitude twenty-one in ten seconds, over a one-degree field. The instrument has a pointing accuracy of one arc second. We no longer need equatorial mountings now that we can use computers to update the altitude and azimuth of the target star. The slew rate, galaxy to galaxy, is less than a second. It is probably the best supernova hunter in the business.'

It was an impressive instrument.

Sacheverell tittered. 'Forgive me, Doctor Kowalski, but it has as much chance of finding Nemesis in six days as I have of winning the lottery.'

'Will you cut out talk like that,' Noordhof said.

Kowalski smiled politely and said, 'Now let me show you the other telescope.'

They made for the monster dome. By now the sun was down and Kowalski switched on the light to reveal a telescope about sixty feet tall, on a classical equatorial mounting. He led them up metal stairs to a circular balcony. They spread themselves around the balcony and looked across at the giant, battleship-grey instrument. A metal plaque said 'Grubb Parsons 1928'; it had been shipped over from the UK or Ireland at some stage. Mounted piggy-back on the main frame was a secondary telescope, and next to it a mobile platform, with a guard rail, which would raise and lower the observer depending on where the big telescope was pointing in the sky. Attached to the bottom of the telescope, at the location of the eyepiece, was a metal box about four feet on each side, from which cables trailed across the metal floor to a bank of monitors clear of the instrument. At the prime focus of the telescope, far above their heads, was a cylindrical cage. The cage contained the secondary mirror. It also came with a chair and harness; the observer had to supply the steel nerves.

It was twenties technology, a masterpiece of precision and power, updated for the new millennium with cutting edge instrumentation. As a tool for discovering Nemesis, Webb would without hesitation have gone for a pair of binoculars.

'This is of course the ninety-four-inch reflector,' Kowalski said. 'As you see we have set up a spectrograph at the prime focus. The atmospheric seeing at this site is excellent. In good conditions it can be sub-arcsecond, and I've even seen it diffraction-limited.'

'I hope you don't expect to find Nemesis with this,' Sacheverell said in a tone of incredulity.

Webb said, 'The Grubb Parsons will be very useful if we do find Nemesis. We can use it for astrometric backup to get a high-precision orbit, and we'll need it to get a spectrum.'

'What do you want a spectrum for?' Noordhof asked.

'Nickel iron or shaving foam, Colonel? We'd be able to work out the surface mineralogy which might be vital in formulating a deflection strategy. However, first catch your hare.'

Noordhof gave Webb a look. 'That's what you're here for, Mister.'

Kowalski said, 'The Grubb can only be operated from up here. If you want broad-band spectrophotometry you have to change the optical filters, which means you have to go into the cage. But we can control the supernova patrol telescope from down below. It can sweep the whole sky to magnitude twenty-one in a month.'

Sacheverell's head shook inside his fur cape. 'It's not nearly good enough. Nemesis is a moving target.'

By now the desert was black; the sky was dark blue and stars were beginning to appear, unwinking in the steady air. Far below, Base Camp was a tiny oasis of light in the dark. The little car swayed in space as Sacheverell, Webb and Noordhof squeezed in. The cable car lurched and Kowalski ran out of the wheelhouse, jumping in just as the car launched itself into space. He pulled the door shut with a tinny *Clang!* and in a second they were sinking fast.

Sacheverell was looking at the dark cliff drifting past a few yards away. His breath misted in the freezing air. In a tone of exaggerated casualness, he asked: 'About this accident. What happened?'

'It was a lightning strike. The car stopped half-way down with one of our technicians in it, and it was three days before anyone noticed. This was last winter.'

'He survived?'

'Heavens no. We had to thaw the corpse out on a kitchen chair before we could get it in a body bag. You should have heard him cracking.'

A look of pure horror came over Sacheverell's face, and Kowalski grinned. He'd had his revenge.

Eagle Peak, 24^{h}00, Monday

The red door was solid and heavy – or maybe, Webb thought, he was just feeling fragile. It had a small brass label marked 'Conference Room'.

The conference room was brightly lit, like a stage, and measured about twenty feet by twenty. There was a heavy dark blue curtain on the left, a long blackboard on the right, and an old-fashioned circular clock, looking like railway station surplus, on the wall straight ahead. Its hands showed three minutes past midnight. Otherwise every foot of wall in the nerve centre was taken up with desks, computer terminals, printers, scanners and deep bookshelves stuffed with scientific journals, books and gleaming brass instruments from an earlier era.

The centre of the room was taken up with a long pine table, already scattered with papers. There were deep leather armchairs scattered around, their dark blue matching the curtain, and working chairs around the big table, and seven colleagues on these chairs awaiting Webb's dramatic entrance, and vertical, disapproving wrinkles above Noordhof's lips. 'Webb, you're three minutes late. I'll say it again: this isn't some cosy academic conference. If Nemesis is coming in at twenty miles a second, you've just cost us three thousand, six hundred miles of trajectory. Half the diameter of the Earth. The difference between a hit and a miss.'

Webb flopped down at the end of the table. 'I'm feeling

a bit fragile.' The soldier shot Webb a venomous look and then turned to Sacheverell. 'Let's get into this. Herb, what's the state of play in the hazard detection arena?'

Sacheverell leaned back in his chair. 'As you'd expect, the big players are the Americans. We have four main civilian programmes, one in New Mexico, and two right here in Arizona. Lowell Observatory have a point six-metre Schmidt at Flagstaff, just a few mountains to the north of us, and the University of Arizona have Space-watch Two on Kitt Peak, to the south. The fourth American civilian programme is on Maui, one of the Hawaiian Islands: JPL are using a one-metre telescope operated by USAF personnel.'

'Is that it?' Noordhof asked.

'There are photographic programmes but if you don't have a CCD you're not in the game. Put a charge-coupled device at the eyepiece of your telescope and you'll get as much light in two minutes as you would with a two-hour exposure hour on a Kodak plate. In that two minutes Flagstaff can cover ten square degrees of sky down to magnitude twenty. Spacewatch Two covers only one square degree, but it gets down to twenty-one in half the time.'

'Sacheverell has overlooked the rest of the world,' Webb pointed out. 'For example, the Japanese have a private network of amateurs and they've also started with a pair of one-metre class telescopes. The Italians have a small-scale network centred round their instruments in Campo Imperatore, Asiago and Catania. The French and Germans have a one-metre Schmidt on the Côte d'Azur.'

Sacheverell waved his hand dismissively. 'I don't want the survival of America to depend on a bunch of Japanese amateurs. As for the Italians, they're penniless. Half the time their telescopes are lying idle. Flagstaff is detecting thirty Earth-crossers a night over half a kilometre across, the new Spacewatch even more.'

Kowalski said, 'And we have our upstairs telescopes. We operate our Schmidt remotely, as a robotic telescope, from this room. Normally we feed in a pre-selected list of galaxies over there but we could just as easily scan the sky looking for a moving object.'

Noordhof tapped the table. 'Like I said in New York, you people have every conceivable facility at your disposal.'

'You mean GEODSS?' McNally asked, round-eyed. 'The whole system?'

'Ay-firmative.'

Sacheverell nodded his satisfaction. 'Space Command controls a network of one-metre, wide-field satellite trackers. They process about fifty thousand observations a day and keep an orbital update on seven or eight thousand artificial satellites. They have a station on the Flagstaff mesa, next to the Lowell instrument, and they've revamped the old STARFIRE suite at Albuquerque. These are one-metre Schmidts. They've already been using Maui for asteroid hunting. GEODSS is one powerful system.'

Noordhof said, 'And with immediate effect, it's yours.'

'What are their CCD chips like?' Webb asked.

Sacheverell waved sheets of paper. 'While our token Brit is feeling fragile I'm downloading from Albuquerque, with the Colonel's help. They're large format, high quantum efficiency, fast readout. They perform close to the theoretical limit.'

Shafer was scribbling furiously on a yellow notepad. He had dispensed with his ponytail and his long grey hair was swept down over his shoulders. 'What's the sky coverage with these GEODSS telescopes?'

Sacheverell said, 'Two square degree starfields, reaching mag twenty with twenty-second exposures. They don't go as faint as Spacewatch Two but like I say their CCDs have fast readout. They can carry out a saturation search in half the time of Spacewatch. Spacewatch has depth; Albuquerque has breadth.'

Webb said, 'I'm impressed. Herb, impress me even more. Tell us what you've got in the southern hemisphere.'

Sacheverell hesitated. 'Okay, we're weak there.'

'What's your point, Oliver?' Noordhof asked.

'We have almost no coverage of the southern sky. Nemesis could sneak up on us from south of the celestial equator when all our telescopes are scanning the sky to the north. Maui can look south to a limited extent, and the ESO Schmidt in Chile might have picked it up serendipitously if they hadn't shut it down.'

'The British closed down the UK Schmidt in Coonabarabran,' Sacheverell accused Webb, pointing a skinny finger in his direction. 'Why did you guys leave yourselves with no asteroid-hunting capability?'

'The giggle factor. Our MOD thought the impact hazard was a joke.'

'Are you telling me half the sky is uncovered?' Noordhof asked in dismay.

'It's worse than that. I'm thinking of the Atens.'

'Excuse me?'

'I hate to add to our troubles, but there's a blind spot about thirty degrees radius around the sun. Anything could be orbiting inside it. An Aten is an asteroid with an orbit which puts it inside the Earth's orbit, and therefore in the blind spot, most of the time. Only a handful have been discovered but nobody knows how many there really are. Now say the Russians discovered one on a near-Earth orbit.'

Noordhof acquired a thoughtful look. Leclerc had been writing in a little red leather Filofax. He looked up and said, 'The probability that we would independently discover it is remote. It would hide in sunlight until it pounced. An Aten makes a lot of sense as a weapon.'

Webb continued, 'Sacheverell's telescopes are all geared up to search the sky around opposition. They're pointing high in the night sky, far from the sun. But if an Aten is coming at us, it won't be there. It will come at us low in the sky, close to the sun. Most of Herb's telescopes can't even reach that low. If Nemesis is an Aten you might see it before dawn, or just after dusk, a few days before impact. Binoculars would do.'

Noordhof took a cigar from his top pocket. 'I need a consensus on the detection issue. Can you people deliver or not?'

Shafer had finished his scribbling. Now he stood up and moved over to the blackboard. He picked up yellow chalk and started to write in a fast, practised scrawl. 'The way these telescopes are operated, sure there's a strong selection effect acting against the discovery of Atens. But I disagree with Ollie about Atens as weapons. For precision work the Russians would need something they could track for a long time, maybe years, and you can't do that with The Invisible Asteroid. I say Nemesis is reachable with Spacewatch and GEODSS. There are 4π steradians of sky and each steradian is $180/\pi$ degrees on a side. That gives us forty-three thousand square degrees of sky over the whole celestial sphere. How much of that can we cover? For a start these things are faint, which means we have to go deep. But we can only do that in a pitch black sky. Okay so there's no moon this week. But to avoid twilight the sun has to be at least twelve degrees below the horizon, and to avoid atmospheric absorption the sky we're searching has to be at least thirty degrees above it. I reckon we have maybe only five or six thousand searchable square degrees of sky on any one night.'

'Declining to zero if it's cloudy,' Judy Whaler pointed out.

'The five-day local forecast is good,' Kowalski said. 'Except for the last day.'

Shafer continued: 'Okay, from Herb's figures I reckon the whole of the world's asteroid-hunting telescopes will cover no more than two or three hundred square degrees of sky an hour. That means say a month to cover the whole sky once.'

'And we've been given five days,' said Whaler. 'Six to one against.'

'Not even remotely,' Shafer disagreed. 'Look at square A on Monday, and by Murphy's Law Nemesis is in square B. Look in B on Tuesday and it's moved to A or C. Apart from which, most of the time it will be too faint to be seen, because it will be too far away, or hidden in sunlight like Ollie's Atens, or camouflaged against the Milky Way.'

'So how long, Shafer?' Noordhof asked impatiently.

Shafer drew a graph. He measured off tick marks on the axes and labelled the horizontal one 'diameter in km', and the vertical one, 'p % per decade'. Then he drew an S-shaped curve, copying carefully from his paper. Webb saw what the physicist had been calculating and was awestruck at the speed with which he had done it. Shafer tapped at the blackboard. 'Assume Nemesis is a kilometre across, with the reflectivity of charcoal. That gives it absolute magnitude eighteen at one AU from Earth and sun.' He drew a vertical line up from the 1-km tick mark on the x-axis to its point of intersection with the curve, and then moved horizontally across to the vertical axis, where he read off 0.85. 'You want to discover Nemesis with eighty or ninety per cent probability, with all the world's asteroid telescopes going flat out? Assuming it's not an Aten? It will take us ten years.'

'We have five days,' Noordhof reminded Shafer in a flat tone.

'So consult a psychic,' said Shafer, going back to his chair.

The tense silence that followed was broken by the loud crackling of cellophane as Noordhof unwrapped his cigar.

'Willy, I think your calculation is flawed,' Webb said, knowing this was a rash thing to say to the mighty Shafer.

'If it's coming at us in a straight line out of a dark sky then it's already close and bright. We don't have to spend ten years looking.'

The physicist gave Webb a disconcertingly hard look. 'Ollie, if it's close and bright and coming at us in a straight line out of a dark sky, we're about to be history.'

'It's our only chance to find it.'

Sacheverell shook his head sadly. 'It must be the jet lag. Willy has just told us that by the time it's close enough to be found it's too late to be stopped.'

'We can harden up on this.' Webb crossed to an empty bit of blackboard. 'Say Nemesis is going to hit us in thirty days. There are 86,400 seconds in one day. If it's coming in at fifteen kilometres a second then it's only $30 \times 86,400 \times 15=39$ million kilometres away now, a quarter of an AU, which makes it sixteen times brighter than it was at one AU. Herb, what's the brightness of a one-kilometre asteroid at one AU?'

'Eighteen for a carbonaceous surface. Everybody knows that.'

Shafer was tapping at a pocket calculator. He said, 'Inverse square brightness, forget phase angles. Yes, if Nemesis is a month from impact it could have magnitude fifteen. We should be able to pick it up now.'

Webb said, 'Go for sixteen or seventeen visual and we cut the exposure times to seconds. We might even have a continuous scan. We could cover the sky in a week. It's then down to bad luck, like coming at us out of the sun or approaching from the south.'

McNally's slim fingers were agitatedly drumming on the table. 'Can we inject some realism into this? If we're a month from impact what am I supposed to do about it? Call up Superman? I need a year minimum, preferably two or three, to build some hardware.'

'But if Nemesis is a year from impact now, we'll still only detect it in eleven months' time, when it's on the way in. A last-minute deflection is the only scenario you can work on.'

'Let me understand this,' Noordhof said. 'If you guys are right, the chances are hundreds to one against our finding this thing in the next five days. Unless it's so close that it's maybe a month or two from impact. And even then maybe not if it's coming at us out of the sun.'

There was a silent consensus around the table.

'Shit,' Noordhof added, looking worried. He turned to the Director of NASA. 'McNally, you have to come up with a deflection strategy based on the month-from-impact scenario.'

'For Christ's sake, that's just off the wall.' The NASA director's face was flushed.

Firmly: 'You have no choice in the matter.' Noordhof was playing nervously with his unlit cigar. Webb had a momentary vision of Captain Queeg rolling little metal balls in his hand.

'Jim,' Shafer's tone was conciliatory. 'We're the A team. Maybe you and I can come up with something.'

McNally shook his head angrily.

Leclerc asked, to break the tension, 'What would happen if say somebody in Japan found an asteroid?'

'The whole astronomical community would know it within hours,' Sacheverell said. 'Civilian discoveries go straight to the Minor Planet Center which has electronic distribution to all the major observatories. But look, forget Japan, Europe and Atens and crap like that. The action is at Lowell, Spacewatch and Hawaii' – Kowalski winced slightly, but said nothing – 'and we're linked in to these places here. We'll see the exposures build up in real time.'

Webb said, 'Detection isn't enough. If we don't follow it up, we lose it. We have to track it long enough to get a reliable orbit.'

Sacheverell said, 'Follow-up means we come back to it

every few hours, using the interval in between to search for other asteroids. An interval of a few hours gives you its drift against the stars enough to pick it up again the following night. To get a believable orbit, you need to track it for at least a week. To get decent precision, say to launch a probe at it, you have to update over months. There are follow-up telescopes in British Columbia, Oak Ridge Massachusetts and the Czech Republic. Also at Maui.'

Kowalski nodded. 'We're well placed for follow-up here. Our Grubb Parsons has a long focal length and its point spread function is small. On a good night we can do very high-precision astrometry.'

'The Grubb Parsons is vital,' Webb agreed. 'Without it follow-up would double the load on the discovery telescopes.'

Leclerc, pen hovering over his Filofax, asked again: 'Suppose you find an asteroid and follow it up. What then?'

Webb said, 'Nearly every one we find will be harmless. We're looking for a needle in a field of haystacks. Old Spacewatch could pick up six hundred moving objects on a clear winter's night, and overall twenty-five thousand asteroids a year. Out of all that, fewer than twenty-five were Earth-crossers. The rest were main belt. Now with all the new systems combined the detection rates are fifty times higher. But that means we have also fifty times more junk to be sifted through. With the CCD mosaics you people are talking about I reckon we need to interrogate about a billion pixels every ten seconds. We have nothing like enough computing power on site to handle the data.'

Noordhof attempted a smile. 'We have the Intel Teraflop at Sandia. It makes your hair stand on end. That too is yours, a personal gift from a grateful nation.'

Judy said, 'That's Wow, but how do we transfer the

data over? Ordinary cable transmission can't handle the flow.'

'We have satellites that will.'

'In that case,' she replied, 'Problem solved. I'll download the CCD processing software from Spacewatch and transfer it over to our magic machine.'

'We have orbit calculation packages at the Sorel,' Sacheverell said. 'I'll pull them over to your computers. I presume it's all Unix-based?'

Noordhof nodded. 'All communication between here and Albuquerque must be secure. I'll get a key encryption package installed when I'm fixing access to our computers. Judy, work at it through the night. Let's be operational by dark tomorrow. Herb, when can you give me a damage profile for Nemesis?'

'Two or three days, if I can access the Sorel.'

'Have you been listening, Herb? At that rate we might as well wait for the field trial. I want a report over breakfast. O seven hundred sharp, all present, and nobody feeling fragile.'

Webb said, 'We're doing this all wrong.'

Shafer said, 'Oliver, I was joking about a psychic.'

DAY TWO

Eagle Peak, Tuesday Morning

The smell of scrambled eggs and coffee drifted into Webb's room, and sunlight had found weak spots in the heavy curtains' defences. He reached for his watch with an arm made of lead, focused on the little hands, and knew he was in for another of Noordhof's special looks. He rolled on to his stomach and looked longingly at the laptop computer and the crumpled sheets of paper scattered over the floor, which had shared his journey from Glen Etive. But there was no time. He skipped shaving and made it with minus two minutes to spare.

Breakfast things were laid out on the kitchen table and Shafer was dithering around the microwave oven. Judy was in an easy chair; she was into a severe white blouse and black skirt, a plate on her lap, and she was using her sharp, red-painted nails to carefully peel a hard-boiled egg. Sacheverell sat next to her with a plate on his lap. He was also pouring her a coffee and she flashed him a smile. McNally, Leclerc and Kowalski were at the window, sipping coffee and looking out over an expanse of desert from which the occasional tree-covered mountain protruded like an island in the sea.

Noordhof was busy on a croissant. A row of cigars protruded from a shirt pocket. He made a show of looking at his watch as Webb entered.

Webb poured himself coffee from a big percolator, heaped a plate with sausage and scrambled egg, and settled down at the farmhouse table. 'You're giving me a hard stare, Colonel.'

'Please God, deliver this man unto my sergeant,' Noordhof prayed.

A screen on a tripod had been set up and an overhead projector on the end of the kitchen table was throwing white light at it. The soldier nodded to Sacheverell, who had a stubble and looked a bit ragged.

Sacheverell put fork and plate aside, wiped his fingers with a handkerchief, took a pile of transparent overlays to the projector and moved them on and off the machine as he spoke. The first one showed three teddy bears of different sizes, with bubble text coming from the mouth of each, like a comic. One bear was saying 10^4 *Mt*, another 10^5 *Mt* and the third 10^6 *Mt*. 'I examined three scenarios which straddle the likely energy range. I'm calling them Baby Bear, Mummy Bear and Daddy Bear. As you see Baby Bear is ten thousand megatons, Mummy Bear a hundred thousand and Big Daddy is a million.

'First I had a look at Baby Bear, deep ocean impact. I had the idea that maybe the aggressors – the Russians? – might want to take out the UK or Japan while they were about it. Anyway, the Atlantic and the Pacific are big, easy targets. Okay. So half a minute into impact we have a ring of water three or four hundred metres high. Wave amplitude falls as it moves out but you're still looking at a fifteen-metre wave a thousand kilometres from the impact site.'

'In the open sea?' Shafer asked.

'In the open sea. Tsunamis are long-range, because the ocean is a surface and specific energy drops linearly with distance rather than inverse square. An earthquake in Chile in 1960 created ocean waves which travelled over ten thousand miles and killed a lot of people in Japan.'

'What was its wave height?' McNally asked, coming back from the window.

'In the open sea, twenty centimetres. The wavelength is hundreds of kilometres.'

'An eight-inch wave killed people?' McNally asked, bewildered.

Sacheverell winced. 'No. When the wave runs into shallow water the same amount of energy is being carried by less and less water. So when it approaches a shoreline it rears up. The twenty-centimetre wave became a metre or two high. Killed a couple of hundred people, if you count the ones that just went missing.'

'So what's the run-up factor on your fifteen-metre wave, Herb?' Shafer asked.

'Ten to forty, depending on the shoreline. If we say twenty, the wave is three hundred metres high when it hits land, assuming the impact was a thousand kilometres offshore.'

'The height of the Eiffel Tower,' Leclerc said. 'How far inland would a wave like that travel?'

'Again it depends. Topography, roughness of surface. Flat agricultural land would flood for ten or twenty kilometres inland. When I say flood, I mean the wave is still two hundred metres high maybe five kilometres inshore.'

Webb said: 'An Atlantic splash of that order would take out nearly all the major cities in Britain.' Although he was actually trying to visualize a half-mile tsunami roaring up Glen Etive.

'Europe is protected by a steep continental shelf,' Sacheverell informed Webb. 'It reflects about three quarters of the energy back into the ocean.'

'Great,' Webb said. 'Really great. Now I know that when I turn into Piccadilly the wave coming at me is only a hundred metres high.'

Noordhof went to the percolator and came back with a refill. 'And if Baby Bear hits land?'

'Blast, heat and earthquake. The blast is a pressure

pulse followed by a hot wind. The nuclear weapons people use an overpressure of four psi to define total devastation although there's huge damage to buildings even at two. Little Bear would flatten everything within a couple of hundred thousand square kilometres, say an area the size of California.'

'Or Britain,' Webb interrupted, still doing his patriotic bit.

'Who would want to zap your feeble little island?' Sacheverell asked. 'I've taken the threshold for fire ignition to be about a kilowatt applied to a square inch for a second. It turns out you ignite everything flammable within a couple of hundred kilometres. Anyone within four hundred kilometres in the open air would sustain first-degree flash burns.'

'That must depend on whether the asteroid hits the ground or breaks up in the air,' said McNally.

'No. The heat comes from the hot wake trailing the fireball. Lastly, earthquake. I've taken Gutenberg-Richter Nine as defining total devastation, and I've assumed five per cent of the kinetic energy goes into shaking the ground. We're looking at Nine over a region about a thousand kilometres across.'

Noordhof took a sip at his coffee. 'So Baby Bear takes out a few states or floods one of our seaboards. But it doesn't totally destroy the USA and it leaves our nuclear potential intact. So let's turn the screw a bit. Herb, take us to Mummy.'

'Wave height scales as the square root of the impact energy, and the flood plane extends as the four thirds power of the run-up wave. These are approximations. They're beginning to crumble when you get to the really big numbers. Mummy Bear makes an open ocean wave fifty metres high a thousand kilometres away. The run-up factor stays the same so you hit the coast with a wave a kilometre or two high. I guess the Rockies or

Appalachians would protect the central USA. For an Atlantic impact, I don't know how much of Europe would be left.'

Shafer said: 'I guess you would submerge whole countries, like Denmark, Holland and Belgium. And what about Manhattan, Washington, . . .'

Noordhof interrupted: 'Our Kansas silos stay intact.'

Shafer said, 'But you're not expected to shoot back. This is just a great natural disaster, right?'

'And a land impact? Blast, heat, earthquake?' Noordhof's voice had an edge to it.

'The blast only scales as the cube root of the impact energy so Mummy just triples or quadruples the range of Baby Bear. So the blast would just flatten a few states. But now there's something new. The fireball. It rises to the top of the atmosphere and everything along its line of sight burns up. Anything within a circle two thousand kilometres in diameter is fried. It would be even worse but the curvature of the Earth acts as a shield.'

'I don't like the sound of that,' Noordhof said.

'Also Richter Nine now extends coast to coast: as well as burning up, the whole of the States would be levelled by earthquake.'

'You want to tell us about Big Daddy?' Noordhof asked, his voice grim.

'Give me an extra power of ten and I'll shower the States with ballistic ejecta. At the impact site, everything as far as the horizon vaporizes. It gets thrown above the atmosphere, recondenses as sub-millimetre particles at a thousand degrees and falls back over an area equal to the USA. Allowing for heat lost to space etcetera I find that the thermal radiation at the surface is about ten kilowatts per square metre for an hour or more after impact. It's like being inside a domestic oven. Try to breathe and your lungs fry. The whole of the United States turns into one big firestorm. I guess nothing would survive.'

Sacheverell tidied up his papers to show he was finished. There was a thoughtful silence. Webb broke it by saying, 'These computations all have big uncertainties. My reading is you'd have less earthquake and more heat. You'd burn the States even with Mummy Bear. Partly I'm thinking of the Shoemaker-Levy 9 comet fragments which hit Jupiter in 1994. We had a coherent stream of material which gave us twenty impacts on to the planet. The heat flashes from the fallback of ejecta were a hundred times brighter than those from the fireballs themselves.'

Shafer stirred his coffee. 'Big Daddy is good news.' There was an astonished silence. Noordhof's cup stayed poised at his lips.

Webb nodded. 'I believe so, Willy. There are maybe a couple of a million cometary asteroids out there, any one of which could give us a hydrogen-bomb sized impact. They probably happen every century or two. This century we had Tunguska in the Central Siberian Plateau on June 30th 1908. It came in low from the sun at about 7.15 a.m. That was ten to thirty megatons. Hundred megatonners come in every few centuries. They've been recorded as celestial myths in Hesiod's *Theogony* and the like. If you go to a few thousand megatons, you're probably into the Bronze Age destructions: the climate downturn, Shaeffer's mysterious earthquakes in the Near East.'

'What has this guy been smoking?' Sacheverell asked.

'Do you accept your own impact rates? The ones you keep re-publishing?'

'What of it?'

'With a decent chance of a thousand megatonner in the last five thousand years?'

'Sure,' Sacheverell sneered. 'Probably at the north pole.'

'So we had ten megatons in Siberia in 1908, a megaton in the Amazon in 1930, another few megs in British Guyana in 1935, but the five thousand years of civilisation before that were missile-free? And what about

Courty's Syrian excavations showing Bronze Age city destructions caused by blast? And when Revelation talks about a great red dragon in the sky throwing a burning mountain to earth, and the sun and moon darkened by smoke, and the earth ablaze with falling hail and fire, and a smoking abyss, and the same celestial dragon keeps appearing throughout the Near East, in Hesiod in 800 BC, Babylon in 1400 BC and so on, and Zoroaster predicts a comet crashing to Earth and causing huge destruction, this is all poetic invention, drawn from a vacuum, based on no experience? You are aware, Herb, that comets were described as dragons in the past? That a great comet has a red tail? You have actually heard of Encke's Comet and the Taurid Complex?'

Sacheverell's face was a picture of incredulity. 'I can't believe I'm hearing this. You are seriously telling us that responsible policymaking should be based on a Velikovskian interpretation of history? You want to throw in the Biblical Flood? Maybe von Däniken and flying saucers?'

'This is breathtaking,' Webb said. 'We're dealing with a threat to hundreds of millions of lives, and you think you can responsibly ignore evidence of past catastrophe just because you don't have the balls to handle it?'

Sacheverell stabbed a thin finger. His voice was strident and the eyes behind the thick spectacles were angry. 'You want to identify gods with comets and combat myths with impacts? What sort of a scientist do you call yourself? I say you're a charlatan.'

'That's it, Herb, go with the flow like a good little party hack. I say stuff your cultural hang-ups and your intellectual cowardice.'

Judy had frozen, mouth wide open to receive a hard-boiled egg. Shafer was grinning hugely. Noordhof, his face taut with anger, punched a fist on the table. 'Enough! Now get this. I could spend hours listening to you guys at each other's throats. Unfortunately we don't have hours to spend. Now simmer down. Ollie, get to the point. Explain to those of us down here on Earth why Big Daddy is good news.'

Sacheverell sat down heavily, flushed and rattled. Webb said, 'Because we could spend two or three thousand years looking for Herb's Little Bears. Because we have a better chance of detecting Big Daddies further out. And because we can maybe hit a big one harder without breaking it into a swarm.'

Shafer brushed his grey hair back from his shoulders with both hands. 'And because the actuarial odds are that we've been hit by a few Tunguskas and maybe even a Baby Bear or two in the historical past, but civilization survived. The damage is relatively local. If you want to utterly destroy America, you have to go for bodies between half a kilometre and two kilometres across. Too little, and you leave the surviving States with lots of muscle and fighting mad.'

'You guys are wrong,' McNally said. 'We're only fighting mad if we know the impact was an act of war. And like Herb said, we're not supposed to know that. Look, even with the Baby Bear scenario you have an America with half its population wiped out, its industrial base gone, no political infrastructure, probably just chaos and anarchy. This is a gun society. We'd destroy ourselves, finish the job the Russians started. Zhirinovsky could do what he liked, where he liked and we'd be too busy to care.'

Shafer said, 'Jim, you just want a Baby Bear because it's easy to shift.'

Noordhof lowered his head pensively. Then he said, 'I go with McNally. The uncertainties are too large for confident statements about the political intentions of the enemy, whether to incapacitate us or utterly destroy us. We conduct the scope of our search to encompass the full range from Baby Bear to Big Daddy.'

'Forgive me, but that is utterly impractical,' said Kowalski. 'If you want to go down to ten thousand megatons you have to reach extremely faint limiting magnitudes. Which means very long exposures even with quantum-limited CCDs. You could wait a hundred years, as Oliver says. Upstairs, in zero moonlight, we can only go to magnitude twenty-two visual at solar elongations more than seventy-five degrees.'

Shafer said, 'If you're drunk and you lose your keys you look under the street lamp. Not because they're necessarily there, but because that's where you have the best chance of finding them. Meaning, we go for what's practical. Extremely faint magnitudes take too long.'

Webb piled on the pressure. 'You're wrong on this one, Mark. The important thing is to cover the whole sky as fast as possible, and keep covering it until Nemesis swims into the field of view. Let's just hope Nemesis is a big one. That way we have a chance of finding it while it's still far out. And we get maybe months of warning. I say we aim for full sky coverage in a week. We should go for ten-second exposures on Kenneth's supernova hunter, limiting magnitude seventeen.'

Noordhof looked at Sacheverell, who nodded reluctant agreement. The soldier said, 'Okay I guess I've been flamed. Forget the Little Bears. For now.'

Shafer asked, 'Can you fix GEODSS for us, Colonel? Give instructions for a magnitude seventeen search?'

'I'll do better. We'll control the FIRESTAR telescopes remotely from here. We'll use encryption in both directions.'

'We can spread it around,' Shafer suggested. 'Route it through half a dozen sites.'

'Flagstaff and Spacewatch Two have preset sky search regions to avoid overlap,' said Kowalski. 'I'll set up the patrol to do likewise. Christ knows we have plenty of unmapped sky.'

Noordhof took a cigar out of a top pocket and started to unwrap the cellophane. 'Right. We now have an observing strategy. We know what we're facing if we can't find this thing, and we know we're fighting hellish odds. It's a start.' He produced a match, struck it underneath the table, glanced at his watch, lit up and carried on speaking all at once.

'I know we all need a break but time's moving on. So we'll split into teams. Kowalski and I will set up liaison with GEODSS and the other observatories. McNally and Shafer will come up with a deflection strategy. Do it, I don't care how. Webb will tell us why we're going about this the wrong way. Liaise with Leclerc, as he suggests. Sacheverell, you're due to brief the Chiefs of Staff and the President on the impact scenarios later today.'

'*What?*'

Noordhof grinned sadistically. 'What's the beef, Herb? You have five hours and maybe you'll even find time to shave. Prepare something non-technical, maybe a movie. This is your schedule: At thirteen hundred, you're collected upstairs by chopper and transferred to a jet at Kirtland Air Force Base. You arrive Cheyenne Peak at fifteen hundred and brief the brass. They're fixing up a little simulation and want your help. At twenty hundred you sit in on a DCI briefing in Washington and at twenty-one hundred you brief the President.'

Sacheverell, looking stunned, appealed to Judy Whaler. He tried another angelic smile. 'Can you help me? Maybe with some simulations.'

Judy gulped down the last of her boiled egg, gave Noordhof a look of disbelief and said, 'Give me an hour, Herb. I need to talk to Ollie.' Sacheverell scurried out of the room, shoulders hunched, heading either for the conference room or a toilet.

'Please can I have a helicopter too?' Shafer asked.

'Within the hour. Just keep your mouth firmly shut and

that includes chatting to the pilot. And make damn sure you're back here with answers at twenty-one hundred precisely. That applies to all of us.' Webb got a heavy stare.

'I've been going through the kitchen cupboards,' Webb said. 'Kenneth, you're brilliantly stocked with spices.'

Kowalski grinned. 'Doctor Negi is a regular observer here.'

'We have to eat. This evening I'll take an hour and make a curry that will transport us straight to heaven. I didn't mean it that way,' Webb added.

McNally said, 'I don't seem to be getting through to you, Mark. No hardware exists that will enable me to deflect Nemesis a week or a month from today.'

Noordhof blew one of his smoke rings. 'I'll tell you why you're wrong, Jim. Because if you're right, we're dead.'

Judy brushed eggshell from her well-filled blouse. She looked at Webb with wide eyes and said, 'Didn't Herb do well.'

Webb displayed his teeth. The oaf hadn't uttered a single original thought. He'd missed out on nuclear reactors scattered to the winds; catastrophic chemical imbalances in the atmosphere; invisible, scalding steam sweeping over doomed seaboards. He'd missed out on the typhoid and the bubonic plague which would surely sweep through surviving populations, deprived of the most basic amenities. He'd missed out on the fact that the big tsunami would hit again and again as the ocean sloshed, maybe half a dozen times or more over a few hours. Most of all he'd missed out on the cosmic winter: the darkened post-impact sky, below which nothing would grow; the freezing gales which would turn what was left of America into a blasted Siberian wasteland in the weeks following the crash; and the terrifying risk of a climatic instability which would close down the Gulf Stream and switch off the monsoon, bringing calamity far beyond American shores.

On the other hand, Webb thought, quite a few of these things had been missed by others; and he had to admit Sacheverell had done a moderately competent internet search. For an idiot.

And now, Webb thought, everybody knows what to expect and it's simple. There will be little warning. A huge burning mountain will be thrown to earth; it will set the earth ablaze with falling hail and fire; it will darken the sun and moon; and it will plunge us into a smoking abyss.

Vincenzo's Woman

The sky was still dull blue, and a light early morning mist was hugging the Tuscan fields, when the soldiers of Christ came for Vincenzo.

The monk was awakened by a violent shaking of his shoulders. His woman was over him, her grey hair brushing his face and her eyes wide with fear. 'Vincenzo! Robbers!'

He threw back the sheets and ran to the window, pulling open the shutters. Horses were clattering into the courtyard below.

There was a heavy thump from below. It shook the house, and came again. The woman screamed, but the thump-thump continued, and then there was the sound of splintering oak, and running footsteps on the marble stairs. A youth of about sixteen ran into the room. He wore a white jerkin, a white cap and striped black and white tights. He was breathing heavily, had an excited gleam in his eyes, and he was carrying a short, broad-bladed sword. It looked new and unused. He stared at Vincenzo and then turned his eyes to the woman. He seemed uncertain what to do next. He was staring excitedly and kept swinging the sword.

An older man, stocky and bearded, followed him into the room. 'Get dressed!' he ordered Vincenzo, ignoring the woman. More men ran in. They started to haul open drawers and cupboards, flinging clothes on to the floor and overturning chairs and tables which got in the way. Vincenzo's woman threw on a woollen dress, and then grabbed the young man's arm. Flushing with humiliation, he turned to hit her but stopped as a man, dressed in a long dark cloak embroidered with golden crucifixes, stepped into the bedroom.

The man approached the old monk. 'Vincenzo Vincenzi, son of Andrea Vincenzi of Padua, you are under arrest.'

'Why? What have I done?'

'You are being taken to Bologna, where you are to be tried for heresy.'

The woman screamed in fright, and settled down to a torrent of abuse delivered in an increasingly excited voice. The old monk tried to pacify her and finally persuaded a terrified maidservant, peering round the door, to take her down to the kitchen.

The monk had hardly finished buckling his tunic when they bundled him downstairs. An open carriage was waiting. Early morning dew was beginning to steam off the red pantiled roofs where the sunlight touched them. A cluster of servants, some of them half-dressed, gaped from the shadows of a cloister. As the carriage clattered out of the courtyard, Vincenzo looked back and glimpsed a cart into which his notebooks and instruments were being tossed – including his perspective tube which, they were later to say, had been invented by the heretic Galileo if not by Satan himself. Minutes later the soldiers, clearly in a hurry, mounted up and galloped out of the courtyard, the cart rattling noisily over the cobbles.

Vincenzo's mistress had dashed out of a back door from the kitchen just as the soldiers were leaving the front, fleeing along a broad gravel path through a garden scattered with cypress and myrtle trees, statues and tinkling fountains. She ran the two kilometres to her brother's house and arrived in a state of near collapse. Her brother, a prosperous wool merchant, had a stable with half a dozen horses. A servant saddled one up and she set out for Florence, forty kilometres away, trailed by her brother whose horsemanship was constrained by age and gout. Entering the city through the Gate of the Cross, with the exhausted horse slowed to a trot, she headed for the city centre. She used Brunelleschi's cathedral dome and the tall bell-tower of the Old Palace as landmarks to find her way to the *Ponte Vecchio*. Across it, at the Grand Ducal Palace, she dismounted and tied the horse to an iron ring next to a window.

A soldier with a pikestaff, his tunic bearing the fleur-delys of the Medici family, stood at an archway. She approached, almost too breathless to speak. 'I must have an audience with His Highness.'

The soldier stared with astonishment, and then laughed. 'Franco! Come here. Your grandmother wants a word with the Duke. Maybe he didn't settle up last night.' A stout man appeared from within, his mouth stuffed and a thick sandwich in his hand. He took in the work-worn hands, the wrinkled face and the cheap woollen dress at a glance. 'Try the back entrance. He's helping out in the kitchens.'

The woman held her hand to her side in pain. 'Deny me access, with what I have to tell him, and he'll have you disembowelled and tossed in the Arno.'

The sandwich man's amused expression gave way to an angry glare. 'Don't talk to me that way, bitch. Just what do you have to tell him?'

'The words are for His Highness, not his dogs.'

The soldier's expression of anger was replaced by one of fear. 'Franco, is this a witch?'

'Shut your mouth, Steffie. You, wait there.'

'And be quick,' the woman said. 'If you want to keep your fat belly.'

Fifteen minutes passed before a tall, thin man of middle age, dressed in black, appeared at the lodge. She curtsied.

He beckoned, without a word, and she followed him into the interior of the building, through a large courtyard and under another archway; a door was opened and Vincenzo's woman followed him into a small anterooom.

'I am the Altezza's secretary. And you will now explain yourself.'

'Sir, Vincenzo Vincenzi has been taken by soldiers.'

The man sat upright. 'The Altezza's mathematician? What soldiers? When did this happen? And who are you?'

'Sir, I am Vincenzo's woman . . .'

'Ah!' Recognition dawned in the man's eyes. 'Of course, I have seen you in the Poggia. Proceed please.'

'It happened an hour, two hours ago, at dawn. The soldiers came. They took Vincenzo and all his books and charts, and his instruments.'

'These soldiers. Describe them.'

'What can I say? They all wore white tunics and caps, and—'

'Soldiers? So far you have described strolling players. Their weapons?'

'Pikestaffs, daggers, arquebuses.'

'Common bandits. If they think they can demand ransom from His Excellency . . .'

'I thought so at first. But then their leader said that Vincenzo was being taken to Bologna to face trial for heresy.'

The man stood up, staring at the woman in astonishment. 'Impossible!' he said to himself. Then: 'Wait here.'

Minutes later Vincenzo's woman was standing outside a door. The secretary turned. 'You will curtsy on introduction and dismissal. Address the Grand Duke as Altezza or Serenissimo, and speak only when spoken to. Now, compose yourself.'

Through the door, along a high-ceilinged room and on to a broad verandah where a man and woman sat at a breakfast table with milk, bread, and a bowl of apricots and apples. Servants hovered around, one of them holding a baby. The man was about thirty. He had a bulbous nose, a thick, turned-up moustache and bags under his eyes. The woman was fat and double-chinned, and stared at Vincenzo's woman with open disdain. The man waved Vincenzo's woman over. Awestruck but determined, she forgot to curtsy and without invitation launched into the tale of the abduction. The man showed little emotion other than a raising of his heavy eyelids, and waited patiently until she had finished.

'You have done well to inform me so quickly. Enzo, see that she has a ducat or two.'

'Highness, I need only the return of my Vincenzo.'

'At least you will accept an escort back to the villa. And my household will repair the damage these men have done.'

The woman gone, the Grand Duke threw a napkin angrily on to the table. 'Barberini?' he asked.

The secretary nodded. 'Who else?'

The Grand Duke snapped a finger at a trembling servant. 'Get that fat pig Aldo out of his bed.'

The fat pig appeared in a minute, his white hair dishevelled, pulling an indigo-dyed cloak over his red tunic.

'Sit down, Aldo. And use that contorted mind of yours to tell me what game His Holiness is playing.'

'Your Grace, this is an outrage.'

'Do you refer to the abduction of a scholar under my sanctuary, or to the fact that you have been roused from your licentious bed?'

'Sire, the law is clear on this matter. The Holy Office is not free to arrest a heretic outside the papal states without the permission of the secular authorities, who in this case are embodied in the person of Your Grace. This need for permission is particularly so if extradition is involved. This arrest is a gross violation of accepted procedure and an unlawful intrusion on your authority and property. An insult compounded by the fact that this Vincenzo is under Your Grace's patronage and protection.'

'I have not yet had an answer to my question: what game is Prince Maffeo Barberini playing?'

Aldo continued. 'I can think of only one reason.' He paused.

'Well?'

'The one actually given. The Church does not tolerate heresy.'

The secretary butted in: 'Serenissimo, it is a warning. If I may speak frankly?'

The Duke nodded, but his expression warned against too much frankness.

'I too have warned you,' the secretary said. 'Your patronage of the arts and music is renowned, and it gives many of us joy to see you continue in the great tradition of your family back to Lorenzo. To praise man is to praise his Creator. But this Vincenzo? He is suspected of magic and worse. And Your Grace – forgive me – I have often suggested that you are too tolerant towards Jews and visiting foreigners. There are more Jews in Livorno than any other city in Italy. And many of the foreigners are suspected of being Lutherans.' The secretary hesitated, wondering if he had already gone too far, but the Duke, peeling an apple, encouraged him with a gesture.

'Worst of all, sire, is the clandestine book trade. You allow it to flourish. In the past year, in the streets of Pisa, Lucca and Pistoia, I could have bought prohibited books by arch-heretics like Melanchthon, Bullinger, Brenz and Bucer. I have even seen, with my own eyes, peddlers selling Calvin's *Institutes*, Castellio's *De Haereticis*, and Luther's *Small Catechism* in streets not a stone's throw from the Duomo. These godless men bring them down over the Alps from the Reformationist printing presses in Geneva and Basel. The abduction of Vincenzo is a warning, sire.'

The Grand Duke stood up and approached to within a foot of his secretary. He was plainly angry, but his voice was controlled. 'My dear Enzo, in promising religious toleration I merely continue the tradition set by my grandfather. Through it Florence has flourished; Livorno is a jewel in the Medici crown. And must I remind you that my own father invited Galileo to Florence where he spent the last years of his life. Am I to be denied the same? And why have they taken Vincenzo's works? To be burned? Will they never be added to the great Library which Gian Carlo, Leopoldo and I have devoted our lives to creating? And are we to stand here discussing my political philosophy while horsemen ride off with a scholar to whom I have offered patronage and sanctuary?'

The secretary bowed. 'So, Altezza. Let us intercept Barberini's mercenaries before they reach Bologna, and hang them at the roadside.'

The Grand Duke turned to Aldo. 'Aldo, you are chewing your lip.'

'I expect they are taking him to Rome: why else say Bologna for all to hear? But that is not why I chew my lips. Your Grace, we must be careful here.' Aldo paused, as if gathering his thoughts.

'Note our magnificent patience, Aldo, while we await your words of wisdom and the horsemen flee with my scholar.'

'The Church sees erosion. Erosion of faith. It is being questioned not only by the northern Lutherans but right here in her midst, by men who look at the sky. She has already pronounced on the Copernican heresy. Only last year, when Galileo died, a heretic patronized by your father, the Church forbade you to erect any monument in his memory.'

'Nor did I.'

'Indeed. But what did Your Grace do instead? Buried the heretic's remains in the Novice's Chapel at Santa

Croce. It is dangerous to provoke a wounded animal.'

'The man who discovered the small bodies which orbit Jupiter, and named them the Medicean planets, deserves honour in return. And the Pope is the lawbreaker here,' the Grand Duke pointed out. 'In any case, what can he do?'

'He could induce his unruly relatives to go to war with you . . .'

'—God preserve me from these Barberinis . . .'

'. . . and he could excommunicate you. In that eventuality the citizens of Florence are also bound to be excommunicated unless they remove you from office. Without pardon for their sins, they risk an eternity of damnation. It could create a dangerous situation for the House of Medici.'

The secretary concurred. 'Some day this city will sink under the weight of its sin.'

'So. I allow Barberini to tweak my nose? My legal authority to be flouted?'

Aldo said, 'Better than blood in the streets, Altezza.' He added slyly: 'And His Holiness will not live forever.'

'Aldo, you have the mind of a poisoner. I do not wish to hear more.' The Grand Duke paced up and down in thought. Then he turned to his secretary. 'Go to Rome. Ask His Holiness to bless me. Wish him a long and happy life. Aldo is right, as always. I do not seek trouble with the Holy Office. But do what you can for Vincenzo. I do not want him to burn.'

The secretary bowed and turned to leave. The Grand Duke called after him. 'Enzo, I do want the return of Vincenzo's works. Some day they must take their place in the Palatina.'

'And if the cost of saving Vincenzo is a quarrel with the Holy Office?'

The Duke sighed. 'Do not bring me back a quarrel, Enzo.'

Piñon Mesa

Noordhof, sensing an atmosphere, said, 'Okay you people, take a short breather. Then break into our agreed teams. Reconvene here at sixteen hundred.'

Webb and Whaler noisily transferred dishes to a dishwasher. Sacheverell came back from the toilet. He jacked up a radiant smile. 'Hey, Miss Nukey, how about some ping-pong?'

Webb experienced a moment of pure distilled hatred. Judy, however, just shook her head politely. Sacheverell shrugged, and shortly he and McNally were thrashing a ping-pong ball in the common room. Shafer had put some frozen packet into the microwave oven and was watching it intently. Noordhof and Kowalski went into an intense discussion over more coffee.

Webb interrupted them. 'Colonel, I have a friend, Scott McDonald, with a robotic Schmidt on Tenerife. I could operate it from here.'

Noordhof's eyes showed surprise. 'You don't say?'

'I didn't know it was operational,' Kowalski said.

'It isn't. It's still being commissioned, which means there's no pressure of time on it. It should be free over Christmas. I can link in to Scott's Oxford terminal, with his permission, and control it from here.'

'I'll think about it, Oliver.'

It was Webb's turn to show surprise. 'What's to think about? We need all the eyes we can get on the sky. With a

83

nine-hour time difference we can seriously extend the night sky coverage.'

'There are security considerations.'

'Mark, let's not get too paranoid. Operating a telescope remotely is what you're supposed to do with a remote telescope. The control signals will route through Oxford.'

'I said I'd think about it.'

Webb sighed. 'It's your country.' He retreated to his room, had a quick shower and then rummaged in the dormitory cupboard. There was a heavy Shetland wool pullover, left by some visiting observer. Red and yellow lightning stripes weren't his fashion statement but it was warm.

'Oliver.' Leclerc startled him. The Frenchman was looking worried. He spoke quietly, almost conspiratorially. 'Oliver, we have to talk.'

'Sure.' Webb took him into his room and closed the door firmly.

Leclerc looked at Webb uncertainly. 'Oliver, there is something very strange going on here.'

My opinion exactly, Webb was tempted to say, but instead waited for him to continue. But Leclerc was judging his man, clearly in an agony of doubt as to how far he could trust Webb.

A brisk knock at the door. 'Join me in a run, Oliver? Or are you still feeling fragile?' Judy, bouncing up and down outside Webb's door.

'One minute!' he called out, and there was the sound of retreating footsteps.

'We'll talk later,' Webb said quietly.

'We must. But only you and me. Nobody else.'

Judy, in a grey tracksuit, jumped up and down outside the building, waiting for her colleagues. Webb emerged. She beckoned him over, taking advantage of their eye contact to assess him with a swift female intuition. His muscular frame and untidy, curly brown hair gave the impression of an outdoor type rather than the quiet academic he clearly was; subtle lines around his jaw suggested a determined streak, and around his blue eyes an unusual intelligence; but at the same time there was a sort of naivety about him. She sensed that he could be humorous, but that he was also shy, even awkward in company. It made for an interesting and unusual colleague.

Webb trotted over to Judy, stretching in the crisp fresh air and the sunlight.

'This is a working run, right?' Webb said.

'Absolutely!' Judy exclaimed, jumping. 'We need it to clear the cobwebs.'

Leclerc appeared a minute later, taking no chances: he was wearing last night's Eskimo suit. Parisian elegance peeked defiantly over the fur-lined collar in the form of a spotted red bow tie. Webb had never before seen a jogger in a bow tie; unaccountably, the minor eccentricity put Leclerc up in Webb's estimation.

'*Wagons Ho!*' she called out. They took off on a slow trot down the road.

She smiled broadly at Webb. 'That was fun. What gives with Sacheverell and you?'

'Herb is a mafia hit man. He's a bully, a megaphone, a weather vane, a party apparatchik of the lowest order . . .'

'But Oliver,' Judy laughed, 'He's our top man in the field.'

'Sure, if you measure scientific excellence by media coverage.'

Leclerc was taking it wide at the hairpin bend, puffing. 'Why the seething hatred, Oliver? Academic rivalry? Or did he reject some paper?'

Judy was beginning to speed up. Webb let her get ahead. 'Not at all, it's because I care about truth. Herb rewrites history in a way that would make Stalin blush. He rigs conferences, stuffs his own people on committees, manipulates opinion . . .'

'Ah, now we're getting to it,' suggested Leclerc. 'He succeeds where you have failed to communicate your . . .'

'. . . but his scientific talent is minimal. He's never had an original thought in his life. He's put the field back a decade.'

'Oliver,' Judy called over her shoulder, 'we don't need stunning new insights for this one. An identification will do.'

'Herb will try to take over this show and if he succeeds we'll screw up.'

Judy was now loping. In spite of her shorter legs Webb, beginning to pant, was having difficulty keeping up. Leclerc was beginning to trail. 'I think you just like a good fight.'

'My dear Doctor Whaler, you malign me. I'm a quiet academic taken away under protest from an important piece of research.'

'More important than the planet?'

'So, they kidnapped you too, Oliver?' Leclerc asked, catching up with an effort.

'It was more like an offer I couldn't refuse. What about you, Judy? Don't they abduct people in flying saucers in this neck of the woods?'

'No abduction. I just drove here from Albuquerque. The Pontiac is mine.'

'Oliver, how many objects are we dealing with out there?' Leclerc was red-faced.

'The known Earth-crossers? About five hundred. And Spacewatch are finding new ones at the rate of two or three a night.'

'I didn't know interplanetary space is so crowded. I'm surprised life on Earth has survived.'

'It nearly hasn't. It was almost wiped out at the Permo-Triassic. Big Daddy's a mouse compared with some of the stuff out there. Hephaistos and Sisyphus are ten kilometres across. They'd yield a hundred million megatons. But it's not a simple impact thing.'

Judy was now well ahead. The men were gasping. 'Bear track!' she called over her shoulder, and the men followed her off the road on to a narrow path through the trees.

'Not a simple impact, Ollie. Meaning?' The ground under the snow was a soft carpet of pine needles. They had adopted a loping motion and were descending at a fair pace, but it did leave Webb wondering about the return trip.

'Chances are the big ones come in as part of a swarm.' Webb was weaving through low, snow-covered branches. 'It's more in the nature of a bombardment episode, with supercomets disintegrating to dust and choking off sunlight for thousands of years at a time. We think the planetary system is surrounded by a huge cloud of comets, reaching nearly to the stars. The whole solar system, comet cloud included, orbits the Galaxy in a two hundred million year cycle. But as it goes round and round it also goes up and down like a carousel. So, we go up and down through the plane of the Galaxy. Every twenty-seven million years we hit the Galactic disc.'

'Which disc we see as the Milky Way,' Judy said, scarcely out of breath.

'I saw it last night. From here it's brilliant. Anyway, because the Galactic disc has a concentration of stars and massive nebulae, every twenty-seven million years when we go through it we get gravitational tides which perturb the comet cloud. The comets are thrown out of their old orbits, they come flooding into the planetary system, the Earth gets bombarded and we have great mass extinctions. Therefore life goes in twenty-seven-million-year cycles. Old life is swept away to make way for the new.'

'Not so fast!' Leclerc shouted. They stopped. Leclerc leaned forward, resting his hands on his knees and taking big gulps of breath. Webb looked up. The observatory was out of sight. Their voices were muffled in the snowy woods.

'*Alors!* All those years you mock the astrologers, and now you tell us our fate does lie in the stars. Where are we now, Oliver, in this great cycle?'

'We're slap bang in the disc now, and we're due for another mass extinction.'

'This Galactic connection,' Judy mused. 'Is it relevant to Nemesis?'

'Could be. Some of the Earth-crossers are just strays from the asteroid belt. Herb will tell you they all are, but there are also serious people who think that. However I reckon that, because we're at a peak of the extinction cycle, maybe half are degassed comets. A comet comes sunwards and grows a nice tail so you can see it from a hundred million miles away. But after a time so much dust from its tail has fallen back on to the nucleus that it chokes off. The comet becomes blacker than soot and almost undetectable. It becomes a soft-centred asteroid.'

'I see the relevance,' said Judy, panting a little. 'If it's a main belt stray it's a cannonball. If it's a degassed comet it's a snowball disguised as a cannonball. Get it wrong when you try to deflect it and we have ourselves a nice little mass extinction. If we have no time to drill holes in Nemesis, the big picture becomes part of the equation. Up or down?'

Leclerc pointed downhill, and they set off again, Judy still leading. After five minutes the snow began to thin and the Ponderosa pines were giving way to scrub oak, through which they caught glimpses of sunlit Arizona desert in the far distance.

'Oliver, how should we be short-listing for Nemesis?' Leclerc asked.

'Whatever asteroid the Russians used, it had to be reachable. What could they reach, André?'

'For deep space missions the Russians launch from

Earth orbits two hundred kilometres high. Even with Proton boosters, their cosmonauts could not rendezvous with and return from any asteroid with an interception speed of more than' – Judy was leaping over a fallen tree, light as a gazelle '—say six kilometres a second.' The men took it together like a couple of Heavy Brigade chargers.

'That means we're looking for asteroids in Earth-like orbits, that's to say low eccentricities, low inclinations and semi-major axes close to the Earth–Sun distance. There are at least half a dozen Nemesis-class asteroids which interweave with the Earth's orbit. They have plenty of launch windows with δV in the range four to six kilometres a second, round trip times three months to a couple of years.'

'In energy terms they are surely easier to reach than the Moon,' Leclerc suggested.

'Much. The Japanese have already rendezvoused with Nereus. You know, we could check out the orbits of these in short order.'

'Maybe the cosmonauts weren't bothered about returning,' Judy called back.

That hadn't occurred to Webb. 'A suicide mission?'

'Why not? Save on re-entry fuel, put it into reaching a more distant asteroid. Would you die for your country, Ollie?'

'My love of country is undying. André, say Judy is right. What δV will you give me?'

Leclerc exhaled, 'For a one-way ticket? We must relax the criteria to twelve kilometres a second.'

'That means they could have reached anything in the inner planetary system.'

'*Merde!*' They pounded on down, exhaled breaths steaming.

'There's another tack,' Webb said. 'Very few kilometre-sized asteroids *could* be diverted on to us. It has to be a near-misser, a potentially hazardous asteroid that already passes within maybe 0.01 AU of the Earth.'

'So what does that do to your list?' Judy asked. They were now half loping, half scrambling down the steep mountainside at speed; by unspoken consent they had abandoned thought of the return climb.

'Depends how big a punch the Russians could deliver and how long a start they had. If they had summoned up a hundred-megaton punch say five years ago they could have gone for quite a few hazardous objects in the kilometre class. Midas has a minimum possible encounter distance of zero, Hermes has 0.003 AU if we ever find it again, Asclepius has 0.004 AU, and so on. I'll have to check but most of these turkeys will be out of it. Their orbits intersect ours but when we cross the intersection point we're well clear.'

'Like two trains going round intersecting tracks, Oliver,' suggested Leclerc, puffing. 'You only have a collision when they reach the point of intersection at the same time.'

They slowed; Judy went down on her backside, and edged down some scree. Webb said, 'What you and I ought to do, André, is match past Russian interplanetary probes to asteroids along their track. The further in the past they deflected it, the bigger the shift they could have achieved by now.'

'Good, Oliver. You draw up a hit list of near-missers and I will see whether any of the Phobos and Venera series could have passed close to them, maybe even with a side probe fired off.'

Now they were off the scree and running together down lightly wooded hillside. Inside his Eskimo suit, Leclerc was sweating, red-faced.

'Even a fast flyby,' Judy suggested. 'Our kamikaze cosmonauts could have—' she raised her hand and they stopped, almost cannoning into each other. 'Did you hear that?'

Webb strained his ears.

'Gunfire,' Leclerc said, and sure enough there was a crackle of shooting down and to their right. It seemed as if several weapons were being fired.

'Hunters?' Leclerc wondered, gasping for breath.

'The survivalists,' Webb suggested. 'How far have we come?'

'We must have dropped a couple of thousand feet.' Suddenly, even after their exertions, the woods seemed chilly.

'Maybe we should cut off to the left and find the road,' Judy proposed.

'Let's take five minutes,' Webb said, glancing in alarm at Leclerc's beetroot face. They sat down on the pine needle carpet and, joy of joys, Judy produced a large bar of chocolate. The gunfire had stopped. They munched quietly for a while, a little uneasy. Leclerc got up and strolled in the direction the gunfire had been. He vanished into the gloom of the woods.

A couple of minutes later Whaler and Webb were relieved to see him strolling back.

'See anything?' Webb asked.

Leclerc gave a Gallic shrug before flopping down again. 'I am not sure. Perhaps some animal.'

'Let's get out of here,' Judy suggested.

They stood up. 'What about this Midas?' Leclerc asked, Webb suspected to make conversation. The Frenchman glanced nervously back in the direction he had come.

'I doubt if it will be on the final list. A bit of supercomet, very fast-moving and therefore unreachable. No probe could catch it.'

'And Hermes?'

'It's lost, like us,' Webb replied.

'Somebody knows where we are,' Judy said looking into the trees on the route they had just come down. A man of about twenty, wearing khaki and green battledress and carrying a long-barrelled rifle with a telescopic sight, emerged from the shadows. A country boy, overweight but with an abnormally thin face smeared with black. The dark eyes in the face were set close together. Webb recognized the eyes as he approached. They were xenophobic eyes, intolerant eyes; they were eyes filled with ignorance and suspicion and the superstition of centuries.

'Mo'nin'. You folks from the Fed'ral Gov'ment?' Spoken through tight, disapproving lips.

'No, we're just visiting,' Webb said, slipping into an exaggerated Oxford accent. Leclerc would lay on the Parisian and Judy would keep her mouth shut.

'But y'all from up top, right?'

'The observatory, yes.'

The man contemplated that, his close-set eyes flickering from Webb to Judy to Leclerc and then back to Judy. He rested his rifle on his forearm.

'One thang I kin shorely tail is y'all ferners.' He paused, his face expressionless. 'Y'ain't bin spyin' on us, have you now?'

The Barringer Crater, Northern Arizona

The man stood in shadow, on the floor of the giant bowl, shivering in the cold desert air. Six hundred feet above him, sunlight was illuminating a thin strip of clifftop and creeping down the rock face. He willed it to go faster, but the laws of celestial mechanics remained unmoved. A green lizard looked at him from an eye at the side of its head, and then scurried along an abandoned girder where men long dead had once tried to reach down to the nickel-iron meteorite they had believed to be buried far under the ground. The chopping sound of the helicopter high above faded as the small, bright blue machine disappeared over the rim of mountain.

The man turned to his companion. 'Are there snakes here, Willy? I hate snakes.'

'Welcome to the Barringer crater, Jim,' said Shafer. 'Ever been here?'

McNally looked around at the bowl surrounding them. 'Seen pictures of it. Please say there are no snakes here.'

'Snakes are not an issue here, Jim. Not like they are in New York, where they smoke crack and carry guns.'

McNally looked relieved. 'I believe you, my feel-good index has just gone up.'

'Now the scorpions, that's another matter.'

'Thanks a million. Why are we here, Willy?'

'I thought a big hole in the ground might lend a little spice to our deliberations. Anyway, genius makes its own rules. We're a small club, the rest of you can only look on and wonder. Let's do the tour.'

McNally turned slowly like a lighthouse, gazing at the circular wall of rock which rose six hundred feet above him on all sides. Then he set out after the physicist, making for the base of the wall a few hundred yards away.

'Some impact,' McNally said.

'A penny firecracker,' said Shafer. 'A few megatons about forty thousand years ago. There may have been people around.'

'So where are we at, Willy? Do we smash it to rubble with H-bombs?' McNally asked.

'Where did you get that from, Jim, your Los Alamos Workshop or a bad movie? Say you tried that and you ended up with a thousand fragments. Each one maybe a hundred yards across and coming in at maybe seventy or eighty thousand miles an hour. The bits would drift apart slowly but they'd keep close to the old trajectory. By the time they reach us they'd come in as a spray, countrywide. Instead of a rifle bullet you get buckshot, coming in over a few hours. So you don't get a million megaton shot, you get a thousand impacts instead, each one with fifty thousand times the energy of the Hiroshima bomb. Ungood.'

'I'm still trying to get a handle on this,' McNally admitted.

'Think of America on the receiving end of a nuclear attack. Then multiply by fifty.'

'So let's take it a stage further, literally pulverize it. Could it be done?'

Shafer started to scramble up the steeply sloping inner wall. 'Depends who you listen to,' he called down. 'One school of thought says the Earthcrossers are just dried-out comets, maybe even just dust balls. In that case, maybe you could. That's the Webb line. Sacheverell thinks otherwise. He says they're strays from the main belt asteroids between Mars and Jupiter. In that case they could be rock or iron and no way could we deliver the energy to smash one up into dust.'

'What's your view?' McNally asked.

'There was this Crusader,' said Shafer, sitting down. 'He wants to show off his strength to a Saracen. So he gets this iron bar and swipes it with his two-handed sword, and the iron bar breaks in two, and he says beat that if you can. So the Saracen gets a silk handkerchief and he throws it up in the air. He holds the blade of his scimitar upwards, and when the handkerchief floats down over the blade it splits in two.'

'That is very poetic, Willy. I like poetic stuff, I didn't know you were a poet as well as a genius. Maybe if I had a Nobel prize too and a head full of parables I would get your drift, but you see just being an ordinary Joe with an ordinary-sized hat who's frantically trying to save his country, the significance of this poetic story passes me by.'

Shafer grinned and threw a fist sized stone playfully down at the NASA administrator. 'That comes from running big bureaucracies. Loosen up, Jim, think lateral. So if the asteroid is rocky, when it comes in it hits us like a two-handed sword and we're blasted to hell. If it's a dust ball, and we turn it into a powder with bombs, the dust floats gently down like a Saracen's handkerchief and cuts off our sunlight. We could end up with a few billion tons of dust dumped into the stratosphere. If it's sub-micron, like condensation from vaporized rock, it blocks out sunlight and we go around in deep gloom. It takes a year for dust to settle out and meantime we've killed off commercial agriculture. So our food chain collapses. Experience shows that people without food eventually die. That's your Saracen option, Jim.'

'If I could corner the market in canned beans . . . is that lateral enough?'

Shafer clambered down and the two men began a circuit

of the Barringer crater. 'Forget about pulverizing Nemesis,' said the physicist. 'The only way we can handle this is to knock Nemesis off course the same way it was knocked on. We need a controlled explosion.'

'You mean use the debris from the explosion like a rocket exhaust?'

'You got it.'

'How much would we need?'

Shafer glanced at his watch. 'I'll be showing some calculations. If we had ten years' advance warning, we'd only need to shift Nemesis by a centimetre a second, about the speed of a fast snail. The long-term orbital drift does the rest.'

'Snail's pace,' repeated McNally. 'I like snails, right from the time I was a boy I liked them. My feel-good index has just jumped again. Tell me what you need from NASA. Maybe we could just smash a heavy spaceship into it.'

'Depends how big Nemesis is. I think we have to assume a one-kilometre asteroid, enough to take out the States comfortably. In that case you could do it with a three hundred ton spaceship. It would be a kamikaze mission, crashing into the asteroid at twenty kilometres a second.'

'Three hundred tons!' McNally exclaimed. 'NASA doesn't run to the Starship *Enterprise*, Willy. And we don't have ten years, right? Say we reach Nemesis a couple of months before it's due to hit us.'

'Then you have to shift it at a brisk walking speed.'

'What would that take?' McNally asked.

'Forget kamikaze. Hitting it with the Starship *Enterprise* fails by a large margin. We'd need to eject billions of tons of asteroid. For medium-strength rock or hard ice, we'd need maybe ten million tons of high explosive.'

'Or its nuclear equivalent. Ten megaton bombs surely exist. So we bury one at some optimum depth . . .'

'There you go again, Jim, getting your ideas from old movies. Truckloads of mining gear, diesel engines running on oxygen, engineers holding on to a spinning asteroid like the Keystone Kops. No, on any timescale likely to be available to us, burial is not a practical option. We'll have to be guided by Judy on what a surface burst can achieve. And we still need to know what the asteroid is made of. Say it had the strength of cigarette ash? You're back to the Saracen option.'

'So test it on the hoof. Zap it with a laser as we approach and get the composition from the spectrum of the vapour, like the Russians did with the Martian satellites. Then use an on-board computer to work out your bomb-placing strategy as you close.'

The physicist shook his head doubtfully. 'Even with a nanosecond-pulse laser you'd be lucky to vaporize anything at over a hundred kilometres' range. That gives your spacecraft maybe three seconds to analyse the spectrum of the vapour, work out the size and composition of the asteroid, calculate the optimal position for the bomb and then actually get itself into a corrected position which might be miles away. Forget it. We need to land on the thing.'

Sunlight was now halfway down the crater wall and a light dew was steaming off, but down at the floor, the bowl was still in shadow and the desert air was freezing. McNally was beginning to feel a sense of oppression, as if the walls were closing in on him.

'How can we?' asked the NASA Director. 'You're telling me Nemesis might be approaching at twenty kilometres a second. We have no launch vehicles which could get out there fast and then slow down to match an approach speed like that.'

'In which case America is about to be exterminated.'

'Damn you Willy, I have six grandchildren.'

'I'm just as fond of my dog.'

They paced on in silence. After some minutes Shafer said: 'What about your big heavyweight, the Saturn Five? As I recall it could just about match the Soviets in booster power. I know you phased it out when the Shuttle came on line, but you must still have the blueprints and the launch infrastructure.'

McNally pulled the collar of his jacket up around his neck. 'Sure. The blueprints are on microfilm at Marshall, and Federal Archives in East Point hold three thousand cubic feet of old Saturn documents. And sure, the old launch pads were converted for Shuttle use, but we might convert one back again with a little help from Superman. But Willy, where do we find firms to supply sixties vintage hardware? It would take so long to redesign for modern hardware and modify a pad, we'd be as well starting from scratch with a clean sheet design. You're talking years.'

Shafer kicked thoughtfully at a stone. 'By which time we're dead.'

'Willy, there are two ways we can approach this. With an unmanned module, or a manned one.' Shafer nodded encouragement, and the NASA Chief continued: 'We could build fast from an existing manned module design, or even revamp one from the Smithsonian Aerospace, and get it aloft on a Saturn/Centaur combination.'

'How long?'

McNally pondered. 'The moon landings were a child's game by comparison. The Phase A study alone would take nine months in normal circumstances. I might cut that to three or four. Acquisition planning a month, systems engineering and testing another year. Life support systems are a lot of sweat. Absolute minimum a year to launch.'

'By which time we're dead,' Shafer repeated. They walked on. The silence in the big bowl was becoming tomblike.

'A shuttle carries people,' said Shafer. 'Stuff its cargo bay with fuel. Once the astronauts are in low Earth orbit they could blast themselves into interplanetary space.'

McNally shook his head. 'The Mark Three can lift eighty tons of payload into a low orbit. Even if that was pure fuel it still wouldn't be enough. Look, Willy, ideas for boosting the lift capability of the baseline shuttle are coming out of NASA's ears. Liquid boosters, carrier pods under the external tank, carrier pods above it, extra side-mounts etcetera. They all need more time than we've got.'

Shafer persisted; his voice was beginning to acquire an anxious edge: 'Half a dozen shuttle launches, each time with a booster tank in the cargo hold. Fix it so the crews can take the boosters and join them on to a single shuttle like Lego. Skip the test phase' – McNally's eyes widened with disbelief – 'that way you use off-the-shelf systems all the way and all you need is a plumber.'

They were halfway round the circumference. Another lizard scurried away from them, its reptilian legs a blur of speed. McNally threw a stone after it and missed. 'I'm sorry, Willy, but you're now into fantasy.'

The familiar egg-beater sound began to echo off the crater walls as the helicopter appeared, and sank down towards them. McNally waved it away with a grand sweep of the arm, and it tilted alarmingly before veering out of sight. The sunlight had almost reached the floor of the crater.

Suddenly McNally froze. He raised a hand to silence Shafer, an unformulated thought just out of reach. Then he nodded his head, and he said, 'I have a very bad idea.'

'Let's hear it,' Shafer encouraged him.

'The Europeans have a comet soft lander. It's called the Vesta. It could reach the asteroid.'

Shafer stopped. 'That's a bad idea?'

'ESA killed it. It was a Horizon 2000 Cornerstone some years back, but they resuscitated it after the Rosetta fiasco. The project's well along and we're lending them our telemetry systems. Trouble is, their Ariane Five isn't powerful enough for a soft land.'

'Oh no,' said Shafer.

'Oh yeah. ESA are shipping Vesta to Byurkan. The Russians are launching it for them with a Proton booster.' McNally narrowed his eyes. 'They're building Vesta at Matra Espace in Toulouse. If we could somehow get our hands on it, without arousing suspicion, we might lift it with a Saturn–Centaur combination.'

'I agree,' said Shafer excitedly. 'It's a terrible idea. A new procurement policy for NASA. Theft.'

'My career would be ruined. I might have to commit suicide,' said McNally happily, his eyes gleaming.

Shafer stopped and let McNally walk on. The NASA Chief Administrator paced slowly up and down for some minutes, muttering eccentrically to himself. He came back, his eyes narrowed. 'Willy, we could bring a bomb up on a Shuttle to save payload on the Saturn. The crew would rendezvous with Vesta two hundred miles up and transfer the bomb over before the space-craft goes hyperbolic. Goddard and JPL could handle the trajectory planning if we ever find Nemesis. Law-rence Livermore have experience with mission sensors and the bomb. I could get the Naval Research Lab to look at the overall mission design. We have our Deep Space Network . . .'

'Don't use it,' Shafer said sharply. 'The Russians would pick up the ionospheric backscatter. Once this thing leaves the ground it's on its own.'

'Where am dat chopper?' McNally started to perform a sort of war dance, whooping and staring up at the crater rim. 'If it gets me to Phoenix I could connect with New York this afternoon and then a Concorde to Paris . . .'

'Hey, Jim, calm down. Even if you reached Nemesis you wouldn't know what to do with it. And something else.

Try to acquire Vesta from the Europeans and the Russians will realize we're on to them. If you're seen within five hundred miles of Toulouse you'll trigger a nuclear strike. I'm sorry, Jim, and I'm sorry about your grandchildren, but we're screwed up before we start.'

Eagle Peak, Tuesday, Late Afternoon

'Let me get this straight,' Noordhof said. 'First, the West's finest brains have so far failed to come up with a strategy to find Nemesis in any reasonable timeframe. Second, even if you do find Nemesis, you have come up with no practical means of delivering a punch to it.'

'Be reasonable, Mark, we're barely in the door,' said McNally. There was a collective murmur of agreement round the conference table.

Noordhof sighed. 'But you only have until Friday night. Where are Kowalski and Leclerc?'

'Kenneth's gone to bed,' Webb said. 'He'll be observing all night.'

'We left André taking a walk round the grounds,' said Judy. 'He said he was meditating.'

'Gone to bed; taking a walk; meditating. Jesus wept, do you people understand the situation?'

'Maybe you should shoot one or two of us, to encourage the others,' Shafer suggested.

'You probably meant that as a joke,' said Noordhof grimly.

'I'm here,' Webb said happily. The backwoodsman from Deliverance, the one with the Fenimore Cooper rifle and the intolerant, ignorant eyes full of medieval superstition, had turned out to be a philosophy student from the University of Arizona in Tucson, in his final year of an MS and writing a thesis on the Influence of the Platonic

School on Aristotelian Cosmological Doctrine, a fact which had reminded Webb that you can't always go by appearances. The astronomer's backside was still sore from the metal floor of the student's suspension-free Dodge.

Noordhof stared angrily at the astronomer. 'That was an unbelievable breach of security. What right do you people have to endanger this operation by wandering off over the mountain?'

'Nobody ever comes here in the winter, Mark. You said so.'

'Has it occurred to you that the Russians might have feelers out? That a place like this might be under surveillance?'

'Astronomers visit observatories, Mark. It can be Hawaii one week, Tenerife the next, Chile after that. No security breach was involved.'

'Allow me to judge that. As of this moment nobody steps more than one hundred metres from this building without my permission, except to go up to the telescopes.' The soldier turned to Shafer. 'Okay. You don't know where it is. You don't know how far away it is. You guess it's a kilometre across and closing at maybe twenty kilometres a second. But now the good fairy comes along and she waves her fucking wand and you find Nemesis some time in the next few days. Then she waves it again and McNally rustles up a launcher and gets a probe out to it. Okay Willy, now it's up to you. Your mission, should you decide to accept it, which of course you do, is to find some way to stop this frigging thing.'

Shafer rubbed a day-old stubble. 'Say it's coming in on a bullseye geocentric orbit. To miss the Earth, we have to deflect it so that by the time it gets here its orbit has shifted by at least one Earth radius. Six thousand kilometres.' He moved to the blackboard and picked up chalk. A blackboard was the logical way for everyone to follow his logic, but Webb suspected it was also the way he liked to work. 'Say we intercept it a week from impact.'

'A week!' McNally gasped incredulously.

'If $R_{\oplus}$ is the radius of the Earth and t is the time before deflection, you need a velocity increment $\delta V = R_{\oplus}/t$ if you want to punch it sideways. A transverse movement of say seven thousand kilometres in seven days comes to one thousand kilometres a day, or forty kilometres an hour.'

'But Nemesis won't be going in a straight line. The Earth's gravity will curve it in,' objected Sacheverell.

Webb joined Shafer at the blackboard and they both started to scribble. Webb got there first. 'Hey, Herb finally got something right. Gravitational focusing will add to the Earth's target area. The gravitational target area exceeds the geometric one by $1 + (V_E/V)^2$ where V_E is the escape velocity from the Earth and V is the Nemesis approach speed.'

'But we don't know V,' McNally complained. 'We don't know how fast Nemesis will come in.'

'We guess. V_E is about eleven kilometres a second and a typical Earth-crosser might hit us at twice that speed. That adds twenty-five per cent to Willy's estimate. Intercept Nemesis a week out and you need to deflect at over fifty kilometres an hour.'

'Okay,' Noordhof said. 'So what does Nemesis weigh?'

Webb and Shafer scribbled, and this time Shafer got there first: 'Pretend it's a rocky sphere a kilometre across, say with density 2.5 grammes per cc. Okay, that means we're dealing with about – yes, 10^{15} grammes. A billion tons.'

'To be knocked sideways at 30 mph,' said Noordhof.

'Without breaking it up,' Webb added. 'We can't

shower the Earth with fragments.'

Noordhof said, 'Nuke it.'

McNally was looking worried. 'That's what I said. But I've been wondering about the legalities of that. As I recall Article Four of the Outer Space Treaty forbids the placing or use of nuclear weapons in space.'

'So how do you think the Russians deflected Nemesis? With a pea-shooter?'

'But the ABM Treaty of 1972. . . .'

'Jim, hear this. Screw all treaties. I include in the screwing thereof the Outer Space Treaty of 1967, the Nuclear Non-Proliferation Treaty of 1968, the Convention on Registration of Objects Launched into Outer Space of 1978 and any other protocols and codicils I haven't thought of or don't know about. Let's just find Nemesis and nuke it.'

Judy Whaler said, 'That's the kind of talk I've been waiting to hear. We can blow a big hole in its side, and use the recoil from the ejecta to deflect it. A rocket effect.'

Noordhof said, 'You people tell me how big a hole we need.'

McNally said, 'With a week's notice, nobody outside a Bruce Willis movie is drilling holes in it.'

Noordhof said, 'In that case you have a surface burst. We surely have empirical data from the Nevada H-bomb tests.'

The NASA Director asked, 'With a one megaton bomb, what weight are you asking me to launch?'

'A ton,' Judy replied without hesitation, moving over to a terminal. McNally nodded his satisfaction. They waited as she tapped her way into a web site. 'My home page. It's full of goodies.' She moved the cursor to an icon and clicked the mouse. A table of numbers appeared.

'Here we are. The Nevada tests.'

Bomb	yield (kilotons)	Depth of burst (metres)	size of crater (metres)	depth of crater (metres)
Jangle S	1.2	1.1	14	6.4
Jangle U	1.2	5.2	40	16
Schooner	35	108	130	63
Teapot	1.2	20.0	45	27
Danny Boy	0.4	34.0	33	19
Johnnie Boy	0.5	0.5	18	9
Sedan	100	194	184	98
Palanquin	4.3	85	36	24
Buggy	1.1	41	76	21
1004	125	180	200	100

'But these are tiny explosions,' Leclerc said, looking over her shoulder.

Judy nodded. 'Schooner was 35 kilotons, Sedan a tenth of a megaton. But I agree, mostly like Jangle or Teapot they were just a kiloton or two. You don't want the neighbours screaming when you set off your A-bombs.'

'Can you do a least squares fit?' McNally asked.

'It's been done.' She clicked again, and a graph appeared on the screen. Shafer got there first: 'So, if we believe the fit, a one-megaton surface bomb excavates a crater six or seven hundred metres across. The crater could be as big as Nemesis. We'd shatter it.'

'Maybe, maybe not,' Sacheverell said.

'Let's run with a megaton for a while,' Webb proposed.

'It is not enough to know the size of the crater,' Leclerc pointed out. 'We need also to know its depth before we know the volume excavated.'

Back to the table. A red-painted fingernail traced along

a row. 'Jangle S was a surface burst. It had a depth about half its diameter.'

Sacheverell said, 'These bomb craters were made in terrestrial gravity. How can we trust these results on Nemesis?'

Leclerc was scribbling on the back of an envelope. 'Shall we ignore details like gravity? If we extrapolate Judy's figures we find we could excavate maybe fifty million tons of Nemesis with a megaton bomb.'

'We can also get at it from the crushing strength of rock,' Webb said, 'Assuming Nemesis is made of rock. If it takes 5×10^8 ergs to crush a gramme of medium-strength rock, and a megaton is 4×10^{22} ergs, Willy's bomb has the energy to excavate eighty million tons.'

Shafer frowned. 'Once again making a hole as big as the asteroid. Meaning we probably break it into thousands of fragments, and shower America with super-Hiroshimas.'

'Now hold on,' said Sacheverell. He sat down next to Judy and rapidly typed in an instruction. A coal-dark, pitted surface filled his screen. 'I'm into JPL and this is Mathilde, a near-Earth asteroid. It has a crater practically its own size and it held.'

'Okay say for now that we blast a hole in its side and Nemesis stays in one piece. Would it hit or miss?' Noordhof wanted to know.

'We still need to know the speed of the ejecta,' McNally said.

'So let's work it out. How fast do your nuclear explosions take place, Judy?' Shafer asked.

'The energy release is over in about a hundredth of a microsecond. It comes out as an X-ray pulse. Ground heating is complete in less than a microsecond. The trouble is, it gets so hot in that microsecond that the ground just reradiates most of the energy back. Only about five per cent goes into making a crater.'

Shafer said, 'We hit Nemesis with a one-megaton bomb.

It stays intact. A twentieth of the energy goes kinetic. So use $1/2mv^2$ and believe André's fifty million tons of ejecta to get at v.' He scribbled rapidly and Webb let him get on with it. The physicist turned back from the board. 'The debris recoils at a hundred metres a second.'

'In all directions,' Webb reminded him.

Shafer nodded his agreement. 'The horizontal components of motion just cancel. The actual orbit shifting is done by the vertical velocity component, which will be fifty metres a second. Are you still with us, Jim lad?'

NASA's Chief Administrator said, 'You're telling me that if I deliver a one-megaton bomb I can blast about five per cent of the asteroid's mass into space at 50 m/s. Times 3,600 gives me 180 kilometres an hour. So how fast does Nemesis recoil?'

Sacheverell said. 'That's high school stuff. From momentum conversation Nemesis itself is deflected at five per cent of fifty metres a second. Two metres a second.'

'Now hold on,' McNally said. 'You've just told me we need thirty metres a second.'

Noordhof said, 'Hit Nemesis a week before impact and you fail by a factor of fifteen to deflect it with a bomb. It looks like we need to catch this asteroid at least six months or a year out, Willy.'

Leclerc raised his hands in a Gallic gesture. 'But for all we know it is only weeks out, maybe even days.'

Sacheverell said, 'The Colonel's right. We need an early warning.'

Shafer shook his head in disagreement. 'We need ten or twenty years to map out the near-Earth environment.'

Noordhof's voice was beginning to border on desperation. 'Are you listening? You have to find Nemesis a year out. Your own figures say so.'

'Mark, how do we know it won't come in next week or next month?'

Noordhof rubbed a hand over his face. 'This is bad news.'

Webb rubbed off the equations and scribbled some more on the blackboard. He came back and sat down heavily at the conference table, puffing out his cheeks. 'It gets worse.'

Inquisition: The Witnesses

'Are you comfortable, Fra Vincenzo?' the secretary asked.

Vincenzo encompassed the room with a wave of the arm. 'I have rarely seen greater luxury outside the Palace of His Serenissimo.'

The secretary smiled. 'Better than the cells of the Sant' Angelo. I suspect they are showing deference to your age.'

'I suspect your own hand in the matter, sir. Not only do I have this fine apartment in the Holy Office itself, I am allowed access to a wonderful library downstairs. If I need to, I may call on the wisdom of St Thomas Aquinas, Scotus and other great scholars in preparing my *Apologia*.'

The secretary lounged back on a sofa. 'So. They tell me you had a rough journey.'

'I contracted a fever. We had to put up for three weeks in Orvieto. They say I almost died, but I remember little of it.'

'The Altezza is of course concerned for you. He is also anxious that your works should not be lost.'

Unexpectedly, the old monk burst into laughter. 'And faced with a choice between my life and my works, which is it to be? No, do not answer, my son. Ferdinand's love of his library is known to all. And he is right. Human life is ephemeral, but my work – it may be of little consequence, but it will surely outlast these bones by many centuries. To be read and studied by men yet unborn. Can there be a closer approach to immortality on this Earth?'

'I fear they may end up on the Index.'

'I have another fear. Something I fear more than death.' Vincenzo poured a glass of red wine for his distinguished guest, and one for himself. His hand was unsteady. 'And that is the torture. I do not believe I could withstand the strappado.'

There was a moment's silence. The Medici secretary sipped the wine, and changed the subject. 'All Florence is talking about your forthcoming trial. The students of Pisa set fire to the Inquisitor General's carriage with the Inquisitor still inside. There was fighting at the University of Bologna between supporters and detractors of the new cosmology. The authorities called in the mercenaries.'

'That is bad news for freedom of thought.'

'And worse news for you, Vincenzo. The Church may feel that it has to make an example.'

'Is there no place in Europe where a thinking man can be safe? They say that Calvin even set aside Geneva's laws to have Servetus burned alive. Bruno met the same fate in this city forty years ago.'

'And you repeat not only the Copernican heresies, but also those of Bruno. What a foolish old man you are, Vincenzo Vincenzi.' The secretary stood up. 'I will be at the Villa Medici in the Pincio for a few weeks. I have asked His Holiness to bring you to trial within days if possible. You have the right to an *advocatus*, which the Duke will pay for. I have made enquiries. You will be defended by a man of good family. He is young, but already well spoken of amongst the business community of Rome.' He turned at the door. 'If you fear the torture, Vincenzo, put yourself in his hands.'

⧗

On the second day of his nominal imprisonment an earnest, round-faced young man, wearing lenses in a wire framework perched on his nose and curled behind his ears, knocked and entered Vincenzo's apartment carrying a pile of papers.

Keenly aware of his rising reputation, Marcello Rossi regarded the defence of Vincenzo as both an honour and a hazard. The honour lay in the fact that the great Medici family had chosen him. The hazard lay in the fact that the defence of an obviously guilty heretic, if pursued too vigorously, could lead to his own arrest on suspicion of holding the same forbidden beliefs. Between Medici and Pope he would have to exercise extreme care, or be crushed like a fly between two colliding rocks.

Vincenzo's new advocate came with bad news: the Grand Inquisitor for the trial was to be Cardinal Terremoto. A massive, heavy-jowled man with small piercing eyes and tight, thin lips, his face was so fierce that its appearance was said to have struck terror into a visiting Spanish conquistador. Terremoto was an arch-conservative, a distinguished Jesuit theologian who had studied at Louvain in Belgium in order to familiarize himself with the heresies which prevailed in the North. A man of formidable intellect, he had shown himself zealous in rooting out the heresies which increasingly threatened the Mother Church.

The facts, Marcello Rossi quickly established, could not be disputed. Vincenzo openly declared his belief in the Copernican system whereby the Earth orbited the Sun and was not at the centre of the Universe. The charge against Vincenzo, that he held these opinions, was therefore no more than a plain description of the truth. And since the Holy Inquisition had, in the trial of Galileo some years before, established that the aforesaid beliefs were heresy, denial of the charge would be futile. Vincenzo's only hope was to abjure the heresy, believe all that the Holy Catholic Church told him, and throw himself on the mercy of the Inquisitor. This the young man strongly advised the old one to do.

His reasoning was sound; but he had reckoned without the stubbornness of his client.

Succinctly, Marcello explained the procedures of the Inquisition to Vincenzo. The trial will be held in secret. Evidence will be presented through prosecution witnesses. You will not be permitted to question these witnesses. You will then be interrogated. If by the end of the interrogation you have not confessed, or disproved the charges, you will be given time to prepare your defence. At that stage, you may call witnesses. But if at that stage you still persist in denial, the young advocate told Vincenzo, nobody will dare enter the courtroom to defend your heresies. The only witnesses who might be persuaded to appear will be those attesting to your upright character and piety. Do you have such? Vincenzo requested Fracastoro of Pisa, an old friend who had known Foscarini of Calabria, the supporter of Galileo. The advocate wrote the name down, and said he would submit it to the Grand Inquisitor.

In what circumstances would the trial proceed to torture? Vincenzo asked, in a voice tinged with fear.

You will be tortured if the evidence indicates guilt which you continue to deny, or if it is thought that your confession is not wholly sincere. Since your guilt is transparent, Marcello said, your only recourse is to purge your soul of the false doctrines and embrace the true beliefs as laid down by the Fathers.

But, said Vincenzo, I believe that the Earth orbits the Sun.

But can you then withstand the torture? Countless thousands of witches, under torture, have confessed to casting spells and curses, to night-flying on broomsticks, to attendance at witches' sabbaths; and amongst these thousands of confessions, at least a few must have been false and made only to escape further suffering.

Vincenzo stayed silent, and Marcello left him to his thoughts.

⧗

That evening, Marcello returned and pleaded with Vincenzo for an hour to confess heresy and throw himself on the mercy of the Holy Congregation. Vincenzo said simply that the Earth is one of the planets, and it orbits the Sun. At the end of the day, with the room darkening and an evening chill drifting in the windows, the young man marched out in despair.

⧗

The Pope's mercenaries came for him an hour after sunrise, when the city was already alive with the clattering of cartwheels on cobbles and the cries of bakers selling their merchandise. They conducted him down broad marble stairs and along corridors to a small chapel, where he received the sacrament from a cardinal who would shortly become one of his judges.

At the very first sight of the assembled cardinals, Vincenzo's heart sank. There were five of them, five red-robed cardinals, with facial expressions ranging from solemn to grim, seated at a long table made of polished oak.

After the opening prayer, and ceremonies which had no meaning to Vincenzo, he was instructed to sit on a low bench facing the table. The monk was shaking with nerves, and had difficulty drawing his eyes away from Cardinal Terremoto's face. A notary sat at the end of the table: everything would be recorded, even Vincenzo's cries of agony should the trial proceed to torture. The courtroom itself was a tall, airy room, its high, embellished ceiling supported by pillars. On the wall behind the notary was a life-sized representation of Christ on the Cross, and next to it a window which, each afternoon, would send sunlight slanting into the great room. Through the window Vincenzo could see the tree-covered hill of Monte Mario, framed on a light blue sky. Sheep were scattered over the hillside; a couple of shepherd boys were playing some game. It was a tranquil picture, far removed from the dark clash between world systems being played out in his own small world.

The first witness of the trial wore the pill-box hat and long cloak of a professor. He had a neat white beard, and he carried himself with the appropriate air of authority. He announced himself as Andrea Paolicci, Professor of Natural Philosophy and Theology at Padua University.

Terremoto opened the questioning. The Cardinal had a deep bass, resonating voice, as if it came from the depths of a crypt. He hunched forward slightly as he spoke, his small dark eyes glittering intensely. 'Doctor, do you accept that the use of eye and mind is a legitimate route to the interpretation of Nature?'

'We may approach the Mind of God through all His Works. That is, not only the Sacred Book, but also through His Architecture.'

'And that there cannot be a contradiction between the two, the Book of Scripture and the Book of Nature?'

'Clearly not.'

'You have studied the Copernican beliefs?' Terremoto asked.

'I have, from the perspectives both of natural philosophy and of faith.'

'It is your philosophical perspective which we seek. Doctor, do you find it tenable that the Earth is a spinning ball, a planet like Jupiter and Saturn, orbiting the Sun, with the Sun at the centre of the Universe?'

The Doctor smiled slightly. 'I do not. The Copernican system is impossible. The world is fashioned as described in the Bible and as it was understood even before the days of Our Lord, by men of the greatest wisdom and

115

enlightenment. I refer in particular to the teachings of Aristotle.'

'But you reach this opinion on the evidence of natural philosophy, and not simply of faith, or from the opinion of scholars from antiquity?'

The Doctor bowed affirmatively.

'Perhaps we can begin with the hypothesis of a rotating Earth,' said Terremoto. 'What is your objection to this?'

The Doctor explained, glancing at Vincenzo from time to time as if justifying his position to the old monk. 'If the Earth truly rotated, what would happen to the air? There would be a violent, endless wind. All bodies not in contact with the ground would rush off in one direction. A falling stone would shoot off to the side as it left the hand. And yet, to the greatest precision which the eye can detect, and from the highest towers which we have, a stone falls straight down. There is no perceptible deviation from the vertical. The Earth must therefore, of necessity, be stationary, in accordance with the evidence of our own senses.'

'And the Sun as the centre of all things? With the Earth orbiting it?'

'If the Earth truly orbited the Sun, as Copernicus claimed, then the stars above would reflect this motion. Over the course of a year, each one would seem to move in a small path in the sky. A star at right angles to the zodiac would trace out a circle. One in the zodiacal plane would be seen to move backwards and forwards in a straight line. At intermediate celestial latitudes the stars would trace out ellipses. No such motion can be seen. Therefore the Earth cannot possibly be orbiting the Sun.'

'What of the hypothesis that the stars are like the Sun? That they are not confined to a sphere but scattered through infinite space?'

'If this were so, the stars would be at different distances from us. In that case the parallax effect which I have described would result in the constellations changing shape over the course of a year. They clearly do not. The Bear, Cassiopeia and Orion are unchanging in the sky. The eye and the mind are thus in harmony with the sacred teachings. The outermost limits of the World are set by the crystalline sphere in which the stars are embedded.'

'What then is your opinion of the structure of the World?'

'The structure of the Universe reaches its most perfect description in the *Summa Theologica* of Thomas Aquinas. The greatest imperfection exists here on Earth. But when we die, the souls of the blessed travel upwards through the heavenly spheres, each sphere of heaven being more perfect than the one before. Heaven, and God, with Christ at His right hand, lies beyond the sphere of fixed stars described by Aristotle. Three orders of angels exist here on Earth, three in the intermediate region, and three in the outermost heaven.'

Another cardinal, Mattucci, asked: 'But are the complicated wanderings of the planets over the sky not best explained by the heliocentric doctrine? Do they not account for the retrograde motion of Mars as an optical illusion caused by an overtaking Earth? And is the system of Ptolemy not inferior in this respect?'

The professor said, 'I cannot deny that in calculating the positions of the planets the Ptolemaic system is complicated. But even as a mathematical contrivance, the Copernican system works poorly. Copernicus created it on the basis of only a handful of observations. Further, my studies reveal that those observations are not reliable. Many of them have been corrupted by frequent copying from Ptolemy. The latter's records are a mighty river to Copernicus's trickling stream. The worst aspect of the Copernican hypothesis is the introduction of a moving centre for the Earth's orbit, a completely arbitrary device whose sole purpose is to save the hypothesis.'

Mattucci persisted: 'But the system is improved, is it

not, by the invention of Johann Kepler that the planets move in ovals?'

'Have I a friend in court?' Vincenzo whispered.

Marcello wrinkled his nose sceptically.

The professor said, 'That postulate can be made, but only as a computational device, not as a description of reality. Ellipses lack the appeal of circular symmetry. They destroy the harmony of the spheres. And for the planets to pursue these shapes, Kepler postulates the existence of occult forces proceeding from the Sun whereas, of course, the stars and planets are moved by angels.'

The Cardinal Mattucci leaned back to show that he was finished with the questioning. Terremoto took it up. 'Doctor Paolicci, apart from the deficiencies of the heliocentric doctrine, which you have so clearly described, do your eyes and mind give you positive reasons for adhering to the Ptolemaic system?'

Paolicci allowed himself a brief, sly glance at Vincenzo. 'It follows logically from the rational nature of the Creator. It cannot be denied that a rational, omnipotent Creator will build a perfect Universe. Of course the Prince of Darkness then induced the Fall from Grace, which is an imperfection, but that exploits the weakness of Man and does not affect the structure of the Universe. Only one object has perfect symmetry, in the three dimensions of length, breadth and height which we inhabit. That is a sphere. A perfect Universe built by a rational Creator must therefore be spherical. And only one type of motion is natural in a spherical universe, and that is circular motion. Otherwise the symmetry would be broken. That is why, of logical necessity, planetary motion must comprise circles, and circles upon circles.'

'You do not, then, accept the Bruno hypothesis that the Universe is infinite?'

'An infinite Universe is unthinkable.'

'And the plurality of worlds? Men on Bruno's planets?'

'Such could not have been descended from Adam, nor could they obtain Christ's redemption.'

Cardinal Borghese took up the questioning. He looked at the prisoner and his lawyer with open hostility before turning to the professor. 'Doctor, you have told us that no contradiction is possible between science and faith.'

'No Christian can believe otherwise.'

'And if a contradiction were to arise?'

'Eminence, with respect, since no such contradiction is possible, your question is without meaning.'

'An apparent contradiction, then?'

'Since actual contradiction is impossible, the appearance of it can only arise in the mind of the Turk, or the Jew, or the heretic.'

Borghese turned to the notary. 'Let it be recorded that Vincenzo is neither a Turk nor a Jew.'

A succession of witnesses from universities in Bologna, Pisa, Naples and Venice was then summoned, all saying much the same thing. By midday the room was becoming hot and stifling, and the court was adjourned for four hours.

In the apartment, the young advocate flopped on to the same settee which the Grand Duke's secretary had occupied the previous week. 'You have an impressive list of enemies,' he said.

Vincenzo gestured with open palms. 'Academics are prone to jealousies. And much is at stake. But I also have many supporters.'

'Unfortunately, Father, your supporters dare not support you in court, while your enemies appear to have gained the ear of Boniface. Why else would you be on trial?' Marcello reached for an apple in a bowl and started to toss it playfully in the air. 'Your old friend Fracastoro – the acquaintance of Foscarini.'

'Yes?'

'He is refusing to testify on your behalf, even on the

matter of your piety and character. My courier tells me the man is terrified.'

'Have I no friends?' Vincenzo asked in despair.

'Perhaps one. The Cardinal Terremoto was told of your predicament with regard to witnesses. At once he instituted a diligent search and has at last found someone willing to testify to your character. I did not find your friend's name.'

'Thank God for a small blessing. But it seems I will have to make the scientific case myself.'

The advocate took a bite at the apple. 'A case which has already been rejected by this same Congregation when Galileo tried to make it a few years ago. Confess to error, Vincenzo. The alternatives are too horrible even to mention.'

'Can I retract the truth, my son?' Vincenzo headed for a small bedroom off the apartment. The advocate put the apple core in the fruit bowl, loosened the belt around his stomach and stretched out on the couch.

The court convened again in the late afternoon. A clerk awakened them and led the old astronomer and his lawyer down the stairs and along the corridors.

There was only one witness. A small, stooped man in priest's habit, with a hooked nose and dark, blotchy skin, hurried into the room. Vincenzo turned to Marcello Rossi in alarm. 'Grandami!' he whispered. 'What is that man doing here?'

'He is your character witness.'

'What? But this man is my sworn enemy. He hates me. Who has done this to me?'

'Terremoto.'

At that moment, Vincenzo knew he was doomed.

The Martians

Then it reached them.

The two generals and the civilian watched from the comfort of their brown leather armchairs as the combat crew frantically checked through their systems, mag tapes spinning and a babble of messages flooding in. The winking red lights had vanished from the map. The lists of refuelling points and aircraft aloft reappeared. The Blackjacks were almost home. The MiGs were far out over the Sea of Japan. The Kola peninsula was deserted. Winton was cool, Pino was grey and sweaty. Hooper, the Chairman of the Joint Chiefs of Staff, noted with disapproval that someone was hyperventilating.

A telephone rang, the pink one. Wallis observed his own hand trembling as he picked it up.

General Cannon was looking down, telephone to his ear. 'Put me on loudspeaker.' Wallis pressed a button and the general's voice boomed round the room. 'April Fool,' it said.

'Sir?' said Wallis, looking up at his commanding officer. Mortified, Wallis found that his voice was as shaky as his hand.

'Somebody just stamped on the mountain. Roof sheared clean off and fell on you. You're dead, son.'

'General Cannon, what was that?'

'Martians,' the voice boomed.

'Men from Mars?' Incredulously. The combat crew, to a

man, stared up at the general.

'Affirmative.'

'Sir, Martians aren't allowed. They're not in SIOP.'

'Foggy, how do you know there are no little green men out there? We wanted to test how the system reacted to something crazy and the only way was to spring it on you. Operation Martian Scenario. Y'all did just fine. We have you on home movies and it's a whole lot of use to us upstairs. You and your crew'll have a full debriefing at the end of this shift. Then maybe you'll want to get drunk.'

Wallis was aware of the eyes of his combat crew on him. In the confines of the steel office, the rage, fear and bewilderment were tangible. He took a deep breath and a chance with his career. 'General Cannon, sir, with respect. Damn you to hell.'

There was an electric silence. Then a deep, genie laugh echoed round the office. 'Son, I'm already there.'

⧖

'Doctor Sacheverell, your assessment?' Cannon asked.

'I'll need to run a few Monte Carlo simulations. But at a first guess I'd say prompt casualties two hundred million. Dead that is,' said the civilian. 'Two sugars, please.'

'Nice one,' said Cannon, pouring coffee. 'You've solved the population explosion.'

'We'd be looking for a few survivors in freak conditions,' Sacheverell continued. 'People down mines, stuff like that. Material devastation with this scenario is quite severe though. Maybe cities reduced to dust or rubble over fifty per cent of mainland USA.'

Hooper and Sacheverell might have come from different planets. Whereas Sacheverell was thin and stooped, Hooper, the Chairman of the Joint Chiefs, was almost as wide as he was tall. Where Sacheverell had a greasy complexion, Hooper had a deeply wrinkled, tanned face. Where the astronomer had a shock of vertical red hair and a headband, the soldier's hair was short, white and fine. Where Sacheverell dressed like a basic slob, with an untidy grey suit and garish red tie on a turquoise shirt, the soldier was immaculate. And where Sacheverell was stirring coffee, Hooper banged a fist angrily. Coffee spilled into the saucers. 'Almighty Christ, am I supposed to believe this? Rubble? *Dust?*'

'And there's no question of any industrial or political infrastructure surviving,' Sacheverell added, hastily picking up cup and saucer.

'Cool it, Sam. Doctor, talk about the C-cubed systems,' Cannon said.

'With this particular scenario, they collapse. But it is a bit way out and in general I can't be sure. I'd have to get into some heavy analysis on ionospheric plasmas and I don't have time for that.' Nor the competence, Sacheverell added to himself. 'I guess you have to expect a big electromagnetic pulse over most of the country.'

'This is pure crap,' Hooper said, flipping through the pages of Sacheverell's hastily constructed scenario. 'Our command systems are nuclear hard.' In a flash of inspiration, Judy Whaler had laid the report out like a film script, fictitious descriptions of fireball impacts linked together with phrases of the 'Meanwhile in San Diego' type. Appended to the Hollywood scenario, and bearing as much resemblance to it as Dr Jekyll to Mr Hyde, was a spartan appendix written in the measured language of science, liberally sprinkled with equations, tables, ifs and buts. The CJCS, Sacheverell noticed, was sticking to the film script.

'Not hard enough,' Sacheverell said. 'A successful Russian first strike only delivers five thousand megatons, most of that near the ground. For all we know there's a million megatons on the way in. Even at one per cent efficiency, that's like a million amps under a potential of a million volts flowing overhead for ten seconds.'

Cannon stirred his coffee thoughtfully. 'That would melt your fillings, Sam.'

Hooper shook his head angrily, as if rejecting the whole concept. 'PARCS and PAVE PAWS would have picked your asteroid up on the way in.'

Sacheverell shook his head too. 'Your radar software filters out signals with long delay times, so you only pick up stuff very near the Earth. It wouldn't have shown up on the radars until the last minute.'

'So? We'll re-programme.'

'You could, at the risk of swamping the computers with small space junk. Even so military radars have a limited range. By the time they detected the asteroid it would be a couple of hours from impact, far too late to stop it. Anyway, you have practically nothing covering the southern sky.'

Cannon said, 'Look, Sam, anything we got into the air would get its wings ripped off even if we were C-cubed operational. This applies to TACAMO as much as Bomber Command. I can't even guarantee we could contact Mitchell's Trident fleet in time.'

'Let me get this right,' said Hooper, bewildered. 'Are you seriously telling me that if this thing hits we're wiped out and we can't hit back?'

'Mitchell's fleet would mostly survive,' said Cannon, 'But so what? The point is, the thing would just be a great natural disaster. You heard Wallis on the phoney NORAD circuit: there was no attack, no enemy, nobody to hit back at.'

The Chairman, JCS, stood up. He walked over to the window and looked out through the Venetian blinds. The rasp of a Prowler penetrated the triple glazing and the room trembled, very slightly. He turned, his back to the window.

'Realistically, how much warning do we get?'

Sacheverell put down his coffee. 'If it approaches the night hemisphere you might see it in binoculars an hour before impact. Assuming you knew exactly where to look. It would be visible to the naked eye maybe fifteen minutes from impact.'

'Mister, what I want to know is, when do the phones start ringing?'

'When you see it as a bright moving star. Say twenty seconds from impact.'

Hooper sat down again, and stared into the middle distance for some moments. 'Well it sure beats the hell out of Star Wars,' he said at last.

'Sam, it's beautiful,' said Cannon. 'The thing is undetectable, practically into our air space before we know what's hitting us. When it does hit us, we're obliterated. There's no point in hitting back even if we could because, like you say, it's just a freak natural disaster. Sam, you know I'm due to meet some senators from the Appropriations Committee in a couple of hours. I'm trying to get final approval for Batstrike.'

'Which we're selling on Middle East scenarios.'

'Fifty billion bucks down the tube, along with the new Grand Forks, our Navy, SAC, brilliant pebbles, C-cubed, all our surveillance systems, the whole BMDO. Everything we have, this thing beats it. And they don't even have to worry about retaliation.'

'I don't believe it,' repeated Hooper, grey-faced. 'This is fantasy stuff.'

'And we reckon they set the whole thing up for a day's defence budget.'

'What's the timescale for this?' Hooper asked harshly.

'Heilbron thinks the Russians have pulled it off already,' said Cannon. 'It's somewhere out there now, on the way in.'

Downstairs, the shift was nearly over. The normally ebullient Pino had been unusually quiet, wrestling with some inner problem. Finally he said: 'Colonel, do you know anything about astronomy?'

'Not much Pino. What do you want to know?'

'Well, are we sure there are no men from Mars?'

'Relax, Pino, there are no Martians. Vince Spearman said it on TV.'

Pino seemed to be examining the arcane names on the screen in front of him. Then: 'This guy Spearman – he's okay?'

'AOK. He's been checked out real good.'

The sergeant relaxed.

Eagle Peak, Tuesday Evening

Webb said, 'If Nemesis is more fragile than a rock . . .'

Sacheverell groaned. 'You're not still on that comet crap. Ever heard of the asteroid belt?'

'Which fails to give us the periodicity in the extinction and cratering records.'

'What periodicity?' Sacheverell sneered. 'There is none. And how come Toutatis, Mathilde, Eros and Gaspra are rock?'

'Mathilde has the density of water. It's a friable sponge.' Webb turned to Noordhof. 'Colonel, Herb will tell you to plan on diverting a solid rock. But if it's a degassed comet and McNally fires an H-bomb at it, we'll end up with a dust ball heading for us. When the ball comes in it will incinerate the upper atmosphere as it slows from cosmic speed to zero. It'll remove all the ozone. Then it'll take a year to sink through the stratosphere and during that year the Earth will be wrapped in a highly reflective dust blanket. Down here we'll be in twilight. We'll have a major climatic upset. Freezing gales will blow from sea to land. The continents will end up looking like Siberia. We might cut the thermohaline circulation in the Atlantic and switch off the Gulf Stream. If we do, that will feed through to a permanent snowfall in Eurasia. That will switch off the monsoon. Nobody in Asia will eat for a year or so. You'll shift masses of water to the poles as ice and change the spin rate of the Earth. Maybe you'll flip the geomagnetic field, and set off seismic faults and vulcanisms worldwide. Then when the dust clears you'll be exposed to the full unshielded UV of the Sun, and you'll have a global catastrophe on top of a global catastrophe. Herb's certainties could do us in.'

'Maybe we want to get it right before we launch a bomb at it,' suggested Shafer.

Leclerc was looking puzzled. 'I always thought comets had tails.'

'Not when they've degassed, André. They may crumble to dust but there are plenty of well-authenticated cases showing that they sometimes turn into asteroids.'

Leclerc said, 'If we find Nemesis, could we tell its internal constitution by looking at it? Using Kenneth's monster telescope? What do we actually know about the reflectivities of the Earth-crossing bodies?'

Sacheverell said, 'We don't. But the museums are stuffed with meteorites. They're fragments of asteroids and they're rocks.' He shot Webb a venomous look.

Webb said, 'You don't have comet debris in the museums because it breaks up in the atmosphere. Nemesis could be like Halley, with a crusty exterior and a fluffy inside.'

'Fluffy snowballs, right?' Shafer asked, narrowing his eyes. 'Dust and ice in equal proportions?'

Webb nodded. 'Give or take. Try to nuke it and you end up with a billion tons of dust. Look, if we get this wrong we could reduce the species to foraging bands.'

McNally's face was a caricature of dismay. He said, 'I go for Sacheverell's theory.'

Noordhof spoke, in a thoughtful tone. 'Ollie. Do you realize what you've just said? That if Nemesis is a comet, the interests of the world at large are best served by letting the USA take it? Are you saying we're on opposite sides, Ollie?' Noordhof asked softly, playing with another cigar. Suddenly the air was electrically charged. Judy, at a terminal, stopped typing and swivelled on her chair to face them.

McNally broke the stunned silence. He gulped, 'Hey, if the Russians changed its course without turning it to dust, so can we.'

Webb shook his head tensely, his eyes locked with Noordhof's. 'They probably had years of a start, letting them push it a few centimetres a second, without setting up big internal stresses.'

Judy Whaler turned back to the terminal. 'A standoff burst! With neutron bombs!' she sang out over her shoulder, and carried on typing.

Webb blew out his cheeks with relief. 'Thank you, Judy. Colonel, we just handle Nemesis with the utmost care. We use a standoff burst. Ablate a skin with neutrons.'

The relief was palpable. Shafer was scribbling. 'Maybe yes, maybe no. Even a neutron bomb emits X rays and they get to the asteroid first. If they create a sheath of plasma the neutrons might not get through. I don't know that neutron bombs would help.'

She swivelled on her chair. 'We do bombs at Sandia, Willy. We can handle the computational side. Neutron bombs are the ultimate capitalist weapon, remember? They're designed to irradiate people, not destroy structures. Suppose instead of positioning a bomb on the surface of Nemesis we detonate it during a flyby, say a few hundred metres up. Instead of forming a crater, the top few centimetres are vaporized and blown off. The stresses are spread over a hemisphere instead of concentrating around a crater.'

Shafer said, 'So we bathe the asteroid with neutrons and X-rays. And if it turns out to be a comet, we might still do it gently enough to preserve its structure.'

Noordhof asked, 'Can we do it? Can we do it?'

Webb suggested, 'Try a one-megaton burst at five hundred metres' altitude and suppose the bomb energy is all in neutrons.'

Judy unconsciously swept her blonde hair back over her shoulder and said enthusiastically, 'Neutrons get absorbed within twenty centimetres. If they just passed through you they wouldn't do damage. It's because they get absorbed within your body that they make such brilliant weapons. The energy will be deposited in a top layer of Nemesis around the thickness of a human body.' She turned back to her terminal.

You're a bundle of fun, lady, Webb found himself thinking.

Shafer drew a circle and a point some way off, and tangent lines from point to circle. Webb saw what was coming and tried to keep up on a sheet of paper. Shafer said, 'Give Nemesis a radius R and put the bomb a distance d from its centre. We need to know how much of the bomb's energy is intercepted by Nemesis.' He scribbled rapidly and said, 'Seen from the bomb Nemesis fills $\pi R^2/4\pi d^2$ or $1/4(R/d)^2$ of the sky.'

McNally said, 'If we explode the bomb five hundred metres up, like Ollie says . . .'

Shafer continued, 'Then we have $d = R$ and a quarter of the bomb energy is dumped on the facing hemisphere of Nemesis. That's good. Now let's skip the detailed trig and suppose the irradiation goes to a mean depth of five centimetres.'

Webb took up the story. 'So we're imagining that over the hemisphere facing the bomb, a surface skin maybe five centimetres thick takes twenty-five per cent of the blast. The concentration of energy will be prodigious.'

Shafer rapidly substituted numbers for symbols in a formula. 'Okay so about half a million tons of surface regolith is exposed to a quarter of a megaton of neutron energy, coming in at a third the speed of light.'

Sacheverell asked, 'Can we turn that into a speed?'

'Easy. Each exposed gramme gets a few times 10^{10} ergs, about the same energy as dynamite. So the surface goes off like dynamite. It turns into a vapour expanding at five kilometres a second.'

'Now you're talking,' said Noordhof. He was leaning forward intently, trying to follow the rapid exchanges between the scientists.

'It's as if you've spread a three-inch sandwich of dynamite over a hemisphere,' McNally repeated, his eyes gleaming. 'A puff of vapour expanding at five kilometres a second from one side of Nemesis. It's Christmas after all.'

Webb said, 'Hey, imagine exploding like dynamite when one of Judy's bombs goes off.' Noordhof shot him a cold glance.

McNally returned to an earlier formula. 'On the week-before-impact scenario, that would shift Nemesis at two metres a second. We're still well short.'

'But we've gained a power of ten,' Shafer said. 'Maybe we could even use a bigger bomb.'

'No,' said Webb. 'You'd bust it up.'

'I agree with Ollie,' said Judy, turning back again from the terminal. 'Hit the asteroid and it rings like a bell. If you hit it so hard that its velocity change is more than its escape velocity then you'll break it up.'

'Now you've lost me,' said Noordhof.

'Imagine the asteroid as a fragile bell, made of glass or something. The Russians tapped it with a pencil years ago and made it ring. But now it's rushing at us and we're having to shift it with a hammer.'

Shafer said, 'You're forgetting that it might have internal strength. Jim, if you can rendezvous with Nemesis a hundred days before impact we might be able to deflect it in principle, maybe even if it's one of Ollie's degassed comets. Fifty days, maybe. Ten days or less and we're in trouble whatever it's made of.'

McNally sounded as if he was in pain. 'A hundred days? Willy, can we get back to the real world here?'

Sacheverell said, 'Cracks and fissures in rock could change the whole story.'

Judy turned to them, a satisfied smile on her face. 'We're in.'

'Where?' Webb asked, startled.

'Welcome to the wonderful world of teraflops, Ollie. While you people are handwaving I log on to God. I fix up a simulation algorithm using Sandia's own shock physics hydrocode, and they run it for me.' McNally pulled the curtains half shut to cut down on stray light, and they clustered round her terminal. She logged in through a series of gateways, each one with a different password. 'I'm using fifty million finite elements and all nine thousand processors. Give me the internal constitution of your comet or asteroid, cracks, fissures and warts, and I'll tell you what happens when you neutron it. Look on my works, ye Mighty, and despair!' She paused, a finger over the keyboard.

'Hey, you read Chaucer?' McNally asked.

Judy raised her eyes to heaven and then pressed the carriage return button with a flourish. 'Even the Teraflop will take some minutes.'

Noordhof, looking at the blank screen, said, 'It seems to me, people, that the critical thing is the internal constitution of this asteroid. Is it rock, iron, ice or what?'

'That's the sharp end of the debate,' Webb agreed.

Noordhof said, 'I get the impression you guys don't know a lot about what's out there.'

Webb agreed. 'Here be dragons. But it's vital.'

The screen came to life. Judy said, 'I want to show you three simulations. Here's number one. I'm exploding a megaton four hundred metres above a one-kilometre rock with the tensile strength of a carbonaceous chondrite.' On the little screen, a potato-shaped, black mass appeared. It rotated slowly for a few seconds, as if being viewed from an exploring spacecraft, and then froze in position. A brief flash filled the screen. The rock shuddered. Black fingers spread out in a cone. When the debris had left the screen, a sizeable hole had appeared in the side of the rock, which was drifting slowly off to the left. 'This is very satisfactory. The nuclear deflection has worked.'

A second potato appeared on the screen, identical to the first. 'Okay, this one is stony, silicon oxide. I've made it a fragment of a large asteroid which has been pounded over geological timescales: it's been weakened. It has internal fissures. It's just a rubble pile.' This time, when the debris had cleared, the rock had fragmented. Half a dozen large fragments, and dozens of smaller ones, were drifting slowly apart.

Noordhof said, 'That looks like trouble.'

Judy nodded. 'Deep trouble. It depends how early we could deflect Nemesis.'

'If we ever find it,' said Leclerc.

A third potato materialized. 'Now the last one, this is a comet with the tensile strength of the Kreutz sungrazer. Let's see what happens.' The bomb flashed briefly. Instantaneously, the potato disintegrated. But there were no fragments to fly apart. Instead, a white amorphous mass gradually filled the screen, apparently growing white hairs as it approached. 'All we've done is generate a dust ball.' The simulation ended. McNally opened the curtains and bright daylight streamed into the room.

Shafer moved over to the window and looked out. 'I seem to remember the Sandia people carried out Tunguska fireball simulations some years ago,' he said over his shoulder. 'And the 1908 data were best fit by a rocky asteroid.'

'But there were counterarguments,' Webb reminded him. 'For example the lack of rocks spalling off along the trajectory, and the coincidence with the Beta Taurid comet swarm. And with a small change in the assumed trajectory they could accommodate a comet.'

Shafer asked, 'What do the spectra say about the Earth-crossers?'

'There are hardly any available. They're too faint.'

'Okay,' said Noordhof, resuming his place at the head of the conference table. 'From what you people are saying it seems to me that I can come to an immediate decision. There's too much at stake here to take chances. We have to invent something that will work whatever Nemesis is made of.'

'We could play with all sorts of deflection scenarios,' Judy said. 'Solar sails, laser propulsion, kinetic energy impactors and so on. Either they take far too long to develop or they can't deflect in the time available. Only nuclear weapons stand a chance, but as you've seen they could give us a cluster of debris or maybe even – if Nemesis turns out to be an old comet – a blanket of dust and a cosmic winter.'

'Hell,' said Sacheverell, 'even a pure rock asteroid would give us that after it fried us.'

Noordhof put his hands on top of his head. 'Am I going mad here? You are telling me the following: One, you will have to deflect Nemesis at less than a metre a second or it will break up and shower us with fragments. Two, you will have to deflect it at more than ten metres a second or it will hit us.'

'Depending on how far out it is,' Shafer said.

'And you can't even guess that?' the Colonel asked.

'How can we?' Judy raised her hands. 'We need to discover the thing.'

'Which brings me to Three. You have no hope of finding it on any timescale likely to be useful.'

'Pending discovery, we could adopt a hundred-day guideline for interception,' suggested Judy.

McNally was in pain again. 'This hundred days you keep bugging me with . . .'

Noordhof reminded them: 'It's not the hundred days. The White House, in their infinite wisdom, have given us until Friday night. And this is Tuesday night, and so far you people have come up with zilch.'

Wisconsin Avenue, Tuesday, 20ʰ00 Eastern Standard Time

The *Salem Witch* screamed as she hurtled along the runway, her headlights picking up only snow rushing out from a point in the dark, and her wheels throwing arcs of slush high in the air. The screaming faded as the little executive jet slowed to a crawl. The pilot taxied bumpily along to a slipway and turned, slipping the Gulfstream in between the parked jumbos and 707s; an inconspicuous dwarf amongst the giants flying the flags of all the world.

They were in a dark corner of Dulles International Airport.

Human forms flickered in silhouette beyond more dazzling headlights. Three men stepped down from the aircraft. Two were in uniform; the third man, a civilian, was clutching a shiny new briefcase to his chest. A sudden gust caught the leading officer's hat and he cursed briefly as he snatched it back from the bitter wind.

Traffic was light and the black Lincoln Continental took them fast and skilfully into town. The driver wore a naval uniform. There was no conversation. Along Wisconsin Avenue the car slowed, turned and halted, its headlights illuminating a wrought iron double gate straddled by a metal spider eight feet wide. The spider's legs were white with snow. A second car, which had followed them discreetly from the airport, drove on. They waited while a camera appraised them from atop a gatepost. Then there was a metallic click, the spider split quietly into two halves and the car sighed on to the inner approach road. They drove through a grove of white-laden trees, lit up by red, white and blue spotlights, and effectively shielding the CIA Director's home from curious eyes and laser microphones.

The avenue curved round to the back of a large, dark house and stopped at the door of a conservatory, lit up from within and throwing an orange glow into the surrounding woods. The three men climbed wearily out of the car, which drove off, its tyres scrunching over the snow. The leading officer opened a glass door and they were met with a surge of hot, foetid air. They walked, single file, along a narrow paved path taking them through dense jungle foliage, past a tinkling fountain and over a small bridge. Colourful fish with long diaphanous fins swam in the pond below. There was a strong smell of narcissus. A slice of Guatemala, preserved in the Washington winter.

There was a sandy, cactus-strewn clearing in the jungle and an elderly man, wearing an oversized grey pullover, was sitting at a circular table, smoking a pipe. He waved them towards white garden chairs around the table. A moth was throwing a giant frantic shadow on the table as it circled to its doom around the light overhead.

The Director's wife came out with a tray of iced tea and biscuits. She had long blonde hair and the slim, elegant frame mandatory for the Washington hostess. The civilian, Sacheverell, guessed she was about fifteen years younger than her husband. She could have been on the cover of *Vogue*, he thought, about twenty years ago.

A breast brushed lightly over his shoulder as she leaned over him with the tray; the light physical contact tingled his nerves. She said, 'Don't forget your tablets, honeypie.' The Director growled and Sacheverell watched her slim form disappear through the French windows. The moth sizzled briefly overhead.

Sacheverell took stock of the evening's company. There

was Honeypie, alias Richard Heilbron, the Director of the CIA, tapping out his pipe on an ashtray and looking like a professor in some provincial university. There was Samuel B. Hooper, Chairman of the Joint Chiefs of Staff, a small, burly, white-haired man who looked as if he had been born radiating authority. And his companion, the gaunt, self-effacing Colonel Wallis who, with his combat crew a few hours earlier, had been tossed in a fire and grilled like the moth.

'Gentlemen, welcome,' said Heilbron. 'How was your Martian Scenario, Sam?'

'A catastrophe. Foggy here manages a threat assessment conference with NMCC and Offutt, they deduce that there's a blast coming from Mexico, and then they're dead. There was no counterstrike, no nothing.'

'You got nothing away? Not even a Trident?'

'Not even a frigging rowing boat. If the Russians have pulled this off . . .'

'As you know we're due to brief the President at twenty-one hundred. I understand we'll be in the East Wing theatre and I've had your movie set up there, Doctor Sacheverell. What I want to do is go over the CIA evidence with you in advance.'

'Rich,' said Hooper, 'I still think this is the most crackbrained tale I ever heard. I hope I'm about to hear some damned hard evidence.'

'What you're about to hear, Sam, is guesswork. Open the folders in front of you, gentlemen. Look at the top two pages. Now this is a translation of a conversation in Russian intercepted by Menwith Hill a couple of weeks ago. It's an exchange between the cosmonauts aboard Phobos Five and their mission control in Tyuratam.'

'Phobos Five?'

'Is a deep space probe which the Russian Republic launched six months ago with three men aboard. Their declared intention is to head for Mars, get into a low parking orbit, launch a couple of probes and come back in one piece. It's a two-year round trip. Ever since the days when there was a Soviet Union we've known they would try for a manned landing on Mars early in the millennium and this looks like a prelude. It all fits nicely.'

The declaration of a nice fit, Sacheverell thought, came with a hint of world-weary scepticism.

Heilbron nodded towards a small cassette tape recorder on the table. 'In this tape the cosmonauts are one week out. Three point three million kilometres away. Speed of light is three hundred thousand kilometres a second. Listen, and try to follow the transcript.'

There was a lot of static. Every few seconds a metallic bleep cut through the sound. Then a voice, speaking in Russian. Putting their weariness aside, Sacheverell and the officers followed the script intently:

00.17.27 GROUND CONTROL. Phobos, this is ground control at 173 hours Ground Elapsed Time. We have readings that the charge in cell 7 is fluctuating. Will you check this please? (Long pause.)

00.18.01 COSMONAUT. Phobos. We're all asleep here. (Background noise.) Control, this is Stepanov. I can report that cell 7 has no malfunction that we know of. All our readings are, ah, normal.

00.18.12 GC. We may have a telemetry malfunction. As a precaution will you go through the check routine on page 71 of the manual? (Long pause).

00.18.48 COSMONAUT. (Expletive.) If you insist. Ah – a moment – (garbled conversation) – Vyssotsky tells me he checked the fuel cells this morning, while I was asleep. He says there were no problems.

00.19.00 GC. Thank you, Toivo Stepanov. I have a (garbled) display now. It says we have a minor telemetry problem here on the ground. You can go back into hibernation. What is that horrible noise? (Long pause.)

00.19.30 COSMONAUT. Vyssotsky is singing.
00.19.36 GC. Glad to hear you're all happy. We await your systems report at 175 hours GET. Ground control out.

Heilbron rewound the tape. Hooper picked a winged insect out of his tea and flicked it into the shadows. He said: 'It's a bit late for quiz games, Rich.'

Wallis said: 'The guy on board answered pretty damn smart.'

Sacheverell, who had also noticed the fact, looked at the colonel with respect. He said: 'Distance is 3.3 million kilometres. With a speed of light of three hundred thousand kilometres a second, that gives a round trip, from the question asked at Tyuratam to the answer intercepted at Menwith Hill, of twenty-two seconds. It fits with all the pauses except the last one.'

'I can see we're in smart company tonight,' Heilbron said. 'Excellent. We can use all the brains we can get on this one. Yes Sacheverell, all the pauses except the last one. What is that horrible noise? Then there's a *nineteen*-second delay and the reply, 'Vyssotsky is singing'.'

'Meaning?' Wallis asked.

'Now hold on, Heilbron,' General Hooper interrupted. 'Are you trying to tell me the cosmonaut answered the question before he got it?'

'Precisely.'

'Christ, Sam, maybe Menwith just screwed up their tapes.'

'Negative. We've checked out the technical side.'

'What's your conclusion, Mister Heilbron?'

'Patience, Colonel Wallis, there's more, much more. We hadn't paid a lot of attention to the Phobos launch until then, you understand. Plenty of stuff on tape etcetera but processing it wasn't a high priority. The timing hiatus had been picked up by one of my bright young geniuses, a guy by the name of Pal. So I put him in charge of a small team, a sort of Operation Phobos. They found this – listen. This is from a conversation three days later. I haven't bothered with a transcript. Listen to the timing pulses.' They listened to the high-pitched, frightened bat, coming between the deep Slavic tones of the man in the spaceship. Heilbron replayed it several times. The military men shook their heads. Sacheverell frowned.

'It's impure,' he said, 'Structured.' He was beginning to feel light-headed, whether from tiredness or the narcotic effect of the scented narcissus he couldn't tell.

Heilbron nodded encouragingly. 'Another Brownie point for our young friend. Now here's the same timing pulse slowed down ten thousand times.' He wound the tape on, missed the start, wound it back again and then played it. Sacheverell felt the hair on the back of his neck prickling as the clandestine message came over, a clear, Morse-like, intelligent signal spreading out from the circle of light, through the Guatemalan jungle, over the big lawn and into the dark woods beyond. Heilbron let it run a minute and then stopped it. He said:

'They've slipped in a burst transmission. It goes on for hours. I've had my best people on it for a week, fifth-generation machines trying to talk to it. It even beat the NSA's Cray T3D at Fort Meade.' Sacheverell recalled that more mathematicians were employed at the National Security Association's Maryland headquarters than anywhere else on Earth. Heilbron went on: 'The consensus now is that it's some sort of one-way encryption system, unbreakable unless you have the key. And the conversation is phoney – the voice people tell me the acoustics aren't quite right or something. What's up there on Phobos Five is a tape recorder. They're playing some sort of charade, ground control asking questions in anticipation of the answers on the tape. Only the tape carries messages and the guy on the ground mistimed, just once.'

'What are you telling us? That the Soyuz is unmanned?' Hooper asked.

'Three cosmonauts climbed on board. We took pictures.'

'Jesus, Rich,' said the Chairman, JCS, in exasperation. 'First you tell us some machine on the spacecraft is answering pre-set questions, then you say there are people on board. Why don't they just do their own talking instead of playing an answering machine?'

'Because they're not there any more.'

Hooper gave the CIA chief a sceptical stare. 'They jumped out?'

Heilbron said, 'Take a look at Exhibit B.' There was a rustle as envelopes, about a foot square, were opened. Sacheverell, baffled, helped himself to more iced tea. The CIA Director produced a small red pill from a packet and swallowed it with his tea.

'Like I said,' Heilbron continued, 'nobody was paying much attention to Phobos at the time and the pictures you're going to see were just filed away at first. Look at the first one. This came from the French. It's an unclassified Spot picture. What you're looking at is the Baikonur cosmodrome. The scale's about a hundred miles. Aral Sea's off the picture to the left. The river' – a thin blue ribbon wandered left to right across the picture, passing through a city – 'is the Sar-Daya.'

'What's the town?' Wallis asked.

'The former Leninsk. It's a hundred miles east of the Aral Sea. Following the Red Army takeover, the whole region has been closed again to Westerners. Leninsk is one of the new science cities: cinemas, culture palaces, sports stadiums and so on. They've built it on to Tyuratam old town – that's the darker colouring on the left.'

'What are the arrows?' Wallis again.

'The one in the middle is the Cosmonaut Hotel. We've a first class source there, a lady who's been with us since the old days.' Heilbron's pipe gurgled and he poked at it.

'Now look at the next few pictures, Sam, and despair.'

There was a rustle and Sacheverell found himself looking at a large black and white photograph with a 'classified' stamp on its border. Heilbron continued: 'You can just see the railway line and the highway next to it coming in from the bottom. It's a busy line, all the way up from Leninsk. The big grey squares you see in the middle are the Soyuz assembly buildings. We think the ones on the left are for type G and Energia assembly – the brute force boosters. Now the tracks go further north and the railway line carries on. The next photo' – more rustle – 'shows the launch complex. The little arrows show what used to be their ICBM silos before Salt Two. Mostly the old SS-X series. Forget them. It's the Energia facility that's got me running to the john. You see it in the next picture. We'd taken routine high-level reconnaissance pictures of the launch, and this was taken by a big Bird on a perigee passage. The thing that's circled' – there was something like a full stop with a white circle round it – 'is a military transport. You see the launch vehicle just to the right. On the next photo you see them putting up netting over everything. They've got something to hide.'

A cluster of tiny dots, each one a man, was scattered around between the vehicles. They seemed to be pulling something over the ground. 'The netting's up in the next picture. Perspective has changed a bit; we're using a different satellite.' The same pattern of buildings was there, but now they were throwing long evening shadows. Cloud had edged in and some of the ground was obscured. A solitary dot threw a long shadow on the ground, arms and legs clearly visible. Sacheverell thought he could detect a moustache.

'They screwed up. Look at the next one.' The next one showed the netting in place, hiding truck, rocket and launch pad from prying satellite eyes. The sun had almost set.

'What am I supposed to see?' asked Hooper.

'Look at the shadows,' said Heilbron. 'The sun was shining under the netting. My geniuses used the outline of the shadows and the angle of the sun and they got the next picture.' They stared uncomprehendingly at a large Roscharsh ink blot; Sacheverell thought he saw a squid with a huge quill pen.

'Now to me this looks like an ink blot,' said Heilbron, to Hooper's evident relief. 'But my geniuses tell me these are the shadows of four men, the rocket, launch gantry, and a lifting crane. Use the computer to deproject and subtract out everything but the thing they're lifting and *Voila*!'

'A carrot!' exclaimed Hooper, staring in bewilderment at the final, blurred computer picture.

'That's right, Sam, it's a carrot,' said Heilbron triumphantly. 'It's two metres long; they're loading it under netting and they're taking it to Mars.'

Wallis said, 'I have it.' He pushed back his chair, stood up and paced up and down, staring into the middle distance. Then he came back, staring at Heilbron, and nodding his head in agreement.

'Well?' Hooper snapped.

'Some carrot, sir,' said Wallis.

Heilbron half-smiled. 'Got it in one. Let me tell you about the carrot, Sam. Look at the last picture. It's a nice present from our lady in the Cosmonaut Hotel.'

It was a black and white photograph. It had been taken through a door slightly ajar, the camera had been held about two feet back from the crack. Three men, dressed for a Russian winter, their fur hats and coats fringed with snow, stood at the reception desk.

'The little guy with specs is local, just reception for the other two. The guy with the Astrakhan hat we haven't yet identified. But the other guy we do recognize. His name is Boris Voroshilov, former lecturer in physics from Tbilisi, now employed at Chelyabinsk-7. He designs nukes.'

'Richard . . .'

Heilbron raised his hand and continued. 'Phobos Five is a cover. Somewhere out there the cosmonauts have sent an automated probe with a tape recorder on to Mars on the old orbit. Meanwhile our heroes have slipped their moorings and set out into the blue yonder on a new orbit, complete with carrot. Only it isn't a carrot Sam, it's a ten megaton hydrogen bomb.'

Sacheverell said, 'I know of only one application for a hydrogen bomb in deep space. Deflecting an asteroid.'

Heilbron pointed the end of his pipe at the JCJS. 'Tell me something. Why would Zhirinovsky want to do a thing like that?'

Hooper's face was like an executioner's.

The CIA chief hammered it home: 'Sam, we're going to get it right in the Kansas breadbasket.'

Inquisition: the Interrogation

The priest settled into the witness's chair. The notary said: 'Identify yourself to this Congregation.'

'I am Jacques Grandami, of the Jesuit Order. I teach theology and natural philosophy at a number of colleges in France.'

Terremoto began the questioning: 'You are acquainted with Vincenzo Vincenzi?'

Reptilian eyes flickered briefly in Vincenzo's direction. 'I know him from the school of theology in Paris, and later in Bologna.'

'What is your opinion of the man?'

'He claims to be devout.'

'Claims to be?'

'I cannot say that he is not. He has the outward appearance of piety. In Bologna he took part in the choral recitation of the divine office, and in the daily recitation of faults.'

'Why then do you seem to hesitate over his piety?'

'He is extremely disputatious, lacking the spirit of humility. He scorns reasoned argument which does not fit his opinion. He thus shows manifest contempt for the arguments of Scheiner, Ciermans, Malapert and other Jesuits against the Copernican system, which he advocates even though, as this Congregation knows, it has been condemned as false. Komensky of Prague, in his *Refutatio Astronomiae Copernicianae*, has written a brilliant refutation of the heliocentric doctrine. But Vincenzo refuses to acknowledge its intellectual force. Instead he has spoken to me, with approval, of the Bruno heresy that the Universe is infinite and that the stars are suns, with planets and living creatures on them. In addition to his false advocacy, he is not, I regret to say, true to his order. He belongs to the Order of Preachers but does not preach. He has taken a vow of poverty and yet lives in a villa provided by the Duke of Tuscany. He has taken a vow of celibacy but shares a bed with a woman.'

Terremoto made to dismiss Grandami but one of the cardinals, a man with a light freckled skin and an accent which seemed to place him in the far north of the country, stopped him. 'One moment! You have said that you are a theologian.'

'I am, Your Eminence.'

'Then perhaps you can answer this question. What is the basis, in the Holy Scriptures, for belief in a stationary Earth?'

Grandami smiled unpleasantly. 'How could Joshua have commanded the Sun to be still if it was not moving in the first place? Does the Psalmist not describe the Sun as going forth in a circuit to the ends of heaven? Does Job not write of the pillars of the Earth trembling?'

The cardinal bowed. 'Thank you, Jacques Grandami. The Peace of our Lord go with you.'

⧖

The interrogation began on the second day, without preliminaries. A row of grim faces met Vincenzo as he was guided to his bench. Cardinal Terremoto opened the proceedings. His piercing eyes were fixed on Vincenzo, and the corners of his mouth were turned down in an unconcealed scowl. Vincenzo felt his legs shaking and his stomach in queasy knots.

Terremoto looked right and left. 'This Holy Congregation is now prepared to question the prisoner. Before we proceed, does the advocate have anything to say on the prisoner's behalf?'

Marcello turned to his client. He whispered, 'Recant, Vincenzo.'

The monk shook his head.

'Recant and throw yourself on the mercy of the court. All these people want is a public abjuration.'

Vincenzo's head was lowered. Almost imperceptibly, he shook it again.

Marcello stood up. Terremoto's small eyes were glaring into his own; the hostility was undisguised, bearing down on the young man like a physical force. The lawyer, fear gnawing at his heart, took an instant decision which he knew would affect his future career and forever change the life of his client. 'Your Eminences, I regard the guilt of my client as sufficiently well established by these proceedings. As he persists in denying his guilt, and shows no sign of contrition for his erroneous beliefs, I must ask to be relieved of the duty to defend him.'

The cardinals murmured between themselves. There was some nodding of heads. Then Terremoto said, 'Your duty to the prisoner is discharged. Leave us with good conscience.'

'Marcello!' Vincenzo cried out in shock. But the lawyer avoided the astronomer's gaze, and Vincenzo could only watch as his former advocate picked up a sheaf of papers and scurried out of the courtroom, eyes to the ground and bent almost double. He momentarily buried his face in his hands.

The lawyer had hardly left the room when Terremoto began the questioning. 'On whose authority do you state that the Earth rotates?'

'My lawyer has sold his soul.'

'Answer the question.'

148

'Authority? That of my eyes and brain, Eminence.'
Vincenzo's voice was shaking.

'I ask of written authority.'

'Your Eminence, the English monk Bede stated that the
Earth is a ball floating in space a thousand years ago.
Nicolas Oresme, over three hundred years ago, stated that
the Earth is round and rotates about an axis. And the
same was said by Cardinal Nicholas Cusanus over two
centuries ago. They even say that Aristarchus and Eratos-
thenes . . .'

'Do you read Greek?'

'No, Eminence.'

'You therefore rely on hearsay, do you not?'

'I rely on generations of scholars produced by the
Mother Church, from Reginbald of Cologne to the Jesuit
writers of today and even such as Fra Paolo Foscarini of
the Carmelites.'

'But amongst the heathen scholars of ancient times,
does Aristotle not stand head and shoulders above the
rest?'

'Eminence, you know that is so.'

'And have you studied his *Physics and Metaphysics*?'

'I have, in translation, and there he commits himself to
a belief in an Earth around which the universe rotates. But
I believe that view to be in error.'

'But did not Thomas Aquinas, four centuries ago, show
that Aristotle's system is compatible with the Christian
doctrine? And is not Aristotle the foundation of natural
science throughout the Christian domain? Is it not then
possible that the error is yours?'

'Aristotle did not have the benefit of the telescope. Nor
the record of centuries of planetary motions which we
have.'

The Inquisitor looked down at some notes. The room
was silent. The sound of a chirping cricket drifted in from
the garden. And then Terremoto suddenly sprang a trap:

'Do you deny that the Bible is the supreme authority in the affairs of philosophy?'

'I believe that the Bible is intended to teach men to go to heaven, not how the heavens go.'

'*Ebbene!* What presumptions are hidden in that neat phrase! Are you also qualified as a theologian?'

'I did not say that, Eminence.'

'You have, however, just seen fit to make a theological pronouncement. The Council of Trent, in its Fourth Session, was explicit about where authority lies: the Word of God is to be interpreted strictly according to the unanimous consent of the Fathers. I repeat my question.' Terremoto looked across at the notary, who read out in a high-pitched voice: 'Do you deny that the Bible is the supreme authority in the affairs of philosophy?'

Vincenzo, colour drained from his face, said, 'Eminence, I do.'

There was an audible gasp from one of the younger cardinals. Terremoto continued: 'Is it also your opinion that the Holy Spirit has allowed the Holy Mother Church to be misled for the nineteen hundred years since Aristotle?'

Another trap, this one with steel teeth.

If Vincenzo replied yes, that the Church had received no guidance from above, then this was akin to denying the Virgin Birth or even the existence of God. If he said no, that the Holy Spirit could not have allowed such an error, then he was admitting to a wilful disregard of the teachings of the Church. Either answer would surely lead to the same fiery end. The notary leaned forward, his face screwed up in anticipation of recording the reply. The cardinals waited. The cricket outside the window chirruped on.

Vincenzo's voice was little more than a murmur: 'Your Grace, that is a theological question. I am incompetent to answer.'

Terremoto was relentless. 'And yet you claim to be a

devout Catholic. Did you not consider it your pious duty, even before meddling in hypotheses which attempt to revise the received wisdom of the Church, to ask such a question?'

'I believe with Doctor Paolicci of Padua that the mind of the Creator can be read in His Creation.'

'Do you accept that man was created in God's image?'

There was an expectant silence. After the heresies they had heard, the cardinals did not know what to expect of the wretched old man who faced them. But Vincenzo simply said, quietly, 'Of course, your Eminence.'

'Then how can he be otherwise than at the centre of the Universe?'

Vincenzo murmured something, wringing his hands as he did. The notary asked him to speak up, but the monk remained silent.

'The alternative diminishes mankind, does it not? And opens the door to unthinkable heresies?'

'God has two books, that of Nature and that of Scripture. They cannot contradict each other. I read the book of Nature. It says what it says.'

The remainder of the morning was taken up with a close interrogation on technical matters, on the precision of the Alfonsine Tables, the precession of the equinoxes, the motion of the eighth sphere, the angular sizes of the fixed stars, their lack of parallax and the fantastic stellar distances then implied in the Copernican system, and on the meaning of Christ's sacrifice to creatures on the supposed other worlds of Giordano Bruno. Terremoto dominated the questioning throughout, his deep-chested voice booming through the courtroom. He showed himself to have a remarkable grasp of the scientific issues. Only the cricket outside the window seemed uncowed: unimpressed by the Cardinal's powerful voice, it chirruped incessantly. By the time the court recessed, it was early afternoon and Vincenzo was drenched with sweat.

That evening, Vincenzo was offered the chance either to confess and recant or take five days to prepare his defence. To the Grand Inquisitor's astonishment, Vincenzo refused both options. Instead, he made a simple statement. It was brief and to the point. He hesitated briefly, feeling the weight of the Inquisition's hostility crushing down on him like a collapsing house, but then began to speak, his voice quavering but determined.

'I deny the *simplicitas* of Aristotle's universe, whereby the sun, moon and planets orbit in epicycles upon epicycles about the Earth. Through the Galilean tube, we see that the Moon is imperfect. It is pitted with craters. With our own eyes we see mountains and valleys like those on Earth. If the Moon is like the Earth, then the Earth is like the Moon. It is therefore just one of the heavenly bodies. The four Medicean planets, revolving around Jupiter, are the clearest proof that not everything revolves around the Earth. We see too, with the tube, that Venus goes through all the phases of the Moon, with the illuminated crescent always turned towards the Sun, and so clearly orbits the Sun and not the Earth. If our Earth is a heavenly body like the Moon, and also a planet like Venus, then we too must orbit the Sun.

'This Holy Congregation has referred to Aristotle, Ptolemy and the Holy Scripture as witnesses for the central position of the Earth. Aristotle also stated that the heavens are immutable. But did we not see a new star in 1572, one which was born, rose in brightness and then died? And if he was wrong in one astronomical matter why can he not be wrong in others? As for Ptolemy, have the new discoveries of the great navigators not made his geography obsolete? Why then should his chart of the heavens not be equally so? Many wise philosophers throughout history have believed that the Earth moves and the Sun stands still.

'As to the Scriptures, we should heed the warning of

Saint Augustine, who tells us not to be concerned when the astronomers seem to contradict the scriptures. It implies only that another interpretation must be sought for the Sacred Texts. Pererius, of the Collegio Romano, tells us that *non potest Sacrarum Literarum veris rationibus et experimentis humanarum doctrinarum esse contraria*. In any case, what are we to make of the words of Job: "Who moves the earth from its place"? Your Eminences are not trained in natural philosophy and are not competent to make judgements in that realm. In the interpretation of the world, it is the book of Nature which we must read, not that of the Holy Scripture.'

A tangible ripple came from the cardinals' table. Vincenzo, his die cast, carried on. 'I believe that the stars are made of fire. There are many more stars in existence than those we see. The perspective tube of Galileo resolves the light of the Milky Way into myriads of stars. These must be suns like our own, at immense distances. That is why the constellations do not change and the stars do not trace out ellipses in the sky as the seasons progress: the stars are at such immense distances that the parallax is too small to be seen. You declare that the Earth is stationary as a matter of faith, and that I am therefore a heretic to hold otherwise. But suppose that, in years or centuries to come, the astronomers prove beyond doubt that it is the Sun which is stationary and that the Earth moves around it? Then you who try me, the cardinals of this congregation, will be seen as the heretics. The Mother Church will be exposed to scandal, and forced to reverse Her doctrine, and Her enemies will delight in exposing Her to ridicule. Eminences, you commit a grave error in making matters of faith out of astronomical questions.'

The old man flopped down, drained. The cardinals, virtually accused of heresy, sat stunned. Terremoto's expression had gone through all the stages of amazement, horror and finally outrage as Vincenzo's audacious statement had proceeded. Their Eminences filed out without a word.

That night, Vincenzo slept not in the luxurious apartment of a Holy Office official, but in a damp cell in the Castel Sant' Angelo. And while he slept, his judges discussed his case by candlelight, and decided on their next step: the *territio realis*.

The White House, East Wing Theatre, 21^{h}00

Sacheverell sat, his stomach churning, in the front row of the little theatre. The door opened and a tall, elderly man peered in. His shirt sleeves were rolled up and he was wearing an outrageously multi-coloured waistcoat.

'Coffee, son?' the old man asked.

'Thank you, sir. Two sugars.' The man shuffled out. Minutes passed, while Sacheverell's mouth dried up. Then the door was opened with the push of a foot and the man reappeared, a paper cup in each hand. He sat down beside Sacheverell and passed a cup over. The astronomer noticed that the old man had one sock black, one blue.

'Two sugars. Now before we get started. We're farmers; we're bankers; we're lawyers. Me, I'm just a country boy from Wyoming. So keep it simple.'

'Will do, Mister President.'

'Okay. This will be new to most of the people here. I've had a preliminary briefing from the Secretary of Defense and he tells me this asteroid thing will devastate us when it hits. But what does he know? You're the horse's mouth, son, and that's where I want to hear it from.'

'I'll do my best, sir,' Sacheverell gulped.

The President grinned. 'What is an asteroid anyway?'

'An asteroid is a lump of rock, sir, going round the Sun just like the planets. They're a few miles across and blacker than soot, very hard to find. Maybe there are a thousand or two big ones in orbit between the planets but only three hundred have been found so far. It could be a hundred thousand years before one of them hits the Earth but when it does you get a giant explosion.'

'How giant?'

'Say one landed in Mexico City. The blast wave would hit us here at a thousand miles an hour. Now with an ordinary explosion, say from a bomb, the blast is just a sudden wind, over in a fraction of a second. But with this one, the blast would go on for hours. Air temperature while it's blowing would be four or five hundred degrees Centigrade, more or less like the inside of a pizza oven.'

'That was quite a speech, son. But I thought you said these things are only a few miles across.' The President's country-boy grin had faded as Sacheverell had talked.

'It's their speed, sir. You have to think of it as a big mountain covering twenty miles every second. When it hits the ground it vaporizes in about a tenth of a second. You could get half a million megatons easy. I've prepared a movie which should give an idea what to expect.'

The door opened and half a dozen men wandered in and spread themselves around the little theatre. Sacheverell had spoken to two of them, Heilbron and Hooper, only a few hours previously. Heilbron caught Sacheverell's eye and nodded. The Secretary of Defense sauntered over and sat down beside Sacheverell. He was about fifty. Away from the television cameras, Sacheverell noticed, Bellarmine had a slightly jaundiced complexion and a receding hairline. 'Hail!' he said. The Chief nodded amiably. Sacheverell, wedged between the President of the United States of America and the Secretary of Defense, felt his skin tingling.

Heilbron walked over. 'Mister President, I've got a movie.'

'Okay let's get into this,' said President Grant. He finished the coffee and crumpled the paper cup, letting it fall to the floor. 'Seems we're in for a matinée performance.'

Heilbron stepped up on to the dais and picked up a short pointer. The lights went down. Maps and photographs appeared in succession on the screen. Heavy-jowled Slavic faces appeared under fur hats. Heilbron kept waving the pointer flamboyantly. A shaky amateur movie showed a military transporter leaving some camp surrounded by a tall barbed-wire fence; another showed tarpaulin-covered train wagons being hauled across an icy, blasted landscape. When the dark conical shape of the hydrogen bomb appeared the President said 'Stop!' and the movie froze, the black shape filling the screen in blurred close-up.

Grant stood up, the picture of the bomb illuminating his face and chest. 'Jesus, is that it?'

'Just about, Mister President. We've intercepted a coded message from Phobos but it's got us beat.'

'Rich, this strikes me as paper thin.'

'Sir, we've often had to act on less. I believe the balance of probability is strongly tipped towards a hostile act against us.'

'By whom?' The Russians alone? Khazakhstan? The whole damned Federation?'

Heilbron shrugged.

'Just what is the significance of this?' the President asked, turning grimly to Sacheverell.

Sacheverell put down his cup and walked nervously to the dais. Heilbron sat down wearily in Sacheverell's chair, and the President sat on the edge of the little platform, his knees crossed. Suddenly, in the half-light, the astronomer found himself facing men who had shed their homely television faces, men with calculating eyes, and ice in their veins, and powers beyond those of the gods. He fought back a surge of near panic.

'Sir, it is technologically possible to divert a near-Earth

asteroid on to a collision course with any given country.' Sacheverell realized with horror that his mouth had dried up, he was almost croaking. 'It would take state of the art technology and extreme precision. The technique would be to blast some material off the asteroid at an exact place and time, diverting its orbit. The problem would be controlling the devastation, which could spill over into neighbouring countries. My movie illustrates a range of possibilities. Movie, please.'

The projector whirred quietly at the back of the room. Mysterious numbers and crosses appeared on the screen. A black and white title read

Impact: 5×10^5 Mt, vertical incidence.
Assailant: Nickel iron, tensile strength 400 MPa, $H_2O=0.00$ by mass.
Target: Bearpaw shale, tensile strength 0.2 MPa, $H_2O=0.14$ by mass.

The title disappeared, replaced by a grid of lines covering the bottom half of the screen. The only movement was a tumbling of numbers on the top right of the screen, next to a label saying *Lapsed time* =. The audience waited.

A green spot came in rapidly from the top. It struck the grid. The lines buckled, and formed a hole with a raised rim. Green splodges hurried off the edge of the screen. Away from the hole the grid of lines was vibrating at high speed, like a violently shaken jelly. The lines vanished and there was an old movie taken at the Nevada test site. There was a timber-framed, Middle America house. At first, nothing was happening. But then the paintwork started to smoke, and curtains were burning. And suddenly the house was splintered wood and smoke streaking into the distance and Sacheverell was saying this is what to expect two thousand kilometres from a half million-megaton impact.

Now there was a coloured map of the USA, with cities marked in bold font. Circles were radiating out from a spot in the middle of Kansas, like ripples on a pond, as if the map were under water. The numbers were loping along in minutes now, rather than seconds, and Sacheverell was saying you expect Richter Nine up here on the Canadian border and down here in Chicago. The map disappeared and more old footage followed; this time the camera was panning over horribly flat rubble. A few dazed individuals in Arab dress stared at the camera. Others were crawling over a mound of debris, like ants over a hill. Sacheverell was saying of course these are stone houses and we can't be sure this applies exactly to New York or Chicago but you would surely level skyscrapers. He was aware that he was beginning to gabble but he couldn't help himself. His voice was now a croak.

Then of course there's the fire, he said, rising to the tension he sensed in his audience. About thirty per cent of the land area of the States is combustible in the summer and twenty per cent in the winter. You would expect thousands of fires over an area the size of France. They could merge into one giant conflagration so you would take out the whole of central USA with flames from the exposure to the rising fireball and this is Hamburg during a firestorm only with red hot ash thrown over the whole country you might set the whole country alight and then of course there's the biomass the biomass yes especially as fat melts at forty-five Centigrade I mean Celsius but they're the same really you expect living people to fry in their own fat over most of the States your skin will bubble and peel off in a few seconds and then your blood and water will boil and then your fat will combust and you will just carbonize while the blast is sweeping you along at the speed of a jet.

The audience sat riveted.

Now the movie was showing something that looked like

one of the more lurid products of a Hollywood studio. An ocean was boiling. Now the boiling green lines formed into a pattern; they reared up into a wave, a tumbling, foaming breaker which washed over little cartoon skyscrapers like a wave over pebbles, and Sacheverell was saying we're not sure about the stability of waves that big but we're working on it with the Sandia teraflop but a splash like this off the Eastern seaboard would wash over the Eastern States but the Appalachians would stop it and you would be okay in Bozeman, Montana. Then there were more flashing symbols, the projector stopped whirring and the lights went up. Sacheverell swallowed nervously, blinking in the light.

His audience remained frozen.

'You got casualty estimates for this, son?' The President finally asked, quietly.

'Hard to judge, sir. Most of the USA is less than two thousand kilometres from Kansas. A half million-megaton bang on Kansas I reckon would leave two hundred million casualties from the prompt effects.'

'You mean injured?'

'No sir, dead.'

'What about survivors?' the Vice-President asked.

'With this scenario one to ten per cent of North America would survive the initial impact. But they would have big problems. Mainly lack of food, medical care and sanitation. I reckon most of them would be taken out with starvation, typhus, cholera, bubonic plague, stuff like that.'

'Comment, anyone?' the President asked, turning round.

'What you're saying,' said the Secretary of Defense, his features drawn tensely, 'Is that the technology is available to create a weapon a million times more powerful than a hydrogen bomb?'

Sacheverell nodded.

'You're some sort of nut,' the Secretary of Defense said.

'It only takes a gentle push, sir. There are plenty of these asteroids around. The trick is to find one that passes close to the Earth. Then you soft land a small atom bomb on it. If you explode the bomb on the right place at the right time, you nudge the asteroid into an Earth-crossing orbit. It doesn't need much. With a mid-course correction – a second explosion with a small atom bomb or even conventional explosives – you could target the asteroid to within a couple of hundred miles.'

Grant turned to Heilbron. 'You say they've pulled it off already?'

'In my opinion it's on the way in now.'

A slim, hawk-nosed man in his late fifties, wearing an expensive, dark three-piece suit, was standing at the back door of the theatre. He spoke angrily. 'In the name of God, Rich, you're telling us we're at war.'

Grant raised his hand quickly. 'Not here, Billy.' He turned to the DCI. 'How many people know about this?'

'The seven of us in this room, two of my staff, and one of General Hooper's aides. On the European side, about an equal number. About twenty people in all. And a team of eight trying to find the thing. They're hidden away in a mountaintop observatory in Arizona.'

'Doctor Sacheverell, we know where to reach you?'

'Yes, sir. I'm one of the team, in Eagle Peak Observatory.'

'Don't even discuss this with your dog. Gentlemen, that applies to us all. I want no apocalyptic statements, no veiled hints, no unusual moves. Nathan, Sam, the Green Room at 3 a.m.'

'With respect sir . . .'

'Nathan, I'm about to entertain guests. Like I said, no unusual moves. What do you want me to do? Send him out for a pizza?'

DAY THREE

The Green Room, Wednesday, 03^h00

Grant and his wife, accompanying King Charles, Camilla Parker-Bowles and His Britannic Majesty's Ambassador, walked along the long Entrance Hall, the sound of Liszt's *Hungarian Rhapsodies* coming from a dozen violins still entertaining a hundred guests in the State Dining Room. The President's head was fuzzy from Chateau Latour and his cheeks ached from hours of enforced smiling. By protocol, he led them to the elevator taking them up to the residence for a private talk.

An hour later Charles and Camilla, looking exhausted, were being escorted by Secret Service men to Blair House, across the road from No. 1651. Grant gave it another hour and then came back down by the stairs to the Entrance Hall. He turned through the colonnade into the Cross Hall. Adam-style chandeliers and bronze standard lamps threw a warm glow on to the marble walls. Images of past presidents looked down at him. The violins were now silent. Somewhere three chimes of a clock cut into the stillness.

A door was ajar and he turned into the Green Room. Logs crackled in the fireplace, and a whiff of woodsmoke unexpectedly evoked a distant memory: a camp fire, sausages sizzling on a stick, smoke stinging his eyes, young men and women laughing. But before he could place the image in time, it had gone forever.

The Secretary of Defense, Nathan Bellarmine, was

sprawled in a Federal-period chintz armchair at the fire. He had smooth, black hair, was slightly balding, and wore a dark three-piece suit. The dark waistcoat and Brylcreemed hair made him look slightly like a snooker player.

Occupying the chair at the other side of the fireplace was a small, hook-nosed, middle-aged man with white hair and eyes like dark pebbles: this was Arnold Cresak, the President's National Security Adviser and a long-standing confidant.

The third man in the room was Hooper, sitting upright on a hard-backed chair, underneath Durrie's nostalgic *Farmyard in Winter*. There were dark shadows under the soldier's eyes. Grant waved them down as they began to rise, tossed his dinner jacket on to the carpeted floor and himself sank with a sigh into deep upholstery.

'Is the room clean?'

Cresak nodded. 'It's been swept.'

The President loosened his black tie. 'I don't like this early hours stuff but what can we do? What are we doing?'

Bellarmine said: 'I informed the British Prime Minister, and the Presidents of France and Germany, as you instructed. They sent us a couple of specialists Monday morning. I now have a team of seven trying to locate the asteroid. They're being run by a Colonel Noordhof, who's with USAF Space Command. I assigned him to 50 Wing, Falcon Colorado. Special Projects, which covers no end of sin.'

'Look, one whisper and we're fried. Who are these seven samurai?'

'We have McNally, the NASA Administrator. The rest are top scientists, for example Shafer, the CalTech genius.'

'Shafer. The hippie scientist?'

Bellarmine said: 'With two Nobel Prizes. He was on the cover of *Time* last month.'

'I don't trust these superbrains: you don't know what

they're really thinking. And what are we doing with Europeans on the team? That sounds to me like a couple of loose cannon.'

'We want the top people whoever they are. We're in a life-or-death situation here.'

'They know the timescale we're working to?'

Bellarmine nodded. 'Consensus is the chances of success are very slim.'

The President held the palms of his hands towards the fire. 'Sam, where in your opinion will the Russians hit us?'

'Kansas. First, they maximize their chance of hitting land. Second, they get Omaha, Cheyenne Peak and the re-vamped silos. If you believe this Sacheverell they'll roast the States in less time than it takes to roast a chicken.'

'Kansas is a reasonable guess,' said Cresak. 'But so is California. Maybe they're going for our economic base. They don't even care if they miss because a Pacific splash would submerge the West Coast.'

'And an Atlantic one would decapitate us,' said Hooper. 'But who cares? We're dead wherever it hits.'

'Okay.' Grant took a deep breath and visibly tensed. He looked like a man about to jump off a cliff. 'Now say we don't find Nemesis in time.'

Hooper said, 'Sir, in that case the parameters define a very narrow envelope.'

'Sam, I'm a tired old man. If you mean we have limited options just say so.'

'We have to assume the worst-case situation.'

'Which is?'

'A blue sky impact. The asteroid comes in from daylight. The first we know about it is when it hits the upper atmosphere at sixty thousand miles an hour and we get a two-second warning.'

'Excuse me, but did you say a *two-second* warning?'

'Yes sir. Two seconds.'

'As His Royal Majesty expressed it to me, in his very British way, it would freeze the balls off a brass monkey in here.' The President poked at the fire and threw in a couple of logs. 'Anyone want a hot chocolate?' Cresak leaned over to a work table next to the fireplace, pulled a telephone from a drawer and muttered an order.

'Now in those two seconds,' Hooper continued, 'while it's punching our air away, it seems it will also generate a massive electric current overhead. So it screws up our C-cubed systems.'

'I thought we had fibre-optic cables from here to Omaha,' the President said.

'A few, not a complete network. The real trouble is, the optical links still need electronic relays to boost the signal every so many miles. If the EMP zaps the relays, then the optical links go dead. Of course our satellite links collapse and we get cut off, isolated from everything at the critical moment.'

'Well now that's just dandy. A few thousand engineers spend a few gigabucks of public money trying to fix it so we maintain integrity of command while the nukes are falling, only when it comes to the crunch you tell me what we really need are smoke signals.'

Hooper remained impassive. 'The links might survive through a nuclear war, Chief, but the asteroid, now that's a new ballgame.'

Bellarmine said, 'So we lose contact with our counterstrike forces at the moment of atmospheric entry, and impact takes place two seconds later?' The Chairman of the Joint Chiefs of Staff nodded.

'I like your technique, Nathan,' Grant said, turning his palms once again towards the rising flames. 'I like the casual way you slipped the word *counterstrike* into the conversation.'

An elderly man, wearing a dark blazer with the presidential seal on the breast pocket, came in, followed by a young maid. A table was set up with four steaming mugs. They left without a word.

Bellarmine turned to Hooper. '*Could* we counterstrike?'

The soldier shook his head. 'Not effectively, Mister Secretary. When Nemesis cuts loose we'll turn into a snake without a head. Even at Detcon One we couldn't contact our silos, and our bombers would be torn to bits even if we got them aloft.'

'We still have our submarines,' Bellarmine said.

'How do we contact them? VLF, blue-green lasers and ELF. Very Low Frequency needs a wire a kilometre long trailed behind a TACAMO bomber. But all our command posts would be overwhelmed even before we contacted the bomber. The blue-green lasers beam down from the ORICS satellites. But' – Hooper checked off the points with his fingers – 'One: the subs and satellites have to be in the right positions. Two: you have Kansas up there in the stratosphere giving us an umbrella of red-hot ash over the States. Three: you have an ionosphere gone crazy. So the signals don't get up to our satellites in the first place.'

'And ELF?'

'We use a forty-mile antenna buried under Wisconsin. The radio pulses vibrate the whole Laurentian Shield. The vibration can be picked up from anywhere on Earth.'

Grant grunted. 'So? That's Nemesis-proof.'

'We still have to be alive to send messages.'

Bellarmine said, 'Not necessarily. If we keep broadcasting Condition Red with the ELF, and other communications channels break down, standing orders are for submarine commanders to launch their nuclear weapons.'

The soldier leaned forward intently and said, 'There's a problem with that.'

'You may as well lay it on, Sam,' said the President.

'If we launch missiles they'll run into Kansas on the way up and disintegrate. It's like Brilliant Pebbles in reverse, a sort of natural Star Wars destroying our own counter-strike. Anyway, our submarine fleet carries only a small fraction of our megatonnage. Even if we get off a few Tridents the new ABM rings round Moscow, Kiev, Leningrad and so on could handle them. Mister President, it's simple. If they get Nemesis in first our capacity to respond is smashed. Russia will incur acceptable losses, but we'll be dead and gone.'

The President sighed. 'Okay Nathan, get it off your chest. What are our options?'

'They're stark. We can accept the annihilation of America and do nothing about it. We can wait for the impact and then try to hit back with our offensive capability smashed. Or we can beat them to the punch. Launch a nuclear strike now.'

'Uhuh.'

The President closed his eyes. Hooper wondered what thoughts were running through the old man's head. The soldier said, 'Only the third option has military credibility.'

A surge of fear suddenly went through Cresak's nervous system like an electric shock. It was more than the fact that the unimaginable prospect of a nuclear war had entered the discussion; it was the fact that it had slipped in, by stealth, almost without conscious reasoning. 'Crap,' he said, his voice unsteady. 'The Russians would hit back. Then Nemesis would come in and finish off whatever was left of us.'

'The time for the Major Attack Option has never been better,' Bellarmine said. 'They don't expect it, their political system's in chaos, and we have a dozen Alpha lasers in orbit to handle any Russian missiles that do get launched.'

'You're insane,' said Cresak. 'What about Carter's PD-59? They could survive a strike long enough to obliterate us.'

'Nuclear war is winnable,' said Hooper emphatically.

'The situation has moved on since McNamara and Carter; we have the Alpha shields now. The winner is the one who hits first. Central Command computers show that a first strike will be decisive and that's why our command and control systems are geared for a first-strike capability. We've always known that a second strike, one under attack, would fail utterly. Sir, we'll never get another chance like this.'

'This is lunacy,' said the National Security Adviser. His voice was shaky but determined. He ticked the points off with his fingers, one by one. 'The Russians kept their C3 system intact through all the political upheavals. Even with SALT and START they still have fourteen hundred ICBMs and a thousand submarine-launched missiles. They have two thousand bomb-proof bunkers to protect their top leadership. The situation has changed in Russia too. They've now got a streamlined chain of command, straight from their General Staff to their missile units. The new leadership have thrown away the old safeguards. They've obtained the unlock codes from the old KGB. The political officers have long gone from the system. They've taken away the electromechanical switches for sealing bomb doors.'

'Get to the point, Arnold. What are you driving at?' asked the President.

'Sir, they could respond in seconds. And if even a handful of their Sawflies got through, America would be finished.'

'Hell, Arnold, we can handle it,' Hooper said. 'The Alpha lasers. And the leadership would be fried before they even reached their bunkers.'

The President sipped at his chocolate. It was too sweet. 'What's the modern view on nuclear winter?' he asked.

Hooper pulled a thin blue document from a battered briefcase at the side of his chair. 'Our climate modellers have looked at all sorts of smoke injection scenarios.

Mostly they darken the sun for about three months and could wipe out agriculture in the growing season. That's another reason for an early strike, to let the sky clear by July.'

Grant said, 'Sam, let's not get too excited. There may not even be an asteroid. All we have is a string of circumstantial evidence that Heilbron has woven into a pattern. We can't go levelling the planet just because the DCI has an overactive imagination.'

'With respect, sir,' Bellarmine insisted, 'if there is an asteroid, chances are the first we know of it is when it hits, by which time we're too late for an effective counter-strike. The only realistic option is Number Three.'

'I believe we're seeing a sort of collective insanity here,' Cresak said, his fear betraying itself in his voice.

'Okay, let's get down to basics,' said Grant. 'What's the strategic purpose of your third option, Sam?'

Hooper put down his mug of chocolate. His face showed real bafflement. 'I must be missing something, sir.'

'What purpose is served by destroying Russia?'

'Retaliation,' said Hooper, the bafflement giving way to incredulity.

Bellarmine sensed something. He said, 'Mister President. It's been the official policy of every administration since World War Two that a Russian attack on mainland America will be met with the Major Attack Option.'

'Public policy, yes,' Grant replied. 'And you know damn well our true policy is that if the diplomatic game ever gets hot we hit first. Hooper's right. It's the only chance of winning a nuclear exchange.'

'So!' Bellarmine raised his hands in an Italian-like gesture. 'For fifty years mutual assured destruction has kept the West safe. What's the difference between this asteroid thing and a big missile attack? The logic's identical. We play it out.'

'Why?'

Bellarmine stayed silent. His expression was an exercise in suppressed bewilderment and outrage.

Cresak drove the point home. 'I guess maybe the Chief thinks it's pointless. Two big dust bowls instead of one.'

Bellarmine said, 'Arnold, your jaw has got disengaged from your brain. Responsibility for the Russian people lies with their leadership, not with us. Our policy has been spelled out, clear as crystal, ever since World War Two. We serve future generations better by following through than by just backing off when the chips are down. The lesson will be remembered for a thousand years.'

'No doubt the cave dwellers for the next thousand years will be grateful for the lesson,' Cresak replied, his voice heavy with sarcasm. 'And the two hundred million innocent people you burn will see the point too. We don't seem to have progressed since the Salem witches.'

'Sure!' Bellarmine snarled. 'Our ancestors thought they were doing right and they got it wrong. And if we get entangled in moral problems now we'll get it just as wrong as they did. This is the White House, not a department of moral philosophy. Our business is to respond, according to publicly laid-down policy, to circumstances imposed on us by the Russians.'

'It's getting hot in here,' said the President.

Hooper said, 'Look. We're under attack, so we defend. Period. Like any country, man or creature since time began. The only live issues are targeting policy and battle management.'

'What targets do you have in mind, Sam?'

'I've arranged a murder session with JSTPS in Offutt at twelve hundred hours. You'll have our prepared options within forty-eight hours. The target sets will depend on whether we launch under attack or go for pre-emption. Mister President, I'm pushing for pre-emption. We have to finish this East–West thing once and for all. The prime target will be Russia but we should also take out Armenia, Belorussia, Moldavia, Kazakhstan, Georgia, Uzbekistan, Tajikistan and Estonia. We may also want to think about Cuba, Vietnam and China while we're about it. I'm thinking of updating the old SIOP-5D list.'

Grant peered into Hooper's eyes. The soldier stared unflinchingly back. 'Some shopping list,' the President said. 'What, specifically, do you mean by take out?'

'I mean destroy all nuclear and conventional military forces, the military and political leadership, the major economic and industrial centres, and all cities with more than 25,000 population.'

'LeMay would have been proud of you, Sam. Why China?'

'We'll be so weak after Nemesis that we can't afford to leave potential enemies around. Mister President, I want your unconditional assurance on this matter. That in the event of an asteroid strike on America becoming a proven eventuality, you will order a retaliatory counterstrike.'

A log collapsed in the fire, sending a little shower of sparks up the chimney. Grant lowered his head, strumming his fingers lightly on his knee. The others stared at him, frozen like models from a tableau in a wax museum. Thirty seconds passed, each one a century long.

'At this moment of time I will give no such assurance.'

'I don't believe I'm hearing this,' said Bellarmine. His tone was aggressive. 'Massive retaliation has been the backbone of our defence posture for generations, endorsed by successive administrations. It can't be capriciously set aside by one individual. Not even a President. Your first duty is the defence of America. If you fail in that, you fail in your duty as President of these United States.'

'Why thank you, Nathan, a homily on my duty as President is just what I need at this time of night.' President Grant stretched and yawned. 'Well, I've enjoyed

174

our little fireside chat. Could this thing hit tonight?'

'Unlikely. Of course we don't know for sure.' Bellarmine was trembling with anger.

'What's the warning time for a night impact?'

'We think ten to forty minutes, sir,' said the Chief of Staffs.

'Better than two seconds. Nathan, Arnold, I want you guys to come up with a joint memorandum on the policy options facing us on the assumption that Nathan's team fails to identify Nemesis or can't find any way to stop it. I want it in time for the extraordinary NSC meeting on Friday midnight.'

The President stared into the fire for some moments. Then he seemed to come to a decision. 'We must keep our options open. I'm prepared to go some way with you, Sam. Increase our state of alert. Let's go to Orange.'

Bellarmine nodded his agreement. 'Sam, upgrade to Defcon 3 worldwide.'

The President stood up, and the men followed him into the hallway. 'Oh by the way, gentlemen. Merry Christmas.' He made his way towards the secret stairway at the East Hall which would take him to the third floor and the Family Quarters, an old man longing for rest. Cresak went back into the Green Room and sat down, staring into the leaping flames. Hooper went off, heading for the back exit. Bellarmine paced up and down the long corridor for ten minutes, feeling stunned. Then he too went towards the rear of the building.

The air was sharp and cold, and there was a bitter breeze. The grounds were white with a foot of freshly fallen snow. A pine tree, its coloured lights swaying in the breeze, stood on the central lawn. Hooper, wearing a long army coat and a white scarf, was standing on the steps of the North Portico, flapping his arms against his sides. A few Secret Service men hovered in the background; they looked frozen stiff.

'Was I hearing right in there, Mister Secretary?' asked Hooper, his breath misty in the freezing air.

'Give me a lift,' said Bellarmine grimly. 'We have to talk.'

'Too damn right. Where you heading?'

'Virginia.'

'Big place. Defcon Three can wait awhile.'

⧗

Hooper pressed a button and a glass partition slid up, cutting them off from the army driver. The general lit up a small cigar and its tip glowed red in the dark.

'You have to smoke these disgusting things?' Bellarmine asked.

'Privilege of rank,' Hooper replied, exhaling a dense smoke cloud. 'Anyway, these disgusting things just happen to be fine Havana cheroots. Heilbron gets his field people to bring them in from Cuba.'

They passed on to the Ellipse. A group of youths stood shivering, scarves round their necks and woollen hats pulled down almost to their eyes. Bellarmine just caught the words 'Say No To Torture' on a placard as the beam of light from the car swept across it.

'A pacifist for a president, at a time like this,' said Hooper. Now the headlights were picking up the broad swathe of Constitution Avenue.

'What do you want – Rambo?'

'Rambo we could handle.' Hooper inhaled the cigar smoke. 'Nathan, we can't let it happen.'

'Meaning?'

'You know what I mean.'

The car was driving past the Vietnam War Memorial. Beyond it the rotunda of the Lincoln Memorial was lit up with a ghostly glow. Bellarmine began to feel his lungs outlined by cigar smoke. 'Grant's mother was a Quaker,' he said. 'Can it be relevant?'

Hooper took another big draw. 'No pacifist should hold the office of president.'

'Sam, talk like that is highly dangerous.'

'Uhuh.'

The car crossed the Woodrow Wilson Memorial bridge; little ice floes on the Potomac reflected orange in the street lights. Snow, compacted by earlier traffic, covered the Beltway. The driver pulled out to pass a truck and grit pattered briefly on the windscreen.

After twenty minutes, marked by a stunned silence and a rapidly increasing smoke density, a sign said Langley and the car turned off the highway. They drove along a tunnel of light. Soldiers stopped them at the gate of the CIA Headquarters, and then they drove past the conference centre. The headlights picked out the imposing central doorway of the main building, but Bellarmine tapped at the glass partition and guided the driver on to the broad sweep of road connecting the five main buildings of the Headquarters. It pulled to a halt at a back entrance, lit up by spotlights hidden in bushes. The car behind them stopped.

Hooper repeated, grimly, 'No pacifist has the right to hold the office of president.'

'So you said.' The driver opened the door and Bellarmine stepped out into the icy air. After Hooper's smoke-filled car, the fragrance of the night was delicious. While the driver held the door, the Secretary of Defense turned back and leaned in to the car. 'The question is: *what are we going to do about it?*'

Eagle Peak, Wednesday

Webb rummaged in a cardboard box in the dormitory cupboard, and found a woollen hat to match the multi-coloured jumper. He pulled the hat on and headed for the kitchen, intending to make a hot chocolate before facing the chilly outside air once more. Shafer was staggering into the kitchen with a rabbit-sized boulder, coated with snow. Noordhof opened the door of the microwave cooker, and Shafer heaved the boulder in, setting the timer for five minutes.

Webb rattled a saucepan on to the cooker and added milk. 'It won't work,' he said, looking for a tin of hot chocolate in a cupboard stuffed with the detritus of past visiting observers.

'Mark's idea,' said Shafer. 'He's just shown me a *Newsweek* article by Broadbent from some months back. Mark can't confirm without clearance, which would take time, but listen to what this guy says.' He picked up the opened magazine from a kitchen work surface:

'In the euphoria of the First Cold War thaw, and with the easing of security in government laboratories around the States, previously tight-lipped administrators appeared to confirm what many academic scientists outside the system had long claimed: that Star Wars was a spectacular, and highly expensive, failure. A year of investigative reporting by our team, however, has turned up a different story.

'Blah blah blah. The guy goes on to say there was an element of disinformation in the "Star Wars Failed" stuff. He says the Army have an array of antennae not too far from Albuquerque. They call it the Beta maser, and it's arguably in contravention of the ABM Treaty. You'll note that Mark isn't contradicting me. Broadbent even says that on one experimental run the Beta maser destroyed a warhead they'd launched from Mid-Pacific, the moment it appeared over the horizon. So if the Beta exists maybe it could do something to the asteroid, but Mark has the right to remain silent, which right you'll notice he's exercising.'

Noordhof said nothing, but he was looking pleased with himself.

'That is one impressive zap,' said Kowalski, looking up from a sheaf of papers. 'Assuming there's truth in the story, maybe it's the answer to our prayers. Colonel, you must cut through the tape. Get us clearance for this stuff right away.'

'No need,' said Shafer. 'We can work out what we need from the article. If these guys can really vaporize a warhead at say five thousand miles' range, it means they penetrate the ablation shield and raise the missile's internal temperature to a thousand degrees within two or three seconds. So let's see how hot this rock gets in five minutes with a miserable kilowatt and use it to get its thermal conductivity.'

The milk was coming to the boil. Webb pummelled hard-caked chocolate powder in a tin. 'It won't work,' he repeated, stirring in the chocolate. Noordhof scowled.

The microwave oven pinged and Shafer put his hand on the rock. 'Warm to the touch. It went in at zero Centigrade so it's gone through thirty degrees in five minutes, say five or six degrees a minute.'

Webb took a sip at the hot chocolate and sighed happily. 'I expect your rock is still cold inside.'

Shafer nodded. 'So is Nemesis. And if it's rock the maser heat will get conducted down quickly. Okay, say a kilowatt gives us half a degree a second on this little stone, and the Beta maser heats a target at five hundred degrees a second.' The Nobel man counted fingers. 'Hey, these guys must be beaming one megawatt per square metre at five thousand miles' range, can you believe that?'

Noordhof radiated happiness. 'Nothing could withstand it. And laser beams don't spread out with distance. We'll ablate Nemesis clean out of the solar system, punch boulders off it. Hey, who needs the eggheads? I thought of this all by myself.'

Shafer shook his head sorrowfully. 'No dice, Mark. Laser beams do spread out. Imagine two mirrors at the ends of a tube, reflecting light back and forth, one of the mirrors with a pinhole. You generate fluorescence inside the tube, and the light reflects and gets pumped up to huge intensity. The only light that makes it out through the hole has travelled the full length of the beam, but there's still an angular spread. It's the wavelength of the light divided by the diameter of the gun.'

'Maybe it's a very big gun,' Noordhof interrupted, 'Giving a very small dispersion.'

'You have the Alpha lasers in orbit. They're hydrogen-fluoride, emitting at 2.7 microns. I guess their peak power can reach ten or twenty megawatts, but they can't be more than a few metres across.'

Noordhof waved the magazine at Shafer. His tone was a mixture of triumph and desperation. 'But this guy is talking about masers, not lasers. Everything is much bigger at radio wavelengths.'

Shafer shook his head again. 'No way can you guys be hiding an array more than ten kilometres across, not even in the New Mexico desert. *Ergo*, if you're beaming centimetre waves the angular spread is at least one part in a million.'

Noordhof spread his hands. 'So? Nothing!'

'Nothing at five thousand miles. But if you catch Nemesis a million kilometres away the centimetre wave beam is spread out over one kilometre, the whole size of the asteroid. With attenuation like that you couldn't boil an egg. Uncertainties in thermal conductivity or internal temperature will make no difference. I'm sorry Mark, but your top secret, Darth Vader, gigabuck, Space Dominance, missile-zapping Star Wars supermaser is as useful as a peashooter. We're back to nukes.'

Webb couldn't resist it: 'I told you it wouldn't work.'

'Where the hell do you think you're going, Webb? Are you looking for Nemesis in the woods?'

'I'm looking for inspiration, Colonel. From the performance I've seen here, I'm more likely to find it with the squirrels.'

Noordhof opened the microwave door angrily. 'Well, you might take the friggin' rock out with you.'

Shafer was still laughing when Webb left the building.

At the far end of the little car park there was a gap in the trees which, on closer examination, turned out to be the beginning of a natural path. It was close to a cluster of garbage bins and Webb suspected that it might be a raiding route for some animals. He took off along it, and found that the path skirted the foot of Eagle Peak, rising gently as it went, with the cliff easily visible to the left through the heavy ponderosa trees. After about twenty minutes, far beyond Noordhof's hundred-metre limit, he turned off to the base of the cliff, brushed the powdery snow off a broad boulder and sat down on it. There was the merest hint of cable rising above the trees about a mile back; otherwise there were no signs of human artefact. For the first time since he had been snatched from another snow-covered mountain, halfway round the planet, Webb had time to stop and think.

A last-minute asteroid deflection was a crass thing, a hefty punch with a barely controllable outcome. A punch on the nose, slowing Nemesis down long enough for the Earth to slip past, was more effective than a sideways swipe. But as the warning time dwindled so the punch became increasingly desperate, to the point where either you risked breaking the asteroid into a lethal swarm or you could do nothing to ward it off. Just which side of the threshold they were on they wouldn't know until they had identified Nemesis.

The Russians, however, had had a different problem: that of precision. Probably, Webb thought, they had used a standoff explosion of a few megatons to give a crude impulse of a metre a second or thereabouts. The bigger the bomb the more potential asteroid weapons were available, and the Russians had hundred-megatonners in their arsenal. For every asteroid liable to hit the Earth they would have a hundred or more potential weapons in the form of near-missers.

But after that they would have had to finesse. A hit within a few hundred miles – or even a thousand miles – of Kansas would be adequate to obliterate the States. But a thousand miles is *precision*! After the initial big explosion, possibly years in the past, they would have required a series of small shepherding explosions, maybe little more than Hiroshimas, to guide the asteroid in.

All of which implied a fair amount of clandestine space activity, maybe using the Phobos or Venera series as a cover. Leclerc's knowledge of past Russian space trips was the key.

There was a movement in the woods. A couple of crows were cautiously dropping from branch to branch about fifty yards away. And something small was scurrying through the trees. A white fox popped its head up and looked at Webb curiously. In a flash of inspiration, Webb suddenly realized that there was another key. He jumped up and the fox and crows disappeared.

In passing he looked in the kitchen and the common room, and knocked on Leclerc's door. He threw off the hat and jumper. Back down to the conference room. 'Where's André?' he asked. Judy looked up briefly from a terminal and shrugged.

Webb picked up a pile of blank paper and made his way to the common room. It was empty. Warm afternoon sunlight was streaming in through the panoramic window. A green leather chair had a worn, comfortable look about it. He settled in. The sun was warm on his thighs and a light scented breeze was coming in through the window.

In some anonymous galaxy near the boundaries of space and time, two neutron stars had collided. With collision velocities close to the speed of light, the stars had annihilated their own matter, transforming it into a flash of radiation of incomprehensible intensity. Before even the Sun and Earth had formed, the radiation was spreading out through the Universe as a thin, expanding spherical shell. And then came the Sun and planets, and life evolved in the oceans, and then the reptiles had crawled on to land and the big archosaurs had ruled the Earth until the solar system entered a spiral arm, whence they had died in a massive bombardment of dust and impacts. It was an episode which had left the mammals and the insects, in their turn, to inherit the Earth. By the time the first primates had appeared the gamma rays were invading the Local Supercluster of galaxies; when *homo sapiens* was learning to carve on rocks the radiation was sweeping through the cave man's own galaxy; and finally, at the very instant the apes had learned how to throw little metal machines around the Earth, the shell had momentarily rushed through the solar system, on its endless voyage to other stars and other galaxies.

But as the energetic photons swept past, a tiny handful had been picked up by the satellites which the apes had just developed; a millisecond gamma ray burst was duly recorded; theoreticians speculated; papers were written and debated; and arriving from cataclysms scattered through the cosmic wilderness, other gamma ray bursts were being picked up, recorded, discussed and debated, and catalogued.

And this was Webb's problem. The Universe snaps and crackles across the whole electromagnetic spectrum. Neutron stars collide; massive stars run out of thermonuclear fuel, collapse and then destroy themselves in a gigantic thermonuclear explosion; red dwarfs dump their atmospheres on to white dwarf companions; relativistic jets squirt from the nuclei of galaxies and stars. Somewhere in this tremendous background of noise was a local event. A sprinkling of X-rays, perhaps, from an illegal nuclear explosion; or a brief flash of light in the sky. An explosion on Nemesis would throw hundreds of thousands of tons of debris into space. Maybe ice, maybe boulders, but surely dust. A cone of dust, fanning out into space and sparkling in the sunlight; a beacon in the dark interplanetary void.

Amongst the thousands of X-ray flashes picked up by ROSAT, there might just be a signature of a different sort. Or maybe even the wide-angle camera on IRAS had picked up a fading infrared glow as the debris from the crater dispersed into the zodiacal dust cloud. Or the Hubble had picked up something.

The first thing was to calculate the signatures that would discriminate between natural astrophysical processes and the effects of a bomb. He would have to investigate a wide range of physical processes. Maybe the hefty thump of 14 MeV neutrons from the thermonuclear fireball yielded a characteristic signature; or the timescale for dispersal of the dust yielded a light curve unlike that from any eclipsing binary. Webb sighed and pulled over a coffee table with a dish of Liquorice Allsorts and jelly babies. It was going to be a long session.

Lunch came and went unnoticed. Colleagues came and went through the common room; Webb was not disturbed. The level of the sweets in the dish next to Webb slowly declined. Around six in the evening Judy went into the kitchen and the smell of curry soon wafted around the common room. Kowalski appeared shortly afterwards, dressed in his Eskimo suit, and then Shafer and Noordhof emerged from the conference room, arguing about something; their voices changed to a low murmur but Webb appeared not to notice. Someone handed Webb a coffee and switched on a lamp. The sun set. Papers scrawled with formulae piled up on the coffee table. The sweets disappeared.

Around midnight Webb completed his calculations: he had his electromagnetic signatures. The best bet had turned out to be the simplest: an unexplained flash of light, seen in the telescope of some amateur comet hunter somewhere on the planet. It might just have been recorded in the IAU Circulars, the electronic clearing house for transient and unexpected astronomical phenomena.

He looked at his watch in surprise, and realized that he hadn't eaten. There was a plate of chicken curry, boiled rice and a Nan bread in the microwave oven. He fired it up, was tempted by the can of Redstripe on the kitchen table but decided against it. He gulped the food down and then went straight through to the conference room along the now darkened corridor. The room too was dark apart from the light from the terminals. Judy and Sacheverell were sitting at terminals. Starfields were drifting across their vision.

'How did the briefing go, Herb?' Webb asked.

'No sweat,' Sacheverell said without looking up.

'We're filtering out the main belters automatically,' Shafer said, 'Otherwise we'd snarl up.'

'And between Spacewatch, Flagstaff and ourselves we've found thirty Earth-crossers already,' Judy said. 'Thirty-one,' she added as the terminal beeped.

'How are you handling them?' Webb asked.

'No sweat.' Sacheverell again. 'The Teraflop is coping with everything we throw at it. We come back to the new ones after an hour or two. Look.' He pressed a terminal key and the single picture was replaced with a dozen small squares, each centred on a bright spot. The little pictures, like frames from a movie, showed clearly that the spot was drifting against the stellar background. 'Usually they've moved several pixels, sometimes dozens. We might not get an orbit but if it has a strong tangential drift we know it's not an immediate hazard.'

'Where are you searching?' Webb asked Shafer.

'Where you expect to find them,' Sacheverell interrupted. 'In and around the ecliptic plane. I hope you're not going to start on crap about high inclination dark Halleys.'

'They're not practical weapons, Herb. Anyway it doesn't matter where you look, you haven't a hope.'

Sacheverell looked up from the screen. 'Hey, we finally agree on something.'

'But don't tell the Colonel what we're agreed on. He's already had a bad day.' Webb sat down at a spare terminal and quickly typed into the Internet. Once into the IAU Circulars, he began to read every one, starting from the most recent and going back through time. Each unexplained flash of light, each gamma ray burst, each surge of X-rays reported in the sky, had to be matched against the theoretical expectations he now carried in his head. It was a slow, painstaking, tedious grind.

⧗

Around 3 a.m. Judy disappeared, and half an hour thereafter Webb too felt he had to take a break. He wandered across the darkened hallway to the dimly lit common room and flopped down in an armchair. The urge to sleep was almost irresistible. There was a smell of perfume. 'Hey, Mister!' Judy said in a soft voice. 'Not even Superman could keep that up.' Startled, he saw that Judy was in the armchair opposite. In the dim light he could just make out that she was wearing a long green dressing gown; her hair was tousled and her blue eyes were strained with tiredness.

Without thinking, he said, 'What's a nice girl like you doing in nuclear weapons? You should be having babies.'

She bristled, but then burst out laughing when she detected Webb's sly grin. 'Webb the sexist! I'm sure. I'm in nukes for the same reason you're in astrophysics, Oliver. I love the subject.'

He felt unable to think. When he spoke, the words were slurred with exhaustion. 'So the lady loves nukes. I still can't think why.'

In spite of her exhaustion, enthusiasm came through in her voice. 'Think of a nuclear fireball in the first microsecond of its formation. The power to devastate a small country in something the size of a beachball. There's a wonderful purity about a nuke, Ollie. It sweeps away everything; even elements are transmuted. It's as near as we can get on Earth to the Creation.'

'You make getting nuked sound like a religious experience,' Webb replied, hardly caring what he said. 'But you want to destroy things, and I want to understand them. I happen to think we were created from something like your fireball.'

'The Big Bang?' she asked.

Webb shook his head. 'The nucleus of the Galaxy. This is something that nobody in their right mind believes. But I still say women are for childbearing. They're supposed to create, not destroy.'

'All females defend their young. Having had our babies

we need to protect them. I do create, Oliver, I create peace. Is that not a noble pursuit in a barbaric world? You have the nerve to sit there and bask in the purity of your subject, with Nemesis on the way in? We can only manage miserable ten-megaton firecrackers, but you? You go cosmic.'

'I also love dogs,' said Webb.

'I prefer cats. And cars. I can strip a Pontiac to its gudgeon pins and reassemble it in a day.'

Webb said, 'You can strip me to my gudgeon pins any day. I'm a fair cook, and I climb mountains.' He thought, this conversation is getting surreal.

She shook her head. 'I'd rather fly over them in my Piper. But maybe you can cook me a dinner some time.'

Webb's skin tingled at the invitation and he thought, hell I must still be alive. 'Which brings me to boyfriends. Got any?'

'Lots of them, all strictly platonic. So far I find nukes more interesting.'

'Are all nuclear physicists as beautiful as you?'

'Only the females.' She stretched her slim legs out on the coffee table between them, nudging papers aside with her bare feet. 'What about you?'

'The ladies? I have an effect on them. But haven't had time to explore the subject. I notice you paint your toenails, ma'am.'

'I hope you paint yours, Oliver. Otherwise we have nothing in common.'

Noordhof marched in and switched on a light. He took one look at the exhausted scientists, blinking in the light, and said, 'You two. Get to bed before you collapse, and that's an order. You're no damn use in that state.'

Judy waved and more or less staggered towards the dormitory. Webb felt his way along the pitch black corridor and stepped outside. The snowy landscape glowed softly in the light of the Milky Way and the stars.

He breathed in the scented air, letting his eyes, strained by hours of terminal-staring, adapt to the dark.

The IAU circulars had revealed nothing.

Mars was high in the south, a bright red, unwinking beacon which, in a couple of hundred years, would hold a teeming human population, a population which would marvel at the havoc their ancestors had wreaked on the beautiful blue planet. A few lights were scattered over the desert far below.

He strolled on to the road which, that morning, he had pounded down with Leclerc and Whaler. Some animal screamed in the distance, a prolonged scream which set Webb's nerves jangling.

The next step would be the IRAF catalogue and maybe some ultraviolet stuff, maybe even going as far back as the IUE which had closed down in 1997. But he knew it wouldn't wash; these were shots so long they had to be a last resort.

Something.

Something; a new idea trying to climb out from his subconscious. But what?

The animal screamed again, closer; or was it another animal? And what makes an animal scream in the night?

Suddenly cold and nervous, Webb turned back towards the observatory. He was asleep within two minutes of collapsing into bed.

⧗

Webb was in the cloister of a monastery, hiding behind a potted palm. In the cobbled central courtyard, hooded monks were building a scaffold. The carpenter, a monk with Noordhof's face, had a row of six-inch nails protruding from his grinning mouth. They were hammering the scaffold together at superhuman speed, only the scaffold turned out to be a big wooden cross and the hammering was overwhelming and it transformed into an urgent tapping at Webb's door, dragging him from his lurid subconscious world into the real one. The dream faded and Webb thought that perhaps Judy had overdone the chillies.

'Oliver!'

Feeling drugged, the astronomer heaved himself out of bed, put on a robe and opened the door, blinking in the subdued light of the hallway. Judy; still in her dressing gown, still with tousled blonde hair and tired, strained eyes. 'Kenneth called. They think they've found something. He's gone up in the cable car with Herb.'

Webb followed Judy down to the darkened conference room. Noordhof and Shafer were clustered round a terminal, the light from the screen giving a blue tinge to their faces. Shafer was in boxer shorts and singlet, and his hair was drawn back into a ponytail by an elastic band. Noordhof was fully dressed. The colonel moved aside and Webb looked at a hundred thousand stars. A wisp of nebulosity crossed the bottom of the screen, probably a remnant from some past stellar cataclysm. The starfield wasn't drifting: someone had set the telescope for a long exposure.

'You see the little triangle of stars near the middle? The top one has moved.' Judy said.

'What's its angular rate?' Webb asked.

'Extremely low,' Shafer said. 'About a pixel an hour.'

'So it's either heading away from us or straight at us.'

'It's coming at us,' Shafer informed Webb. 'It's slowly brightening.'

'Have you any orbit at all?'

The physicist pointed to an adjacent terminal. The centre of the screen showed a coin-sized disc. A series of near-parallel lines criss-crossed the screen, the longer ones going from edge to edge; each line passed through the centre of the disc. 'This is one of Herb's programmes. We're projecting the two-sigma error ellipses on to the target plane.'

'Only you don't have distance information so the ellipses come out like lines.'

'That's the problem. You see they've been shrinking as the data accumulate, but they still pass through the Earth. Collision is a definite possibility.'

'I agree, Willy, but so is a miss. These are still long lines. We need an accurate orbit and we're not going to get that with a one-hour time base.'

'You said it yourself, Ollie. The Earth's gravity pulls things in when they get close. In the last stages these lines will shrink to a point.'

'What are the chances, Ollie? Is this Nemesis?' Noordhof asked anxiously.

'At a minimum, it's going to be a very close encounter.'

'What does that mean? Do I wake the President or not?'

Another elongated ellipse suddenly appeared on the screen, shorter than its predecessors. Its centre still passed firmly through the coin-sized Earth.

'This is it, right?'

Webb lowered his head in thought. 'Mark, we're not going to answer your question with the orbital dynamics to hand.'

'But we can't wait. Not if this is the big one.'

Webb asked, 'Do we have brightness information?'

Shafer nodded. 'Herb says its magnitude has gone from twenty-one point five to twenty-one point two in the last hour.'

'I thought we weren't looking fainter than seventeen?'

Shafer shrugged. 'Mark ordered it. He's still fixated with Baby Bears.'

Noordhof said, 'Screw you, Willy. I made the right call and there's the living proof.'

'Kenneth and Herb are trying to get its spectrum with the ninety-four-inch,' Judy volunteered.

Webb said, 'At m equals 21? Full marks for effort. Look, the orbital accuracy is horrendous but we might be able to use δ*m*. Anyone got a calculator?' Shafer thrust one into Webb's hand. 'Point three magnitude change translates into a roughly thirty per cent brightening in the last hour.'

'Maybe it's just a rotating brick,' Shafer suggested.

'Too much light change in too short a time. Chances are the bulk of it is due to its approach. With inverse square its distance from us has decreased by fifteen per cent in the last hour. A spectrum is pointless. It'll be on us in seven or eight hours.'

Shafer said: 'Jesus.' The tone sounded more like a sudden conversion to Christianity than an oath.

Noordhof had an unlit cigar between his fingers. 'If this is Nemesis we're dead. Is it Nemesis?'

'Willy's point about rotation is partly right. We just don't know the approach rate precisely enough to be sure.'

'Wonderful!' Noordhof snarled. He crushed the cigar and threw it to the floor.

'Let's guess it's approaching at twenty kilometres a second. In six hours that puts it' – Webb tapped buttons on the calculator – 'Crikey. Less than half a million kilometres away. What's the time?'

Noordhof looked at the big railway clock. 'Four fifteen.'

'From the way you guys have been operating I guess Kenneth's supernova telescope has picked this thing up near the meridian. We're probably looking at an eighty per cent sunlit face rather than a night-time crescent.'

'Make this quick, Webb,' said Noordhof. 'The White House are going to need every second we can give them.'

Webb crossed to the blackboard and used his sleeve to wipe a clear space. There was just enough light to scribble. 'A one-kilometre carbonaceous asteroid has magnitude 18 at one AU. This thing is 0.003 AU away which with inverse square luminosity would make it a hundred thousand times brighter than that, size for size.

Use the magnitude/brightness formula

$$m_2 = m_1 + 2.5 \log (L_1/L_2)$$

Put $m_2=18$ and $L_1/L_2=100,000$. At that distance, a one-kilometre asteroid would have magnitude 5.5. You could see it with the naked eye.' Webb stabbed the air with a piece of chalk. 'But this one is 20.5, fifteen magnitudes fainter. For every five mags you go down, you lose a factor of a hundred in brightness. Ten mags down gives it only one ten thousandth of the intrinsic luminosity of a one kilometre asteroid, ditto the surface area. This beast is less than a hundredth of a kilometre in diameter. Hey, we can relax. It's only ten metres across.'

Shafer laughed. 'A glorified beachball!'

'Are you sure?' Noordhof wanted to know.

Webb nodded. 'At the ninety-nine per cent level. Even if it hits it'll just be a brilliant fireball in the sky. We get these all the time. Colonel, you're a fool. You've thrown away priceless hours of observing time. Forget the Baby Bears.'

An expression close to terror crossed Noordhof's face. 'I was about to waken the President.' A collective outburst of laughter relieved the tension. Judy headed for the kitchen and started to fill the coffee percolator.

'By the way,' Webb asked, 'Where's André?'

'He's not in his room,' Judy called through.

'And he's not up top,' Noordhof said.

Shafer put his hand to his mouth. 'Ollie, I haven't seen Leclerc since lunchtime.'

Webb looked at Noordhof. 'Mark, it's been a bad day. First a blind alley with your laser. Then a false alarm with this beachball. And now it seems that one of your team has gone missing.'

The Tenerife Robot

Judy pulled her dressing gown lapels round her neck and made for the dormitory. Webb, swaying with tiredness, headed in the same direction.

'Where do you think you're going, Webb?'

'I'd have thought that was obvious, boss.' Webb saluted ironically.

'I've given thought to your friend's automated telescope. The one in Tenerife. You say you can work it from here?'

'I can work it from here. The instructions go to Scott's Oxford terminal and get routed through. Anyone sniffing cables at Tenerife would believe the operator was in Oxford.'

'With an external phone line? And an open modem?'

'Yes, for direct access. But it's password protected and I have the password.'

'And your friend?'

'Scott's in Patras. His wife is Greek and they're with her family over Christmas. I have an open invitation to use the robotic telescope until it's properly commissioned.'

'So, with half a million megatons coming in, and a telescope sitting idle, your action plan is to fall asleep.'

'I was waiting for your authorization, remember? Are you telling me you're getting over your paranoia?'

'I have to balance risks here. Go ahead with it.'

'The sun's up over Tenerife by now, Mark, but I'll check

that I can access it from here. Meantime, Herb and Kenneth must be turning into icemen, trying to get the spectrum of your beachball. Why don't you call them back down?'

Webb sat heavily down at the terminal Judy had been at. The chair was still warm. Another small ellipse had appeared on the screen, the disc representing the Earth still firmly inside it. By the time the bolide arrived the Pacific would be in darkness, and a brilliant shooting star would light up the night sky, to be seen only by the uncomprehending eyes of flying fish. He routed the picture over to an empty terminal, and typed in a file transfer protocol. Immediately, the terminal asked for his username and password. He gave these and a fresh window appeared on screen: he was now in effect sitting at his own computer in Wadham College. He asked for a second FTP to be opened up, the one linking him to the robotic telescope. Webb was asked for a pin number. He supplied it and found himself in effect in Tenerife, at the console of Scott's telescope, in little more time than it took to say Beam me up Scottie. The whole procedure had taken less than thirty seconds.

Webb could now use the mouse to control the movement of the telescope, little numbers at the top right hand of the screen giving the celestial co-ordinates at the centre of the starfield. The shutters of the telescope dome were closed in daylight hours, but he had confirmed that he could contact the telescope from here.

Then he switched to the external camera, mounted on a pillar about fifty yards from the main instrument.

The picture came through immediately. The camera was looking back at the telescope, whose silver dome was gleaming in the morning sunlight. He rotated the telescope dome and saw it swivel immediately. He scanned slowly, and the camera panned over the rocky foreground. A cluster of telescopes came into view, the massive William Herschel conspicuous amongst them.

Someone was walking outside the big dome. He carried on scanning, and the camera picked up the tops of clouds further down the mountain; they were above the inversion layer, and the atmosphere was likely very dry. He pressed another button and temperature, pressure, humidity and prevailing wind at the site were displayed. Then he swung the camera over the Tenerife sky; it was cloudless. Everything was operating smoothly. Tonight he would use the robot to search for Atens. As the signal came in to Eagle Peak it would automatically be reproduced a few hundred miles away, at Albuquerque, and the Teraflop would interrogate each picture element on the screen, comparing it with a digitized star chart and the co-ordinates of known asteroids. Any discrepancy would be recorded as a flashing point on the terminal VDU.

The thing would be to get as close as he could to the horizon, close to the sun but before the dawn light flooded the CCDs. Experimentally, he typed in an altitude and azimuth. Again the telescope's response was swift.

In fact, remarkably swift: there was something odd.

Webb felt his scalp prickling.

His exhaustion suddenly lifted. He typed in another celestial co-ordinate. He tried a third and a fourth, each one with the same amazingly fast response.

He took a surreptitious look around. Shafer was at a terminal, leaning back in his chair, arms flopped at his side. With his eyes half shut and mouth half open, and with his stubble and ponytail, he looked more like a moron in a gangster movie than one of the sharpest scientists on the planet. Noordhof was at the conference table reading some report. Both men seemed past the point of exhaustion. Quietly, Webb logged on to the Internet and navigated his way to an infrared satellite image of Europe and North Africa. The image was less than ten minutes old. Tenerife and La Palma were covered with cloud. No mountain tops protruded above them. And yet the Tenerife camera was showing a clear, sunny sky.

Slowly, a fact almost beyond comprehension sank into Webb's mind.

The observations from the robot telescope were a fake.

Lake Pepsi

Wallis rolled one of the general's Havana cheroots from one end of his mouth to the other, spat, and heaved again on the oars. Little whirlpools spun away from the boat and it lurched erratically forwards.

Wallis thought he might as well be rowing a corpse. The CJCS lay back, motionless, a hand trailing in the water. His small mouth gaped open and a strip of hairy stomach lay exposed between his Hawaiian tunic and the top of his trousers.

The corpse was calculating. From time to time Wallis thought he saw the fat man's eyes briefly studying him from behind the reflecting sunglasses. They were about half a mile out from the shore, the general's jeep a little splodge of fawn next to the jetty.

The lake, set in a ring of wooded hills, was like the caldera of some ancient volcano. A flock of snow geese flew in formation, honking high overhead, preferring the winter in Baja California to the one in Siberia: voting with their wings.

He needs an opening, Wallis decided. He said: 'Quite a place you've got here, as they say in old movies.'

The corpse stirred. 'Margaret's,' said Hooper. The comment was unnecessary: his marriage into one of the wealthiest families in America, with both showbiz and dubious New York family connections, had long been a staple of tabloid gossip. 'This particular land was bought on some killing with Pepsi futures. You're practically rowing on the stuff. Foggy, feather your oars and stow your barnacles or whatever it is matelots do. Now we're going to drink a little beer, catch a coupla fish and have ourselves a friendly little talk.'

The Chairman of the Joint Chiefs of Staff sat up and opened the lid of the wicker picnic basket. He moved aside a six-pack of Red Stripe and the small black briefcase which never left his side. He struggled with some fishing tackle; it looked new and the general gave the impression of a man who couldn't tell a fly from a spinnaker. A little white worm wriggled in silent agony as a hook was thrust through it, and then it was whipped through the air into the water. The geese vanished behind Jacob's Mountain and the honking faded away.

'Margaret likes her barbecues, good chance to meet people. Probably Teddy, the Clinton people and a few of her showbiz friends, maybe the Newmans. Oh, and some Mexican band. You may not want to come after you've heard me out.'

'General, I've long since deduced that I'm not here for the fishing.'

'Son, what you are here for will blow your mind apart. First I want to ask you a few questions. All on a hypothetical level, none of it's for real, if you get my drift.'

'I get your drift.'

Hooper gave a half-smile. 'Sure you do, you're a bright boy. How come they call you Foggy?'

'It goes back to Parrot Island, sir. I guess I go around in a kind of haze.'

'Which haze doesn't fool me. You're bright enough to know that if you report this conversation I will deny that it ever took place. Talking about boys, how's your one getting on? He's on some sort of camping trip in Allegheny, ain't he?'

Wallis's heart gave a jump. It was a distinct thump in

the chest. 'Didn't know you knew about it, sir,' he said casually. His son had arranged it with a teenage friend only the week before. *Nobody* outside the family circle had known about it.

'Real mountain man country up there. Straight out of Deliverance. You got balls letting your boy go out there. Still, I reckon they've got to find their own feet some time.' Below the sunglasses, Hooper's mouth had formed into a prim smile, and the incredible fact dawned on Wallis that his commanding officer had issued a threat.

'General, why are we here?' Wallis threw his half-smoked cigar in the water with a nervous gesture. The atmosphere was suddenly tense.

'Nemesis.'

'The Martian scenario.'

'A tiny handful of people in America know about it. You're one of them.'

'No doubt for good reason, sir.' Wallis waited, an unformed sense of dread washing over him.

'Colonel, in what circumstances would you commit treason?'

Wallis stared, aghast, but all he got was his own distorted image, bulbous in the fly's eyes of his commanding officer's sunglasses.

'Sir, the question is an insult. I don't want this conversation to continue.'

'The honour of your country is at stake.'

'If you put it that way.' Wallis retreated into his shell, slipping into a formal, military-style tone. 'As you well know, sir, my oath of allegiance calls on me to serve my country, and to obey the orders of my superior officers to the limits of my conscience. If there's something in the book about treason I guess I missed it.'

Hooper's eyes showed approval. 'Sinews of an army, son. Without loyalty and discipline and obedience, some-times even blind obedience, you don't have an army, you have a rampaging horde. Trouble is, obedience is morally neutral – it serves all sorts of masters. But this man's army is based on values. Cripes, the lettuce Margaret puts on my sandwiches. 'Kay, let's start easy. Suppose your superior officer was under some incredible strain, to the point where he was cracking up, couldn't think straight? If he gives some wacky order, or even worse, if he fails to act when he should, what would you do about it?'

'It's in the book, sir. I'd go over his head.'

'Uhuh. And if said superior officer was right at the top?' Hooper opened a Red Stripe; he tossed the ring into the water, and it glinted as it spiralled down to oblivion. He held out a sandwich to Wallis but the colonel shook his head.

'Excuse me, but the man at the top is the President.'

Hooper didn't reply. He sipped froth off the top of the can. Wallis said, quietly, 'I advise you to proceed with extreme caution, General. You're on a minefield.'

'Who isn't these days? I repeat my question.'

'I get the drift, General, but we serve a democracy, not some banana republic. If the man at the top gets it wrong the people throw him out, not the Army.'

'Sure.' The general re-cast the line. It whipped through the air, and fresh ripples spread over the smooth lake surface. 'A hypothetical, like I said. Suppose Eagle One has cracked under the strain. Gone pacifist, can't fulfil his duties, whatever. So he has to be removed. But say the act of removing him leads to a nuclear strike against America?'

'How could that situation arise?'

'Simple. What do you impeach the President with? Failing to counterstrike against the Russians? Do we go public with Nemesis? And what would our Kremlin friends do then? Wait for us to zap them? Fact is, they would—'

'Now hold it there, sir. The only thing you go public with is that the President is unfit for Office because he's ill.'

'Get real, Wallis, there are intelligent men in the Kremlin. They would read the signs. They would have to pre-empt our strike. You want to gamble America on the Russians being dumb? That's some chip to put on the table.'

'The fact remains that the National Command Authority rests with the President, not with traitors.'

'Colonel, your head is stuffed with mush. Remember your school history? Remember how the good guys always won, eventually? How can this be? It's not God, it happens by definition. The winners shape what later generations believe to be good. *By definition*, retrospective definition, the patriots are the guys who win and the traitors are the guys who lose. Maybe it's okay for Eagle One to let our country be attacked and do nothing. Maybe he can waive his Oath of Office. Maybe our Peacemakers and our B52s and our entire defence posture, they were always a big bluff, we never intended to retaliate when the nukes were pouring down on our frigging cities. Is that your line, Colonel? Who's the patriot – the guy who supports his country or the one who brings it down by supporting faulty constitutional structures?'

'General, I would like for us to go back now.'

'They'll bite, Foggy, give them time. Deal with the facts. Fact One, Nemesis is coming in: we're under attack now. Fact Two, the Chief is psychologically paralysed: he's unable to discharge his duty to defend America. Fact Three, any appeal to the people by way of Senate or Supreme Court or any constitutional mechanism alerts the Russians and exposes us to nuclear annihilation. That's why you're here, that's the problem, and I still haven't heard your solution.'

'Are you asking me to join a conspiracy?'

Hooper paused, then he grinned slyly and said: 'Hell no, Foggy, this is a purely hypothetical discussion, remember? You're being asked to think. For the first time in your life, to judge by your performance so far.'

'Sure. Hypothetical like the man from Mars.'

Hooper forced the point relentlessly. 'What we have here is a flaw built into the Constitution. Say your Commander in Chief is abandoning his responsibilities, betraying his Oath of Office. Now say that public impeachment of said Chief would alert the enemy and bring forth the Day of Judgement. What I need from you is an answer: what would you do about it?'

'Not my problem.'

'On the contrary, Foggy, for reasons which will emerge this evening, you're the key. Answer my question.'

Wallis felt as if doors were closing all around him. He said, 'I'll have that beer now.'

Hooper tried another tack. He wedged the fishing rod between his knees and reached for a can, tossing it to the soldier; water lapped against the underside of the boat with the slight movement. He opened his briefcase and pulled out a sheet of paper. 'Typed it out this morning. Listen:

A strict observance of the written laws is doubtless one of the high duties of a good citizen, but it is not the highest. The laws of necessity, of self-preservation, of saving our country when in danger, are of a higher obligation.

Okay so far? Now listen to this:

To lose our country by a scrupulous adherence to written law would be to lose the law itself, with life, liberty, property and all those who are enjoying them with us; thus absurdly sacrificing the end to the means.

Straight from the horse's mouth, boy, from Thomas Jefferson. The guy who *wrote* the frigging Constitution. You know, reading this, Jefferson practically anticipated Nemesis.'

'I know what you're asking me. I need time.'

'Time, laddie, is the one commodity we do not have. Hey!' The line went taut. Hooper began to pull at the rod, reeling it in. 'Hell, Foggy,' the CJCS went on in a more conciliatory tone, 'we've all been programmed with particular values and these work for us nearly all the time but democracy is only a tool. It has limits like any other tool and sometimes you have to do things for the public good that the public would lynch you for if . . . damn you, I'm trying to talk to this guy . . . look, this is a new game and you need new rules . . . stop wriggling . . .' Hooper stood up and the boat rocked dangerously as he reached out for a writhing fish.

'Steelhead, General, it's a beauty.'

'Time's running out, Colonel, and we need to know where you stand.'

'We?'

'Party starts about eight o'clock. We'll be looking for answers.' Hooper, grimacing horribly, held up the squirming fish. 'Now what the hell's bells do I do with this?'

The Party

[Extract from testimony before the Defense Appropriations Sub-Committee of the House of Representatives in relation to USAF budget. John Chalfont, Utah Democrat, presiding.]

Chalfont: Well, what I'm asking is, say the President has a heart attack or something and he doesn't relinquish authority, who then can make the decision to launch if the situation requires it?

Hooper: Sir, that is not an area we like to talk about much.

Chalfont: But the word has to come from someone, is what I'm getting at. We can't just be a headless chicken.

Hooper: No sir, it has to come from the Vice-President. We are at all times available to respond.

Chalfont: Well, say SecDef walks into your office and tells you to launch your missiles, you don't need codes or stuff like that and he has the authority because the President is sick. Do you do it?

Hooper: The policy is that the President makes that decision.

Chalfont: But he's sick.

Hooper: I don't believe I can answer that.

Hamilton: What my colleague is getting at is, with the new Russian threat, we can't afford another Haig fiasco, we have to get the right finger on the button.

Who has the authority to press the button if the Commander-in-Chief is out of it? Say the national interest suddenly required a launch.

Hooper: The Vice-President has the authority.

Chalfont: General, I don't want to sound as if I disagree with that, but is it not still the case that the CJCS needs to be consulted?

Hooper: He's subordinate but yes, he has, that hasn't changed from the First Cold War days.

Hamilton: He holds the appropriate codes?

Hooper: A lot of us hold the codes, down to the Brigadier-General on the Cover All plane.

Hamilton: A hypothetical, General. Say the President and the Vice-President are killed in a plane crash and Zhirinovsky sees his chance . . .

Hooper: We could respond.

Hamilton: Are you then telling us that a military authority exists for launching nukes separate from the civilian one?

Hooper: I did not say that, sir.

Hamilton: What does that mean? Is that a denial?

Hooper: Well, there's no actual military authority as such but look, the Situation Room is soft and Raven Rock is hard. Say Washington is wiped out and nukes are pouring down on our country. What would you expect military commanders to do in that situation?

Hamilton: So authority to launch passes from the President to the Vice-President, with CJCS in consultation, and what we're trying to get at is, what does the decision handbook say if they're both incapacitated. What is the civilian authority?

Hooper: It has to be the Secretary of Defense, in consultation with the Joint Chiefs.

Chalfont: And if SecDef was in that plane crash?

Hooper: Well, that's a pretty hypothetical scenario, if I may say so, sir.

Chalfont: But what if?
Hooper: You're into a massive decapitation there, but there are still procedures. [Remainder of reply deleted.]

There's a conspiracy to overthrow the President, maybe kill him. They want me to join it, and I'm thinking about it.

The gorilla leaned precariously backwards, mouth agape, scratching its armpits and making what it imagined were gorilla-like noises. A French whore, her slim legs straddling the neck of her onion-selling companion, stretched her arm over the gorilla, unsteadily trying to pour a glass of red Martini down its throat. The onion seller staggered, the whore screamed, Martini arced through the air and a little crowd cheered as they collapsed on to the grass and the gorilla jumped up and down shouting *Ooh! Ooh! Ooh!*

God, I hate these people.

Wallis had another problem. She was a dusky, blonde, man-eating southern belle, full of pouting coyness; she was dressed in a red crinoline dress of alarming cleavage; and she was also, Wallis had learned with increasing desperation, persistent to the point of obtuseness. Ten minutes of guttural snarling in response to her subtle probing had failed to dislodge her.

'What exactly do you do, honey?' she finally asked outright, in an Alabama drawl.

'I'm a sanitary engineer,' he said in a sudden inspiration.

'You mean you're not in movies?' she asked in dismay, the demure pout vanishing and the accent becoming pure Bronx.

'Hell no, I'm in excrement, Miss. You know the Chinese have been spreading sewage on their fields for thousands of years? Well a bunch of us thought, why can't we do the same here? So we've got a pilot plant going, trying to turn the sludge into little pellets for fertilizer. It's working fine except the stuff smells, but we're working on that too. Say, that guy near the marquee – oh, he's just gone in – wasn't that Hal Brooker?'

'Hal Brooker the movie producer?' she asked, turning.

'Yeah I think so. They tell me he's casting for some costume piece about the Civil War. Anyway, the beauty is, we extract the methane from the crap and use it as a fuel to operate the process. So the plant costs nothing to run, isn't that exciting?'

'Real exciting,' she said. 'Listen, it's been nice talking to you.'

'But there's more. Methane is a greenhouse gas,' Wallis called after the retreating figure. 'By burning it up we're helping the environment.' But Miss Low Cleavage had vanished along the flight path to the marquee.

God, I hate these people, Wallis thought again. He drifted casually across the lawn, drink in hand, judging the ebb and flow of the crowd. Past the pool. Don't catch anybody's eye. Expensive bridgework sparkled at him out of a tanned face; Wallis pretended not to see it. People were dancing. The Tijuana Brass were sending soft, metallic notes over the rich, the beautiful and the Mexican waiters in short red jackets and tight black trousers.

Report the conspiracy and condemn my son to death. A boy of sixteen, somewhere in the Alleghenies.

Down the steps to the patio, where a large pig was covered in banana leaves, with its body cavity stuffed and its alimentary canal replaced by a long metal spit. The pig rotated unhappily about its horizontal axis while flames roasted its flesh and its fellow mammals nibbled at canapés and drank tequila from salt-encrusted glasses. The smell of burning charcoal and flesh hovered over the party. Wallis passed by.

Report it to whom? How deep does the treason go?

About fifty yards out from the lodge, the crowds began

to thin. Little clusters of people chattered and laughed under the floodlit magnolia trees and the monkey puzzles. The trees were draped with tinsel and linked by long chains of multi-coloured lanterns; but the Christmas lights were more for effect than illumination, and here the shadows were dark. An overheated Santa Claus, his face flushed, was into a serious discussion with a Barbary pirate. Wallis nodded to them but he passed by unnoticed. Then he was at the edge of the lawn, marked out by bougainvillaea. He glanced behind, and casually strolled through them, into the shadows and the fir trees.

He went steadily on, the carpet of pine crackling under his feet. A couple of hundred yards in he stopped. There were shafts of light through the branches, but no human silhouettes: he was alone. Latin American rhythm was still in the air, but the night sounds of the forest were beginning to compete.

But what if the President is the traitor, and the conspirators are the loyal Americans? Are the patriots really the guys who win, by definition?

He came across a track, just visible in the darkness. Whether made by humans or large animals he could not say, but he followed it. It climbed steeply up. About half a mile from the lodge, panting with exertion, he cut away from the path and wandered randomly, still climbing. He came to a clearing about twenty yards wide, and sat down. The ground was bone dry and covered with moss. Pinewood scented the air. There was a gust of laughter and a woman's scream from far below. Someone had fallen or jumped into the pool.

I don't need to think about stuff like that. The President is my commanding officer. I obey his orders. Period.

A half moon had risen over the mountains to the right, and it was reflecting off the snowy peaks, and the roofs of the Mercs and Porsches parked behind the lodge. The Pacific was a huge black hole over to the left.

The classic Nuremberg Defence. I vass only obeying orders.

Wallis had a brief, fantastic urge to get out of it, find a freeway, hitch a lift to anywhere. But not at night, in flowing Arab robes. Not even in California.

There was a metallic glint from far along the approach road to the lodge. Wallis could just make out a shadowy figure, standing. The man might have been speaking into a walkie-talkie.

I'm not cut out for this frigging moral dilemma stuff.

The soldier lay back, his eyes by now dark-adapted. The broad swathe of the Milky Way was overhead, dazzling, amazing. The filmy ribbon was divided by a great black rift; it swirled across the sky, a highway for gods and ghosts and creatures of the mind.

Was Jefferson right? Country before obedience? But who sets the acceptable limits on obedience? The guys giving the orders?

Something came into his vision, approaching from the Pacific. It was a moving star. It grew brighter and Wallis sat up. A faint chopping sound came over 'Stranger on the Shore' and the shrilling cicadas. A helicopter. Two miles out from the lodge, its lights were extinguished. It was just visible in the moonlight. It flew low over the trees, descending. The soldier lost it behind a hill but it reappeared, sinking towards the lodge. It touched down about three hundred yards back from the car park. A solitary figure came out, bent double, and moved briskly towards the back of the lodge. The chopper revved up, rose and soared away, following the line of the approach road and disappearing from Wallis's sight.

Wallis wondered about that. He was startled to find himself wondering about the beliefs, quietly held and strongly cherished, which had guided his life.

Maybe everything I've ever believed is junk. Maybe patriotism and loyalty and morality are just brain implants, devices put in my head from the age of five for purposes of control. Maybe it's all just a game and there's no right and wrong beyond my own sense of right and wrong. So follow my private conscience and screw the rules?

He lit up a small Jamaica cheroot, his match throwing a brief circle of light around him. He was still thinking in confused circles, a cigar later, when the hairs on the back of his head began to prickle. There was the faintest crackle of breaking pine needles, somewhere behind him. Casually, he stood up and turned. A young man, standing in the shadows. Twenty yards away. Smart, dark suit, close-cropped hair. Motionless as a statue.

'Sorry to startle you, sir. General Hooper's compliments. He requests that you rejoin the party.'

'Evening, fella. Now how the hell did you find me way up here?' With a gut-wrenching start, Wallis realized that he must have been under surveillance from the moment he had left the party.

'If you'll follow me down, sir.'

The party was three drinks noisier. The Tijuana Brass were into some frenetic number, but a young couple were dancing, waist-high in the water, to some private music of their own. Wallis followed the young man across the lawn, past the pool and over the patio. The young man nodded farewell and made off in unparty-like, military strides. A fat man in dark glasses and a blue sombrero had a slice of pork wedged between two thick slices of bread in one hand, and a large cigar in the other. He saw Wallis and detached himself from a group. Silver sequins covered the man's sombrero and extended down over his black suit, as if he had been showered with sticky confetti. Wallis recognized him first by the whiff of Macanudo cigar smoke.

'Ah, there you are, Foggy. Great party, huh? Saw you and the Farmington girl. Should've stuck in there, boy, that family owns half of Texas.'

'Which half?'

'The one Margaret doesn't own.'

'I'm an old married man, sir,' said Wallis.

'Sure you are, yes sirree. Son, you can't just hide away like that, the world's too small and we're too smart. You want to mix mix mix. We got a visitor. Follow follow follow.'

Hooper, wriggling his fat bottom energetically, rumba'd his way past the now half-eaten pig. He gobbled the last of his sandwich and lifted two red Martinis from a passing silver tray, leaving the smoking cigar. He blew the waiter a kiss, but the man's Aztec features remained frozen. Then the soldiers were through the open French windows of the lodge. A log fire crackled in the downstairs room, throwing its flickering light over a dozen hugging couples.

Wallis followed his leader up the pinewood stairs and along a corridor whose floor was soft with Chinese carpet and whose subdued lighting showed walls lined with paintings signed by de Heem, Marieschi and Laurencin. They passed Wallis's bedroom and turned left into a small study, all red decor and mock colonial furniture. The band had started up on 'Rudolf the Red-Nosed Reindeer' and the door shut it off with a pneumatic clunk.

A werewolf, in a dark three-piece suit, was lounging back in a grey swivel chair behind a desk, the hairs of its face bristling. A lamp and a thin, red book were on the desk, which was otherwise bare. Eyes assessed Wallis from behind the mask. The werewolf indicated chairs and the soldiers sat down. Hooper took off his sombrero and dropped it to the floor, and the bonhomie went off with it. The soldiers put their drinks on the desk.

'The Ayrab – is he with us or not?' the werewolf asked.

'We have a definite maybe,' Hooper replied.

'What's his hangup?'

'Some crap about his oath of allegiance.'

'Look,' said Wallis, 'what General Hooper tells me is that I have two duties, one to my President and one to my country. The two have always coincided. Until now. What we have now is a President unable to act because he's frozen by cowardice or pacifism or whatever, and I have to ask, which comes first, President or country?'

The werewolf nodded encouragement, but its eyes were filled with caution.

'My oath of allegiance is to the Constitution, not the President. But, we have procedures. Remove him constitutionally, I tell the General here. But he tells me that the act of so removing the President is too dangerous. The Russians will cotton on to what's happening and try to nuke us, out of fear for themselves. The story he's trying to sell me is that the price of constitutional action is the obliteration of America. Which would make the Constitution a bit pointless in the first place.'

'He's grasped the issue. I told you he's a bright boy,' said Hooper.

'But what the General forgot to mention,' Wallis continued, 'is that the Chief might act at the last. Maybe he's praying for a miracle. When the Almighty fails to oblige the President might still come up with the Major Attack Option. We just won't know until Nemesis is practically in our air space. Any removal of the Chief before the last seconds is blatant mutiny.'

Hooper made a noise like escaping steam, and gulped down the second of his drinks. Bellarmine took off his mask and said: 'Colonel, it's the only way we ever thought to operate.'

'I don't know why I'm listening to this. This chatter is about treason. The decision to nuke belongs to the President of the United States and him alone.'

'I don't believe so,' the Secretary of Defense replied calmly. He opened the book in front of him. 'Truman document NSC memorandum number thirty invests the authority to launch nukes with the President. Okay. But there's an answer,' he continued. 'Listen to this. Here is Section Four of the twenty-fifth amendment to the Constitution:

> Whenever the Vice-President and a majority of either the principal officers of the executive department or of such other body as Congress may by law provide, transmit to the President *pro tempore* of the Senate and the Speaker of the House of Representatives their written declaration that the President is unable to discharge the powers and duties of his office, the Vice-President shall immediately assume the powers and duties of the office as Acting President . . .'

'Now hold on, sir,' said Wallis. 'Who are the executive department? Surely at least the Cabinet? What about presidential aides?'

'Why not the whole frigging civil service?' Hooper interrupted. 'Let's wait for the cruise missiles to swarm out of Chesapeake Bay like Venus arising and then get the Speaker out of his bed, assemble Congress for a nice cosy debate and have the typists standing by for the written declaration. The missiles will get here faster than you can read it never mind type it but hell, I'm just a soldier, I guess we have to get the Supreme Court in on the act while the bombs are falling.'

'Ease off Sam, you're on too much choke,' said the Secretary of Defense. 'Wallis, I respect your need for a legal basis, but it exists. The authority for launching nuclear weapons passes through the President, the Vice-President and myself as SecDef. The procedural requirement is that a decision to launch is made in consultation with Hooper here as Chief of JCS.'

'That means two against two,' said Wallis, 'with the President carrying the ultimate authority.'

'There's a loophole,' said Bellarmine. 'In the context of the Situation Room, with a nuclear strike in the balance, and each and every second of huge importance, Hooper and I alone are the principal officers of the executive department. On the issue of presidential fitness to discharge his powers and duties, Hooper and I alone make the decision. We don't consult the cabinet, and we dispense with written declarations. The guys who wrote this stuff just didn't have this situation to handle.'

'Seems to me that, by the Twenty-fifth, if you remove Grant you end up with the Vice-President,' said Wallis. 'Where does McCulloch stand?'

Bellarmine said, 'He hasn't been briefed. He knows nothing about Nemesis.'

'Come on, pal, McCulloch's a chimpanzee,' Hooper interrupted. 'Fat wino shopkeeper with an IQ about sixty. He couldn't even grasp the issues. Everybody knows Grant just chose him for the Southern vote. You want a chimpanzee to make the decision for a nuclear strike? Is that what you want, Wallis? The decision left to a chimpanzee?'

'Yes, sir, if it's next in the chain of command.'

Bellarmine tapped his fingers on the table. 'McCulloch won't be available for consultation.'

'What does that mean in plain English, sir?'

Hooper said, 'Foggy, you might want to consider whether that's an appropriate tone to address the Secretary. What you've just been told is all you need to know. McCulloch won't be available for consultation.'

'But by the Twenty-fifth, you need the Vice-President to remove the President.'

'He won't be available for consultation,' Hooper repeated in a voice which closed the matter.

Bellarmine continued. 'Our problem is this, Colonel Wallis. Suppose we remove Grant by wielding the Twenty-fifth. Would the Communications personnel then accept my authority as President *pro tempore*? The big enemy is the clock. The whole transfer of command has to be over in seconds. There will be no time for long explanations. Or even short ones.'

'The swiftest rebellion in history,' said Hooper. 'It has to be over and the new chain of command in place in the seconds between the asteroid entering our air space and the blast reaching our silos.'

'Which is where you come in, Wallis, you and your Signals background,' Bellarmine continued. 'A transfer will come through for you in the next day or two. You will be given command of the communications room. Briefing sessions are being set up for you. You will be in charge of the personnel at the crucial moment. The decision that Communications accepts my authority will be made by you. Our counterstrike will then be enabled.'

'You're trying to slip one over on me,' Wallis insisted. 'If the President is removed you still have the Vice-President.'

Hooper banged a fist on the table. 'We have here the most doggone stubborn soldier in this man's army.' Bellarmine raised a hand to silence the Chief of the JCS.

Wallis bowed his head for some seconds. Then he said, thinking as he spoke, 'I suppose if the Vice-President is out of it, and the President is legitimately removed by the Twenty-fifth, and SecDef at least is the only relevant principal officer in the circumstances, then yes' – he seemed to come to a decision – 'the SecDef does become the Acting President. Gentlemen, I can't connive in the removal of the Vice-President from the decision-making process. But if for whatever reason he is absent at the crucial moment, I can then follow your orders with a clear conscience.'

In a moment of panic, Wallis realized that with these words he had become a party to a plot to overthrow the President of the United States and launch a nuclear strike in which the dead would be counted in the hundreds of millions. 'Oh Holy Christ,' he added, suddenly feeling nauseous.

Bellarmine half-smiled.

'Margaret's fixed up for a fireworks display about now,' Hooper said, picking up his sombrero.

'I'll want to bring some of my own people with me, people who know me,' Wallis said, cold sweat developing on his brow.

Hooper stood up. 'Sure and begorrah. Just let me have their names. We shouldn't miss it.'

Bellarmine turned into a werewolf again.

The crowd Ooh'd and Aah'd as rockets whooshed into the night sky, exploding with a *Whump!* into multi-coloured stars, while a dazzling waterfall of silver flame poured expensively on to the far end of the lawn. Wallis thought of the shadowy figure he had seen on the approach road, and the polite young man who had known just where to find him in the dark woods.

If I'd made for the freeway, I would probably now be wrapped in chains, and spiralling down towards the bottom of Lake Pepsi: an act of patriots, for love of country.

Soft flesh was pressing against his arm. Another starlet-in-waiting, hormones awash, dark eyes staring up into his; she said isn't it exciting; and he slid an arm around her waist and said Yeah sister, cool, like I'm glad I slipped out of the AIDS hospice for the night.

PART TWO

ITALIAN MASQUE

masque [<Fr. <It. *masquerata*: see MASK] 1. a masked ball. 2. a disguise, pretence. *vi.* 1. to take part in a masquerade. 2. to act under false pretences.

DAY FOUR

Eagle Peak, Thursday Morning

Webb wakened with a jerk around 7 a.m., having had two hours' sleep in the past twenty-four. The memory of that morning's unsettling discovery came to him – but something else, an inspiration, was speaking to him like a voice inside his head. The Tenerife question would have to wait.

Fearful that the thought would fade as he came to, he focused on it single-mindedly, visualizing it in an assortment of bizarre contexts. He staggered to the bathroom and shaved off a two-day stubble under a shower, his eyes closed. He then dressed quickly, by now fully awake and easily able to resist the fatal inner voice telling him to stretch out again for a couple of minutes.

He tapped on Noordhof's door, Number Four with a desert view, and tapped again. Noordhof appeared in underpants, swimming with sleep. The soldier, Webb noticed, had the beginnings of a pot belly.

'Colonel, I need to make a call to Europe.'

Noordhof scratched under his armpit. 'Telephones are death, Oliver.'

'I've had an idea. It's a long shot and it's probably dead in the water. But if it's right it leads us straight to Nemesis.'

Noordhof was instantly awake. 'Okay. We'll use the secure cable to Albuquerque. I'll ask our Communications hotshots to route your call via some innocuous address. Who are you calling?'

'An old friend. She's not in the asteroid business, not even in science. Nobody would have reason to connect her with Nemesis.'

'Give me ten minutes, then join me in the common room.'

Webb put on a heavy pullover and went outside, running around the building in sheer frustration. Judy's Firebird was tinged with frost, and the tracks of small animals criss-crossed the car park snow, concentrating around the garbage bins.

'Join me, Oliver?' Judy asked, emerging from the main door in her grey tracksuit. 'Ten minutes' aerobic.'

'Thanks, Judy, but not this morning. You'll stay within Noordhof's hundred-metre circle, of course.'

She smiled enigmatically. Webb followed her trim, lithe frame as she took off through the trees at a fair pace, blonde hair bouncing. In spite of their weird heart-to-heart of only a few hours ago, she was still, to him, an enigma. Either she hadn't grasped the responsibility she was carrying, or there were nerves of steel underneath that bouncy exterior.

Noordhof, now dressed in smart casual style, was waiting for Webb at the telephone. Shafer was in an armchair, covering a sheet of paper with equations; he gave Webb a friendly wave without looking up.

'Right. This call can't be overheard at the US end but we can't answer for Europe. We had to give you a local address because of the transatlantic delay. If your friend asks, you're phoning from the Ramada Inn in Tucson. We're reserving a room there in your name as a precaution. You're doing the Grand Canyon, the Painted Desert, whatever. Dial out as usual. Just be extremely careful what you say. I'll be listening on the kitchen extension.'

Webb dialled, and a few seconds later a male voice answered, 'Western Manuscripts,' as clearly as if it came from three feet away.

'Virginia Melbourne, please.'

'She's at home today.'

'Thank you.' Webb dialled her Bicester home number. It rang for nearly a minute; and then a contralto, somewhat husky voice said 'Virginia Melbourne.'

'Hi, Virginia.'

A transatlantic pause, and then: 'Ollie! How are you? Are you calling from Oxford?'

'Actually I'm in the States. What mischief are you up to, Virginia?'

'For starters, I'm standing here naked and dripping wet.'

'I'll try not to think about that.'

'I'd rather you did, darling. Whereabouts in the States are you?' Noordhof, looking through the open doorway from the kitchen, visibly tensed.

'Arizona, doing the tour. I thought I'd treat myself to a warm Christmas for a change but I'm beginning to twitch. You remember that manuscript I was translating? Volume Three of *Phaenomenis Novae*, by Father Vincenzo?'

'Remember it, darling? We scoured the Bod looking for it. Did your lost photocopy ever turn up?'

'No. What about your original?'

'No. It's still missing. And you just can't steal a manuscript from Western Manuscripts: our archives are a hundred per cent secure. It's the oddest thing.'

'Virginia, I need a favour.' Webb ignored the wicked chuckle in his ear. 'You told me there's an original?'

'*The* original. Our Bodleian copy was a Late Renaissance transcription made in Amsterdam. Looking at myself in the mirror, I'd say I have a pretty good figure.'

'Where can I get my hands on it?'

'The manuscript, you mean? It's somewhere in Italy. I can't be sure. Vincenzo's not one of your big names, Ollie, not like Galileo.'

'Please, Virginia!'

'Well now, I might be able to rustle up a contact for

you. I think one of the Jesuit priests at Castelgandolfo could point the way. Shall I look into it?'

'Please. Send me as much information as you can about the historical background to *Phaenomenis*. I'm preparing a monograph on comets, and I thought I'd say something about the Renaissance theories. Maybe draw up a chapter outline while I'm at the Grand Canyon.'

Virginia's contralto voice dripped with unconcealed envy. 'Some people have all the sodding luck. Can you access a terminal?'

Noordhof was tensed up again.

'Yes, I'm due to drop in on a colleague at the University of Arizona.'

'In that case I'll scan things in and type something up, and put it on anonymous ftp. You should be able to access it through my home page within a couple of hours. But it'll cost you.'

'Name your price.'

'A weekend in Paris?'

'Agreed.'

'A naughty one?'

Noordhof's eyeballs were rolling.

'Virginia, I'm forever grateful. Byee.'

Elated, the astronomer turned to Noordhof. 'Mark, I must get to Rome right away. I want to get my hands on a four hundred-year-old manuscript.'

Noordhof was about to reply but the glass door banged open and there was the sound of running footsteps along the corridor. Judy entered the room panting, flushed and shaking. 'Come quickly.'

The men left Kowalski and Sacheverell asleep and followed her at a fast trot to the cable car shed. She pointed upwards. A wisp of cloud was swirling around Eagle Peak; but then it cleared, and they could just discern a man dangling from the cable car, his arms at full stretch, legs waving.

Webb sprinted back to the observatory building and reappeared with a coastguard telescope and a tripod. They quickly set it up. In the eyepiece, Webb traced the cable up to the summit. The top platform almost filled the field of view. The car had stopped about twenty feet down from it. There was a clear three thousand feet of air between the man and the ground below. 'It's André. The door's open and he's hanging on to the edge of the floor. By the tips of his fingers, I think.'

'How the bloody hell?' Shafer asked.

Judy's fists were at her mouth, clenched in fright. 'How long has he been like that?'

Noordhof ran into the cable car winch house. Judy and Shafer followed him in, staring up through the big plate glass window. Webb stayed at the eyepiece. Noordhof moved over to the panel. It was on a gunmetal grey desk, with a large On–Off switch and a lever marked Up and Down.

'What are you doing, Mark?' Webb called in.

'I'm sliding the car up. He can't hang on like that for more than a few minutes.'

'You'll knock him off. He'll hit the concrete platform.'

'It's up or down. And his grip won't last the trip down.'

Shafer was holding his head in his hands, looking up. 'How long has he been hanging like that?'

'Try it slow,' Webb shouted in to the winch house.

Noordhof pulled the big switch to On. The motor whined and gears clashed. He turned the lever slowly from neutral towards its Up position. In the eyepiece of the telescope, Webb saw the little car jerk alarmingly, and Leclerc's feet wave frantically in space. It edged up towards the platform. The Frenchman's body drew alongside a concrete wall; it seemed to be scraping his back.

'Slow!' Webb shouted in. Then 'Stop! He's not going to make it. It's the Eskimo suit. There isn't the space. If we try to drag him through he'll lose his grip.'

Noordhof sprinted out and put his eye to the telescope. Leclerc's head seemed almost to be jammed in the space between platform and car. His arms were stretched full length above him, as if he was grasping for something almost out of reach. He was about one unattainable metre from safety.

The soldier ran back into the building, and reversed the direction of the lever. Webb saw the Frenchman drifting clear of the narrow gap, and then he was into open space. 'He's clear!' Noordhof put the lever to its maximum. The engine whine rose in pitch and the steel cable vibrated tautly, winding swiftly on to the big drum. They ran out and watched the little car sink towards them.

Leclerc was hanging motionless, his legs no longer waving. He was now well out from the cliff. Webb thought he was looking down. For the first few hundred feet the descent of the car seemed to be agonizingly slow; as it approached the halfway mark it seemed to be descending marginally faster, and although Webb knew that to be an illusion of perspective, he began to think that Leclerc might make it. But two thirds of the way down, at about a thousand feet above ground, the Frenchman lost his grip.

Judy screamed. Webb shouted No! Leclerc hurtled down with terrifying acceleration, arms and legs waving helplessly in the air. He hit a projection of the cliff a few hundred feet up and as many feet away from the horrified group. The muffled 'Thud!' came above the whine from the winch house, and a shower of little stones and earth followed the body which bounced high before disappearing into the treetops.

Judy ran back to the main building without a word. Noordhof, Shafer and Webb ran through the trees. They found Leclerc without difficulty, a path of broken branches marking his flight path. Noordhof and Shafer paled, and Webb turned away. He found a quiet corner.

His body tried to vomit but his stomach was empty.

Noordhof took off his blue anorak and covered the Frenchman's head with it, stepping to avoid the dark red snow near the corpse. They searched around for heavy stones to secure the anorak in position.

Judy had coffee on the boil when they returned. Her eyes were red. Noordhof disappeared momentarily and returned with a half bottle of cognac which he emptied into the coffee percolator before Judy poured. Webb crossed to the kitchen sink and splashed icy water over his face, drying off with a dish towel. He felt reasonably calm inwardly and was surprised to find that he could not lift his mug without spilling the coffee. After the third attempt he left it on the table.

Shafer drank down half his coffee in one draught. 'Okay Mark, talk about it. How could that possibly have happened? And what was he doing up top, anyway? He's not an observer.'

Noordhof said, 'This is how I see it. He goes up top for whatever reason, maybe just for the view. He pulls the lever but trips up when he gets to the car. End of our rocket man.'

'Truly an accident?' Judy asked in a shaky voice.

Noordhof shrugged. 'What else?'

Murder, Webb thought to himself.

Judy's hands were trembling and her eyes were tearful. So, maybe she was a good actress. He glanced at Noordhof. If he was an actor he was underplaying his hand: the soldier was cool and self-controlled. Webb was startled to find Willy Shafer looking at him closely, as if the Nobel man was reading his mind. *Or maybe he's wondering about me*, Webb surmised.

Shafer said, 'This is a police matter.'

'Sure.' There was a long silence.

Judy came back from the cooker and joined them at the table. Her speech was unsteady but composed. 'You don't have to say it, Colonel, we all know we can't realistically involve the cops. There's just too much at stake for questions. But if we don't report this we put ourselves on the wrong side of the law. And the more we try to conceal this accident, the more we dig ourselves into a hole. We have to dispose of a body. How do we do this?'

Noordhof said, 'We have to keep our eye on the ball here. This is arguably a military police matter but, Judy I'm glad you see it that way. Frankly, the legalities don't matter a damn. We just have to find Nemesis in the three days remaining to us, which includes today. That's our overriding goal and nothing, not even death in the team, can be allowed to deflect us.'

Shafer spoke to Noordhof. 'But we still have a body out there, Mark. And Leclerc must have relatives, maybe a family.'

'Leclerc was a widower with no family. His secretary was made to think he'd taken leave. Nobody in France knows where he is.'

Shafer looked as if he was trying to read the soldier's mind. 'You have access to people who can handle this type of situation, right?'

Noordhof sipped thoughtfully at his *caffè corretto*. 'I'm amazed at your perspicacity, Willy, but I don't suppose I should be since you're on this team for your brains. Yes, I understand there are guys on the payroll who can handle this type of situation all the way from the scene of the death to the coroner's report. I'll make a call.' He toyed with a spoon. 'I'll let Kenneth and Herb sleep on, and inform them when they get up. McNally is due back from Toulouse later today. Look, we can't let ourselves be paralysed by this. Some people will arrive in the next hour or two but they won't come in and you'll have no contact with them. Once they've left, Leclerc will have gone and it will never have happened.'

Noordhof changed the subject abruptly. 'Oliver, what

were Leclerc and you cooking up?'

Webb briefly wondered how much to tell. 'I wanted to exploit André's tremendous knowledge of Russian space capabilities. Particularly their launch hardware, degree of electronic sophistication and details of past space enterprises. We were going to liaise to find out what asteroids they could conceivably have reached and diverted in the past.'

Shafer said, 'NASA and Space Command must be stuffed with people who know things like that.'

'SecDef requires a European involvement or two for political reasons. He was very clear about that. It'll take a day or two to identify, brief and transport someone suitable over.'

'That's too late,' said Webb. He was trembling. 'I needed Leclerc today. This morning.'

'Are we coming apart here?' Shafer asked.

'Oliver,' said Noordhof, looking agitated. 'Think of something. You must have a Plan B.'

'André was Plan B. Plan A was looking for something unusual in the sky, some signature of the Russian deflection of Nemesis. It wasn't working as of three o'clock this morning.'

'Can you pick up on it again?'

Webb hesitated. 'I can but we're into the long shots. That phone call I made earlier.'

Noordhof said, 'Long shots are all we have left. Yeah, what gives with that manuscript thing?'

Sacheverell wandered in, bleary-eyed and barefooted, wrapped in a white towelling gown. He poured himself coffee, pulled out a chair and sat down at the table. He sipped at his coffee and gave it a startled look. He looked around, eyes blinking. He seemed to sense an atmosphere but said nothing.

Webb found that he could now just lift his coffee without spilling it. He gulped the hot liquid down.

Shafer said, 'Out with it, man.'

'It's thin. A manuscript went missing a couple of months back. A notebook by Vincenzo.'

'*The* Vincenzo?' Sacheverell asked sleepily.

'Yes. I was hoping to translate the eighteenth-century transcription in the Bodleian. I had a photocopy made but it went missing from my apartment before I had a chance to look at it. Nothing else was touched. I had a Chubb lock and secure windows and there was no sign of forced entry. Whoever took it (a) knew exactly what they were after, and (b) were highly skilled thieves. But now it gets really weird. I go back to the Library to get another photocopy, to be told that in the meantime their original too has gone missing. Now that just can't happen. Understand, Herb, that we're talking about security like that surrounding the Crown Jewels.'

Sacheverell looked baffled. 'I guess I'm still asleep. What has a seventeenth-century monk got to do with anything?'

'Someone has gone to a lot of trouble. Maybe there's something in Vincenzo's notebook that people don't want us to see.'

Sacheverell blinked. His gaze wandered towards the big window. When he spoke, there was a weariness in his voice. 'I'm still asleep. This is a weird dream. Ollie's brain is still wired up to ancient history only now he's turned it into some kind of intellectual game for his personal amusement.'

'Just drink your coffee, Herb.'

'He's freaked out by the responsibility we're carrying here.'

Noordhof tapped the kitchen table. 'Hey, you two. Don't start.'

Webb said, 'I've been thinking about the precision needed to guide Nemesis. You don't just need to get a precise deflection, you also need to know where you're deflecting from to six or seven decimal places. Very few Earth-crossers are known to that degree of accuracy. They wouldn't dare plant radio beacons on it, for all to detect, and the chances are it would be out of radar range even if the Russians had a sufficient deep space radar facility. It seems to me they'd have to derive the pre-deflection orbit using optical data just as we do. Okay so maybe the cosmonauts sat on Nemesis for a year, navigating and computing until they got it all worked out. But there might just be a much easier way.'

Noordhof poured more coffee into Webb's mug. The astronomer emptied it and Noordhof replenished. 'Most of these orbits are chaotic, meaning that tiny uncertainties – just a few kilometres – build up so that after three or four hundred years the asteroid could be just about anywhere. But the converse is this.' Webb raised a finger in the air. 'Suppose you did know precisely where it was four hundred years ago. That would give you a time base maybe fifty times longer than anything you could get with modern observations. Now if you had such an observation, even a very coarse one, you would tie down the modern behaviour of the orbit to a tremendous degree of precision. It would be just what you needed to target the asteroid.'

Sacheverell spoke to the sugar jar on the table. 'There has to be an explanation for this and it can only be that I'm still dreaming. In case anyone hasn't noticed, we can hardly find these things with wide aperture Schmidts and CCDs, never mind the lousy toys they had four hundred years ago.'

'I'm in no mood for an argument, Herb, but there's precedent for this. Uranus was recorded over twenty times before it was finally recognized as a planet in 1781. I was looking for pre-discovery observations of Encke's comet in old star maps and manuscripts. You need a strong telescope to see it nowadays, but it was seen a dozen or more times with the naked eye in the nineteenth century. Anything capable of a close encounter with the Earth could have been picked up with a two-inch refractor or even the naked eye.'

Sacheverell took another sip. 'I might have known it. You're into the old Clube and Napier rubbish. Did I get out of bed for this?'

'So what about the manuscript, Ollie?' Shafer asked. 'If it's gone what can you do about it?'

'My contact at the Bod tells me that one copy still remains. It's the original, and it's held by someone somewhere in central Italy. I want to find that manuscript and see what's in it.'

Noordhof's voice was dripping with incredulity. 'Let me get this straight. Your conjecture is that information vital to the survival of the United States could be in this ancient manuscript.'

'All copies of which were quietly and systematically removed. There had to be a reason for that.'

'Ollie . . .' Noordhof was starting to play with a cigar. 'I have to go with Herb on this. We're almost out of time here. We can't afford the luxury of eccentric diversions.'

'Now hold it right there, Colonel.' Shafer's tone was firm. 'We have to let Ollie run with this. Okay it sounds crazy to us. But he's on this team because he knows his business and sometimes crazy ideas are the best.'

'Anyone got a match? I bow to your wisdom as exemplified by your Nobel Prizes, Willy. But I still think Ollie's time would be better spent giving us a list of known near-missers that we could check out. And what if we pick up a suspect asteroid in Webb's absence? We'll need him here, not wandering around Europe looking for some missing ancient manuscript.'

Webb took this as a coded recognition that Sacheverell wasn't up to it. He said, 'I'll be giving the team a list of known close approachers this morning. It's still dark on

Maui and some might be accessible from there right now. Others could be checked out on Kenneth's telescope tonight. If all goes well I'll be back before the deadline and no way will irrevocable decisions have been reached before then. Nor, I predict, will you have found Nemesis.'

Judy had found a box of matches in a kitchen drawer. Noordhof lit up. He fixed an intense stare on Webb and adopted a grim tone. 'Ollie, I repeat what I was authorized to tell you. That if we don't find Nemesis by the prescribed deadline the Administration will go on the working assumption that it won't be found before impact, and will then adopt the appropriate posture.'

Webb said, 'I know what that means, Colonel. But I'm convinced that this is something that has to be checked out.'

The soldier sighed. 'We're into the Christmas period, Oliver. Transatlantic flights will be booked solid.'

'I'll bribe somebody off a flight if I have to.'

'I don't like it. We need tight security for this operation, and we don't get that with people wandering around Europe.'

'This is my last throw. I don't have anything else.'

'Jesus.' Noordhof blew a contemplative smoke ring. 'Okay. We're having to take risks all the way here. Cross the Atlantic by the fastest possible route. Willy, take Judy's car and give Webb a lift to Tucson. Judy's not up to driving.'

'But I'll go along for the ride,' she said. 'I'm nearly through the bomb simulations.'

Webb asked, 'What day is this?'

Noordhof groaned. 'Ollie, it's now Thursday morning, ten hundred hours Mountain Time. Our deadline is set in Eastern Standard Time, that is, the time on Washington clocks. Deliver Nemesis by midnight tomorrow EST. Which is to say, you have one day and twelve hours. If you don't make it back here get this Royal Astronomer guy to endorse your identification. No offence, but for something like this I need confirmation.'

They stood up. Sacheverell shambled towards the refrigerator. Over his shoulder he said, 'This is a joke. So far as I'm concerned Webb's now out of it.'

'One last thing, Ollie. The Secretary of Defense wants a personal briefing from the team tomorrow evening at a secure location. We'll need to know how you've progressed. You'll be in Italy but contact us at Willy's beach house, which is in Solana Beach, California. As before the line will be secure at the American end but just remember that telephones are death. It's a question of balancing risks. Use a public booth, and if you have a shadow of doubt don't phone.'

'I'll give you my number to memorize in the car,' said Shafer.

'Herb,' Noordhof said, 'I've got some bad news.'

Back in his room, Webb put his laptop computer into its case and squeezed clothes and papers into odd spaces. He stepped out of his room and moved down the stairs, along the corridor and out the front door.

Into the winch house. The car had locked into place, its door half open. Webb ignored it and crossed to the control desk. A vertical metal panel below the controls was held in place by four simple screws. He took out a pen and bent the clip, using it as a screwdriver, glancing back at the main building as he did. The panel came off easily.

Webb stuck his head inside, keeping well clear of the thick, live cable which rose from under the concrete and disappeared into the On–Off switch. A slight crackling of his hair told him that he was dangerously close to a high voltage. The design of the switch was simple. When the switch was moved to On, two metal prongs would make contact with two metal studs and so close the circuit. However at the back of the studs were two strong electromagnets, placed in such a way that, if current flowed through a second cable, the studs would be pulled back and no contact made whatever the position of the On–Off switch. This other cable, Webb assumed, went all the way to the upper platform. It was a device to ensure that the cable car could be moved only from whatever platform it was currently at.

But someone had earthed this second cable: a shiny new wire had been wrapped tightly round it and joined on to a metal rod freshly driven into the concrete. Which meant that the cable car was now controlled from the ground. Which meant that an ill-disposed individual on the ground could wait until Leclerc had stepped halfway out of the car and then suddenly pull it away, leaving Leclerc, off-balance, to fall into the gap between car and platform. Webb's scalp began to tingle and he couldn't have said whether it was his discovery or the electricity.

Webb pulled his head out just in time to hear the observatory door close. He had been in plain view; but had he been seen? Hastily, he screwed the panel back into place. He walked briskly back to the observatory. Kowalski, in the corridor, was looking stunned. He shook his head without a word. Sacheverell's voice came from the common room; it was raised in anger. Webb passed by to the Conference Room and logged in to Virginia's home page. And while he transferred her Vincenzo files into his laptop computer, he pondered. There was a lot to ponder:

1.   Fraudulent signals from a telescope;
2.   a murdered colleague;
3.   Leclerc's disappearance before his murder;
4.   a missing 400-year-old manuscript;
5.   somewhere out there, a billion-ton asteroid, closing at twenty or thirty kilometres a second; and now
6.   someone determined to make sure they didn't find it.

Tucson, Thursday Afternoon

Shafer took the wheel and Webb flopped into the passenger seat, the lack of sleep suddenly catching up on him. In a moment Judy appeared. Webb scrutinized the contours of her tracksuit as she approached. She caught him at it and gave a bleak smile as she settled into the back seat. The curves, Webb decided, didn't leave room for a pencil, let alone a weapon. He began to wonder if exhaustion was bringing out some latent paranoia.

They took off smoothly, Shafer taking the big car down round the hairpin bends with ease. Webb found himself peering anxiously into the trees. As they dropped below the snowline, the temperature rose marginally, and by the time the Pontiac had stopped at the gate separating the survivalists from Piñon Mesa, the air was mild. A smell of woodsmoke met Webb as he pulled the gate open.

They drove through the settlement, past a couple of dirty red Dodge trucks. An elderly man was sitting at a porch with a pipe and a gallon jar of some brown juice at his feet. He raised his hand in a friendly gesture as they passed. Shafer said that, given Nemesis, maybe the survivalists had the right idea, and Judy said that wasn't funny.

Down the last stretch of hill; turn left; and put the foot down on the open road. Webb began to tremble; he couldn't analyse the reason, but thought it was probably relief. Shafer turned on the radio and they listened to a rabid evangelist for a minute before replacing him with dentist's waiting room music: Country and Western, easy on the mind, brought to you by Jim Feller and his Fellers.

A helicopter flew high in the opposite direction, its twin rotors glinting in the sunlight. Webb wondered if it was Leclerc's hearse, with its specialist undertakers, but kept the thought to himself. Judy's perfume was beginning to intrude again.

Some twenty miles to the south of Eagle Peak they pulled into a little cluster of shops and a café. Shafer bought Judy coffee in a paper cup while Webb disappeared into a nearby camping store. He emerged minutes later in a Hawaiian shirt, purple-rimmed sunglasses and Bermuda shorts, carrying a big brown paper bag.

They stared, astonished. Judy tried not to giggle. 'Are you changing your personality, Ollie?' Shafer asked.

'You should see the underwear,' the astronomer replied, climbing into the Firebird. 'No, I'm just trying to confuse the enemy. Who would connect Mister Showbiz with the quiet academic who arrived at Tucson Airport three days ago? So you're the man who blew the Standard Model. A cool insight.'

'Hey, a theory screaming with singularities and eighteen free parameters? There had to be a better way.' Shafer thundered past a posse of bikers.

'But an electron as a Mobius strip? And what about your new stuff, a mind/vacuum interface? That is *weird*.'

'It'll take a generation to become mainstream. Now listen to words of wisdom from your Uncle Willy. These days, Einstein wouldn't get a job as a lab technician.'

'You mean . . .?'

'You have two possible career routes, Oliver. The easy route is this. Don't stick your neck out, keep to beaten paths and get on lots of committees. In a word, look and act like Establishment Man. And in no circumstances, whatever – I emphasize this – step outside the mainstream. Don't get any new ideas.'

'And the hard route?'

'Get a new idea. But one thing above all.'

'I'm gasping, Uncle Willy. More wisdom, quick.'

'Find Nemesis. Or your generation's cancelled.'

Judy leaned forward, speaking to both men. 'What are our chances?'

Webb said, 'I'm scared to think about that.'

'You have less than two days to play your hunch, Ollie, and a big hunk of that will be spent flying,' she pointed out.

'Something bugs me about this,' said Shafer. 'It's the Zhirinovsky factor. The guy's been in power for a couple of years, right? Say you were in his position. How long would it take you to get something like Nemesis going?'

'A lot more than two years,' said Webb thoughtfully. 'To track an Earth-crosser with enough precision would take at least that long.'

'And we'd need to know just what we were pushing around,' Judy added. 'Look at how variable the responses are in the simulations. It would mean a lot of spectroscopy, maybe even a soft-landing. Only then could you shepherd the asteroid in.'

'I guess it would take ten years and a lot of clandestine space activity,' Shafer proposed. 'Which puts its origins right back in the Yeltsin era. Well before Zhirinovsky.'

'So?'

'So all Russia wanted before the food riots was peace to develop their capitalist experiment.'

'What are you saying, Willy?' Webb asked.

'Something bugs me is what I'm saying.'

Judy suggested, 'There was always an undercurrent of dissatisfaction in the Red Army. Maybe a small group has been cooking this up for years, without knowledge of successive Russian Presidents.'

'Is it possible?' Webb asked.

'Undoubtedly,' she replied. 'Big countries have mechanisms for keeping secrets, Ollie. A group of high-level conspirators could pull these levers to hide the Nemesis project from their own leadership.'

'For ten years?'

'It bugs me.'

Soon, they were speeding along broad streets and through prosperous Tucson suburbs. Shafer followed signs for the airport. They pulled over briefly at a trash can where Webb dumped the brown bag containing his RAF-supplied suit and Glen Etive pullover. At the terminal entrance, Shafer and Webb shook hands. Whaler gave him a wave from the back of the car, and then they roared off.

At the terminal, Webb found reassurance in the teeming crowds. He bought a psychedelic pink backpack with a Save the Whales motif and a few toiletries. The American Express card seemed to be an infinite source of funds and he momentarily played with the idea of a one-way ticket to Rio de Janeiro.

He joined a long line at a TWA reservation desk. After fifteen minutes of increasing frustration it became clear that the queue was static. He gave up and crossed to a cluster of telephones. A parcel-laden woman with a mouthful of keys made it just in front of him. She started to look for coins and Webb muscled her aside. A passing man let loose a stream of outraged invective. Webb literally snarled and the man backed off hastily. He dialled through to the TWA desk. A mechanical voice said please do not hang up you are on hold and he was treated to Mantovani's 'Music of the Mountains' for one, two, three minutes. Then one of the girls picked up the phone and he watched her as she typed at the computer terminal and said No sir, the Concorde is fully booked likewise all our flights to Rome this being the Christmas period but if Sir is really that desperate there is a flight to Paris in an hour and forty minutes and you might be able to connect from there except that everything is choc-a-bloc in Europe too and Air France are on strike oh it doesn't leave from here, didn't I say? Phoenix. Have a good day, sir.

Webb ran gasping to the taxi stand. A fat taxi driver was reading a newspaper. Webb said, 'I'll give you a hundred dollars for every minute less than a hundred minutes it takes you to get me to Phoenix airport. Plus the fare. Your time starts now.'

A wide range of human emotions expressed themselves in the taxi driver's face, culminating in a delighted grin. Webb jumped in. The driver did it in ninety-five minutes, with cold desert wind streaming around Webb's face from an open window and heavy metal blasting from the rear loudspeakers. At Phoenix, Webb handed over a fat wodge of notes to the grinning driver. Boarding was in progress and he made it with two minutes to spare.

First class on the BA flight to Paris via London was, incongruously, half empty. A Sophia Loren lookalike offered to tuck him in under a blanket but Webb, his head spinning with exhaustion, resisted the temptation.

Hello Ollie!!

You finally phone me! From sunny Arizona! When I'm naked!! I always knew you had hidden depths, Ollie, but WOW, what psychic timing!! And all that heavy breathing. So, will you teach me some new stuff when you get back? I still haven't got past bondage and leather knickers. Anyway, here's your historical background to *Phaenomenis* and I hope you rot in hell you cold unfeeling miserable robot fish on a slab.

Saving myself for you alone (but not for much longer),

Virginia (still).

PS. These big-breasted cowgirls. They sag after forty.
PPS. They all have AIDS.

She likes me, Webb told himself. He looked down on a range of snow-covered mountains, golden in the sun, wondered briefly where Nemesis would hit, and settled down to the story of Vincenzo.

THE LAST DAY

Advanced Concepts

'We have nearly fifteen thousand nukes. Nine thousand active, and another six on the reserve list.' Judy was wearing large gypsy earrings, a white T-shirt, classic Levi 501's and Nike trainers. Dark sunglasses protected her eyes from the strong sunlight which streamed in through the cockpit window. Incongruously, she was wearing a pearl necklace.

McNally's tone revealed his surprise. 'The USA still has fifteen thousand bombs?'

'But they're mostly the W-series, just a fraction of a megaton each. Great for knocking off cities and the like but no way do they have the punch to deflect a small asteroid. Not on our hundred-day guideline. No, Jim, if you're looking for real action you have to go for the old B-53s. And we only have fifty of these.'

'One will do,' McNally declared.

'I don't believe so. They're not neutron bombs.'

'Let's run with your B-53s for a moment anyway.' The NASA Administrator glanced at the compass and made a tiny adjustment on the joystick. Desert drifted below them. He had flown straight from Toulouse to Tucson where Judy and the jet had been waiting. He was now *en route* to the Johnson Space Center at Houston, first dropping Judy off at the Sandia National Laboratories, twelve square miles of nuclear wisdom tucked securely inside Kirtland Air Force Base near Albuquerque. Judy was briefing him as they flew.

She produced a bar of dark chocolate, broke off a couple of squares and offered them to the NASA chief, who accepted happily. 'Okay,' she said. 'They're the oldest nukes still in service. They've been operational since 1962. But they're also the largest and they're pretty lightweight for their power. That's one of the nice things about nuclear weapons: the yield to weight ratio increases with power. The bigger the bomb the more punch per pound.'

'These B-53s – just how much punch are we talking about, Judy?'

'Nine megatons. Now that is destructive enough for any conceivable military target, but the bomb itself weighs only four tons. It's a three-stage weapon. That's classified information, by the way, but in the circumstances . . .'

'Don't you people have anything bigger? I seem to recall the Russians exploded a fifty-megatonner once.'

'The *Tsar Bomba*. A wonderful thing,' Judy smiled. 'It was really a hundred-megatonner but they configured it for fifty when they exploded it in Novaya Zemlya. Even then you could pick up its pressure wave on ordinary domestic barometers anywhere in Europe. We think it weighed thirty tons.'

'So, what have we got to match it?'

'Zilch. Our military asked permission to develop sixty megatoners way back in the fifties, but this was denied. We've always gone for precision targeting rather than massive zaps.'

McNally slid his sunglasses down his nose and looked over them at Judy. 'We lack the nuclear punch to deflect Nemesis? Are you serious?'

'If it needs more than nine megatons.'

McNally took a few seconds to absorb this startling new information. 'Tell me about your neutron bombs.' A small town was drifting about twenty thousand feet below them, narrow white roads radiating from it through the desert. A plume of smoke rose from a farmhouse some miles to their left.

'Jim, they're just tactical tank-busters. Artillery shells with no more energy than a Hiroshima. Armoured personnel are hard to kill, but neutrons penetrate armour. Some tanks, like our M-1, are reinforced with depleted uranium, which is very dense and hard to penetrate with explosives. But listen, this is really smart. If you set off a neutron bomb you activate the depleted uranium so the soldiers find themselves cocooned in a radioactive tank at the same time as the neutrons from the bomb are penetrating it. At a few miles' range their blood drains out from every orifice in a few minutes. Closer up and they just dissolve into a hot ooze. Closer still and they explode. More chocolate?'

McNally declined. He loosened his tie.

'But as a Nemesis killer, they're far too small. They're made that way so you don't have military commanders wiping out too many towns at a time when they're hitting Russian tank brigades in Europe. I don't believe our stockpiles include neutron bombs in the multi-megaton range.'

The NASA Administrator responded to some chatter on the radio. 'By the way, we're now in New Mexico. What's a three-stage weapon, Judy?'

She hesitated. 'I guess I can say. Start simple, with a gun firing two sub-critical masses of uranium together. That's fission for you, a straight one-stage atom bomb. The trouble is, it has limited power. The fission reaction is slow to develop and the bomb blows itself apart before all the fissile material is used. The Hiroshima bomb was only 1.4 per cent efficient, for example. You can't get much more than a critical mass to explode. But fission bombs do give you a plasma a metre or less across with a temperature of about fifty million degrees, and that's hot enough to start you on the fusion route, transmuting four hydrogen atoms into one helium one with the mass deficit emerging as energy through $E = mc^2$.'

'I've never been clear what form of hydrogen you use,' McNally said.

'That's classified too, but what the hell. It varies. Liquid hydrogen is best but you can use compressed gas and we've even used a hydrogen-impregnated solid. Anyway, more than eighty per cent of the energy from a simple fission bomb comes out as X-rays. Teller and Ulam got the bright idea that, because the X-rays are moving at the speed of light – they *are* light – maybe you could use them to compress a large capsule of hydrogen at very high speed, before the assembly got disrupted. The fastest reaction at fission temperatures is between the heavy hydrogen isotopes, deuterium and tritium. So you stir these isotopes into the brew, light the touchpaper and retire a long way back. Four hydrogens fuse to give you one helium, as per undergraduate physics courses, but this leaves surplus mass in the form of a 14 MeV neutron and an eighteen MeV photon which is an impressive quantum of energy.'

'That's a two-stage weapon, the touchpaper being an A-bomb.'

Judy finished the chocolate bar with a satisfied smile. 'Correct. Not only Teller and Ulam, but also Sakharov in Russia got the radiation implosion idea. So let us give thanks unto these gentlemen for the hydrogen bomb. But why stop at two stages? If you want a bigger bomb, use the fusion explosion to compress and explode a third, fission stage. It makes for a dirty bomb but a powerful one, and no new scientific principles are involved. Each stage can be ten or a hundred times more powerful than the one before. No question, *Tsar Bomba* – King of Bombs – must have been a three-stager. There was even a Soviet design for a layer cake at one stage.'

'The mind boggles,' said McNally, his mind boggling.

More radio chatter. McNally explained, 'We're now entering restricted airspace. Let's hope Noordhof fixed it like what he said he would.' He spoke into his mouthpiece and trimmed the aircraft. Far above them, two Tomcats passed swiftly across their bows, right to left. A third fighter appeared from nowhere and started to probe inquisitively, looking at them from all directions and keeping a safe twenty metres away. They flew on for some minutes. Then the pilot waved, and the jet tipped its wings and hurtled into the sky above.

'Judy, it seems to me you're going to have to tart up a B-53, turn it into a neutron bomb.'

She brushed little flakes of chocolate off her white sweater. 'But Jim, the way a neutron bomb works is that you let the neutrons escape during fission instead of absorbing them to create more energy. That means a neutron bomb will always be a low-energy device. If we're going on a last-minute deflection, meaning we need energies in the megaton range, the neutron bombs we need don't exist.'

'Make one, very very fast.'

She shook her head emphatically, setting her earrings swinging. 'Jim, where is your sense of realism? Whether it could be done even in principle I don't know. But it absolutely can't be done in the time available.'

'Hey, that's my line,' McNally complained. He nudged the joystick forwards and the altimeter needle began to drift slowly down.

'Jim. Just how much weight can you push into inter-planetary space?'

'Depends where you're going and how fast you need to get there. The old Galileo probe weighed about 750 pounds and it had a 2,500-pound spacecraft to push it around. But we used several gravitational slingshots to get it out to Jupiter.'

'Give me a number.'

'At the extreme? Think of four thousand pounds.'

'Six B-61s, each seven hundred pounds, ten feet long and a foot wide. A third of a megaton each if we use the Model Seven version. Could you launch those?'

'Maybe. But it's not enough.'

Judy fingered her necklace thoughtfully. Suddenly her mind seemed to be elsewhere.

⧗

The Sandia Corporation's newest building, Number 810, took up about 8,000 square metres of the centre of Technical Area One, deep inside Kirtland AFB. With the love of acronyms which characterizes large corporations everywhere, the building was labelled CNSAC: the Center for National Security and Arms Control. Security began with its physical layout, which had been designed so as to guarantee secure communications within and between the four elements of its programme: Systems Analysis, Advanced Concepts, Systems Assessment, and Remote Monitoring/Verification.

Judy loved Advanced Concepts. Its remit was to investigate new technologies whose development might threaten the defence of the USA, and to propose countermeasures in the event such techniques were identified. She loved the Group because of its creativity, the wonderful and wacky ideas which it tossed around, the sheer fun of it, like the vacuum bomb concept which they had been running with, pre-asteroid. There were no fools here.

Not even Advanced Concepts could stop the unstoppable. But at last, depending on answers she got here, Judy thought there might just be a way. An extremely long shot, longer even than Ollie's deranged story about a manuscript. She turned into the secure building. Her slim fingers were still running over her pearl necklace.

Vincenzo's Manuscript

We, the undersigned, by the Grace of God, Cardinals of the Holy Roman Empire, Inquisitors General throughout the whole of the Christian Republic, Special Deputies of the Holy Apostolical Chair against heretical depravity.

Whereas this Holy Congregation has found that you, Vincenzo Vincenzi, son of the late Andrea Vincenzi of Florence, aged seventy years, have been found to advocate the proposition that the Sun is at the centre of the universe and immovable, and that the Earth moves and is not at the centre of the universe; which propositions, due to Copernicus and Galileo, are contrary to the authority of the Holy and Divine Scriptures, and are absurd and erroneous in faith; and whereas it has also been found that you embrace the belief of Giordano Bruno that the stars are suns scattered through infinite space, and that living creatures may inhabit planets orbiting these stars, which opinion is also absurd and erroneous in faith; and that you instruct pupils in the same opinions contrary to the Holy Scriptures; we find, pronounce, judge and declare, in the name of Christ and His Most Glorious Virgin Mother Mary, that you have rendered yourself guilty of heresy.

So we the undersigned cardinals pronounce.

F. Cardinal of Cremona
F. Cardinal Mattucci

M. Cardinal Azzolino
Cardinal Borghese
Fr. D. Cardinal Terremoto

Webb thought, *plus ça change*: I meet little cardinals at every conference. He looked out of the little window. The 747 had now entered the dark hemisphere of the Earth, somewhere over the Atlantic Ocean.

Ollie darling. Okay so the Holy Roman Inquisition gets a bad press but Vincenzo can't really complain. If he'd been tried in Germany or the Alps he'd have been tortured and executed, no question. The good Doctor Karpzov of Leipzig, a contemporary of Vincenzo, managed to procure the deaths of twenty thousand witches in the course of his saintly life. Such was his virtue that, in between carbonizing old ladies, he read the Bible fifty-three times.

Was the Holy Office paving the way in this Madness? It was not. On the contrary it was often accused of being soft on witches. An accused witch in the custody of the Holy Office had protection, in the form of the *Instructio pro formandis processibus in causis strigum, sortilegiorium, et maleficiorum*. This little document puts women in their place: *genus est maxime superstitiosum*. The silly things are prone to vivid imaginings, false confessions and the like (my vivid imaginings would set your kilt on fire). The *Instructio* therefore insists on caution in proceeding to an arrest, accepting testimony and so on. Torture was applied only after the suspect had had a chance to mount a defence. Even when *maleficio* was established, first-time offenders who repented were only banished, or made to abjure on cathedral steps, or put under house arrest or whatever.

There were, however, three classes of felon who

risked being barbecued: second offenders (two strikes and you're out), hard core heretics (*e.g.* denying the Virgin Birth), and the stubbornly impenitent, like Vincenzo. Policy was to burn the first lot and have a go at last-minute conversion for the other two.

Anyway, what are a few hours or days of pain measured against the everlasting torment of Hell? If those few hours or days will persuade a heretic to recant, and so attain Heaven, then surely true cruelty lies in withholding the services of the torturer? To flinch from applying a little unpleasantness is to fail in one's duty to the Blessed Virgin, to the Church and to the heretic him/herself. It's all spelled out in Masini's *Sacro Arsenale* 2nd ed., Genoa 1625.

You have to be cruel to be kind, as Miss Whiplash said to the bishop.

So where does that leave our Vincenzo? Read on, sailor.

Remarkably, given the ferocious attack on them by Vincenzo, the cardinals had provided him with an escape clause. Perhaps the Grand Duke had thrown a long shadow, and there had been a nod from His Holiness; who could say? At any rate, on condition that he recanted, cursed and reviled the said opinions, the Inquisitors declared, he would be sentenced only to life imprisonment.

Vincenzo now had a choice. He could die for his beliefs, like Giordano Bruno before him, who had gone to the stake convinced in the plurality of worlds. Along that route lay the rack and the strappado; and beyond that the stake. Or he could adopt Galileo as his role-model, and abjure on his knees, his hand on a Bible held by the Inquisitor.

Vincenzo recanted. The *territio realis* – showing him the horrific instruments of torture as a prelude to using them

– had done the trick. He was duly sentenced to *carcere perpetuo*. Whether by nudging from the Grand Duke's emissary was unclear, but the sentence was commuted to confinement, for life, to the estates of the Duke of Tuscany. Since the Duke owned much of northern Italy the sentence was, finally, nominal. Vincenzo and his mistress had spent the remainder of their days in obscurity, under the Duke's protection.

⧗

The Grand Inquisitor had taken vows of poverty. However the small print, had there been any, did not forbid the possession of a wealthy brother. And like many wealthy Romans from the Emperor Hadrian onwards, the Inquisitor's brother had a villa in the hills near Tivoli. It was a place to escape the hot, stinking, malaria-ridden plain of Rome during the summer months. And shortly after the trial, Vincenzo's books and instruments were delivered, for disposal, to the Inquisitor, who was then in residence at his brother's Tivoli villa.

The Cardinal recalled that Copernicus's *De Revolutionibus Orbium Coelestium* had been placed on the *Index Librorum Prohibitorum* in 1616, whereupon, the following year, the Dutch heretics had published an Amsterdam edition. And Elzevirs of Leyden had been quick to publish the works of Galileo. He would allow no such embarrassments to fall on the Church again. Across the front cover of each of Vincenzo's ten volumes, he wrote *cremandum fore*: they would be consigned to the flames.

What happened next is unclear, Virginia wrote. Maybe the Grand Duke's Secretary had applied a little pressure. Whatever, Terremoto scored out *cremandum fore* and replaced the words with *prohibendum fore*: they were not to be burned, merely not to be read. A few copies were made but were lost, all but the one which had found its way to the Bodleian. Virginia had appended a surviving letter from the period:

> Reverend Father. His Holiness has prohibited a book in octavo entitled *Phaenomenis Novae*, in ten volumes, by Vincenzo Vincenzi, son of Andrea Vincenzi of Florence. The book contains many errors, heresies, and pernicious and schismatic propositions. I am informing your reverence so that you may promulgate an edict prohibiting the book, ordering booksellers and private individuals to surrender whatever copies they possess, on pain of established penalties. I note that your reverence discovered copies of the *Republic* and *Demonomania* of Jean Bodin, in a bookshop of your city. These were indeed, by order of Gregory XIV of blessed memory, condemned. All copies of the above book are to be burned on seizure. Your zeal in these matters is well known to His Holiness and to the Congregation, and we do not doubt that you will apply it to the matter in hand, in the service of our Lord God. May He preserve you in His holy grace. I commend myself to your prayers.
>
> Rome, 30 August 1643.
>
> Of your reverence, fraternally,
>> The Cardinal Terremoto

The Grand Duke never succeeded in adding Vincenzo's works to his great library. The Cardinal put them in a dark basement room in his brother's house, hidden amongst the junk and detritus of a large family home; and there they remained, forgotten, for over a hundred years.

⌛

In 1740, a librarian from Florence by the name of Dr Tomasso Bresciani was passing through a marketplace in

Rome. He bought a sausage at a stall and took it away wrapped in an old paper. Unwrapping the sausage in the Triano park overlooking the Colosseum, he found the wrapper to be a letter from Vincenzo, now long dead. Webb imagined the good librarian choking on his sausage. The paper was traced to a junk collector and thence to a house belonging to the grandsons of a nephew of one of the Grand Inquisitors, who were selling off waste paper from their basement. Bresciani recovered the notebooks, which found their way to the famous Riccardian library in Florence, where they were indexed, filed, restored, bound, and once again forgotten.

⧗

They next turned up two hundred years later, in 1924, in the attic of a farmhouse in Provence. Another footnote: 'Almost certainly Napoleon's troops. They were forever looting museums and libraries from Italy and carting stuff over the Alps. Women too, I expect. Ollie, when are you coming back?'

Three thousand crates went north, some of which fell into Alpine torrents. Many of the remaining manuscripts, with a value beyond money, were turned into wrapping paper in Paris. Most were shredded and sold as scrap, an unparalleled act of vandalism by greedy Parisian businessmen. *Phaenomenis* was a lucky survivor.

They were then purchased from the farmer for pennies by the famous monk Helinandus ('copy of receipt scanned in if you're interested'), and so they came back down the road, all the way to Rocca Priora, south of Rome, becoming part of the Cistercian monk's famous collection of astronomical manuscripts.

A fact which made Webb sit up.

⧗

Unfortunately, Virginia's note continued, along came the

Second World War. While the Allies were advancing inland from Anzio, trainloads of good things were being taken north by the retreating Germans. One of those trainloads got stuck in a tunnel between Frascati and Rome, and in a bloody fight the partisans reclaimed the booty which included, but of course, a collection of manuscripts hastily taken from the monastery by some German officer. Unfortunately, in the confusion of *Nacht und Nebel* which is battle, some of the sacred relics, art treasures and rare manuscripts simply disappeared. Vincenzo's manuscript has never been seen since.

There is of course the Bodleian transcript of the original by some anonymous Dutchman. Or was, darling. But as that too has now gone missing, along with your photocopy of it, it seems that the works of Vincenzo have vanished from the face of the Earth.

And at this point, Virginia stopped. She had scanned in her flowery signature; it took up almost the entire screen of his laptop.

Webb stared into the dark night. For the first time since Glen Etive, he fully believed that the task was hopeless. To find a manuscript which had gone missing in some forgotten skirmish almost a lifetime ago? In twenty-four hours?

He decided that he would send Virginia, the librarian with the steamy hormones, some flowers. He looked at his watch. He'd have to be quick: a planet without flowers was due along.

He had almost overlooked the last page, assuming it would be blank. But now he clicked the return button on his laptop and saw that Virginia had added a postscript to the end of her file:

'Ollie dear – you might want to get in touch with that Rocca Priora monastery. There are rumours.'

Monte Porzio

The short Atlantic night was drawing to a close, and a pale sun was beginning to illuminate a solid sheet of cloud which hid the ocean below.

Webb put his laptop aside and stretched. He tried to gather his thoughts.

Maybe, Webb wondered, I'm being paranoid. Maybe in my excited state I'd misunderstood the wheelhouse circuitry. If so, Leclerc's death made for a very strange accident; but an accident nevertheless?

And what about the fast response of the robotic telescope? Perhaps that's all it was: a fast response, made possible by the quietness of the electronic flow across the Atlantic at that time of night.

On the other hand, Webb speculated, what if Leclerc's death was murder, and the Tenerife observations were a fraud? It would have to mean that Leclerc had been getting close to Nemesis, and that someone on the team didn't want it to be identified. That is, someone on the team wanted an asteroid to wipe out their country. Family, friends, home, community, even their dog if they had one, someone wanted the lot to go.

Webb was vaguely aware of being less worldly than the average street trader; but even allowing for his own limited insight into the human condition, he could not believe in a folly which plumbed such depths. The proposition made no sense.

Webb thought about his colleagues on the team. Six Americans – Mark Noordhof, Judy Whaler, Jim McNally, Willy Shafer, Herb Sacheverell and Kenneth Kowalski.

Noordhof had been chosen by the Secretary of Defense or the President, because of his knowledge of missile defence technology. Judy worked in a corporation at the heart of the nation's defences. Both these individuals needed the highest possible security clearance and must have been vetted to death at various times in their careers.

McNally was NASA's Chief Administrator, for God's sake.

That left Shafer, Sacheverell and Kowalski. But these were all in a sense accidental choices. Willy Shafer was chosen for his eminence as a physicist. Sacheverell because he was conspicuous in the asteroid business (okay he's an incompetent loudmouth but that didn't alter the fact). Kowalski just happened to be director of a remote observatory with the facilities they needed. None of these people could have even known about the Nemesis threat, let alone manipulated themselves on to the team.

Okay, Webb thought, everyone is squeaky clean.

Therefore exhaustion is making me paranoid. Leclerc's death must have been an accident, and the robot telescope just has a remarkably fast response.

It was just odd that, at the moment he had been panning the robot camera over the bright, sunny Tenerife landscape, the Spot satellite had shown the island to be thick with cloud.

⧖

The twelve hours of flight, coupled with the loss of another eight hours due to the contrary motion of aircraft and sun across the Atlantic sky, meant that the Jumbo landed at de Gaulle at nine o'clock, local time, on a grey, stormy Friday morning. Webb adjusted his watch. It was now 3 a.m. Friday in Washington. He estimated that he'd had about three hours' sleep in the last three days.

No Monsieur, the flights to Rome are fully booked. There is, however, a flight to Nice, laid on by some small company capitalizing on the Air France strike. There is one remaining seat but it is a standby and it is for Monsieur to turn up before somebody else gets it. Oh, did I not say? Not from here, from Orly. Monsieur is most welcome. Monsieur took a taxi whose driver was as responsive to the promise of a huge tip as his Tucson cousin.

The standby seat was taken.

Yes, Monsieur, Quai d'Orsay Aviation do operate an executive air taxi but Monsieur appreciates that we cannot fly him into Italy without the necessary paperwork and at this time of year the Italians would simply file their flight plan away for days. Monsieur's fastest route is to fly to Chamonix, on the French side of the Mont Blanc tunnel, and proceed from there.

He used the twenty minutes they needed for flight preparation to telephone Eagle Peak, where it would be about one o'clock in the morning. Noordhof came on the line almost immediately. The conversation was terse:

'I'm in Paris, just about to leave for Chamonix, arriving at L'Aèrodrome Sallanches in maybe three or four hours. Can I be met?'

'I'll fix it.'

The office of Quai d'Orsay Aviation was about the size of a broom cupboard, dingy and empty. Webb fumed for about five minutes until a handyman, a small man with a handlebar moustache, entered carrying a tool box and a polythene sandwich box. He led Webb to the entrance of a hangar. Webb almost fainted at the sight of the tiny, two-seater Piper Tomahawk. He froze at the open door of the little toy, but someone heaved on his backside and he was in. The 'handyman' turned out to be the pilot and Webb thought what the hell, I died trying.

They were a full half hour on the slipway waiting for clearance, during which time the pilot kept looking at the low clouds and making increasingly dubious noises about the flying conditions, while gusts of wind shook the aircraft. By the time the Tomahawk was bumping its way into the dark clouds, propeller racing, Webb reckoned he had attained some new plane of terror.

They jiggled and bumped their way across France, passing first over fields laid out like a patchwork quilt, and then over the white-covered Massif Central, occasionally glimpsed through snow-laden cumulus. Webb declined the offer of a sandwich although Monsieur would find the pig's brain filling quite delicious. Low, white clouds ahead turned out to be the Alps which, as they approached, increasingly dominated the field of view. The pilot pulled back on the joystick to gain height. Soon they were flying bumpily over the Mont Blanc massif. Through the clouds they glimpsed needle-sharp peaks, icy blue lakes, and isolated villages in the snow. Circling L'Aiguille du Midi, the pilot tilted the aircraft on its side so that Webb could look straight down at the crevasses and banded glaciers falling away from the big mountain. Then the Tomahawk righted itself, and the pilot took it unsteadily down through heavy snow. Webb glimpsed the tops of pine trees just below their wheels; then there was open ground and an orange windsock, and the pilot managed a brief '*Zut!*' as a gust of wind caught the wings at the moment of touchdown.

Alive on the ground, Webb inwardly swore that his feet would never leave solid earth again. He resisted the urge to kiss the snow and instead settled up with the pilot, whose eyes lit up with simple joy at the sight of so much ready cash. The pilot disappeared into a wooden hut at the edge of the runway, and ten minutes later was taken off in a taxi.

Webb waited, shivering in Hawaiian shirt and Bermuda

shorts as the snow gusted around him. Through occasional patches of blue he could make out formidable, jagged peaks towering all around. He looked at his watch. He was attracting the amused attention of a plump girl inside the hut. He was about to head for Chamonix when a bright red sports car gurgled on to the airport road. A man emerged with green Tyrolean hat, complete with feather, and a long green trenchcoat.

Webb climbed in. 'I'm in a bit of a hurry.'

'I know,' Walkinshaw replied. 'That's why I hired the Spyder.' Bulls bellowed; a giant thrust Webb in the back; and in seconds they were on to the main road and moving at a speed which he associated with a race track.

They skimmed past a clutter of chalets and high-rise hotels on the left. On the right more chalets lay below an icy citadel, clouds swirling around its summit. Passing over a bridge Webb glimpsed turquoise, surging meltwater. Survival time two minutes, he thought for no reason.

'These chalets – aren't they built in an avalanche zone?'

The civil servant shrugged. 'What do rich foreigners know?' He turned on to a steep Alpine road whose route up the mountain towards the Mont Blanc tunnel was mapped out by crawling lorries. A notice advised snow chains and extreme caution. It came in several languages but to judge by his driving Walkinshaw seemed not to understand any of them.

⧖

Rain.

Rain, beating hard against a window.

Swish-swish.

The rhythmic swish-swish of windscreen wipers, and the hiss of tyres on a wet road.

The hum of an engine.

Heavy rain, driving hard. Powerful engine.

Webb drifted back to sleep.

NEMESIS

The car slowed and turned. Headlights flickered in from outside. The car stopped and Walkinshaw stepped out, the door closing with a satisfying Clunk! Webb listened to his receding footsteps, the steady drumming of rain on the roof, and the thermal ticking from the cooling engine. There were voices outside.

Webb struggled up to a sitting position. His arms and legs were made of lead. An illuminated sign said *Pavesi*, and above it was a picture of a plump, smiling chef holding a roasted turkey on a tray. The clock on the dashboard read just after three, and the autostrada cafeteria was busy. The voices were coming from a group of truck drivers at the entrance of the cafeteria, one of whom made a dash for his truck, holding a newspaper over his head.

Walkinshaw appeared and ran towards the car with a paper cup, water streaming over his dome like head. Webb lacked the energy to open his door. He handed a hot chocolate carefully to Webb, before settling into the car.

Walkinshaw sipped at his drink. 'I have never seen anyone so exhausted.'

'I'm more concerned about you, Mister Walkinshaw. I don't believe you're a civil servant.'

'Actually, I'm a pianist in a brothel,' said Walkinshaw. Webb assumed it was a joke.

'And there is no Walkinshaw at the Department of Information Research. I checked.'

Walkinshaw's face was a picture of injured innocence. 'So? There might have been. Sir Bertrand is disappointed in you, Webb. He thinks you're off on some eccentric tangent.'

'I probably am. I also believe someone on the team is trying to screw us up.'

'Don't be ridiculous. Finish your chocolate.'

Webb had scarcely done so before, once again, he flaked out.

He wakened again in the late afternoon, stretched out on the soft leather. The morning rain had gone and the sky was blue. Webb sat up. The terrible exhaustion had eased but he felt as if his blood had been drained off and replaced with water.

They were speeding over a cobbled road, with Trajan's Column on the left, the Roman forum to their right and the Colosseum straight ahead. There was a mechanized chariot race around the Colosseum but Walkinshaw took it in his stride. They stopped at traffic lights, the lights turned green, and the traffic made a Brand's Hatch start. Walkinshaw weaved swiftly up to the head of the traffic. The Appia Antica appeared ahead but they suddenly screamed off round a corner.

In minutes they had cleared the suburbs of Rome and were hurtling towards a large hill town some miles ahead. 'Frascati,' Walkinshaw said. 'The Embassy have given us the use of a house just beyond there.'

They trickled through the town and then started to climb through a winding road. There were signs for Tuscolo and Monte Porzio. Ahead, Webb glimpsed a cathedral dome straddling the summit of a hill some miles ahead, with ancient houses clustered around it like cygnets around a swan. The Spyder cannoned up the narrow road, and Webb's knuckles showed white against the dashboard, and his scrotum thought it was being squeezed by a gorilla. At last the car growled and slowed, and they stopped at the large metal gates of a white villa.

Walkinshaw searched under some stones and triumphantly produced some keys. Then they were up a short, steep drive. There was a balcony, big enough to hold a party on, looking down on a panorama which probably had not changed in a thousand years.

'This belongs to one of the Embassy staff. It's probably a safe house, and in any case we only need it for a few hours. However you are still Mister Fish, and you still look like a corpse in a freezer. Would you like to rest awhile?'

'I daren't.'

He was aroused by sunlight on his eyes. He was in a king-sized bed. Cherubim hovered over him, and a saintly, bearded figure in the ornate ceiling had raised a glass of wine. A chandelier of pink Venetian glass was suspended almost overhead. Twin dragons guarded a wardrobe about twelve feet long underneath a mirror of similar size. He had a quick shower in an old-fashioned bathroom about the size of his Oxford flat, and found his way to a downstairs lounge. Walkinshaw was contemplating a lurid female photograph in a magazine. He stood up as Webb approached.

'Ah, much better. You no longer look like death warmed up.'

'What time is it?' Webb asked.

'Just after five o'clock. You've been out for an hour.'

'Oh my God. I have to get to a monastery. It's not too far from here.'

'I'll come with you.'

'No. I'm a solitary scholar researching a manuscript. And you look like something out of MI5.'

'At least I'll give you a lift, time being what it is.'

Webb opened the car window and glanced at his watch. The plain of Rome stretched into the distance on his left, with its wonderful city shimmering in the haze. Beyond, the long spine of the Abruzzi Hills stretched to the south. The air blowing in the window was warm and scented, and the sky was blue.

And he had fifteen hours.

The Apiary

It was a fifteen-minute drive up a steep, narrow, tree-lined road. The monastery was contained within a wall about fifteen feet high, part of which was also the front of a church. A white marble saint with a lightning conductor running down his back stood atop its steepled roof. Behind the wall a tall bell-tower dominated the skyline.

There was a crowded car park. Walkinshaw put the seat back and covered his eyes with his ridiculous Tyrolean hat. Webb followed a family into what seemed to be a porter's lodge, and passed through it to a shop, where he was met by the scents of a thousand flowers. A brisk trade in honey, royal jelly and some translucent green liqueur was under way, while the Virgin Mary, captured on canvas, stood with her eyes raised to Heaven and arms crossed on the wall behind the counter. Webb tried out his Italian: 'I'd like to speak to the Father Abbot, please.'

The white-robed monk behind the counter raised his bushy eyebrows in surprise. 'You have made an appointment?'

'Yes,' Webb lied. 'But I'm only in Italy for a few hours.'

'*Un àttimo.*'

A few minutes later the monk reappeared. With him was an older man, nearly bald, with a ruddy face and a smile which, Webb thought, was less than wholly welcoming. 'I'm Father O'Doyle,' he said in an American English with a strong hint of Irish. 'The Father Abbot is in chapel but I'm responsible for visitors. No visitors are pencilled in to my diary for today. When did you write?'

'About six weeks ago,' Webb lied again. 'My name is Fish. I'm from Cambridge. I'm trying to trace a book.'

'Ah, that explains it. You want the Father Librarian. Come with me.'

Webb followed the American monk out to the car park and back in through the church. About halfway down he led Webb off to a transept, produced a large key and unlocked a door. There was a short stretch of corridor. Webb noted a door, with an alarm and lights over it, protected by three locks. The monk caught Webb's curious stare. 'Our sacristy,' he said.

Through another locked door, Webb found himself outside again, in a large, square cloister. Father O'Doyle led the way along the covered cloister-walk. Webb was surprised to find Christmas lights and decorations strung between the pillars lining the walk. Faces looked down at them from barred windows. 'Oblates,' the monk said, waving up.

They turned off and climbed some stairs. A handful of white-robed monks, hoods down, passed silently. Through a door, Webb found himself in a modern library. A few teenage students were scattered around desks. 'I will leave you in the capable hands of our librarian.'

The librarian had the physique of a rugby player, but the muscle was turning to fat and his face was pale.

Webb tried out his rusty Italian. 'My name is Larry Fish. I'm from Cambridge in England. I'm doing some historical research and have been directed to your library. I wrote some weeks ago.'

'I do not recall your letter. Did you not receive a reply?'

'I don't know. I've been travelling.'

The monk bowed. 'What do you seek, my son?'

'My informant was uncertain, but she thought that you might be in possession of the works of Vincenzo Vincenzi.'

A look of surprise passed over the librarian's face, but quickly vanished. 'A moment.' He disappeared momentarily through a door and returned with a set of keys. He said, 'Follow me.'

Webb followed the monk out of the neon-lit, computerized library back down the stairs to the cloister and past a refectory with a long, heavy table and a small lectern. At the end of the cloister-walk was another set of stairs and the monk led the way down them and along a cool, dark stone-lined passage which ended in a massive wooden door. The monk used two keys. From the push he gave it, Webb inferred that, underneath the wood veneer, the door was basically a slab of steel. The monk punched in a number on a keypad and then locked the door behind them. 'To control humidity and temperature,' he said. 'I must remain with you, but also I must attend compline in an hour. And tonight, of course, we celebrate the birth of our Saviour.'

Webb took a moment to wander while the Father librarian stood at the door. Some of the books predated Gutenberg; many could have bought a Rolls-Royce, or a yacht, or a house. Here, handwritten, was Vitellio's medieval compendium on optics, and next to it Kepler's 'supplement to Vitellio,' his *Dioptrice*, in which he described the principle of the camera centuries before Daguerre. Here, unbelievably, was Nicolas of Cusa's 1440 *De docta ignorantia* of 1440, asserting that the universe is unbounded, and that all motion is relative, almost five hundred years before Einstein and the modern cosmologists. There was a little cluster of seventeenth-century comet books – Rockenbach, Lubienietski, Hevelius and others. And there was Copernicus's *De revolutionibus orbium coelestium* – the 1617 Amsterdam edition – which had ushered in the painful birth of the scientific revolution. It was Aladdin's cave, but Webb had no time to explore it. He turned to the monk, who simply said,

'*Opere di Vincenzo, qui*' and took Webb to a shelf.

And there, indeed, were the *Opere* of Vincenzo; all but Volume Three.

'Volume Three, Father?'

'We have fifty thousand titles here, but unfortunately not the one you seek. It has been missing from our collection for sixty years.'

Webb's heart sank. 'How can I have been so misinformed? Volume Three was the one I sought.'

'And after sixty years, you are the second man to have asked for it in a week.'

You don't say. 'To be frank with you, Father, I'm desperate to see it. I'm involved in a scholarly dispute which only the works of Vincenzo can resolve.'

The librarian lowered his voice conspiratorially. 'Perhaps you should speak to our Father Abbot. At this time of day, after chapel, he is often in his study. Follow me.'

The librarian left Webb facing the Abbot across a large desk. A computer terminal on the desk struck the astronomer as somehow odd. Unmonklike, he imagined Noordhof saying. The man was middle-aged, with a thin face and a classical Roman nose. He spoke with easy authority, in English, and had bright, alert eyes.

'So, Mister Fish, you are from Cambridge. Which college is that?'

Webb tensed. 'Churchill.'

'On Madingley Road, as I recall. It is many years now. Tell me, that little coffee shop on Silver Street – what was it called?'

'There are a few,' Webb guessed.

'Lyons? Was that it?'

With a start Webb realized that he was being tested. He avoided the trap: 'Rings no bells, I'm afraid.'

'How odd. Everybody knew Lyons in my time at Cambridge. I wasted my youth there.' Webb raised his hands expansively, Italian-style, and the Abbot dismissed the matter. 'It was so long ago. Perhaps it no longer exists. However, it is not part of our Rule to engage in idle gossip. You seek the works of Vincenzo, Mister Fish. You see that our collection is incomplete. Are you aware of their history?'

'I understand that the partisans rescued them from the Nazis, along with sacred artefacts and works of art, at the end of the last war.'

The Abbot nodded. 'It is also widely believed by local people that these things were returned to our monastery whence they were looted. Alas, Mister Fish, that persistent rumour is only partially true. Some treasures, some works of art, were not returned. The volume you seek is amongst them.'

Webb, feeling gutted, closed his eyes in despair.

The Abbot continued, 'Vincenzo was a very minor actor in the great drama which was played out so long ago. Now had it been Galileo, great efforts would no doubt have been made to recover his works. But Vincenzo? Few have even heard of him.' The Abbot looked at Webb with curious intensity. 'Is it so important, this scholarly dispute?'

'If only you knew, Father Abbot.'

'You can tell me no more?'

Webb shook his head.

The Abbot leaned back in his chair and looked at Webb thoughtfully over steepled hands. 'I am left wondering what possible scholarly dispute can require such secrecy and lead to so much despair in your face.'

'I'm not at liberty to say. And I don't come from Cambridge and my name isn't Fish.'

The Abbot chuckled. 'I thought as much. But we all have secrets to keep. I too have constraints on my freedom to talk.'

This guy knows something, Webb thought, maybe from the confessional. He toyed with the mad idea of blurting out the whole Nemesis story but immediately dismissed the thought. It would be seen as the ravings of a lunatic. He also suspected that the Abbot, faced with a choice between betraying a confession and permitting a holocaust, would tell the planet to get stuffed.

'You are leaving Italy soon?' the Abbot asked.

'I must. I came only for the manuscript.'

'All this way for a missing volume! If only I could help. Before you leave us, perhaps you should take the opportunity to see our monastery. There is an unusual mixture of styles here. You will have seen that our basilica is made in the style of a Greek cross, that is square, rather than in the medieval plan which has a long nave so as to represent the shape of the cross of Christ. The craftsmen who built our monastery were influenced by the Doric, which is simple and strong, rather than decorative. And yet our chapel is entered through a porch with a horizontal entablature supported by columns, more in the style of the decorative Corinthian order.' The Abbot smiled. 'But I agree with your expression, Mister Fish. If you prefer, we can satisfy more bodily needs. We have many products. I recommend our liqueur, which is made of over thirty aromatic herbs according to a secret recipe which even I do not hold.'

Webb stood up. 'Another time.'

'And our honey is famous. You must see our apiary.'

'Thank you. Unfortunately I have to get away.'

'Our beekeeper is Father Galeno. He is very old, and wanders a little, but he is a most interesting man to talk to. I said as much to your colleague.'

My colleague? Webb made for the door. 'Thank you. Time doesn't permit.'

The Abbot said again, 'Our apiary, Mister Fish. Father Galeno is a very interesting man.'

God I'm thick, Webb told himself. The Abbot made the

sign of the Cross and Webb said thanks for your help.

The Apiary was a square of grass the size of a small field beyond the bell tower. It was lined by dozens of box-shaped hives painted in bright primary colours. A monk, wearing a plastic hat with a protective veil, was bent over a hive with a metal bucket and a long, flat piece of metal. The air buzzed as Webb approached.

'Father Galeno?'

The Father Apiarist turned. He was a tall, thin man, in his middle eighties. He spoke in Italian and Webb was grateful for the six months he had spent in Rome some years previously. Bees were crawling over the monk's white robe and his veil. His sleeves were tied with string at the wrists. 'Would you like to buy some honey?'

'Not today.'

'Then you are here to be shown the wonderful life of the bee.'

'Unfortunately I have no time,' Webb said.

'No time. Now that is sad. We can learn much from the world of the bee.'

Behind the veil, Webb saw dark eyes, a curious mixture of vacancy and sharpness. Instinctively, he felt that an oblique approach was called for. 'Tell me, Father,' Webb asked, 'In your experience, is a bee conscious of its own existence?'

The man's eyes lit up. 'Undoubtedly. While the bee can see and hear, its real world is one of chemistry. It responds to smell and touch. Its mind cannot therefore be understood by us, whose world is sight and sound. True, it is deeply controlled by instinct in its daily toil, but yes, of course God in His wisdom has given it the ability to experience life in its own way.'

'But it has no reasoning power. It hasn't the brain.'

There was a high-pitched cackle. 'In that respect, does it differ from most of humanity? Only human arrogance makes us even try to understand the world as perceived by the bee. The essence of its consciousness will forever be a mystery to us, but not to the bee, and not to the Almighty.'

Webb tried to look pious. 'Father, I'm here because of a book.'

'The bee does not learn its dance. It has been given to it by the Creator. Could blind evolution have taught a bee how to dance? What chemicals could combine to make a small insect dance an intricate code?'

'A book, Father.'

'Could blind chance make flower and bee come to depend on each other for their very survival? The functions of queen, worker and drone interlock so perfectly?'

'It's a very old book.'

The voice became truculent. 'You must speak to our Father Librarian.'

'It was taken from a train by partisans at the end of the Second World War.' Webb tried a shot in the dark: 'And you were one of the partisans.'

The old man looked at Webb with surprise. 'Now that is very strange.'

Webb waited. Bees were crawling over his exposed legs.

'This book: it is a volume by the heretic Vincenzo?'

Webb spoke quietly. 'Father Apiarist, where can I find this book?'

The shutters came down, the eyes became vacant. 'I cannot say.'

'Cannot?'

'Will not. I said this also to the other.'

A honeybee was crawling up Webb's thigh. He tried to ignore it. 'Why not?'

'Discussion of the matter is impossible.'

'Father, I don't want to take it away, only to study it for a few hours. It is of the utmost importance.'

'No.'

'I have to see it.'

A bee had found its way under the old monk's veil and was crawling over his lips. He had a face like a stubborn child. 'Memories are long in the hills.'

'Memories?' The bees were thick on Webb's shirt.

'It is your bright colours. They think you are a flower. Stand still or you will make them angry and they will sting your eyes.'

Webb tried again but he knew it was hopeless. 'Father, please. I ask only to see this book by Vincenzo.'

The apiarist shook his head and turned to a hive. He pulled out a frame dripping with honey. The air filled with angry bees and Webb moved hastily back. 'A young man with no time? Nonsense, you have all the time in the world. Come back when you can spare some for the bees. They can teach us much.' He banged the hive with the bucket and the sky blackened with insects.

Crazy old fool, Webb thought, flying for his life, with the high-pitched cackle of the Father Apiarist almost drowned out by the angry buzz of the honeybees swirling around his head.

Johnson Space Center

The taxi dropped McNally at the main gate. He spoke briefly to the security guard, who provided him with a visitor's badge, and so NASA's Chief Administrator entered the Johnson Space Center unannounced.

The Center was almost deserted; it was after all the day before Christmas. He was gambling on workaholism amongst the senior staff, but if necessary he would simply summon them from their families. He strolled alone through the rocket park, sparing the Saturn V booster a longing glance as he passed, and continued on along the Mall, past the administration buildings, the simulation and training facilities, the laboratories and warehouses which he ultimately controlled. At the far end of the mall was the Gilruth social and athletic center; it was a long walk. He entered the Center unrecognized and extracted a can of icy Coke from a machine. Then he climbed some stairs and looked down with pleasure at two teams of fifteen-year-olds playing basketball. A white-haired grandmother in a blue tracksuit was running around, whistle in mouth.

McNally made a couple of internal calls and returned to the game.

The Chief Engineer, a bulky, bearded man, appeared in two minutes and twenty seconds. They shook hands and he sat on a chair next to the NASA boss. 'You into basketball Jim?'

'I hate all sport. No, I'm into security. We can't talk in our offices just yet.' The Engineer pulled a face.

Twenty seconds later the Deputy Administrator arrived, looking bemused, and sat on the bench in front of them. 'My secretary told me you're on vacation, Jim.'

McNally dispensed with social preliminaries. 'I intend to mothball Deep Space Four. I expect to replace it with the European Vesta, which should arrive at White Sands in a C-14 within the next few days. The Albuquerque people will reconfigure it to be launched on an Air Force IUS, probably the same booster which we used for the Galileo probe. Frontiersman will take it up to two hundred miles. I want the Shuttle astronauts retrained. At least two Mission Specialists will be on board, a nuclear physicist and an astronomer. Neither will have any background in astronautics. I'm not yet at liberty to tell you what this is about. What I can say is that Vesta will go through as a Defense item. This package has to be ready to go in one hundred days maximum.'

'How many was that?' the Chief Engineer asked.

'One hundred. Maximum.'

Lesser men would have howled in outrage, protested the obvious impossibility. But the instruction was so preposterous, the autocratic decision so out of keeping with the consultative spirit of the NASA hierarchy, that the executives, senior and experienced men, immediately realized that only some grave situation could lie behind it.

'The Russians are supposed to be launching Vesta. What do they think about this?' the Assistant Administrator asked.

'They don't know yet.'

The Chief Engineer stroked his beard thoughtfully. It was a mannerism which had started many years ago as a joke and had gradually become second nature. He itemized the points with his fingers. 'Let's look at this, Boss. Suppose we divide the problem into (1) crew training, (2) mission planning and (3) hardware development.'

McNally nodded.

'Take Item One. You know how the Mission Operations Directorate works. Crew training is so meticulous they practically tell the astronauts when they can go to the john. You're well aware that training in a hundred days is impossible even for an experienced pilot, and that you can't let a couple of rookies loose on a Space Shuttle.'

McNally bowed his head to indicate agreement.

There was an outburst of shrill screaming from below, echoing painfully from the gymnasium walls. The Chief Engineer let it die out before he continued: 'Okay, now look at the broader mission-planning aspect, Item Two. For example, think about the documentation alone we need to create for the operational support. Transportation and flight rules, command plans, communication and data plans, mission control and tracking network plans, system operating procedures, operations and maintenance instructions, flight control operations handbooks, new console handbooks, software documentation. Hell, I'm running out of fingers and that's just the documentation.'

McNally bowed his head again.

The Assistant Administrator said, 'A lot of the MOD's load will fall on their Flight Design and Dynamics division.'

McNally bowed.

'So. In a hundred days you expect them to carry through a flight design analysis leading to the development of flight design ground rules, develop the guidance, navigation and control software as well as design and construct any new hardware required, rig the MCC and the SMS's for the flight in question, come up with performance analyses for the ascent, orbit manoeuvring, payload deployment, proximity operations – with rookie specialists carrying out EVA – plan the descent and landing phases, create new in-flight programmes for

SPOC and develop integrated checklists for all of this. In a hundred days.'

'Maximum.'

The Engineer scratched his head. 'What payload accommodation category are we talking about? Dedicated, standard, middeck?'

'We'll be launching Vesta plus IUS plus four or five tons.'

'Jesus. Dedicated.'

The Assistant Administrator attempted reason. 'Okay Jim, since we're in Wonderland, we may as well take a broad-brush look at Alex's Item Three, the hardware timescale. Look at the performance milestones for Cassini, starting say from the moment the Huygens probe was delivered. It took three months to test and integrate the probe with the spacecraft, right? Another four for JPL to integrate and test all the instrumentation. The probe was in our space simulators for another seven months. Then after it was delivered at Kennedy it took another six months to complete integration with the Titan/Centaur launch vehicle. If I've counted my fingers right that's twenty months. And you're looking for the same progress in three. Let's inject some realism into this, Jim.'

McNally brushed the monstrous problems aside. 'Look at Clementine One. From concept to system design was three months. Acquisition planning overlapped with that. Sure it was another year for the systems engineering and test, but the Europeans have done most of that work for us already. We had the spacecraft integrated with the ground subsystems in a couple of months. Look, the only thing that matters is the integration of Vesta with the launch vehicle, a standard Air Force IUS which will go up with the Shuttle. All it needs is a launch vehicle adaptor. We can do it in three months.'

The game below was getting noisy. McNally added,

'For reasons of security I want to confine this to Johnson and Canaveral.'

'Where is this Vesta headed?' the Chief Engineer wanted to know.

'I don't know.'

The Assistant Administrator laughed outright. McNally had now crossed the boundary from the preposterous to the insane. The Chief Engineer tried to keep his voice level, but it had an angry quiver to it. 'Jim, I'd like you to explain something to me. How are we supposed to plan a mission if we don't know where we're going?'

McNally opened his mouth to reply, but the Deputy cut in. His eyes were icy: 'Alex is right. What do I tell my MOD? With no destination, what is there for them to plan?'

'They plan for a high-speed, maximum precision flyby of an as yet unspecified interplanetary target, using the on-board radars for last-minute course correction.'

'You'll never get off with this, Jim,' said the Chief Engineer. 'MOD will refuse to issue a commit-to-flight certificate. Or somebody will trigger the yellow light system and force an internal review. And rightly so. This could be shaping up to another Atlantis disaster.'

'The responsibility for technical readiness is yours. I expect you, and your Safety and Mission Assurance Office, to deliver.'

'Jim, you're asking me to send up half-trained astronauts on a string and sealing wax lash-up. I won't do it. I won't be responsible for the deaths of five or six people and the loss of a Shuttle.' The Chief Engineer stood up. 'You're forcing me to resign.'

McNally looked the engineer squarely in the eye. 'Some guys who look like telephone engineers will be fixing your office phone shortly. That's so the phone call you're about to receive from the President of the United States is secure. That call will have three consequences. First, you'll find out what this is about. Second, you'll wish you hadn't. And third, you'll make the deadline if it kills you and I mean that in its literal sense. Similar calls will be going to Art and Jackie this afternoon. Until these calls are made, I have no authorization to tell you what this is about.'

If McNally had slapped the Engineer, the effect could hardly have been more startling. The man stared, amazed. He seemed to have lost the power of speech.

The Assistant Administrator recovered first. 'If some major disaster happened at Byurkan, and Vesta had to catch a gravity assist window, that could justify our stepping in to help with a crash programme. Either that or a target of opportunity. It would have to be a joker, like a new comet. There would be no case to trigger a yellow light; they're usually for cost overruns anyway. Which is it, Jim? Is Byurkan about to have a big disaster, or does some comet have to be intercepted real soon?'

That's the trouble with these Princeton types. Too damn smart. McNally tried to adopt a poker face.

The Engineer had recovered sufficiently to talk. He sat down again and stared at the AA. 'But a hundred-day timescale?'

McNally glanced at his watch. Eight hours. *If Webb doesn't deliver . . .* Unconsciously, his mouth twisted in tension.

A whistle blew. The grandmother, red-face, was waving her arms around. The sharp squeaking of trainers on wood came to a stop. An outburst of youthful cheering was followed by a tribal chant: the girls' team had won.

The Engineer asked, 'What instrumentation will be on board?'

McNally tried not to smile. Knowledge of the instrumentation would provide a strong clue to the nature of the mission. He finished his Coke. 'A spectrometer for inflight target analysis. A short-pulsed laser for ranging: eight bursts a second and it only weighs a kilo. A high-resolution camera with a light CCD coupled to the laser. The setup has ranging accuracy of one metre and believe me we're going to need it. There will be a military package on board.'

'You said this is a flyby?'

'A flyby. No slowdown, no soft landing. Vesta will do what it's going to do on the hoof. The ranging is coupled to some megasmart electronics, and the probe will have to carry out some very sophisticated decision-making in maybe 0.1 of a second.'

The Engineer stared up at the high wooden ceiling. Finally he said, 'I see resemblances to the Galileo project. JPL handled the overall project and Ames managed the probe system. So why not use the experience gained at Pasadena and Mountain View? Maybe we could even use the Galileo flight plans as a template. I'll bring over key people from the JPL flight design team and get them working with our MOD. Get me your Mission Specialists right away and I'll throw them into our flotation tanks on their first day. The moment you can specify their tasks I'll configure the Mission Simulators. If you can get clearance to bring a few Vesta people over . . . and a target would be useful, Jim, when you're ready to give me it.'

Engineers. Always finding obstacles until they smell a challenge. I'm not on top of these guys for nothing. McNally smirked.

The AA's eyes narrowed thoughtfully. 'The onboard military package. Should we be thinking of something like a bomb?'

Screw all Princeton smartasses to hell.

Santa Maria della Vittoria

The telephone was ringing as Walkinshaw opened the door. Webb had picked up the receiver before the civil servant could stop him.

The voice at the other end spoke in Italian. It was a second or two before Webb recognized it.

'Mister Fish?'

'Yes.'

'You have an interest in a manuscript?'

'Yes.'

'I think I can help you.'

Webb's heart jumped. Instinctively, he tried not to sound too enthusiastic. 'I'm very interested. Where is it?'

'The matter is not straightforward. Do you know the amphitheatre in Tuscolo?'

Webb had a fleeting vision. A picnic. A day out of Rome. Giovanni, and a couple of girls, and wine and sunshine, and Italian bread and cheese. 'Yes, I do know it. It's up the hill from Monte Porzio.'

'Time is very short, Mister Fish. Please be there in twenty minutes.' The receiver went down.

Webb looked at Walkinshaw in amazement. 'I have a contact.'

Walkinshaw shook his head. 'That's impossible. This is a safe house. Nobody knows you're here.'

Webb headed back to the door. 'We'll have to shift. The car will only take us so far and the rest is a climb.'

Walkinshaw held up a restraining hand. 'Not so fast, Webb. Are you listening to me? Nobody is supposed to know you're here.'

'Walkinshaw, I absolutely must have that manuscript.'

Walkinshaw followed the astronomer out to the car. 'Are you listening to me, Oliver?'

The ignition keys were still in the car. Webb stood at the car door. 'I don't care. Look, we're talking about the planet. Do you want to be fried? With your family? And your country? If this asteroid hits America what do you think they'll do about it? I say they'll launch a nuclear strike in revenge. The Russians will hit back in turn and we'll be back to the Dark Ages even before Nemesis gets here. The world's run by madmen, Walkinshaw, not rational people.'

'Webb, will you calm down. You're exhausted and not thinking clearly. You are my responsibility. I can't have you rushing bull-headed into this meeting. I need to know who knows you're here and what you're getting into.'

'There's no time for stuff like that, you idiot. I have to take risks. I'm going. Stay here if you want.'

The car was smelling of hot plastic and the heat was deadly. Walkinshaw took the wheel, and they put the windows down. 'Who was it?'

'The librarian.'

'Did you give him – or anyone – the villa's phone number?'

'Of course not. I don't even know what it is.'

'The address, then?'

'Absolutely not. Turn right.'

'Oliver, something is badly wrong here.'

'So you said. Left up here.'

The road took them up past villas with big wrought-iron windows, swimming pools and dobermans wandering the grounds, and then they were into woods. There was an empty car park. The *guard'auto* had gone home.

The sun was low in the sky. Memories came flooding back. Franca, that was her name; and Giovanni's lady had been called Ambra.

'Stay put, Walkinshaw. I'm a solitary scholar, remember?'

Walkinshaw looked into the surrounding trees. His face was dark. 'This is getting worse by the minute. Look around you. Why would he want to meet you in a place like this?'

'He doesn't want to be seen talking to me, that's all.'

Walkinshaw's civil service urbanity was gone. 'You lunatic. You don't know what you're walking into.'

There was a path through grass leading up to the little Roman amphitheatre a quarter of a mile ahead. A burly, white-robed figure was standing motionless on the stone steps. As Webb approached the man moved away and disappeared into a nearby wood. Webb ran up to the amphitheatre. The undergrowth was dense but the monk's path was clearly visible in the trail of bent and broken twigs. Puffing, Webb followed the trail and found himself in a broad Roman road, the big flagstones still in place after two thousand years. The trees formed a wide overhead canopy, and the road went steeply back down the hillside. The monk was standing motionless, about three hundred yards ahead. Webb walked smartly towards him.

At about a hundred yards, the monk walked off to the right, disappearing amongst the trees. It was getting dark and Webb ran forward, risking a fall on the ancient cobbles. Turning off along the librarian's route, he found himself back at the car park.

Walkinshaw was standing at the car. He was peering at the monk alertly, as if sensing that something was wrong.

Something was wrong. From close up, the man had the wrong build for the librarian; he was too thin, the hair was not in the style of a monk's tonsure. Walkinshaw shouted 'Webb! Run!' and then there was a sharp *Crack!*

and the civil servant, open-mouthed in amazement and pain, flopped down in a sitting position with his back to the car, with a red spot welling up from his chest.

Terrified, Webb turned to run but a pale, freckle-faced girl had appeared from the trees, and she too was carrying a pistol. She approached to just outside arm's length and pointed the gun steadily at Webb's chest.

They did Leclerc and now they're going to do me.

Walkinshaw was sliding slowly sideways; his eyes were swimming in his head; he was gurgling; bright red, frothy blood was trickling from the corner of his mouth. The girl waved Webb back towards the car. He ignored her and moved towards Walkinshaw. The monk hit him in the face with the barrel of the gun. 'You can't leave him!' Webb shouted in English. 'He needs help!' The monk understood. He fired into Walkinshaw half a dozen times, the civil servant's body jerking and the pistol shots cracking into the dark woods, while Webb yelled obscenities and the girl gripped his hair tightly and held her gun at his head.

Then Webb was thrust into the back of the car while the man threw off the monk's habit. He turned out to be an unshaven youth with the expressionless face of the psychotic. He turned the key and took off down the Tuscolo road. Through his fear and rage, Webb thought that it hadn't been necessary to run over Walkinshaw's body and that the civil servant might still have been alive when the wheels went over him.

⧗

In Rome, the youth sped through EUR along the Via del Mare, which transformed into the Via Ostiense, and then they were through the Ostiense Gate, passing a white pyramid and rattling along the Viale Piramide. The woman was breathing heavily. Her pupils were dilated, and from time to time she would giggle for no clear reason. She kept the gun hidden under Webb's buttock and the thought of an accidental sex change, which recurred whenever the car rattled over cobbles, wasn't funny. He began to shiver uncontrollably, going alternately hot and cold, and a monstrous headache threatened. Strangely, to Webb, the emotion beginning to dominate in him was anger. He was angry at being pushed around, angry at being struck in the face, and angry for Walkinshaw and his family if he had one. It was a seething sense of outrage which he kept firmly in check.

They hurried along the side of the Tiber before cutting away from it, and Webb found himself orbiting the Victor Emanuele before speeding up the Via Nazionale. The man turned into the Street of the Four Fountains and pulled the car to a stop.

He turned and snapped his fingers in Webb's face. '*La chiesa. Vai indietro. Subito!*'

The urge to slap the youth's face was almost beyond Webb's power to resist. He pushed open the car door, slammed it shut violently and crossed to one of the *quattro fontane*. The car horn hooted and the man gestured menacingly, waving him towards the church. Webb thrust a middle finger in the air. He splashed his face with the cool water and then sponged down his legs. There was nothing he could do about the dark patch on his shorts. He tossed the pink-stained handkerchief on to the road and looked at the inconspicuous little church with the flight of stairs leading up to a dull green door. Above the door, '*Santa Maria della Vittoria*' was written in gold lettering.

There was a brief gap in the flow of traffic and he crossed the street. He felt barely able to walk. On the steps he looked back; the young assassins were watching him intently. He pushed open the outer door. Assorted church notices; a collection box for 'the deserving'; an inner door, brown and old. He went inside. The door closed behind him with a sudden pneumatic hiss and the Roman traffic switched off.

There was a musty smell, like a cellar or a second-hand bookshop.

Webb let his eyes adjust to the gloom. Rows of pews stretched to an altar, draped with white linen. Cherubim on the ceiling; crucifixes and statuettes; candles burning. And one human being, a young woman near the front sitting motionless, head down. She crossed herself and walked smartly off, her high heels clattering loudly in the confined space. Their eyes met briefly; she gave no sign of recognition.

Take it as it comes.

He stepped warily down the left aisle, heart thumping in his chest and leaning on the pews for steadiness. In a small transept was a white marble sculpture. The sun was streaming down on it from a high window and the sculpture seemed to glow, floating in space. A white marble woman was lying back and a half-naked youth stood over her, holding an arrow poised to plunge. The woman's eyes were half-closed and her lips were parted. Around this couple were what looked like theatre boxes. Assorted gentlemen occupied these, their faces leering and gloating, eternally congealed.

It was bizarre.

'The Rapture of Saint Teresa.'

Webb whirled round. Elderly man. Iron grey hair, greying goatee beard, metal-rimmed spectacles. White linen suit, dark tie, expensive shirt; black ebony walking stick. Thin lips drawn into a smile. If he was an immediate threat, Webb couldn't see how.

'She is three hundred years old and, as you see, very beautiful. Many regard her as Bernini's finest work. And this church, being one of the best examples of late baroque in Rome, is a worthy setting for her. What do you think?'

Webb said it to hurt: 'It looks like a porn show in a Berlin nightclub.'

The man winced. 'What we are seeing, Mister Fish, is the climax of Saint Teresa's mystical union with Christ. I believe that Bernini is telling us about a spiritual experience of such intensity that it can only be described to the herd, even remotely, by comparison with the sex act.'

Webb said, 'You could read what you liked into it.'

The man sighed. 'That is the way with much great art. But you disappoint me, sir. I see that you are a superficial man, a child of your time, just another mass-produced product of a technological Reich.'

Webb was trying hard to control his anger. 'Was I brought here for this?'

The man's smile broadened. 'That's the spirit! Actually, you are here because my instructions are to kill you.'

⧗

They emerged into the sunshine and walked arm in arm along a noisy, bustling street. Webb, in spite of himself, was glad of the support. The young assassins had vanished. At a small piazza a traffic policeman, dressed in white, stood on a raised pedestal, around which cars flowed like lava. An articulated truck was having difficulty negotiating a corner and the policeman was waving at it furiously.

'This way, cavaliere,' said the elderly man, pointing his ebony stick. 'We shall have a beer at Doney's.'

They turned up into a broad, gently sloping promenade, the Via Veneto. The street was reassuringly busy. Webb let himself be guided to a pavement table under a blue and white-striped awning. A dark young man with long, shiny hair approached. The older man casually placed his stick on the table, its metal tip pointing in Webb's direction, and ordered a beer. Webb asked for *un'aranciata*.

A whistle blew, back down the hill. The articulated

290

lorry wasn't making it round the Piazza Barberini. Further up the Veneto, Webb saw a crop-headed marine with an automatic weapon; he was standing at the main door of the American Embassy, and he looked in a bad mood.

The man sipped at his beer. 'I should have asked for a German lager. You are wired up like a cat about to spring, Mister Fish. Do try to relax. You must know that if I had wished it, you would by now be dead.'

'Who are you?'

'I think of myself as a surgeon.'

'I assume you set up the surgery in the Tuscolo woods,' Webb said.

'Overzealous amateurs. One must work with the material to hand.'

A girl in a short, lime-green skirt sat down at a nearby table, facing Webb. She had an uneducated, Sicilian peasant look about her. She scanned the menu without once looking in his direction.

Webb said: 'Society has rules.'

Little wrinkles above the lips disapproved. 'Mister Fish, you increasingly disappoint me. The rules are for herd control! To obey them, it is enough to have a spinal cord. The free man makes his own rules.' An outburst of car horn blaring came from the piazza down the hill.

The waiter left a little printed bill. Webb waited until he had gone. 'Why am I still alive?'

The man sighed. 'You remain alive, for the moment, because of my greed. It seems that you are proving troublesome to some people. You seek a manuscript. I have found out where this manuscript is; in fact, I have held it in my hands. My instructions were to liquidate you before you got your hands on it. A simple enough task, for which I was offered a sum of money. I can now access the book whenever I please and well, here you are. As for the sum of money, it was strikingly large. So large that it made me wonder.'

Webb stared at the man in open disgust. 'A man died so that you could have spending money? I regret even having to breathe the same air as you.'

'If that is a problem for you, it can easily be remedied.'

'What do you know about this manuscript? How did you know where I was?'

A hand waved casually in the air. 'The details escape me.'

'Where does the Father Librarian come into it?'

'A naive fool, sold a plausible story.'

'And your overzealous amateurs?'

'They too were easily manipulated, like all young idealists. Told they were striking a blow for the people, they were eager to believe it.'

Webb sat back. He eyed the man speculatively. 'What am I worth?'

The man fingered the ebony stick absent-mindedly. 'One million American dollars. And in cash, the only medium of exchange I recognize. Already I have received half.'

Webb sipped at his orange juice. He was beginning to feel nauseous, and found himself taking deep breaths. 'That's a lot of money.'

'Indeed. And the question I have to ask is, where does the value lie? In your death, or in the book? If in the book, then perhaps I now have in my possession something whose true value is, shall we say for the sake of a figure, ten million dollars.'

'I begin to understand.'

'Are you in a position to offer me ten million dollars for it?'

'No,' Webb lied.

The man's face adopted a disapproving expression. 'That is unfortunate, Mister Fish.'

'And I intend to steal the book back from you.'

The man laughed incredulously. 'I admire your honesty,

if not your sense of self-preservation. How do you propose to do that?'

Webb finished off his drink.

The man continued: 'I have seen this book. The how and why need not concern you. I have pored over its pages, every line, every letter. But it has defeated me. In its pages I see no hidden treasure, no secret diamond mines, no plans of invasion. But, Mister Fish, you know something about this manuscript. Something which may allow you to unlock its secret. You may therefore succeed where I have failed.'

'That is possible, given your level of intelligence.'

'It is also possible that you will insult me once too often.'

Webb said, 'I think not. Because you're going to let me walk away from here.'

The man nodded. 'It is in my interests to do so. If the value lies in your carcass, I will never see you again. But if it lies in the book, you will risk your life to return for it. I am gambling half a million dollars by letting you walk free against ten million dollars if you come back for it. A reasonable risk to take, is it not?'

'Let me anticipate your proposition. I'll unlock the secret of the book. In return you will promise to leave me alone and sell or blackmail your paymasters with whatever I come up with.'

'You have a formidable intelligence, young man. That is dangerous. I will have to take great care.'

'No, I'm thick. That's why I'm in this position. Why don't you just throw me in a cellar and force me to decipher it?'

'Because you would invent some story even if you found nothing. Only if you return for the book will I know for certain that it truly contains something of greater value even than your life.' The man finished his beer, patting his mouth with a handkerchief. 'I doubt if you intend to keep your part of the bargain. When you return, if you do, you will attempt to steal the book.'

'I doubt if you intend to keep your half. Once I've given you the information I'm out of bargaining power.'

'Life is a risk, my friend. Consider the one I am taking with my paymasters.'

'May they meet you, one dark night.'

'I will leave you here. You will remain seated for ten minutes, after which you may do as you please. If you attempt to leave before ten minutes have passed, your day will turn into everlasting night.'

'The manuscript?' Webb asked.

'You and it will connect. If you attempt to escape with it you will be killed without warning, and I will settle for the other half million dollars in exchange for your carcass. But enough talk of death, my unworldly friend. Tonight is *Natale*, a celebration of birth. Why not proceed to the Piazza Navona, where the crowds are already gathering, filled with the joy of Nativity? Find a seat at the Bar Colombo if you can, and enjoy yourself. Be alone and carry nothing electronic.'

'Do something for me,' Webb asked. 'It will complete the bargain.'

The man raised his eyebrows.

'Kill the bastards who murdered my companion.'

The man laughed, exposing a row of gold fillings. 'You see! Under the veneer we are not so different! I advise you to change your clothes before the police start making connections. And then come to the Colombo within the hour, young man, and find me the hidden message, and live to enjoy your grandchildren.' The man picked up his walking stick and handed a ten thousand-lira note to the waiter, before sauntering down the hill. Near the Barberini, Webb lost him in the crowds.

Webb turned his chair slightly to get a better view of the tables. About nine feet away a silver-haired man, perhaps a banker, was reading *Il Giornale*. A young man from the north, in Levi's and a black sweatshirt with Princeton University written across it, was staring openly at the Sicilian girl. She was throwing occasional sly glances at him. Two workmen with vast bellies were sharing a joke. A middle-aged nun was sipping a cappuccino. Their eyes met and she smiled coldly at him.

Surely not the nun?

No, the young man.

An elderly priest came through from the back of the café and the young man rose. They went off, arms linked Italian-style. Webb played with the toothpicks for ten minutes, then got up and headed down the hill, trembling, nauseous, and light-headed with relief. At the piazza, the articulated truck was jammed halfway round the corner, unable to move forwards or back. The street echoed with the blare of car horns and the traffic cop had disappeared.

Before he turned the corner, Webb glanced back up the hill. The banker was folding away his newspaper.

⧗

Webb knew the geography of Rome. He had spent six productive months with colleagues from the university, two years – or was it two million years? – ago. Some instinct told him to head for the Trastevere, the territory of *noialtri*, the people apart, who did not always speak freely to the law. He turned right along the Viale del Tritone, and headed across the city by foot. Once over the Garibaldi Bridge, he quickly lost himself in a maze of narrow streets, avoiding children on mopeds and three-wheeled *motofurgoni* loaded with big flagons of wine.

In a small square a *frutteria* lady was setting out her wares for the evening, heaving a massive box of tomatoes on to a table. A white-haired flower lady, an espresso perched on a cobble at her feet, stared with hypnotic fascination at Webb's beachwear. Through an archway into a busy little square, cluttered with tables where men with wrinkled faces sat nibbling, drinking, watching the world go by. Wonderful smells drifted out of a hosteria.

A woman was sweeping out the doorway of a clothes shop. She *buongiorno*'d and followed Webb in. He tried the word for 'underpants' in three languages and ended up, red-faced, surrounded by a gaggle of women trying to help. Half an hour later he emerged in a neat dark suit, in the style of an Italian businessman. He crossed the square to a tiny little cobbler's shop. The man looked at Webb's mass-produced sandals with polite amusement. Webb waited another half hour while the sun set and the cobbler tapped away at a last, a row of little nails projecting from his mouth. When the black leather shoes eventually appeared, they were of fine quality, and a quarter of the price Webb would have paid in Oxford. He had a coffee in a bar, letting the trembling in his body subside, and watched two youths playing a noisy game of pinball. Fifteen minutes later, he exchanged lire for a pile of *gettone* and fed them into the café's telephone.

While he waited to connect, he looked at his watch. Walkinshaw had been dead for less than two hours.

And Webb had only ten left.

Casa Pacifica

The President faced Noordhof across the Oval Office desk, gazing at the soldier without a blink. 'Let's hear it again, Colonel,' he said over steepled hands.

'Sir, there is the possibility of a leak.'

'I must be going deaf. For an unbelievable moment I thought you said there was the possibility of a leak.'

'Leclerc is on a marble slab pending disposal,' said Noordhof in an unsteady voice. 'He had an accident with a cable car.'

The President raised his eyebrows in disbelief. 'He's your rocket man?'

'Yes, sir. He and Webb, the other European, were supposed to identify Nemesis.'

'So what does this Webb have to say?'

'We can't find him,' said Noordhof.

The President's tone was flat. 'My hearing's gone again. Would you repeat, slowly and clearly, what you just said?'

'He's missing. We've lost him.'

Grant pursed his lips and gave the soldier a long, steady stare. He finally said, 'Okay, Colonel. Now tell me how you pulled off this amazing feat.'

'Sir, I don't know how. He's just disappeared.'

The President let a full minute pass while Noordhof prayed for a great earthquake to swallow him up.

'We lost a strategic H-bomb in Alaska once, a B-43 as I recall,' Grant reminisced. 'And it wasn't inventory shrinkage either. Turned out some Alaskan Command Air Defense guys thought they'd found a way round the Permissive Action Links. They tried to blackmail Uncle Sam with it. Not that the Great Unwashed ever got to hear about that little escapade.'

'What happened, sir?'

'We couldn't go through the courts with a thing like that, of course. There was an unfortunate air crash. But you, Colonel, you do things on the grand scale; you're on course to lose the planet. We face annihilation if we don't find this frigging asteroid and nuclear holocaust if we're seen looking. And so far you've managed to spring a leak and lose half your team in four days. Magnificent.'

A red blush spread over Noordhof's face. The President turned to the CIA Director. 'You got light to throw on this farce, Rich?'

The CIA Director stuffed tobacco into his pipe from an old black pouch on his lap. 'Nope.'

'But someone knows about your team,' said the President.

'That's impossible. These are just accidents,' said Heilbron unconvincingly.

'This is beginning to sound like the last message from the *Titanic*,' the President said.

'You can't scare me, Mister President, I'm too old. We're doing our human best.'

'If that's your best, I'd hate to see you people on a bad day.'

⧖

They drove out of Casa Pacifica in a cramped little Fiat with tinted windows, and joined Interstate Five heading south. The Stars and Stripes fluttered over Pendleton Marine Corps base to the left; to the right, half-naked bodies lay sprawled out on Red Beach or splashed in the Pacific shimmering beyond. Late-afternoon traffic was pouring up from San Diego. The Secret Service man drove carefully, watching the ebb and flow of traffic around him, searching with practised eyes for the anomaly in the pattern, the car which lingered too long, the strangeness in the proportion. But there was only the Buick in the rear mirror, a steady forty yards behind.

'Okay, Colonel, fill me in. What's the word on your team?' asked Bellarmine, removing his dark glasses.

'We have more on the Leclerc–Webb thing,' said Noordhof. 'I've had Nicholson from our Rome Embassy nosing around. This is weird, sir, but it seems the story starts in a monastery, in some mountain area south of Rome. It's run by monks.'

'A monastery run by monks?' Bellarmine asked sarcastically.

'Yes, sir. It seems they have this famous library of old books, called the Helinandus Collection or something. All very securely held, fire-proofed, steel doors, smart electronics and so on. Local rumour has it that they are holding loot which was taken from the Germans at the end of the War, including a lot of books. One of them might be a manuscript written by an Italian called Vincenzo. But it's just local folklore.'

'Do I know this guy Vincenzo?'

'I doubt it, sir, he's been dead three hundred and fifty years.'

The Secretary of Defense sounded perplexed. 'How does this connect with anything whatsoever?'

'This Webb guy gets it into his head that there's something in this missing ancient tome that will let him identify Nemesis. Naturally everybody assumes he's just flipped.'

The driver was looking at something in his rear mirror.

'Well, has he or hasn't he?'

'That's the thing, Mister Secretary. We tell the Brits what's going on, they send out one of their people to nursemaid Webb, and the last thing we hear is that Webb's minder gets seven rounds from a Beretta 96 pumped into him and is then run over with his own hired car. Now if Webb has been chasing some chimera, how come his minder gets bumped off?'

'Unless he did it himself,' suggested Bellarmine. 'What's the word on him?'

'He's just disappeared. Nobody knows where he is.'

'And how does that leave the great asteroid hunt?' Bellarmine asked.

A decrepit white car sailed by them, filled with students. A long-haired girl blew a kiss and then the car was past. Bellarmine's driver blew out his cheeks in relief.

'In chaos.'

The driver slowed down and turned off at a sign saying 'Solana Beach'; the Buick followed. He manoeuvred a few turnings and drove along a street with notices on pavements and in windows saying 'No Vacancies', 'Real English Beer', 'Debbie's Delishus Donuts $1.50'. Bellarmine stared out at this other America, at the little holiday groups on the sidewalks eating delishus donuts and wearing kiss-me-quick hats, strange people who were content to stroll aimlessly, without benefit of sharp-eyed protectors or jostling reporters.

Then the driver skimmed past an elderly woman with thick spectacles trying to reverse an orange Beetle, and turned into a quiet row of shabby beach houses. He drove slowly along for fifty yards and pulled to a stop at one of them. The street was absolutely quiet. No signs of life came from within the house. Heavy lace curtains hid its interior. A window shutter was dangling half off; the next storm would finish it. The driver frowned.

'Stay put, sir. That's an order.' In the driving mirror, he watched the manoeuvrings of the orange Beetle. It eventually kangaroo'd off round the corner. 'Okay, sir. Let me check out the house.'

'Clem, it's okay. You're strung up like a violin string,' said Bellarmine.

'Sir, this is irregular. I'd be a lot happier if one of us checked it out.' Clem saw waiting assassins, Bellarmine dying in a pool of blood on the sidewalk, terrifying congressional inquisitions.

'Forget it. Come for me in a couple of hours. And cheer up, man. If the golfball buzzes you know where I am.'

The cars drove off and Bellarmine waved Noordhof on into the house. The Secretary of Defense stood on the sidewalk, alone. He felt a strange exhilaration. The second most powerful man in the world had an overwhelming but unfulfillable urge: to go for a stroll.

Bellarmine walked up the concrete driveway and round the side of the house. There was a dirty white side door, half open, facing into a small hallway, cluttered with buckets, sacks of dog meal, logs and boots. A deep-throated baying came from within the house. A voice shouted 'In here, Mister Secretary.' Bellarmine, who hated all dogs, stepped into the untidy hallway. A door opened and he froze with fear as the Hound of the Baskervilles rushed for him, baying excitedly.

'Get down, Lift-off! Welcome to my beach house, sir. I'm fixing us up with a royal concubine.'

Solana Beach

Bellarmine followed the ponytailed scientist along the corridor and through slatted swing doors. The kitchen was brightly lit, surgically clean and chaotic. Rows of gleaming sharp knives dangled from hooks on a wall. On a worktop next to a large stove was a half-empty bottle of Jack Daniel's, a supermarket chicken and a clutter of spices and unopened bottles of wine and liquor. A small balding man of about fifty, wearing an apron which made him look like a big Martini bottle, was chopping spring onions. His movements were slow and deliberate, as if the process was unfamiliar to him.

'Do you guys know each other?' asked Shafer, disappearing through another set of swing doors. The Director of NASA put down the vegetable knife, wiped his hands on the apron and shook hands with the Secretary of Defense. Bellarmine nodded; the NASA Director said I guess we sing for our supper here and Bellarmine said he'd do a fan dance if it got him answers. Then a voice from next door shouted 'Help yourself to a drink!' Bellarmine poured two large sherries, emptied one and filled it up again.

Shafer reappeared with a wodge of papers stapled together. There was a knock at the door and the Great Dane started a deep-throated baying. Sacheverell walked into the kitchen. 'Get down, you slobbering idiot!' Shafer yelled.

'Nice friendly dog, Shafer,' said Sacheverell, while it eyed him, growling, from under the swing doors.

'Yeah,' said Bellarmine. 'Makes for a nice secure house. Anyways, the media think I'm on vacation at Nixon's old place. Right. I'm here for a briefing. Get started.'

Shafer said, 'Jim, drop that for now. Let's go next door.'

Next door was a large living room. One wall was taken up by a long blackboard covered with equations. At the far end of the room a bay window looked out over the sea. Books and papers were scattered over wicker chairs, television, computer, couch, floor.

Bellarmine made his way through the clutter to the big bay window. The floor creaked and SecDef felt it give a little. On the beach below, a few girls sat topless, drinking wine and chattering. A hundred yards out at sea some young men were skilfully balancing on surfboards while big Pacific waves rolled under them and broke up hissing on the sand, or hit an outcrop of rock over to the right with a *Whump!* and an explosion of spray. Shafer appeared through the swing doors with a bottle of Jack Daniel's. 'Sir, come back from the window. We had a landslip and you're overhanging the cliff. We're propped up by timbers, but I don't know how long my beach house has got before it slides into the sea.'

Bellarmine turned from the window and shared a couch with a clutter of journals and books. The others settled down on casual chairs, except for McNally, who shared a cushion with the Great Dane in front of a wood fire.

The Secretary of Defense spoke slowly and clearly, as if to make sure his words were fully assimilated. 'In just over ten hours' time I report to an extraordinary meeting of the National Security Council. The President, the Chiefs of Staff, myself and others may take certain decisions on the basis of information given me here. I need three things from you people. First, do you confirm the damage estimates given us by Sacheverell? Some of us had difficulty taking his stuff on board. Second, have you come up with some means of nullifying this threat? Third, have you found this asteroid? Now, Colonel, what exactly has your team delivered? What about the simulations Sacheverell here showed us? Is he serious?'

Shafer, standing at the swing doors, poured himself a whisky. 'They sent me your little cartoons, Herb, and I've done a few runs of my own. Of course we don't know what they've posted us but I've guessed we're in the hundred thousand-megaton ballpark, give or take. I broadly agree with your calculations. If and when Nemesis hits, America will be incinerated.'

Bellarmine looked blankly at the Nobel physicist.

'You missed out on a few little details,' Shafer continued. 'Nuclear reactors scattered over the countryside, petrochemical smog from burning oil, coal deposits set on fire for a few centuries, stuff like that. And you weren't quite right on the fireball. It's primarily the blanket of fire spreading over the top of the atmosphere that will set us alight down below: Ernst Öpik saw that way back in the fifties. Another little oversight, Herb, was the counterflow, the air rushing to fill the vacuum left by the rising fireball. Still, since we're all dead by then I don't suppose we care.'

Bellarmine pointed dumbly at the Jack Daniel's. Shafer crossed the room with the bottle and filled his glass, continuing the critique as he did. 'And I guess you used a pretty coarse grid for your ocean simulations, Herb. It's not just the tsunami you have to worry about. It's the plume of water thrown forty miles into the air, and the superheated steam shooting around. The sea bed would crack open and you'd get a rain of molten boulders thrown for one or two thousand miles. God knows what would happen to coastal areas. In your San Diego scenario people would have broiled before they drowned. And if you'd used an ocean-wide grid you'd have found that the coastal areas don't get hit by one wave. They get hit by a succession, at more or less fifty-minute intervals. You'd replace seaboard cities by mudflats.'

'Okay,' said Bellarmine, 'I believe you. If it hits we're finished. Now the sixty-four thousand-dollar question and I want to hear a good answer. Colonel, have you found Nemesis?'

Noordhof said, 'No, sir.'

There was a heavy silence.

Noordhof broke it. 'Mister Secretary, the scientists here tell me it could take ten or twenty years to discover Nemesis by telescopic search. You gave us five days. It's unreasonable. And we have almost no chance of picking it up by telescope until collision is imminent.'

'Why haven't you people been tracking these rocks as a matter of routine?' Bellarmine asked angrily. 'If you've known all along that these things are out there, that strikes me as a matter of duty.'

Shafer shot back: 'Zero funding. Some of us went blue in the face trying to warn you people, but you didn't want to know.'

Bellarmine continued as if Shafer had not spoken, 'And because of this dereliction of duty, we're now in a situation where an asteroid is heading for us and all we can do is wait to be hit.'

'We're down to Webb,' said Noordhof.

'Forget it,' said Sacheverell, sounding peeved.

Shafer said, 'Look, we're not even sure of the major types of hazard. We just don't know what's out there. The British school think that fireball showers or dark Halleys or giant comets are an even bigger risk than your Nemesis-type asteroids.'

'Unmitigated crap,' declared Sacheverell.

'So what now?' Bellarmine asked.

The Nobel physicist moved some books and sat down on a wicker chair. 'Another drink, I guess.'

There was a knock and the sound of footsteps. Shafer

roared at the Great Dane, and disappeared through the swing doors. Someone was saying 'Oh Jerusalem! City of Joy! I made it!' Judy Whaler walked into the room.

'You're five minutes late, Judy. Mister Secretary, may I present our nuclear weapons expert?' Bellarmine nodded.

'Carburettor trouble,' Whaler explained, sinking into a wicker chair. 'Kenneth's looking after the shop but I have bad news about that. The forecast for tonight is thickening cirrus over southern Arizona.'

Bellarmine's voice was grim. 'Let me be clear about this. Are you saying the Nemesis search is over?'

'The telescopic search, yes. We won't make your midnight deadline, Mister Secretary.'

There was a silence as they absorbed Judy's words.

'You heard about the Rome thing?' Noordhof asked, thrusting a large Jack Daniel's into her hands.

She nodded and took a big gulp. 'Kenneth told me. First André and now Ollie.'

Noordhof said. 'We don't know what's going on over there.'

'Where does this Webb's ancient manuscript come in?' Bellarmine wanted to know.

The Colonel answered. 'It's gone missing, which drew Ollie's attention to it in the first place. His idea was that if you had an observation hundreds of years old it would give you a long time base and a very accurate orbit, which is what the Russians would need to target the asteroid. If there really is a moving star recorded in the book, we could use it to work out which asteroid it refers to, and so identify Nemesis.'

Sacheverell said, 'Mister Secretary, it's a fantasy thing. We can forget it. Webb should never have been on the team.'

Shafer shook his head. 'I disagree. The Italian business suggests that Ollie is on to something.'

The Colonel asked, 'With only ten hours left to identify

Nemesis, and Arizona clouded over, we're just about finished. Can't you give us more time?'

'No. Because every day carries the risk that Nemesis will hit before we've had time to take appropriate action. Because the longer we delay the greater the risk that Zhirinovsky learns that we know about Nemesis and decides to pre-empt any punch we might want to deliver. Because no matter what time you're given you'll always want more. The NSC want answers by midnight tonight. Your failure to deliver does not buy you more time.'

Shafer poured Bellarmine his fourth drink of the evening. 'And nullifying the threat?' SecDef asked. 'Say you magically identify it in the next few hours? Presumably you hit it with the Bomb?'

'We got those coming out of our ears,' said Noordhof.

'If my experience as Secretary of Defense has taught me anything, it's this. There is no problem that can't be solved with the use of enough high explosive.'

Noordhof said, 'Sir, we need to know what we're targeting. The Bomb is no good if we create a shower of fragments or a big dust ball heading for us.'

'I think I've found the solution to that,' said Judy, her voice betraying satisfaction. She put down her drink and walked over to the blackboard. She drew a string of dots joined by a straight line. Next to it she depicted an irregular shape with an arrow pointing towards the line. 'We make a necklace from small atomic bombs, maybe neutron bombs. We fire the probe at Nemesis, as nearly head-on as we can. As the probe approaches it shoots off little neutron bombs in such a way that they're strung out in a line. The line cuts in front of Nemesis like so, and we set the bombs off in sequence, each one bursting just as it reaches the asteroid, say a kilometre or two above its surface.'

'Nemesis has to run through a bomb alley,' said Shafer.

'Yes. They're just toys, each one no more than a dozen

Hiroshimas, so that each one gives a gentle push to Nemesis, not enough to break it up even if it's made of snow. But the cumulative effect is a big push, the same as if we'd given the asteroid a single hefty punch. We're going to explode the bombs directly in front of Nemesis, to brake its forward motion so as to let the Earth get past before the asteroid reaches our orbit. That's more energy-efficient than a sideways deflection.'

McNally said, 'In the frame of reference of Nemesis it's just peacefully coasting along and suddenly bombs appear out of space and start exploding in its face. It's simple.'

'All truly brilliant ideas are simple,' Shafer asserted. 'And we can space the neutron bombs thousands of kilometres apart so they don't interfere with each other.'

'Simple in principle but extremely difficult in practice,' she said. 'I have a detailed design study under way at Sandia. One way or another, we'll have something workable within the hundred-day guideline.'

Bellarmine clapped his hands together in satisfaction. 'Well done, Doctor Whaler. McNally, what you have to do is deliver her atomic necklace. What do you have to say about that?'

It was McNally's turn to use the blackboard. 'Willy and I have identified a route. It's extremely difficult.' He scribbled on the board with yellow chalk. 'The Russians are due to launch a comet probe built by the French. It's called the Vesta. We thought if we could get hold of it without arousing suspicion . . .'

'McNally, the Reds must have their antennae at full stretch. What in Christ's name do you suppose they'll think if we grab this probe from them?'

'Mister Secretary, we think we've found a way. The French have built a duplicate, for electronics testing and the like. We often do the same. It's not up to full specification but it might do for the purpose. If we could get our hands on this duplicate probe along with the detailed plans we might configure it to deliver Judy's necklace. We'll need to bring over the French engineers under an oath of secrecy.'

'But Vesta is too heavy for anything but the Soviet booster,' objected Sacheverell.

'That was for a long interplanetary trip, soft landing on several comets as it went. Most of that weight is in the fuel tanks and the metal darts for penetrating surfaces. We're going to strip all of that out along with the scientific instrumentation. We'll use four Shuttles in two pairs, two carrying Judy's atomic necklace and two carrying Vesta duplicates, the French one, and one we'll knock up ourselves from their plans. Or we might use one Shuttle four times. We'll have specialists on board to mate the necklace with its Vesta clone. Then we'll launch from 200 miles up with inertial upper stages like the one we used for Galileo. It's just about possible to get a dozen of Judy's bombs up that way. But we're talking very smart system development, navigational equipment and so on. We're cannibalizing existing systems all the way. I have teams on it now. We might – I say might – do it inside the magic one hundred days.'

'I'll ask the CIA Director to come up with some cover story for your launches,' Bellarmine promised.

'Point him in the direction of Venus probes,' suggested Shafer.

The SecDef put his glass on the floor and wandered back to the bay window, picking his way over books. A gust of young laughter came up from below. Someone was tuning up a guitar and a bonfire was getting started, pieces of driftwood being thrown on to the flames, and faces flickering red around it. Someone had lit a cigarette and it was being passed around after each puff. Kids these days, Bellarmine thought.

Shafer said, 'I hope you're not too hungry, Mister Secretary. Royal Concubine takes an hour to prepare.'

Bellarmine came back, flopped on to the couch and leaned forward, resting his chin heavily on his hands. He said: 'The sharp end is that we haven't found Nemesis.'

The telephone rang. Shafer picked it up and said 'Ollie!' The effect was like pulling the pin of a hand grenade. Everyone rose to their feet. The Great Dane, sensing atmosphere, leaped up.

The conversation was one-sided and carried on for some minutes, Shafer interspersing the occasional grunt. Finally he said, 'Hold the line, Ollie.'

'What's going on, Willy?' asked Noordhof.

Shafer spoke rapidly, his hand over the mouthpiece. 'Webb's phoning from a public box in the boondocks. Some guy was paid to bump him off. This hit man has the manuscript. He works out that it must have something valuable in it but can't see what. So he makes a pact with Ollie. He lets Ollie go to see if he'll come back for the book. If Ollie does, thereby risking his life, that proves to the killer that the manuscript is worth more than the contract price on Webb. The deal is that Ollie agrees to decipher the manuscript and the hit man then lets him go. The guy figures he can then sell the manuscript to his paymasters or blackmail them with its secret message.'

Bellarmine was aghast. 'This is a highly dangerous situation.'

McNally said, 'Ollie hasn't a hope.'

Shafer's hand was still over the mouthpiece. 'He can kill Webb when he's got the information out of him, collect his blood money and then proceed to the blackmail. Ollie knows this but he still has to go for the manuscript in the hope of getting away with it.'

Judy was looking agitated. 'He's going straight to his death. Tell him to pull out.'

Noordhof took the telephone from Shafer. 'Webb. You have to make contact with the killer . . . use your initiative . . . of course he expects you to try . . . look, there's no other way . . . Mister, get this: you have no choice in the matter.'

Bellarmine took a turn. 'Webb, this is the Secretary of Defense. I'll give it to you straight. The White House requires the identification of Nemesis within ten hours, failing which we shall proceed on the assumption that Nemesis will not be identified before impact.'

Bellarmine listened some more. His mouth opened in astonishment, and he turned, aghast. 'He's thinking of pulling out.'

'I'll fix the yellow bastard,' said Noordhof angrily, but Shafer grabbed the soldier roughly by the arm and hauled him back.

The physicist took the phone again. 'Hi Ollie. Yes we have the picture here . . . that was a brilliant insight . . . I warned you: what did your Uncle Willy say about getting a new idea? . . . Listen, we have a problem here, in the form of high cirrus. It's beginning to creep in over Southern Arizona . . . two magnitudes, five, who knows? . . . it'll slow us to a crawl . . . yes, I agree . . . it's down to you, Ollie, you must follow through on your insight . . . yes, he means it . . . he won't say . . . my interpretation is that you have ten hours and then they feel free to nuke Russia . . . I don't know, two hundred million or something . . . you and I know that, Ollie, but what do politicians know? . . . they couldn't handle the concept . . . they like certainties . . . sure, none of us asked for it . . .' Light sweat was beginning to form on Shafer's brow. Judy poured him half a tumbler of Scotch. There was more conversation, then 'Ollie says that as a British citizen he needs to get his instructions direct from HMG.'

Noordhof nodded his head fiercely. 'Yes! Tell him I'll fix it. And tell him I'll see what help we can give at the European end.'

Bellarmine said, 'No, no, no. Webb must be seen to act alone.'

Shafer spoke quietly into the telephone, and then replaced the receiver. He looked round the group. His eyes half-closed with relief and he exhaled. 'He's going through with it. Judy, I know how you feel but look what's at stake.'

'He must be helped,' Judy insisted.

Shafer looked at the Secretary of Defense with raised eyebrows. Bellarmine looked grim. He said, 'If covert American action is spotted by the Russians . . .'

'But if Oliver fails . . .'

Poetry unexpectedly entered McNally's soul. 'We're stuck between the Devil and the deep blue sea.'

'We're clouding over,' Judy reminded them. 'And Hawaii's out of it. Ollie's our only hope and he surely has no chance on his own.'

'He meets the hit man in a couple of hours,' said Shafer.

'Oh boy. Do we know where?' Noordhof asked. Shafer shook his head.

The soldier raised his hands helplessly. 'So what the hell can we do?'

The Abruzzi Hills

Webb, feeling like a rag doll, drifted with the crowds.

It was now dark. He crossed the bridge and walked in the general direction of the Piazza Navona. He made a determined decision to relax and enjoy his last hour, and came close to succeeding. The air was caressingly warm; the smells wafting out of coffee shops and trattorie were exquisite; and the ladies, it seemed to him, were exotically beautiful.

He wandered randomly along a cobbled side-street and into a little church. There was a Nativity scene, with little hand-painted donkeys and people. The straw in the stable was real which made the stalks about forty feet tall on the scale of the figures. It was simple stuff, a childlike thing in a complex world. Someone had put a lot of love into it. It brought him close to tears, and he didn't know why. Webb the sceptic, the rational man of science, sat quietly on a pew for half an hour and, unaccountably, left feeling strangely the better.

He passed by the Navona and walked along to the Spanish Steps. The throng was nearly impenetrable. Italian chatter filled the air. Kilted shepherds were on the steps, playing some sort of thin, reed-like bagpipes.

Time to move. Webb started to push his way through the crowd.

A tap on the shoulder. '*Taxi, signore.*' A dark-skinned man with an earring.

Nice one, Webb thought. A precaution in case surveillance had been set up for him in the Piazza Navona. He realized that he must have been followed from the moment he left Doney's Bar.

Webb followed the taxi driver away from the piazza along the Via Condotti. A red carpet stretched the length of the street. There was a sprinkling of couples, and families with tired children, and ebullient groups of youths. A yellow taxi was waiting at the end of the lane and the driver opened the rear door for him.

The taxi sped through town, heading south past the floodlit Colosseum. Webb assumed he would be heading for some suburban flat but the driver was speeding past tall tenements and heading for the ring road, out of town. The astronomer didn't attempt conversation; the night would unfold as it would.

The driver turned on to the ring road and off it again in a few minutes. He slowed down as they approached a *lampadari*, a two-storeyed glass building filled with lampshades of every conceivable style, every one switched on, and forming an oasis of blazing light in the darkness. The driver took the taxi at walking pace round to the back of the building, the car lurching over rough pot-holed ground. A dark saloon car was waiting, and a short, tubby man was leaning against it with a cigarette in his mouth. Webb got out, and the man ground his cigarette under foot.

'*Piacere*,' said the man, shaking Webb's hand. He led Webb to the saloon and politely opened the back door. The taxi driver reversed and drove off the way he had come, while the new driver took off with Webb, still heading south. The road was straight but the surface was poor. There were bonfires at intervals along the side of the road, and shadowy figures flickering around them, and parked cars. Fields lay beyond, in darkness.

They stopped briefly at an autostrada toll. A policeman

was chatting to the toll official. Webb could have touched his gun. The driver collected a ticket and then they were off again. They passed under a large illuminated sign saying *'Napoli 150km'*. The tubby driver held out a packet of Camel cigarettes over his shoulder. Webb declined. They passed villages atop hills, lights blazing, looking like ocean liners suspended in the sky. Over to the left Webb could make out a spine of mountains; these would be the Abruzzi, whence came the shepherds and the werewolves. They drove swiftly along the autostrada for about half an hour, far from Rome, heading south.

A green illuminated sign in the distance resolved itself into a sign saying 'Genzano', and the driver went down through the gears and turned off. A solitary, weary official at the toll took a note from the driver and then they were winding along a narrow country road, heading towards the hills.

The road started to climb, steeply. The driver went down into second, the transmission whining briefly. They passed between houses in darkness, along a cobbled street little wider than the car. Then the car was through the village and still climbing steeply, its headlights at times pointing into the sky.

The road turned left and there were poplars on either side. Left again, through a wide gateway, and the sound of tyres rolling over loose stones. The driver stepped out, slamming the door. Webb could make out the outline of a villa. There were low, rapid voices. Then footsteps approached the car and stopped. The driver opened the door, grinning.

'Ivrea, Pascolo. Please to come with me, *professore*.'

In the near pitch-black, Webb followed the sound of the driver's footsteps. There was a smell of honeysuckle. As his eyes adapted he began to make out a two-storeyed villa. It looked as if it might have a dozen rooms. There was a garden on three sides, two or three acres of lawn dotted with low bushes. A little spray of water arced into the sky from a fountain, sparkling in moonlight. Behind him were poplars and beyond that the stony slopes of a mountain: as far as Webb could tell in the dark, they were maybe a thousand feet from the summit. The fourth side of the little estate was bounded by a low wall with stone urns along it. Beyond the wall was a black sky, ablaze with the winter constellations, every one an old friend.

'This house is so isolated that not even thieves come here. Okay?'

'I get the message.'

Suddenly floodlights illuminated the grounds, dazzling him. Two dark shapes bounded round from the back of the villa. They looked like small, swift ponies except that they turned out to be large, swift alsatians. They leaped playfully up on Pascolo who, Webb thought, should have gone down like a skittle by the laws of Newtonian mechanics.

'*Ciao, Adolfo, come stai?*' Ivrea cried, pulling at their ears. '*Ed anche tu, Benito!* and now, *professore*, I take you to my aunt. *Basta, ragazzi!* She is a grand woman. You stay here with us.' The dogs were bounding excitedly around Webb now, and beginning to snarl. Pascolo roared at them and they fell away obediently.

She was waiting for them at the main door, in a flood of light. She was tall, dressed in the traditional black, with bright, alert eyes set in a deeply wrinkled face. She smiled courteously and raised her hand in the fascist salute. '*Buon Natale*,' she said in a firm voice. Educated Florentine accent, Webb thought, not the coarse peasant dialect of Pascolo Ivrea.

'Ah, Merry Christmas. How do you do?' Webb replied in his best Italian. 'You are very kind to let me come here,' he added, as if he had a choice.

The woman smiled. 'The English are good people. Pascolo, the dogs, must I teach you manners? Now, professor, please let me show you my home.'

Mussolini was a good man. *Il Duce* stared at Webb from every square foot of the hallway. Old photographs showed him looking noble, looking thoughtful, looking inspirational. Here he was, the great horseman, the great poet, the bluff countryman. *Il Duce* and her father went back to childhood. Papa had looked after the countryside for the *fascisti* and the Leader. Everyone was with him. In the good times Benito would come here to relax, when he had to get away from the plotters and the schemers in Rome.

And here am I with Papa, the old lady said with quiet pride, pointing to a slim, attractive teenage girl standing beside a horse and a tall thin man with riding crop and boots. Next to them was a relaxed and smiling Mussolini, looking quite human, Webb thought, when he wasn't posturing. Benito, Papa used to say, whatever happens anywhere else, do not worry about here. Here in the hills the people are with you; they understand you. That was before the traitors and the partisans, of course.

Of course, Webb said.

Then there were the slippers of some pope in a glass case, more faded pictures of Mussolini looking noble, a brick from some holy place, and a tiny private chapel, candles freshly lit. Then the old lady excused herself, disappearing along a corridor, and Pascolo explained that he would be taking her to her beach house at Terracina in the morning but please to follow me *professore*.

Webb followed Pascolo up marble stairs to a landing. The man opened a solid oak door. The room was large, plain and comfortable. It had a double bed, a chest of drawers and a large desk, and a shower room led off. The desk came with an Anglepoise lamp, a pile of paper and a couple of pens, but not, a quick scan revealed, with *Phaenomenis Novae*. French windows led out to a broad balcony.

'*Va bene?*' Pascolo asked.

'First class, Pascolo. Do you leave early tomorrow?'

'*Si.*'

'Do you have something for me?' Webb kept his voice casual.

There was no hesitation. 'Sure, *professore*. I go with my aunt now to collect it.'

⧗

At least, Webb thought, he could contemplate the business of escape. Webb wandered round the big empty mausoleum. A Christmas tree about nine feet tall, decorated with illuminated bells, looked lost in the big sitting room. There was no telephone. He went out to the grounds. Adolfo and Benito leapt around playfully enough and then chased each other around the house. Over the low balustrade the ground swept down for about three thousand feet to a plain which stretched into the haze. Webb thought he could see a thin glimmering strip on the horizon, like the sea reflecting moonlight, maybe fifty miles away. He could see that the village was dominated by a cathedral, lit up for Christmas.

The motorway, the one along which Webb had been taken, was the *autostrada del sole* connecting Rome and Naples. Lights were drifting up and down it. He reckoned he was about fifty miles south of Rome, probably north of Cassino, south of Frosinone. That put him high in the Abruzzi Hills. Down on the autostrada, modern Italy flowed briskly past; up here, they ticked off the calendar in centuries.

He went out the main gate and set off down the hill. The village seemed deserted. He passed a big white building, like a cantina, which had open ground in front of it and wooden benches and chairs laid out, damp with dew. He walked down the narrow, steep street. Wizened faces looked out of windows. Conversations stopped as he approached and started up again as he passed.

The cathedral was a masterpiece of frescos. Its high altar was a blaze of candles. It was also empty. Webb went back up the street.

'Il padre?' he called up to an ancient hag, wrinkled and nearly toothless. There was a voice from the back of the room, and an outburst of gabbling from other houses. Then a stream of something incomprehensible was aimed at Webb from several directions at once. He heard 'solo domenica' a few times.

He tried 'Servizio postale?' There was an outburst of cackling; he'd said something funny. Someone told him to collect it at Genzano. More faces were appearing at windows.

Webb had one last shot, a throwaway to which he already knew the answer: 'È un telefono qui?'

More merriment. The Man from Mars was proving an endless source of fun.

⧗

In an hour the dogs started barking and a small, blue, rusty Fiat turned into the drive and disgorged Pascolo, a little fat wife and an amazing brood of children. The children swirled around the house, teased the dogs and threw things over the garden wall and into the fountain.

Dinner in the big kitchen seemed to make no allowance for Christmas. It was an affair of huge steaming pots, huge plates of spaghetti al sugo, huge tumblers of cold white wine and tiny humans leaping off in random directions without warning. Pascolo's wife smiled and nodded and chattered away in some thick dialect of which Webb caught about one word in ten. They told him the wine came from his fascist aunt's vineyards and he declared it to be superb which explained why he was drinking so much. After dessert – a massive, cream-covered treacle tart – Pascolo vanished.

Webb, his nails unconsciously digging into the table-cover, waited for the manuscript. After twenty minutes he gave up and plodded up to his room. He kicked a chair in frustration and flopped on to the hard mattress. Pascolo had radiated simple honesty for the entire evening, giving nothing away – maybe because he had nothing to give.

There was a knock at the door. Webb stood up apprehensively, dreading the appearance of Walkinshaw's killers. But it was only the old lady. In her hand was a small red leather book. Webb sensed that she wanted to talk; he indicated a chair and sat on the edge of the bed.

'You are a scholar. You study history.'

'That is so.'

'How did you learn that I have the book?'

Webb tried a lie. 'The Father Apiarist.'

She smiled with pleasure. '*Ebbene!* At last Franco has spoken. That was a bad night.'

'A bad night?'

Her eyes seemed to look beyond Webb. 'Many terrible things were done, all those years ago. You are sure that he did explain?'

'Yes, but not in detail. Perhaps you could tell me more.'

As she began to pour out her story, he sensed that it was something she had bottled up for years, that a ghost was being laid to rest. He listened attentively. 'My brother was a partisan. His father disowned him and so this house has come to me. It happened in 1944. The Allies had moved inland from Anzio and already they were shelling Grottaferrata. Kesselring had summoned forces out of nothing and the battle was a hard one. But by May the Germans were streaming north. And then we heard that they had filled a train with munitions and guns, but also with wine and sacred relics from the Monastery. This was too much. Our own former Allies robbing us as they fled. And then God created for us a miracle. The train with the holy relics and the wine and the guns was stopped at a tunnel. One of their big guns was too wide to go through. For the first time the *fascisti* and the partisans joined forces. In the dark we attacked. We killed Germans.

'And then was the great tragedy. While the Germans were still being killed, and we were quickly unloading the wagons, we started to fight amongst ourselves. In the dark I ran away along the railway track, with my arms full of whatever I had snatched. But then two partisans jumped out from the ditch of the embankment. They had machine guns. They raised them to shoot me. The air was full of noise and smoke. In the half dark I recognized my brother and he recognized me. There was only a second to act. He turned his gun on his friend, a boy from the same village. He killed his friend to save me, his sister and enemy. We did not say a word. I ran into the dark.

'We have never spoken of this. As to what I had rescued from the train, it was worth little. Communion wine, silver cups, candlesticks, and a few old books. I never dared to return them.'

She smiled. 'I am glad that Franco has decided to speak at last. He must believe that after all this time the boy's family will forgive him.'

A small boy appeared at the door, followed by his even smaller, dark-eyed sister, finger in mouth. The old lady continued: 'Your colleague tells me that you will need peace and quiet to study the book. The children are excited by *Natale*, but will be in bed soon. *Non sul letto, Ghigo, tu sei senza cervello?* The children ran off giggling. She stood up.

'I'm very grateful to you, Signora. I wish you good night and every happiness.'

Webb opened the French windows. He was light-headed from a mixture of relief and exhaustion. A cool breeze flowed into the room, bringing some sub-tropical scent with it. Car headlights were drifting up and down the distant autostrada. Some animal cry came up from the olive groves below, and he could hear the wind rustling through the poplars at the side of the villa.

He had the book.

He looked at the ancient leather cover. Faded gold lettering said *Phaenomenis Novae*. Underneath was printed *Tomo III*.

It was old and faded. It had a musty smell. On the flyleaf was a date, 1643, and a neatly written dedication in Italian

To the Most Illustrious, Esteemed and Generous Leopoldo, Granduca di Toscana

And below that, the name of the author, Father Vincenzo of the Order of Preachers.

Across the top of the flyleaf someone had written *cremandum fore* in a thin, neat hand, then scored out the *cremandum* and replaced it with *prohibendum*.

Webb flicked through the pages.

It was more of an astronomer's working notebook than a manuscript. There was page after page of a faded spidery crawl in Latin and Italian, page after page of drawings – the moons of Jupiter, sunspots, lunar craters – hot off the eyepiece of Vincenzo's telescope. The bold new frontier of science, of nearly four centuries ago.

The key to Nemesis, in his hands.

So run off into the dark night?

Pascolo: mine host, or a jailer?

The dogs: friendly, or killers on a snap of the fingers from Pascolo?

Webb looked at his watch. 10 p.m. Two in the afternoon in Arizona, 4 p.m. in Washington.

Eight hours.

A twinge of pain in the jaw warned Webb that he had been unconsciously clenching it. His hands trembling, he picked up the typescript and began to read.

Io, Europa, Ganymede and Callisto

22^h00

A hundred pages. Drawings, charts, notes. Written in a scrawl both flowery and spidery, the ink little faded after four hundred years. Webb had no way of guessing what the Grand Duke had thought of Vincenzo's work, if indeed he had ever set eyes on it.

The apparent lack of supervision had to be an illusion: somewhere, a mechanism for control was in place. But the identification of the crucial text was going to take the same length of time wherever he was, and at least here he wasn't fleeing over mountains and could study *Phaenomenis*. Webb looked at his watch. He would give himself until midnight, and then make his break.

Resisting the urge to rush at it, he started slowly and methodically through the pages of *Phaenomenis*. It took him half an hour.

Nothing.

He rubbed his eyes and slipped quietly down the darkened stairs to the kitchen. Childish sleeping noises came from one of the rooms as he passed. He found the light switch and went into the big kitchen. He made himself a sandwich with salami and a rosetta, and tiptoed back up to his room with it. Of jailers or dogs, there had been not a sign.

Back in his room, Webb went through it again, a line at a time.

He was beginning to see a problem with Vincenzo: there was nothing *Novae* about his *Phaenomenis*. He had always come second. Sunspots, craters on the Moon, the satellites of Jupiter: they were all there, but they had all been seen earlier by somebody else. Galileo, Huyghens, Schroter – these were the sharp men of the new age, and they had all been there before him. Vincenzo had tried; but at the end of the day, he was a failure.

And still nothing.

Webb started on it a third time.

Line one: *Observationes an 1613*.

Line two: *oriens   Januarius   occidens*

The remaining page was taken up by a simple drawing:

The page was completed by a couple of lines at its foot: *Die 2, h.12 a meridie. 1 et 3 conjuncti fuerunt secundum longitudinem.*

So. On 2nd January 1613, at midnight, Jupiter had satellites 4 and 2 (that would be Callisto and Europa) on its left, with 1 and 3 (Io and Ganymede) to the right. Io and Ganymede had then changed places in the early hours of the third.

All of which could be worked out in minutes on a modern computer.

He nibbled at his sandwich; it was painfully spicy. Every page was turning out much the same as the last. None of them connected with hysterically screaming terrorists and determined killers, let alone Nemesis.

⧗

23ʰ00

Webb took another break; he was beginning to have a problem with keeping his eyes open.

He put out the lamp and walked on to the verandah. A half-moon hung low in the sky, and the fields and hills glowed a gentle silver. Far to the north the horizon was tinged with orange; that would be Rome and the villages of the Castelli, and the towns scattered over the Campagna. He took five minutes to breathe in the honeysuckled air.

A solitary car was hurtling down the autostrada. Probably, someone heading back for a long weekend with his family in Naples or Palermo, escaping from a car factory in Turin or Milan where the young men of the *mezzogiorno* went to make big money. He went back in, switched on the lamp, and started on his third read of the book.

⧗

23ʰ30

Charta 40.
Die 28, h.6.

Fixa A distabat a Jove 23 semidiametres: in eadem linea sequebatur alia fixa B, quae etiam precedenti horam observata fuit.

Something.

Webb stared dully at Vincenzo's scrawl.

Take it slow.

A star had moved. Vincenzo had shown it in position A, whereas in the previous hour it had been in position B.

By now Webb had looked at this drawing several times. Jupiter, the orbiting planet, is a moving target seen from Earth, itself an even faster-moving platform. The giant planet therefore drifts against the stellar background. Centre a telescope on Jupiter, and any nearby star will seem to drift past it from one night to the next, reflecting mainly the Earth's motion.

But that rate of drift was maybe one degree a day. On the scale of Vincenzo's drawing, this star had moved about ten Jupiter diameters. Vincenzo would probably have been looking at Jupiter near opposition, when the disc of the planet was not quite resolvable by eye, maybe fifty seconds of arc. The star had therefore moved five hundred seconds of arc, or eight minutes of arc, or about one eighth of a degree, in the course of an hour. Three degrees a day.

This star was moving.

A moving star, seen in a small telescope nearly four hundred years ago.

An asteroid, tumbling past the Earth.

Through his exhaustion, Webb smiled. Nice one, Vincenzo.

And good evening, Nemesis.

Martini, Bianca, Giselle and Claudia

Webb looked at his watch through unfocused eyes.

Half an hour to midnight. At midnight, Bellarmine's 'aggressive posture' would come into play, a stance based on the working assumption that America was destined for annihilation. But that was midnight in Washington: to get there, the meridian had to cross the Atlantic, a journey taking six hours.

Six hours and thirty minutes to get out of this time warp, away from medieval Italy, back to the real world with real people, and computers and telephones; and then identify Nemesis from Vincenzo's little sketch, and make the vital call.

Six and a half hours, six of them drawing on the curvature of the Earth.

He put the book securely in his inside pocket and fastened the little button. He crossed to the bedroom door and opened it quietly. Harsh light flooded on to the stairwell. There might have been a faint scuffle downstairs, like a dog turning on its side: probably from the kitchen. The smell of the evening's spaghetti sauce met him faintly as he passed. A dog's head in outline rose under the kitchen table, ears raised in silent curiosity: Benito. The Führer would be around.

Quietly, Webb opened the main door and then he was out, on a warm starry night, with a ten million-dollar manuscript.

There has to be a catch.

The light from Webb's bedroom illuminated the grounds as far as the wall. The half-moon was rising, and there were dark, still shadows which might contain anything. He stood next to the fountain, listening to it tinkling down and holding his face up to the delicate spray. Then he strolled round towards the back of the house. To Webb's taut nerves, his footsteps were jackboots on gravel, crashing through the still of the night. He reached the wall and leaned on it, looking out over the valley. The stone was cold on his hands, the countryside asleep. The fields were dark too, and filled with gnarled old witches frozen in grotesque shapes: olive trees, barely visible in the dark. And beyond was a black mass, the cathedral, a still giant lowering over a jumble of shadows.

Just getting some fresh air.

He lay on the wall, put a leg over and rolled. It was an alarming drop and he hit the earth with a solid thump, then rolled some more into a perfumed bush. He jumped up, gasping, and ran into the dark, keeping low against the wall. The wall curved away and there were twenty yards of open field to the road.

The road was too open. He changed his mind in mid-flight and turned through a right angle, charging down the field, towards the witches, not daring to glance behind. It took him into the light from his bedroom, a billion-candlepower searchlight flooding the field like a football stadium.

Webb weaved from side to side, hearing stretched to the limit and expecting at any second to hear the noisy panting of running dogs. His back muscles ached in agonized anticipation of a bullet smashing its way through his backbone.

He reached the trees and dodged wildly through them, but he was now out of sight of the villa and the mountain beyond. He stopped, puffing, and looked fearfully back up, leaning against a tree while blood pounded in his ears.

No dogs, no riflemen, and it can't be this easy.

Webb suddenly realized that he could be under surveillance from right here, amongst the trees. Time passed, as he let his eyes adapt and his breathing get back under control. Time to peer into the twisted black shapes surrounding him.

A faint scuffling, maybe thirty yards away. No doubt some animal.

Again. Closer.

Far, far away, he heard the whine of a car. It passed.

Webb turned and stumbled towards the village. A thin branch hit him painfully in the face, scratching his cheek. Through the trees he could glimpse lights twinkling on the plain beyond the autostrada. The olive grove came to an end at what seemed to be an ancient defensive ditch about thirty feet deep. The ditch stretched off to the right and merged with a steep, rocky slope in the distance. To his left, Webb could make out the rear of the cantina, about fifty yards away, with the road just beyond it.

No sound of pursuit. No scuffling from the shadows.

Stealthily, he moved to the edge of the trees. He literally felt weak at the knees. There was a low wall and on the other side of it the road leading into the village. Inky, jagged shadows lined the cobbled road. Moonlight reflected brilliantly from a small open window in the village.

He climbed the wall and stepped quietly on to the cobbled road. He kept in the shadows as much as possible on the way down to the village, and stopped in the shadow of the first building, a derelict wine cellar. The smell of sour wine drifted out of a grilled window.

Too many shadows; but quiet. Quiet like a cemetery.

A dog howled, the sound coming from about fifty yards ahead. Webb froze, terrified. Another one, back up the hill, took up the wolf call. He looked behind: underneath his bedroom – that would be the kitchen – another light had come on. The animals subsided. He padded hastily along the medieval street, almost tip-toeing on the cobbled stones, and almost within arm's length of the houses on either side. If a trap had been set, this was the place. Into the cathedral square. Light was flooding out of the open cathedral doors.

The cathedral bells crashed into life. Webb literally jumped in fright. He flew across the square. A final short stretch of houses. People were coming out of doors. He almost ran into an elderly couple in the near-dark '*Buon Natale!*' he shouted, and then he had cleared the village, the cobbles giving way to a rutted track with vines and olives on either side.

He loped down, and then he was running full pelt down the deserted track, with the sound of the bells in his ears. About half a mile down from the village the track joined on to the slip-road for the autostrada and he slowed, puffing and laughing with relief. The man at the autostrada toll was reading a newspaper, cigarette dangling from mouth. Webb passed unnoticed.

He crossed the deserted autostrada and sat on a low wall, baffled. It had been too easy. In a minute a car's headlights appeared, approaching from the south. He stepped on to the autostrada, still breathless. The headlights flooded him; he waved his hands, suddenly realized that the car had appeared suspiciously on cue, and stumbled back off the road, crouching behind the wall in an agony of uncertainty. The car passed at speed, its exhaust roaring into the distance.

Safer to wait for a truck.

He waited. A couple of cars drove past on the opposite carriageway. Webb used the passing headlights to check the time and wondered if he had been right to let the first car pass.

Fifteen minutes went by, during which, with increasing

desperation, he tried willpower and prayer. But no car came.

A voice? Maybe; but it was on the limit of hearing. Webb put it down to an illusion caused by pounding blood and overwrought senses. And then, distinctly, there was the low sound of a female laugh. He walked along the emergency lane, catching occasional murmurs of conversation as he approached, although not enough to make out the sense.

A car was parked in a police layby about a hundred and fifty yards from where he had been waiting. Human figures were just discernible in its red tail-lights.

'*Buona sera!*'

A woman of about thirty emerged from the shadows. Her mini-skirt was leather and absurdly short, and her legs were skinny. 'Good evening,' Webb said.

'*Chi sei?*'

'*Sono un Inglese.*'

'*Ma che ci fai qui?*'

'*Mi sono perso.*'

The woman turned to the shadows behind her. '*Dice di essere un turista che si è perso. Forse sta cercando un letto per la notte.*' Somebody laughed, short and sharp.

'My name is Claudia,' she said to Webb, in heavily accented English. 'Can we do some business? Look, I'm clean.' She delved into her blouse and pulled out a little card. Webb held it to the tail-light of the car. There was a photograph of herself and a warning in several languages. The English one said

If the stamp is red don't take her to bed
If the stamp is blue it's up to you

There were a lot of stamps. They looked red but presumably that was the tail-light.

'Actually, I was looking for a lift to Rome.'

The woman laughed and said something incomprehensible over her shoulder. 'You have to pay for our time, *bell'uomo*. And there are four of us.'

'There's no problem with that.' Four ladies of the night, services rendered. Webb almost smiled at the reaction in Accounts.

The car was small, two-door and smelled of stale cigarettes. Webb found himself squeezed into the back between Claudia, who turned out to be red-headed, and a girl with long dangling earrings and smooth skin who announced herself as Giselle.

The front seats went back and another two women slipped in, into the front. Claudia said, 'We were just going anyway. Business is *cattivo* at Christmas.'

The driver turned to Webb. She had short hair in tight curls; she was wearing a black choker and her eyes were heavy with mascara. 'This is Martini and my name is Bianca,' she said in educated English. 'I'm a criminal lawyer. I make a lot of money.'

'How do you do? I suppose these are your clients.'

'What about you, Englishman?'

'*Un professore matto.*'

She laughed. '*In cerca della pietre filo sofali.*'

Webb's credentials as a mad professor established, the little car eased itself on to the autostrada and then took off briskly; and four whores, a nerve-shattered scientist and the secret of Nemesis headed swiftly towards Rome.

The Werewolf Club

Il Lupo Manaro, the Werewolf Club. A part of Rome which Christmas had not reached, and where white light was the only taboo.

The small car turned out to have a powerful engine, and on the trip back to Rome the speedometer needle hovered at a deeply satisfying one hundred and fifty kilometres an hour. There was a lot of repartee in a strong local dialect, most of which went over Webb's head. Wedged between Claudia and Giselle, he was treated to their bony thighs pressing against his. Claudia's hand kept straying to his knee.

Within an hour and a half the great plain of Rome was glittering below them and soon they were rattling noisily into quiet suburbs, and down towards Cinecittà. There were still crowds promenading at 1 a.m. in central Rome. Webb tried to keep his bearings from monuments and places he knew.

An alarm bell began to ring in his head.

They cut left at the Colosseum and seemed to be heading south; but then they made a sharp turn north. A sign said *Circo Massimo* and there were tall floodlit ruins on a hill to the right; and then the criminal lawyer was taking them past the Mouth of Truth, over the Palatine Bridge, across the dark Tiber, and into the maze of narrow crowded streets of the old ghetto.

This was no good: he needed the airport, fast. He said,

casually, 'You can let me out anywhere, ladies.'

Claudia sniggered, Martini laughed wildly, and Webb's heart sank, his growing suspicion that he had never escaped hardening up.

The car turned off at a triangular piazza and drove some way into a narrow lane, pulling into the kerbside. The five of them tumbled out. Martini and Bianca were into some noisy exchange, all Italian exuberance, Bianca's long earrings swinging like pendulums. Claudia was having trouble with her stiletto heels on the cobbles, and Webb's legs were in agony with returning circulation; they linked arms for mutual balance.

Ditch her and run? Webb reckoned he might get ten yards.

A group of young men and their ladies approached, singing and giggling, and receded into the dark.

A lane leading off a lane, and there was *Il Lupo Manaro*, strobing the dark corners with green and pink neon. A notice at the entrance told them that

Mephisto
Performs
A Nite of Magic
With the Sounds of
The Meathooks

There were photographs of a rotund middle-aged man, attempting to give an air of mystery to his unmysterious features with beard, top hat, cape and wand. Even at one o'clock in the morning it was antiquated corn.

Webb said, 'Thank you for the lift. I ought to go now.'

Claudia was smiling with her mouth. 'But you have to pay for our time, remember? Settle up in here.'

'Five minutes?'

'Ten.' Claudia took Webb by the hand and led him in. Cones of ultraviolet light, thrown down by spot lamps in the ceiling, interspersed the deep gloom. Synthetic fibres passing through the beams glowed a deep purple, and diamonds, if they happened to be real, sparkled and fluoresced. There was, Webb noticed, a lot of fluorescence around. He was startled to see Claudia's lips and eyelids glowing a brilliant green.

A mature woman with an air of having seen and done it all, once too often, said *'Buona sera!'*, and it was *buona sera* all the way through a maze of perspex doors into the heart of the club. A luminous purple shirt front and cuffs approached from the shadows like the Invisible Man, and materialized at the last into a figure of oriental features and indeterminate age.

They were ushered to a low table near the centre of the room and lay out on settees, Roman style, Claudia and Giselle flopping down on either side of him. They seemed to be well known in the club, Bianca in particular being on the receiving end of a lot of greetings.

Candles were lit at the table; they burned red and blue and gave off a strange herbal smell, which mingled with the already dense smell of Havana in the air. Expensive minks were scattered casually over the backs of settees, occupied by couples in various degrees of intimacy and angles to the horizontal. Martini and Bianca shared, Martini casually stroking the lawyer's legs, which were draped over her own. Webb began to wonder about them. A waiter approached and Martini ordered gin fizz all round. The warmth, the narcotic perfume and his exhaustion were like heavy chains.

A small transparent dance floor was lit up from below by a moving kaleidoscope of primary colours. Half a dozen couples were on it, and a phallic rhythm was being banged out by four seasoned characters in an illuminated corner near the stage, their leader's sweaty face leering into a microphone and more or less singing while his big hairy hands flickered between cymbals and kettle drums.

Big hairy faces with canine teeth glared down from the walls, in glowing pictures which interspersed with sketches of nubile maidens in varying degrees of Eastern promise.

Bianca leaned over towards Webb. 'The police keep closing this place down,' she said over the music. 'But it keeps opening up again under new management. Different names up front.'

'I expect you have one or two clients here.'

'A few tourists and provincials apart, they are all my clients.'

Webb suddenly realized that in the Lupo Manaro he could be dismembered with an axe, and nobody would notice a thing.

'Look, I need to pay you and go.'

Bianca smiled and shook her head. 'First, we have a surprise for you.'

Martini waved into a dark corner of the club. A fat man in a dinner suit leaned over Claudia and, ignoring Webb, made some remark. Claudia laughed and kissed the man, who vanished into the gloom. Webb was startled to catch the eye of a black-bearded character in a velvet tuxedo at a table a few yards in front of him. The man blew a kiss. 'Not you, stupid!' he said, waving to someone at the back of the club.

A slow melody began to ooze out of a saxophone; Martini and Bianca wandered on to the floor and started to dance, hugging each other closely.

'*Sei stanco*?' Claudia asked Webb, entwining her skinny arms around his neck, her luminous lips almost touching his. 'Are you tired?'

'Ah, maybe I need some fresh air.' He grabbed his gin fizz.

She pulled back and laughed. 'You are so inhibited, Englishman. But tonight, for you, love is free. Why not relax and enjoy life? While you can,' she added enigmatically.

Webb had a desperate inspiration. 'Teach me to tango, then.'

The woman squealed with delight and led Webb on to the dance floor. As they reached the floor she whispered something to the man with the sax, who grinned; and the tempo was suddenly sharp and bouncy.

'Popcorn!' cried Claudia, wriggling her bottom, flinging her hands above her head, gyrating and shaking her breasts all at once. It resembled no tango Webb had ever seen. The stage cleared apart from the two of them. His desperate inspiration, to make a break for the rear, had died the moment he saw the heavies off-stage, watching his performance with dispassionate eyes. He concentrated on Claudia, clumsily trying to match her pitching and yawing, while sweat wet his brow and lurid visions of holocaust grew larger by the minute.

After a frenzied minute the tune slowed to a halt like a train coming into a station, there was a smattering of applause and Claudia, grinning and perspiring, led him by the hand back to the settee, where two men and a woman were now seated. The older man Webb had last seen at Doney's; his grey hair was now reflecting pink in the club lighting. The other two he had last seen viciously murdering Walkinshaw in the dark Tuscolo woods.

Webb took the indicated space between the young ones. Claudia, suddenly aloof, joined Giselle on another settee. Martini and Bianca were deep in some woman talk. They paid him no attention.

The pink-haired man pulled round a chair to face Webb. 'Good evening, Mister Fish.' His spectacle lenses were reflecting the reds and blues from the spotlights and candles. 'You have been successful?'

'Yes.'

'We have a bargain, remember?'

'How do I know you'll keep your half of our deal? The moment I tell you what I know, you could finish me.'

'That was what made our bargain so interesting. Neither of us seemed likely to keep it. You might try to steal the manuscript, I might decide to kill you. But if you do not now tell me – *allora*, my friend has a stiletto in his pocket, only a few centimetres from your kidneys. I have seen him at work with it. It is a particularly distressing death.'

Sweat was coming out of every pore in Webb's skin. 'There is something in the manuscript.'

There was a roll of drums. A little fat man came on and jabbered into a microphone in Italian, and then on strode Mephisto, complete with pointed black beard, top hat and a long black cloak with red inner lining. There was whistling and laughter as a short-haired peroxide blonde in a sequined bathing suit wheeled on a table. The magician bowed and got into his act, which involved the appearance and disappearance of lighted cigarettes, glasses of water, doves . . .

'Something in the manuscript,' hissed into Webb's ear.

Webb fumbled with the button on his inside pocket and produced *Phaenomenis* with shaking hands. He flicked to a page and pointed to Vincenzo's Latin script. 'Here. In this paragraph. A coded message. Renaissance scholars did this. Instead of announcing a discovery in plain Latin they made up . . .'

'The message?' the man said harshly, every line of his face contorted with greed.

Applause. A guillotine was being trundled on to the stage, one of its wheels squeaking. It was a heavy wooden structure, twelve feet tall, topped by a massive steel blade which gleamed red, white and blue in the strobing lights. The blade hissed down and a water melon split into two with a heavy thump. Mephisto was calling for a volunteer, to general high-pitched merriment. A Scotsman, a fat Glaswegian with a Gorbals accent, was shouting garbage as three of his equally drunk friends hustled him on to the stage. The blonde seized his arm and his friends staggered off, laughing wildly.

'Must I force everything past your teeth?'

'The Duke of Tuscany hid part of his wealth. I suppose for insurance against a rainy day. But it seems he didn't trust his courtiers. Vincenzo was unworldly, and he owed his life to the Duke.'

The Scotsman had used rope and chains to tie Mephisto on a plank, with the help of the magician's assistant; now he was sliding it on a metal hospital trolley until the magician, face up, had his neck under the blade. The Scotsman clattered off the little stage at speed.

'Speak, Fish!' But now the little fat man was on stage again, patting his brow with a handkerchief and demanding total silence due to the perilous nature of the experiment. The peroxide blonde looked solemn. A curtain was pulled, and the audience went still. The blonde pulled a string. The blade accelerated rapidly down. There was a slicing noise which shook Webb's already jangled spine. A bloody head, eyes bulging and veins stringing from its neck, rolled out from under the curtain. The blonde screamed hysterically, the audience rose in pandemonium and then the curtain was pulled back and Mephisto was standing, head in place and chains at his feet. There was an outburst of relief and laughter and the audience thundered their applause.

'My patience is exhausted.'

'It seems Vincenzo hid some part of the Grand Duke's treasure on his behalf, recorded the location in his notes in code, but then died before he could tell the Duke where he'd hidden it.' Webb had scarcely slept in days; it was the best he could do at that hour in the morning.

'And now, my good friends, one last illusion. Another volunteer, please.' His eyes ranged over the audience and settled on Webb. 'You, sir!' he said, pointing dramatically. Forty pairs of eyes turned.

'Stay in your seat.' But the man in the velvet tuxedo grabbed Webb's arm, laughing, and pulled him to his feet. The hit men hauled at his other arm. The audience laughed and clapped at the tug-of-war which was rapidly becoming bad-tempered. Webb shouted 'Okay! I surrender!' and there was more applause as he picked his way between settees and climbed the steps. He slipped the book back in his pocket. From the stage Webb could just make out, beyond the footlights, Martini and the assassins forcing their way hastily towards the exit.

'Try to stay calm,' Mephisto murmured in English, and Webb's heart jumped. 'My friends,' the magician addressed the audience theatrically, 'you see before you a man.' There was a snort from somewhere beyond the footlights and someone giggled. 'There is one thing wrong with a man. And that is, he is not a woman. It is a fault which we in our world of illusion can put right. God created woman by removing a rib.' The blonde gripped Webb's arm firmly as the magician leaned down and swiftly produced a bright orange chainsaw from under the table, trailing an electric cable. The audience roared.

'Do we dare to repeat God's experiment?' Cries of *Yes! Si!* came from forty throats. The chainsaw burst into life. Mephisto produced a half-bottle of some spirit from an inside pocket and drank it in a single draught, the blonde jumping as the saw swung towards her. More laughter. 'Now Doctor Mephisto is drunk enough. Let the surgery begin. Let us remove a rib from this man. I ask someone to inspect this box.' The saw waved erratically towards off-stage.

A box was wheeled on, and the velvet tuxedo man, keeping a weather eye on the buzzing chainsaw, tapped the walls, jumped up and down on the floor and declared that this was an okay box no nonsense. The blonde led Webb into the box and the door closed. He stood in pitch black. The sound of heavy chains being wrapped round and round the box came in magnified. The sound from the chainsaw rose in pitch and then there was the deafening racket of splintering wood. He backed into a corner before realizing that somehow the saw was not penetrating the box. There was another sound, a panel sliding at ground level. Light flooded in from the floor. A hand was beckoning urgently and Webb climbed down a short wooden ladder. A light-skinned man, dressed in blue overalls, put a finger to his mouth. Another one, with the face of a patrician Roman, was wearing the full uniform of a Colonel of the Carabinieri. He nodded curtly to a woman of about twenty-five, her eyes covered with a red Venetian mask and a sequined red cloak draped around her shoulders, and she climbed the short ladder unsteadily in red high-heeled shoes. Little bells tinkled around her midriff as she brushed past Webb.

'They'll be waiting for me at the back,' Webb whispered, blinking in the light. 'I saw them run out.'

'I know. The name's Tony Beckenham, by the way, from Her Britannic Majesty's Embassy. And this is Colonel Vannucci of the SDI, the Italian Security Service.'

'How do you even know about me?'

'Your American colleagues. And Walkinshaw's people.'

'But how did you find me? Nobody could possibly have known where I was.'

'Nonsense. We just followed the manuscript trail. The old bat in the hills has been telling that story for the past fifty years.'

The colonel was looking agitated. 'Mister Fish, this is not-ta time for talk. The danger is extreme. We recognize at least seven wanted criminals in the club. It is amazing good fortune for us. But they will kill you without a thought and shoot their way out. Until the *squadra* arrives I have only three people here and we cannot return fire in a public place.'

'What then?'

'Hide! Back on stage!'

'Beckenham, I want you to open up the Planetological Institute in the Via Galileo and I want a car standing by to take me there.'

'Don't be a bloody fool.'

The sound of whistling and clapping penetrated through the stage floor. A wooden panel opened from above and a pair of long sequined legs in red high heels emerged, climbing unsteadily down the steps.

'Go, go!' Vannucci said, pushing Webb back to the ladder.

'I want to be in Oxford in three hours maximum. I don't care if you have to charter a Jumbo.'

Vannucci was forcing Webb up the ladder.

'And I need a fast laptop computer on board. I left mine in the safe house.'

A scared look came over Beckenham as it dawned on him that Webb was serious. Vannucci was practically lifting the astronomer upwards.

'With a Linux interface,' Webb shouted down, disappearing.

'A what inner face?'

Inside the dark box again, Webb felt himself being trundled some yards, he guessed to just off-stage. The band started up on some sleepy tune, rose to a finale.

Footsteps approached. Webb fell against the side of the box as it was tilted up. It was wheeled for maybe ten yards and then a tremendous *Crack!* erupted within it. A man shouted, angry and frightened; a woman screamed; running footsteps.

Somebody kicking hard at the base of the box. Webb, drenched in sweat, took two feet to it and it burst open. Beckenham, the policeman and a woman in a black cocktail dress dragged him out and on to his feet. All three with guns and the woman, in addition, with an evening bag. A walrus-moustached janitor in a glass booth crouched, quivering, behind a chair, eyes wide with fear. It could have been a scene from a comedy.

Webb was about to speak when the woman grabbed him violently by the hair and hauled him down on to his knees. At the same instant a bullet smacked into a whitewashed wall next to his face; Webb actually glimpsed it, spinning and buzzing, on the rebound. Then the policeman was hauling open a red emergency exit door, and an alarm bell screamed into life, and Webb was being thrust into the narrow lane outside. He fell heavily.

The woman appeared, hauled Webb to his feet and pushed him ahead of her along the lane. Webb got the message and took off like a hare. He sprinted round a corner and almost collided with the young Tuscolo killers rushing out of the Werewolf Club. Webb dived to the ground. The hard cobbles knocked the breath out of him. From behind he heard two sharp bangs, and two bright yellow flashes briefly lit up the neon-strobed lane. The young ones fell like sacks. The lane emptied, people stampeding into the club or disappearing into doorways. The Tuscolo woman's face was a foot from Webb's. She had long black hair, her eyes were half-closed and quite lifeless, and something like porridge was oozing from a neat black hole in the centre of her forehead; the youth was clutching a long, thin knife, but he too was lifeless. The alarm was deafening in the narrow lane.

Webb got up and swayed, on the verge of fainting. The woman, about ten yards away, was calmly putting her high-heeled shoes back on. He said, 'Can we get a move on here?' but his voice came out as an inaudible whisper.

Oxford, the Last Minutes

A *squadra volante* car whisked Vannucci, the woman and Webb across the city to the *Istituto di Planetologia* in four minutes. The doors were already open and a tousle-haired caretaker was engaged in an animated exchange with two *Carabinieri*, his hands waving dramatically. He unleashed a stream of Italian at Webb as the astronomer ran past, into the lighted building.

He ran up a flight of stairs and along a dark corridor towards Giovanni's office. He had used a visitor's password two years ago and there was no chance that it would still be valid; he would just have to rouse Giovanni at home. He tried his old username and password anyway and – joy! – it worked: the Linux window appeared.

Webb looked at his watch and, yet again, converted to the Eastern Standard time zone. He had been in the Werewolf Club for nearly an hour, and he had four hours left to identify Nemesis.

What he had to do was run the known Earth-crossers backwards in time, perturbing their orbits with the gravitational pull of the planets, and seeing how close each asteroid had been to the Earth in the Year of Our Lord 1613, on 28 November.

He took a minute to think. They would have fast orbit integrators here but he wouldn't know their names or modes of operation. The one he used at Oxford, developed by the celestial mechanics group at Armagh

Observatory in Northern Ireland, was based on Bulirsch-Stoer and symplectic routines and probably as fast as anything on the planet.

The future orbit of an asteroid or comet can be approximated by a series of straight-line steps. Each step takes so much time to compute. The greater the length of the stride, the fewer are needed in total, and so the faster the orbit is calculated. However large strides, although fast, lead to unreliable results: no real asteroid ever moved in a series of straight lines. An orbit computed with very large steps deviates more and more from reality. A computation with very small steps is highly precise but takes a very long time. Webb's quandary was that he needed high precision but had very little time.

A message on the terminal wished him a Merry Christmas but regretted that the Oxford Institute mainframe was down for maintenance over the festive season.

He had no access to the Armagh computers.

He dialled in to the Observatory's home page for the telephone number and called through. Paolo, luckily, had been prevented by poverty from joining his family in Turin this Christmas, and as usual he was working late. The Italian student immediately arranged to put the programmes on to anonymous ftp, which would allow anyone to gain access to them. Webb had them into Giovanni's machine in minutes and then transferred them on to half a dozen floppy disks, along with the planetary ephemerides for the past four hundred years, and the orbital elements of all known near-Earth asteroids.

He now had what he needed. Everything but time.

He typed in a brief e-mail message to Eagle Peak:

The Navigator has reached the New World.
Natives friendly.

It was Enrico Fermi's coded wartime message announcing

that the atom had been split. Willy Shafer would understand it, but not a casual hacker.

He ran back out of the building to the police car, which took off, blue light flashing, through the town.

Vannucci glanced at Webb in the flickering light from the streets. 'I would love to know what this is about.'

Webb stayed silent.

'A countryman of yours is brutally killed on Italian soil. I do not like that. If I had my way you would now be answering questions in *La Madama*.'

'But you're prevented by instructions from above, right?'

The policeman lit up a Camel cigarette. 'Your little book. Was it worth it?'

Webb thought of Leclerc hurtling to his death, and Walkinshaw riddled with bullets, and the young ones with holes through their brains. He nodded. 'Definitely. Was anyone hurt in the club?'

'You mean apart from the people who died in front of your eyes? One of my men is in the San Salvadore, undergoing emergency surgery.'

'The people who died were the ones who killed Walkinshaw. The older man with me in the club set it up. They were after the book. That's all I can tell you. A grilling in the *questura* would yield no more.'

Vannucci took a reflective puff at his cigarette. 'I would not be so sure of that.'

'Your lady – what a brilliant shot.' She looked back at Webb from the front passenger seat and gave a cool smile. Her English was good: 'Given the poor light, I thought I did well.'

This one won't need counselling, Webb thought. He looked out at the scenery speeding past and suddenly felt cold. 'This isn't the way to the airport.'

'We're taking you to the military airfield at Ciampino.'

They reached it in ten minutes. The police car drove

straight on to the runway. An executive jet was waiting, door open, headlights on, engines whining, Beckenham at the steps with laptop computer in hand. Webb grabbed the little computer from Beckenham, shook hands briefly, and then the door was closed and the aircraft accelerated swiftly forwards.

As the jet curved into the sky, Webb glanced down at Rome by night, a great luminous spider's web divided by the Tiber. But there was no time for the luxury of terror. He fed in the programmes from the floppy disks.

Beckenham had done well at short notice. It was a fast little machine, with a P5 chip and solid architecture; it might take say ten minutes to explore the past history of each Earth-crosser back to 1613. There were five hundred known Earth-crossers. So, the identification process could take up to eighty-five hours. Three and a half days, day and night.

He had three and a half hours.

A supercomputer would do the job in minutes. He could have tried to download the Armagh programmes across to the Rutherford-Appleton HPC if he had had access, but he hadn't. It might take days to get into the supercomputer from the outside, and they probably had batch jobs booked up for days after that. He could attempt to muscle in now by wielding the AR of the Chairman of Council, but that could attract attention, and that attention could lead to a nuclear attack.

He could e-mail the information through to Kowalski. But there were no encryption arrangements between Eagle Peak and either Oxford or the aircraft. An e-mail message could circle the globe and touch down in half a dozen states before it reached its destination. Too dangerous: he might as well use a loudhailer.

And if the traitor on the team – if there was a traitor on the team – got to the message first, there was no telling what mischief might be done.

Having exhausted every alternative, Webb turned to the little toy on his lap.

The trick, as he saw it, was to go for the candidates most easily diverted. Leclerc would have fed in knowledge of past Russian probes and given him a more targeted list. Still, he could use the standard list of potential hazards, starting with 1997 XF11, Nereus and other obvious choices. With luck, Nemesis would be on the list of known potential hazards and he would have it within a few hours. That was the theory.

He clicked on an icon, and the machine asked him a few questions. Are you integrating the orbit forward or back in time? How long would you like the integration to go? What positional accuracy (in AU) would you like on the termination date (the more accurate the required position, the slower the integration)?

The preliminaries over, the machine got down to specific orbits. First it asked him for the semi-major axis of the orbit; then its eccentricity; and then the three angles defining the orientation of the orbit in space: inclination, longitude of ascending node, longitude of perihelion. The orbit's size, shape and orientation in space defined, it finally requested one last number: the true anomaly, a precise date at which the asteroid was at its point of closest approach to the sun (Julian date, please).

There was care to be exercised. In 1582 Pope Gregory XIII, on the advice of his Jesuit astronomer Clavius, had taken ten days out of the Christian calendar which had, over the centuries, gradually drifted out of phase with the seasons. The Catholic nations had taken this up at once. By the time the English had reluctantly joined up in 1752, eleven days had had to be taken out of the Protestant calendar and the peasantry had duly rioted, being reluctant to pay double rent. Vincenzo's observation, having been made in seventeenth-century Italy, was therefore 28 November by the Gregorian calendar. But Webb then had to convert this to the Julian date, a steadily ticking clock used by astronomers to bypass the vagaries of peasants and politics. This is reckoned from 1 January 4713 BC. Julian days start at noon. A Julian day is therefore shifted by twelve hours relative to the civil day and twelve hours at twenty-five kilometres a second is the difference between a million-kilometre miss and a hit.

He dug into the *Astronomical Ephemeris* and converted Vincenzo's Catholic date to the appropriate Julian Day. From then on, Webb hoped, it would be plain sailing.

He started with Nereus.

Two little spots on the screen, one yellow and one blue, began to whirl rapidly around a fixed central disc, eventually coming to an abrupt halt with 28.11.1613 (Greg.) showing in the top right-hand corner of the screen. The process had taken about twenty minutes. The spots were nowhere near each other. On to the second asteroid on the easy-to-shift list. And then the third.

Over the English Channel, as the little jet sank along its approach path, and Webb punched in a succession of increasingly implausible candidates, it began to look as if Nemesis was not amongst the known Earth-crossers. At the moment the wheels made screaming contact with the runway he scored off the last candidate in his list of possibles. None of them had fitted Vincenzo's observation. Either good men had died chasing a phantom, or Nemesis was an asteroid known only to the Russians.

Webb settled into the back of a ministerial Jaguar and started on the Mission Impossibles, the asteroids which could not realistically be shifted in orbit. The car sped him along the M25 at a hundred miles an hour; either the driver was taking a chance or the police had been asked to turn a blind eye.

There was nothing else to be done. They were impossible because they were too fast to shift, but deadly – because of their speed – if somehow diverted nevertheless.

He made the identification just as the car turned off on to the M40. He ran the program again, pushing the accuracy as far as he dared. The program now took thirty agonizing minutes to complete, but the result was identical, and suddenly the multiple insanities which had dominated his life these past few days – the Inquisition, the mad bee-keeper, the crazy old fascist lady, the greedy assassin and his weird and wicked companions – all were sloughed out of his mind and dumped in the dustbin of history. *I've beaten the lot*, he thought triumphantly. He picked up the carphone, tingling with excitement, and dialled through to the Astronomer Royal's ex-directory home number.

'Sir Bertrand, I have it. I'm about fifteen minutes from the Institute.'

'Say no more.'

Webb stood at the front door of the Institute, flapping his arms in the early morning cold. Traffic was non-existent. He exchanged hellos with a group of noisy revellers, the young men in dinner suits, their ladies shivering in ball gowns, dinner jackets covering their bare shoulders. After half an hour a dark Rover turned off Broad Street, the wet road glistening in its headlights. The car mounted the pavement outside the Bodleian and stopped, its headlights switching off. The figures inside made no move to leave the car, and he couldn't make them out; they might have been lovers.

Ten minutes later the Astronomer Royal's Jaguar also turned off Broad Street and drove past the Rover, along Park Road. The AR emerged, wrapped in a long black coat, a Homburg and a heavy white scarf. A gust of icy air blew round the corridor as the AR opened up, locking the door behind them and putting the bolts into floor and ceiling.

Webb led the way without conversation to his basement room. He cleared a space at his desk and they leaned over Vincenzo's manuscript, opened at the page with the moving star. The AR, his breath misting in the unheated air, looked at it and then at Webb, eyebrows raised.

'Well?'

'The Latin says it's a moving star.'

'Laddie, I was reading Ovid when you were still in nappies. What's the significance of this?'

'The point is, nothing else in Vincenzo's notes stands out. Apart from the moving star, all he records are Saturn's rings, star clusters, Moon craters and so on. This can only be a close encounter with a celestial missile.'

'Did you get me out of bed at four o'clock in the morning for this?'

Webb's heart sank. 'I did.'

'I was rather hoping that your identification, when you made it, would be based on a solid foundation. You seriously claim that this identifies the asteroid?'

I don't believe I'm hearing this. 'Yes sir, I do.'

Sir Bertrand looked at Webb incredulously from under his bushy eyebrows. 'Yes, Webb, I'm afraid that is your style, the inverted pyramid. I have long been aware that solid groundwork, on which this Institute has built a world-class reputation, is too tedious for you. I am also aware that you are given to flights of, shall we say, speculative fancy. However, on this occasion you have excelled yourself. You build a superstructure which would have us identifying an asteroid, panicking half the planet if it got out, firing spacecraft into the blue and triggering incalculable political repercussions. And you do it on the basis of two points on a four hundred-year-old manu-script.'

'Sir Bertrand, I grant you I sometimes feel as if I'm wading through treacle in this place, but would you like to tell me what else it could be?'

'A simple misidentification of a star. Or an internal reflection in a flawed lens. And they were all flawed four centuries ago. A comet unconnected with the asteroid in question. Or even a couple of variable stars which winked on and off on successive nights.'

'Men have killed for this manuscript.'

'I don't want to know that.'

'It's relevant information. They haven't killed because Vincenzo saw an internal reflection.'

'Utter bilge. I cannot endorse your identification.'

'I don't know why people are even bothering with your seal of approval. What do you know?' Webb was past caring.

'Perhaps because high officials in America would rather place the future of their country in a pair of safe hands, rather than those of some immature young maverick. From what I am now hearing, they were wise to do so.'

'I'm about to give you the name of this asteroid, Sir Bertrand. And when I do, keep in mind that its orbit is chaotic. A chaotic orbit means two things. One, a tiny perturbation applied early enough can yield a huge change in orbit. Two, to exploit the chaos you need to know the orbit with fantastic precision. *Phaenomenis Novae* not only identifies the asteroid, it gives a four hundred-year time base, exactly what they needed for high-precision manoeuvring.'

'Webb, do you not understand?' The Astronomer Royal's tone was despairing. 'We need solid, hard-headed evidence, not wild speculation.'

'When they decided to use this particular asteroid, they must have known of this close encounter. They must have raked through every manuscript they could find covering the period, and then decided to get rid of the only two copies of Vincenzo in existence. The one at the Bodleian, and this one, stolen from the Helinandus Collection sixty years ago.'

'You are deranged. Perhaps you should take to writing cheap thrillers.'

'Take a look at this,' Webb said. He fed in a disk, typed at the keyboard and stood back. The Astronomer Royal sat down heavily on Webb's chair and watched the two little spots rapidly trace out orbits. 'I'm running time backwards in the Solar System. The blue one is the Earth, hence the circular track. The yellow one, that's the suspect.'

While the little blue Earth whirled on its circular orbit, the yellow spot representing the asteroid traced out an elongated ellipse; two trains, each on a different track. The tumbling digital calendar measured the progress of the Wellsian time machine as it hurtled back through the internal combustion era, the wars and revolutions, the fall and rise of kingdoms, backwards through the years in minutes. And as time passed, it became clear that the yellow ellipse was not fixed in space, but was slowly rotating as the asteroid sped round it. On several occasions it happened that, unknown to the creatures inhabiting the blue spot, the yellow one passed dangerously close overhead, and that the things which mattered so much to them – wars, treaties, revolutions, history – were within an ace of being swept aside in a single, incinerating half-hour. The yellow and blue spots approached more and more closely and then, finally, touched. The whirling spots stopped, fused together on a single pixel of the screen, and the calendar froze. On the twenty-eighth of November, 1613 AD.

'The same night Vincenzo saw the moving star,' Webb said. 'I've also checked the background constellation and the angular rate, and they fit. It's beyond coincidence.'

The Astronomer Royal expelled a great lungful of misty breath. He tossed his hat on the desk and wandered over to Webb's bookcase, pretending to read the titles. Webb gave him time.

'We had a near miss then?' the AR finally said, flicking through the pages of *Methods of Mathematical Physics*.

'Yes, sir. It passed within seventy thousand kilometres of the Earth.'

'What?' Putting the book down. 'That's treetop level!'

'And easily seen in Vincenzo's telescope, especially if it's an old cometary sungrazer, maybe slightly outgassing a few centuries ago. The surprise is that others didn't spot it.'

'Which asteroid is this?'

'Karibisha. Eccentricity point seven, orbital inclination just 2.5 degrees, which guarantees a succession of close encounters over the centuries. Semi-major axis just over 2.1 AU.'

'Is it hard to detect?' the AR asked.

'Practically impossible. By the way, "Karibisha" is a Swahili word of welcome.'

'A word of welcome. How beautiful, even at four o'clock in the morning. With an eccentricity like that no wonder it's hard to see.'

Webb nodded in agreement. 'It's coming at us out of the Sun. It will be invisible right up to the last few days or hours.'

Sir Bertrand put the book back and ran his hands through his white hair. He picked up a telephone. 'The perfect weapon. We're in the nick of time. If you're wrong, Webb . . .'

'Unfortunately there's a problem,' Webb said.

'Yes?' Tension suddenly edged into the Astronomer Royal's voice. His fingers hovered over the telephone dial.

'That impossible hundred-day guideline which NASA are using for the rendezvous project.'

'What of it?' The AR steeled himself like a man waiting for a punch.

Webb delivered it. 'Nemesis hits in forty.'

PART THREE

MEXICAN CARNIVAL

Carnival [<Fr. <It. <ML < *carnem levare*, to remove meat] 1. the period of feasting and revelry just before Lent. 2. a programme of contests, *etc*.

Cape Canaveral

Forty days.

Catch Karibisha a minimal five days from impact. To achieve this, spend ten days getting to it (the spacecraft's speed is optimistically half that of the death asteroid; therefore ten days of travel by the spacecraft on the way out is covered in five by Karibisha on the way in).

Subtract those ten days of travel time from the forty to impact.

The balance is the time which remains to prepare and launch the spacecraft.

It's simple: cut the one hundred days of spacecraft preparation to thirty, or die.

⌛

'Doctor Merryweather? I'm sorry to disturb you at this hour . . . my name is Rickman, Walt Rickman . . . no, we haven't met, sir . . . Chairman of Rockwell Industries, the Aerospace Division . . . I have a problem . . . it's pretty late here too – I'm calling from Downey, California.'

'Is that your sister, honey?'

Merryweather struggled up to a sitting position on his bed. 'Okay, Mister Rickman, I guess I'm awake. What can I do for you?'

'I'm told you're the best weather man in Texas.'

'Not at three in the morning.'

'That's right, sweetie, tell her to take a taxi.' Merryweather waved his wife to silence with an annoyed
gesture.

The Rockwell Chairman's voice had a worried edge to
it. 'I've just been wakened by my engineers at Canaveral.
You know the Venus probe we're launching?'

'Of course.'

'They're catching a launch window in six hours.
They've broken out of the *T* minus six hour hold and have
started on the tank chilldown and propellant loading.'

Merryweather scratched his head. 'So what, Mister
Rickman?'

'Something bizarre is going on out there. The MMT at
Johnson are ignoring the Weather Launch Commit Criteria. My engineers think they've gone mad.'

'Who is the Flight Director at Johnson these days?'

'A guy called Farrell.'

Merryweather's wife was poking his ribs. 'Joe Farrell.
He's rock solid, Mister Rickman.'

'Doctor Merryweather, that's a five billion-dollar bird
out there and they're ignoring the wind criteria and my
people tell me that if they attempt a launch the Shuttle will
hit the gantry on the way up.'

'Mister Rickman. There are ten first-class meteorolo-
gists out at JSC and an equally good team at Canaveral.
On Shuttle weather support they have about a hundred
years of corporate experience between them. If they say
it's okay to launch, believe me, it's okay to launch.'

'It's the SMG who've asked for you. They want you at
Johnson. You're expected and authorized. I spoke to
Senator Brown.'

The statement brought Merryweather up short. The
chief of the Spaceflight Meteorology Group, after he
himself had retired from the post, was Emerson, a young,
slightly anxious but highly able man. If George Emerson
was asking for his former boss, something bizarre was

indeed going on. Merryweather had one last shot: 'If FD is violating the launch commit criteria he'll be overruled by his own MMT.'

'Except that it's not working out that way. The Mission Management Team seem to be hypnotized or something. Look, my engineers are a hard-nosed bunch and they're telling me something weird is going on out there.'

Merryweather said, 'This is a joke, right?' There was a silence at the other end of the line. 'Okay, maybe I should get on over.'

'A helicopter is on its way and should reach you in five minutes. You have no overhead wires or other impediments in your back garden? Restricted entry to the prime firing room begins in two hours but I've fixed you up with a badge. I'm grateful, Doctor.'

'Don't be. I have no official standing now and I can't influence events. I'm just curious.'

⌛

Cut an improbable one hundred days to an impossible thirty. How?

In an organization as open to public scrutiny as NASA, internally and externally, with an ethos of safety and careful, meticulous planning drummed into its soul following the Challenger and Atlantis disasters, how?

First explain to your top managers and your celestial mechanicians and your flight design analysts that sleep is hazardous to their health. Then, with due authorization and swearings to secrecy, tell them why. Then step back; get out of their hair.

Abandon flotation tanks and prolonged astronaut training. Stick the inexperienced mission specialists into existing Hamilton Standard space suits, show them the oxygen switch and the waste management facility, and tell them to touch nothing else.

Use experienced Shuttle pilots and arrange it so that the

mission specialists, safely inside the orbiter, tell them how to prime the nukes during EVA. Don't get that bit wrong.

Abandon all thought of spacecraft environmental testing, simulated mission environments and the like.

Use big hunks of old interplanetary mission and operational support planning. Tear out the pages that don't apply. Do likewise with the computer programmes on board and on the ground.

Improvise.

Pray.

⧗

KSC press release no. 257-02

The Venus probe passed an important milestone today when it was hoisted atop the Air Force inertial upper stage, prior to being loaded into the Frontiersman Space Shuttle. The operation was begun at midnight precisely and it was on the upper stage by 1 a.m. Until now, IUS and the probe it carries have been undergoing integration and testing at the Payload Hazardous Services Facility (PHSF) at Kennedy Space Center. Verification tests will begin immediately and are expected to be complete within twenty-four hours. Probe close-up activities will begin on the following day, February 13, leading to its encapsulation inside the Shuttle cargo bay. The long crawl to Launch Complex 39-B on Cape Canaveral Air Station will then begin.

'In this weather? Idiots.'

'Sir?' The young Air Force pilot, startled, looked across at the white-haired meteorologist.

'Just talking to myself, son. It happens when you get to my age.'

'Yes sir. I talk to my teddy bear.'

Merryweather put the press release back in his brief-case. He glanced down at the chalets and villas of the NASA executives over which they were flying. The familiar outline of the Johnson Space Center, a sixteen hundred-acre sprawl, appeared ahead. Merryweather tapped the pilot's shoulder and indicated a spot near the warehouses at the edge of the site: he wanted to walk. The helicopter sank over warehouses and test facilities, flew low over the astronaut isolation HQ, and settled gently down on to a field at the edge of the site.

Merryweather collected his badge and shook hands with a young, plump man. 'Hi George. It's gusty out there, prevailing west-nor'west, humidity eighty per cent. Cloud ceiling moderate.'

'Am I glad to see you, sir. I'm going nuts. Come along to the Weather Room.'

A bank of familiar terminals faced Merryweather. He went straight to one of them, and looked at a set of black lines covering a map of North America. Over Canada, the USA and Mexico the lines seemed to meander aimlessly. Further out they wandered over Cuba and the islands of the West Indies. But just outside Mexico, they formed into tight, concentric circles.

'Ho hum. Anything from GOES or the DMSPs?'

'Over here.'

For the next forty minutes Merryweather immersed himself in a complex mass of data from geostationary satellites, polar orbiters, radars from Cocoa Beach to Melbourne, sixty-foot towers scattered around the launch pad, buoys in the heaving seas up to 160 miles from Cape Canaveral, balloons at 100,000 feet in the stratosphere and lightning detection systems at over thirty sites around the Cape. Telephone exchanges with the USAF 45th Space Wing Commander and the Weather Team at Canaveral confirmed what Merryweather clearly saw: the weather pattern was unstable and deteriorating.

Two sets of weather criteria have to be satisfied before a Shuttle launch is permitted. The weather has to be right for launch, and it has to be right for landing. The launch criteria need only the observed weather at the moment of launch; but the end-of-mission criteria require a forecast. Merryweather concurred with his worried colleague: neither set of conditions was satisfied.

⧗

Merryweather entered the third-floor Flight Control Room, the one used for Department of Defense payloads. The Flight Director was sitting on the bench with his back to a console, in conversation with the CAPCOM, Gus Malloy, a former astronaut.

'Jim, heard you'd turned up. Good to see you.' The FD's expression did not match his words of welcome.

Without preliminaries, Merryweather leapt into the attack. 'Joe, what's going on here? They tell me you're overriding your Weather Team. The landing criteria will not be satisfied. You need a cloud ceiling more than eight thousand feet and you'll have six. You need visibility five miles and you'll have four. You know crosswinds have to be less than twenty-five knots and you'll have forty. There's an even chance of strong turbulence at the point of landing, and I couldn't rule out a thunderstorm in forty-eight hours. You want to fly your Shuttle back through anvil cirrus? Maybe in a thunderstorm?'

'Jim, at the worst we can put down in Morocco instead of Edwards. You guys are all the same. You know the standard weather parameters are conservative. We're just giving a little flexibility.'

'A little? There's a storm heading in from the Gulf. I practically guarantee precipitation at Kennedy within the next four hours. You'll be gusting well over the thirty-four-knot peak. The damn thing could hit the gantry on the way up.'

'Jim, you're retired, remember?'

'You'll never get this through the poll.'

If only I could explain, the FD thought. But he simply shrugged and said, 'We've taken an executive decision. And the final decision to launch or scrub is mine.'

'I have no official status here but I want it noted that I concur with your SMG. The Flight Rules are not satisfied, neither LCC nor RTLS criteria. And the downrange weather advisory gives seas in excess of five: there are twenty-foot waves out there, Joe. Launch Frontiersman in this and I'll personally crucify you at the congressional inquiry.'

'So noted. We're tanking up now and we GO in four hours and twenty minutes.'

'If I recall the routine, the astronauts are due a weather briefing in fifteen minutes. They'll refuse to fly.'

'You'll see.'

The prime firing room at the Kennedy Space Center has its own code of discipline. Conversation is limited to the business in hand: there is no place for idle chatter between the serious professionals who man it. No personal telephone calls are made except in an emergency. No reading material unrelated to the business in hand will be seen therein. The professionals do not wander about; each man (and they are nearly all men) remains at his assigned station, concentrating on the task in hand.

The vocabulary of the firing room is terse, technical and laden with acronyms. This clipped conversation is not used to exclude the uninitiated; rather, by stripping away non-essential verbiage, the language yields precision of speech and concept; and the vital outcome is that, in a complex, changing and highly technical environment, individuals understand each other perfectly. As a sub-set of the English language it serves its purpose even though, to the outsider, there is something faintly absurd about describing a lavatory as a waste management facility, or a stranded astronaut's fate as an ongoing death situation.

Three hours before launch, entrance to the firing room is restricted; movement within the room is minimized. Twenty minutes before launch, while the 'ice team' are making a last check on the ice which builds around the liquid hydrogen and liquid oxygen tanks, and the white room close-out crew help the astronauts into their little vehicle, the door of the firing room is locked. And fifteen minutes before launch, readiness polls are conducted amongst the Shuttle Launch team. These polls ensure collective responsibility, and protect the system against eccentric or arbitrary decisions by highly placed officials.

Launch Director: Russ, on the weather, we have an update.

Spacecraft: Shoot.

LD: SMG confirm exceedence on the landing crosswinds at Edwards.

Spacecraft: Badly?

LD: Gusting up to forty knots, six over limit. You could always put down in Morocco. The main problem is Ailsa. She's moving our way faster than predicted. Giving us a high gust situation now and 45WS tell us we're close to violation of the weather LCCs. And it's going to get worse. We either break out of hold now or abort.

Spacecraft: Roger. We can feel the shaking in here. What gives with the MEC?

LD: Our programmers are still on it.

Spacecraft: What's the time factor on the crosswind?

LD: We have a Jimsphere up and your old pal Tony is now overhead in the T-38. SWO has issued a down-range weather advisory.

Spacecraft: I copy. Look, Zeek, why don't we just break

out of hold and launch? Give us a mark at *T* minus five minutes and one minute prior to exit. JSC can play with the Mach attack angles and get a fresh load profile while we're counting down.

LD: Patience. JSC are polling now. Let's wait for verification.

Spacecraft: The guys in the spacesuits say yes.

LD: Russ, you don't even have a vote.

Spacecraft: We can manual override on the tank separation.

Houston Flight: NTD, this is Flight on channel 212.

LD: Go ahead.

Houston Flight: The KSC Management poll is in. Prime Launch Team report no violation of the LCC.

That was a lie.

Engineering verifies no impediments to continuation of the count. MMT Chair verifies that continuation is approved by the senior managers. What is the KSC poll?

   LD: We agree with continuation and are loading up a new *I*-profile.

   Spacecraft: What's happening on the tail computer?

   LD: Still trying, and we'll initialize the IUS before we pick up the count.

   Houston: Launch Director, Operations Manager here on 212 circuit. LSEAT have made a final recommendation. We're permitting some flexibility in the LCC wind criteria.

But they had just said the criteria were met. Someone was attempting the old CYA: Cover Your Ass.

We confirm you are GO to continue the count.

The voices were as calm and controlled as ever. But to

Merryweather, sitting aghast in the discretionary chair next to the Flight Director, the firing room had been hi-jacked by maniacs.

LD: Ah, copy. Thank you.

NTD: The countdown clock will resume in two minutes on my mark. Three, two, one, mark.

NTD: The countdown clock will resume in one minute on my mark. Three, two, one, mark.

NTD: Stand by. Four, three, two, one, mark. Ground Launch Sequencer has been initiated.

Orbiter Test Conductor: Commence purge sequence four.

OTC: You have go for LOX ET pressurization.

OTC: Flight crew, close and lock your visors. Initiate O_2 flow.

OTC: *T* minus one minute thirty seconds.

OTC: Minus one minute.

OTC: Go for auto sequence start.

OTC: Fifteen seconds. Ten. Main engine start, three, two, one. Ignition.

The light, when it reached the dark-adapted eyes of the spectators, was painful in intensity. A blowtorch flame thrust down from the rockets in a kaleidoscope of shock waves and swept out from underground tunnels in a carnival of steam.

The thunder, when it reached them, bellowed out over the swamps, tore at sinews, shook ground and bones and flesh. Then the retaining clamps swung back and Frontiersman surged upwards.

It almost made it. A sudden squall of wind and rain, a freak thing, tilted the ship and swung it away from the tower. Rapidly, the on-board computers tried to compensate; the sudden angry roar would reach the onlookers twenty seconds later. But then the freak gust dropped at the very second the computers were compensating and the huge fuel valves were trying to respond. Frontiersman flung itself against the tower like a man pushing against a door which suddenly opens. It just touched. A collective *Aah!* went up from thousands of people braving the wind on the hoods and roofs of their cars. A loud *Bang!*, like a metal hatch being slammed shut, would reach them, but disaster was already plain to see.

The Shuttle began to spin. The flaming tail disappeared into the clouds half a mile above, but the direction was wrong. Seconds later the clouds lit up as if a giant flashbulb had popped, and shock waves ripped overhead, with a deep *Thud!* which was more felt than heard. And then there was a luminous, spreading yellow ocean, and the heat on the face even at five miles, and the fragments of tank and booster raining out of the illuminated clouds, and crashing to the ground along with the debris was the hope, the only hope, of averting Nemesis.

Not that Merryweather, staring horrified at the sight on the giant screen in the Houston firing room, knew it. But the Chief Engineer knew it; and the Flight Director knew it; and a small group of powerful men, clustered grimly around a television in the Oval Office, knew it too.

His Majesty's Treasury

It was a brief paragraph, tucked away in page two of *The Times*:

Cresak flies in and out

Mr Arnold Cresak, President Grant's National Security Adviser, flew into London this morning and had lunch with the Prime Minister. He flew back on a regular commercial flight in the afternoon. The meeting was concerned with mutual security matters of a routine nature.

Routine like a nuclear strike, Webb thought, sipping his second tea of the morning.

Graham bustled importantly into the Hall carrying a pile of papers which Webb recognized as the new publicity drive forms from Central Office. He spotted Webb and adopted an 'I want words with you' expression before joining the self-service breakfast queue.

Screw that, Webb thought. He quickly folded away *The Times*, slipped out and made his way to the Common Room. A smokeless coal fire was glowing bright red and his favourite leather armchair was empty. He picked up *Icarus* from the coffee table, sat down with a sigh of pleasure and swore quietly when Arnold tapped him on the shoulder. Webb followed the janitor across the drizzling quadrangle to the Lodge.

'Sorry about the mess, Doctor,' Arnold said, clearing the *Sun*, the *Sporting Life* and a half-eaten slice of toast from a spindly wooden chair. Webb sat down and found himself facing a pouting nymph with enormous breasts. She was wearing only torn, thigh-length jeans and was straddling a giant spark plug. The calendar was two years old and it was too early in the morning for busty nymphs.

'About time,' the Astronomer Royal growled over the telephone. 'The Houseman would like to know the right ascension of Praesepe. Another damned freebie for you, Mister Kahn.'

Webb had been dreading it for weeks, he felt himself going pale. He went smartly back to his flat and quickly stuffed clothes, toiletries, papers and false passport into his backpack. A casual eavesdropper would probably not know that a Houseman was a fellow of Christ Church College; nor that Praesepe, the Beehive, was a star cluster. He took down a perspex star globe from the top of a wardrobe, blew off the dust and found Praesepe: its right ascension – its longitude in the sky – was nine hours and thirty minutes. His watch read ten minutes past nine. That gave him twenty minutes to reach Christ Church College, presumably the main entrance at St Aldates. Enough time for Webb, but not for the casual eavesdropper to work out the AR's message even if it had been recognized as coded. The fact of speaking in code was itself disturbing information. As an afterthought, Webb grabbed his laptop computer on the way out.

Feeling slightly foolish, he took a side door and trespassed through the Warden's back garden, not daring to look towards the windows of the house. He climbed over a garden wall, half expecting an outraged shout, and found himself in the college car park. He crossed Parks Road, looking back at Wadham, and had a near-miss with a female cyclist wearing a long scarf and a Peruvian hat. Nobody was hanging about the college; there were only the usual motley students coming and going. He walked briskly north, away from Christ Church, before turning left on Keble Road and back south on a parallel track along Giles Causeway. A black Jaguar was parked on the double yellow lines outside Christ Church, its motor purring. The chauffeur opened the rear door of the ministerial car and Webb sank into the red leather seat.

They joined the M40; the traffic moved smoothly enough along the motorway and through the endless grey suburbs of Ealing and Acton, but in Kensington the flow began to congeal like water turning to ice. The chauffeur looked worried. He drummed his fingers against the steering wheel. He picked his nose. He switched on Radio One and switched it off again.

'Where am I headed?' Webb asked.

'I have to get you to the Treasury Building by noon sharp, sir,' said the chauffeur, looking in the rear mirror.

'Relax. I'll walk.' Webb left the chauffeur to the traffic jam. He walked along busy streets to the Mall, where he cut off through St James's Park. In Horse Guards, men dressed in red were responding with wonderful precision to the sharp, echoing commands of a sergeant major with a superb repertoire of insults. He moved quickly along Whitehall and turned into the Treasury building as Big Ben started to chime.

'Name?' said the thin man at the desk.

'Mister Khan.' The man gave Webb a look but ticked his name off. Webb waited in the inquiries office for some minutes, until a tall, cheerful man not much older than himself came to collect him.

'Tods Murray,' said the man, in an accent which Webb connected with polo and country clubs in Henley. The man's handshake was weak and clammy. There was an impressively grand staircase but they squeezed into a small lift, and emerged on to a broad circular corridor with a red carpet. There was a smell of expensive coffee, probably Jamaican Blue Mountain. Tods Murray knocked at a door and led Webb into a small, comfortable office. At a heavy table sat the Astronomer Royal and the Minister of Defence. The AR wasn't smoking and Webb thought he looked a bit wild-eyed.

'Coffee?' asked the Minister, waving at a chair.

'No thank you, sir.'

'Something stronger, perhaps?'

'No.'

The Minister looked at Sir Bertrand, who shook his head, and then poured black coffee into a Worcester cup. 'Would normally have held this meeting in Northumberland House, but we don't want you wandering in and out of the MOD. Not that we think anyone's keeping an eye on you, nothing so melodramatic. Just a belts and braces thing.'

'That's good to know, Minister. I recall the last such reassurance.'

The Minister gave him a look.

'Is that a complaint, Webb?' the Astronomer Royal asked.

'Your theory,' the Minister said.

'Which one is that, Minister?'

'These suspicions about the signals from the robot telescope, a traitor on the Nemesis team and so on. We sent it all on to the CIA. They have reported that every American on that team had been thoroughly vetted and each one was regarded as loyal beyond question. Yankee White was the term used.'

'But Minister, a determined attempt was made to keep that manuscript from me. One of your own staff died in front of my eyes in Italy. Someone paid these people to kill me.'

Tods Murray responded. 'If there was a leak, it didn't come from the Eagle Peak team.'

The Minister said, 'For all we know your assassin was a

pathological liar. The whole business could have been local private enterprise. After all, you let it be known that you were very keen on that manuscript.'

Webb said, 'But the Tenerife telescope. From the outset it was responding too quickly. Transatlantic connections aren't that fast.'

'Webb,' said the Astronomer Royal, 'you made the connection during the graveyard watch. Transatlantic communication would have been quiet.'

Tods Murray added, 'And the CIA telecommunications experts checked the routing. It's fine.'

Webb shook his head stubbornly. 'But La Palma was clouded over. I saw it myself.'

The Astronomer Royal picked up on that. 'The Met Office tell us that the cloud was broken at the time of your observations, Webb. You just happened to log on to the Spot satellite at a moment when everything was overcast.'

'I was being fed false pictures.'

The Astronomer Royal sighed. 'That is ludicrous.'

'And Leclerc?'

'There was no sign of tampered switches in the wheelhouse. It was an accident.' The Minister's tone was final. 'Let's not get obsessive about this. Your suspicions were exhaustively investigated and found to be without foundation.' He pretended to read a sheet of paper. 'However, you were not invited here for a discussion about your latent paranoia, Doctor Webb. We have other plans for you. But first, I'll hand you over to Bertrand for some news.'

The Astronomer Royal said, 'There is good and bad. The bad news is that the Americans have given up trying to reach Nemesis. There's just no time.'

He gave Webb a moment to assimilate the information, and then added: 'The good news is that Karibisha might miss. There's an even chance. I'm afraid it's going to be a cliffhanger right to the end.'

'They've seen Karibisha, then?'

'Yes. The US Naval Observatory managed to pick it up pre-dawn. They only have a short arc to go on. NASA's best estimate is that its perigee will be one Earth radius. We will have either an extremely close encounter or a grazing collision.'

'What do the errors look like on the target plane?' Webb asked.

'A very elongated ellipse, almost a narrow bar, passing from the Pacific through central Mexico to the Gulf of Mexico. One sigma on the long axis is two thousand kilometres, on the short one a couple of hundred.'

'We could still have an ocean impact, then?'

'Or a miss. The asteroid came within range of the Goldstone radar some hours ago and they should be sharpening up on the orbit now.'

The Minister interrupted the technical exchange. 'It says here it's approaching us at fifteen miles a second and is four million miles away at the moment. It will pass the Earth in three days and' – he looked at his watch – 'eight hours.'

'Can you imagine the public reaction if this gets out?' Tods Murray said.

The Minister looked as if he could. He added brown sugar crystals to his coffee. 'I don't know how much longer we can keep it quiet.'

Webb said, 'With Karibisha's orbit it will be the devil to detect until the very last hours. But once it clears the solar disc it will be visible even in binoculars, just immediately before dawn.'

'We'd like you to go to Mexico,' said the Minister, stirring. 'To the point of closest approach.'

Webb puffed out his cheeks.

'Of course our satellite intelligence should let us know immediately whether this Karibisha has hit, but GCHQ do worry a little bit about signal failure at the critical moment due to electrical disturbances in the ionosphere. They're not sure they could immediately tell the difference between a freakishly close encounter and a hit.'

'EMP, Webb,' Sir Bertrand explained.

'Frankly,' the Minister continued, 'we want as many channels of communication as we can get, including old-fashioned transatlantic cable. It has been agreed with the Americans that there will be two scientific observers, one from America and one from Europe. On a matter of this supreme importance, HMG prefers to have a hit or miss verified not only by remote sensors but also by our man on the spot. You will understand that, depending on the outcome of the event, certain actions may be taken within minutes of it.'

Tods Murray said, 'We're asking you to take an even chance of being obliterated.'

The Minister adopted a tone of excessive politeness. 'It doesn't have to be you. Would you prefer we found someone to take your place?'

Webb felt the Astronomer Royal's eyes on him. 'I insist on going,' Webb said, heart pounding in rib cage. The Minister grunted his satisfaction.

'Do I know the American observer?' Webb asked.

The Minister looked at a sheet of paper. 'A Doctor Whaler.'

'I know her.'

'The centre of the two-D error ellipse is somewhere over central Mexico, according to NASA,' said the Astronomer Royal. 'Close to bandit country.'

The Minister peered at Webb closely. 'You remain convinced that there was some sort of conspiracy to keep you from identifying Nemesis?'

'I do, sir. That's why I insist on going. I want to keep my ear to the ground.'

'Mexico, Webb,' said the Astronomer Royal, for no discernible reason.

Webb said, 'I'd like to see the NASA report.'

The Minister added more sugar, slurped and closed his eyes briefly with satisfaction. 'That's better. I'll see you get it, Doctor Webb.'

Tods Murray said, 'The Americans are setting up a link from the epicentre and we will be waiting for your call. Should you, for whatever reason, not be in a position to use their link, then we can alternatively be reached through this number.' He slid a card across the table. 'Of course we can't imagine how such a situation would arise.'

'Don't let this simple precaution feed your fantasies about a conspiracy, Doctor Webb,' said the Minister.

'I'm being reassured to death here,' said Webb.

'Your flight leaves from Heathrow in ninety minutes,' said Tods Murray. 'The same need for security applies, and you are still Mister Fish from the moment you leave this building.'

'Phone in from Mexico the instant the asteroid has passed overhead,' the Minister said as Webb reached the door.

'What if it hits?'

The Minister showed surprise. 'We'll know. You won't call in.'

Judge Dredd and the Angels of Doom

Outside the Treasury building, Webb found a telephone and made a brief call. Then he went to a Barclays Bank and drew two thousand pounds in the name of Mr L. Fish, and took a taxi to the Natural History Museum in Cromwell Road. In the atrium he stood underneath the jaws of the long-necked *Diplodocus* which greets visitors to that great museum, while Japanese tourists and school parties swilled around him.

In five minutes, Judge Dredd emerged from the Japanese tourists and the school parties. He was red-eyed, skinny and stooped, had long, black, filthy uncombed hair and was dressed in Oxfam cast-offs. All he lacked, Webb thought, was the anorak.

They shook hands. Webb noticed the slightly red-rimmed eyes of his old friend. *He hasn't changed*, Webb thought. *Still living in the virtual world while the real one passes him by. I was like you not so long ago.*

'Jimmy! How's life treating you?'

Judge Dredd shrugged. 'You know.'

And as socially clueless as ever.

'Jimmy, I need some help. Look, I don't have any time as I have a plane to catch. Would you mind sharing a taxi with me to Heathrow and I'll explain as I go? I'll pay the return fare, don't worry. It's worth a hundred pounds to me to have you even listen to my problem.'

'A hundred? In the name o' the wee man where do ye

get money like that, Ollie? Are you cracking banks these days?'

Webb laughed. 'No, still at the Oxford institute. They actually pay me to pursue my hobby.'

They random-walked their way through the crowds and on to Cromwell Road. Webb waved down a taxi, asked for the airport, and closed the window connecting them to the driver. He passed over a hundred pounds in small denominations.

There was a certain honesty about Judge Dredd. He took the money with pleasure, without feigning reluctance or asking why. 'Well, Ollie, I'm listening with both ears.'

'I need to break into a highly secure American installation.'

The Judge sniffed. 'America's neither here nor there. But if you're talking about the Milnet, that's a big problem. And if it's air-gapped there's nothin you can do unless you're on the inside. Is it VMS, Unix, Win NT or what?'

'It's Unix-based.'

'You need a name and a password. Usernames are nae bother. But ye'll no get in without a password.'

'I need access to the Sandia Corporation in Albuquerque.'

Judge Dredd displayed rows of yellow teeth. 'So that's where the money's coming from? You've got in with the KGB, right?'

'Come on Jimmy, you know I'm a peace activist.'

'Aye, and I'm Napoleon Bonaparte.' He paused thoughtfully, drumming his skinny fingers lightly on his knee. 'The Holy Grail is the password file.'

'Which you can't access because you need a password to log in, in the first place.'

The man looked at Webb with amusement. 'You always were a bit of a lamer, Ollie. If it was an ordinary business it could be easy. The Citibank job wasn't even clever. The number of Freds and Barneys I've come across in passwords would crack you up. If there's a modem at the other end we could just keep dialling and hanging up automated-like.'

'Transatlantic, isn't that expensive?'

Judge Dredd giggled. 'I never paid for a transatlantic call yet. It would be unprofessional. But it's crass 1980s stuff and it takes ages. And these days most places automatically block you after a few misses.'

'Jimmy, I need an answer within thirty six hours.'

'Thirty six hours! Ye're away wi' the fairies, Ollie. These jobs take weeks.'

'Is it beyond you?' Webb asked to provoke.

Judge Dredd thought about it. 'I'm thinkin, I'm thinkin. Sometimes ye can get the password file from FTP or CGI scripts. You don't even need to log in, you just do an anonymous download. The CIA and NASA were cracked that way through ordinary web browsers, exploitin a programme called PHF.' A dreamy look flitted across the man's face, as if he was reliving some past triumph. 'But after the Rome Lab job the military started installing a lot more firewalls. A decent packet-level firewall restricts you to a couple of machines inside their network. Mind you, there's ways round that now, with packet fragmentation and the like. Of course you spread the probes and attacks around, and nothin is traceable. The Rome Lab attackers leapfrogged their way in through phone switches in South America.'

He paused again. Webb took that as a cue. 'Jimmy, I'll pay you a thousand pounds for a successful penetration.'

The man's bloodshot eyes widened, and alarm flickered over his face. 'You're intae somethin heavy here.'

Webb nodded. In the confines of the taxi, a sour, unwashed smell was quickly building up.

'It's your business why ye want in, I guess. Okay let me

think.' The man was silent for a minute. Webb looked out at the congealed traffic. Then Judge Dredd was saying, 'These high security places sometimes have a soft underbelly. They rely on outside systems like suppliers, research labs, civilian phone networks and so on. Somebody in Argentina tunnelled into Los Alamos via a legitimate university connection. It might be worth a try. But even when you get the password file you still have another problem.'

Webb waited.

'The passwords are encrypted. So you have to run a cracker on it.'

'You mean a decryption package?'

A pained expression crossed the Judge's face. 'You cannae decrypt a password once it's encoded, not in Unix. It's a one-way system. However what you can do is run a dictionary file. What this does is apply the encryption routine to thousands of words, crap like Fred and Barney high on the list. You end up with millions of possibilities for thousands of words. It compares this encrypted output with the encrypted passwords in the file. When it finds a match, bingo, ye've got the password.'

The taxi had cleared Central London and was moving briskly; signs for Hounslow, Staines and the airport were appearing at intervals. The taxi was reeking of unwashed body.

Webb knew that with his next words he would be in grave breach of the Official Secrets Act; but he saw no alternative. 'Jimmy, it's important that you keep quiet about this. I have to know the source of messages going in to a place called Eagle Peak Observatory in Arizona. There's a telescope in Tenerife. It can be controlled remotely through an intermediate node and I can give you the pin numbers to do it. When I operate it from Arizona I see signals which look as if they come from the Tenerife telescope. I need to know whether they really do. I suspect they don't.'

Webb pulled a fat brown envelope from his backpack, keeping it out of sight of the driver's rear view. The man stared incredulously at it.

Jimmy asked, 'Where is this intermediate node?'

'The Physics Department, Keble Road, Oxford University.'

'And where does the military come intae it?'

'I suspect the signals really originate from the Sandia Laboratory.'

'You don't mean yon Teraflop?'

'I do. Can't you do it?'

'In thirty six hours? It's a megachallenge, no question.'

Webb slipped the envelope over. Judge Dredd riffled the banknotes as if he couldn't believe it, and slipped it into a pocket. The smell was turning into a stench and Webb wondered when Judge Dredd had last had a bath.

'But it might be done. I'll no be able to penetrate the whole Teraflop Box, yon iron's too big for that. But with root access I could install a packet sniffer at some network switch. A desktop PC will do. You just sit quietly watching the data and biding your time. Like a crocodile watching the comings and goings on a river bank. If you keep seeing the same sequence of signals near the start of a message you might be on to a password. Then you pounce. Once you're in, you get out before anyone even notices. But you hide away a few lines of code that lets you get in the back door again whenever you feel like it.'

'Jimmy, I don't care how you do it, so long as it's done surreptitiously,' said Webb.

'This is a big job, ye appreciate. If I cannae hack it in time I might get the Angels of Doom on to it. Surreptitious-like. They say their latest SATAN scripts will find holes in almost anything.'

Webb scribbled down a set of numbers. 'I'll call you at midnight tomorrow. I'll see you get the other half within a week.'

At the airport, Judge Dredd directed the taxi back home without stepping out, and Webb made his way through the crowds to Terminal One, gulping fresh air and feeling like Klaus Fuchs.

⧖

Shortly after Webb's Jumbo had hauled itself into the air, an unknown, but clearly disguised, man entered the secure London office of Spink & Son wheeling a tartan shopping trolley and carrying a brown paper bag filled with breakfast rolls and tins of beans. He made a purchase extraordinary even by the standards of that office, paying a fortune in cash in return for gold coins. In the main he bought the 'old' sovereigns, with 0.2354 of a Troy ounce of pure gold. These he weighed in heaps of ten on his own scales, before loading them into the trolley. He then placed the rolls and beans on top of the coins, and wheeled the trolley out on to the street, towards some destination unknown. The transaction took up much of the afternoon. Also that afternoon, Albemarle, Samuel and other coin dealers in the London area likewise found heavy runs on the Krugerrand, the maple leaf, the US Eagle and the Britannia.

And in Zurich and London, the world centres for the exchange of gold, the price of the yellow metal moved imperceptibly upwards. It was the merest nudge, barely detectable above the random tremors of the global market.

⧖

The huge aircraft started the big haul and dwindled to a tiny flying insect skimming just above the Atlantic. Webb travelled first class. And while the sun stood still in the sky outside, and air of lethal coldness hurtled past inches from his head, he dined six miles high on smoked salmon and champagne, and he watched Loren and Mastroianni in love, and he worried.

⧗

While the tiny insect skimmed over the water, gold kept drifting up; still a whisper all but lost in noise. The exchanges in Hong Kong and Singapore had closed for the night; but clever men and women in London and New York, people who spent their days alert for tiny fluctuations in the jagged curves on their monitor screens, had noticed the trend on their monitors; they worried too, but about different things. But then these markets too closed, and waited for the Earth to turn, for the sun to rise and pierce the Tokyo smog.

⧗

There was a thunderstorm over Newfoundland and congestion in the air over JFK, and the turbulence played with the huge aircraft like a cat with a mouse. At each bump Webb, in a state of terror, peered backwards into the dark; he could just make out the engine trying to shake itself loose from the flapping wing. He tried not to weep with relief when the Jumbo landed smoothly and taxied off the runway. A tired lady with a bright floral display in her lapel kept saying 'Welcome to New York' to the ragged passengers pouring into Customs & Immigration. Webb sat worn out on a plastic seat while world travellers were whisked in limousines to Manhattan or took the helicopter, still flying in this weather, to East 60th Street.

An hour passed before a tall Indian appeared, black hair sweeping down his shoulders. 'Mister Fish? Mexico bound? Would you follow me, please?'

Almost past caring, he followed the Indian on to a

walkway and into the dark New York night. The air was bitter outside the terminal and snow was fluttering down.

'I'm Free Spirit,' said the man, ushering Webb into a Cadillac. 'It don't mean free liquor either, it's my tribal name and I'm proud of it.'

'Right on,' Webb said.

Free Spirit stopped to pick up an old woman who should have been meeting her son at St Louis by now are you a stranded passenger too, four boys they have and still trying for a girl he should cut it off and pickle it if you ask me you did say you're a stranded passenger? Webb tried to nod in the right places.

The car stopped outside the Plantation Hotel and the clerk, a balding man of about sixty, gave the woman a ground floor room and took Webb up to the first floor. The man hovered. Webb told him he had no dollars. The man said he took the other stuff too. Webb said he didn't have any of that either and the clerk left shaking his head. Webb locked the door, had a warm shower and collapsed into bed.

He lay in the semi-dark and listened to the night sounds of New York and the elevator disgorging the late-night arrivals.

He worried because something didn't fit. He was still worrying when he drifted into a confused, restless, dream-filled sleep.

⧖

While Webb slept, the quiet little run on gold continued, a trickle slowly gaining strength. More ominously, the dollar began to drift down against other currencies.

The meridian drifted at a thousand miles an hour across the Pacific, the vast, empty, watery hemisphere of the planet. Twelve thousand miles across the ocean, dawn touched the Sea of Okhotsk and the northernmost islands of Japan. An hour later the sun pierced the morning fog over Tokyo; an hour later again and Singapore awoke; and once again clever people, this time in glass-fronted towers overlooking Kowloon and Clearwater Bay, began to worry. They made precautionary moves.

The dollar's drift became a slide.

Just before 1030 GMT, in London, three taxis drew up in New Court, a small courtyard in a narrow street close to the Bank of England. Three men emerged from the taxis and, as they entered the offices of N.M. Rothschild, were joined by a fourth man arriving on foot from the direction of the Bank tube station. As happened every morning at this hour, they were ushered into a small, quiet, wood-panelled office. The walls were lined with portraits of past monarchs, like hunting trophies: a reminder that, historically, even kings had needed the moneylenders. Each man had a desk on which was a telephone and a small Union Jack. The chairman of Rothschild's was already seated, and he welcomed the arrivals with a nod; it was a routine repeated twice daily, at 10.30 a.m. and 3 p.m.

The five constituted an inner circle of the London Bullion Market Association. They traded gold between themselves without ever physically exchanging the yellow metal. On their word, the twice-daily 'fixing' of the price of gold, the value of gold was decided, and so the wealth of the world's central banks, holding vast gold reserves, was determined.

The chairman of Rothschild's (N.M. Rothschild, founded in 1804) opened the proceedings. He spoke in a soft, colourless voice, almost a monotone: here, gold and money, the most emotionally charged subjects known to man, were traded in an atmosphere from which all passion was ruthlessly expunged. 'Gentlemen, we are faced with an extraordinary situation. My office informs me that there has been a sharp upwards movement in bullion within the last few hours.'

The man from the Standard Chartered Bank (a subsidiary of Mocatta and Goldsmid, founded 1684) nodded. 'It's small, but quite distinct. However, my office can find no reason for it.'

There were murmurs of assent. The man from Montagu Precious Metals (Samuel Montagu, a relative newcomer, having been founded in 1853) tapped a folder in front of him. 'It is very mysterious. My buying orders from our Middle East offices alone amount to nearly a billion dollars at last night's Comex rate.'

The man from Deutsche Bank Sharps Pixley (Sharps, founded 1750 and merged with Pixley in 1852) raised an eyebrow. 'But what about security? Can you physically export so much gold from London to Saudi?'

Rothschild's gave Sharps Pixley a disapproving look: the tone of surprise had been a tad too strong, too colourful, for this office.

The man from the Republic National Bank of New York spoke in a measured, cultured American accent. 'My office feels that this is being driven by a small number of individuals who, for whatever reason, are trying to capture as much of the private gold market as they can. The market has spotted this and is responding irrationally.'

'We must not have panic,' Deutsche Bank Sharps Pixley said, looking worried.

Rothschild's almost smiled. 'Panic can be profitable. As one of my predecessors said, the time to buy is when blood is running in the streets.'

And with what passed for social chit-chat over, the five began the serious business of fixing the price of gold, of resolving the age-old tension between buyer and seller. Each man had a portfolio before him, and referred constantly to his office through the telephone. As the prices began to converge, each dealer lowered his little flag to indicate agreement with the fixing price. The man from

New York was the last to agree. The flight from the dollar would be catastrophic, but the force of the market was overwhelming. As soon as he had lowered his flag, a messenger was summoned and the price of gold was published worldwide. Overnight, it had almost doubled.

Immediately after the Rothschild's morning session, encrypted information began to flow along the Highway from Midland Global Markets to the offices of the Hongkong and Shanghai Banking Corporation, whose assets under management were four hundred billion dollars. Midland Global owned the Corporation and four hundred billion dollars was a lot of responsibility. The Corporation began to offload its derivatives market, quietly tried to go short on the Nikkei.

For South Africa, the world's largest gold producer, the news was good. Barclays de Zoete Wedd contacted their owners, Barclays Bank, for instructions, but the message was already on its way from London: somebody knows something, thinks the future is bad news. Some unspecified calamity may be on the way; maybe the greenhouse is beginning to run, or the Arctic ice cap is about to break off. Whatever. So reduce exposure to the future; get out of leveraged currency swaps. And do it quietly, always quietly. No panic selling.

The Nikkei 225 Index faltered. By the close of day it had begun to plunge. On the Square Mile, the Bank of England raised interest rates, and raised them again, but the slide was becoming uncontrollable, the strain on currencies intolerable.

As the sun moved round, rumours began to sweep the markets. Whatever the calamity, somebody knew it was going to hit the States; maybe the big one was about to hit San Francisco and Silicon Valley. Whatever.

Panic. The slide on shares and currencies, now out of control, accelerated towards a precipice. Gold, the one certainty in an uncertain world, went stratospheric.

NEMESIS

All this without knowledge of the nature of the impending disaster. But in the early hours of the morning, Eastern Standard Time, while Webb tossed and turned in a stifling hotel room, that information reached the offices of the *New York Times*.

The Situation Room,
T-49 Hours

The Admiral was a six o'clock riser. At six fifteen, as on most mornings excepting Thanksgiving, birthdays and the like, hot water was spraying on his head and down over his scrawny, suntanned neck. He turned and shut his eyes, letting the stream hit his face and run down over his chest and his trim stomach. He groped for the shower switch, turned it off and was just turning to the shower door when his wife opened it.

'Robert. Were you expecting a car this morning?'

The Admiral showed surprise. 'No I was not. What's going on?' Hastily, he dried himself off. Only once, in his ten years at Washington, had he been summoned from his home, and that had been at the outbreak of the Second Korean War.

He dressed quickly, ran a comb through his grey, wiry hair, grabbed a briefcase, sipped in passing at the coffee which his wife held for him and made for the door. A young ensign was waiting, and a black limousine was parked on the street outside.

The car took off smoothly, the ensign taking the Admiral quickly on to Columbia Pike and past Arlington Cemetery before turning right on to the Jefferson Davis Highway. The ensign, Admiral Mitchell soon realized, knew nothing beyond his orders to transport him to the briefing chamber on the third floor of the Pentagon as quickly as possible.

The Emergency Conference Room was as large as several tennis courts. Mitchell looked down on it through the glass partition with alarm. The room was a hive of activity, the focus of the 'battle staff' being four duty officers at the head of the enormous T-shaped table, peering at consoles, talking into telephones, taking messages, giving orders.

Hooper, on a telephone, beckoned the Admiral over with a wave of the arm. 'Mitchell, over here.' For some reason lost in the mists of time, nobody but his wife ever addressed Mitchell as anything other than Mitchell.

'What gives, Sam?'

Hooper put down the telephone. 'Take a look at this. Your office just relayed it through.' Hooper thrust a sheaf of papers into the Admiral's hand.

Mitchell felt himself flushing as he skimmed through the reports. 'What are these guys playing at?'

'The Bear's on the move, what else?'

'But why? What precipitated this?'

The Chairman of the JCS gave the Admiral a strange look. 'Mitchell, you're about to be told a story which you simply will not believe.'

Something like fear flickered across Mitchell's face. 'I saw a Sikorsky on the helipad. That can't mean what I think.'

Hooper nodded grimly. 'We're gathering up the JEEP-1 civilians. They'll be dispersed to Site R and Mount Weather. And we're stocking the civil defence bunkers in Denton with bureaucrats.'

'*What?*'

'Like I said, there are things going on that you just won't believe. Let's get to the Gold Room – Bellarmine's waiting.'

The Gold Room should have been filled with senior officers and their aides. The Admiral was astonished to find it empty except for the Secretary of Defense, who waved him impatiently into a chair.

'What is this?' the Admiral asked.

'Mitchell, we're heading for the Sit Room in a few minutes. But first, pin back your ears and listen to this.'

⌛

'They say Nemesis will miss with fifty per cent probability,' Heilbron informed the President.

Grant scowled. 'Meaning it will hit with fifty per cent probability. An even chance that we're history. Anything more on that probe?'

'They've abandoned the attempt. They needed more time.'

'We're helpless, then.'

The Situation Room was low-ceilinged, small and cramped, with dark wood panelling on three of the walls, and a large curtain covering the fourth. The Secretary of Defense, the CIA Director, the National Security Adviser and the Chairman of the JCS were sitting around a large teak table which dominated the room. Admiral Mitchell, not a member of the NSC, was nevertheless seated at it, on Hooper's right.

'Mister President,' the CIA Director added, 'As the asteroid approaches they'll be able to sharpen up the orbit. Meaning we'll move towards certainty one way or another over the next forty-nine hours.'

President Grant opened a drawer in the table and took out a telephone. He spoke briefly into it and the curtains behind him parted. A large screen covered much of the wall. The land masses of the United States and Russia faced each other across the North Pole. 'Admiral Mitchell, what gives with these naval movements?'

Mitchell stood up and walked over to the screen. 'Mister President, the Russians are mobilizing. They're moving their entire Baltic Fleet.' His hand waved over the screen. 'They appear to be evacuating the Kola peninsula.

And their ships are pouring out here, through the Kattegat. Northern Command tell me the Swedes are lining the roads to get a view. Normally they have only a third of their Northern Fleet at sea, but they seem to be dispersing almost their whole surface fleet into the Atlantic. And down here, sir, they're moving an abnormal tonnage through the Bosphorus.'

Grant said, 'Tell me about their submarines.'

'I'll remind you, sir, that Navy Operations Intelligence Center have been logging a sharp increase in submarine movement over the past few days. SIGINT have been picking up the communications activity that goes on when their subs slip out of berth. Over here at Petropavlosk, we believe they have maybe sixty subs out, three of them Akula class. Now we can make it hot for them in the Pacific as necessary, but over here, in the Polyarny Sea and around the Motovskiy Gulf, they can give their undersea craft reasonable air coverage. As you know, sir, we have SOSUS cables round Murmansk and the Kola Inlet. They've been picking up exceptional traffic for some days at these locations too.'

'Exceptional traffic – what does that translate into?' Grant wanted to know.

'We think they may have put eighty submarines in that area, half of them strategic. Not to put too fine a point on it, Mister President, they're dispersing their whole submarine fleet.'

'Thank you, Admiral Mitchell. Now that you're in on Nemesis, perhaps you'd like to sit in on this session.'

Mitchell sat down. 'Sir, are we going nuclear?'

Bellarmine had been bottling up the same question. Now he could contain himself no longer. 'Mister President, these submarine movements are as clear a signal as you can get. Do you finally agree to a counterstrike?'

Cresak cut in. 'What we're seeing is a defensive reaction to our State Orange.'

Hooper tapped the table. 'This is it, gentlemen. They know we're wise to the Nemesis game. They're aiming to get theirs in first.'

Bellarmine cut in. 'Mister President, we have to conduct the war from a secure location.'

Grant looked stunned. 'War? What are you talking about, Bellarmine? The asteroid could miss and Cresak could be right. This is not necessarily a prelude to a nuclear strike.'

Hooper's eyes had a glazed look. 'Can you possibly be serious?'

The telephone in front of the President buzzed. He picked it up and listened. 'Yes, bring it in.'

A door opened and a military aide stepped in smartly. He handed the President a sheet of paper and left. Grant felt light-headed as he read it. He passed it to Bellarmine, and the paper was circulated round the teak table, ending up with Hooper.

FLASH
FROM: CINCEUR VAIHINGEN GE
TO: JCS WASHINGTON DC / /J9 NMCC
TOP SECRET PEAK
(T1/S1) SIGINT REPORTS BARRACKS EVACUA-TION BY RUSSIAN FORCES IN KIEV, GOMEL, VITEBSK, MINSK AND WEST MOSCOW. TANK MOVEMENTS NEAR SLOVAK BORDER AT TAT-RANSKA LOMNICA IN HIGH TATRAS. LARGE-SCALE CALL-UP OF RESERVISTS. TANK MOVEMENTS REPORTED EAST OF PRIPET MARSHES AND (UNCONFIRMED) THROUGH CARPATHIANS. RECOMMEND IMMEDIATE UPGRADE OF DEFCON AND DECISION ON EUCOM REINFORCEMENT OF SLOVAK AND GERMAN FORCES. DETAILED REPORTS WILL FOLLOW.

Hooper said, 'It figures. We know they've been evacuating barracks and bringing up troop-carrying helicopters all the way from the Ukraine to Chechnya. In my opinion the dispositions are shaping up to a mass movement through central Slovakia, converging on the Pilzen area.'

'Pure speculation,' said Cresak.

The buzzer went again. This time Bellarmine went to the door and took the papers from the aide. The Secretary of Defense turned, grey-faced. 'Mister President, that's the least of it.'

'Go on,' said Grant.

'They're bringing Backfires into Kola from their eastern airfields. Maybe a hundred of them.'

'Um-huh.'

'Mister President,' said Hooper, 'they don't aim to hang about. Just as soon as Nemesis zaps us they'll roll over Europe. We no longer have tactical stuff in Europe and the Brits and French wouldn't dare use their strategics without us to back them up.'

Bellarmine said, 'The temptation must be irresistible. When the asteroid hits us, Europe will be plunged into chaos. The Russians will roll their tanks in faster than decision-making machinery in Europe can assess policy. With us dead and Europe overrun they've got the world.'

Cresak said, 'Our scenarios assume a two thousand-second nuclear war. If they're planning to hit us with nukes what's the point of starting a mobilization that would take a month to complete? Anyway the dispositions aren't right for a European incursion. We've always looked to a thrust across the plains to the north. Why all the tank movements on the Slovak border?'

'So they've had us fooled,' said Hooper.

'The pattern in Europe doesn't fit an imminent invasion,' Cresak insisted. 'Where are the Spetznaz attacks? Where are the airborne forces? They should be setting up to take Bremen airfield and move towards the Weser and the Rhine. Backfire bombers in Kola make no sense for a European attack.'

'The first and oldest rule of warfare,' said Hooper. 'Deception. You're talking the orthodoxy they put into our heads. The Kola bombers are aimed at us over the polar route. They're going to finish us off in all the confusion. And with us gone who needs commandos? They don't need to alert anybody with D-1 incursions. It's safer to roll over Europe without any softening up.'

'But the Slovak border movements . . .'

'A lead-up to a flank attack through Bavaria or even a thrust through Frankfurt. Hell, if we're out of the way they can take Europe any which way they please. Leave soldiering to the soldiers, Cresak.'

'They're sabre-rattling. What we're seeing is a defensive reaction to our State Orange,' Cresak insisted. 'Nobody's going to invade anybody.'

⧗

What wakened Anton Vanysek was the shaking of his bed.

At first, it sounded as if an unusually heavy lorry was passing below his seventh storey flat. But the rumbling went on and on. He threw back his blankets and opened his window. Bitterly cold air wafted into the room. The street below was empty, but then he saw, between the high-rise flats, dark shapes rumbling on the road about a kilometre away. It was impossible to say what they were in the early morning gloom. He was tempted to go back to his warm bed, but the whole building was vibrating. He quickly dressed, ignoring the sleepy questions from his wife, wrapped up warmly, and ran down the stone stairs.

Trnava was typical of many middle-sized towns in Slovakia. A picturesque old town was surrounded by high-rise flats, white identikit monstrosities built in the days of the communists, whose concrete cladding had long cracked and crumbled. The whole district was connected by a network of cracked and crumbling roads. Interspersing these great rabbit warrens were factories and chemical works whose outputs left strange smells in the air and brought out mysterious rashes in children, nervous complaints in the middle-aged and lung problems in the old.

Anton Vanysek had, for over twenty years, been irregularly paid small sums of money to report on local political activity, gossip, anything at all which might interest his controllers who, he assumed, passed it on to the CIA. Almost always, apart from the heady days of the bloodless revolution, his information was banal, but then the sums of money were pitifully small.

This morning, however, as he nervously approached the main road which cut through the centre of the town, he was astonished to see that the dark green shapes were tanks. His astonishment turned to fear as he approached closer in the dull light and made out the red stars on their sides.

This information would either earn him a great deal of money or a firing squad.

For the third time in fifty years, Russian tanks were rolling into Slovakia.

The Road to Mexico

In the pale morning light, the hotel looked not so much seedy as tottering. There were a dozen motley guests in the dining room, looking like last night's collection of stranded travellers; the room smelled of cheap waffles and bacon frying in old fat; but there was something else in the air. Webb joined a little group clustering around newspapers on a table, and looked over shoulders.

The *Examiner* said

KILLER ROCK THREATENS AMERICA

and followed it up with a lurid and largely fictitious piece about astronomers huddled at secret meetings. Unbelievable words were being put into the mouths of sober colleagues. Only that well-known British expert Phippson, Webb thought, might actually have spoken the words attributed to him. More soberly, the *New York Times* ran

NEAR-MISS ASTEROID APPROACHING

with the sub-headings

But No Danger, say NASA Scientists

and

Financial Markets Plummet

NASA, of course, had long since taken control of the Minor Planet Circulars. To ensure the public were not unduly disturbed by false alarms, the orbits of close encounter asteroids were routinely put through a refereeing procedure, with guidelines for media contact. A few scientists had long worried about a process which allowed an American Government Agency to decide what was good for the world to know. And now the procedure was being tested under fire and There is No Danger, say NASA Scientists. He scanned the news reports briefly over the shoulder of a young black girl with coloured beads in her hair. It was desperately short on specifics and it left him wondering how this closely guarded secret could have escaped Big Brother's reassuring control. He found a table with a semi-clean cover and asked for bacon, eggs and tea. The waiter, a hunched man with Greek features, came back after some minutes with scrambled eggs and coffee. 'Seen the nooz?' he asked.

'Media hype.'

'I reckon. I got shares in Chrysler. Say, you sure you're the scrambled egg?'

⏳

Free Spirit drove Webb back to JFK. The traffic was nose to tail and eventually slowed to walking pace on the approach road to the airport. A group of men and women were parading with hastily constructed placards near the entrance, ignored by the police. A white-haired man with a sandwich-board proclaiming *Behold I Come Quickly* stepped in front of the car and Free Spirit slammed on the brakes.

'Did you see that, Mister? Did you see that? That's my problem too,' Free Spirit laughed, clapping his hands.

Within the terminal, chaos ruled. The reassurances of

NASA scientists notwithstanding, it seemed that half of New York State had suddenly decided to take a New Year vacation in Europe.

By contrast, the international departure lounge for the flight to Mexico City was a haven of solitude: apparently there had been about two hundred early morning cancellations and a similar number of no-shows. Webb had a coffee and shared the lounge with about twenty families of Hasidic Jews, the men with big beards and broad black hats. Why they were going to Mexico he couldn't guess. Apart from the Jews and Webb, there was only a scattering of Mexican business types, presumably returning to families back home, and a blonde female wearing a slightly old-fashioned dress with a black shoulder bag. She looked up from her magazine, glanced at him and resumed her reading. Webb took his cue and ignored her.

Eastern Airlines hauled them into a bright sunny sky. They tilted up over Manhattan and the Hudson River and turned south, still climbing. When the plane had levelled out the blonde woman moved across the aisle and sat beside him; they were the only two travelling first class. 'Oliver! The hero returns.' Unexpectedly, she kissed him on the cheek. She was still into cheap perfume.

'Hi Judy, they told me you'd volunteered for this.'

'You know how it is. Some politicians use moral blackmail as a tool of the trade.'

'What were you doing in New York?' Webb asked.

'Briefing some UN people. Have you heard the latest about Karibisha? They've got the probable error of perigee down to – wait for it – five hundred miles. And it's still fifty-fifty whether it will hit.' She smiled. 'I'd make a will but who'd collect?'

'So, what's been happening at Eagle Peak?'

'I wish you'd been there when your word came through. Noordhof and Herb took off like bats out of hell and haven't been seen since. No doubt they've been doing the rounds of Washington briefings. And no word from Willy. Either he's in his beach house or else he's quietly emigrated to Antarctica. The truth is, there was nothing much to be done there before Karibisha emerged from the blind spot. Kowalski stayed on as a caretaker.'

'And when they pick it up?'

'Mighty will be the panic. Herb and Kowalski will be getting high-precision astrometry.'

'From the 94-inch?'

'And the Hubble. They've been testing a direct link.'

'Did you come up with a means of deflecting Karibisha?'

'They didn't tell you? Staggered explosions. The idea was to deploy a dozen baby nukes, strung out along Karibisha's path like beads on a wire and each one going off in its face to slow it down; kind of like stopping an express train by gently puffing at it.'

'How baby were they?'

'A third of a megaton each. We needed four Shuttle launches, in two sets of two. One Shuttle in each pair carried an upper stage rocket in its cargo bay, the other half a dozen bombs. Mission specialists were supposed to connect the bombs to the upper stage in orbit. Six bombs weren't going to be enough on their own which is why we needed a second dual launch. The Shuttle accident killed the scheme.'

'Of course it was carrying a Venus probe, ha ha. What was it actually carrying?'

'Unfortunately, half a dozen of my B61s, modified with neutron generators. They're clearing up an awful lot of plutonium at Cape Canaveral. Take my advice, Oliver, don't eat tuna for the next million years.'

Webb looked around at the empty cabin. 'How close are we to war?'

'Who can say? But I'll tell you something,' Judy leaned towards Webb. Her tone was conspiratorial. 'The Teraflop has been real slow recently.'

'You mean . . .?'

She was almost whispering in the big empty aircraft. 'They're gearing up for something.'

⧗

Over the Florida swamplands Webb could make out tiny clusters of houses in little clearings; and then a stretch of sand was cutting across their line of motion. A few boats trailed long white wakes and then there was nothing but blue water: the Gulf of Mexico. A menu appeared. Webb ordered *mignons de filet de boeuf Rosini*, and Judy had poached salmon with a mousseline sauce. She studied the wine list closely and four half-bottles of champagne took them merrily across the Gulf.

In the early afternoon the engine sound changed and Webb felt his ears going funny; the Lockheed was dropping. They flew over tree-covered mountains. Broad highways apparently led nowhere into the hills. Minutes later they were weaving a path between hills covered with houses and roads. Mexico City, an unplanned sprawl stretching to the horizon; bigger than Tokyo, London, Singapore, New York City; Sacheverell's 'irrelevant puff of smoke'. Some boys were kicking a football on grass at the edge of the runway as the plane hurtled past, wings flexing. They didn't look up.

The pilot expressed the hope that y'all enjoy your stay in Mexico and that y'all will fly with Eastern Airlines again soon. The hostesses at the door were smiling, but Webb had the feeling that it was a bit forced. The sounds of a riot were coming from the direction of the terminal.

'You're not staying over in Mexico?' Webb asked the cabin steward at the aircraft door.

'No way, sir. It's fuel up and get the hell out. This is our last flight in.'

As they approached the luggage terminal the sound intensified. It was like an angry football match. Round the

400

last corner of the corridor, and there was the main hallway
and a brawling, bellowing mob. Between the mob and the
international arrival lounges was a thin, ragged line of
teenage soldiers.

A steady trickle of passengers, life-giving boarding cards
tightly clutched, was filtering through, ducking under the
arms of the soldiers. There was no question of passport or
security checks. A lieutenant was in the rear of the line,
pacing nervously up and down.

Webb, Judy and the orthodox Jews approached. The
lieutenant turned in astonishment. He raised his hands.

'You cannot get through!' he shouted above the baying.

'We must!' Webb shouted back. 'Our business is
urgent.'

'But señor, you see it is impossible.'

'I'd like to speak to your superior officer.'

'So would I. He has not been seen all morning.'

'We're here on diplomatic business. We have to get
through.'

He pursed his lips, marched over to his men, issued
some order and then turned back, nervously fingering the
holster of his gun. 'I can spare only a dozen men. You
must keep together. If you stray you are lost.'

The soldiers formed up into a thin wedge; they were
plainly scared. At an order they began to push into the
crowd. Webb and Judy huddled together with the Jewish
families, following behind the wedge.

The soldiers began to use their rifle butts in a violent,
panicky fashion. Slowly they pushed away from the
check-in area where the staff, faces lined with tension,
seemed to be taking bundles of money or tickets at
random from a sea of thrusting hands. A well-dressed
businessman was punching someone repeatedly on the
head. The other party was kicking at the businessman's
shins. Webb glimpsed a woman on her knees.

Midway to the main exit, an arm emerged from the

crowd and grabbed at Webb's sleeve. It was rifle-butted away. It came back, tugging. A dark-suited, pock-faced little man. 'Doctor Webb?' he shouted. 'Signorita Whaler? My name is Señor Rivas. Welcome to Mexico. Please can you come this way?'

They left their protective wedge, the little man muscling his way through the crowds and Webb taking up the rear. For a few panicky moments he lost his orientation, half fell and was unable to breathe, but then he forced himself to his feet and glimpsed Judy's blonde hair some yards ahead. Over to the right he caught sight of a solid phalanx of black hats and beards, and then the crowd had swallowed them up.

The crowd density fell away at the entrance to the airport. An official with a green suit and impassive Aztec features was, by some miracle, loading their suitcases and Webb's laptop into the boot of a car, a black Lincoln Continental with darkened windows. Rivas opened the front passenger door for Judy. Stepping into the back of the car, Webb caught a glimpse of a holstered gun under the man's armpit. The interior of the car was cool.

There was a sudden roar from the direction of the terminal. Webb glanced back; the crowd had broken through the line. It was surging towards the departure lounges.

'Good to see you again, Oliver,' said Noordhof, paying little attention to the riot developing yards from them. His handshake was firm and businesslike. He was wearing light tan trousers and jacket. 'It's prudent to wear civilian clothes in Mexico City just now,' he said without explanation.

'Why are you here, Mark? For the same salary you could be tucked away in a deep limestone cave somewhere.'

'I'm responsible for you people. But I won't say the thought didn't cross my mind.'

Rivas took the wheel and they pulled away in silence.

He took them along the airport boulevard, past unbelievable slums, and on to the Avenue Fray Servando Teresa de Mier, heading downtown.

The car swept them silently along broad streets. Away from the airport there was something like normality apart from the occasional machine gun poking over sandbags at strategic corners; and for all Webb knew, that too was normality in Mexico City.

Judy, a child in a magic garden, kept looking back at him, enthusiastically pointing out street markets and mosaic-covered buildings designed by architects from Mars.

'You're looking a bit strung up, Oliver,' said Noordhof. 'Why don't you relax?'

Webb put a hand to his brow. 'Relax? By this time tomorrow we could be little stars twinkling in the sky.'

The colonel put his hands together in an attitude of prayer.

The Mexican whisked them along the broad Avenue Insurgentes. Apart from a lot of broken glass, there were still few signs that things were crumbling. All the same Rivas was visibly tense, looking up and down roads as they passed and generally wasting no time.

'University City straight ahead,' said Noordhof. 'Once we're through that we're in the clear.'

'In the clear?'

There was a queue of traffic ahead, and flashing lights in the distance. An army truck raced past, overtaking them on their right. Noordhof said, 'Yeah. Mexico City is being sealed off. Something to do with the roads north being jammed.'

'But we're going south.'

Ahead, soldiers were jumping out of the back of a truck. Barbed wire was being stretched across the street. An officer looked up sharply and then jumped as the big car squeezed through the gap, but then the Lincoln was round a corner and the cameo had vanished. A sign showed a little yacht on waves; below the yacht were the words 'Acapulco 400 km'.

The road was starting to climb; soon they were winding through a countryside of tall mountains, rearing out of stubbled fields yellow with corn. Noordhof looked at his watch. 'Step on it, Rivas. You're racing an asteroid.'

Rivas stepped on it. Unfortunately it turned out that, while he had a great deal of speed, he had very little skill. Taking one corner too wide, the car had a hairsbreadth miss with a red bus, stacked to the roof with straw-hatted Mexicans. Rivas shouted something colourful; there was an exchange of hooting, and then the bus had vanished in a trail of blue smoke.

They roared through a dusty little village. A wedding procession scattered. Angry shouts and the barking of a dog receded into the distance.

An hour on, Rivas slowed down. They came to a turning, an open parking area, and a lodge house. The car braked to a halt. Rivas and Noordhof held out identity cards. Judy and Webb produced passports, which were closely scrutinized by an American GI. The soldier checked their names against a list and waved them in.

'Oaxtepec,' Rivas said. 'I get you here in time, yes? This is a government recreation centre. The American soldiers and yourselves are our guests until the asteroid flies past. At least I hope she flies past.' Rivas was driving them, now at a leisurely pace, along a well-surfaced road. Acres of lawn were randomly broken up by swimming pools and colourful flower beds. The road climbed, and finally stopped at what seemed to be a big ranch house.

Noordhof excused himself, explaining that he had a chalet bungalow down the hill. Rivas was escorted towards a room in the main building. A man of Indian extraction, wearing a white jacket and dark flannels, led Judy and Webb along a cloister to adjacent rooms.

Webb's room was spacious and the furniture was ornate and solid. One wall was a French window leading out to a lawn dotted with palm trees and sub-tropical bushes. A fan took up half the ceiling. He threw his backpack and jacket on a chair, walked over to the window and looked out at the swaying trees.

The phone rang. Noordhof said, 'They've picked it up at Gran Sasso, Nice and Tenerife, and the HST are locked on. Goldstone have it on radar.'

'Orbit?'

'The Harvard-Smithsonian, JPL, Finland and Palomar all agree on perigee. It's somewhere in an east–west narrow arc about ninety miles wide. A fair drive south of here.'

'Collision probability?'

'Still fifty-fifty.'

Webb put the receiver down and looked at his watch. It was just past three o'clock. Nemesis, alias Karibisha, would come in at 06:15, in just over fifteen hours.

If it existed.

⧗

Webb wiped sweat from his eyelids. He took a few deep breaths, and tried to keep his voice steady. The sweat on his palms made the receiver slippery.

Judge Dredd answered with a tired 'Yeah.'

'How did it go?' Webb asked.

'Ollie! It's a bummer. I just could not get root access to the Teraflop. It's no often I'm beat but there you are.'

Webb groaned.

'I'm awfie sorry about that, Ollie.'

'You tried. Thanks, Jimmy.'

'Real sorry. Mind you, I got your answer.'

'What?'

'Oh aye, it was easy. I just gave the Tenerife telescope instructions through Eagle Peak and the Oxford terminal at one and the same time. I got different pictures from both. Either yon telescope points in two directions at once or the Eagle Peak pictures are a barefaced fraud.'

Webb felt himself going light-headed. 'Jimmy, you'll never know how grateful I am. I'll see you next week. Meantime remember the second half of our deal.'

'Which is?'

'Keep quiet about this or I'm in trouble.'

The reply was pained. 'You're in trouble! What about me? If the Social found out I was earning on the side . . .'

Webb put the receiver down. The light-headedness was worse; a feeling of detachment began to wash over him, as if his soul was outside, looking down on his tormented mind from a point just below the ceiling. He went to the toilet and sat on the lid with his eyes closed and his head in his hands.

Xochicalco

Judy was tapping at the French window. She had a bright yellow towel under her arm and was wearing a crocheted, cream-coloured bikini with a matching shawl draped round her shoulders. Webb hauled himself from his exhausted sleep into the conscious world.

She put her arm in his. Webb let himself be led down a long hill, past swimming pools and through acres of landscaped garden. Her arm was trembling slightly. The touch of her skin, the inflexion of her voice, the intimacy of her presence, even the hint of perspiration from her body, all these he found both delicious and disturbing.

He sensed that she had something to tell him.

A jellyfish on stilts, as they approached, turned out to be an enormous geodesic umbrella underneath which was a small sub-tropical jungle of orchids and palm trees. They stood on a little hump-backed bridge under the umbrella and watched the volcanic spring water bubbling below. The air was acrid and sulphurous, and the woman led him along a narrow path through the tropicana. Away from the hot spring the air was heavy with scent. Butterflies the size of handkerchiefs were flitting around the palm trees and the orchids. Judy looked around conspiratorially, and they sat down on a bench. 'I've something to tell you.'

She paused. A jeep was approaching down the hill at speed.

'Yes?'

The vehicle braked to a halt outside the dome, a little American flag fluttering on its bonnet.

'Spill it, woman!' Webb swallowed a lump in his throat.

She put a protective hand on Webb's. 'Oliver, we're both in great danger here.'

A squat GI with a head like a bullet was clambering out. Judy leaned forward. 'Later. We mustn't speak of this in the hacienda.'

The soldier was on the hump-backed bridge. 'Compliments of Colonel Noordhof, folks,' he said in a Brooklyn accent. 'He would like you to join him for a light snack. Gee it stinks in here.' The soldier took them briskly back up the hill, in a straight line which shaved swimming pools and ploughed through flower beds as necessary.

They met up in the big restaurant, all wood and tall ceilings with an enormous empty fireplace. Aztec descendants wore white jackets and hovered around with impassive expressions. Their calmness mystified Webb. Either they believed their government's reassurances about Nemesis or they were indifferent to vaporization; neither seemed likely. Judy had reappeared in a short denim skirt, white cotton top and walking boots. She wore long dangling silver earrings and was carrying a canvas shoulder bag. After the frantic exit from Mexico City, Noordhof seemed in a good humour, and if the astronomer's nerves had been less taut he would have missed the occasional appraising glance in his direction. The soldier kept cracking jokes about Jane Fonda; from their content, Webb assumed they had a military circulation. They had enchiladas stuffed with chicken and a sauce with little jalapeño peppers in it, and candied sweet potatoes for a side dish. Two dishes of sauce, one red and one green, were placed in front of Webb.

'The waiters use this as a test of virility,' Noordhof explained. 'The green sauce is for ladies and wimps. The red one is for real men.'

'I don't hold with these stunted concepts of masculinity,' Webb declared. He dipped a thin slice of a turnip-like vegetable into the green sauce, nibbled it, turned red, spluttered and then tried to swallow the Orinoco River. The Aztecs smiled their approval.

'Or was it the other way round?' Noordhof wondered.

They finished off with a dessert of baked bananas with egg whites and sweet condensed milk poured over them, washing it down with coffee spiced with vanilla and cloves, poured over cream and crushed ice.

Finally, Noordhof looked at his watch and said, 'You want to check out the setup at ground zero, Doc?'

'What about my siesta?' Webb asked, bloated.

They heaved themselves up the wooden steps of the hacienda. The jeep was waiting at the front door. Judy and Webb sat in the back. Bullet Head revved the engine and they took off smartly down the hill and out of the complex, driving towards the sun, and the hinterlands.

The road was narrow and dusty. A few family homes, little more than corrugated iron huts with three walls, were scattered around the fields, with scraggy children playing happily enough, or heaving buckets of water. The soil was thin and stony, and broken up by outcrops of rock. Eventually, even the houses petered out, and the cacti took over, tall, emaciated giants standing like motionless triffids. Buzzards were gliding in big lazy circles high in the mountains. Sacheverell's scenario again; but it hadn't described the hot, humid air which streamed past the army jeep. Webb's shirt was sticky with sweat. Metal was painful to touch. Judy wore dark sunglasses and her vaquero hat. Ahead of them, low on the horizon to the south, dark clouds were building up.

As they drove steadily south, towards the dark horizon, the temperature rose inexorably. For a mile behind them, a long billowing wake of dust marked out their trail. Webb's throat turned into a hot, desiccated tube, and he felt his face going the colour of beetroot. Noordhof's conversation began to wilt, and then died, and they headed out, into the deserted inferno, in a mood of grim endurance. Still jet-lagged, Webb tried to stretch out, laying his head back on the seat.

There was a blonde, Nordic maiden. Her eyes were glacier-blue and she was wearing a white gown. She was up to her waist in a pool of turquoise meltwater which cascaded down from Buachaille Etive Mor, spraying them both. She smiled enigmatically, and waded forwards carrying an ice-filled tumbler of Coke on a silver tray. She held the tray out to Webb. He stretched out for the cold drink, but there was the sudden roar of an avalanche, and a rock struck him on the head, and there was a crash of gears and a heavy lurch, and the ice maiden was gone, and a pitiless sun was burning into his eyes. The jeep was slowing, the driver turning off the road. They started to bump and grind along a little donkey track. The track snaked its way upwards through foothills, weaving its way around boulders. The soldier worked hard on the wheel, cursing and begging your pardon ma'am, while the jeep's suspension squealed in complaint. Ahead of them was a wooden hut, an anomaly in these primordial surroundings, like a telephone booth on a mountain top. The jeep reached it and stopped with a groan. A red-faced soldier emerged hastily and came to attention. His shirt was sticky with sweat.

Noordhof stepped out of the jeep and stretched himself. His brow was damp with sweat. He grinned wolfishly. 'That was the easy bit. Epicentre dead ahead. From here on in we walk.' He returned the soldier's salute smartly, and led the group off in single file.

The air was even hotter, and it was scented. As they climbed up, they were surrounded by the drone and clicking of a billion invisible insects. Irrationally, Webb began to feel hemmed in, overwhelmed. We are the true rulers of the Earth, they were saying; you are the temporary guests; we were here a billion years before you, will be here a billion years after you have gone.

They scrambled upwards over boulder-strewn ground in grim silence. Once a twin-rotor helicopter passed, thundering overhead, a jeep swinging below it on a long cable. It disappeared over the horizon ahead and the insects returned. After half an hour of it, the ground began to level out and they began to see signs of ancient cultivation. The path was taking them through terracing. There was a hilltop ahead and as they approached it, structures began to appear in silhouette against the sky. Reaching the summit, they found themselves looking out over a small city. Some community long gone had levelled the ground. Stone pyramids, temples and walls were everywhere. Hundreds of camouflage-green tents were laid out about half a mile to the right, and the city was swarming with soldiers.

Noordhof waved an arm around. 'Ground zero. The place of decision.'

'My feet are killing me,' Webb said.

'I have to see the boss,' said Noordhof, leaving them; he had slipped into a brisk, military style, marching rather than strolling. Judy and Webb had simultaneously spotted a van with an open side and an awning. The woman who handed out tumblers of iced Coke was middle-aged, wrinkled and wore a shapeless khaki overall, but to Webb she was the Ice Maiden of his dream. They downed two each in quick succession and Webb thought that maybe there was a God after all.

A GI sidled up. He looked about sixteen. He was small, freckled and had ginger hair cut almost to the scalp. 'You the Brit?'

Webb nodded.

The soldier licked his lips nervously. 'Say, this asteroid

thing – the line is it's going to miss. Or we wouldn't be here, right?'

'Right,' Webb said reassuringly.

The young soldier wasn't reassured. 'You can give it to me straight, sir. We really are okay?'

A tall, thin bespectacled sergeant approached. 'Are you in pain, Briggs?'

'No sarge.'

'That's strange, because I'm standing on your hair. Get it cut.'

The soldier hurried off. 'Say, can I show y'all around?' the sergeant asked, nominally nodding in Webb's direction before fixing a grin on Judy. Webb wandered off with a wave.

There were bas-relief carvings around the sides of the squat, stony buildings: armed warriors, human sacrifices, arms and legs and dismembered trunks. Waiting for the sky-god. On one side of a truncated pyramid Webb recognized a stylized cosmic serpent, winged and feathered, the ancient symbol of catastrophic skies from the Norse lands to Ceylon, from China to Mexico: the ancient giant comet, father of a hundred Karibishas.

He climbed the ancient steps of a pyramid. A thick black cable trailed up and on to the observing platform, and wound its way into the base of a big shiny paraboloid staring fixedly at a point on the blue sky. The blue lightning logo of Mercury Inc. was painted near the top of the dish. The Valley of Morelos, flanked by steep-sided mountains, stretched to the southern horizon. Whoever once controlled this ancient hilltop also controlled the valley, and passing traffic, and probably territory far beyond. The thunderclouds to the south were building up rapidly. Big Daddy, when he came, would approach from there.

'You're looking at thirty megabytes a second, son,' a voice said. A short, white-haired man in a khaki shirt, with a belly overhanging his belt, was looking up at Webb. Small blue eyes were set back in a round head.

'I'm impressed.'

'We use it to patch straight into the White House via one of our geosynchronous DSPs. You also link straight in to your Whitehall number through this selfsame dish so once the Holy Passover occurs you just pick up that phone over there and let 'em know. So you're the Brit who identified Nemesis. General Arkin.'

'How do you do, sir?'

'I do fine. What'll we see?'

'At two hundred miles impact parameter? A rapidly rising moon. It'll cross the sky in a few seconds, going through all the phases of the moon as it passes. My guess is Nemesis will have a rough, pitted surface.'

Arkle nodded thoughtfully. 'And if it's a bit closer?'

'Say it touches the stratosphere. It'll leave a black smoky trail, and tomorrow will be dark.'

'Closer still?'

'In that case, General, Nemesis won't seem to move much. We'll see a small crescent, very bright, low in the morning sky, coming from over there.' Webb pointed in the direction of the thunderclouds. 'The crescent will grow very fast – in a few seconds it will form a yellow arch straddling the sky from horizon to horizon.'

'And what then?'

'The sky will go incandescent, but I doubt if our brains will have time to register the fact.'

'And then goodbye America. We should have zapped the bastards long ago.'

'There's a lot riding on your communications, General, and there's a thunderstorm on the way,' Webb said, pointing south. 'What if your system is struck by lightning?'

'We got two of everything in this man's army. Two backup systems, two generators' – the soldier's hand swept over the plateau – 'and the best communications men in the world, all here just so you and I can make a ten-second call.'

'Maybe the Russians know about this. Maybe they'll try to knock you out, for the sake of confusion. What about spetsnaz activity?'

Arkin laughed. 'Son, you're talking to Task Force One Sixty here, from Fort Bragg, Carolina. You want to know about behind-the-lines activity? Ask us, we wrote the book. The nearest Russians are a hundred and forty miles away in Mexico City and we got them monitored. We're a full brigade, with the blessing of the Mexican Government who are proving highly co-operative on account of they object to being vaporized.'

The Sun flickered briefly, and Webb felt a sudden downdraught. A helicopter whispered overhead and lowered itself into a clear space a few hundred yards away.

'You see that, son? That is a McDonnell-Douglas MH Sixty Pave Hawk. Quiet as a mouse on account of it's for infiltration. It has all-weather vision, seven-point-six-millimetre machine guns and two-point-seven-five-inch rockets. It can do a hundred and eighty-five miles an hour and fly to Mexico City and back twice without refuelling. We got two of them too.'

'General Arkin, you seem to have two of everything.'

'Believe it. Anything you need?' The general looked appraisingly at Webb, then produced a large cigar and proceeded to light up. About a hundred yards over his shoulder Judy was having the intricacies of a diesel power generator explained to her by about a dozen GIs.

'I'd like to get back. Can I commandeer a jeep?'

'Sure, and a driver. Tell 'em I said so.'

'There's an old joke, General Arkin. "Ladies and gentlemen, you are now flying in the first fully automated aircraft. There is no need to worry as nothing can go wrong nothing can go wrong nothing can go wrong . . ." '

The soldier laughed again, and blew a smoke ring. 'Boy, you sure are a worrier.'

Low, dark clouds overtook the jeep on the way back, blotting out the hot sun. Noordhof had stayed put, still having business with Arkin, and Webb had finally prised Judy away from her enthusiastic technical instructors before commandeering the little fat driver to take them back. The landscape, already primeval, took on a dull, alien look, as if it belonged to another planet. Out here, the brooding atmosphere was almost tangible.

The driver put on his headlights and assured them that Jesus begging your pardon ma'am we're in for Sumthin that's for Shore. He pulled over and stopped, the brakes squealing. The humidity was terrific and his short thick neck glistened with sweat. The silence was unnatural. He began to haul at the tarpaulin hurriedly, as if anxious to get away. Webb jumped out to help just as the first hailstone clanged noisily off the bonnet of the jeep, and they barely had time to scramble back in before an avalanche of hail poured down from the sky.

The first flickering blue etched a brilliant Christmas tree on Webb's retina, and a deep electrical crackle rumbled round and round the mountains. Judy cried with delight, and after that the powerful echoing *Boom!* of one thunderclap after another merged with the solid roar of hailstones on the jeep, while wind tore at the canopy and lightning strobed the landscape so that it looked as if they were part of a jerky old movie. Conversation was futile, but the driver managed a steady stream of profanity.

Once the bouncing and mud-sliding got out of hand; the driver had mistaken the road. He put on the brakes but the jeep started to slither and they found themselves in a terrifying, out-of-control slide taking them sideways down towards a gorge. They were about to jump for their lives when the jeep hit a rock about three feet from the edge and stopped with a bump. Webb had a nose-down view of a surging, yellow river forty feet below them, and a fallen tree wedged between black rocks.

Judy and Webb jumped out and heaved on the jeep while the driver, white-faced and shaking, reversed slowly on to the real road. Arcs of mud flew up from the spinning wheels and they all turned a sodden, yellowish brown and their fear released itself in hysterical laughter.

They eventually reached the real road, where the driver pushed his nose up to the windscreen and called up some Special Reserve language which took them safely back to Oaxtepec.

Judy stopped Webb as he was about to enter his room, mud and water forming spreading pools around them. She spoke softly. 'That was not an accident, Oliver.'

Webb stared. 'Come on Judy, the driver misjudged the road.'

'Warning posts had been pulled up. Recently. The sockets were still filling with water. The posts were probably thrown in the river. And there were footprints in the mud. Not ours.'

'How can that be? Nobody overtook us on the way back.'

Judy wiped water from her eyes. 'The helicopter could have.'

'The helicopter? Do you know what that implies?'

She put a finger to her mouth. 'Not so loud. We must talk.'

'Not in this state. Later.'

Webb had a shower, feeling badly rattled. It was too humid for comfort and he wrapped a towel around himself. He lay under a sheet, watching the rain pour down the French windows and listening to it hissing down on the grass, while the sky beyond crackled and flickered.

He fell into an exhausted, nightmarish sleep. When he

awoke it was dark. He dressed quickly and walked hurriedly along to the reception area. Apart from the lady at the desk, the big ranch-like place was deserted. Rain drummed down on its roof. She had taut curves and black hair pulled back in a ponytail, and a white frilly blouse with a low cleavage guarded by a golden crucifix. The receptionist smiled as Webb approached.

'Ah, Señor, there is a message for you. It came before the storm.' She handed over a fax:

WHEN IS A CUSTARD PIE NOT A CUSTARD PIE?
UNCLE WILLY LUMPARN.

The address was c/o a newsagent in Coolidge, Arizona.

'I'd like to make an international call, to London.'

'But the lines, they are all down.'

'Mexico City, then?' The woman picked up the receiver, listened and shrugged.

'Does this happen a lot?'

'Always, when we have thunder.'

'When will they be open again?'

'When the thunder is gone. Maybe.' Webb nodded and strolled thoughtfully on to the covered cloister.

Between Oaxtepec and Mexico City, there was only one road, and General Arkin's enthusiastic little story about the awesome gunships suddenly made a lot of sense. Suddenly everything was beginning to make sense.

Between two hundred million and a billion lives, he thought, depended on his making a telephone call. But he was isolated, in remote bandit country, and hemmed in by an elite task force.

And no way would they let him make that call.

Tinker Air Force Base,
T-9 Hours

Vice-President Adam McCulloch settled himself into the front left seat of the passenger capsule and looked at his watch, which he had not adjusted since leaving Washington DC in order to avoid troublesome subtractions. It was 22:15. A two-hour flight to Andrews, from where, he thought, he would board *Nightwatch* and disappear into the blue yonder. His head still reeling from the Presidential Counsellor's briefing, he wondered where *Nightwatch* could go to be safe from the blast from this flying mountain thing. Or maybe they would bundle him into the Presidential helicopter and take him to some subterranean command post.

Through the little oval window he watched the generals and the military specialists climbing the steps into the converted C-130, each man an inky black shadow rimmed with floodlight from a battery of harsh lamps. Admiral Tozer and his aide settled themselves down in the seats across the passageway. Tozer nodded amiably across at the Vice-President, who was beginning to think about the hip flask which his assistant carried for him in the Vice-Presidential briefcase.

The door below was closed, the big lever turned by a stocky man in Air Force uniform. A light came on overhead and the Vice-President clicked on his safety belt. A man was down below, waving from the runway. It was General Cannon. McCulloch unbuckled, got up quickly, climbed the three steps to the cockpit door and hauled it open. He tapped the co-pilot on the shoulder. 'Hold the plane. And get the door open.'

The door was pulled open and McCulloch shouted down over the roar of the giant engines. 'Ain't you s'pposed to be coming with us?'

The general cupped his hands over his mouth. 'I'm going on ahead. Things to do. Got a jet waiting as soon as you take off.'

McCulloch put his thumbs up and went back inside. He put his jacket into the overhead hold, buckled up again, and the door was again secured. One of the propellers started to race, and the transport swivelled around. Then all four engines revved up and the massive aircraft lumbered towards the runway, its wings vibrating as it moved.

⧗

Cannon watched dispassionately as the transport aircraft, lights strobing the dark, aligned itself on the runway. Then the sound of the four engines rose in a powerful crescendo, the huge propellers spun up to a grey blur, and the aircraft started forward. 'Goodbye, McCulloch,' Cannon said, as if to himself. Then he turned to his aide. 'Right, Sprott, let's get up there.'

⧗

The control tower personnel watched the Hercules transport hurtling along the runway and rising past them into the air, carrying the Vice-President, six generals, four admirals and a couple of dozen aides and experts. Fifteen minutes earlier two Cessna security planes, loaded with night vision and radar detectors, had probed a corridor fifty miles east-north-east of the base and reported in. It was a routine precaution against the possibility of terrorists with missiles. Now the

Cessnas were circling the airstrip, waiting to land, red lights flashing from their underbellies; otherwise the airspace was quiet. It was just a case of giving Cannon's jet the signal for takeoff.

McCulloch watched the control tower, an oasis of light in the black, pass below him, and then there was the flat panorama of rural Oklahoma, barely visible in the moonlight, sprinkled with lights from farms.

While the huge aircraft climbed, the Presidential Counsellor climbed up the steeply tilted passageway, leaning into the acceleration and holding a maroon briefcase. He tapped the Vice-President on the shoulder. McCulloch nodded and indicated the seat next to him, and the man virtually fell into it.

The Vice-President was looking puzzled. 'Bozo, maybe you cain tell me somethin'. If this hyar mountain from space hits us, what in hell's name am ah s'pposed to do about it?'

⧗

'Balls Niner, you are cleared for takeoff.'

'Balls Niner. Roger.' The pilot pushed forward the throttle and the aircraft whined quickly along the runway, climbed nimbly into the air and went into a shallow, banking turn. The pilot took it steeply up to forty thousand feet and levelled out.

⧗

McCulloch looked up from the briefing paper the Counsellor was explaining to him. He shook his head, as if to clear it, and glanced out of the window. A solitary car was moving along some solitary road. 'That's strange,' he said.

'Sir?'

'You got ahs, Bozo, take a look. We're kinda near the ground.'

The Counsellor glanced out and smiled indulgently. 'I don't think so, sir.'

⧗

The pilot exchanged some comments with the tower. He glanced back, looking worried, at General Cannon. 'Sir, there may be a problem.' Cannon moved up to the vacant co-pilot's seat.

The pilot said, 'Eagle Five aren't responding to Tinker.'

Cannon put headphones on. The pilot leaned over and pressed a switch. 'Who am I speaking to?'

'General Cannon?' a young voice replied anxiously. 'We can't raise the Vice-President's plane.'

'Explain, that, please.'

Another voice came on, older, carrying an edge of authority. 'General Cannon, Lieutenant Commander Watson here. Tower asked Eagle Five for their position three minutes ago. They gave us their ETA for Washington and a stand-by for present position, then, nothing. We've patched in a civil radar. They're on course and due to pass into Missouri at fifteen thousand feet in four minutes. But they're at twelve now and losing altitude. Make that eleven.'

'Have they given a mayday?'

'No sir, that's the problem. We're getting nothing. But at this rate they'll soon be in the grass.'

'Give us a vector and we'll head over.'

⧗

The Vice-President was staring intently out of the window. The Counsellor looked across the passageway. Admiral Tozer was reading a report and his aide was asleep, mouth open. The Counsellor leaned over McCulloch. The aircraft was ploughing solidly on, the huge propellers, illuminated by an underbelly light, were spinning reassuringly, and the muted roar of the engines was rock steady. But the light from the scattered farms below seemed brighter, and the C-13 had a definite backwards tilt. Quietly, he unbuckled and climbed the three steps to the cockpit door.

The first thing which the Counsellor noted was the sheer size of the cockpit, which looked not so much like a cockpit as the bridge of a ship. An array of multi-coloured lights moderated the gloom.

The second thing he noted was that the flight crew were either unconscious or dead. They were slumped forwards or sideways, held in their places by the safety harnesses.

The third thing to impinge on the Counsellor's senses, as he turned to shout, was a brief, overwhelming dizziness as he breathed the poisoned air, followed by a tremendous spasm in his carotid artery, and the sensation of floating down towards the cabin floor.

An automatic mechanism in the tail of the Hercules detected the nose-up configuration of the aircraft and applied a correction. In fact it overcorrected and the plane, manned by lifeless pilots, began to head towards the ground two miles below. The mechanism, detecting this, pulled the plane back up, and the cycle was repeated, more steeply this time. It was on a downward cycle when, pushing aside the corpses of the Counsellor, an Air Force captain and his own aide, Admiral Tozer took his turn in the poisoned air. The port wing of the aircraft touched a steeple, sending a spray of stonework and a thirty-foot fragment of wing spiralling over the town of Carthage, Missouri. He pulled on the joystick, his lungs bursting, and there was a moment of blackness. He seemed to be floating towards the cockpit ceiling. A cluster of orange lights approached rapidly from the sky above. Disoriented, it was a second before he recognized them as the lights of a town. The lights shot over his head and then there was more blackness.

⧗

Fox One circled the fierce orange fireball at a safe height.

Cars were beginning to stream out of Carthage towards the flames just beyond the town.

Cannon looked down without emotion at the fiercely blazing remains of the aircraft he had been scheduled to fly in. 'I've got a schedule to keep. Carry on to Andrews. And ask Tinker to patch me through to the White House. We'd better let them know the Vice-President has just met with a tragic accident.'

The Whirlpool

Webb walked along the covered walkway, tingling with nerves. To his left a small waterfall poured off the roof.

The call to his old friend had converted ninety-nine per cent certainty to one hundred per cent. Nemesis was a deception and a fraud. It was a monstrous conspiracy.

He thought he knew why, and the answer terrified him.

Webb's door was unlocked and the light was on. The sound of churning water came from within. Adjoining the bedroom was a long washroom with a vanity unit and a whirlpool tub. Judy was up to her chin in soap suds.

'Hi Oliver!' she waved a soapy hand as the astronomer passed.

Noordhof was straddling a heavy chair in the middle of the bedroom. His arms were folded on the back of the chair.

Webb kicked off his shoes and sat on the bed, at the pillow end, with his back to the ornate wooden headboard.

The churning stopped.

The colonel moved to the telephone, lifted the receiver and dialled. 'A-okay here. Ten minutes.' He returned to his chair, and folded his arms again on the back, only this time he was holding an ivory-handled Colt revolver.

'What happens in ten minutes?' Webb asked, his mouth dry.

Judy emerged from the bathroom in a white dressing

gown, her blonde hair wrapped in a towel. She sat down at a dressing table and started doing something to her eyelashes.

Noordhof said, 'There's nothing personal about this, Oliver. I like you. You're just a little man way out of your depth. But before the squad turns up, I want to know how much you know. Do you know *anything*?'

'I know that Nemesis doesn't exist.' Webb kept his eyes on Noordhof; but he sensed that Judy, at the dressing table, had suddenly frozen.

Noordhof showed surprise, then a flicker of admiration. 'How in Hell's name did you work that out, Doc?'

'Gut instinct.'

'Was that all?'

'Leclerc's death was the first real thing. I think André got there before me. He came to me worried but didn't live long enough to say why. I believe he'd worked out that the Russian deep space programme has a history incompatible with the multiple visits that would have been needed for a high-precision deflection. I also guessed that in the hours when he went missing, before he died, he realized it was a setup and he cleared out of Eagle Peak.'

'He tried. You were all under constant surveillance from the woods, Oliver. My people saw André, he saw them and took off in the cable car. Considering it had to look like an accident, I thought they showed real initiative at short notice.'

The soldier waved the pistol encouragingly, and Webb continued. 'Item Two was Vincenzo's manuscript. Quite a coincidence that I was translating it just before I was dragooned into your team.'

'You were slow on the uptake, Oliver. We thought we were going to have to ram the book down your throat.'

'I couldn't understand why, if *Phaenomenis* had real information in it, the Russians would draw attention to it by stealing it from under my nose. What was it with these thefts? I began to suspect that I was meant to get hold of Vincenzo's book, meant to identify Nemesis from it.'

Judy had finished with her eyelashes; she moved her chair next to Noordhof's.

The Colonel scratched his head thoughtfully with the barrel of the revolver. 'Good thinking, Oliver.'

'But a couple of things really got the alarm bells ringing.'

Noordhof waited politely.

'Karibisha. It's too big. As a killing machine, it's over-enthusiastic. At a million megatons it would set the whole world alight. The fireball would poison the atmosphere with nitric oxide. The Russians would have suffered tremendous damage along with the rest of the planet. They have first class people in this business and they would know that a Karibisha impact is global suicide.'

Noordhof tried to sound casual. 'So did you share your suspicions?'

'Wouldn't you like to know.'

Judy said, 'I doubt it. He wouldn't know who he could trust. Anyway, I believe he was out here before his suspicions crystallized.'

Webb kept talking. 'I knew I was being manipulated. I went along with it because I had to know who, and why. Somebody *wanted* me to get that book, *wanted* me to find an asteroid in it. Now who would want that, and why? I thought long and hard about that.'

'Is that it?' Noordhof asked.

'There were other things. No way could Karibisha have been seen that close to the sun with the claimed precision. The NASA report you showed me yesterday had to be a lie. After that, things have been falling into place quickly.'

The Colonel shrugged. 'Yeah, the NASA report was a rush job. You threw us by asking for it. All those phoney US Naval Observatory observations, Goldstone radar data and so on. What the heck, you gave us less than a day.'

'Why me, Mark? Why choose me for your team?'

'We chose you with care, Oliver. We knew you were set on finding some comet in old star charts. So we supplied you with an asteroid instead. We got rid of all copies of Vincenzo but one to raise its profile in your thick head and to make sure you didn't go making comparisons. You were supposed to be a pushover but you turn out to be a giant headache. I knew you were trouble when I saw you checking the switching circuit in the wheelhouse. You weren't supposed to do that, Ollie. And your damn robot telescope had us in a real panic. I had to stall you for a full day while we got a team to rig the circuitry. And still you saw through it.'

Judy had unwound the towel from her head and was rubbing her hair with it.

'I'm glad I was a pain but you still had me fooled up to a point. I thought you were trying to stop me identifying the asteroid. It was some time before it dawned on me what you were really about, that you were actually trying to stop me finding that there is no asteroid.'

Noordhof said, 'The manuscript thing was CIA false flag recruitment at its best. They used a real artist, the best Renaissance document forger in the business. Even the nib of the pen was right for the period in case somebody thought to use neutron activation analysis on the ink. Vincenzo's book, of course, was the genuine article. All this guy had to do was add the moving star. It had to match the orbit of a real Earth-grazer, it had to be good enough to fool the manuscript experts, and like you say we had to get rid of every copy except the one with the insert in case anyone thought to make comparisons.'

'I suppose he had an unfortunate accident?'

'The forger? Yeah, he swallowed hydrochloric acid, can you imagine?' Noordhof shook his head sorrowfully. 'Don't worry, Ollie, I'll be more humane. And you've still got five minutes.'

'I'm curious about one thing,' Webb said, to keep the conversation going. 'Where did my so-called assassin come into it?'

Noordhof looked glum. 'A sideshow that went wrong. I fixed it so you would have to buy the lousy manuscript. Uncle Sam was supposed to pay a couple of million bucks for it; half for me, half for my Italian counterpart – not that he'd have lived to collect it. But the guy gets greedy. He guesses the manuscript might be worth a lot more so he sells you a story about a contract on you and tries to jack up the payment for himself.'

A thunderclap shook the room and the light flickered briefly. Webb asked, 'What's the story when I don't report in at *T* equals Zero?'

'Another accident, of course.'

'You expect to get away with that?'

Noordhof's eyes glinted. 'Ollie, we expect to get off with a nuclear strike.'

Webb let it sink in slowly. 'I was afraid of that.'

'Yeah, and with a few thousand nukes pouring into the Evil Empire, who's going to notice some Brit going missing in Mexican bandit country?' The soldier glanced at his watch. 'By the way, you've got four minutes. How time flies when you're enjoying yourself.'

Now Judy was patting her legs dry with the towel. She looked around and dragged over a coffee table with a box of paper handkerchiefs and a heavy marble ashtray.

'Is the President in on this?' Webb asked.

'Poor Ollie, still on planet Mars. Things don't work that way, friend. If the Chief knew about it, how could he deny it? We're protecting him. Nemesis is the nuclear button, but if it's going to work the Chief has got to believe in it.'

'I think I can see how it works,' said Webb. 'The non-existent asteroid grazes the atmosphere. An electro-magnetic pulse shorts out your electronic systems and you lose all contact with the White House. So the President thinks the non-existent asteroid has hit, the shock wave is on the way in and America is on the way out. So he gets the nukes away while he can.'

'Got it in one,' Noordhof said with genuine admiration. 'We will have total control over everything coming into the President's War Room, wherever it is. There will be a perfect simulation of an asteroid strike, and when the smoke clears, it turns out it was all a grazing encounter like you say but tears of joy and ring out the bells, America is still with us and the Bear is dead.'

'And Karibisha?'

'We were going to shift perigee into the Gulf at the last minute but in this weather ain't nobody going to see it here, so why bother.'

'Post-encounter?'

'The Earth has deflected it back into the sunlight.'

'But the EMP! You can't take that over the whole of America.'

'No but while we're zapping Russia a couple of our nukes will go off prematurely and give us the real thing. Who's going to tell the difference?'

'And Russia just lets it all happen.'

'BMDO tell us they can handle the response. Provided we get in an overwhelming first strike, our losses will be acceptable. And if a couple of their nukes get through, we have even more EMP to add to the confusion.'

'Acceptable losses,' Webb said thoughtfully. 'I have one question.'

'Sure.' Noordhof waved the Colt invitingly. 'You still have three minutes.'

'Why? Zhirinovsky, right?'

'Zhirinovsky, right. We have an overwhelming nuclear advantage now. But he's catching up fast. In a few years we'll be back to the old parity only this time we'll be facing a raving lunatic and it's only a matter of time before he decides to zap us except that on account of some of us love our country we're trying to do something positive about that.'

'The guy is just bombast. And he probably won't survive the next Russian election.'

'Thank you, Oliver, you're full of surprises, I didn't know you included political analysis amongst your talents.'

Noordhof leaned forward to say more, waving the gun at Webb. There was a crackle and a tremendous bang, and the lights went out. Webb froze in the pitch black. When they came on a second later Noordhof's eyes were wide and he was holding the Colt at arm's length, and it was pointing straight at Webb's chest. The soldier re-folded his arms.

Webb glanced at Judy, but her eyes betrayed nothing. 'One last question.' He suppressed an urge to panic. 'What about the New Mexico scorpion here?'

Judy gave a cold smile.

'We needed an ear in the team. A scientist to make sure things went smoothly, to make sure y'all got the right ideas at the right times and nobody started getting any wrong ideas. Doctor Whaler came on the personal recommendation of right-thinking people at the highest level in the National Security program.'

'After all, Oliver, my job is to preserve peace through revolutionary and visionary means,' Judy said.

'Revolutionary? I don't think so. Nemesis is a hoary old ploy, a border incident created to justify war.'

She continued. 'But what a wonderful challenge! And morally justifiable, contrary to what you seem to think. What's the point of a short-lived peace if it's just an interlude before annihilation? What we're facing is a Ghengis Khan with nukes. The threat posed by his weapons of mass destruction is just too great. Surely Mark's philosophy is right? Seize the moment, and settle the issue for all time.'

'Skipping the tedious legalities,' Webb suggested. A thunderclap shook the French windows.

The Colonel said, 'You know the old saying, Ollie. My country, right or wrong.'

'Respect for the tedious legalities is what separates men from monkeys. And you from me.'

The soldier faked a smile. 'Negative, Oliver. The vital difference between us is that I'm holding the gun.' He glanced again at his watch. 'Anything else you want to know?'

'You're not going to shoot me.'

Noordhof raised an eyebrow.

Webb took a deep breath. He could hardly speak. 'I have protection.'

'Sure you have. I can't wait to hear about it.'

'A couple of hours ago I was sent a fax. '*When is a custard pie not a custard pie?*' The desk will confirm it.'

'He's right,' Judy said.

'Yeah, we know. It got us puzzled. It should have been intercepted but the stoopid girl . . .'

'It's signed by my Uncle Willy Lumparn, who doesn't exist,' Webb said, trying to put a confident edge into his voice. 'But look up Lumparn in an atlas. Check it out. It's a circular lake a few miles across in Aaland, which is a Baltic island, property of Finland.'

'Maybe you should get to the point quickly, Ollie. Your time's up.' Noordhof raised his gun, pointing it at Webb's chest. Uncertainty was flickering across the soldier's face.

The dark nozzle of the gun was filling Webb's universe. 'I'll keep it simple, Mark. Lumparn is an old impact crater. Custard pies get thrown as in Laurel and Hardy movies. The fax is asking me whether we're in a custard pie situation. They're asking me whether an asteroid is being thrown, whether Nemesis is real. I'm here to find out. You surely don't think I kept my suspicions to myself? And if I don't give the right coded reply at the right time, Project

Nemesis blows up in your face, your President doesn't launch and you try to find some part of the world where you can hide from the Mongoose squad, say like the bottom of the Marianas Trench. You're coming apart at the seams, Mark, you and your insane plot.'

Noordhof stood up, his composure gone. He paced up and down the room, glaring uncertainly at Webb. Then he kicked the chair aside and marched up to the astronomer, and pointed the Colt at his head, and Webb felt himself yielding to terror. Noordhof spoke harshly over his shoulder. 'You know this guy, Judy. What about it? Is he bluffing?'

She stood up and stretched, and gazed speculatively at Webb. 'Who sent the fax, Oliver?'

'Willy Shafer.'

Judy's smile broadened, while Noordhof gasped with relief before throwing back his head with laughter. 'I guess you haven't been reading the news, Oliver. Willy's beach house finally slid over the cliff, with poor Willy inside it. Oh man, either he sent the fax two days after we killed him or you sent it to yourself after you got here, for insurance. Great try, man, you had me scared to death!' And he laughed some more, but not enough to make the gun waver. Webb felt his face going white.

Judy yawned and approached the head of the bed. 'I'm truly sorry. It's not the way I'd have wanted it. But when you consider what's at stake there's really nothing else we can do. Mark, I'm tired and ready for sleep. Why wait for your death squad? When the next thunderclap comes, pull the trigger. Goodbye, Ollie.'

The Situation Room, T-1^h30^m

The telephone at the side of the President's bed in the First Lady's Bedroom never rang before 07:30, at which time a White House operator would wish him a good morning. The Nemesis emergency necessitated an earlier call, which had been arranged for 03:15.

But it was ringing now, an hour early, at 02:15.

'Mister President.'

It was Billy Quinn, the White House Chief of Staff.

Something in his voice. Grant, drugged with sleep, struggled up to a sitting position.

'Billy? I thought we were moving to Site R at four o'clock.'

'Sir, leave the residence immediately.'

'What?'

'Please don't argue. You may be in danger. Leave now, quickly.'

The line went dead.

Grant threw back the blankets and headed quickly through the President's Bedroom – in fact a study with a deep red decor – to the shower room. He dressed rapidly, dispensing with jacket and tie. Back through the red room. Toby, a mongrel saved by his children from death row many years ago, watched from the foot of the bed, ears pricked up. The President looked at his sleeping wife uncertainly, then left her alone. Toby followed him into the kitchen and climbed back into his basket with a sigh, and Grant headed out across the hall.

The elevator door was open. Jim Greenfield, his personal assistant, was waiting. They went down into the corridor where they were joined by a bleary-eyed Quinn. The three men marched without conversation along the corridor towards the Oval Office, Greenfield slightly ahead of the other two. They carried on past it, Greenfield, still leading the way, crossed over to the Executive Building and down some stairs. Light was shining under a door. It opened and a Secret Service man, his face lined with tension, seized the President by the arm and pulled him in, looking out before closing the door again. Hallam, Cresak and an army officer were standing at the head of the bowling alley. Hallam came over quickly.

'Thank God,' he said emotionally.

'What the hell?' Grant asked.

'Sir, Vice-President McCulloch is dead. We got the news only ten minutes ago.'

'How?'

'A plane crash near Carthage Missouri. He was on his way here from Tinker. Mister President, it may not have been an accident.'

Grant tried to assimilate the information. 'Not an accident? Is this Zhirinovsky?'

'No sir, your own people.'

The President felt a dull pain developing in his chest.

The army officer said, 'Sir, there's a conspiracy to remove you.'

'Who the hell are you?'

'Colonel Wallis. I'm in charge of the DCO Unit.'

'The new man. I've seen you around.'

'Mister President, General Hooper and Secretary Bellarmine see you as failing in your duty on the retaliation issue. They intend to remove you from office when the asteroid hits, unless you immediately order a counterstrike against the Russians.'

'Who else is involved in this?'

'I have no hard information on that.'

'Want to speculate?'

'It may involve all three service chiefs. There may be CIA involvement, probably going up to the Director.'

'Heilbron? Never.' Grant's voice was grim.

Quinn said, 'Chief, they've isolated you. With McCulloch out of the way . . .'

'I carry the final authority.'

Quinn continued: 'They could have sold Wallis the wrong story as insurance in case he crossed them. I just don't know what their real tactics are.'

The President turned again to Wallis. 'When did you learn about this?'

'When they asked me to join them. A month ago.'

'You've been sitting on this for a month?'

'I said I'd join them.'

'You played them along?'

'No, sir. I thought they were doing the right thing.'

'But you had a last-minute change of heart.'

'Yes, sir. I think maybe I should be shot.'

Grant surprised Wallis: 'Don't worry about it, son.' He turned to his National Security Adviser, whose mouth had developed a nervous twitch. 'Arnold, you got something to say?'

'Only that you can't risk going back to your quarters.'

Grant rubbed his face with his hands. 'Billy, in the last resort it may come down to firepower. Have some standing by discreetly. Arnold, get over to the Sit Room and keep your mouth shut.' Grant looked at his watch. He picked up a bowling ball and took aim at the distant pins.

Hallam said, 'Sir, Nemesis arrives in five hours.'

The President sent the ball skimming along the wooden alley. 'Hey, didn't Francis Drake do this before the Spanish Armada?'

⧗

Bellarmine was pacing agitatedly up and down in the corridor just outside the Situation Room as Grant approached. His face was white and he was unconsciously tensing his mouth. He closed his eyes with relief when the President appeared.

'Jesus Christ, sir, where have you been? We turned the Cottage inside out looking for you. Vice-President McCulloch was killed in an air crash an hour and a half ago.'

'I know. What about his replacement?'

'Caroline Craig's on her way in from Seattle, sir. They're briefing her in-flight, but she won't get here in time.'

'Okay, brief me. And Nathan, this is a good time to keep calm.'

A soldier emerged smartly from the Situation Room, carrying a wad of paper. 'Mister President, we have reports of further tank and troop movements into Slovakia. They're massing on the Czech side of the Black Forest.'

'Okay.'

Another aide approached. 'Sir.'

'Well?' said Grant roughly.

'The Pentagon say the hotline is dead. They can't get through to the Kremlin.'

'Watch your feet, sir,' a technician warned as President Grant picked his way over a mass of cables. Technicians bustled around, none of them paying much attention to the entry of the Chief. Foggy Wallis approached. The two men exchanged looks.

'This way, Mister President. Your team's all here. Watch your head.' The President ducked his head and they went through an open door, following the route of more cables stretching across the floor like long shiny black snakes. The room was brilliantly lit with studio lights. About a dozen men, some in uniform, were seated around the big central table. They stood up as the President entered.

Grant's place at the table had two telephones, red and black, and two books, one red and one black. He stared dully at the books, and sat down in the chair with as much enthusiasm as a man about to be electrocuted. The curtains had been pulled back from the end wall and the large screen was exposed, with speakers at either side of it. The walnut panelling had been removed from the walls to reveal banks of television screens. Desks and terminals had been crammed into the little room since he had last used it two days ago, and it now looked like a miniaturized version of a Star Trek set. About a dozen men and women, some in uniform, stared at television screens. Two men, shirt sleeves rolled up, stood in a far corner of the room, one with a video camera, the other holding a boom with a microphone, recording for whatever posterity there was going to be.

The room was cramped and stuffy. It was also claustrophobic.

'How long to impact?' Grant asked.

'Ninety-five minutes,' said Hooper. 'Mister President, where have you been?'

The President sat down. He turned to Hooper. 'Silo activity?'

'We wouldn't expect to see anything until their missiles take off,' said Hooper. 'We got a couple of Cobras out from Shemya to look at the Kamchatka area an hour ago. The pilots report they've been blinded with laser beams. We're trying to talk them back in.'

Grant turned to Cresak. 'What's the diplomatic situation?'

'The Security Council are calling an emergency meeting in a couple of hours. Ambassador Thorp went into the Kremlin three hours ago and we haven't heard from him since.'

'What does Kolkov have to say?'

Cresak shot Hooper a baleful look. 'He's upstairs now.

He accuses us of gearing up for a first strike. He says his people are just positioning themselves for defence.'

'This from the men who gave us Nemesis,' Bellarmine said. 'The creep, the hypocritical creep.'

A woman in Air Force uniform approached the President. Grant looked at her. 'Falcon are downgrading the GPS's, Mister President.'

The global positioning satellites could be used by an enemy in a precision attack on American targets. The standing plan was to downgrade them in the event of a threat. Thousands of Jumbo jets, aloft at any one time, depended on them for navigation. But around the world, the last Jumbo jets were now landing; nothing would take to the air until Karibisha had come and gone. The downgrading, however, would send an unmistakably dangerous message to the other side.

Grant nodded.

'Mister President, Silk Purse is airborne in Europe. We need the British Prime Minister's permission to use our F1 11s at the English bases. Their Minister of Defence is stalling us. Sir, we're running out of time for a decision. We have to release the permissive action links.'

'No way.'

'Sir.' Hooper opened a handbook at a book-marked page. He was attempting a matter-of-fact, legalistic tone. 'I refer you to JSOP/81-N. Our destruction is imminent, and you must now therefore proceed to State Scarlet. If our B 2s are going to beat the blast from the asteroid they have to get out over the polar cap now.'

'Past their failsafes? Sam, the decision to nuke stays with me, not with a bunch of one-star generals. We don't even know if the asteroid will hit.'

'We do, however, know that the use of Nemesis as a weapon is an act of war. It is our right and duty to respond to that act of war. Mister President, I want some cold logic on this. Our duty is to serve the interests of the American people. If we're hit, we'll be too shattered to defend ourselves against any subsequent hostilities. American interests are best served by destroying future potential enemies while we can. That's why we gave you only the Grand Slam targeting option.'

'So much for flexible response, Sam.'

'Grand Slam is the only option that preserves some sort of future for our children.'

The President turned to Wallis. 'Colonel, give me a rundown on our communication links.'

'We have three independent links from the ground station at the Xochicalco epicentre. One by satellite, one by shortwave radio, one a direct cable link. The cable link we had to patch in to the Mexican commercial land lines. We've got some of the best communications men in the army on site. The whole thing is protected by Special Operations Command. A couple of MH6 gunships in case of any monkey business.'

'Sir,' a soldier interrupted, 'the *Carl Vincent* has reached its co-ordinates. They're getting Phantoms aloft now.'

Wallis said, 'Apart from Xochicalco, sir, we have the Navy about a thousand kilometres off the Atlantic seaboard. The asteroid will be coming from sunward but it's pre-dawn out there and the Naval Observatory tell us a visual sighting should be possible and the thing should pass right over their heads. There's an Atlantic storm out there, lots of low cloud and rain. Xochicalco's washed out but communications aren't affected.'

'I must know on the instant if we have a hit or a miss.'

'A French Spot satellite will be over central Mexico at the critical moment. If Nemesis hits we'll see plenty. The pictures are being relayed in from Goddard and we'll see them as they arrive.'

'Where do I press the button?' the President asked calmly.

'The helicopter is standing by. You'll be at Raven Rock

in less than fifteen minutes. MYSTIC is activated. It just needs your word.'

'Nothing from the Kremlin?' Grant asked Wallis.

The soldier shook his head.

'Okay, let's head for the Rock.'

The Hacienda

Webb was shaking so much he could not put his feet in his shoes. Judy had slipped back to her room to dress, and Noordhof was raising himself to his knees, groaning, holding his ear while bright pink blood oozed between his fingers. The marble ashtray lay on the floor, split in two after Judy's powerful blow. The gun was on the bed beside Webb, within arm's length.

Noordhof struggled up to a sitting position on the bed. He was clearly dazed and in great pain.

The net curtain billowed briefly as Judy came back, dressed in black trousers and sweater. She slid the glass door closed. She looked dispassionately at Noordhof and said 'Kill him.'

The lights failed again. A sharp cry of pain, male or female, came from the pitch black. Webb cursed and flopped down on the bed, groping for the gun. There was a crash of glass at the instant he felt its cold metal barrel. Wind and rain were suddenly gusting in the room. He sprinted towards the window and collided bodily with Judy. She fell back with a gasp and then he was running over broken glass in his socks. A flash of lightning, a brilliant celestial tree momentarily implanting on his retina; a vision of Noordhof frantically trying to shake off a net curtain. Webb rushed forwards, firing into the darkness. He had never used a gun and the first round jerked his wrist painfully. In the weapon's flashes

441

Noordhof appeared as a series of stills, snapshots of a man weaving and turning. Then the soldier had fallen face down about fifty yards ahead, and the gun was clicking empty, and there was only rain, and wind, and blackness.

'Oliver!'

'Over here! I think I've killed him.'

'Noordhof's squad is on the way. We must run.'

Webb sprinted back into the room. 'I need a telephone!' he shouted, forcing his bleeding feet into shoes.

'A telephone? Where?'

'In the hacienda. At the reception desk.'

'You madman!' Judy shouted in reply. A flicker of light threw her face into harsh relief, revealing wild eyes and water streaming down her sodden hair: a witch from *Macbeth*.

'I have no choice.'

'They'll cut you off with bullets.'

'No time to discuss it. Look, we'll go on a wide circle round the back and approach the ranch from the front. That way we don't bump into the squad. Do you know cars?'

'I've been around them since I was fourteen.'

'So steal one. Bring it round to the front.'

'Ollie, enter the hacienda and you're dead.'

'I have to try. Go!'

They sprinted across the sodden ground, away from the ranch, and took a wide curve towards the front, risking exposure from a single flash of light; but for the moment there was only a distant flickering on the horizon. They made for the dark, squat outline of a small building. It turned out to be a football shelter and they arrived, gasping, just as a thunderbolt lit up the landscape and hammered on the ground. They stood at the back, puffing, and looked out through a waterfall streaming down from the corrugated roof. A dull glow came from the hacienda entrance.

'I don't think we were seen,' Judy said breathlessly.

'Two red lights, about thirty yards to the left of the entrance.'

'Soldiers smoking. I think I see a jeep.'

'Don't even think about it. It's hardly twenty yards from them.'

'There are three wires behind the steering column. Two must be joined together. When you touch them with the third, the engine starts.' The sky flashed blue and there was an instantaneous glimpse of three caped soldiers huddled under a clump of trees. Three jeeps were parked not far from them. But the thunderbolt had shown something new, a tableau of four soldiers striding purposefully along the covered verandah, in the direction of the rooms.

'Oliver,' she said quietly, 'Your death squad.'

Webb felt the old scrotum contraction, and this time his scalp shrank with it. He said, 'A jeep, front entrance, ninety seconds,' and ran into the dark. At the hacienda, he strolled casually out of the shadows, an eccentric foreigner walking in the rain, sodden. Dice were clattering on the hard wooden floor. Half a dozen GIs were shouting incantations and exchanging paper money. At the far end, Arkle and a few officers were lounging in armchairs, drinking coffee. Arkle looked up startled, but recovered quickly and gave Webb a wave. He returned it, casually, wiping wet hair back from his eyes. A longfaced, weary corporal at the desk was reading *Playboy*.

'Are the lines open yet?' Webb asked.

'Sure. Where do you want?'

It would be the early hours in London. Webb gave him the Astronomer Royal's ex-directory number. The corporal started to dial. The squat, bullet-headed sergeant left the game and wandered over.

'Hi Doc,' he said, with exaggerated casualness. 'Problem?'

'Not really.' Don't give him a handle. Arkle had left the

443

officers and was striding over. Webb was light-headed and sweating, and Arkle's face told him what he had feared: that he would never make the call.

'Ringing for you sir,' the corporal said, holding out the receiver.

Arkle reached them. The sergeant stayed within arm's length.

'Hi Doc, you're up early,' the general said.

Webb took the receiver. 'Couldn't sleep with all the noise.'

The Astronomer Royal, sounding tired, said: 'Waterstone-Clarke.'

Arkle killed the connection, a chubby finger going down on the button. 'Can't let you make the call, Doc. Security.'

'Security?'

'That's right. Security.'

The sergeant sensed an atmosphere, stepped back nervously.

'First I've heard of it, General. I need to speak to my London contact.'

'This is an open line, son. We don't know who could be listening in. London contacts are out until Nemesis has passed.'

Webb nodded, mentally setting a new priority: *Get out of this alive.*

'By the way,' Arkle added, 'Colonel Noordhof's been looking for you.'

'I'll keep an eye out for him,' Webb said, moving towards the stairs.

'He'll be along. Join us for coffee.'

'Thanks, but I need to dry out. I'll just get to my room.'

'I insist,' said Arkle.

'Okay.' Moving to the stairs. 'Join you in a minute.'

'I reckon you're not hearing too good, son. Join us now.'

'Sure. I'll join you now in a moment.'

Games with words. The sergeant glances uncertainly between them, his lips twitching. A few yards away the GIs play their own esoteric word game as the dice clatter along the floor: don't come, baby's new socks, it's a natural. Arkle stands, baffled and tightlipped. Slowly up the wooden stairs. Slowly along the short stretch to the door. Almost there. Don't run, for God's sake don't run. Slowly open the door. Turn to Arkle: a final wave. Casual, unhurried. Don't blow it now; don't run.

On to the verandah. Rain teeming down. Somebody shouting. A jeep without lights roaring up. From behind, Webb senses the ranch door opening. Shadowy figures rushing along the verandah, boots clattering on stone flagons. Another shout, this time from Arkle. The loud assertiveness of command.

'Stop them!'

Webb takes a running jump into the vehicle. Somebody seizes him by the collar. Webb punches him hard on the nose and cries out with the unexpected pain in his knuckles, but the sergeant staggers back, covering his face with his hands.

'Hit the boards!' Webb yells.

She hits them.

⧗

The pilot sprinted the hundred yards from the Portakabin to the helicopter, splashing through puddles and bent double against the rain. He quickly climbed in, threw off his baseball cap, put on his headphones and went through the check routine at superhuman speed. As the rotor started to chop he checked the radar; the other ship was ten miles to the south, six hundred feet above ground and following the prearranged perimeter patrol. There was a brief exchange on the radio. The pilot pulled on the collective and the gunship rose above the pyramids and the paraboloids. From above, the whole complex was lit up like some bizarre Alcatraz. He did a hard banking turn over the ancient city, switched on the thermal imager and followed the road north.

Ten minutes later he picked up the lights of Xochicalco, every detail of the ranch complex visible, pale and ghostly, like a snowscene tinged with green. The roof of the main building glowed as if aflame. He drifted over the complex and picked out Noordhof's bungalow. A man was standing outside it and the pilot switched on the Night Sun as he descended, to be seen.

Noordhof ran unsteadily towards the gunship, like a drunk man. He was holding the side of his head. The pilot leaned over and opened the side door. The Colonel buckled himself in; blood was oozing out of a three-inch gash in front of his ear.

'You should get that seen to, sir.'

'The road to Mexico City. They've got a jeep.'

The gunship soared rapidly into the air.

'How much of a start, sir?'

'Christ knows.' Noordhof's words were coming out strained; maybe concussion, the pilot thought, or maybe pain, or maybe the giant bruise at the side of the soldier's jaw made speech difficult. 'I was out maybe ten minutes. It took you ten to get here. I guess they have a twenty-minute start.'

'No problem, sir. All we have to do is follow the road. We'll have them in five.'

⧗

'We have to get off the road!' Webb yelled above the screaming engine. Judy, hunched forward like a short-sighted old woman, ignored him. Swathes of rain streamed across the cone of the headlights. The jeep's speedometer was hovering at around eighty miles an hour independently of the curves in the stormswept road. He tried again, putting his wet face close to hers and holding grimly on to the dashboard. 'The helicopter at Oaxtepec – it has thermal imaging. All he has to do is follow the road. Can you hear me, you crazy witch? Even if you switch off your lights the heat from your exhaust will show up like a whore in church.'

'You have a map, stupid? Where do we leave the road?'

'Another ten minutes on it and we're dead. Watch that corner. Oh My God. Why did you wait until the last second to move on Noordhof? You had me worried.'

'A New Mexico scorpion, am I? Anyway, how did you know I wasn't on Noordhof's side?'

Another glistening corner rushed up and Webb grabbed her arm to stay on. Arcs of mud and water shot past his head. The jeep hammered into a deep pothole and he was momentarily in free-fall. 'That slide into the gorge. If you were in with them you wouldn't have told me it was a murder attempt. Anyway, if God had meant you to fool me he'd have given you brains.'

'And the pigs thought I was expendable,' she shouted furiously.

'They recruited you and . . .'

'. . . and I went along with them to see how deep it went. Like you, Oliver, I didn't know who I could trust.'

'Get off the road in five minutes or we're dead . . .'

'The pigs, the lying, treacherous pigs!'

'. . . and half the planet with us!'

Mexico, the Last Hour

They flew six hundred feet high in pitch black, the machine bucketing in the wind, but in the infrared the road below was easily traced even through the torrential rain.

A brilliant green spot appeared at the top of the HUD and drifted slowly down. The pilot grunted in satisfaction. 'Contact. Two miles ahead.'

Noordhof peered through the driving rain into the blackness ahead. He thought he saw a hazy light but it disappeared. In a second it reappeared, more strongly now, at first seeming to move unphysically fast over the ground before it resolved itself into the reflection of headlights sweeping from side to side as the driver manoeuvred round corners.

'I see them,' said Noordhof. Then: 'Take them out.'

'Sir?'

'You having problems with your hearing, Mister?'

'Sir, is that an authorized order? This is Mexican territory. We're not at war with Mexico, sir.'

'Ay-ffirmative it's legal,' Noordhof lied. 'Ay-ffirmative you're in Mexico. And if you question my orders again ay-ffirmative I'll stick your head up your ass.'

The pilot pulled the collective up and the gunship soared into the clouds, stabilizing at two thousand feet. The storm played with the machine like a child with a rattle. They flew blind, the infrared increasingly useless against the water and the pilot increasingly nervous about mountains. Finally he lost his nerve and dropped the machine below the cloud base. Noordhof looked behind; they were well past the headlights.

The pilot took the machine on for a minute and then turned it round, pushing the stick forward to decrease the lift, and settled gently down to the road, facing back towards a corner. He loaded a single rocket, pressed a key to arm it, and put his thumb over the fire button, with his free hand ready to switch on the searchlight when the jeep appeared. At this range there would be no need for a guidance mode: it was just switch on, take a second to line up and then, fried gringo.

Light scattered off a stony field. The pilot tensed. The headlights came into view about three hundred yards away. He began to press his thumb against the firing button, switched on the searchlight, and the wet bodywork of a melon truck glistened brilliantly in the beam. With a single curse the pilot switched off the light and soared away, leaving the driver standing on the brakes and frantically crossing himself.

They flew on for another five minutes, following the curving road.

'Okay,' Noordhof finally said. 'So they're cute. They've left the road.'

'Where, sir? It's all mountains.'

'They ain't on the road. So they must be off it.'

'I'll go back and do a to-and-fro sweep, sir.'

'Just don't hit any mountains.'

It seemed incredible, but the weather was getting worse, the sheer mass of water cutting down transmission through the normally optically thin infrared window and degrading the imager's range. The radar was a mass of snow. He pulled the stick to the left, veering off the road, and began to fly low, in narrowly spaced sweeps about five miles wide. He began to wonder if maybe they weren't so crazy after all.

⧗

Webb sat awkwardly on a melon and put his back up against a thin metal girder entwined with ropes, spreading his legs wide to maximize lateral stability. He could see Judy in silhouette, jammed in a corner, knees almost round her ears.

He looked at his watch, and could just make out 4.59 a.m. on the luminous dial. It might take the pilot half an hour to find the empty jeep and check out the surrounding countryside before he cottoned on. It might be more, and it might be less.

Judy and the driver had talked in Spanish and Webb understood there was a village with a telephone which they said worked quite often. If Julio's lazy son had done a proper job on the carburettor they would be there in maybe half an hour, otherwise who could say? From there we could phone a garage for a repair. He could recommend his cousin Miguel, who would not object to being wakened for gringo business.

But if the rain stops, Webb thought, the pilot's IR range will expand and he'll find the jeep in minutes. The hammering of the rain on the tarpaulin was deafening and brought joy to Webb's heart; the occasional faltering of the engine, however, was having the opposite effect.

⧗

He hadn't expected it would be at the bottom of a gorge and he almost missed the faint, fuzzy blob on the imager. He dropped to a hundred metres above the ground, hovering over the spot. He switched on the Night Sun and a cone of driving rain swept through the brilliant beam.

The jeep was lying on its side, three quarters immersed in black surging water. The gorge was about thirty feet deep and the ground on either side sloped steeply upwards. He lowered the gunship as far as he dared, the blades whipping the water below into a spray.

'No sir!' he shouted but it was too late, Noordhof had opened a door and leapt into space. The Colonel disappeared under the water with a splash and immediately reappeared, drifting rapidly towards the jeep. He grabbed at it in passing and held on firmly with both hands, his face more under the water than above it. Then he vanished. The pilot, alarmed, took the gunship down until the runners were almost touching the water. The blades were hardly a foot from either side of the gorge. In the confined space, the roar from the quiet gunship was painful.

Noordhof re-emerged, gasping, and went under again. He stayed under. Unthinkingly, the pilot began to hold his breath. He was almost panicking when Noordhof appeared once again, his hands reaching up for a runner. The Colonel missed and the current immediately swept him downriver, into the blackness beyond the light. The pilot took the machine along, picked up a bobbing head and dipped the runner into the water, moving with the stream. Noordhof grabbed the runner and this time heaved himself on to it. The pilot took the machine out of the gorge and lowered it on to flat ground. Noordhof, water pouring off him, heaved himself into the gunship.

'The melon truck!'

Angrily, the pilot jerked open the throttle, tilted the machine and flew along the line of the road.

Impact

Around five fifteen the hammering of the rain on the canvas roof began to ease, and by five forty-five the storm had passed. The sky was still black except to the east where, looking through a cut in the tarpaulin, Webb could see the horizon outlined against the sky. The countryside was flatter here, and there were houses dotted around amongst the fields. Once or twice they passed by a cluster of adobe houses, and once a couple of trucks roared past, going in the opposite direction. At this latitude, Webb reckoned, it would be light in another ten or fifteen minutes.

The engine faltered, picked up for a few hundred yards, and then died. The truck slowed down and bumped to a halt, its brakes squealing. The driver, his elderly face decorated with a grey moustache, tapped at the glass and shouted something derogatory about his son-in-law Julio. Judy struggled over melons and there was a noisy exchange of conversation in Spanish. She clambered back. 'This happens after a lot of wet. The ignition goes. He says to wait until the engine heat dries out the electrics.'

Webb pulled the canvas aside and they jumped out. The driver stepped down from his cab and lit a cigarette, leaning against the door.

They were in rough, open terrain, strewn with boulders and cacti. There were no habitations.

'Oliver, there is no place to hide.'

Webb looked at his watch. He said, quietly, 'The time for hiding is over, Judy. Either I make contact and expose Nemesis as a fraud, or the Americans start launching nuclear weapons.'

'God in Heaven. How much time have we left?'

'Twenty-four minutes.'

'I'll say a little prayer. But Oliver . . .'

'Yes?'

'What if the pilot has found the jeep?'

'We did the best we could.'

Judy stepped smartly over to the driver and engaged in a short conversation. She came back and said, 'There's a little town ahead, about twenty minutes' drive. The driver will finish his cigarette and try the engine.'

'Do you have any money?'

'I'll speak nicely to him.' There was more animated chatter and Judy returned with a handful of coins. Webb waved his thanks to the driver, who nodded cheerfully, threw away his stub and pulled himself into his cab. Webb and Judy climbed back in. The driver left the cab again, stretched and lit another cigarette. Then he relieved himself noisily at the roadside, into a puddle. Then he climbed aboard once more. Then he tried to find a radio channel, muttering loudly as he scanned the airwaves. Then he gave up, and tried the ignition.

⧗

Luck was smiling on the pilot. As the rain eased the range of his imager extended. He increased altitude. To the right, flecks of red were appearing on the horizon; in a few minutes it would be light. He sensed that the chase was nearing its climax. He kept up the full throttle, tilting the machine forwards for maximum speed.

⧗

'Can't you get him to go any faster?'

'This is Mexico. If I ask him, he'll stop to talk about it. We're only minutes away.'

Webb scrabbled to the back of the truck and pulled the flapping tarpaulin aside. The sky was grey, with lurid red and black stripes to the east. Already the air was warm. He leaned out and looked in the direction of motion of the truck. They were passing between a few houses; and there was a town, about two miles ahead.

'There's a town about four minutes ahead. We could just make it.' Webb paused, suddenly aware that the lady's attention was elsewhere.

'Oliver, behind you.'

⏳

The pilot switched off the imager. The occasional house, large cacti, even brushwood could all be made out.

He saw the dust trail before he saw the truck itself. It was the same truck; the same grey, the same flapping tarpaulin cover. It was about two miles from a small town, dead ahead. He smiled primly, made a small course correction with the rudder, and pushed the stick forward in its collective mode. He began to lose altitude, moving directly towards the lumbering vehicle.

⏳

'When the driver slows, jump and run for cover.'

'He'll kill you, Oliver. You will die.'

'The light's not perfect. I'm hoping he'll hit the truck,' Webb said. The helicopter was a mile away, cruising slowly in; the pilot, no longer in a hurry, was savouring the moment.

'But the old man . . .'

'. . . has had it. I need my phone call.'

The melon truck began to slow. Webb looked round. Narrow crossroads ahead. A row of adobe houses, brightly painted. A green-painted cantina, shuttered, at the corner. Thirty yards from it, the entrance to a street.

The truck slowed to thirty-five miles an hour ... thirty ... twenty-five ...

'What are you doing?' Webb shouted. 'You have to jump!' But she stood, legs askance, scowling.

'Judy, come on. I have to go!'

'Then go! I'll distract the pilot and make him think we are still inside. Jump, Oliver, jump! You'll remember me?'

Webb left her to die. He leapt out of the truck, fell with a thump and rolled breathlessly on compacted earth, clutching the money. He jumped up, his ribs in pain, and dashed for the street. He sprinted round the corner and along the road. It was lined with small shops, closed and shuttered. There was no telephone booth. He hurled himself along the street.

He felt the wind from the rotor before he heard its whispering chop-chop. He glanced behind and dived to the ground as the dark gunship swooped past. He got up and ran the way he had just come. The machine tilted and flew backwards. Its rear rotor scythed the ground to and fro, whipping up dust. Terrified, Webb weaved and dived flat. The whirling vertical blades passed inches from his skull. The force of the wind was like a blow on the face, and then there was unbelievable pain, a frightful slash in his thigh and blood spurting from a ripped trouser leg. He saw a narrow lane, crawled underneath the machine and staggered towards it, trying not to faint. There was a tremendous bang and a wave of heat, and he was floating through the air, and then a pile of polythene bags and boxes was rushing up from the ground and he was rolling and tumbling amongst kitchen rubbish. Dazed, he hauled himself up. The street he had just left was a mass of fierce yellow flame. He felt as if his face was in an oven. There was a fearful pain in the back of his head.

He ran limping along the lane and took off along another one, mercifully away from the heat, and then another: he was in a warren of narrow streets, cluttered with tables and chairs, with washing strung overhead. A thin mongrel barked excitedly at him as he passed. A pall of black smoke was drifting over the rooftops. His watch said three minutes to Nemesis and only will power lay between him and a faint. His leg was warm and sticky but he didn't dare to look at it.

The lane ended and there was a wide open square. A few people were running towards the source of the smoke. There was a white church, and a cantina, and outside it a telephone booth. He looked at the sky. There was no sign of the gunship. He ran across the square to the phone booth. He grabbed the receiver, not knowing what sounds to expect; he stared stupidly at the coins, trying to match them with the slots, dropped them, picked them up, shoved in a few which seemed to fit, and started to dial the international number with violently trembling hands.

The black gunship appeared over the rooftops. There was a little dust storm as the pilot lowered himself into the square. Webb wondered if he would use the machine guns or the rockets. A telephone was ringing, a familiar sound, a final reminder of home in this distant and alien land.

The pilot was hovering now, about thirty yards away and six feet above the road, in the middle of the ochre dust. He was lining up in leisurely fashion, chewing gum. Noordhof, alive and well, seemed to be urging him on. Webb sensed that the pilot would use a rocket and wondered what his death would be like.

'Northumberland House,' said a well-bred female voice. The melon truck shot into view. The pilot, startled, tried to rise up, but the roof of the truck caught one of the runners and the gunship flipped over on to its back. Shreds of tarpaulin and melon showered into the sky.

'Ah, Tods Murray, please. This is Oliver Webb calling from Mexico.' Webb watched hypnotized as a melon approached from nowhere. It smashed into a corner of the phone booth, turning into a red mushy pulp and spraying shards of glass into Webb's face. A helicopter blade was boomeranging high, high in the air. Its course was erratic and Webb saw it turn lazily and start to fall towards the phone booth. The truck stopped. Judy was out and running for her life, hair streaming behind her.

'Trying to connect you.'

There was a sudden *Whoosh!* and a ball of flame enveloped the truck; the blade had turned over and was picking up speed, plunging directly towards the booth. Webb dived out just as the blade sliced through it. Something sliced deep into his already injured thigh and he found himself lying on the dusty ground crying with pain. There was the smell of burning fuel and a pool of flame was spreading around from the remains of the gunship. Globules of blazing plastic were dripping down to the ground and the cockpit was filling with black smoke. The pilot seemed to be unconscious; Noordhof was upside down in his goldfish bowl, kicking desperately at a door with both feet.

The phone booth was a mangled wreck of glass and plastic, but the receiver was on the ground.

It still had its wire. Was it possible?

There was a surge of flame and heat, too hot to endure; one of Webb's eyes was closing up with blood; machine gun bullets were beginning to bang like firecrackers; a pool of blue flame was spreading out from the machine. Webb crawled towards the receiver, willing himself not to faint. He put his ear to it. Big red ants were scurrying along in the dust, fleeing from the approaching flames. The telephone receiver was crackling. From the gunship came the ferocious roar of a missile exhaust rising in an unpredictable crescendo.

'Webb! Where the hell have you been? And what's that noise? Are you at a carnival or something?'

⧗

In a bunker deep under a granite mountain, a handful of ordinary men were deciding the fate and future of life on the planet, in conditions of buckling emotional stress which guaranteed preconception, information overload, groupthink, hallucination, delusion, cognitive distortion and old-fashioned stupidity.

The Secretary of Defense stood up. 'Everybody stand away from the door,' he said loudly. 'Mister President, gentlemen.' There was a stupefied silence, as if someone had pulled the pin of a grenade. Admiral Mitchell rose angrily but Grant waved him back down. Only Bellarmine and Grant remained standing, facing each other across the table.

'Mister President, sir. You are respectfully relieved of your post as Chief Executive and as Commander-in-Chief of the armed forces of the United States of America. This action is taken by myself and the Joint Chiefs of Staff. As of this moment General Hooper will direct military operations with myself as acting president. We have the gold codes.'

Grant's face was grey. 'The fairies run away with your brain, Nathan?'

'THREE MINUTES,' came from the next room.

'A detachment will be along to escort you from here in a few moments, sir. Meantime the Rock and the Communications Personnel are under our control, and we have a lot to do.'

'You're under arrest, Bellarmine. Sit down.'

The National Security Adviser rose, white-faced and trembling. He virtually snarled: 'If I had a gun I would shoot you. What is your authority for this outrage?'

A telephone near the back of the room rang and kept on

ringing, cutting into the hush which had gradually blan-
keted the room as a stunned awareness of what was
happening had spread. Someone lifted the phone and was
talking urgently into it. Then the corporal was saying 'Ah,
it's the *Carl Vincent*'.

'TWO MINUTES.'

'I'll take it,' snapped Bellarmine.

'No. Put it through to the table,' said the President
grimly. The corporal froze, as suddenly and completely as
if he had turned to stone.

'Your authority?' Cresak barked.

'The Twenty-fifth. The President is refusing to defend
this country when under mortal attack. He is failing to
fulfil his Oath of Office and has therefore disqualified
himself from holding that office.'

'You can't make that judgement,' the Admiral snapped.
'This is plain treason.'

'We're zapped in two minutes and you want to assemble
the Senate?'

'The *Carl Vincent*!' the corporal said, his voice coming
out in a strangulated croak.

'I said give it here,' said Bellarmine, sweating. There
was the brief, angry chatter of a gun. A cry of pain came
from the other side of the door. Then there was a thump,
and the sound of someone slithering down it.

'You heard me, soldier,' Grant snapped. 'Through to the
table, now!'

'ONE MINUTE.'

The corporal, breathing air in big gulps, turned to
Wallis. 'What'll I do, sir?' he begged.

Hooper snapped, 'Cut out the snivelling, boy. You
heard. The President has been relieved of his command.
You take your orders from . . .'

'Ignore that,' Wallis cut in. 'Your supreme commander
is the President. This is an attempted coup devoid of legal
authority.'

'You treacherous bastard,' Bellarmine snarled.

The corporal, eyes rolling in his head, moaned, 'Oh Holy Mother of God!'

'We're losing Xochicalco!' Fanciulli shouted. 'There's a whole lot of static.'

A red light flashed over the oak door.

'Stay where you are,' the Secretary of Defense snapped. He strode to the door and flung it open. He recoiled in horror as the inert body of a Secret Service man fell back against his legs, a round, ruddy face staring upwards up, prim round mouth half open, with a white shirt stained by a row of red patches. A young marine, breathing heavily, blood trickling down the side of his head, stepped over the body into the room and saluted the President.

'What's going on here?' the President asked.

Hallam followed the marine in. His cheek was grazed and swollen. 'We're more or less on top of it, Sam. Somebody's monkeyed with the switchboards but we're working on it.'

'Oh Christ,' said Hooper. Bellarmine looked as if he was about to faint. He sank into his chair, burying his face in his hands.

'Sir!' Wallis shouted, leaning over a screen. 'The Backfires are twelve minutes from Canadian airspace. Eighteen still on a Kansas azimuth, two have broken away for Alaska, the Purdhoe Bay area.'

'Sir!' a soldier shouted, 'We may have an intruder in Californian airspace, flying low north of Pendleton. Nothing on radar.'

'The sneaky bastards. While we watch the Kola build-up they send Stealths on ahead from the Urals,' said Hooper. 'We're out of time as of now.'

'The *Carl Vincent*,' the President shouted, 'On the blower, NOW.'

'Sir,' the corporal whooped, 'I've been trying to tell you. We lost her twenty seconds ago. All I'm getting is static.'

The speaker on the table crackled into life. There was a voice, hidden under layers of static, distorted beyond the possibility of decipherment.

'Does anyone understand this?' Grant shouted.

'It's the asteroid,' Bellarmine said in exasperation. 'It's hit. Don't you see we have to hit back?'

'Sir!' a soldier shouted, 'NORAD say another eighty Backfires have taken off from Kola.' He pointed to a television screen.

There was a tiny strip of runway, and a desolate snowy landscape, and a clutter of buildings. Little black moths were gliding along the runway or strung out in black moving silhouettes against the snow. Grant said 'Oh please God, not that.'

Hooper said 'What does it take, Sam? The blast is on the way in now!'

The black girl waved and pointed. 'Mister President, we have the picture from Goddard. On the screen.'

'Sergeant, Hooper and Bellarmine are under arrest. Anyone who reaches for the red phone is to be shot. No warnings, just shoot.'

'Yes *sir*.' The picture was a shimmering, irresolute haze.

'What the futz is this?' Grant snapped. 'Has it hit or not?'

'They're doing a maximum entropy, sir.'

'A what?'

'They're trying to sharpen it up.'

'Wallis, what gives with Xochicalco?'

'The channels are full of static, sir. We're getting nothing.'

'Mister President,' said Hooper, 'whatever the legalities of our action, we'll be scattered to the winds any time now. Whatever your reasons for inaction, you can't hold off any longer. America is under attack now. Get our missiles away now. We only have seconds.'

'Mister President, I beg you on my knees, launch!' Bellarmine implored.

'So it's hit?'

'Sir,' said a man in naval uniform, 'It could just have grazed the upper atmosphere. That would give us EMP but no impact.'

'Where's the frigging Kremlin?'

Wallis said, 'Sir, every damn channel to the Kremlin seems to be out. We're going to try a straight commercial phone line.'

'Why aren't Goddard delivering?'

'Sir, they say the picture needs to be processed.'

'How long, woman?' the President shouted at the top of his voice.

She shrank visibly and spoke quickly into the phone. 'Five minutes, sir.'

'Five *what*?' Grant yelled, and the girl crumpled, tears welling up.

Wallis said, 'Sir, if you want an effective response you're down to maybe a minute, maybe less.'

'Get them away, Grant!' Hooper bellowed, his fist raised. He half-rose from his chair, as if he was about to lunge for the telephone. The marine, a look of pure terror on his face, raised his rifle towards the general. Hooper lurched back and smashed his fist repeatedly on the table.

The President raised his arms like an old-fashioned preacher. The room fell silent. Someone next door began to recite an ancient prayer, in a calm Southern accent:

Our Father which art in Heaven . . .

He picks his way over the cables and stares at the video camera following him. It stares back indifferently. He stands at the flag, hanging by the door. The black girl next to him is sobbing quietly. He puts his hand on her shoulder. The flag begins to blur and to his surprise Grant realizes that he too is weeping.

He looks around, unashamed, the tears trickling down his chin. He is no longer in a command post deep under the ground: he is in a wax museum. And somehow the museum is also a sea, an ocean of faces stretching around the globe, faces born and unborn, all awaiting the decision of this one man, this country boy from Wyoming. Insects crawl under his skin. They have tearing forceps for jaws. A crab in his stomach is tearing its way out, devouring his intestines as it does. Acid trickles down his throat, burning his gullet. The dull pain in his chest has long since grown to a tight grip.

Of course it's obvious. Has been all along.

A voice whispers, 'Mister President, we have maybe thirty to sixty seconds before the blast hits us.'

'Hell of a decision for a Wyoming ploughboy, Nathan.' The voice whispers again. 'Sir, we need your word.'

'I don't know how we got into this state – maybe it's beyond human control. Maybe the world goes in cycles and it's my luck to be in the hot seat when the time comes to crash out. You didn't need your rebellion, Mister, I was getting round to my planet of ashes. So goodbye my children, and hail to the mutants.'

Deliver us from the Evil One . . .

'Wallis, get on with it. Hooper, proceed with Grand Slam. Mitchell, fire your Tridents.' The soldiers quickly move to terminal screens and begin to speak into telephones. Grant reaches out for the red phone. Wallis breaks open a sealed envelope.

For Thine is the Kingdom . . .

Someone, a woman, says nervously 'Mister President, it's the British Prime Minister.' Her voice is lost in the immensity.

The Power and the Glory . . .

'Can't someone stop this?' another woman asks. 'I have children.'

Forever. Amen.

Wallis sits down at a desk, near the back of the protected room. A camera swivels round to follow him. He starts to read numbers into a telephone, one at a time, in a clear, decisive voice. The President picks up a red phone, and the camera quickly swings back towards him. But Grant's vision is blurred, and his hand is shaking. He tries to talk but words won't come. Bellarmine's eyes are staring, willing the President on. Hallam stands in the midst of it, hand over his eyes like a child keeping out some fearful monster. Hooper's jaw is clenched to the point where he can hardly speak.

An ancient telex machine, a comedy thing, a museum piece amongst the Silicon Valley technology, bursts into life, chattering. 'Oh sweet Jesus oh sweet Jesus. Sir, it's President Zhirinovsky.'

Simultaneously, the British Prime Minister's voice comes over the speaker, as clearly as if he is calling from the next room. 'Ah, good morning, Mister President. Have I called at a bad moment?'

Sonora Desert

The meteor comes in high over the Sonora desert, trailing a long, luminous wake and throwing moving shadows on the ground far below. Near the end of its flight it flares up, splits in two and then it is gone from the star-laden sky.

'Did you see that?' Judy asked, appearing from around the porch of the house.

'A sporadic, I think,' said Webb. 'There are no showers at this time of year.' In the starlight, Webb could just make out that she was wearing the same crocheted shawl he had seen her in at Oaxtepec, and the same crocheted bikini; and she had the same elegant bodywork. She was carefully carrying two tumblers filled to the brim with a liquid which seemed to glow orange-red. She handed him a drink and sat cross-legged on a rug laid out next to the tub. To Webb she looked like a satisfied Buddha.

He shifted his leg. The hospital nurse had finally removed the swathes of bandage. Judy had left her Pontiac Firebird for him with a map and he had gurgled the big psychedelic car along the I-10 through Tucson and then along Gates Pass before turning north into a narrow road cutting through the Saguaro National Park. The six-inch gash in his thigh still ached from the journey, but the warm water of the big whirlpool tub was beginning to ease the pain. Big Saguaro cacti stood around them in dark outline, like silent sentinels, or triffids.

She sipped at the drink. 'How's the leg?'

'Better, Judy. Thanks for the invitation, by the way. I'm impressed.' He waved his hand to encompass the Sonoran desert, the cacti, the dark, snow-tipped mountains and the huge celestial dome which dwarfed it all. Out here in the desert, the stars were a lot brighter. Here and there the lights of houses were scattered, like candles in a dark cathedral.

'Well, you were told to rest. This is a good place to do it. I call it Oljato, which is Navajo for the Place of Moonlight Water.'

'Although the company is boring.'

She raised her eyebrows in surprise. 'Be careful, Oliver. There are rattlesnakes out there.'

Webb sipped at the drink. It was chilled, and had a distinctive flavour which he associated with Mexico but couldn't otherwise place. 'So what does your Fort Meade mole say?'

'The investigation's still under way. It seems the operation was planned by a small group of clever people in the NSA. It was a sort of Cyberwars in reverse.'

'Cyberwars?'

'Information warfare. Look at the damage single hackers have done when they penetrated a system's computers. Now think of a planned attack by hundreds of them, based in some hostile country, penetrating thousands of computers. They could build up undetectable back doors over a long period of time and then strike all at once. They could crash planes, erase files from businesses and laboratories, penetrate rail networks, cause financial chaos, destroy the command and control of weapons systems, all from the safety of their own country and using nothing more than computer terminals.'

'But surely that's a recognized problem,' said Webb.

Judy nodded. 'But what people had in mind was an external enemy. Nobody thought there might be an enemy within.'

'And because they protect the systems, they know about them,' Webb suggested. 'And they know all there is to know about information warfare.'

'Which knowledge was used by a small group within the National Security Agency against the American leadership. The Chiefs of Staff, the President, the Secretary of Defense, they fooled everybody.'

'The old problem,' Webb said. 'Who protects us from our protectors?'

'These people weren't traitors, Ollie. They were patriots. They had a clear-headed view that the country had to protect itself against a perceived future attack by taking pre-emptive action. That action could not be taken by an administration proclaiming peaceful co-existence.'

'And the CIA was in on it too?'

'Again, my mole thinks only a small clique within the organization. They only needed a few guys. The upper echelons were taken in just like everybody else.'

Webb leaned back and sank up to his neck in the warm water. 'I like the way they're trying to handle the aftermath. Actually selling the conspirators' story to the public. A straightforward near-miss asteroid, the Naval Observatory observations a mistake etcetera. They'll never get off with that.'

'Don't be so sure, Ollie. Nemesis has supposedly rushed back into the blind zone, deflected by Earth's gravity.'

'Forget it.'

Judy drew the shawl closer around her shoulders. 'The *Enquirer* said it was a CIA plot to make the President zap the Russians, did you see?'

Webb grinned. 'And not a soul believes them. What's the line on the palace revolution?'

'In the Kremlin? The analysts don't know. My guess is the Russian Army decided Zhirinovsky was just too dangerous to have around.'

'It was close. I'm glad the driver's ignition worked.'

'But now they've pulled out of Slovakia, and they're getting back to some semblance of democracy. We'll see what the elections bring.'

Webb's eyes were now fully dark-adapted. A little lemon tree, almost next to the whirlpool tub, glowed gently. At this latitude his old winter friend Orion the Hunter was high in the sky; Sirius, a white-hot A star, lit up the desert from nine light years away; the Milky Way soared overhead, bisecting the sky. And Mars beckoned from the zodiac, unwinking and red. A strange feeling came over him, the same one he had experienced in a little church in a cobbled lane in Rome a million years ago. It was unsettling, a one-ness with something; he didn't understand it. The desert at night, Webb felt, was a spiritual experience.

'The world's getting dangerous, Judy. Some day we'll build a Noah's Ark and move out. A little seedling, the first of many, to scatter our civilization and our genes around the stars. Once we're spread around a bit nothing can extinguish us.'

She was smiling. 'I guess I overdid the tequila. But I can't make up my mind about you, Oliver. Are you a visionary or a screwball?'

'I'm just a quiet academic who wants to get on with his research.'

She put her drink on the ground, stretched and yawned like a cat. 'What about your people?'

Webb said, 'I heard the Minister on the World Service, speaking to the House. Our diligent watchers of the skies etcetera. What a blatant old hypocrite! He'd been closing us down left, right and centre.' He finished the tequila sunrise. His head was spinning a little, but the sensation was pleasant. 'So how did you get involved in this business, Judy?'

'One merry evening with Clive – that's my boss, now under suspension – I got the feeling I was being probed for my politics. I thought at first he was just curious. Then I thought maybe there's some question over my loyalty. It carried on over a few days. Nothing obvious, you understand, just the odd remark. I could easily have missed it. I began to think there's something strange going on here and so the more he probed the more outrageous the opinions I expressed. At the end I looked so right wing they must have reckoned I thought J. Edgar Hoover was a communist. Then one warm evening in La Fuente, with soft lights, sweet Mariachis music and Bar-B-Que ribs, Clive introduces me to Mark Noordhof. The whole plot was spelled out on a what-if basis. I must have made the right noises, because at that point Mark tells me the Eagle Peak team has to include someone who knows their way around nukes, and would I like to join them to make sure you all stayed on track. I agreed.'

'But you kept all this to yourself.'

'I was trying to find out how high it went,' Judy said. 'Like you, I didn't know whom I could trust. But enough about me, Ollie. You've resigned from your Institute.'

'Broken free, is the way I'd put it. I never did fit in with the groupthink.'

'It's getting cold.' She stood up, dropped her shawl and climbed into the tub, making waves. 'What will you do?' she asked, slipping off her bikini under the water.

Webb thought, Is this really happening to me? He said, 'They've fixed me up with a scholarship at Arizona University.'

'It's the least they could do.'

'This is a wonderful place. How often do you come here?'

'To Oljato? Whenever I can. Most weekends. In New Mexico I have a small downtown apartment.'

Webb screwed up his courage, and said it. 'I was wondering if I might rent this place from you. It's only half an hour from the University.'

Judy laughed delightedly. 'Ollie!'

'A strictly platonic arrangement, Judy. You're basically uninteresting.'

Judy's mouth opened wide. She splashed water at him. 'What gives with these insults?'

'I'm trying out a new technique. I got it from the master of a charm school, an old friend who calls himself Judge Dredd. It's supposed to dazzle women. First you ignore them, and then you insult them. And after that, so Judge Dredd assures me, they're eating out of your hand. Is it working?'

'Brilliantly.'

Once again, he thought, Webb the Rational is baffled. If I'm a blind machine in a pointless Universe, how can I feel these emotions? Can computer software feel pain? Could an assembly of wires fall in love?

He suddenly realized that of all the mysteries he had explored, the most baffling was here beside him, her blonde hair backscattering the starlight, her toe casually exploring, her very presence dissolving him.

Judy reached over the side of the whirlpool tub to a switch. He caught a glimpse of breast. The water began to swirl powerfully. They sat back awhile, letting the warm jets pummel their bodies. In the near-dark he could just make out her expression; she seemed amused by something. Her toe explored some more. He lifted it aside but it came back.

Now she was half-swimming towards him.

She lifted a bar of soap and straddled him. Her breasts were glistening wet and her nipples were standing out, dark circles against white, round flesh. 'Your chest or mine, Ollie? Strictly platonic, of course.'

⧗

'Teresa, Teresa, what are you doing out here?' Vincenzo asked, scolding.

In the starlight he could just make out that his woman was wearing a cotton cloak over her nightwear, but her white hair was uncovered and the air was chilly.

'When are you coming in, Vincenzo?' she asked, handing him a glass of hot mulled wine.

'Soon.'

'When will you start coming to bed at a reasonable hour? You're not a young man any more.'

'Mind your own business, woman. Now get yourself out of this cold.'

Vincenzo heard the woman's footsteps retreating along the gravel path. He put the glass down at the side of the flickering candle, enjoying the momentary warmth of the flame near his hand. He returned to the eyepiece of the little telescope, mounted on a tripod which sat on a marble bird table. He glanced along the brass tube, took his bearings from Aldebaran in the Hyades cluster, and moved his telescope towards a faint star to the left of the Bull's Eye. The faint, fuzzy star was still there, barely visible through the eyepiece of his instrument. It had moved a full degree since last night. It had no tail but otherwise looked cometary.

The eleventh, secret volume of his notebook was almost full, and it was opened at a page near the back. He always found it hard to judge the sizes of the stars; indeed, they even seemed to vary from night to night. But he estimated the position of the fuzzy star. He labelled it 'A', and drew a line to another star which he labelled 'B'. Underneath, he wrote a few lines of explanatory text in Latin.

A voice came out of the dark: 'Vincenzo. You will die of cold. Either come to bed now or I will lock you out for the night.'

Vincenzo Vincenzi sighed. The ways of God are mysterious, he thought, and none more so when they manifest themselves through a woman.

He snuffed out the candle and took a sip at the spicy

wine. The old man closed the notebook, the last volume of his life's work, and shuffled along the broad gravel path, through the garden scattered with cypress and myrtle trees, statues and tinkling fountains. Orion the Hunter guided his path; Sirius glittered over the roof of the villa; the Milky Way soared overhead, bisecting the Italian sky. A shooting star came and went. He wondered if men would ever reach the stars. Cardano of Pavia had said that Leonardo the Florentine had tried to fly, but had failed. Momentarily, the reality of his own insignificance overwhelmed him; he felt crushed by infinity.

Near the door, his woman was holding a lantern. She took him by the arm and looked at him as if tolerating a foolish child. Vincenzo smiled. Why fear the infinite? Is God's love not equally boundless?

And perhaps, Vincenzo thought, I am a foolish child. Nobody will ever care about my feeble attempts to chart the timeless wonders of the sky, or the wanderings of the little comets.

Will they?

⧗

Fixa A distabat ad Aldebaran 37 semidiametres: in eadem linea sequebatur alia fixa B, quae etiam precedenti nocte observata fuit.

Revelation

This book is dedicated to Fabbio Migliorini

Prologue

At the mention of memoirs, the Minister threatens me with everything from Section Two to the Chinese water torture. Naturally, since all I want is a quiet life, I back down. To his credit, he tries not to smirk.

'You can't stop me writing a novel, though.'

The Minister turns puce but then he's known to be heavy on the port.

So here it is. Of course it's only a story, and if pressed I will deny that it ever happened. And deny it I have done, consistently, in all my conversations with those people with polite voices and calculating eyes.

To me, as a polar ice man, there's nothing odd about a tale of fire which starts in an Arctic blizzard. The planet is an interconnected whole; I measure the burning of rainforests in the thinning of the pack ice I walk on, and of fossil fuels in the desperate hunger of the ten-footers which raid our camps. The Arctic, in turn, is biding her time, quietly stoking up her revenge . . . but I digress.

The key to unlocking the secret of the diaries was Archie. My old friend Archie was the fatal miscalculation

1

of the puppet masters. They had correctly assumed that I wouldn't understand the material I was handling, that I lacked the arcane knowledge which was the key to the secret. But if this particular puppet cut its strings, if I didn't do what my manipulators expected me to do, well, I give the credit to Archie.

We went back to the Creation, Archie and I. As boys we'd wandered around Glasgow's Castlemilk district in the days when it was run by real hard men, not the sham jessies you see now. Young buccaneers in search of trouble, which we often found. And if that seems an unlikely start to a couple of academic careers, I could tell you some juicy tales about quite a few distinguished Glaswegians. In fact our current Scottish Prime Minister . . . but there I go, wandering again.

Then there were the ladies, and then I went to Aberdeen and we drifted our separate ways until we met by chance years later at a Royal Society dinner in London. Archie the buccaneer was now a respected nuclear physicist, renowned for his work on superstring theory. I was into Arctic climate, looking for signs of trouble ahead. New Age monks, we had disdained commerce, despised the worldly, and devoted our lives instead to the search for greater truths.

As to how this unworldly pair reacted when wealth beyond calculation came within our reach, well – that's part of the story.

The rest of it has to do with blowing the planet to hell.

1

The Shadow on the Lake

Thursday, 29 July 1942

Out-of-towners. Men with an intense, almost unnatural aura about them. Come from God knows where to the back of beyond. In his imagination, the station master sees gangsters, Mafia bosses come for a secret confab.

It is, after all, a quiet branch line, and he has to occupy his mind with something.

He has no way of knowing that the three men alighting from the Pullman are infinitely more dangerous than anything his imagination can devise.

First out is John Baudino, the Pope's bodyguard. His gorilla frame almost fills the carriage door. He is carrying a dark green shopping bag. Baudino surveys the platform suspiciously before stepping down. Two others follow, one a tall, thin man with intense blue eyes. He is wearing a broad-brimmed pork-pie hat, and is smoking a cigarette. The third man is thin and studious, with a pale, serious face and round spectacles.

The man waiting impatiently on the empty railway

platform expected only Oppenheimer; the other two are a surprise.

'Hello, Arthur,' says the man with the blue eyes, shaking hands. He looks bleary, as if he hasn't slept.

'You could have flown, Oppie. A thousand miles is one helluva train ride.'

Oppenheimer drops his cigarette on the platform and exhales the last of the smoke. 'You know how it is with the General. He thinks we're too valuable to risk in the air.'

Arthur Compton leads the way to the exit gate.

The station master gives them a suspicious nod. 'Y'all here for the fishing?' he asks, attempting a friendly tone. It is out of season for the angling. His eyes stray to their unfishing-like clothes and luggage.

'No. We're German spies,' growls Baudino, thrusting the train tickets at him. The station master snaps their tickets and cackles nervously.

In Compton's estate wagon, Baudino pulls a notebook and a Colt 38 out of the shopping bag at his feet. He rests the weapon on his knees. He says, 'Do your talking somewhere quiet, Mister Compton. And not in the cottage.'

'Come on, John, it's a hideaway. Nobody even knows I'm here.'

'We found you,' Baudino says over his shoulder. He is already checking car registration numbers against a list.

Compton thinks about that. 'Yeah.' He takes the car along a narrow, quiet suburban road. After about three miles the houses peter out and the road is lined with conifer forest. Now and then a lake can be glimpsed to the right, through the trees. After ten minutes Compton goes down through the gears and then turns off along a rough track. About a mile on he arrives at a clearing, and pulls up at a log cabin. A line of washing is strung out on the verandah. They step out and stretch their limbs. The air is cool and clear. Baudino slips the gun into his trouser belt.

Compton says, 'You know what I'm enjoying about this place? The water. It's everywhere. It even descends from the sky. After the mesa, it's glorious. You guys want coffee?'

Oppenheimer shakes his head. 'Later. First, let's talk.' He leans into the wagon and pulls out a briefcase.

Compton points and they set off through a track in the woods. After half a mile they come to a lake whose far edge is somewhere over the horizon. They set off along the pebbled beach. Baudino takes up the rear, about thirty yards behind the other three, to be out of hearing: what the eggheads get up to is none of his business. His assignment is protection and to that end he keeps glancing around, peering into the forest. Now and then he touches the gun, as if for reassurance.

Compton says, 'Oppie, whatever made you come a thousand miles to the Canadian border, it must be deadly serious.'

Oppenheimer's face is grim. 'Teller thinks the bomb will set light to the atmosphere, maybe even the oceans.'

Compton stops. '*What?*'

Oppenheimer pats the briefcase. 'I've brought his calculations.'

The studious one, Lev Petrosian, speaks for the first time since they arrived. His English is good and clear with just a hint of a German accent. 'He thinks atmospheric nitrogen and carbon will catalyse fusion of the hydrogen. Here's the basic formula.' He hands over a sheet of paper.

Compton studies it for some minutes, while walking. Finally he looks up at his colleagues, consternation in his eyes. 'Jesus.'

Oppenheimer nods. 'A smart guy, our Hungarian. At the fireball temperatures we're talking about you start with carbon, combine with hydrogen all the way up to nitrogen-15, then you get your carbon back. Meantime you've transmuted four hydrogen atoms into helium-4 and fired out gamma rays all the way up the ladder.'

'Hell, Oppie, we don't even need to create the nitrogen. It's eighty per cent of the atmosphere. And we've already got the carbon in the CO_2, not to mention plenty of hydrogen in the water. If this is right it makes the atmosphere a devil's brew.' Compton shakes his head. 'But it can't be right. It takes millions of years to turn hydrogen into deuterium.'

Petrosian says, 'About one hydrogen atom in ten thousand is deuterium. It's already there in the atmosphere.'

'You mean . . .'

'God has fixed our atmosphere beautifully. He's made it so it by-passes the slow reactions in the ladder. The rates are speeded up from millions of years to a few seconds.'

'When does the process trigger?'

6

'It kicks in at a hundred million degrees. The bomb could reach that.'

Oppenheimer coughs slightly and stops to light up a cigarette. 'We could turn the planet into one huge fireball.'

'What does the Pope think? And Uncle Nick?' Compton is referring to Enrico Fermi and Neils Bohr, atomic physicists whose names are so sensitive that they are referred to by nickname even within the barbed wire enclave of Los Alamos.

Oppenheimer takes a nervous puff. 'They don't know yet. I want us to check it out first. We'll work on it overnight.'

Compton picks up a stone and throws it into the water. They watch the ripples before they carry on walking.

'Out with it,' Oppenheimer says.

Compton's tone is worried. 'Oppie, look at the big picture. The U-boats have just about strangled the British. Hitler's troops are occupying Europe from the North Cape to Egypt. Russia's just about finished and I'll bet a dime to a dollar Hitler will soon push through Iran and link up with the Japs in the Indian Ocean. The Germans and the Japs will soon have the whole of Asia, Russia and Europe between them.'

'So?'

'So then Hitler will be over the Bering Straits and through Canada like a knife through butter. By the time he gets there he'll be stronger than us. We have a two-thousand-mile border with the Canadians, Oppie, it's indefensible, and I don't want my hideaway to be five minutes' flying time from Goering's Stukas.'

Oppenheimer's intense blue eyes are fixed on the lake, as if he is looking over the horizon to Canada. 'That's a grand strategic vision, Arthur. But what's your point?'

'Ten minutes ago that grand strategic vision didn't bother me. So long as we won the race to build the gadget, we'd be okay. But how can we take even the slightest chance of setting the atmosphere alight? I'm sorry, Oppie, but given a straight choice we'd be better to accept Nazi slavery.'

Oppenheimer nods reluctantly. 'I've lost a lot of sleep over this one, Arthur, but I have to agree. Unless we can be a hundred per cent sure that Teller is wrong, the Bomb must never be made.'

There is just a trace of sadness in Petrosian's voice. 'I understand your reasoning, gentlemen. I'd probably think the same if I hadn't lived under the Nazis.'

2

Flesland Alpha

The new millennium

Death and destruction entered Findhorn's Aberdeen office in the form of a small, bespectacled, mild-mannered Norwegian with an over-long trenchcoat and a briefcase. He claimed that his name was Olaf Petersen, and the briefcase was stamped with the letters O.F.P. in faded gold.

Anne put her head round the door. She was being a redhead today. 'Fred, there's a Mister Olaf Petersen here.'

The red leather armchair had been purchased for a knock-down price at a fire-damage sale but it was all brass studs and wrinkles and it gave the little office a much-needed air of opulence. Petersen sank into it and handed over a little card. He looked around at the photographs which covered the office walls: icebergs, aurora borealis, a cuddly little polar bear, an icebreaker apparently stranded on a snowfield.

The card read:

Olaf F. Petersen, Cand.mag., Siv.ing. (Tromsø)
Flesland Field Centre
Norsk Advanced Technologies

'Coffee?' Findhorn asked, but he sensed that the man had little inclination for social preliminaries.

'Thank you, but I have very little time. The Company would appreciate some help, Doctor Findhorn.' Like many Scandinavians, the man's English was excellent, only the lack of any regional accent revealing that it was a second language.

'Norsk and I have done business from time to time.'

'This particular task is quite different from anything you have done for us before now. Something has turned up. The matter is urgent and requires the strictest confidentiality. We hope that you can help us in spite of the very short notice.'

Findhorn thought of the empty diary pages yawning over the coming months. Petersen was looking at him closely. 'I had hoped to take a few days' break over Christmas.'

Petersen looked disappointed. 'Frankly, I'm disappointed. You were perfect for this assignment.'

Findhorn thought it better not to overdo the hard-to-get routine. He said, 'Why don't you tell me about it?'

Petersen, smiling slightly, pulled a large white envelope from his briefcase. 'Do you have a light table?'

'Of course. Through here.'

By labelling the door 'Weather Room', Findhorn hoped to imply that further along the corridor there were other rooms with labels like 'Mud Analysis' or 'Core Sample Laboratory' or even 'Arctic Environment Simulation Facility. Do Not Enter', rather than two broom cupboards and a toilet. The light table, about five feet by four, took up much of the room. They picked their way over cardboard boxes and piles of paper. Findhorn switched on the table and pulled the black curtain over the window. Petersen opened the envelope and pulled out a transparency about a foot square. Lettering in the corner said that it had been supplied courtesy of the National Ice Center and a DMSP infrared satellite.

Findhorn laid the transparency on the table. Down the left, the west coast of Greenland showed as a grey-white, serrated patch except where sea fog obscured the outline. Someone had outlined the limit of the pack ice with a dotted line. There was a scattering of icebergs. Little arrows pointed to them, with numbers attached.

'Do you see anything odd?' Petersen asked.

Findhorn scanned the picture. 'Not really.' He pointed to an iceberg off the Davy Sound, just on the boundary between Greenlandic and international waters. 'Except maybe A-02 here. It's pretty big.'

'Unusually so, for the east coast. The big tabular bergs are usually found on the west of Greenland. They break off from the Petterman or the Quarayaq or the Jungersen glaciers, and drift down through Baffin Bay to the Newfoundland Bank.'

'So where is this one headed?'

'It's been caught up in the East Greenland Current. It may round Cape Farewell and join its western cousins or it may break out into the North Atlantic. But size and drift aren't the issue, Doctor Findhorn. Take a closer look.'

There was a little dust on the transparency, overlying the big iceberg, and Findhorn puffed at it. The dust didn't blow away. He brushed it lightly with his finger but again it stayed put. He frowned.

'Try the microscope,' Petersen suggested politely.

Findhorn swivelled the microscope over the big transparency. He fiddled with the knurled knob, brought the photograph into focus.

The iceberg filled the field of view. A pattern of ripples marked its line of drift through the surrounding ocean. It was surrounded by a flotilla of lesser floes, like an aircraft carrier surrounded by yachts.

Findhorn swivelled the front lens holder. He frowned some more, puzzled.

The specks of dust had resolved themselves into rectangles, man-made structures like huts. Other, smaller shapes were scattered around.

He turned the microscope to its highest setting and increased the intensity of the light shining up through the translucent glass. And then he looked up from the microscope, astonished. 'But this is crazy.'

Olaf agreed. 'Icebergs melt. Split. Capsize. No sane individual sets foot on an iceberg.'

'But . . .'

'But a large camp has been set up on this one.' Olaf, leaning over the light table, tapped the photograph with a stubby finger. 'Yes, Doctor Findhorn, this is crazy. These small irregular shapes you see. They're men. On an iceberg which could overturn at any time.'

Findhorn stood up from the microscope. The light from the table, thrown upwards, gave Petersen a slightly sinister look, like a mad scientist in an old horror movie. A vague feeling of uneasiness was coming over him. 'What exactly does Norsk want from me?'

Petersen gave a good imitation of a smile. 'First, we'd like you to fly out to the northernmost rig in our Field Centre.'

'Norsk Flesland?'

'The same. Then, from there, we'd like to fly you out to the *Norsk Explorer*, our icebreaker, which is currently about three hundred kilometres north of the rig, just on the limit of the helicopter's range. The *Explorer* will take you to A-02, which is further north again. We want you to climb that berg.'

And now it was happening again, the old, lurching sensation in the stomach. 'Why? And why me in particular?'

Petersen was still smiling, but he had calculating eyes. 'Perhaps I will have that coffee after all.'

'How you gooin ar keed?'

'Okay thanks. Just a bit nervous.'

'Yow never bin on a reeg before?' The man's voice was raised, to penetrate Findhorn's ear protectors.

Findhorn looked out at the dark sea. In the distance, lights were blazing on the horizon. The helicopter was heading directly for them.

'Nope.'

'Thought so. What's yow job?'

'I'm just visiting.'

'You joost veezeeteeng?'

Findhorn nodded. The blaze of lights was beginning to take shape. As the helicopter approached he began to make out three illuminated giants wading in the ocean, holding hands.

The Brummie was still probing. 'Not that it's any of my business, of course, yow know what I mean?'

Now Findhorn could see that their upper structures were forested with cranes and big metal Christmas trees. There were pipes and strange projections and tiny men on walkways and platforms. The arms joining the giants resolved themselves into connecting passageways. It was a city on stilts. Its lowest deck was thirty metres clear of the Arctic Ocean: the engineers had planned for a once-in-a-century giant wave. As to the icebergs, however, they relied on statistics and prayer. Against a ten-million-ton berg, Norsk Flesland might as well be made of matchsticks.

'I'm impressed,' Findhorn said.

'Ooh ar, you will be. Yow looking at something taller than the Eiffel Tower. With ten decks and three turbines geeveeng us twenty-five megawatts. We get 'alf a million barrels of crude and three hundred million cubic feet of gas every day. There's 'alf a mile of water between the reeg and the seabed and the well penetrates fifteen thousand feet of mood.'

He's close, Findhorn thought. *It's pushing six hundred thousand barrels a day, and they reach it through eighteen thousand feet of Upper Jurassic sandstone.*

'But you know,' the man confided, 'for all its size, there's something keeps me listening in the dark, know what I mean?'

'A big berg?'

The man shook his head. 'A meecroscopic crack. Fatigue in a leg.'

'Which one is Alpha?'

The man leaned over Findhorn and pointed a nicotine-stained finger. 'The platform in the middle, that's Flesland Alpha, the living quarters. Beta on the left is drilling and wellhead, and Delta on the right is the gas process platform. We do twelve hours on, twelve off. They like to keep the accommodation separate. There's about fifty metres of corridor joining them.'

'What's it like, working on a rig?'

'Norwegian reegs are breell. Now on Flesland Alpha, yow've got everytheeng you want, from a ceencma to a sauwna. There's a gymnasium, snooker, leather armchairs, escalators between decks, en-suite rooms, fantastic groob. It's like the Hilton. Only the American Gulf rigs can match them, and they have the weather for barbecues. Now the Breetish exploration rigs, they're roobish. Four men to a room, recreation a grotty TV room, canteen groob worse than a motorway stop.'

'I take it you're a Brummie?' Findhorn asked.

The man bristled. 'Naeiouw. I coom from the Black Country, from Doodley, can't yow tell? There's a beeg zoo there.'

'What's your job?' Findhorn asked. The helicopter was

beginning to tilt. A long pier jutted out from Delta, and at the end of it a flame fluttered in the wind, throwing a thin orange light on the dark ocean below. Findhorn glimpsed derricks, and brilliantly lit walkways, and a confusing mass of pipes, and then the helicopter was sinking down towards an octagonal helideck, the wind from the rotors rippling water on its surface.

'Oi look after the peegs, ar keed.'

Findhorn decided against asking for a translation.

A muffled voice came over the intercom. 'There's a very high wind out there. Keep a firm hold of your baggage and watch your footing. Keep your ear protectors on.'

On deck, the wind threatened to knock Findhorn off his feet. It was cold and wet with sea spray. There was a smell of oil. Men on the helideck pointed toward a stairwell. Findhorn followed the oil men, in their orange survival suits and carrying holdalls, down metal stairs and along a short corridor. Here the air was warm. There was a queue at a desk marked *Resepsjon*; there were lifejackets to hand in, and hard hats and steel-toed boots to collect; there were ID cards to exchange for cabin and muster cards.

For Findhorn, however, the rules were being broken. The platform manager, steel grey hair poking under her helmet, was waiting. Without a word she took him by the arm and led him past the queue. There was to be no trace of Findhorn's visit to Flesland Alpha.

It was so huge that, at first, Findhorn thought he must have imagined it. Eyes straining and nerves taut, it was too easy to see non-existent structures in the whirling grey patterns of the blizzard. But then the helmsman was shouting 'Iceberg dead ahead,' and suddenly it was real, and Findhorn found himself saying, 'Oh my God.'

As it approached, the white turrets and battlements of the Disneyland castle resolved themselves into crevasses and overhanging cliffs and old meltwater tunnels as wide as motorways.

Through the big panoramic window of the bridge, wipers clicking, Findhorn and Hansen watched the ship's forecastle plunging down troughs, with black water and foam and chunks of ice swirling along the deck before smashing against the bridge and pouring over the sides. A foot of solid ice covered davits, ventilation shafts and deck railings.

Even as he watched, visibility was deteriorating. The Captain, clinging on to the engine-room telegraph, had acquired a dour, taciturn expression. His eyes, Findhorn noticed, kept straying to the ship's inclinometer. Every few seconds the clang of little bergs ran through the ship's hull.

Findhorn looked in vain for a route up the grim, lifeless structure; the cliffs were pockmarked and yet smooth; old shorelines were marked out along its length by sloping ridges. Waves bigger than houses were pounding the foot of the berg. He said again, 'Oh my God.'

'Aye,' Hansen agreed, gripping the telegraph. 'Rather you than me.'

'Ice two fifty metres,' the schoolboy called out. His face was almost buried in the cowling of the radar.

His accent had just a trace of Norwegian and he had a cool, nonchalant attitude. The giveaway was the slight tremor in his voice; that, and the grip of his hands on the edge of his desk.

'Are you sure it's the right one?'

Hansen grinned sadistically. 'This is the age of GPS, Mister. But there's one way to make sure.' A blast of sound actually shook Findhorn like a jelly. His heart jumped, and the sound of the ship's horn echoed off a hundred unseen bergs. They waited.

'Would you look at that?' Hansen exclaimed.

A tiny shape was moving at the top of the iceberg. It resolved itself into a man dressed in thick white furs. The man started to wave furiously.

'Is that Watson or Roscoe?' Hansen asked.

'Too far away to say,' Findhorn replied.

To his utter horror, he realised that the berg was swaying. The ice cliff facing them was slowly tilting over. He watched aghast as it just kept on tilting towards them. The man should have fallen off, plunging to a painful death in the icy water far below; instead he quickly scrambled back and disappeared from view. A black wave was rearing up from the foot of the berg, displacing floes as it headed their way.

As the ship entered the lee, Hansen issued more orders, all of them mysterious to Findhorn. The Captain pointed. 'There's your route up, laddie.'

Findhorn made out the thin rope ladder, now overhanging the tilting cliff, its base immersed in the churning water. Little hunks of ice and snow were splitting away from the top of the iceberg and crashing into the sea around the ladder. Thundering echoes came from the bergs scattered around. His mouth was parched and he was beginning to feel petrified with terror.

'I'll not move in much closer, some of these beasts have a wide underwater shelf. And I'll not risk more men than necessary. Findhorn, get up there. Do your job, and get yon people down that ladder ASAP.'

Findhorn stood, frozen. 'Quickly man,' Hansen snapped, 'before she turns turtle.' A practical man, our captain, Findhorn thought, not given to expressions of good luck or similar flim-flam.

'Sub-surface ice one thirty metres ahead, captain. It goes way down.'

'Very well. This is as far as I go.' Hansen lifted a telephone and a shudder ran through the ship.

'Can't you take me closer?' Findhorn was looking at the mountainous waves between him and the berg. The ship was plunging like an elevator in free-fall and fear was distorting his voice.

'Mister Findhorn, sir. Don't push your bloody luck. I shouldn't even be here. I'm breaking icebreaker Rule Number One as it is: you can handle any two of fog, storm and ice, but if you have all three you get the hell out of it. I'm not about to tempt fate with Number Two: don't approach an iceberg closer than its height.' Hansen nodded over Findhorn's shoulder: the execution squad, in the form of Leroy, the Jamaican first officer, and Arkin, the red-faced bosun, ice club in hand and looking like a murderer.

'I've seen this happen before,' Hansen said. 'She's about

to turn turtle. And when she flips, she'll do it without warning.'

Findhorn, out of words, pulled up his fur cape. A sailor pushed the door open against the wind, and the bridge was suddenly filled with whirling snow. The man grinned as Findhorn passed.

On deck, the roar was overwhelming. A *whee!* came from overhead, from ice-festooned cables and wires attached to the masts. The snow was like stinging needles. The ship suddenly rolled. Churning black sea rose towards the deck. Findhorn overbalanced, grabbed a thick white handrail. Leroy snatched at his cape, hauled him upright. They clambered along the deck, Arkin leading and rapidly turning into a snowman.

On the lee of the ship, four sailors dressed like Eskimos were gripping the stanchions connected to the motor launch. Two of them were hammering fiercely at thick ice. Arkin climbed in, and Findhorn felt an indeterminate number of hands heaving him into the boat. Then he was gripping its side in terror as it was hoisted up on a derrick and swung out over the sea, the leverage exaggerating the ship's roll. The Zodiac slapped onto the water and Arkin snapped open the quick-release shackles, almost falling into the water as he did.

Down at sea level, the waves were immense. One loomed high over them. It hypnotized Findhorn. He watch its approach, assumed he was about to die. Instead the wave lifted the boat upwards, like a rapidly rising elevator, and threatened to smash it against the iron hull of the icebreaker; but then Arkin quickly puttered the little boat up and over its crest, towards the ice cliff. The berg seemed to have stopped tilting, but neither was it righting itself. This close to the boiling waves, the water seemed greasy. It was covered with a thin layer of frazil ice, and wisps of frost smoke outlined Findhorn's lungs and penetrated his layers of thermal clothing. The spray and snow assaulting his face were painful.

'You wan' try for the rope?' Leroy shouted, his face pitch-black against his white furry cape. Arkin was steering round an ice flow twice the size of the motor boat.

Findhorn looked at the big waves thundering off the face of the berg. The boat would smash itself to pieces if they approached too close. The ice on the cliff looked as hard as steel. Too terrified to speak, he nodded.

The rope ladder was dangling near a large cave. The water inside it was relatively calm. Arkin puttered them towards it. This close, the berg seemed monstrous. It was hissing, as the melting ice released bubbles of ancient air; Findhorn saw them sailing into the open jaws of a living entity. As they entered the cave the sea water began to churn below them, slapping powerfully off the side of the berg and drenching them with icy salt water. Arkin gripped the tiller with both hands. Then the boat was rising upwards.

Leroy shouted: 'Ice platform rising! Clear off!'

There was a terrifying hiss as the rising berg sucked in water and air. The sea churned. Arkin, eyes wide with fear, revved up the engine and swung the tiller. As they raced out from under the overhanging ice the rope ladder scraped alongside and Findhorn, in a moment of pure insanity, leaped at it. He grabbed a wooden rung and swung dizzily back under the overhang. The boat was racing clear. The noise was terrifying. He scrambled upwards, not daring to look down, but then the berg was pulling him up from the maelstrom. Ice showered from above, a fist-sized lump striking him painfully on the shoulder. He scrambled up recklessly, desperate to escape the hissing monster at his feet.

Fifty metres up, gasping for breath, he summoned up the nerve to glance down. Arkin had taken the Zodiac well clear of the berg. Small, pale faces looked up at him. The snow was closing in again and the *Norsk Explorer* was just a hazy outline. He thought of what he had just done and his whole body began to tremble.

He looked up. The rope ladder ended about twenty metres above him, tied around shiny metal pitons hammered into the ice. Beyond it was a ridge about three feet wide, an old shoreline, and on the ridge was a bearded man. Findhorn, his heart hammering in his chest, climbed up the last few feet of rope. He grabbed the gloved hand tightly and found himself hauled up on to a flat stretch of rough ice, and facing a man with a pinched nose and a worried face adorned by a five-day growth of ice-covered, grey beard. Small hard eyes peered out from behind the snow goggles. Buster Watson: Findhorn knew him from half a dozen international conferences; a pushy little egoist.

'Thank God,' the man shouted into the wind. 'Where the hell have you been, Findhorn?'

'We're lucky to be here at all in this weather. What happened to your radio?'

'We lost nearly everything when the bloody thing calved off.'

You lost the radio but not the huts?

Then Watson was shouting, 'Move it, we have very little time.' Bent almost double against the wind, he led the way across the top of the berg, along a flat plateau about fifty metres wide. Through the driving snow Findhorn glimpsed violently flapping tents and snow-driven huts. A tethered silver balloon was straining horizontally at its leash, rubbing against the ice. They passed a sonar tower whipping in the wind, firing little chirps of sound into the atmosphere overhead. The site looked for all the world like a scientific ice station.

Only the location was crazy.

Now they were passing the charred remains of a hut, a downwind line of soot marking the wind direction at the time of the fire, and the plateau was beginning to slope down. Watson led the way to a rectangular hut about twenty feet long; one of Findhorn's specks of dust. There was a surge of warm air as Watson pulled the door open against the screaming wind. Inside, a generator was throbbing. It was secured to the ice with deep steel pins. There was a smell of diesel. A shiny black cable from the generator was pinned along the ice and disappeared into a shaft about four feet wide.

Watson threw back his fur hood and took off his goggles. 'We started with a steam probe. The hole it made was a guide for a big gopher. It just melted its way down.'

Findhorn stood nervously at the edge of the shaft. Naked lights were spaced at ten metre intervals down its side and there was a long aluminium ladder, converging to a point of light far below. 'How far down does it go?'

'Three hundred feet.'

'*What?*'

'Yes. Below sea level. You first.'

3

Berg

The rungs were covered with smooth, hard ice and the spikes on Findhorn's boots meant that he had to raise his boot away from each rung before placing it on the one below.

Below about twenty feet the blizzard's scream was a whisper. At forty feet there was a sepulchral silence broken only by the metallic clatter of boots on rungs, and Watson's wheezy breathing above. The man seemed in a hurry, his boots sometimes just inches from Findhorn's head.

But then, starting at about sixty feet, Findhorn started to hear new sounds. They were coming up from below, and there were several components. There was something like an intermittent hissing. There were what might have been human voices. Most of all there was an occasional boom, so deep it was almost felt.

The ladder was tilting, a slow, pendulum-like oscillation. It had a period of maybe two minutes. Findhorn thought he could use the period of oscillation to work out the depth of the berg, started the calculation in his head, but another deep *Boom!* scattered the numbers away like crows from a farmer's shotgun. A few seconds after the boom, a blast of cold air swept briefly up the tunnel. The berg was breathing.

In the glare of the lamps, far below, Findhorn saw that the tunnel curved slightly, the ladder disappearing from view. Two hundred feet into the climb, the hissing was loud, and there was the occasional buzz of a chain saw. And then, about three hundred feet down, the shaft was opening up and Findhorn jumped onto flat ice at the end of a short tunnel. Watson pushed past and, bent double, led the way. It opened out to an amazing sight.

The cavern was fifty or sixty feet wide and as high. It was lit up by harsh blue spotlights, some on tall tripods, like a film set. Four men were directing hot, steaming water into a tunnel from a thick white hosepipe connected to a second generator. They were enveloped in the condensing fog which poured out of the tunnel mouth. Two others were shovelling icy slurry into a hop attached to the generator. In the confined space of the cavern, the noise was deafening. Findhorn's arrival created a sensation. A cheer went up, but it died out as the floor continued to tilt.

Findhorn thought, *we're under the Arctic Ocean*. He fought off a panicky moment of claustrophobia.

Watson waved his hands to encompass the cavern. 'We excavated this with hot-water cannons.' One of the men approached, chain saw swinging; in the cavern's weird illumination he looked like a troll stepped out from a Grimm fairytale. He had the wrinkled face of a heavy smoker and he was unconsciously licking his lips in fear. 'How're you doing?' he asked in a tough Dublin accent.

'Right, are we getting off this bloody coffin?'

Findhorn turned to Watson. 'How long has it been like this?'

'Since it calved. It's getting worse. In the last hour it's been tilting an extra five degrees. Look, I've a pension to collect, can we get a move on?'

'Where's Roscoe?'

'Like I said, there was an accident.'

In the circumstances, Findhorn let it pass.

'Along here. Look, we don't have much time.' The fear in Watson's voice was infectious. He led Findhorn towards the end of the cavern. They passed a tall, vertical wall with a six-inch fissure running from floor to ceiling. Findhorn was met with a strong, icy breeze as he passed the crack. To his surprise and horror, another tunnel led from the end of the cavern further down into the bowels of the iceberg. Rough steps had been hacked out of the ice. Watson started down. Findhorn almost refused to follow, felt something close to panic.

The deep, rhythmic bang was coming up from this second tunnel. At intervals along it, long metal rods had been driven into the ice, to various depths. Intense lights shone at the end of the rods, and the ice glowed a brilliant aquamarine blue from within. Each light had melted a little sphere of ice around it, and meltwater was trickling back along the rods and on to the icy floor, making a treacherous, almost frictionless surface.

But the blue glacier ice was far from pure. Stones, boulders, gravel and dust were scattered through its interior. Beyond about fifty feet, their cumulative mass acted as an optical barrier like a wall. Imbedded about thirty feet into the compressed ice, within reach of the powerful arc lamps, were larger, dark shapes. One of them was recognisable as a propellor, its blades twisted backwards. Beyond it, on the edge of visibility, was a jagged section of fuselage, still with its windows, one of them, remarkably, with its glass still intact. Two long strands of cable wound into the blackness.

A man was standing with his face to the ice. As Findhorn approached the man turned. 'Admiral Dawson, US Naval Research Office. What the hell are you doing here?'

'Just passing by. Thought you might want your life saved or something.'

The berg was levelling out.

'Thanks but we're doing just fine.'

Unexpectedly, Watson let forth a stream of profanity. 'This fucking maniac wants us here until the berg overturns. Get us out of it, Findhorn.'

Findhorn pointed at the dark shapes. 'What's that?'

'A Yak Ten. A nineteen fifties Soviet light aircraft.'

With a row of elongated bullet holes along the side of the fuselage.

'What are you trying to do, Admiral?'

'We were trying to cut towards the cabin area. Another hour would have done it, only the way this is going I don't believe we have an hour. The sonar shows more fuselage just in the dark over there. And a wing. And since you're here, you may as well come and see this.'

The berg was beginning to tilt in the opposite direction.

It was minus twenty degrees but Watson's face was beaded with sweat.

Findhorn followed Admiral Dawson further down the sloping tunnel, gripping a red nylon rope which acted as a handrail. Watson took up the rear. The tunnel was narrowing and tilting more steeply down. Findhorn had a brief vision of a grave passage deep inside a pyramid, and as they descended he felt his nerve beginning to crack. But then, a hundred feet down, Dawson stopped at a brilliant blue light. It had been driven a couple of feet into the ice and steam was hissing off it and billowing along the shaft.

Findhorn cleared a covering of frost away to reveal clear blue ice. It was a moment before he recognized the shape.

The corpse had partially mummified. Evaporation had turned it into little more than a skeleton covered with white, smooth, hard-looking flesh. Some of the flesh had transformed to grave wax. The corpse had been partially dismembered, pieces of arm being sheared off, the flesh more or less separate from the bone. Clothes had largely been stripped away. The abdominal wall was opened and the intestines, surprisingly intact, looked as if they were made of brown parchment. He found himself not a foot from a face the size of a soup plate. Dark matter had been squeezed out of the skull and the glacial drift of fifty years had spread it into a fan which stretched beyond the sphere of illumination about six feet in radius around the arc light. An eye was recognizably blue; the other, Findhorn thought, was probably round the back of the squashed face. Teeth had penetrated the leathery skin and the jaw had sheared sideways. The nose was flattened almost down to the gaping mouth. The torn remains of a grey suit were scattered amongst darker chunks of matter.

Findhorn peered closely at the hideous sight. In his imagination, the blue eye stared back at him.

'There's another body in the pilot's seat,' said Dawson. 'No way can we reach it.'

'Why couldn't they have crashed further up the glacier?' Watson complained.

Findhorn was peering into the ice. There was a metallic glitter from a black, rectangular shape about four feet into the ice. 'What's that?'

'It's what this is about, pal,' said Dawson. 'As if you didn't know.'

The awful tilting of the berg had stopped; but neither was the ice mountain righting itself.

Findhorn said, 'Tell your men to get out of here and leave me a chain saw.'

Watson disappeared round a corner and returned with the troll. The Irishman half-slithered down the tunnel, his free hand waving a chain saw and looking like a big crab's claw. Watson pointed his torch and without delay the man started on the ice. The noise in the narrow tunnel was deafening but the saw was cutting quickly into the wall, ice spraying around the tunnel.

'Get your men out of here, Watson,' Findhorn said again.

The berg was beginning to move again, but instead of levelling out, the tilt was increasing. 'Oh Holy Mother of

Christ she's going,' Watson wailed, his eyes wide with fear.

The Dubliner was in to the depth of his elbows. The tunnel had levelled and was now beginning to tilt in the opposite direction.

Now the chainsaw man was in up to his shoulders.

There was a tremendous bang, deep and powerful. The berg shook. Watson shouted, 'What the hell?'

Findhorn slithered back to the main cavern, which now lay below them. A wall had split. The fissure was now a foot wide and as he looked it continued to widen with a horrible cracking noise. Men were at the shaft entrance, fighting and punching to get on the ladder. He ran back to the side tunnel, hauled himself up by the red nylon handrail.

'Abandon ship,' he called out, his voice thick with fear. But Dawson was pushing the Irishman further in.

The Irishman's feet were kicking frantically. He wriggled back out, his face grey. 'Feic this, I'm out o' here,' he said harshly. He promptly slipped, landed with a gasp on his back, and slithered down the tunnel, the chain saw tobogganing ahead of him.

'Give me your ice axe,' Dawson snapped at Findhorn, gripping the handrail.

'Don't be a fool, Admiral. She's splitting. Get out of it.' But Dawson grabbed the axe with his free hand and leaned into the shaft, hacking furiously. Findhorn, gripping the nylon rail with both hands, waited in an agony of impatience and fear.

There was another bang. The berg suddenly lurched.

'She's going!' Findhorn shouted.

The admiral was tugging at something. 'Get me out! Quickly!'

There was a third tremendous *Crash!* from the direction of the main tunnel. Findhorn's feet gave way. He thumped heavily on to the ice, tumbled into the cavern. The fissure was now six feet wide and he tobogganed down towards it. Boxes, lamps, drills, chain saws, men were slithering down out of control into its mouth. Water was surging down the shaft, carrying men with it. The lights failed. In the blackness someone was screaming, high-pitched. Findhorn, on his back and accelerating out of control, felt a freezing wind rushing past him. The screaming was now above him, receding as if it came from a man shooting upwards. From below came a deep, powerful *Bang!* like an explosion. It filled Findhorn's world: and at last he recognized it as the sound of water slamming into a cavity. He was now in near free-fall.

And then he felt a giant hand pushing him up from below, as if the tunnel was accelerating skywards, and ice gouged a painful furrow in his brow, and a patch of light grew rapidly overhead, and in a moment the approaching grey had lightened and bleak daylight was streaming into a crevasse and he was out and fifty metres up and arching through the air, arms waving helplessly. He had time to glimpse a tiny boat with two petrified faces looking up, and beyond it the misty outline of the icebreaker, and dominating all a massive, ice-speckled black wave, a malign, living entity taller than the ship, and in the seconds while he somersaulted towards the Arctic water, Findhorn knew he was about to die.

4

Findhorn's Dream

Findhorn recalled his death in great detail. Mainly, he thought what a stupid way to go.

They'd had a boozy lunch at El Greco's, Hazel, Bruce and he. The *spada* had been first class (sauce-free, grilled to perfection). They'd discussed the Matsumo contract, and had agreed it was amazingly lucrative. Over coffee and ouzo they'd wondered – out of his hearing – about the attractions of Kontos, alias 'Bonkos', the ugly Greek proprietor with the red Ferrari and the endless string of what Bruce enviously described as 'luscious bints'.

Outside the restaurant, Hazel had shouted something to Findhorn as he'd stepped onto the busy street, his head spinning with wine. He'd had only a fraction of a second to follow Hazel's shocked gaze before the Leyland truck hit him, smashing his skull onto the hard London street, a massive wheel crushing his chest an instant later.

The heart monitor sent out its microwave signal and by the time the ambulance had reached the casualty entrance at St John's, the vultures were already awaiting the formal pronouncement of death. The casualty doctor shook his head over Findhorn's smashed chest and the corpse was quickly transferred to the team with no more than a hurried signature. In their grey, sealed van, along the Mall, the body was strapped to a table. A variety of scalpels and a small saw were used to remove Findhorn's head. As they turned up Haymarket, the blood vessels attached to the body were ligatured to stem the flow of blood. At a red light, while tourists and office girls crossed in front of them, Findhorn's carotid arteries were being connected to tubes and the blood in his head was replaced by a cold, cold liquid. Around Piccadilly and up Regent Street, his head was wrapped in foil and immersed, upside down, in a vat of liquid nitrogen, causing a surge of freezing fog to flood the van temporarily before escaping through a vent into the busy street. The metal lid of the vat secured, warm air was pumped into the van and the team took off their masks, goggles and bloody gloves, and relaxed. Somebody opened a Thermos flask; a cigarette was lit; and, over the headless cadaver, the chat turned to the forthcoming match. The van headed swiftly towards the M1, its destination a large, anonymous country house tucked away in the Buckinghamshire countryside.

All this Findhorn saw as if from above, from a camera in the roof of the van.

There was a tunnel, and all that ever had been or would be was imbedded in its walls, and he was moving along the tunnel towards a tiny light marking its end, and the light grew until he found himself in a brilliant white room and he woke up, unable to move. The cold was unlike anything he had ever experienced. It was an intense pain. Something was throbbing gently in the background, like the flow of blood through his ears. The room had no walls or ceiling; it was egg-shaped, white. There was no discernible lighting but it was bright like an operating theatre. A door slid open and a nurse, twentyish, came silently in and bent over him. She was the most beautiful woman he had ever seen.

'I made it,' he said, but the voice came out as a whisper.

'Just.' Her voice was surprisingly rough.

'How long was I dead?'

'A very long time. Very long.'

'I have a body?'

She smiled. It was a strange, mechanical smile, the lips almost curling into a semicircle. 'Of course. Cloning is an ancient art. You are now thirty, perfect in physiology, and will remain so for all time. And your intellect has been boosted. By the standards of your century, you are a superman.'

'Has anyone I know survived?'

'No. Brain preservation was very uncommon in your day. It makes you a very rare specimen. We have plans for you.'

'Plans?' Findhorn felt a twinge of anxiety.

Again the strange smile. Close up, there was something not quite right about her eyes; their shape was odd. 'Did you think you would spend eternity in Paradise?'

'This cold. Can't you get rid of it? Why can't I move?'

'As I said, we have plans for you. The cold is part of it.'

A vague sense of dread began to surge through Findhorn. This wasn't the way he'd anticipated his resuscitation, not the world he'd expected to find. A thought suddenly struck him. 'You're not real, are you? A hologram?'

'Hologram,' she repeated. There was a tiny hesitation. 'Hologram. Yes, I have it, a device from your century.' Findhorn thought he detected a hint of amusement, almost mockery. 'No, Mister Findhorn, I am not a hologram.'

'But you don't exist.' A fresh horror. 'Neither do I. You're feeding impulses into my brain. None of this is real.'

'What did you expect? Space-hungry, resource-greedy people who never die? No, machines supplanted organic life a very long time ago. However we still find a living brain very useful when we can find one.'

Findhorn suddenly envisaged a computer somewhere, eternally feeding dreams into brains stored in some vast, automated warehouse. Simple economics. Much easier to tickle brain cells than re-create living, space-hungry, resource-greedy people who never die.

The throbbing was louder. It was like the engine of a ship. The cold was in his bones. It was causing him terrible pain. 'Look, this isn't what I expected. I don't want an eternity of this.' He took a painful breath and reached a decision. 'It was a mistake. Please switch me off. Let me die.'

The lips curled into a perfect semicircle. The eyes followed the shape of the mouth. She leaned over him and for the first time Findhorn saw something long, thin and metallic in her hand. 'I'm so sorry. You don't have that option.'

* * *

'What did he say?'

'He's coming round.'

'I'll tell the captain.'

Findhorn opened his eyes. The first-aid room was warm; the cold Findhorn felt came from within. He was immobile under layers of blankets. A gentle, steady throb was coming up from the ship's engine below. Leroy, dreadlocks hanging down over his brow, was leaning over him, concern showing in his eyes. The nightmare of immortality fading, he managed to whisper: 'Leroy, you're beautiful.'

The first mate's anxiety gave way to a wide grin. 'You should see my sister.'

Hansen's bearded face appeared round the door. 'Thought you were a goner.'

'What happened?'

Leroy moved aside to make room for the captain in the tiny room. 'How 'bout some nice hot soup?'

'It could kill him,' said Hansen. 'Upset his circulation and flood his brain stem with iced blood. Make it lukewarm.'

When the first officer had gone, Hansen turned to Findhorn. 'We got it.'

Findhorn nodded, almost too weak to speak.

'It was inside a block of ice. They spotted it coming out with Watson. They got you on board first, then went back for it. Took half an hour to find amongst the floes.'

'And?'

'It's in the ship's safe. The admiral seems to think it's his property. I respectfully disagree. If it hit the water it's salvage.'

Hansen pulled out a pipe and began to stuff the bowl with black, tarry tobacco. 'It cost us. The berg split clean in two. Watson, Dawson and you came out of its centre like you'd been shot out of a cannon. Three men on Watson's team never got out, four drowned in the water. Seven dead.'

Findhorn remembered. 'My God.'

'Aye. And another three died on the berg before we got there, but our American guests are being remarkably tight-lipped about that. The Leith police will sort them out.' The captain was managing to speak while lighting his pipe; he was clearly well practised in the art. 'You owe your life to Leroy. Watson, yon Admiral and you were the only ones in reach and you were all sinking down. Leroy goes for you first, but the fur gear weighs a ton in the water. Then he gets the admiral. By the time Arkin and he gets him out, Watson is gone.'

Findhorn sank back into his dreams.

The smell of frying fish drifted into the first-aid room. From below, the throbbing was stronger, more rapid. Bleak Arctic light streamed in through a porthole. The ship was rolling up and down the big waves, and each time it reached a crest Findhorn saw icebergs scattered over the sea like ships in an armada. So Hansen had probably cut west to clear the pack ice and turned south just past Jan Mayen island. But there was still drift ice; they had probably not yet reached seventy north.

Findhorn wriggled an arm from under the blankets and peeled them off one by one. He sat up; it was possibly the most difficult thing he had ever done. His wrist watch, on the table next to him, was still working and it said 7.15. That would be p.m., frying fish being an evening meal even for this cosmopolitan crew; he'd been unconscious for eighteen hours. His bladder was threatening to burst.

Ten minutes later, bladder relieved, dressed in an over-large Aran jumper, jeans and sneakers, he presented himself at the entrance to the mess room, steadying himself against the roll of the ship.

'You raving eejit,' Hansen welcomed him. 'What are you doing up?'

'I'm after Leroy's red pea soup.'

Leroy vanished. While Findhorn was being helped into a chair he caught the eyes of the Dubliner. 'What happened to Roscoe?'

The Irishman's tone became evasive. 'There was a bit of an accident, like.'

'What exactly?'

'A sort of a fire.'

'What sort of a fire?'

'I was inside the berg when it happened.' The Irishman changed the subject. 'Ten men for a briefcase, sir. Was it worth it?'

So much for secret instructions, Findhorn thought. He was conscious of a dozen faces – Chinese, Korean, English, Norwegian, Indian and indeterminate – waiting for his answer.

Leroy stepped over the threshold. He placed crusty bread and a bowl of red soup in front of Findhorn. 'I'll know when I've opened it.'

'You won't be opening anything.' The admiral, in a light blue shirt and navy trousers, had followed Leroy in to the mess. 'The briefcase happens to be the property of the United States Government.'

'I'm fine, thanks,' said Findhorn. 'What business did you people have tunnelling in there? You were way off base.'

A blond crewman said, 'Greenland is the sovereign territory of Denmark. I expect my government may have a claim.'

Leroy clapped his hands in delight. 'Except that the berg had drifted into international waters by the time we got it. Hey, ah reckon it's finders keepers.'

Hansen was looking out of a porthole. His hair, like his beard, was nearly white, with dark streaks. Over his shoulder he said, 'Lawyers could get rich on this one.'

The admiral was in no mood for banter. 'I keep telling you people. The briefcase is American property. On behalf of the United States Government, Captain Hansen, I require that you hand it over to me now. Or take the unpleasant consequences.'

Hansen scraped at the barrel of his empty pipe. It gurgled when he blew through it. He turned and approached the admiral to within two feet. He said, 'Admiral Dawson, sir. With all due respect, awa' and bile yer heid.'

41

5

The Whisky Society

The *Apeiron Trader* drifted through a damp, freezing haar which wrapped itself around Findhorn's neck and trickled down to his shoulders, undercutting jacket, Aran pullover and thermal vest. Port Seton and Musselburgh drifted past a mile to port, their street lights coccooned in an orange haze.

Hansen appeared on the deck and leaned on the railing next to Findhorn, pipe smoking. 'Not a night for brass monkeys. Mind you, after your wee swim in the Davy Sound . . .'

Findhorn nodded, staring down at the flow of dark water reflecting the distant town lights. 'I'm confused.'

'Aye.' Hansen looked at Findhorn shrewdly in the half-dark. 'I've been thinking about this. What do you deduce from the following?' He raised a gloved finger. 'First. They order me to put in at Longyear Island. Why did they do that, Findhorn?'

'To transfer us over to to the *Apeiron Trader*.'

'Aye, but why? And second.' Another finger went up in the air. 'Having put us on to this glorified banana boat, and told us we're bound for Aberdeen, it does a last-minute change and comes down the coast to Edinburgh.'

'They're disorganized?'

Hansen laughed cynically. 'Norsk disorganized? No way. No, Findhorn, this is being done for a reason. Think about it. Longyear Island is about the most desolate, godforsaken hole on the planet. The transfer was carried out with only polar bears for witnesses.'

'I don't get you,' said Findhorn, but he did.

'They're trying to make sure we're not traced.'

Findhorn said, 'You've been too long at sea, Captain,' but he felt a chill: Hansen's story made sense.

'There's something in that briefcase.'

In the half-dark, the captain was looking angry. Findhorn waited, and Hansen continued: 'I've had a fax from Norsk. The crew are being put up in the Post House and flown out to their destinations tomorrow. We've been fixed up at the Sheraton.'

'Why the dour expression?'

'I have reasons. Three of them are wrapped up in sheets in the *Apeiron's* cold room. A few more are enjoying an Arctic cruise a thousand yards down in an iceberg. They'll end up in your fish fingers some day.' The wind caught little sparks from his pipe and blew them out to sea.

'What happens next?'

'Paperwork. And the Leith police and the Lloyds people and the Board of Trade and the Marine Accident Investigation Board. But not you, Doctor Findhorn, not according to my instructions. Our masters don't want you involved in these enquiries in any circumstances. They want you to disappear into the foggy night wi' that briefcase.'

'What do you think about that?'

Hansen took the pipe from his mouth and spat in the water. 'What do I think about it?' he repeated angrily. 'This just happens to be my country, bought and paid for with six hundred years of blood. I'm no' having a bunch of Eskimos telling me what I may or may not say to the lawful Scottish authorities.'

'So what will you do?'

Findhorn caught an eyeful of stinging pipe smoke, but Hansen kept puffing. 'Co-operate with the aforesaid authorities and stuff Norsk. Effing reindeer herdsmen trying to run my country.' Hansen spat again into the Firth of Forth. 'And I'll tell you somethin' for nothin'. There was some funny business went on in that American expedition.'

In the semi-dark, Findhorn could see the captain's shrewd eyes narrowed, staring intently at him. 'Just what is this about, Findhorn?'

'I haven't the faintest idea.'

'Maybe you have and maybe you haven't. And what's in yon briefcase to get the Yanks so excited?'

'Not to mention Norsk. Do you think they've fixed it so the police let me disappear into the night?'

'If they have it's an outrage. By the way, you meet with Company officials on the premises of the Whisky Society. After this little voyage, it strikes me as a damn good rendezvous.' Hansen tapped his pipe out on the railing; little sparks drifted downwind. Then he turned back to the bridge.

Leroy sauntered up and joined Findhorn at the railing.

Now they were within sight of Edinburgh Castle a couple of miles ahead and to the left, astride its basalt plug, floodlights illuminating its massive walls. The *Apeiron Trader* was slowing and heading to port, the automated lighthouse on Inchkeith Island swinging round to starboard.

'Edinburgh is a cold, cold city, mon. Time was when I had a little hot chocolate used t'wait foh me in Constitution Street. Just the thing after a long voyage. Lucinda, that was her name, a real enthusiast.' Leroy's mind was momentarily elsewhere. 'Smooth, dark skin, Jamaican, a lovely girl. But damn me, while I's in Murmansk and points north, if she doan up sticks and go back to her daddy in Jamayca, somewhere up in the Blue Mountains. He's a coffee farmer, mon, which is Jamaica-speak for abject poverty. Some day I will go there and I will rescue her from a life of pickin' coffee beans.'

'Maybe she likes picking coffee beans, Leroy. Which would you rather be, poor and warm or rich and cold?'

'But now my hot chocolate come in a mug,' Leroy complained. 'Choa man, how is de mighty fallen.'

Findhorn, his ears now painful with cold, grinned in sympathy and headed for his cabin.

There was a knock on the door. Hansen, briefcase in hand. 'From now on it's your responsibility, laddie. I take nothing more to do with it.' Findhorn nodded and took the briefcase.

He tossed it on the bed. It was black. On its side the letters LBP were printed in gold. It was in good condition and it was hard to believe that it had been under glacial ice for half a century. Findhorn tried the lock, but it was squashed almost flat. It would take a hammer and chisel to get at the contents.

Who owned it? The USA, Denmark, the Company, or Finders Keepers?

Another knock on the door, this one peremptory. Admiral Dawson, dressed for shore in a heavy seaman's jacket, and with the expression of a man anticipating a fight. The admiral nodded at the briefcase. 'Thanks. I'll have it now.'

'No way, Admiral.'

Dawson tried to push into the cabin but Findhorn put a hand on his chest and shoved. 'Hey, chum, you're a guest on this ship.'

'Get out of my way, Findhorn. That briefcase is United States property.'

'Maybe, maybe not.'

Dawson took a deep breath. He spoke softly, but there was anger in his voice. 'Look, pal, you have no idea what you're getting into here. Just forget the whole business. Hand over the briefcase and walk away. Believe me, it's in your own interests.'

'If that's a threat, can I have it in writing?'

Dawson, red-faced and grim, didn't reply. Findhorn closed the door on him.

Twenty minutes later, Findhorn was down the gangplank while it was still being secured. He had a backpack and carried the briefcase in one hand while holding the gangplank rail carefully with the other. A thrill of pleasure went through his nervous system when he felt solid concrete under his feet. There was the sour smell of yeast in the air; the Edinburgh brewers were emptying their vats. There was no sign of the admiral.

The crew began to trickle down the gangplank but Findhorn went on ahead, towards the customs shed. The Irishman, grim-faced, was standing at it as if it provided sanctuary. Two policemen were approaching him in a businesslike manner. Findhorn passed him with a nod, and then, in the shed, ran a gauntlet of keen-eyed officials; but he went unchallenged back into the dark, freezing fog.

A cluster of high-spirited young sailors passed him and disappeared into the dark; they sounded as if they had a riotous evening ahead. A police car sat on the dock, its driver watching the little flurry of late-night activity with dispassionate curiosity. Tall metal gates a couple of hundred metres ahead marked the end of the docks. More policemen, two in uniform, and more close scrutiny. A nod so imperceptible that Findhorn wondered if he had really seen it, and then he was through the gates and into the streets.

Leroy was standing in conversation with a mini-skirted girl. Beyond lay the bonded warehouses of the big distilleries; and beyond them again was Leith Walk, and pubs and restaurants and crowds and anonymity.

Findhorn walked quickly along the quiet dockside street, past the barred windows of the whisky warehouses. A taxi hooted as it passed; Leroy was grinning and waving, girl in tow. Half a mile ahead a brisk evening traffic was going around Leith roundabout. Findhorn glanced nervously behind him; the street was empty. His footsteps were echoing off the high grey walls and buildings. He broke into a trot, the backpack bouncing heavily on his back. He made it with relief to the roundabout. There were restaurant crowds here, and drunks, and young people hanging about. He turned right along Constitution Street and past the Spiral Galaxy. Close by Leith River was a high wall. Through to a little cobbled courtyard and up a flight of stairs. A man stood at the top, polite, suited, muscular.

'Are ye a member, sorr?'

'The name's Findhorn. I'm expected.'

'Aye, Doctor Findhorn, sorr. Your party's waiting for you.' The door was opened and warm air enveloped Findhorn.

It was a big old tenement room, plush red and gloriously warm after the nip of the Edinburgh haar. It was sprinkled with an odd collection of comfortable, Victorian-style armchairs and tables. Each table had a jug of water: at cask strength, it was advisable to dilute the whiskies on offer. An open fire burned cheerily in a corner and a pot of coffee was on the go next to it. There was an aroma of whisky and coffee, and the air was light blue with tobacco smoke.

The Society was crowded. A woman, at a table near the fire, caught Findhorn's eye. She was tall, about fifty, with trim, greying hair and pearl ear-rings, and was wearing a long red coat. Her companion was squat, bulky and had a far-Eastern appearance; probably Korean, Findhorn thought. The woman waved. As Findhorn approached, it became plain that the Korean's bulk was due to muscle rather than beer. He had a heavily lined face and was smoking a cigarette.

Findhorn suddenly felt uneasy.

'Doctor Findhorn? I'm Barbara Drindle, from the Arendal office of Norsk Advanced Technologies. And this is Mister Junzo Moon. I'm afraid he doesn't speak much English.' Her voice was husky and her accent was good, very good, but it wasn't native English.

Findhorn put backpack and briefcase on the floor and sat down at the vacant chair, next to the glorious heat. The woman smiled: 'After your adventures I should think you need something strong. The Society buys direct from distillers. Because of some strange quirk in the law it isn't allowed to use their brand names, which is why the bottles here are labelled by number. But you'll see a little catalogue on the bar which tells you all you need to know. What would you like?'

'A coffee, I think.' Findhorn helped himself and returned to the table.

'The Company have arranged a room for you at the Sheraton tonight. I expect you'll want to get back to your office as soon as possible.' She slid over an envelope. 'An airline ticket for Aberdeen.'

Findhorn slid the envelope back. 'No trouble. I haven't seen you around at Norsk. Which division is that?'

Suddenly, the Korean's expression was hostile, but the woman's smile didn't falter. 'The Secretariat. I work directly for Mister Olsen. And now, we'll be getting on.' She leaned down for the briefcase.

Findhorn seized her wrist. The woman was surprisingly strong.

'Do I really know you're Company? Some very persistent Americans have been after this.'

The Korean looked as if he wanted to break Findhorn's neck. The woman's smile acquired a chilly edge. She sighed, disengaged Findhorn's hand and produced a sheet of paper from her handbag:

```
TO DR F. FINDHORN.
This is to certify that Ms. Barbara
Drindle is employed by the Directorate
of Norsk Advanced Technologies. She is
to be given the documents retrieved from
the Shiva City Expedition.
```

The paper was letter-headed with the Norsk Advanced Technologies logo of an Earth held in the palm of a hand, it had all the right e-mail, telephone and postal addresses, and was signed with the neat, precise hand of Tor Olsen himself.

'Satisfied?'

Findhorn said, 'Forgive me, I had to be sure. So, you're with Olsen's office in Arendal?'

'Correct.'

She picked up the briefcase and tried the lock. Then she handed it over to the Korean. Findhorn tried to look calm while the Korean hauled at it like a bad-tempered gorilla. He finally snarled and shook his head like a dog getting rid of fleas.

Findhorn said, 'It's been under tons of ice.' Ms Drindle gave him a cool smile once again and gestured to the Korean, then headed for the exit with a wave of the hand. The Korean stood up. To Findhorn's amazement he turned out to be little more than five feet tall which, with his girth, made him look like an orang-utan. He shot Findhorn a look of pure hatred and followed Ms Drindle out.

Findhorn gave them thirty seconds, then went to the exit. A car was taking off smartly on the riverside street and he just failed to catch its registration number. Then he was briskly down the stairs and off in the opposite direction. He trotted smartly up Constitution Street and turned into the Spiral Galaxy. Once in the safety of the crowded, smoky bar, he sat down with a sigh of relief: he didn't want to be around the muscular Korean when they discovered the *Apeiron Trader's* supply of *Playboys*.

6

The Museum

Findhorn held onto one certainty in his uncertain world. In no circumstances was he about to take up his room at the Edinburgh Sheraton. Not with the icy Ms Drindle and her knuckle-grazing companion on the prowl.

He gave himself an hour in the Spiral Galaxy before risking the streets, feeling his lungs silhouetted by tobacco smoke. He plodded up Leith Walk, the backpack heavy on his shoulders, keeping a sharp eye out on the dark streets. Once a car stopped about twenty yards ahead of him, began to reverse. It was probably someone looking for directions. Findhorn ran off up a side road and then into the mouth of a close and stood, heart beating, for about ten minutes, before risking the streets again.

At the top of the Walk, near Calton Hill, he waved down a taxi. He took it to Newington, and trawled half a dozen anonymous B & Bs before he found one with a room and a welcome. The doorbell was answered by the lady of the house, whose long, green Campbell tartan skirt matched the hall carpet. His room was small, clean and had a deep-piled, green Campbell tartan carpet. He dropped his luggage and flopped onto the soft bed, exhausted; the encounter with Norsk's unnerving representatives had left him drained.

He looked at his watch. It was 11 p.m. There was a payphone in the hallway, and a directory. A television was flickering in the lounge as he passed; some football match. He glimpsed a few semi-comatose guests sprawled over armchairs. He dialled through to the Sheraton and asked for a Mister Hansen, just arrived.

It was clear from the slurring in Hansen's voice that his liver was having to cope with something like a litre of Glenfiddich.

'Hansen? Findhorn here. I need your help.'

'Well, well, if it'sh no' the elusive pimpernel. They seek him here, they seek him there, they seek yon Findhorn everywhere.'

'They? They've been looking for me?'

'Desperately. A comely wench, too, ye have hidden depths, laddie. I'd go for two falls, two submissions and a knockout wi' that one any day.' The captain giggled.

'She'd probably strangle you with her thighs. Will you sober up, man?'

There was a long silence. Findhorn visualised the captain swaying on the edge of his bed. Then: 'Whaur are ye?'

'A few miles away. Look, would you phone Norsk in Stavanger? I can't do it from here. Leave a message on their machine if there's nobody there. Tell them I have the papers they're looking for. And tell them I'll hand them over only if given good reason.'

The silence was longer. Findhorn could almost sense

the struggle at the other end. When the captain spoke, he was clearly trying to get a grip on reality. 'Good reason?'

'Yes.'

'What the hell is that supposed to mean?'

'Listen, Hansen. Ten men died in that operation. Shiva were a hundred miles off base. They were carrying out a major tunnelling operation which had nothing to do with Arctic meteorology. There were people on that berg desperate to get their hands on that briefcase and for all I know they have a right to it. For all I know *I* am the rightful owner. I won't hand it over to the Company or anyone else until I know what this is about.'

'You won't hand over – my God, Findhorn.'

'I'm not an employee. There was no written contract, I accepted no payment. Nothing requires me to hand over material found in an iceberg to them or anyone else.'

'They'll cut off your goolies, laddie. Norsk's a giant.' Hansen struggled for an adequate description. 'A Sumo wrestler with three balls and forty foot high.'

'Phone their Stavanger office. I'll call you tomorrow.'

Back in his room, Findhorn slipped off his clothes and slid under the cold sheets. He looked at the material he had emptied from the briefcase: a bundle of letters, bound together with red tape, and about twenty small desk diaries, dark blue, each marked with a year. He opened one at random and flicked through it. It was in good condition. The binding was loose, as if someone had tried to pull it away from the pages; otherwise there were few signs that it had been under the crushing pressure of glacial ice. Water had ruined some of the other diaries, reducing the ink to an illegible smear or removing it altogether.

They were American. On the front leaf of each was written a name in English: Lev Baruch Petrosian. There were no other details. The name sounded vaguely familiar. The diary had been written up in a strange script. It looked Cyrillic but Findhorn knew the Russian alphabet and this wasn't it; neither was it Arabic. He thought it might be some Caucasian or Asian script like Persian. Scattered throughout the pages, and looking incongruous against the ancient script, were equations. There were even, here and there, phrases in English, written in a small, clear hand.

The equations caught his attention. They weren't the familiar ones of meteorology, and he didn't understand them, but he recognized the field in which they were used, and the knowledge gave him a twinge of apprehension.

He fell asleep with the bedside lamp shining in his face.

The following morning the haar had been replaced by a clear blue sky. He had bacon and eggs along with a black, coffee-like liquid, and then risked the streets, unsure whether he was in mortal danger or just paranoid.

The city centre was two miles to the north and he headed towards it, feeling increasingly nervous as he approached over the South Bridge. The Waverley railway station was below the bridge and he thought they might be looking for him there; or at the bus terminus; or the airport; or at Hertz or Avis or Budget. Or they might be cruising the streets; or they might be doing all of these things; or, he thought, I may be turning into a certifiable case of raging paranoia.

Along busy pavements to George Street. He found a business centre and started to photocopy the pages of the diaries. They were a page to a day for twenty years, two pages to a photocopy. It was tedious work. It took him an hour and a paper refill to get to 1940. For a break, he logged on to a computer and checked his e-mail. He'd been at sea for two weeks and he was faced with a long list of messages, mostly low-grade or now time-expired. The most recent, however, made him swallow nervously. It had been sent at three o'clock that morning.

> *Dear Dr Findhorn,*
> *It would be in our mutual interests to discuss the papers which you have in your possession. I do not represent Norsk Advanced Technologies. May I suggest we meet at Fat Sam's at say 1 p.m. today? Their calzone is excellent.*

He looked at his watch and did a quick calculation.

Edinburgh's George Street is stuffed with banks and there was a Bank of Scotland next to the business centre. He entered it and asked to open a safety deposit account. Outside of movies about robberies he had never seen the inside of a safety deposit. He put the diaries and the bundle of letters safely into a little steel box. Then he turned the corner to the post office in Frederick Street, where he put a label on his backpack, leaving it to be posted on to his Aberdeen office.

He emerged from the post office carrying no more than a bundle of photocopied papers: at last he was travelling light. He bought a cheap briefcase from a store with 'Sale of the Century' on a notice in its window and put the diary photocopies into it.

Now Findhorn made his way across Princes Street Gardens and up the Mound to the Edinburgh Central Library. There, in a quiet room occupied by scholars, students and a tramp getting a spot of heat, he looked through *Encyclopaedia Brittanica*. He quickly identified the script: the diaries had been written in Armenian. Then he looked up Petrosian, and it came back to him.

Lev Baruch Petrosian. A 1950s atom spy. He had vanished just before the FBI got to him. It was a long gone scandal, the people involved now presumably old men, or dead. Findhorn thought of the blue eye, imbedded in the gruesome face, staring at him through the ice. Upstairs in the library, he flicked through *The Times* of the period. Petrosian had made it to the obituary columns and the librarian made him a photocopy.

Another short, nervous foray into the streets. He passed by a public phone booth, preferring to use one in a quiet corner of the Chambers Street museum. A grizzly bear contemplated him with small, hostile eyes. It had reared up on its hind legs, it had clawed limbs of immense power and it was displaying sharp teeth, but it was stuffed.

'Archie? Have I disturbed you?' Archie was one of those academics who led a semi-nocturnal existence, often as not turning up at his department around noon and leaving again at some strange hour of the following morning.

'Fred? How are you? Not at all, been up for hours.

Anne tells me you were heading for the north pole. Are you phoning from there?'

'I'm in Edinburgh. I hitched a lift on an icebreaker and came back early. Listen, I need advice. It involves your field of study but I can't talk about it over the phone. Can I meet you, say in a couple of hours?'

'My goodness, Freddie me lad, are you spying for the KGB or something? Okay, I've no classes this morning. I can be in George Square at eleven o'clock.'

'No. I'd like you to meet me in Edinburgh.'

There was a puzzled hesitation, then: 'Aye, okay. Meet me at Waverley station at twelve.'

'No, again, Archie. I don't want to be seen at the station. I'm in the Royal Museum in Chambers Street.'

'This has got to be woman trouble.'

'I wish.'

'Right. The museum it is. I should be there in a couple of hours.'

That was the thing about Archie. He knew when not to ask questions.

Findhorn decided to do this methodically. He'd start with transport, work his way through the armour to the natural history, and then go up to the medieval dress and the Chinese stuff on the first floor, and then points beyond.

He was about thirty, tall with long untidy hair and an untidy black beard. He was wearing an unbuttoned trenchcoat, exposing a large beer belly. The archetypal wild Glaswegian, Findhorn thought, watching nervously from the top floor gallery overhead; and a man who didn't give a damn.

Archie was looking around expectantly. Findhorn gave it a minute, but he saw no signs that his friend had been followed. Feeling like a fool, he called out and waved, and ran down the stairs past the Buddha on the first floor.

They collected coffee and doughnuts at the museum café. Findhorn led the way to a corner table and sat facing both entrances. Archie's eyes were gleaming with curiosity. 'So what gives, Fred? I've been fired up all the way here.'

'I can't tell you what this is about, Archie. Not yet.'

'Och, be reasonable! I hav'nae come a' this way for a coffee. If it's no a wumman, you're in trouble with the polis. Neither of them sounds like Fred Findhorn.'

'What can you tell me about Lev Petrosian?'

Archie raised his eyebrows in astonishment. 'The atom spy?'

'The same.'

Archie's face seemed uncertain whether to show astonishment, worry or delight. 'In the name o' the wee man, what are you getting into, laddie? Petrosian came over here as a Nazi refugee, like Klaus Fuchs. A lot of the top wartime brains did. Fuchs was the big spy in the A-bomb era, but not many people know there were others. Theodore Hall, for example, a Brit also at Los Alamos.'

'What did he actually do?'

A couple of dozen twelve-year-olds trooped boisterously into the café, carrying artist's notebooks and pencils, followed by two adults, both female. The ambient noise level went up sharply. Findhorn eyed the adults nervously.

'He was at Los Alamos twice. Don't know much about what he did. I know the first time round he was involved in a big scare. Teller got the idea that if they did manage to explode an atom bomb the fireball might be so hot it would set the world's hydrogen alight, turn the atmosphere and oceans into one big hydrogen bomb. That would have got rid of Hitler, along with the rest of humanity. Petrosian was involved in the calculations which ruled that possibility out.'

'You'd have to be very sure you got something like that right,' suggested Findhorn.

Archie was studying his doughnut closely, and knowing him, Findhorn thought he was probably analysing its topological properties. 'Aye. They kept coming back to it. Now the second time, when they were developing the H-bomb, I'm even less sure about what he did. There were rumours that the guy went off the heid.'

'In what way?'

'Let me think. Got it. It was the same again. Something about zapping the planet. But since hydrogen bombs were going off like firecrackers all through the fifties and sixties, we can safely say he was wrong.'

'Could he have found something new?'

Archie shook his head. 'Nuclear physics is understood, Freddie. There's no room for new stuff at the energy levels these guys were into.'

The adults were trying to get the pupils into a line and Findhorn thought that the teaching authority should have issued them with whips. He dredged up a distant memory, something he'd seen on a television news item. 'What about cold fusion?'

Archie's voice was dismissive. 'A fiasco. It never came to anything.'

Had the comment come from some establishment hack, Findhorn would have paid it only so much attention. But he knew Archie; okay he was one of life's iconoclasts, but he was sharp with it. The opinion commanded Findhorn's respect.

'Suppose you're wrong, Archie. Suppose Petrosian discovered something. And suppose the authorities of the day didn't want people getting curious about it. Putting it about that he went mad would be an effective cover story.'

Archie said, 'It's coming back to me now. Petrosian escaped from Canada just before the FBI closed in on him. The story is he was picked up and flew over the north pole to Russia. But there's no record that he ever arrived. The assumption was that he crashed somewhere over the polar route while making his escape.' He gave Findhorn a disconcertingly close stare. 'And all of a sudden, fifty years later, Findhorn of the Arctic leaps off an icebreaker, flips to cloak-and-dagger mode and starts asking me urgent questions about Petrosian.'

'A hypothetical, Archie. Suppose something of Petrosian's was found in the ice fifty years after it was lost. Let's say a document. And suppose that some people were very anxious to get their hands on it, would go to any lengths. The question is this: what could be in that document?'

Archie gave his friend another long, searching stare.

Then he said, 'I'm damned if I can think of a thing.'

'Archie, I may need to tap into that giant brain of yours now and then. I can see the wheels turning now. But I can't tell you more just yet.'

'Any time, day or night.'

Findhorn stood up. 'I have to go, Archie. I'm meeting some people.'

Archie's face was serious. 'Fred, you could be getting into something heavy. If you've found something out there in the polar wastes, something that people want to get their hands on fifty years after it was lost, and if that something has to do with Lev Baruch Petrosian, let me give you one piece of serious advice.'

Findhorn waited.

'Keep it damn close to your chest. And trust nobody.'

7

Fat Sam's

Findhorn looked at his watch. He had fifty five minutes until the meeting at Fat Sam's; time enough to complete one important piece of business.

Back at the library, he pulled out a dog-eared Yellow Pages directory and ran a finger down *Translators and Interpreters*. He thought of his overstretched credit card and avoided the outfits with expensive boxes and names like 'School of Modern Languages' or 'International Interpreters', or which offered interpreters for trade missions. German and French translation figured heavily and he excluded these. That left half a dozen two-line entries. He noted their numbers.

Back to the museum. With change from the café he went through the numbers systematically. None of them had Armenian on the menu.

Back to the library. The security man at the entrance gave him a look. Now Findhorn opened the directory at *Clubs and Associations* and ploughed through working men's clubs, the Royal Naval Association, the Heart of Midlothian Football Club, Royal British Legion clubs, community associations, the Ancient Order of Hibernians,

bingo clubs and Masonic Grand Lodges. From this bewildering miscellany he drew two conclusions: one, *homo
sapiens* is a gregarious animal; and two, Edinburgh did
not have an Armenian Club.

And he now had forty minutes.

On an inspiration he took a taxi to Buccleuch Place
and asked the taxi to wait. He dithered between the School
of Asian Studies and Islamic and Middle East, conscious
of his one o'clock appointment and the ticking meter. He
chose the Islamic at random. The building was almost
deserted. He scanned a notice board, ignoring the lists of
examination results and the conference notifications.
There were three cards, pinned on the board. Two were
curling at the edge and offered tuition, one in German,
one in French. The third was new and written in blue ink:

> *Angel Translation Services*
> Hark the herald angels sing
> Our translations are just the thing.
> Peace on Earth and mercy mild
> Our complete service is really wild.
> We do:
> German, Russian, Turkish,
> Arabic, Bulgarian, Armenian.

It was corny enough to be a student enterprise, suggesting
fees he might be able to afford. The address was in Dundee
Street, which Findhorn remembered as a down-market
part of the city. Again suggesting impoverishment.

The taxi passed the Fountain Brewery, a massage

parlour and a sign for Heart of Midlothian FC, and disgorged him at the entrance to a tenement flat. The interior of the close was dingy and there was a faint smell of urine. A yellow Vespa scooter was attached to the metal bannister by a heavy chain. Findhorn made his way up worn steps. On the second floor, the door on the right had a doorbell, a peephole and a card:

```
R. Grigoryan
S.A. Stefanova
J. Grimason, aka Grim Jim
```

Nothing about Angel Translation Services. He hesitated, then pressed the buzzer.

Apart from the over-large gypsy ear-rings, she looked as if she was just out of bed. She was in her twenties, with dark eyes and blonde hair going dark at the roots. She held the lapels of her green dressing gown together and blinked at Findhorn curiously.

'Angel Translation Services?' Findhorn asked doubtfully.

The effect was startling. Her eyes opened wide. 'Oh my gosh! What can I do for you?'

'I'd like a little translation.'

'Romella!' she shouted, without taking her eyes off Findhorn. 'Business!' Then, 'Which language?'

'Armenian.'

'Romella! Oh, please come in. I'm Stefi Stefanova. I do Bulgarian and Turkish. She's having a bath. Are you sure you don't need some Bulgarian?'

Through a hallway with a bicycle, propped up against a table with a pile of mail. Findhorn glimpsed a final demand letter in red. Doors to left and right led to bedrooms. A pile of soft dolls was spread over a bed. A kitchen to the right was a clutter of unwashed dishes and an overflowing pedal bin. Stefi led Findhorn ahead to a small room draped with psychedelic curtains and furnished with a low table, candles and cushions, but no chairs. A football team poster was surrounded by postcards pinned on the wall along with pictures of quaint Irish cottages and dizzying snow-covered peaks. A calendar on the wall showed a hunk of half-naked masculinity flexing his pectorals for the camera.

'Did I hear you say Armenian?'

She was running a comb through shoulder-length brown hair, still damp. She was slim, although with well-rounded breasts, and quite small. She had a small round face and big brown eyes behind John Lennon spectacles. She had delicate facial bone structure and smooth skin. Silver earrings in the shape of two long cylinders hung down from delicate ears. She was wearing a plain pink T-shirt and black leather trousers, and a pair of worn Nike trainers.

'I'm Romella. Romella Grigoryan if you can pronounce it.' The accent was Scottish, melodious, with a tinge of American.

'Fred Findhorn.' They shook hands. Findhorn opened the briefcase and pulled out the photocopies. 'This is just a selection. There will be about two thousand pages in all. What do you think?'

She flicked through a few pages at random. 'The handwriting's clear enough. Some of this is pretty technical, I'd probably have difficulty even in English. But yes, I think it's okay.'

'I'm meeting some people and I'd like to leave this with you for a couple of hours. Now, there might be a couple of problems.'

She raised her eyebrows.

'I need the translation urgently. Can you take it on right away?'

She frowned doubtfully and glanced at the wall calendar. It was a good performance.

'If it's too much you could point me to another translator.' He sensed Stefi tensing at the door.

Romella smiled slightly. 'No, I can squeeze it in.'

'A verbal translation would be quickest. We'd have to go through the diaries together.'

'Okay.'

'And as I say it's urgent. It will mean working long hours.'

'Business is business.'

'There's another problem. The material is confidential.'

Romella bristled. 'Naturally, confidentiality is assured.'

'I mean, highly confidential.' Findhorn glanced at Stefi. She nodded and smiled, taking in every word with open fascination. 'We'll need a separate workplace.'

This time, the frown was genuine. 'I'll have to think about that.'

Findhorn pulled a card out of his wallet. 'You're right to be careful. Actually I'm Jack the Ripper.' She laughed, displaying a row of perfect white teeth, and read the card.

'My secretary Anne's on holiday but I can give you her home number now if you like. My father is Lord Findhorn, a Court of Session judge. He's at home too, in Ayrshire, and if you like we can phone him to confirm that I really am—'

'I wasn't implying—'

'I have to go now. We can discuss terms when I get back. That is if you want the job.'

'Unsociable hours—'

'No problem. You fix a rate.'

Taking the stairs two at a time, Findhorn wondered about another problem: how to tap the old man for a few quid.

Findhorn risked the streets again. It was a straight mile and he heard the sharp crack of the one o'clock gun just as he was turning into Fat Sam's.

A few business types were scattered around, and there was a birthday lunch in progress. Al Capone, king-sized cigar in mouth, was resting a sub-machine gun on his arm. Bogart, Dietrich and other icons of the bootleg era also looked down on the proceedings from posters scattered around the walls. In a corner, a piano was thumping out rhythmic jazz by itself, and a fat fish near the cash register kept bumping its head against the tank. A notice said it was a pirhana.

Two men at a corner table, waiting. One was tall, elderly and stooped, formally dressed in suit and tie. Findhorn could make out a large Roman nose, a blotchy skin over a skull-like face, and a slightly vacant expression which didn't fool him for a moment. The other was about forty, gaunt, with metal-rimmed spectacles, dressed in a formal suit that made him look like a Jehovah's witness. Findhorn saw them in outline: sun was streaming through a roof window, obscuring their faces.

'This place used to be a slaughterhouse,' the skull said, indicating a chair. The accent was English ruling class, Winchester, Eton or the like: a species in decline but still with plenty of bite. 'Hence the roof windows. We can move if you wish.' Findhorn shook his head. The man ordered *spaghetti alle vongole* and Findhorn took the *calzone*. The Jehovah's witness ordered nothing. They all settled for *aqua minerale*: clear heads were the order of the day.

The skull waited until the waiter was out of earshot. 'My name is Mister Pitman, as in shorthand.'

'Of course it is.' Findhorn looked at the Jehovah's witness. 'And I expect you're Mister Speedhand.'

The Jehovah's witness nodded. 'It'll do.' The accent was American.

Pitman said, 'I won't insult your intelligence by pretence of any sort, Doctor Findhorn. You hold certain documents. We represent people who are willing to pay for them.'

'Documents?'

'And please don't insult mine.'

A little bread basket arrived. 'You have a consultancy business in Aberdeen, I believe. You sell weather. You call yourself Polar Explorers to create the illusion that there is more than one of you.'

'There is more than one of me,' Findhorn complained. 'I have a secretary.'

Pitman nodded absently, trying to spread icy butter on soft bread. 'Ah yes, Anne of a thousand hairstyles. And how is your business doing?'

'I'm sure you're about to tell me,' Findhorn said warily.

'As an entrepreneur you are best described as a bad joke. You sell a few sparse grid points for commercial and military climate programmes, which make only miniscule improvements to their forecasting ability. Your turnover pays Anne's wages, and the office rent, and perhaps the coffee money. It leaves you with less profit than a street busker.'

'I could use a few more ice stations.'

The waiters had clustered round the birthday table. A candle-lit cake was presented and they burst into 'Happy Birthday to You' with the help of the piano and electrically powered black mannikins with banjos on a stage. The man waited for the cacophony and the applause to subside. 'Would a hundred thousand pounds help?'

A second-generation Sicilian waiter served up the main course with a flourish. Pitman started to poke at the little clams on his pasta. Findhorn had started on his third glass of water but still his mouth was dry. 'Enormously. But the documents, as you call them – actually they're diaries – aren't for sale.'

Mister Shorthand was concentrating on a clam, dissecting it like a zoologist. Mister Speedhand said, 'One million, then?' The American accent was turning out to be east coast, probably Boston.

Findhorn felt himself going light-headed. He looked at Al Capone, spoke thoughtfully to the gangster. 'If you offered to put a million pounds into my bank account, in exchange for the diaries, I guess I'd have to say no.'

Findhorn, dazzled by the sunlight, hoped he had imagined the look in Mister Speedhand's eyes. Pitman examined a little clam on the end of his fork. 'Someone has been talking to you.'

'No.'

Mister Speedhand said, 'Doctor Findhorn, before you find yourself in an irretrievable situation, just hand over these diaries and walk away. It's in your own interests.'

Findhorn said, 'This is fascinating.'

Pitman said, casually, 'Whoever holds these diaries is a target.'

Findhorn felt light drops of sweat developing on his forehead. He put it down to the warmth of the restaurant. 'Wrong place, wrong time. This is new millennium Edinburgh, not thirties' Chicago.'

Pitman smiled thinly. 'And you have no place to hide.'

Findhorn took a deep breath. 'If I fall under a bus, the diaries will vanish for ever.'

'Believe me, that would suit some people very nicely.'

'I could get Special Branch protection,' Findhorn said. A weird feeling was coming over him, as if he was stepping into some parallel universe: the familiar, Edinburgh surroundings were still around him, but another reality was taking over.

The thin smile widened. 'Are you a Salman Rushdie targeted by Muslim fanatics? A famous film star being stalked? You are nobody. Unless you have a high public profile, the state will save itself the expense.'

Findhorn pushed his plate away, feeling nauseous. 'You were right about the *calzone*.'

'You have a stark choice: a million pounds, or imminent death.' He stared at Findhorn with curiosity. 'For most people, the choice would present no problem at all.'

Findhorn took some toothpicks out of a dish. He started to build a little pyre but found that his hands were trembling. 'Nobody is getting these diaries until I've found out what's in them. And maybe not even then.'

A fleeting dark look; a spoiled child being denied a toy.

Mister Speedhand said, 'Doctor Findhorn, I would like you to trust me on this. You simply cannot imagine what you're getting yourself into here.'

Findhorn asked, 'You represent American interests, right?'

In spite of the sunlight streaming in Findhorn's face, he became aware of a subtle change in the body language of both men. Speedhand hesitated, and then pulled back: 'That needn't concern you. What matters is that you have just been offered an absurd sum of money for documents which you have no right to in the first place.'

'And then there's the veiled threat.'

'Was it veiled? I'm sorry about that.'

Findhorn picked off the points with his finger. 'Ten men died trying to get these diaries. I've just been offered a million for them. I've been issued with heavy threats in the event I don't hand them over. I'm sorry, chum, but until I find out what this is about ... let's just say I'm curious.'

'Curiosity did the cat in,' Mister Speedhand said.

'I'm not a cat.'

'But do you read Armenian?' Pitman asked.

Findhorn side-slipped the question. 'Something has been puzzling me.'

The man waited. Findhorn sipped at his water and continued, 'There were no rescue vessels in the vicinity of that berg. Nothing on radar, at least. But Dawson wasn't behaving like a man about to drown. A man risking his life, yes. But not a man expecting to die.'

Findhorn waited, but the men remained impassive. 'Okay,' he finally said. 'So arrangements were in hand to rescue Dawson. What about the others?'

The older man was twirling spaghetti like a native. 'They were, shall we say, an inconvenience.'

Findhorn felt himself going pale.

'Much like yourself,' Speedhand added.

Pitman sucked up a long strand of spaghetti. 'Perhaps it will help you reach a decision if I tell you that there are other parties interested in these diaries, parties with a less friendly disposition than us.'

With a surge of self-blame Findhorn thought about the Armenian translator, and he wondered what he might be getting her into, and he wondered, *what the hell is in those diaries?*

Pitman was now attempting an avuncular tone. 'Come under our wing, Doctor Findhorn. If you really will not sell us the diaries, at least let us offer you protection, and of course a translator. Solve the riddle of the diaries, thus satisfying this dangerous curiosity of yours, and give us first refusal on the information you find.'

'The endgame should be interesting, when I hand over the information and find myself out of bargaining power. Do you seriously expect me to trust you?'

The man acquired a puzzled look. 'Of course not. But what other option do you have? Unprotected, you will last at most only a few days, perhaps hours.'

Mister Speedhand said, 'A large organization is looking for you now. You cannot use road, rail or airport.'

Pitman said, 'And the streets are very dangerous for you.'

There was a grim silence. Findhorn's toothpick structure collapsed.

'You still don't get it, Findhorn,' Speedhand said. 'We have to have those diaries. Refusal to hand them over is not an option we can tolerate.'

'And if I refuse nevertheless?'

'Without our protection, the other party will find you very quickly.' The man snapped his fingers at a passing waiter.

'Nothing is what it seems here,' said Findhorn.

Pitman's expression didn't change, but Speedhand was acquiring a hostile look.

'Take that pirhana, for instance. Actually it's a big grouper, *Serranid Serranidae*.'

'What do you want?' Speedhand asked. 'A prosecution under the Trades Description Act?'

'No. It just makes me wonder what else is on the level hereabouts.'

As the Sicilian approached, Findhorn suddenly got up and made for the exit. The men, taken by surprise, sat astonished. He ran out and turned left and left again, glancing behind from time to time, and with no plan in mind other than to lose himself. He found himself in Lothian Road. A black taxi cab appeared and he stepped in front of it. It squealed to a halt.

'Bloody hell, mate.'

'I know. Morningside.' It was the first thing that came into his head. The Morningside suburbs were full of doctors and lawyers, and big mortgages, and care homes for the well-heeled elderly.

'You'll get yourself killed, Mister.'

Not in Morningside. Nobody ever gets killed in Morningside. Nasty, rough people beat you to a pulp or knife you in Leith or Craigmillar, but that never happens to people in Morningside. They're too genteel.

'Oh my God!'

The taxi driver stared at his passenger with alarm. 'Are you okay, mate?'

'Not Morningside. Dundee Street. Can you make it fast?' A thought had suddenly hit Findhorn like a punch. *How many translators of Armenian are there in Edinburgh? And how long will it take to find Romella Grigoryan, and through her, me?*

But the Edinburgh rush hour was building up and the traffic lights were consistently against the taxi, and by the time it pulled up at the tenement, Findhorn was being torn apart with frustration. He ran up the stairs and knocked.

And knocked again.

8

Camp L

Findhorn caught a whiff of cheap perfume. He tried to sound relaxed. 'Can we go?'

'Now? Not tomorrow?'

'I'd really like to get started. We can discuss your fees on the way.'

'Can't it even wait until after dinner?'

'Please!'

Romella gave him a slow, suspicious look while Findhorn inwardly fretted. She disappeared, leaving him at the open door.

'On the way to where?' she shouted through from a bedroom.

'My brother's flat. We have to get ourselves to Charlotte Square.'

She reappeared wearing a denim jacket over her pink sweater. She handed Findhorn his briefcase.

'You're sure you're not Jack the Ripper?' She was pulling a Peruvian hat down over her ears.

'Not even Jack the Lad.'

Stefi appeared from the kitchen, wiping her hands on a kitchen towel. It was half past four in the afternoon and she was still in her dressing gown. 'Do you like shish kebabs? My shish kebabs are . . .' She kissed her fingers.

'Another time.'

'You have to eat,' Stefi pointed out.

'I just have, thanks.'

Romella said, 'Okay, let's go.'

Out to the landing. She pulled the door behind her with a click. Someone was coming up the stairs. Findhorn froze.

'Evening, Mrs Essen.'

An old crone with a plastic bag in each hand; she grunted sourly as they passed. Findhorn exhaled with relief, felt weak at the knees.

The sky was dark grey and a light trickle of sleet was promising heavier stuff to come. 'We're about a mile from Dougie's flat. You don't sound like an Armenian.'

'Not surprising, considering I'm frae Glesca . . .' she momentarily affected a thick Cowcaddens accent '. . . I was brought up for some years in California. My folks still live there, in La Jolla. Dad's a lawyer. So your father's a Court of Session judge?'

'Yes. The whole family are lawyers. If you ever see a pink Porsche driving around Edinburgh, that's my younger brother, Dougie. He's with Sutcliffe & McWhirtle.'

'I've heard of them. They're criminal lawyers, aren't they?'

'Dad thinks they're criminals who just happen to be lawyers. They specialise in finding tiny legal loopholes and turning them into gaping chasms. They'll get you off anything – if you can afford them. My sister lives in Virginia Water with a barrister called Bramfield. He's rich, she's miserable and they're both drunk whenever I visit them.'

'But you didn't go in for law. Your card says you do polar research.'

'I've broken with the family legal tradition. Result, poverty.'

'I hope you can afford my fees.'

It was growing dark and car headlights were coming on. The gloom gave Findhorn an illusion of security. They passed Fat Sam's and turned left down Lothian Road. By the time they were crossing Princes Street the rush hour was in full swing and the light sleet had turned into a freezing downpour. They trotted along slushy pavements down to Charlotte Square. Here the grey terraced flats had doors with up-market brass knockers and brass plates proclaiming private medical practices, tax consultants and law firms with bizarre names. Interspersing these were private flats with names ending in Q.C. and enormous lamps in the windows.

Shivering with cold, Findhorn turned up a short flight of broad, granite stairs. He fiddled with some keys, opened a heavy door with a brass plate saying Mrs M. MacGregor, and switched on a light.

They were met by opulence and cold. Pink Venetian chandeliers threw glittering light over a patterned Axminster carpet, a little Queen Anne table with a pseudo-thirties telephone and half a dozen stained-glass doors. Jazz players cavorted among spiral galaxies and naked angels on a high vaulted ceiling. Stairs at the end of the corridor curved out of sight; they were guarded by a big wooden lion, and a scantily draped Eve was eating a marble apple on the first landing.

Romella laughed with delight and surprise. 'The Sistine Chapel!'

'Dougie's into surrealism,' said Findhorn. He turned a knob on the wall and there was a faint *whump!* from a distant central heating boiler. 'He's in Gstaad just now. He skiis there over the winter.'

Into a living room with a hideous black marble fireplace, a floor-to-wall bookcase, and a faded wallpaper effect expensively created with hand-blocked Regency patterns. Light cumulus clouds floated on a sky-blue ceiling.

'Wait till you see the bedrooms,' Findhorn said. He switched on a coal-effect fire and headed for a cocktail cabinet made up to look like a Barbados rum shack.

Romella flopped down on a cream leather settee. 'The bedrooms. A gin and tonic, please, and don't overdo the tonic.'

Findhorn poured two glasses and sank into an armchair. Then he pulled the photocopies from his briefcase and put them on a glass table between them. 'There are people after these diaries. And they're looking for me. You ought to know that before you start because if you help me they might come looking for you too.'

Her low, gentle laugh was captivating. 'That must be the weirdest chat-up line ever. Certainly it's the most original I've ever had.'

'You can come and go as you please, but I'm staying here. I don't want to risk the streets more than I have to.'

'Here am I, all alone in a big empty flat with a weirdo. It's like something out of *Psycho*.' She said it jokingly but Findhorn thought there was a trace of uneasiness in her voice. 'You're kidding about people looking for you, right?'

'No, I'm serious. Maybe you want to pull out.'

'If you're into drugs . . .'

'Look, if it makes you feel safer why don't you ask your friend Stefi to come over? And Grim Jim and anyone else you want – a boyfriend if you have one. You can all stay here. There's plenty of room.'

'Okay, I'll ask Stefi. A little girl company might be good. The phone people aren't disconnecting us until tomorrow.' Romella waved a hand around. 'She'll love this. Jim's on a field trip over Christmas, he's a geology student.' She sipped at the drink. 'Are you going to tell me the real story on this stuff?'

'I am serious. There's something in the diaries. I have no idea what it is. But there are people very anxious to get their hands on them and I have been threatened. What I need is a translator to help me solve the riddle. And I have to stay out of sight while I'm about it. They're looking for me in Edinburgh and I can't risk railway stations and the like. I know I come out sounding like a mad axeman on the run from Carstairs.'

Romella was sitting unnaturally still. Findhorn waited. He added, 'I need your help. Your fees are secondary.'

'Let me phone Stefi.'

Findhorn headed for the kitchen, G&T in hand. He half-expected to hear the front door banging shut as

Romella made her escape. A thirties-style light blue refrigerator held nothing more than a bar of Swiss chocolate, a few out-of-date yoghurts and a wedge of diseased Stilton.

Romella appeared; she had taken off her denim jacket. 'I've given Stefi the story. Wild horses won't keep her away – she's a bit of a romantic. She's Bulgarian and I suspect she has Romany blood from somewhere. She promises to keep out of our hair while we're translating. She's coming over with clothes and food and stuff.'

'Brilliant.' Findhorn saw no point in hiding his relief and he grinned.

'And she loves to cook.' Romella thought of the highest number she dared. 'I think I want to charge a hundred pounds a day for this one.'

'Agreed,' Findhorn said without hesitation. 'And Stefi gets twenty plus expenses for housekeeping.'

'Well now, Fred Findhorn B.Sc, Ph.D., Arctic explorer in a hurry, why don't we get started?'

The big living room was now comfortably warm and Findhorn sank into the settee beside Romella. He passed over the copy of *The Times* obituary. 'By way of background.' She started to read out loud:

Lev Baruch Petrosian, who is presumed to have died in an Arctic plane crash, began his career by making a number of important contributions to the so-called quantum theory which underlies the modern understanding of matter and radiation. He is better known, however, as a physicist involved in the wartime development of the atomic bomb, and later in the development of the hydrogen bomb during the Cold War period. A cloud hangs over his career in that he has been suspected of espionage, although the charge was never proven. Mystery surrounds the fatal Arctic air crash . . .

She paused and looked at Findhorn, eyebrows raised.

. . . in which it is rumoured that he was escaping to the Soviet Union to avoid arrest.

The son of a shepherd, Petrosian was born in a cottage in the Pambak mountains of Armenia on 29 December 1911. His early years were as eventful as his later ones. Orphaned at an early age in the course of a Turkish massacre of Armenian Christians, he escaped as a child with an uncle to Baku on the shores of the Caspian Sea, shortly before that city fell to the Turks, allied to the Germans, in 1918. Smuggled out in a British troop ship, they reached Persia where they stayed until the end of the Great War.

His education began in a private gymnasium in Yerevan, and Petrosian soon distinguished himself as an exceptionally able student. A chance meeting with Ludwig Barth, the German physicist, resulted in an invitation to study physics at Leipzig University. In 1932 the University accepted him as a student for a doctorate, and he began work on the

*quantum theory of matter. It was an exciting time
do do physics in Germany . . .*

'In more than one way,' Findhorn suggested. 'The Nazis
were coming on stream.'

Romella picked up the thick sheaf of papers on the
table. 'And here we are. The diaries start then.'

'He must have been twenty-three. I wonder what
triggered him?'

Romella was flicking through the pages. 'A girl, maybe.
A girl by the name of Lisa Rosen.' And translating in a
low, melodious voice which Findhorn found curiously
sensual, they at last entered the strange world of Lev
Baruch Petrosian.

She was brown-haired, talkative and cheerful. The contrast
with Petrosian's withdrawn, introverted character could
hardly have been more stark.

The diaries recorded the slightly immature recollections
and emotions of a young man finding his way in a
disintegrating world. Lev's world was one of strident
voices at street corners, of unemployed men prepared to
march like robots behind swastikas and martial bands, of
professors introducing seminars with 'Heil Hitler!' and
adopting, either from conviction or self-preservation, the
attitudes and postures of the Nazis.

They also increasingly mentioned the name Lisa.

One evening, Lisa took Petrosian to a social gathering
at the house of her brother, Willy Rosen. The social
gathering turned out to be a meeting of the local student

communists. Lev politely refused the invitation to join. He attended several such meetings, arm in arm with Lisa, but always without commitment.

One snowy day in January 1933, Lisa failed to appear at the laboratory. When he visited her in her little apartment, Lev was horrified to find her in bed, her face black and blue and her eyes almost closed up. The Brownshirts had used fists and heavy sticks to break up one of the meetings. After that, it seemed to Lev the most natural thing in the world to join the communists, the only group opposing the thugs with any degree of effectiveness. On the Party's instructions, he joined in secret. He was strictly forbidden to join the Reichsbanner, the Social Democratic Party groups who fought the Nazi Brownshirts in the streets. You are too talented, he was told, too potentially valuable to the cause, to risk a knife in your ribs.

On 30 January 1933, Hitler came to power. On 27 February the Reichstag was set on fire, and a national outburst of orchestrated thuggery against communists and Jews followed. Lev, this time with Lisa, once again found himself avoiding broken glass and unruly gangs in narrow streets. On 22 September the Reich Chamber of Culture came into being and promptly set about banishing all 'non-Aryan' culture from German life. On 4 October the racial and political purity of all newspapers and their editors was assured by the passing of the Reich Press Law. On that day too, Ludwig Barth summoned Lev: 'I can no longer accept you as a student. Your background is non-Aryan; you associate with Lisa Rosen, a communist and a Jewess. You have been speaking out against the Brownshirts.'

'Is this you speaking, professor, or the University?'

'It doesn't matter; there is no prospect that the University will grant you a doctorate.'

Professor Barth's comments did no more than crystallize thoughts which were already in Lev's mind. German academic life was in free-fall, matching the descent into hell of the country outside. The universities were being Nazified, recalcitrant professors dismissed, some murdered.

That evening Willy knocked on the door of Lev's fourth-floor apartment. Lev let him in. Willy was in an excited state. 'Lev,' he said, 'you are about to be arrested. Why? For speaking out against the Brownshirts. It is the Party's decision that you must leave the country immediately.'

'And Lisa and yourself?'

'Our place is here,' Willy said, 'fighting the fascists, with what outcome who can say? But you are too valuable to lose. You must carry on the struggle for world communism abroad.' Willy gave him the name of a girl in Kiel. 'She will look after you. Now go, quickly.'

Within half an hour Lev was heaving a suitcase loaded with books and little else through dark streets. After an hour, a safe distance from his apartment, he climbed a fence and spent a freezing night on a park bench, listening to the sounds of the dark. Early in the morning he made his way to the railway station. He half expected arrest on arrival, but in fact caught a train to Kiel without incident. He half expected arrest at Kiel too, but again left the railway station unchallenged, and found his way to an address which turned out to be a taxi service. He stayed there for six weeks, never leaving the house, until it was judged safe to transport him across dark fields to Denmark. Once there, he presented himself at the Neils Bohr Institute in Copenhagen where, as it happened, Otto Frisch was looking for an assistant. He wanted to test his Aunt Lise Meitner's quirky idea that perhaps an isotope of a rare heavy element called uranium was an unstable thing, prone to spontaneous fission like an amoeba.

A few months after Petrosian's flight, a mentally unstable Nazi storm trooper by the name of Bernhard Rust became the Reich's Minister for Science, Education and Popular Culture.

Soon after that, another storm trooper was appointed Rector of Berlin University. He promptly instituted twenty-five courses in 'racial science'.

Physics became 'a tool of world Jewry for the destruction of modern science'. Einstein the Jew was 'an alien mountebank' whose prestige proved, if proof were needed, that Jewish world rule was imminent.

And while German cultural and scientific life continued to self-destruct, a great exodus of talent took place. Soon this immense flow would be turned back against the Reich, focussed on its destruction. Some of it was directed into radar, some went into codebreaking. But for Lev Petrosian, far away in the New Mexico desert, it was the Bomb.

Dear Lev,

Yes, your letter did get through on the old Geghard trading route. If you think this isn't my handwriting you're right. I'm dictating to that pious old fornicator Father Arzumanyan. He asks if he can have his arithmetic book back as you've had plenty of time to master it.

Tomas is well. So am I. So are our sheep. That's about all the news here except that I'm seeing a girl. I can't say more as the good Father would refuse to write it down. Let me just say that she has skin as smooth as a baby's bottom and a bottom as . . . oh dear, I'm being censored.

Now here's a wonderful coincidence, but also black news. Aunt Lyudmila told me her friend Karineh — the one with the nose, you remember — knew of someone who'd made it out of Germany through Denmark, just as you did. So I enquired and it turns out he's now a teacher in the Gymnasium. A man called Victor. He says he knows you from Leipzig. It also turns out he was smuggled out through the Kiel underground in exactly the same way as you, with the same Kiel girl. She must be quite something but I must stop thinking like that now I'm in love. Anyway, now for the bad news. He tells me the Gestapo have arrested your friend Lisa. He says nobody knows anything about her fate, and that this type of thing is happening all the time now.

We're all expecting war any day. I want to kill

Nazis, but who would look after the sheep? Tomas is too old to cope alone.

I love your stories about England but of course you're making them up. Tell me more anyway. And will you ever get to AMERIKA?

Your loving brother,

Anastas

Petrosian's diary, Monday, 27 August 1939

War any day.

Hoping my British citizenship application gets through otherwise I'll be an enemy alien and God knows what will happen then. Colleagues very supportive.

Newspapers full of the non-aggression pact between Nazi Germany and the Soviets. I think Russia is trying to buy time, and Germany doesn't want to fight on two fronts again. It won't last. Still, it's hard not to feel let down.

Ph.D. exam next week, Nevill Mott from Bristol the external examiner. Good choice. He's studied at Göttingen, speaks fluent German and has left-wing sympathies. He's my age and a full professor!

Wednesday, 10 October 1939

Citizenship tribunal went OK. Told them I'm full of hate for the Nazis and that I still see Lisa's broken face in my dreams. Max Born had written to confirm I was an active anti-Nazi in my Leipzig days. No mention of any communist ties, but Max wouldn't have known about that. They said I should expect category C, which will mean I'm not subject to any restrictions, Russian pact with the Nazis notwithstanding.

My first paper, jointly with Max: *On Fluctuations in Zero Point Energy*. I feel like the father of a new baby! Great prestige being linked with Max Born, who's talking about getting me a Doctor of Science at Edinburgh.

Sunday, 29 June 1940

Writing this three days after the event. A policeman knocked me up at dawn and told me to pack whatever I could carry. Taken to police station, herded with others on to the back of a lorry and taken to an army barracks at Bury St Edmunds. Then for some reason separated from the others and driven off to Glasgow. Then put on board an old steamship in pitch-black. It sailed us down the Clyde, hugging the coast going south until we reached the Isle of Man. So much for category C – I'm an enemy alien and that's that. The camp is huge. There are about thirteen hundred of us. German offensive has now given Hitler the whole of Western Europe and it can't be long before he crosses the Channel. I want to use my mathematics and physics to defeat him, but how?

I haven't even had time to contact the department.

REVELATION

Thursday, 3 July 1940

The general feeling amongst the internees is that the British are finished. But the British attitude, which we're getting from our guards, is baffling – they don't seem to know when they're licked.

Personally I'm not so sure they're washed up. There's still no sign of a German invasion, a month after Dunkirk. If the Huns couldn't do it then, they can't do it now. Just possibly the war isn't lost.

A big worry. Suppose I'm wrong and that the British surrender. They might have to hand over internees to the Germans as part of the deal. What would the Nazis do to people like me?

Again writing this up after the events. Taken to Liverpool on a steam packet, then herded on to the *Ettrick* with over a thousand German and Italian prisoners of war. Then out into the Atlantic. Swastika flew under the red ensign to show we're carrying prisoners but when we heard that hadn't saved the *Arandora Star* three days earlier the captain did an abrupt about turn. Now the British are putting their trust in a destroyer escort. A bad crossing made worse by having to share it with arrogant Nazis.

Saturday, 29 November 1940

We're being moved to Camp Sherbrooke to escape the Canadian winter. Sad, because we all feel settled in Camp L. I'll miss the wonderful view from the Heights of Abraham over the St Lawrence. Food and washing facilities have been much better than in England, so we've been doing rather well as enemy aliens. Spacious huts, and we could have stuck the bitter Canadian winds.

And the cultural life has been fantastic. Friedlander was even elected a Fellow of Trinity College, Cambridge last month. I've made friends with some terrific people. Hermann Bondi, Tommy Gold, Klaus Fuchs and Jürgen Rosenblum especially.

'Klaus Fuchs?' Romella asked, her brow wrinkled.

Findhorn said, 'The atom spy.'

'What about the others?'

'Some of them ring bells too. I think Bondi became Chief Scientist at the UK Ministry of Defence some time after the war.'

'Not bad going for an enemy alien.'

Findhorn frowned. 'Gold rings a bell too. Yes, got it. Bondi, Gold and Hoyle came up with the steady-state theory of the Universe. I read that in *Scientific American*. Rosenblum I don't know. Do you think the contacts are significant?'

'I'm just the translator, remember?'

'So why have you stopped?' Findhorn asked.

9

The Temple of Celestial Truth

Jesus Christ Incarnate, corporeal vessel of the soul of Tati from Sirius. Transmogrified from the world of the ethereal to that of base matter. Messenger from the Higher Level and conduit to the transcendental. And leader of the Apostles, who alone will attain Heaven.

The executioner was first to arrive. She was a middle-aged, motherly woman, of the type one might associate with coffee mornings and home-made jam. She was wearing a red anorak and a long, black skirt, and was carrying a large but featureless black leather handbag. Her taxi driver turned right at the village of Maybole, away from the traffic heading south for the Irish ferries, and drove for some miles along a quiet stretch of road along almost uninhabited countryside, towards the sea. The entrance to the Castle was blocked by traffic cones, and a notice said 'NO ENTRY DUE TO STORM DAMAGE', but a storm-swept gatekeeper removed the cones and waved the taxi in.

Heaven? The dwelling place of the Angels, located

amongst the awesome halls of the Milky Way. Its specific location, the innermost planet orbiting the white dwarf companion of Sirius.

The extraordinary proof to match this extraordinary claim? Listen to the prehistoric stories handed down by generation after generation of the Dogon, the Saharan tribe contacted by the first wave of extraterrestrials. Listen to them repeat the ancient Dogon myths that describe the white dwarf orbiting Sirius in a fifty-one-year period, a star discovered by the astronomers only last century. How else to understand this except as information given to the primitives by visitors from that binary system?

And how else to understand the Book of Revelation's 'mighty angel come down from heaven, clothed with a cloud, and his face was as it were the sun, and his feet as pillars of fire', except as a visiting UFO, glowing with the heat of re-entry, smoke and flames pouring from its nozzles?

The Castle faced the Atlantic Ocean on an isolated rocky promontory in south-west Scotland. In spite of this isolation, it was only ninety miles from Edinburgh where, somewhere within that city, the diaries were located. Cannons faced landwards from the front of the Castle but to ensure privacy Jesus preferred to rely on men who stood under golf umbrellas in glistening raincoats and spoke to each other through mobile telephones.

The south wing contained private apartments, and these had been prepared by the Outer Circles, the trainees and ordinary faithful, for the arrival of Jesus and the Inner Circle.

By nine p.m., as the evening flights from Europe started to land at Glasgow, Edinburgh and Prestwick, an unusual traffic began to flow along the narrow access road: taxis, hired executive cars, the occasional chauffeur-driven Rolls-Royce.

Jesus Christ arrived at midnight. His helicopter, glistening wet and windblown, landed on the broad lawns outside the castle, on a landing pad hastily improvised from sheets weighed down by stones and lit up by spotlights.

Prophet of Apocalypse, as announced by the Seven Angels from Sirius. How else to understand 'thy wrath is come, and the time of the dead, that they should be judged, and that thou should give reward unto thy servants the prophets, and them that fear thy name, and shouldest destroy them which destroy the earth', except as a second coming, and a call to destroy those whose unbelief is preventing the arrival of the second wave of UFOs which will transport the Apostles to Heaven?

A buffet had been laid out in the nearby stables restaurant and people ate as and when they pleased. Little groups wandered around the armoury, its walls thick with the deadly weapons of two hundred years ago; others preferred to linger amongst the columned elegance of the spectacular oval staircase. With the arrival shortly afterwards of Nan Rice, Warden of All Souls College in Oxford, who turned up in a battered old Ford Escort, the Inner Circle of the Temple of Celestial Truth was at last complete.

Because time was short, the meeting began almost immediately. The Circle had dressed in the long, black, Mandarin-collar robes which they used for formal occasions. Only Tati alias Jesus had an additional adornment, a pendant in the form of a silver Earth symbol – a cross within a circle – hanging from his neck. He was a small, stout man of about fifty with a neat, grey beard and short grey hair. A large Bible and a Pepsi were on the table in front of him.

Tata, the human transfiguration of the woman clothed with the sun and with the moon under her feet, and companion of Tati, sat next to him at the end of the table. She was tall, in her thirties, smooth-skinned and with hair swept back in a bun. She had dark, watchful eyes and a broad, somewhat lascivious mouth. Amongst the faithful, celibacy was encouraged, but there was also a discreet understanding that rank hath its privileges.

The windows of the big conference room were lashed by an Atlantic storm, and the flames in the open fire leaped and flickered in the draught. The Brothers faced each other around a square of polished oak tables littered with carafes of water, and Seven-Ups and Cokes.

'Perhaps Shin Takamara would be good enough to report on our Far Eastern concrete project.'

Shin Takamara was small, sixtyish, with a near-bald head and over-large spectacles. He had a gentle, scholarly air, and he spoke modestly, but with an undertone of quiet pride. 'I am pleased to report that we have made an excellent start. Our pilot trial, as you know, took place in Seoul in the nineties. There we induced a builder to use our sub-standard concrete in the construction of an apartment store. As you know it collapsed with the loss of five hundred lives.'

'A fine achievement,' Jesus agreed.

'How did you get round the quality-control inspectors?' The question came from Ricky Ross, the West Coast American.

Takamara smiled slightly: the American was new to the group and still learning. 'It's much cheaper, in the Korean context, to bribe an official than it is to pay for high-quality concrete. Economic arguments have a powerful influence in the tiger economies.'

'He accepted a bribe knowing that the store could collapse?' the American asked.

Takamara explained patiently. 'The concrete we used was sub-standard, but not enough to make either owner or official believe that the store would fall down. The safety margin was simply shaved away. And our engineers made sure that the air-conditioning design was inadequate for the hot Korean summer. Then, when the store changed hands a few years later, the new owners installed a new air-conditioning unit on the roof. They knew nothing about the weakened concrete. Once the unit – a thousand tons of metal – was on the roof, it was only a matter of time.'

'Not only a fine achievement, but untraceable to us.' Jesus expressed his satisfaction.

'In the last year we have created over a hundred high-rise apartments in Korea and Taiwan in a similar condition. They will all start to collapse within a few months of each other. The scandal may bring down governments.'

'Splendid. Now, our brother from Western Europe.'

Herr Bund, a stooped, middle-aged man, addressed the table. He spoke in BBC English. 'Our infiltration of Aryan supremacy groups is beginning to pay off. All they really needed was intelligent leadership. We have already incited race riots in Austria and Germany. The actual loss of life has so far been small, but a wonderful climate of fear is beginning to spread through many districts of our major cities. Give it another year and I expect the spectre of a fascist revival will begin to dominate the agenda of the European Union.'

'Congratulations, Brother Bund, to you and the West European chapel. We will follow developments with great interest.' Herr Bund smiled his satisfaction, and Jesus Christ turned to a small, weak-chinned man. 'What about the Irish question, Brother McElvaney?'

'The situation needs very little help from us. We have decided that our best course is just to stand back and let it run. We don't even need to advise on channels for the delivery of weapons and Semtex.'

Jesus frowned. 'It is not part of our philosophy to stand back and do nothing. There is no situation so bad that it cannot be made worse with judicious effort. Can't you develop it further? Perhaps even foment a civil war between north and south?'

McElvaney gulped nervously. 'We did look into such a scenario. It involved creating a series of escalating tit-for-tat outrages attributed to each other's security services.'

'Take it from the shelf, Brother, dust it down and revive it; who knows where it might lead? Let us have a detailed plan by our next meeting. And now, the United States?'

Ricky Ross could hardly contain himself. 'Of course my country is a rich source of resources for our purpose. The gun problem has spiralled out of control; crime impinges on every aspect of life; there are countless racial, economic and cultural tensions; the drug problem is overwhelming all segments of society; there is almost no sense of social cohesion; there are many small religious or backwoods groups isolated from the rest of society and hostile to federal government or any government at all.'

'A rich brew,' Jesus agreed. 'And what are you doing with it? I note there have been a few high-profile bombings.'

'I regret that my West Coast chapter can't claim credit for them. But we are spreading our message. We have already, on the internet, circulated simple cookbook recipes for creating deadly nerve gases. Our immediate hope is to repeat the Aum Shinri Kyo Tokyo subway attack, without the errors in preparation and dispersal of the sarin gas which the Supreme Truth made.'

Shin Takamara said, 'Only eleven passengers were killed, although five thousand were injured.'

'But according to expert testimony to the US Senate, if the Supreme Truth had done the job professionally, thousands would have died,' Ross said enthusiastically.

'What do you have in mind?' Jesus encouraged him.

'Simultaneous attacks in all the major cities with

subway systems. I already have a team of chemists in a ranch west of LA preparing the botulism aerosols and sarin gas. We're using hobos and drifters to calibrate the lethal toxin count.'

'I am impressed,' Jesus said. 'The Americans are a young and energetic people. The speed of your spiritual enlightenment is an inspiration to us all.'

Ricky Ross acknowledged the compliment with a broad grin.

'And now, Brother Voroshilov?'

A small, gaunt, grey-faced man nodded. His accent was hardly recognizable as that of an East European. 'With respect to my West Coast Brother, we have achieved far more in my country. In America you are plagued by specialist agents, not least the FBI. Your military machine is under control. Your judiciary is independent and more or less uncorrupt. Our judiciary and bureaucracy, on the other hand, have been almost totally subverted. And our co-operation with criminal power has been an overwhelming success, creating the greatest threat to our peace and economy. The fiscal crisis, which we have at least partly engineered, is undermining the maintenance of our strategic nuclear forces and making criminals out of our most able generals and admirals.'

'We know all this—' Jesus began.

'But I have an even greater enterprise to report. We have a nuclear suitcase operation nearing completion. I had thought to surprise our brothers and sisters with the result. However when we next meet I hope to report a spectacular success, involving a major European city.'

'You need no praise from me, Brother. Your successes speak for themselves. I can hardly wait until our next meeting.' Jesus nodded. 'And now, we come to the climax of our proceedings. Not only of our proceedings, but an opportunity which has come only once in all our history. It is a great moment for us all. Our brother from the United Kingdom will now report.'

Attention focussed on a man sitting across from Jesus. The man was about forty, gaunt, with thick lips, metal-framed spectacles and short, vertical sandy hair. He was unconsciously gripping the sheets of paper in front of him, and his cheeks were flushed. 'I have to report a temporary setback,' he said in a neutral, slightly northern accent.

Tata sensed fear in the man's face, felt her heart beat faster. Under the long oak table, her hand slid over to Tati's heavy thigh, and squeezed it tightly.

There was a heavy silence around the table. The Apostles waited.

'Our quest for the doomsday machine still continues,' he said. His voice was unsteady.

'I don't wish to interrupt,' said Jesus, 'but perhaps we should use plain language here. You were assigned to obtain certain documents. Did you, or did you not, fulfil that task?'

Unconsciously, the man's mouth was twitching. 'In plain language, I did not.'

Jesus spoke quietly. 'Perhaps you should explain the circumstances.'

Sweat was making the man's brow glisten in the light of the chandelier high above the table. He sipped nervously at a Seven-Up. 'As you know certain facts were brought to our attention by one of our brothers in NASA. A routine unclassified surveillance by a French satellite had revealed the presence of aircraft wreckage at the mouth of a glacier in Eastern Greenland. The location of the wreckage indicated that the wrecked aircraft was probably the one which was intended to transport the nineteen fifties atom spy, Lev Petrosian, to the Soviet Union, along with certain documents.'

'Was this information classified?' Takamara asked.

'It was in the public domain, but had attracted very little interest or attention. We had information suggesting that the documents in the aircraft—'

Jesus interrupted, '—were the key to the doomsday machine described by the fifth angel.'

The man gulped. 'Yes. An American scientific team, manning a weather station on the Greenland Ice Cap known as Shiva City, was nearby. Through a large donation by us to the Polar Research Institute which financed the station, we were able to persuade the team, reinforced by some of our people, to head for the wreckage. Unfortunately the glacier calved off and the Shiva City expedition found itself afloat on an iceberg. Although we had succeeded in infiltrating the group, our Brothers went down when the iceberg broke up. An icebreaker, however, had by this time reached the berg.'

'A simple rescue operation?' asked Ross.

'We suspect not. The icebreaker was the property of Norsk Holdings, the oil exploration company. At any rate an individual aboard the ship, a polar scientist by the name of Findhorn, acquired the documents and disappeared with them before we could get to him.'

Jesus snapped his fingers. The executioner leaned down to her handbag, pulled out a syringe and a small bottle with a straw-coloured liquid. The wooden floor creaked slightly as she tap-tapped her way across the room to Jesus. The rain battered the window, and the fire was crackling. And yet the big room was enveloped by a strange silence.

The UK brother licked his lips. His breathing was heavy.

Jesus contemplated the syringe. Then he stood up and walked over to the rain-lashed window. He was a surprisingly small man. The lights of the Castle showed a white-capped sea, merging into darkness beyond. The lights of a fishing boat were about a mile out; they were bobbing up and down: the boat was making heavy weather. Lighthouses flashed from Holy Island, Ailsa Craig and Pladda. On the horizon somewhere beyond, he knew, was Arran, but only an occasional glimpse of light could be seen in the black. Down and to the left was a boathouse; he could make out a dark figure: someone under an umbrella, talking into a mobile phone.

He turned to the UK brother. The man's face was grey. Jesus said, 'As we all know our human bodies are hosting our souls temporarily, pending our completion of the cleansing programme which the first wave initiated over five thousand years ago, when the Egyptians first worshipped our home star. That programme is to be completed within the first century of this millennium. Only by freeing the earth of its unclean souls can those of us who are the

Apostles be freed to enter the bodies which await us on our true home, Tatos, the innermost planet orbiting the white dwarf Sirius B.'

'I know this, Tati.'

'But you need to be reminded of it.' Jesus nodded to Tata. She opened the Bible at a bookmark, and read out:

> *And the fifth angel sounded, and I saw a star fall from heaven unto the earth: and to him was given the key to the bottomless pit.*
>
> *And he opened the bottomless pit: and there arose a smoke out of the pit, as the smoke of a great furnace; and the sun and air were darkened. And there came out of the pit locusts upon the earth . . .'*

Tata paused, threw a brief, mirthless smile at the UK brother and then said:

> *And in those days men shall seek death, and shall not find it; and shall desire to die, and death shall flee from them.'*

A fanatical edge was creeping into Tati's voice. 'What does this passage describe but a cosmic machine intended for the destruction of mankind? We have always understood this prophecy. How to explain the timing of this iceberg event, if it was not caused by the Angels of Revelation? They have clearly used their powers to send the doomsday machine of this Petrosian to us. They have given us the task of fulfilling their prophecy, a task which was delegated to you. You were entrusted with fulfilling our destiny.'

Bund said, 'You have failed not only us, depriving us of our homeward journey, you fail all of the Apostles going back five thousand years to Menes of the First Dynasty.'

'And you fail the Sothic brothers and sisters who await us on Tatos,' the Warden of All Souls pointed out.

Jesus said, 'Look what you have done to us.'

The man looked as if he was about to faint. He stared wildly around the table, but saw no compassion: the faces of his brothers and sisters were uniformly grim. 'It's only a temporary setback. I can find this man. I can get the diaries back.'

The executioner had been standing quietly, away from the table. Now Jesus nodded to her. She filled the syringe slowly from the bottle, approached the man slowly.

'Please . . .' He had seen the liquid at work.

Brothers on either side seized the man's arms. The executioner held the man by the hair. He felt the point of the needle on the side of his neck, at the carotid artery. 'I can retrieve the documents,' he gabbled. 'The man hasn't left Edinburgh. My entire northern chapter has converged there. He can't set foot on the Edinburgh streets without being seen. We know that the documents are in Armenian and we're combing the city for every translator of the language.' The woman was exerting a gentle pressure with the needle; the man felt the skin about to puncture; his eyes were wide with terror. 'He'll be found within days.'

'How many days?' Jesus asked.

'Three. Three at the most.'

Jesus looked around. 'What do you say? Shall we give this wretch another chance?'

There was a murmur of agreement around the table. Tata shook her head.

Jesus looked at her, assessed the opinion around the table. 'Very well, Brother. Find this polar scientist . . .'

'Findhorn.' The voice was a croak.

'. . . this Findhorn, and the documents. Do so within twenty-four hours.'

'Twenty-four hours?' The man's voice quavered incredulously, but then his eyes went to the needle, still only inches away from his neck. The executioner was pursing her lips in annoyance. 'I will!' he whispered. 'I will!'

'One other matter.'

'Say it, Tati. Give me your instructions.'

'Findhorn's theft is an insult to our extraterrestrial fathers. Convince him of this, and have him repent, before you destroy him.'

10

Hot Air

'I believe you!'

It was a moment before he recognized Stefi: a velvet pill-box hat, glistening wet, was pulled down almost to her eyes, a *Doctor Who* scarf was wrapped around her neck and she was wearing a knee-length coat and leather boots. She was holding two large suitcases, and her eyes were shining with enthusiasm. 'I knew there was something about you.'

'Come in, Stefi.' Findhorn looked quickly up and down the street but could see nothing out of the ordinary.

'I won't be a problem. I'll keep totally out of your way.'

'Okay. Maybe I'll get to sample those shish kebabs.'

Beyond the marble Eve, on a landing as large as the Dundee Street flat, a hippopotamus peered at them through reeds. A zebra was drinking on the other wall. Unseen by it, a crocodile watched quietly, its eyes just above the water. The crocodiles on the ceiling, however, had wings and were flying in formation. The African watering-hole motif surrounding them was broken by six pastel-coloured doors. 'I'll take Dougie's room,' said Findhorn, opening a blue door. He heard Stefi Stefanova give a squeal of delight as she opened the pink door next to him. Romella took the green room across the landing.

Findhorn had a shower in a vast blue bathroom and wondered if Stefi's helpfulness would extend to buying him some underwear. When he emerged, wrapped in a bath towel, Romella was sitting on his bed with the papers in front of her, neatly sorted by years.

'Stefi's nipped out for some late-night shopping. I've left the front door unlocked if that's okay. I thought we might carry on.'

'Excellent.'

She riffled through a sheaf of the papers. 'I can't make out forty-one. It's hopeless.' Romella dropped the photocopy of the water-stained diary onto the floor. 'Before we start, what are you looking for?'

'I wish I knew. Maybe some new scientific process.' Side by side on the single bed, leaning against the ornate Mexican-imported headboard, Findhorn was enjoying the warmth of her forearm.

She picked up 1942. 'Why all this macho Arctic explorer stuff? What do you actually do?'

Findhorn looked at his new companion, and decided she was genuinely curious.

'I go out to my ice station and measure things. Cloud cover, wind patterns near the ground, most of all the way the pack ice moves.'

'Why? For weather forecasting?'

'I just do stuff like that to finance my research. What

I'm really about is testing a theory.'

'So what's the great theory?'

'I think we're heading for a catastrophe.'

'A catastrophe,' she repeated tonelessly.

'Romella, I have a confession to make. I'm not a polar explorer, I'm a mathematician. My field is instability in complicated systems.'

She laughed in surprise. 'Well, I'm gobsmacked. What's a mathematician doing at the north pole?'

'Because of something I discovered. On paper.'

'Tell me about it,' she encouraged him.

'Did you know that sea level has risen by ten centimetres in the last century? Half of that comes from melting icebergs, the other half from warming oceans.'

'Fred, I know lots of things, but not that.'

'Ten centimetres isn't a catastrophe, but fifteen metres is and I think that's where we're headed. I think that big hunks of Antarctica are about to break off. Especially the West Antarctic ice shelf, which reaches hundreds of kilometres out to sea. It's sitting on the ocean bed, barely holding onto the continent. Now a little warming to lubricate its contact with the rock and off it goes, an iceberg half the size of Britain drifting into the Pacific and melting.'

She was looking at him thoughtfully. He continued, 'Every city round the ocean rims would end up like Venice. Los Angeles would disappear, New York City would be reduced to a handful of islands and London would turn into a big lake with buildings sticking out of it. All the major financial centres except Zurich would go, and every harbour in the world would be flooded. And the map-makers would have to redraw their atlases. Can you imagine the economic chaos?'

'So why aren't you in the Antarctic drilling holes?'

'Because I think the first signs will appear around the north pole, not the south.'

'How come?'

'The way I think it will go is this. When pack ice cracks it opens up a lead – a long channel of open water. This sea water is at about minus two degrees as against minus thirty-five for the air. So heat pours out from the lead, warming the ice around it. Okay, as things are at the moment the lead will slowly freeze over again. But with global warming under way there will come a point where the leads which open up are too big to be closed again by refreezing. They'll melt more ice, creating more leads and so melting even more ice – et cetera. The ocean will suddenly dump its heat into the ice. The Arctic ice cap will just crack up and disappear.'

'The polar cap will disappear? Suddenly?'

Findhorn nodded. 'Suddenly. But that's just the trigger. The rise in sea level will add buoyancy to the West Antarctic shelf which will just lift off and float away, adding to the mayhem. Cities, islands, countries will be submerged all around the world's ocean rims. And with all that water vapour in the air, even the Greenland ice cap will start to melt. Big hunks of the planet will become hotter than the Sahara. That's why, even if you live in Jamaica or Tokyo, you should still care about the Arctic. We're all wired up together.'

'And you're out there, a lone pioneer trying to save the world. Can't you get government support or something?'

'Unfortunately my funding application was sent to Mickey Mouse, alias Sir David Milton, and that was that.'

Somebody was running up the stairs. Findhorn started.

Romella said, 'Relax, it's just Stefi. You're serious about being hunted, aren't you? Do you think this mad theory of yours has anything to do with Norsk asking you to collect the diaries?'

'I don't see any connection. Petrosian was a different sort of mad scientist.'

Stefi appeared at the bedroom door, holding a plastic bag. She looked at them and grinned slyly. Romella gave her a look and said, 'But what's it actually like, working out there? Disappearing into Arctic wastes with no TV, no fish and chips?'

'And no girls?' Stefi added.

'Imagine being inside a deep freeze day after day, sometimes with a howling wind. It can be so cold you want to weep. But there are compensations. When you fly in you see this tiny cluster of huts next to a ship and all around it is this huge expanse of ice, with long open cracks of sea water. You see these big blocks of ice, all weird sculptures and aquamarine blue. You feel as if you're on solid ground but you know you're on a skin of ice only a metre thick and the water under it goes down for two miles. Sometimes in the night you can hear the ice cracking. I've seen a hut disappear overnight. I've walked two hundred yards to starboard from an icebreaker, worked in a hut for a couple of hours, and come out to see the ship fifty yards away, aimed right at me. There's nothing like it. It's like being an explorer on another planet.'

'It sounds dangerous. All those blizzards and cracks in the ice.'

'The polar bears are the big problem. They're wonderful killing machines. They're clever, and they're especially dangerous when they're hungry.'

'Talking of which,' Stefi said. She waved the plastic bag and disappeared.

Romella flicked through the copy of the 1942 diary. 'There's some gobbledegook in here. Maybe you can make sense of it.'

Petrosian's diary, Wednesday, 28 July 1942

Our much-promised, and badly needed, long weekend.

Collected Kitty early. A joy to see her so happy. She was wearing a long green skirt and a sweater, and the Indian ear-rings I gave her. Loaded up the wagon with camping gear, but about half the car taken up with her easels and canvasses and other painting stuff. Guess what she'll be doing.

Took off eight a.m. and headed west. It was interesting to see the cacti getting smaller as we got higher and then the trees starting to appear and get bigger. Spent a couple of hours in the Petrified Forest and then on to Flagstaff. Nice town, clear air after the furnace heat of Los Alamos. Lots of pine trees around. Found a picnic place and devoured salad sandwiches and lemonade. Sky blue, air warm, and impossible to believe there's a war on. Then turned north and took a long straight road to the south rim of the Grand Canyon. It was dark by the time we got there.

Couldn't afford the restaurant prices in Grand Canyon village so decided we'd have a barbecue, which would be more fun anyway. Went to local store and bought hickory chips, charcoal, matches, firelighter, barbecue skewers, tin plates, mugs, coffee, sugar, milk, two bottles of red wine, T-bone steaks, barbecue sauces, cutlery, salt, pepper and chillies. Worked out twice as expensive as a dinner but who cares! Had a super time. Tried my party trick (reciting π to thirty decimal places). Kitty made me keep repeating it as the wine bottle went down. Think I passed the test.

Then the funny phone call. It makes me wonder how the hell they found me because I didn't know myself we were even going to be in Arizona, never mind the Grand Canyon, south rim. Went back to the store for toiletries and the phone was ringing as I entered. The storekeeper says are you Mister Miller – my code name when I travel – and I say yes. Unbelievable!! It's Oppie. Wants me to go to some lakeside cabin near a place called Escanaba, which apparently is on Lake Michigan. Over a thousand miles away. Wants me there tomorrow as a matter of 'supreme urgency'. I tell him I'm drunk and I'm here with Kitty, but he says dump her and make it anyway.

Got lost on the way back to the tent and wandered around the forest in the dark with visions of dropping into the canyon. Furious row. She can't believe I didn't phone in. Asked her if she'd run me to Flagstaff in the morning and could I borrow the train fare and she nearly hit me.

Thursday, 29 July 1942

I'll remember this day as long as I live.

I slept in the wagon, Kitty took the tent. I love Kitty to distraction and it hurts to have us quarrel. I can't blame her but at the same time can't tell her about the project.

Woke up about six. A racoon was heading for the remains of our barbecue, stopping to go up on its hind legs now and then. Ran off when I went to waken Kitty. Packed up, then zero conversation all the way to Flagstaff. Asked her to stay until Saturday and I'd try to get back and we'd still get our weekend but she took off the earrings and said, 'Give them to your Lake Michigan broad.' Felt sick.

Got to the cottage, which it turns out is being rented by Arthur Compton, also on holiday. We took a car down to a quiet beach overlooking the lake, and there I listened to Oppie's story.

Teller has been calculating the temperature build-up in the fission reaction. He finds that the heat will ignite the atmosphere and maybe even the oceans.

Arthur and Oppie both devastated. Compton says it's better to accept Nazi slavery than take the slightest chance that atom bombs could explode the air or the sea. The gadget must never be made.

REVELATION

Friday, 30 July 1942

Exhausted, having worked overnight on Teller's calculations. He thinks a deuterium/nitrogen reaction will take place and, the air being eighty per cent nitrogen, that we have a massive problem:

$$C^{12}(H, \gamma)N^{13}$$
$$N^{13}(\beta)C^{13}$$
$$C^{13}(H, \gamma)N^{14}$$
$$N^{14}(H, \gamma)O^{15}$$
$$O^{15}(\beta)N^{15}$$
$$N^{15}(H, He^4)C^{12}$$

So at fission temperatures two hydrogens combine with carbon to give a burst of gamma rays, the atmospheric nitrogen combines with the hydrogen in water vapour to create oxygen 15 and more gamma radiation, carrying a thumping great 7.4 Mev of energy. The O^{15} isotope is unstable and beta-decays to heavy nitrogen N^{15} in 82 seconds. A neutrino carries the energy from this clean out of the Galaxy so we forget it. But then the heavy nitrogen so created interacts with more hydrogen. It disintegrates back to ordinary carbon, creating helium and a hefty 5 Mev. It's as if the Earth's atmosphere has been created just waiting for the nuclear match. The bottleneck is the long reaction time for combining two hydrogen atoms with a carbon one. The fireball would cool down too fast to pull it off. But Teller has a trick up his sleeve. He says the two hydrogens are already there in the atmosphere's water:

about one hydrogen atom in ten thousand is deuterium.

I suspect he's wrong. If my overnight sums are right the nuclear reaction rates need one hundred million degrees to be self-sustaining. I doubt if an atom bomb will yield more than fifty million degrees. So we're maybe on the right side of hell. Nice ethical dilemmas: (i) do we have the right to risk humanity on the correctness of our calculations? (ii) with a safety margin of only two, and given a straight choice, should we take a chance on burning the world or submit to Nazi slavery?

Mentally and physically worn out. But I can't complain. Nobody's shooting bullets at me.

Saturday, 31 July 1942

Refined the calculations with the help of better cross-sections. Chance now about three in a million. Compton says this is acceptable. Oppie asked who are we to decide on behalf of humanity what's an acceptable risk. I suggest we stick a notice in the local newspaper asking the public for their opinion. They don't think that's funny.

Flew back to Flagstaff on borrowed money, in desperation borrowed a pick-up from an incredibly kind woodcutter and hammered it all the way to the Grand Canyon. Kitty gone.

'What do you make of that?' Romella asked, rubbing her forearm. 'I'm freezing.'

'An irate girlfriend, and a near-miss on vaporizing the planet. Just another weekend.'

'This formula . . .' Romella asked.

'I haven't a clue.'

'If you say so.'

'If the sums had gone the other way . . .' Findhorn said. 'What's that?' He pointed to a smudged scribble.

She tilted the page and screwed up her nose in concentration. 'It says HMS *Daring*.'

'What has that got to do with anything?'

Romella shrugged. 'How would I know? It's probably nothing.'

'I agree. Probably nothing. Forget it.'

'Standard stuff, Freddie. Teller was discovering what's called the carbon-nitrogen cycle. It's what fuels hot stars, hotter than the Sun. But nothing on Earth can approach that sort of temperature.'

It was three o'clock in the morning and they were using oblique language. Archie had said it didn't matter as he was working anyway, and Findhorn didn't believe him even slightly.

Just a chat between friends.

About nuclear physics.

At three o'clock in the morning.

Nothing unusual about that. No eavesdropper would even notice.

Could Petrosian have discovered some way of getting the necessary temperature, of locking into this cycle to create a powerful new bomb? The question came out as: 'Not even, say, a nuclear fireball?'

'Not even a nuke.'

'It's another red herring, then?'

'Extremely red. But keep digging, laddie. This gets more intriguing by the minute.'

Findhorn switched off the bedside lamp and flaked out.

11

The Gardens

'I know all about HMS *Daring*.'

Romella and Findhorn, loading up a Miele dishwasher with breakfast things, looked up in surprise. Stefi was standing in dramatic pose at the kitchen door, looking like a snow-dusted mummy.

'Well?'

She flung off coat and scarf and flopped, teasing out the moment. She pulled back a kitchen chair and put her leather-booted feet up on the table. 'At least, I know where to go to find out about it. I spoke nicely to a young man in the National Library. It's all in the Public Records Office in Kew.' She read from a little card. 'Admiralty Report Number 26/54, for instance, tells us about the ship's vibration trials. There's lots of stuff like that.'

'When were those trials?'

'1954.'

'Clever girl,' Findhorn said, 'But the diary entry was July 1942. 1954 didn't exist then.'

'Oh.'

The deflation lasted a few seconds. 'Well what about this? HMS *Daring*. British destroyer of 1,375 tons.

Torpedoed by a U-boat on the 18 Feb 1940 off the coast of Norway. Only fifteen survivors. He wrote his entry just four months after it sank.'

'That's it? Nothing unusual about it?'

'It was unusual for a British warship to be sunk by a U-boat, otherwise I can't see anything odd. You Brits are so proud of your Royal Navy, but Bulgaria has a navy too, you know. I could murder a coffee, especially one with two sugars and lots of milk.'

Findhorn was filling the kettle. 'We've seen nothing in the diaries.'

'But we've only gone as far as 1942,' Romella pointed out. 'Black and no sugar.'

'I need to photocopy the rest of them.'

'Where are they?' Stefi asked.

'Tucked away safely.'

'He doesn't trust us. Are you sure you want to risk the mean streets?' There was a slightly sarcastic edge to Romella's voice.

Findhorn was looking for sugar. 'I do not, but what choice do I have?'

'Okay, while you're out risking your life I'll get more girlie things from the flat. It looks as if we'll be here for some days.'

'Be careful, Romella. If anyone asks, you've never heard of me. You're not translating anything for anyone. And make sure you're not followed back here.'

Romella glanced at Stefi. 'Isn't that the most wonderful chat-up line? What do you think?'

Stefi was undoing laces. 'I believe everything Fred tells

me. He's being hunted by bad people. I'll stay here and drink coffee and hope he doesn't get caught.'

Findhorn ordered a taxi and watched for it from an upstairs window. He sat well back on the short journey to the bank, looking out at the normality on the streets and feeling foolish, as if Mr Shorthand and Mr Speedhand were receding bad dreams, with Ms Drindle and her pet gorilla even more remote and unreal.

He emerged from the bank with an armful of diaries. George Street was busy and grey, and a cold, freezing fog had descended. He walked briskly along the street, feeling exposed, and turned into the business centre.

First he phoned Archie. The call was brief.

Then he started to photocopy. The diaries went up to 1952 and after an hour he had reached 1948 and needed a break, and he phoned Archie again. This conversation was even shorter:

'Archie?'

'It's all set up, Fred.'

'Thanks.'

And Findhorn resumed the photocopying. After another hour the tedium became unbearable and he sat down at a terminal. He now had access to an antiquated, unused computer in the basement of Archie's department at Glasgow University. He thought about a password. It had to be memorable, unguessable and in no dictionary. He thought of:

In Xanadu did Kubla Khan
A stately pleasure dome decree

He took the initial letters of the first seven words, replacing the *A* by the number 1 to give iXdKK1s, and concluded it with a couple of nonsense symbols. The final password was unguessable, but mentally retrievable:

iXdKK1s!!

Assume the people behind Drindle and the Korean had access to high-speed computers which they might use in combination to approach cracking speeds of a million characters a second. A six-character password based on a combination of ten numbers would be broken in ten seconds. One based on the 26 lower case letters might take two and a quarter hours. An alphanumeric combination could be broken in forty days and eighteen hours. A password based on all 96 characters on a keyboard, upper and lower case, would occupy the computers for two years and seventy-eight days, day and night. And Findhorn's password had nine characters.

In any case, first find your computer.

The scanning was slower and even more tedious than the photocopying, and it took him well into the afternoon.

Photocopies of the diaries to 1950 were now heaped on the desk in front of him, as were the originals; but their electronic clones lay in a secret machine, accessed through an impenetrable gateway and protected by an unbreakable password.

As an afterthought, Findhorn checked his e-mail. He froze. A terse message stared at him from the monitor:

REVELATION

1. Seafield Cemetery, 4.00 p.m. precisely.
2. Alone.
3. Bring the diaries.
4. Contact the police and the bitch dies.

The source of the message was some Brazilian address, no doubt meaningless. He hard-copied the message. His watch said three thirty.

He phoned Romella's flat, letting it ring for a full minute before giving up. Then he rang his brother's flat. Stefi answered straight away: 'Hello?'

'Stefi.'

'Fred, thank heavens you phoned.' There was anxiety in her voice.

'What's the problem?'

'It's Romella. She should have been back long before now. And she's not answering the phone. Where can she be?'

'Stefi, stay put and don't answer the door. I'll be there shortly.' He hung up before she could reply.

In George Street, a taxi approached on cue and he took it straight to the flat. The driver was happy to park on the double yellow lines. Findhorn thought he saw movement behind a net curtain as he climbed the steps. He heard the Chubb lock turn, and then the big bolt which went into the floor, and then the Yale lock, and then Stefi's eye was peering anxiously round the door.

Findhorn handed the e-mail over without comment. Stefi gave a little scream. He dropped the diaries on the floor and ran for the stairs. 'I have twenty minutes.'

'Will you call the police?' She was running after him.

'It would take me more than twenty minutes to explain and even then they'd never believe it. And if the police get in on the act it will be the end of her.' Stefi caught up with him at the marble Eve and grabbed him by the sleeve.

'Fred, take a minute. Stop and think. What will happen to you if you go there?' She was beginning to tremble.

'Stefi, all I know is that I'm out of time.' He pulled free, ran up to the African watering hole and came back down, two steps at a time, carrying a briefcase. Stefi was standing at the front door. It was locked and she was slipping the key inside her sweater.

'What do you think you're doing?' he shouted angrily.

'Seafield Cemetery in this weather will be deserted.'

'Of course it will. Why else . . .'

'So you'll get a knife in your ribs, you idiot. If you can't think of yourself think of Romella. She's a witness. What do you think they'll do to her once they've got what they want?'

Findhorn hesitated.

'How badly do these people want the diaries?'

Ten dead; a million pound offer; a large organization hunting me. 'Very badly.'

'So. Is that not a great big bargaining chip?'

'Okay. Okay.' Findhorn paced up and down the hallway, his head bowed. Then: 'You're right, Stefi. I'll e-mail these creeps from some cyber café. We'll meet as equals in Edinburgh Castle.'

'Is that safe?'

'It's a military garrison.'

She said, 'I'll come. If you do get her back she'll need female company.'

He hesitated again. Then Stefi was saying, 'I'll stay in the background. Nobody will see you with me.'

'Hell, there's no time to argue.'

Stefi was groping around in her sweater. 'This key is bloody freezing.'

The man was about forty, gaunt, with thick lips, metal-framed spectacles and short, vertical sandy hair. He was dressed in a long black coat, the collar of which was turned up against the icy breeze, and his hands were in its pockets. He was standing next to Mons Meg, looking out over the battlements of the castle. Findhorn joined the man at the wall. Far below, office staff were criss-crossing Princes Street Gardens, looking like amoebae under a microscope. Beyond the gardens, Princes Street was festooned with decorations and crawling with traffic. 'It's a long way down,' Findhorn said.

'But at least death would be quick.' There was something odd about the man's demeanour; Findhorn couldn't specify it. 'The Castle goes back to the fourteenth century. You would think it was impregnable – who could climb walls like these? And yet it has been conquered, twice, in its long history. Once by siege, once by trickery.' The accent had a slight northern English tinge; Findhorn tentatively placed it in Yorkshire.

'Trickery is what's bugging me.'

'Yes.'

'I like it,' Findhorn said, trying to keep the fear out of

his voice. 'No false reassurances or stuff like that. I think maybe I'll be dead in a few hours and you say "yes".'

'A few hours? You are an optimist. Unless you deliver.' The man's eyes flickered towards Findhorn's briefcase. 'You have them, I sincerely hope.'

'What exactly is in these diaries?'

'If we knew that, we wouldn't need them.' The man stepped back from the wall. 'Think what we have achieved in four hundred years. Think of the damage done by a cannonball from this.' He tapped Mons Meg, the massive cannon, next to him. 'Now we have bombs the size of a cannonball which could evaporate the castle, the hill it stands on, the Esplanades and everything within a kilometre of here. Can you imagine what the future will bring?'

'Is this relevant to anything?'

A gleam entered the man's eyes. 'Oh yes, very much. God hath made man upright; but they have sought out many inventions. Ecclesiastes one, twenty-nine.'

'Oh God,' said Findhorn, 'Not a religious fanatic.'

'Take your friend. I could kill her now, by a slight movement of my finger, even although she is miles away.' He pulled a mobile phone out of his pocket and held it towards Findhorn. The little square monitor had a message, easily read even in the fading light: KILL THE BITCH.

'A touch of the button and the message is sent.' The man put his hands, with the mobile, back in the deep pockets of his coat.

Findhorn suddenly felt as if he was walking on

eggshells. 'Why "the bitch"? You've got something against the ladies?'

'Who can find a virtuous woman? Proverbs thirty-one, ten.'

'A woman-hater and a religious nut, all in one. I don't believe you're real.'

'Handle me with care, Doctor Findhorn. I'm real, I'm a religious fanatic, as you put it, and I am deeply irrational by your standards. And now, if you please, the diaries.'

Findhorn, dreading the reaction, unstrapped the buckles of the case and handed over a dozen sheets of paper, then stepped back to give the man a secure space. The man skimmed through the pages and then looked up sharply. 'And the rest?' His tone was suddenly harsh.

'They're not here. What you have is proof that I have them. I'm not about to hand them over without some guarantee that Romella will be released.'

'This wasn't the arrangement.'

'Not your arrangement, chum. But it is mine.'

Cold blue eyes studied Findhorn from behind the spectacles. 'You don't know who you're trying to push around.'

'The Castle's closing, gentlemen.'

The man waited until the soldier was out of hearing. 'You'll be getting her by instalments, Findhorn.'

'Start sending me parcels and I'll start burning the diaries.' Findhorn found himself getting angry, tried to control it.

'Gentlemen, if you please.'

'I'm just looking for a secure exchange. And remember

you need the diaries more than I need Romella. She's just a translator. She means nothing to me.'

'Is that so?' The man hissed. 'Let's take a walk down the esplanade, Doctor Findhorn, while we make a new arrangement and you explain why you're risking your life for a girl who means nothing to you.'

It was six o'clock and the rush-hour traffic was being replaced by late-night shoppers and pantomimegoers.

Findhorn turned off Princes Street down a steep path leading to the darkness of the Gardens. He cut off the path over wet grass, heading for the safety of the shadows as quickly as he could. A couple of giggling girls passed, then a drunk who wished him a Merry Christmas. Findhorn grunted in reply. He found a tree, stood in its shadow, letting his eyes slowly adapt to the dark, and waited.

And waited.

Suddenly, after half an hour, lasers began to probe the sky overhead like futuristic searchlights, coming from some point on the Salisbury Crags about three miles away. Behind Findhorn, Edinburgh vibrated with life; buses sped along a busy Princes Street; shop windows reflected the Christmas lights. He was only fifty yards from safety. In front of him, the Castle loomed high over the Gardens, its turrets and walls reflecting a pale, ghostly light.

A hundred yards to his right the Norwegian pine was draped with lights. Ahead of him two men on ladders were trying to drape a banner across the bandstand. Another was setting up chairs on the stage. Half a dozen musicians were taking instruments out of cases. There was something reassuring about the hammering and the banter. A circle of light about thirty yards in radius surrounded the bandstand; beyond this circle, shadowy forms were moving, on the limit of visibility. They were real, or they were Findhorn's imagination at work; he could not say.

It was so huge that, at first, Findhorn thought he must have imagined it. And then he realised that he had, that the towering black cliff was old lava rather than ice, that the rumble at its base was a passing Intercity train and not the thunder of waves at the foot of the berg. To his horror he realised that he had momentarily dozed; but the return to reality brought back the bitter cold and the terror.

Marooned in an island of dark shadows, surrounded by a sea of light, he gripped the briefcase with both hands and again peered into dark shadows. His mouth was dry. Now and then he looked quickly behind.

Somewhere in the dark, if the man could be believed, was Romella. She would be brought into the light of the bandstand; Findhorn would approach out of the dark with the diaries which he now held; the exchange would be made; and the parties would each melt back into the dark night.

Or so they said.

Something odd about the men on the bandstand.

A cough in the dark, over to Findhorn's right. He shrank back against the tree.

A cigarette was glowing red about a hundred yards to

the left. An occasional arc marked its passage in and out of the owner's mouth.

A torch picked out a group of three, on the bridge crossing the railway. It was the briefest flash; but Romella was in the middle of the group. The grip on his briefcase tightened.

In a minute three figures emerged into the light in front of the bandstand. Two men, one a teenage tearaway in a leather jacket, the other the religious fanatic, still in his long black coat, warmly wrapped up with a red scarf. Romella propped between them, head lolling from side to side. She was wearing a short skirt and a simple T-shirt. Findhorn thought she must be utterly frozen, perhaps even close to hypothermia. The men stood, gazing into the dark around them.

The musicians were hardly ten yards away. They were paying no attention, and Findhorn suddenly knew what it was about them. They weren't testing their instruments.

And no seating had been set up for an audience.

And the men on the ladders were taking forever to set up the banner.

He stepped out of the shadow of the tree and walked towards the three. They spotted him about thirty yards away. Romella went still.

Someone else, a small, plump woman, approached out of the dark like a ghost, and stood beside the two men. She was carrying a large, plain black handbag.

Findhorn walked into the light of the bandstand. The men were watching him intently.

Some of the musicians were climbing down the

bandstand at its far end and walking into the shadows.

Romella was shaking her head in a doped but urgent way.

12

Doomsday

Findhorn is conscious of moving shadows beyond the circle of light. He walks forward, holding up the briefcase. Closer in, he sees that the plump woman behind Romella is holding a hypodermic syringe. Romella says, 'Fred, clear off,' but her voice is slurred and barely reaches him.

He puts the case down on the frost-covered grass about ten feet from the men, and steps back. Everyone's breath is steaming in the icy air. He has never known such an alertness in all his senses; everything around him seems slow. He wonders what is going on behind the circle of light but doesn't dare to turn round.

Mister Religion leaves Romella, steps warily to the briefcase, as if he expects it to explode. He crouches down to open it and pulls out a diary at random. He pulls a small black torch from his pocket and shines it on the book, flicking rapidly through its pages. Then he shines the torch into the case and briefly counts the diaries. The lasers are flickering overhead and Findhorn feels as if he is inside some weird science-fiction fantasy.

'You can let her go now,' Findhorn says. He is judging distances.

The man looks up. 'If only life were so simple.'

'What the hell is that supposed to mean?'

'All men are liars. Psalms . . .'

'Stuff the quotes. We have an agreement.'

The man sighs. He closes the briefcase, stands up and puts the torch in his pocket. 'It's only fair, in your closing moments, that I tell you this. Miss Grigoryan is privileged. Her talents will help to solve a great mystery and enable a great prophecy to be fulfilled.'

'Prophecy?' Findhorn asked, to keep him talking.

'With her help we will be able to turn the key to the bottomless pit.' Mister Religion turns and nods. The syringe woman, and the men holding Romella, move backwards. It is as if they are on wheels. For a moment Findhorn half believes he is in a bizarre nightmare.

He hears movement from behind.

The bandstand lights switch off.

Suddenly there are only the strobing blue lights in the sky, and silhouettes against the Castle wall.

Findhorn rushes forward. He collides painfully with a dark figure who says 'Oof!' Someone from behind grabs him by the arm, shouts, 'Run, you fool! We have her.' He pulls free and sprints in her direction. He catches a whiff of Romella's perfume. She is being hauled along by the hand. Findhorn grabs her free arm; he can't make out the other party. Torches are probing dark corners. Staccato, angry shouts follow him into the dark. Someone runs past, footsteps pounding on the frozen ground. Findhorn whispers, 'Go to the left!' They run wide at the big Christmas tree, keeping away from its radius of light, towards the narrow pedestrian bridge over the railway.

Stefi, gloved and helmeted, is revving the engine of her Vespa. Seconds are lost while Romella climbs onto the pillion. She seems about to collapse. Then Findhorn is shouting 'Hold tight!' and Stefi accelerates away on the footpath, lights out. Findhorn races along the path after them, his companion following. On to a road, with lights and cars, and across it to a multi-storey car park. Footsteps pacing them from behind. Stefi's scooter is disappearing briskly round a corner, Romella clinging like a baby monkey.

The car park will have security cameras and there is is a busy street on the far side. If the Syringe People want to avoid cameras, the car park is a buffer. But now, in the street lights, Findhorn recognizes the other man: Mister Speedhand. He shouts to Findhorn and beckons towards a car, jumping into it.

Four men burst onto King Stables Road from the park entrance. Their faces are concealed under balaclavas. Findhorn knows he has no chance in a race. They spot the car, race Findhorn to it, but Findhorn gets there first and leaps in, slamming the door. It is the sort of car that has in-flight navigation and quadrophonic CD and deep leather seats and air conditioning and twin carbs, and there is a satisfying thrust in Findhorn's back as the driver takes them from zero to sixty in a millisecond. The pursuers shrink to gesticulating dots in the rear window.

Findhorn, his heart thumping, and gasping for breath, wonders about the liquid in the syringe. He looks at Mister Speedhand, and Pitman clinically studying him in the mirror, and he wonders if he should have taken his chance with the religious maniacs.

Along the Grassmarket, with its winos and bistro crowds. He thinks he glimpses a red tail light disappearing up the Candlemarket, a steep cobbled hill ending at a T-junction. The car goes up this hill. The turn, left or right, is going to be crucial. Findhorn is gasping.

Left is down the Mound, skirting the Gardens again; but it is also city centre, traffic lights, evening crowds. Right is no stopping, suburbs, countryside beyond; right is dark lay-bys, and narrow tracks winding into the Pentland Hills.

The big car turns left. Findhorn feels his legs going to jelly which is unfortunate as he intends to jump out at the first red traffic light. He sees Stefi's bright yellow scooter a couple of hundred yards ahead, wonders if Pitman has spotted it, or even if he is following it.

Down the Mound. The traffic lights are co-ordinated so that if they are green at the foot of the hill they are green all the way and he will be swept through the city and on to an unknown destination and an uncertain future.

Don't let them suspect your intentions. You are the Grateful Rescued.

'Thanks. I thought my e-mail was a long shot, especially as I just pressed the reply button. Were the musicians your people?'

'No, they were theirs. You owe us, Findhorn.' Speedhand's tone is icy, but it carries an undertone of seething anger.

'Who are they?'

'You've just lost us the diaries, Findhorn. Why should we tell you a fucking thing?'

Down the hill, the lights are at green. The cars ahead are accelerating through. Pitman is strumming his fingers on the steering wheel, studying the traffic flow, judging a system of vortices and eddies unknown to the authors of the Highway Code.

Stefi has skimmed past the traffic and she is through. Findhorn imagines that Romella, without helmet or riding gear, is being freeze-dried. The scooter turns smartly right then left, speeding up Hanover Street and out of sight.

'You didn't rescue us as an act of charity.' Findhorn's mouth is dry.

The queue ahead is streaming fast through the lights. The lights turn orange but the drivers ahead are chancing it. Pitman accelerates. The streets are packed with Christmas shoppers.

The lights are now red. Still he is going to try for it. An Edinburgh citizen, full of his rights, steps onto the road. Pitman curses and stops.

Findhorn contemplates the crowded pavements. He stays put. 'How did they find us?'

Speedhand said, 'How many translators of Armenian do you think there are in Edinburgh?'

'Okay, I'm an amateur. But I'm learning fast. What do you want from me?'

'You've just created us a mountain of trouble, friend.' The traffic flow has changed; filter traffic is turning off. It won't be long. Findhorn pretends to look out of the window but he is examining the door lock and the handle. A long stationary queue has accumulated behind them.

A horrible thought strikes him. Maybe there's a child's lock. Maybe he won't be able to open the door.

The car is an automatic. It moves off smoothly; the big engine can hardly be heard. Speedhand is saying, 'Unless you're even more stupid than I think, you've made copies of the diaries. We'll have those.' The car is slowing to turn left up Hanover Street. In a department-store window, reindeer with no visible means of propulsion are pulling Santa Claus into a snow filled sky.

People are jaywalking. Pitman swears briefly, idles, picks up speed. Findhorn waits as long as he dares. He snatches at the door handle. The door opens; he jumps out. The car is doing about fifteen miles an hour and he staggers, almost falling, before swerving onto the pavement and muscling his way through the crowds. The car, swept along by the traffic flow, is heading up the street. He looks back and glimpses Mister Speedhand at the rear window. The man's face is out of control, full of surprise and rage. Findhorn gives him a wave but he shows no sign of Christmas spirit.

Romella emerged from the downstairs toilet after half an hour of vomiting. She was chalk-faced, apart from livid bruises around her eye and lips. She waved aside an offer of help and made her way to the leather couch.

Findhorn said, 'I'm sorry. Maybe you should just walk away from this.'

She managed a weak, defiant stare through one eye.

'Don't blame yourself, Fred. You told me the situation and I chose to think it was just a fantasy thing. You're a bit weird, after all.'

Stefi came in bearing hot chocolate.

Romella was whispering again. 'And thanks for turning up. You didn't have to do that.'

'It was the least he could do,' Stefi said. 'Look at you.'

'If you didn't turn up they were going to burn holes in me until I told them where you were. There were three of them.' She managed to pull the blanket from around her knees. 'Look at my tights!'

Findhorn obliged. 'What happened?'

'The bastards dumped me in the boot of a car and drove off. I don't know where we went. They drove for hours and I nearly froze to death.'

'They were keeping you on ice until they set up the meeting with me,' Findhorn suggested. 'They'd have killed us both, me right away. I'd have been just a braindamaged smackhead who overdosed in Princes Street Gardens. They'd have dealt with you later, once you'd translated for them.'

'When they finally let me out, it was dark and I was in a car park. My legs wouldn't hold me at first but when they did I started to struggle. They got alarmed at the noise I was making. That's when the punching began. I don't know what happened next except that they shoved me back in the boot, and next time they opened it they forced some horrible liquid down my throat. I'm sure it was just cough mixture. You know, two teaspoons only, don't overdose, may induce drowsiness.'

Romella's voice was beginning to trail off, and her eyes were beginning to swim in her head.

Stefi put the mug on the coffee table and said, 'That's enough. No more talk.'

'The car was a Mercedes 600 SL. Maybe a year old. Boot smelled new.'

They laid her out on the couch.

'Green Merc. Swiss registration, I think. Didn't get the number.'

Findhorn took off her trainers. Stefi tucked the blanket around her and switched off the lights. The room glowed a gentle red from the stove. 'She needs medical attention.'

Findhorn said, 'With bruises like that, and an overdose of medicine, a doctor would have to call the police.'

'So what?' Stefi wanted to know. 'I'm calling the police anyway.'

'Romella has a say in this. Wait until morning.'

'Any change?'

'She's breathing more easily.'

'You look like death warmed up, Fred. Get some sleep.'

Findhorn staggered off. If men were going to burst into the house waving hypodermic syringes, he hoped they would do it quietly.

Findhorn was awakened by sunlight. A voodoo mask stared at him with empty eyes, on top of a small bookcase devoted to travel books, thrillers and cricket. He looked out over the Edinburgh skyline, with its monuments and steeples. The Castle was less than a mile away, black and dominating. Stefi's yellow scooter was propped up against the wall of the back garden, out of sight from the streets. He dressed, discovering a swollen ankle, and limped down the stairs. Romella was turned towards the back of the couch and an elegant leg protruded from under the blanket; the offending tights had disappeared. Her breathing was normal. Stefi was on the armchair, head tilted back. She was snoring slightly.

In the kitchen, he found a percolator and coffee beans from a small sack stamped Blue Mountain, Mavis Bank, Jamaica. Typical Doug, he thought; no nasty instant powders for little brother. The noise of the coffee grinder was rasping in the still of the house. A couple of minutes later Romella appeared, bare-footed, hair dishevelled and with a colourful yellow and blue swelling surrounding her right eye, and a bruised lip. Her sweater and skirt were wrinkled from a night's sleep.

'The Swamp Thing,' Findhorn said.

'What?'

'An old horror movie. You remind me of something I saw in it.'

'Thanks, Fred.' She winced.

'Shall I get you a damp cloth?'

'I still feel drugged.'

Over tea and toast, Stefi turned up looking like Action Woman in black sweater and leggings. She poured herself coffee, added condensed milk from a tin and flopped down at the kitchen table.

Findhorn broke the silence. 'I had no idea things would get this heavy. I can't have you risking your lives like this.

140

I think you should just walk away. It's me they want, and the diaries.'

'Who are they?'

'I don't know. There are at least two groups after the diaries. One of them offered me a lot of money.'

Romella studied Findhorn over her coffee. He found her steady gaze disconcerting. 'How much money?'

'A million pounds.'

There was a stunned silence.

Stefi eventually broke it. 'A million pounds? Are you joking?'

'I'm very serious.'

'And you turned it down?' Her voice was incredulous.

'Money isn't the primary issue here, Stefi. It's not clear who really owns the diaries, if anyone. But the main thing is, I want to find out for myself what's in there. Petrosian was an atomic scientist, remember. Say he's discovered some way to make a super-bomb, or even some political secret that people don't want out. I might just want to burn the lot.'

Romella touched her bruised eye and groaned. 'Forgive me, Fred, but who are you to make judgements on things like that?'

'Diaries plus conscience equals responsibility. I had no idea what I was getting into but here I am, stuck with it. There's nobody else.'

'And suppose it's something beneficial?'

'Then I'd want to patent it first and become wildly rich.'

Stefi looked at Romella, fixed a look on Findhorn, and

spoke in a tone which allowed for no argument. 'I think you'd better start at the beginning, Mister. Spill the beans.'

Findhorn thought that maybe Stefi Stefanova had picked up some of her English from old B movies. Romella was having some difficulty drinking. She reached into a pocket for a handkerchief and patted her bruised lips. 'Yes, Fred, it's time to spill the beans.'

'You wouldn't believe a word of it,' Findhorn warned.

Stefi and Romella were giving him hard stares. He spilled the beans.

Finally Romella said, 'Right then, we should get on with it.'

Findhorn's heart leaped. 'You mean you're willing to carry on with the translation?'

'Why not? I don't like being knocked around.'

Stefi was looking reflective. 'There could be a lot of money in this.'

'Or none.' Findhorn pointed out.

Stefi said, 'Romella gets fifty per cent.'

'Ten,' said Findhorn.

'Twenty.'

'Agreed.'

'You said that money isn't the issue,' Stefi reminded him.

Findhorn nodded warily. 'Uhuh.'

'Good. So I'll settle for ten per cent.'

'For Heaven's sake, Stefi, why should you get ten per cent?'

She waved a finger at him. 'Because you need me. They

know you and they know Romella. Every time you step out of the house you both risk your necks. But me? They know nothing about me. I can come and go in safety and do research for you, like HMS *Daring*, for example.'

'Good point. You could make all the difference. I've been consulting a friend with specialist knowledge. I'll surprise him with ten per cent of whatever we end up with, which will probably be nothing.'

'How secure are we here?' Romella asked, with a touch of anxiety in her voice. 'They might find out you have a brother in Edinburgh and check up.'

'This is Doug's hideaway. Nobody knows about it. Doug has a Queen Street apartment, but as a criminal lawyer he also wanted some place he could escape to without getting phone calls or visits at strange hours from strange people. So this pad is in our Mum's maiden name – that's the MacGregor on the nameplate. And the phone is ex-directory and under Mabel MacGregor.'

Stefi waved her hands around. 'I could get to like it. All this space, and angels and crocodiles.'

Findhorn said, 'We've assembled a team, and agreed the division of spoils. It's a start.'

'One for all and all for one,' said Stefi, reinforcing Findhorn's suspicion that she learned her English from movies.

Findhorn said, 'My bet is that the value of the secret lies with whoever discovers it first. And I don't know what resources we're up against.'

Romella was dabbing her lips. 'We're in a race? So let's get started.'

* * *

Findhorn was crouching in front of the genuine coal effect Scandinavian stove with the imported Mexican fire surround, trying to understand the controls.

'There's one thing I'd love to read about now.' Romella was carefully applying a skin-coloured powder to her bruise. The photocopies were laid out on a coffee table.

'Well?'

'The first time they set off an atom bomb. How Petrosian saw it. What it was like from the inside.'

Stefi, cross-legged at the table, flicked through a heap of photocopies. Findhorn pressed a button and flames shot up. He joined Romella on the couch.

Petrosian's diary, Thursday, 12 July 1945

Philip Morrison and I took the plutonium core out of the vault at Omega. Of course it was in sub-critical pieces. We put them in a couple of valises especially fitted for the purpose. Sat them in the back seat of Robert Bacher's sedan and set off for Alamogordo, with one security car in front, one behind. Both sweating at the thought of an automobile accident. Very unlikely, but what if we got hit by a truck and the bits went critical? A weird feeling, driving through Santa Fe, a sleepy little one-horse town, carrying the core of the 'gadget' – the atom bomb. If the locals had known what was being driven through their main street!

Turned off on a dirt track and left the plutonium in a

room at MacDonald's ranch house, which had long been abandoned by the family.

Friday, 13 July 1945

Just after midnight, in MacDonald's Ranch, Bacher officially hands over the core from the University of California to Tom Farrell, General Groves's aide, along with a bill for two billion dollars.

Then we wait. Got a little sleep.

At nine a.m. Louis Slotin begins to assemble the core. He has to push the plutonium pieces together on a table to the point where they almost reach criticality. He's carrying a lot of responsibility – if he makes the slightest mistake we're dead, there's no bomb, the war in Japan takes a different turn and so does the future.

His concentration is terrific. He keeps licking his lips. You have to stare to see his hands moving at all and we're all standing like statues and screaming inside. Then Oppie turns up, practically sparking electricity with tension. This has a bad effect on everyone. Boss or not, Bacher tells him to get out. Louis completes the job.

3.18 p.m. We get a call from Kistiakowsky. The gadget is ready for the core. We carry it out on a litter and again it goes in the back seat of Bacher's sedan. We head for the tower at Trinity, Bacher at the wheel driving with extraordinary care.

Working in a tent at the base of the tower. The core goes on a hoist and is raised over the assembly. Lowered down into it with extreme slowness. Geiger counters rise to a crescendo as it goes in. Atmosphere unbelievable – I can't describe it. The tiniest knock could start a chain reaction.

Wind rising, flapping tent. We can't afford dust.

The core sticks. It's the heat from the plutonium, it's expanded compared with the dummy runs. The biggest concentration of eggheads the world has ever seen and not one of us thought of that. What else have we missed?

Equilibrium eventually reached and the assembly is complete by ten p.m. We leave it overnight in the tent. Groves gets some fantasy about Japanese saboteurs into his head and sends an armed guard out to it.

Saturday, 14 July 1945

Deteriorating weather. Freshening wind means the gadget sways as it's raised up the tower. Jams at one point. Eventually it reaches the top and Jerry eases it into the corrugated iron hut a hundred feet up.

Sunday, 15 July 1945

Weather getting serious. Storm clouds, high wind, thunder in the distance. What happens if Base Camp gets hit by lightning? Or even the tower?

Oppie up top, checking the connections. Alone with his creation. What thoughts are going through his head?

Eleven p.m. The General has been on site for some hours giving the weather men hell. Lightning flashing and drizzling rain. What if there's a short circuit? And what will the wind do to the radioactive dust? MPs assembled to evacuate Socorro if necessary. But Amarillo in Texas, three hundred miles away, could also get it. How do you evacuate 70,000 people at a few hours' notice?

The old rumour back again: some of the senior men are predicting the atmosphere will be set alight. Bets being taken on whether all life will be destroyed.

Truman and Churchill due to meet Stalin at Potsdam. It doesn't take much imagination to see that Truman will want a result. I imagine Oppie and Groves are under huge pressure from above.

Midnight. Can't see the Tower for mist. Heavy rain. Storms forecast to be heading this way.

Tension beyond endurance. We're all going insane with it.

Monday, 16 July 1945

Pouring rain throughout the early hours.

In the Mess Hall at Base Camp, Fermi has a new worry. He thinks if the wind changes suddenly we could all be showered with radioactive fallout. Oppie gets all distressed – he's practically weeping. Groves takes him out to the S.10,000 bunker – far too close, I thought.

Then the full force of the storm hits the tower. Lightning dangerously close. They have to postpone. At the same time the gadget has to be fired in the dark for the instrumentation to record it properly. Latest possible moment is 5.30 a.m.

Four a.m. Rain stops. Conditions to hold for next two

hours. Oppie and Groves agree to go ahead at 5.30, the last possible moment. A stream of headlights in the desert – the arming party retreating from the tower at speed.

A bunch of us are on Compania Hill, about twenty miles NW of zero point. Countdown starts at twenty minutes, then warning sirens and people at Base Camp take to trenches.

And then suddenly the sun is shining, and the hills are shimmering in the light. It's a tiny sun on the horizon, too bright to look at until it has grown into a big churning mass of yellow, and then it's floating up from the ground on a long stem of dust. The fireball turns red as it cools and at that point you can see a luminous blue glow around it – ionized air.

This is all in silence. When the bang comes it hurts my ears and then there is a long, long rumble like heavy traffic, and a strong gust of wind.

I can't describe the feeling. It's somehow threatening, as if we had interfered in a part of Nature where we had no business to be. I have goosepimples for hours afterwards.

13

Witch Hunt

Stefi said, 'I have a feeling I can't describe too. We have a piece of living history here. Can't you feel it? Is it not speaking to you?'

Findhorn stood up and stretched. 'Stefi, it's only a photocopy.'

'I'm beginning to learn things about you, Doctor Findhorn. For example, you have all the romance of a cold fried egg.'

'There's nothing in there,' Findhorn complained.

Romella said, 'He keeps coming back to this question of setting the atmosphere alight.'

'I know,' said Findhorn. He was wiggling his strained ankle. 'It preyed on his mind.'

'It's beginning to prey on mine,' Romella said.

'My nuclear physics friend says it has to be a red herring. It couldn't happen unless the bomb was so big it would zap the planet anyway.'

'This religious maniac,' Stefi asked. 'What was it he said in the Gardens?'

'I'll help them turn the key to the bottomless pit.'

'A very useful clue.' Findhorn assumed Stefi was being ironic.

She stood up. 'I'm going to speak to that nice librarian boy.'

'About HMS *Daring*?'

'*Inter alia*. I'll bring back a Chinese take-away. Byee.'

Romella had been flicking through the A4 sheets. Her face was thoughtful. 'Petrosian seems to have gotten into some sort of trouble after the war.'

Findhorn sat down on the couch again. 'Tell me the story,' he said.

At 8.14 a.m. Japanese Time, Monday, 6 August 1945, powerful shock waves ripped across Hiroshima at the speed of a bullet.

News of the explosion was flashed from the *Enola Gay* fifteen minutes after the drop, and was announced at Los Alamos through the Tech Area's Tannoy system. Oppenheimer quickly called the whole staff together in an auditorium, acknowledging the cheers and shouts like a prize fighter. Suddenly, the suspicions of the scientists' wives, that their menfolk had been engaged on something extraordinary, was confirmed. Their children learned that their fathers' work was praised by the President, that their overcrowded little Los Alamos school was being named in great newspapers. In sheer exuberance they paraded through every home in the complex, led by a band banging on pots and pans.

Three days later, Fat Man was dropped from the *Great Artiste*. Nagasaki became an inferno of flames visible for two hundred miles, and another eighty thousand dead were added to the hundred and twenty thousand of Hiroshima.

A couple of days after that, Los Alamos resounded with parties, conga lines, sirens, drunkenness and TNT explosions in the desert. For most, the doubts, the moral questions, would come later; this wasn't the time.

Over the next few weeks, depression settled over Los Alamos. A diaspora took place, as talented young men took up teaching positions in universities around the States. Few of the emigrés returned to their homelands. Fermi joined a new institute at Chicago. Oppenheimer took up his old post at CalTech but, after the daily contact with minds of scorching brilliance, and the creation of a sun which had scorched the New Mexico desert, teaching was an anti-climax. He soon accepted directorship of the Institute for Advanced Studies at Princeton, and continued to advise government on the development of the new weapons until the day came when the witch-hunters finally got to him.

Across the Atlantic the radar men, whose contribution to the victory had been even more vital than that of the atomic scientists, were likewise dispersing, and would likewise enrich scientific life in future years. Lovell, whose airborne radar had finally killed the U-boat threat, went on to create the Jodrell Bank telescope. Hoyle went on from his wartime radar work to become the most influential living astrophysicist. Bondi, an Austrian and former enemy alien, became Chief Scientific Adviser to the Ministry of Defence; and Tommy Gold, a brilliant iconoclast who had likewise fled the Nazis from Austria, would harass a complacent scientific establishment with radical new insights for the remainder of the century.

At the end of 1945 Petrosian gave up his bachelor flat. With the help of a couple of scientists' wives, he loaded cardboard boxes with Indian pottery, cacti and books, and left them in storage to be sent on. He drove his four-door Buick slowly through the weird, wind-sculpted canyons. Occasionally he glimpsed the Sangre de Cristo mountains far to the west, glowing blood-red in the light of the setting sun. The car's progress was soon marked by tracks in a light covering of snow. He reached a small house on a ridge overlooking Santa Fe; and there he stayed overnight with Kitty Cronin. The morning brought a difficult farewell.

He took Route 85 south, running parallel to the Rio Grande, before turning left, skirting the Trinity test site. Somehow Trinity was a psychological boundary. Once past it, he felt he had left one world behind and was entering another. He drove a thousand miles to Arkansas, stopping only occasionally at roadside diners to relieve himself and have an occasional snack.

Others from the Los Alamos days, and from the defeated Germany, were to turn America into a great powerhouse of science and technology; Petrosian, however, took no part in this. In Arkansas, he buried himself in a small-town community college, a position far below what his talents and reputation could have earned him. Almost wilfully, he had returned to the obscurity whence he came.

Petrosian's record as a refugee who'd worked on the

Manhattan Project was soon known locally. He had helped build the Bomb and finish the war in Japan; he had saved thousands of American and Japanese lives; he was a local hero.

Lev quickly established himself as a popular and competent teacher, with a talent for explaining difficult ideas in simple ways. He lived quietly, making only a few close friends. A few Southern girls fluttered their eyelashes at him, but he kept to himself. If asked, he would express clear opinions on anything, and soon became known as anti-segregationist, anti-religious and anti-establishment in outlook. Strangely, in this conservative backwater, these outrageous opinions merely enhanced his popularity, establishing his reputation as a slightly mad foreign eccentric. Lev nominally joined an organization for protecting academic freedom; otherwise, he stayed apart from all organized activity, political or social.

And Romella was now ploughing through year after year of diary whose pages were utterly banal. There was no hint of any drama in Petrosian's life, nothing to suggest that he had invented some new theory, found some novel means of creating energy, or thought of some way to make a super-bomb in a garden shed. He had, in effect, switched off and dropped out. Stefi was singing in the kitchen, and Romella's voice was becoming hoarse, when she said, 'And here comes the trouble.' It started one Wednesday morning in the summer of 1953.

That Wednesday morning started as an ordinary day. Lev

had developed a routine. His internal clock woke him at half past seven. He was showered and dressed by eight. Around then the mail would arrive, and he would read this over a breakfast of cereal, coffee, a boiled egg, orange juice (Florida oranges, freshly squeezed) and marmalade on toast. By nine o'clock, he was on his way to the College, a two-mile walk along a broad, tree-lined suburban road.

They announced their arrival through a letter with an unfamiliar look and a Washington Capitol postmark. With a vague sense of foreboding, he returned to the kitchen table and slit the envelope open with a breadknife. He read and re-read the contents. Then he stood up, abandoning his breakfast, and paced up and down the kitchen, his head whirling.

```
Dear Doctor Petrosian:
Your name has been raised in testimony
before the Internal Security Sub-
committee of the United States Senate
Committee on the Judiciary. This testi-
mony was taken in executive session and
publication of it has been witheld pend-
ing your having an opportunity to give
testimony. We have set Thursday, 4 June
1953 as the day when this may be
released. Accordingly, we are asking you
if you will appear at 9.30 a.m. on that
day, in room 424-C, Senate Office Build-
ing, Washington, DC. In the event that
you do not avail yourself of this
```

opportunity, the evidence will be made
public.

Sincerely yours,

Henry J. Alvarez
Chairman, Internal Security Subcommittee

Petrosian walked his standard route to the College on
autopilot, scarcely aware of his surroundings. But instead
of making his way to the mathematics building, he took a
back path towards the Faculty of Arts and entered the
corridors of the English Department. To his relief, Max
Brogan was in his office.

Max Brogan was an untidy, overweight West Texan,
with curly brown hair thinning on top and a double-
chinned face which managed to be permanently cheerful
no matter what the external circumstances. His chief claim
to fame was his small, overweight wife who ran the Sweet
and Tart, a culinary highspot in the little town. Today
Brogan was wearing a pink, short-sleeved shirt and shorts.
Pencils were sticking out of a pocket. On the face of it the
friendship between Petrosian the thin aesthete, and Brogan
the good-living, corpulent Falstaff, defied analysis; but a
closer examination revealed a common factor: each man
detected in the other, in his own way, a quiet but rock-
solid individualism. The tides of fashion, whether
intellectual or sartorial, ebbed and flowed in vain around
these men.

Brogan was at his desk, or at least it had to be assumed there was a desk somewhere under the pyramid of books and papers in front of him. He looked up as Petrosian entered; his normally cheerful expression had a serious edge to it. 'I heard.'

Petrosian collapsed into a black leather chair. 'Anyone else?'

'Neymeier in French Literature, Sam Lewis in Liberal Studies, but what the hell it's only nine o'clock and there are bound to be plenty more. Maybe even me.'

'Why you, Max? You're as American as turkey on Thanksgiving.'

Max raised his hands. 'Maybe some writer on the reading lists I give my students, maybe I went to a party with the wrong people ten years ago. Who knows with these frigging morons?'

An old, old sensation was gradually creeping over Petrosian, a sensation he thought he had left behind twenty years ago in Germany, and fifteen years before that in Baku. It was the feeling of being a target, of being hunted by some ill-defined, implacable, malevolent force. He felt the fear in the dryness of his mouth as he spoke. 'What will I do, Max?'

'Squeal on your friends. It's a ritual. You confess and give them names, they confer absolution and move on.'

Petrosian said, 'But I've done nothing wrong.'

'I envy you, Lev. You're a single man. A man with a wife and three kids who's done nothing wrong, now that's a whole new ballpark.' Brogan shifted uneasily. Lev waited while his friend plucked up courage. Then the Texan was saying, 'Look, these guys scare me. They only need to name you and you're destroyed. Once you're on their blacklist you'll never work again.'

Petrosian repeated, 'But I've done nothing wrong.'

'But can you prove it?'

'I'm not even a communist.'

'You do your own thinking, right? You're a liberal? Maybe even a New Dealer? That's all they need, pal. They have an agenda, which is to put the American political landscape somewhere to the right of Genghis Khan.'

'Max, I've done nothing wrong.'

Max was all patience. 'You still don't get it, Lev. That's not a defence.'

Petrosian shook his head in bewilderment, and Max tried again. 'Look, Mary has a cousin, an accountant with MGM Studios. The tales he told us would make your hair stand on end. You know these people reduced the studio czars to milksops? They denounced some wartime movie as Red propaganda because it showed the Soviets fighting Nazis. Another one got the treatment because it showed Russian kids being happy. You said something, or you did something. Yesterday, or twenty years ago. Or somebody thinks you did.'

'My instinct tells me to fight these swine.'

'We got an old saying hereabouts, Lev. Those who wrestle with pigs are bound to get dirty.'

Petrosian stood up. 'Okay, Max. But I'm an old Nazi-fighter and I'll tell you this. Those who are led by pigs end up in their slimy mire.'

Back at his office, a message was on Petrosian's desk, propped up on books so that it could not be missed:

Please contact me immediately.
B. Lutyens.

Petrosian crossed the campus lawns towards the Faculty offices, his stomach churning. Janice was typing briskly on a Remington.

'The boss is expecting me.'

Normally he would have expected a smile, or a joke. But today she nodded without looking up or pausing. Lev knocked on Lutyens's door.

The Head of Faculty, Boothby W. Lutyens, was a burly, white-haired and florid-faced man. Of limited talent, his rise in the College hierarchy had a lot to do with an astute nose for office politics, coupled with an uncanny ability to say the right things at the right time. The fact that he came from a rich Southern family which had generously endowed the University was, of course, neither here nor there.

Lutyens was pouring coffee from a machine in the corner of the room. He was wearing a crumpled white suit, the trousers supported by brilliant yellow braces. He was looking grim and Lev sensed that he already knew something. He didn't offer Lev a coffee. He crossed to his desk and put his feet up. Lev remained standing, and without a word passed over the letter. Lutyens glanced at it and tossed it back. 'I have a copy.'

'What's going on?'

'What it says, Petrosian. You have questions to answer.' Lutyens's tone was cold.

'That's not telling me much.'

'It's all you'll get from me.'

'Who are these people?' Lev asked. The hostility was baffling.

Lutyens stared at Lev over half-moon spectacles. 'Don't you read newspapers, son? It may have escaped your attention, but there's a war on. And while the Commies are in Korea spilling the blood of our boys, others right here in their own country are stabbing 'foresaid boys in the back. Infiltrating our institutions, undermining our values, getting at the minds of our young people. I imagine HUAC's questions will have something to do with your own associations in this regard. If I'd known you were a Commie I'd never have hired you.'

'What associations?'

'The American Association for Democratic Information and Freedom, a front organization if ever there was one. You evidently forgot to inform this College about your membership of that society when we offered you the post.'

'Doctor Lutyens, Americans have been forming societies for mutual purposes since America began. The process is part of democracy. The reason I belong is this: I was a student in Germany in the thirties. I saw what cowards academics are. They talk a lot of bullshit about freedom but as soon as a threat like this comes along they head for the hills. It seems to me the only safe organization to join these days is the Methodist Church.'

Lutyens puckered his lips, forming the skin above them

into tight, vertical, disapproving wrinkles. 'Watch your tone, Petrosian.'

'It strikes me that for a man to freely hold and express his beliefs is the American way. Do you have a problem with that?'

Lutyens said, 'There's a point beyond which academic freedom should not be pushed, Petrosian. We're very dependent on federal funding these days. Meaning we are vulnerable to government definitions of loyalty and politically appropriate attitudes.'

'I envy you, sir. I wish I had your moral flexibility.'

Lutyens thumped his coffee furiously down on the table. He stood up angrily, open-mouthed. Lev said, 'Can you at least tell me what testimony the loyalty board are talking about?'

Lutyens glared angrily. 'You got difficulty with your hearing? I told you, I have no more information to give. Now get out.'

Janice didn't look up as Petrosian left.

Over the next few days, subtle changes took place in Lev's professional and social life. The first time a colleague crossed the street, out of greeting distance, Lev put the apparent slight down to his own over-sensitive imagination. The second time it happened, with another colleague, he was not so sure. The third time, it was becoming clear: to be seen with Lev Petrosian was bad news. He met no overt hostility in the common room; it was just that his colleagues were polite and distant. They tended to exclude him from conversation. He was assuredly excluded from

160

the jokes, and more than one outburst of ribald laughter, it seemed, was directed his way. In the classroom, his sophomores stared out the window more, rattled desks more, paid less attention than usual. It might just be, he thought, that the course was getting tough; but the usual banter and repartee which he shared with his students was gone, to be replaced by a sullen and hostile silence.

There was, however, nothing subtle about the unsigned note which Lev found at his feet when he opened his office door one hot, sticky afternoon. The ribbon on the typewriter was worn, and the typist was clearly unskilled. In upper-case letters, it read

    JEWS, NIGGERS, COMMIES, YOU'RE ALL THE
    SAME.
    HITLER DIDN'T FINISH THE JOB.
    WE WILL.

Petrosian found Max Brogan again in a quiet corner of the campus, seated in the shade. About fifty yards away some girls were trying out Hula-Hoops, pausing from time to time to collapse in giggles on the parched grass.

'You're looking pale,' Brogan said as Lev flopped onto the bench.

Petrosian passed over the message. Brogan's lips tensed angrily as he read it.

'What does it signify, Max?'

'*Semper in excretum, solo profundis variat.*'

'And boy, am I up to my neck in it.'

A lithe girl in tight white sweater and shorts was

gyrating her hips and Max paused momentarily. 'Lev, you need representation. I know a liberal-minded lawyer. Maybe you can plead the Fifth or something.'

Petrosian shook his head. 'I don't need a lawyer. I've done nothing wrong. And I'm not even a Communist.'

Max Brogan laughed sardonically. 'Well, that helps. You know what they say.'

'No. What do they say?'

'You don't lynch the wrong nigger, that's not the American way.'

'Don't knock your country, Max. I lived under the Nazis.'

Brogan shrugged. 'You're doomed anyway. The Board of Regents are scared shitless. I hear whispers they're aiming to buy off McCarran with a loyalty oath. That ought to shake a few professors out of their torpor. Lev, are you going to co-operate with HUAC?'

'I guess so.'

Max grinned bleakly. 'Of course you are. You're a baseball-loving, gum-chewing, God-fearing, loyal American. And you have one thing more going for you.'

'What's that, Max?'

'You're white. God help you hereabouts if you'd been born Theodore Sambo Roosevelt.'

14

Inquisition

'Hello FBI, Atlanta, this is Lewis Klein of Domestic Intelligence, Washington. Would you connect me to Don Dilati?' A pause, then: 'Don? Lewis Klein here . . . Fine, thanks, and yourself? . . . It's about this guy Petrosian . . . your very own commie, yeah. The HUAC hearings . . . there's been a change of plan. The guy's college is holding an internal enquiry to root out Reds and HUAC want him shunted onto it on account of they're overloaded up here. Anyway, it's being held locally and I was wondering if we might liaise with you guys down in darkest Arkansas. We have very bad vibes about this Petrosian. We see him as more than just a parlour pink. We suspect he passed information on to Russia when he worked on the atom bomb . . . Sorry, the source is restricted. We have permission from the man upstairs to plant the usual devices and we have a trash can recovery order . . . What do you mean, law and order Arkansas style, we can match you people any day . . . 'Kay, I'll come down with my team and see if we can't stick one on him this time. I mean get something to burn him. I'm deadly serious, that was the word, "burn" as in high voltage . . . Sure, same to you. Good hunting.'

A local junior grade high school had been turned over to the hearings. Petrosian, feeling terribly alone, turned into the main gate and made his way to the entrance, where a black security man was sitting at an uncomfortably small school desk. The man examined Lev's letter, checked his name against a list, and waved him to the left with a sympathetic grunt. In Petrosian's lonely world, a sympathetic grunt was like a mother's hug.

A bare corridor was lined with people, mostly men, smoking, and the air was blue with cigarette smoke. Eyes, some curious, some hostile, followed his route. Black cables snaked from a window into a noisy classroom. A card tacked on the door had 'HUAC INTERVIEW ROOM' written on it in blue crayon, and another blue-collared security guard looked at Lev's letter and led him by the elbow into the room. There was a buzz of conversation as he entered. Some flashbulbs popped. Two movie cameras sat on tripods at the back of the room. The guard ushered him to a seat at the front of the classroom and then went to another one to one side of the door. Two microphones faced Lev on the desk and he thought they were unnecessary for such a small room. He found himself facing a raised dais, on which was a long desk with carafes of water, tumblers, papers and a wooden gavel. Three black, high-backed chairs were at the desk. Each had a small card in front of it: 'Mr Andrew Dodds, Board of Regents, Greers Ferry College', 'Congressman Olaf B. Yates, Arkansas', 'Senator Henry Alvarez, HUAC,

Washington'. On the wall was a blackboard which had been wiped clean, an American flag hanging limply, and next to it another door. Lev assumed that his inquisitors would enter through this second door, which probably adjoined another classroom. Hot, sticky air was circulating from an open window. The morning sun streamed across a stenographer next to the door. She had white, pulled-back hair and was sitting straight-backed in a corner, staring ahead, like a machine waiting to be started.

A couple of minutes passed. The heat was stifling and Lev's mind began to wander. He was wondering about the gavel, whether they'd transported it from Washington or borrowed it from the local courthouse, or bought it from a gavel shop, when the door near the blackboard opened and three men walked in.

They were all in their forties. Lev knew Andrew Dodds, the College representative, by sight. He was small, near-bald, with a weak, receding chin and small eyes which peered out from behind round, steel-rimmed spectacles. Petrosian thought he bore a startling resemblance to Himmler, could hardly separate the two in his mind.

Olaf B. Yates shambled in behind Dodds. The Arkansas congressman looked like, and probably was, a dirt farmer. He was a small, burly man with a rough complexion and a squat nose like a boxer's.

Alvarez was tall and stooped. He had a slightly asymmetric mouth, one corner being pulled down. It soon emerged that this corner of the mouth gave an occasional nervous twitch, which would also contract the senator's cheek. Instinctively, Petrosian felt that he could handle Dodds and the dirt farmer, that he had the intellectual edge over them; but the same instinct made him fear Alvarez, the travelling inquisitor from Washington. Alvarez had fixed a steady, hostile stare on Petrosian, as if he was reading the scientist's mind.

The man from Arkansas, Olaf B. Yates, tapped the gavel. 'This hearing will come to order in the matter of Lev Baruch Paytrojan.'

A few mysterious preliminaries over, mainly to do with the empty lawyer's chair next to Petrosian, Dodds alias Himmler fired the opening salvo. He had a methodical, clipped way of speaking and a slightly nasal, high-pitched voice which soon became irritating to listen to. 'Doctor Petrosian. It has been determined by the Attorney General, and by the Director of the FBI, that institutions throughout America are being penetrated by persons whose purposes are subversive, that is to say, broadly speaking, inimical to the American way of life. Unconstitutional means are being employed, in clandestine fashion, by these people – communists and their fellow travellers – to overthrow the state.'

From the corner of his eye Petrosian was aware that Alvarez's cheek had twitched. It was to become an increasing distraction throughout the long inter-rogation.

Dodds continued, 'They have infiltrated every level and every type of organization and institution. They have infested educational, scientific, governmental, labour and communications establishments, the latter including the entertainment world. The House Committee on Un-American Activities has been active in attempting to root out these subversive elements from American life. Young, idealistic people in educational establishments are especially vulnerable when exposed to dangerous and alien ideas. We in the Greers Ferry Community College are anxious to play our full part in this patriotic enterprise. The purpose of these hearings is to establish the loyalty to America of our staff members. Testimony has been given in closed session to this committee which may tend to call your loyalty into question. You are here to satisfy us that your loyalties do indeed lie with the country to which you now belong. Do you understand?'

Petrosian nodded.

'Please answer yes or no for the record.'

'Understood, sure.'

The Arkansas congressman asked, 'Doctor Paytrojan, where was you borned at?' The voice was almost comically hillbilly.

'Armenia.'

'That's Russia, right?'

'It is now. But Armenia is a country with its own culture, language and even script. The Armenian Church is the oldest established Christian Church. It goes back to 300 AD.'

'You don't say? But yo're still a Russian.'

'I became an American citizen in 1945.'

Dodds picked up the questioning. 'I have here the reading list you give to your sophomore students. It includes a book called *Through Rugged Ways to the Stars*, by Professor Harlow Shapley, Director of Harvard College Observatory.'

'Yes, It's on my recommended reading list.'

Dodds stared at Petrosian through his spectacles. 'Are you aware that Shapley has been co-chairman of the Progressive Citizens of America? That he has asked scientists to, I quote, "answer to a higher cause, and increase the importance of their world citizenship over their local loyalties"? What do you think he meant by that, Doctor Petrosian?'

'I know he has left-wing convictions.'

The hint of a sneer. 'You might say. HUAC have listed him as affiliated to between eleven and twenty communist front organizations.'

Alvarez interjected. He had a heavy, commanding voice, over-loud for the cramped little room and the microphones. 'Let me put it directly, sir. Do you think it right that impressionable young minds should be exposed to ideas from the minds of communists and their fellow travellers?'

'Yes.'

The answer took the panel by surprise. Petrosian added, 'But then, I'm not imposing an opinion, simply exposing students to a range of ideas.'

Alvarez changed tack abruptly. 'How are the Brooklyn Dodgers doing just now?'

It was Petrosian's turn to be surprised. 'I have no idea.'

'And the Cardinals?'

Lev shrugged, bewildered.

'Do you play baseball?'

'No, sir.'

'Football? Basketball?' Alvarez was adopting a tone of incredulity.

'No.'

'Are you physically prevented from so doing?'

'No, I'm in good health. I'm just not interested in sport.'

'Meaning you have no sense of belonging to a team. Don't you think that good American citizenship involves you in social as well as legal obligations?'

'You mean, I should answer to the higher cause of social conformity, like the communists?'

Alvarez glared at Petrosian. 'Before we go any further in this enquiry, sir, let me make one thing clear. Smart talk of that sort is unwelcome at this hearing.'

The Congressman said, 'Y'see, it's like this, Mister Paytrojan. I never knew a ballplayer who was a Communist. Good loyal Americans are team players.'

'Do you attend church?' Alvarez wanted to know, clearly rattled by Lev's defiant reply.

'No.'

'What is your religion exactly?'

'I was brought up as a Christian Armenian.'

'And now?'

'I'm no longer active.'

Mister Arkansas grinned. 'You admit to being an aytheeist?'

'Agnostic is the word. There are things in the natural world I can't explain, like why it exists at all.'

'And do you expose students to this aythecism of yours?'

'I don't expose them to classroom propaganda of any sort, unless you consider doing your own thinking to be propaganda. All they get from me are the ideas and concepts of modern physics.'

'You have a problem with God, country and flag?' Senator Alvarez wanted to know.

'Not at all. But I also think it's my duty to make young people do their own thinking. I don't know how to do that except by exposing them to new ideas. And all new ideas are subversive to some extent.' A light sweat was forming on Lev's brow.

Alvarez again: 'So while our boys are out there in Korea meatgrinding their way back to the 38th parallel, you're back here nice and cosy telling our young people to go easy on the loyalty thing?'

'Did I say that?'

'No sir, you did not. Not in so many words.'

Alvarez leaned back. Mister Arkansas had a mock-puzzled look on his face. 'Did I hear you just admit you teach subversive ideas to students?'

'The syllabus includes some discussion of new ideas in physics. I said that all new ideas are subversive.'

'Subversive.' The congressman paused, to give the impression he was thinking about that, and also to focus attention on himself. 'Subversive. Doan that word mean undercutting the established order of things?'

'Yes.'

'And doan disloyalty involve the same thang?'

'Yes.'

'Well pardon me if I've missed somethang. I ain't had

the privilege of a higher education. It seems to me that you doan give your impressionable young students classroom propaganda but you do just happen to expose them to disloyal ideas.' A triumphant, yellow-toothed grin spread over the Arkansas farmer's face: he had outwitted an atomic scientist, delivered a crushing blow. He noted with approval the busy scribbling of the reporters.

The logic was so unbelievable that Petrosian couldn't answer it. He sat, literally speechless, until Alvarez stepped in. The senator now asked the ritual, and deadly, question: 'Doctor Petrosian, are you now or have you ever been a member of the Communist Party of the United States?'

It was expected, but still Petrosian felt his skin going clammy. 'No.'

'Nevertheless in 1946, you joined the American Committee for Democratic and Intellectual Freedom.'

'Yes.'

'Are you aware that this is a known communist front organization for the defence of communist teachers? That it has been declared un-American and subversive by this very House Committee on Un-American Activities?'

'So I heard. I didn't know that when I joined.'

Alvarez referred to a sheet of paper in front of him. 'On June 30th of 1946 you attended a party at the home of Max and Gill Brogan, who are alleged members of the Communist Party.'

'I don't remember.' Petrosian wiped sweat from his brow.

'Present at that party was Martha Haines. Are you acquainted with her?'

'Yes.' The question puzzled Petrosian. She was the local public librarian, a plump, motherly woman. He saw her every fortnight over the library counter.

'Are you aware that Miss Haines is a member of the Daughters of Bilitis?'

'The who?'

'A lesbian organization, sir. You also attended meetings at the house of Paul and Hannah Chapman, who are known to be functionaries of the Communist Party. Paul Chapman was recently dismissed from employment with General Electric as a security risk. I don't suppose you remember those meetings either.'

'I have a lot of friends from my Los Alamos days. I neither know nor care about their affiliations.'

'Yes, let's go back to those Los Alamos days, Doctor.'

A vague feeling of dread began to suffuse through Petrosian's body. 'Let me say it again. I have a lot of friends from my Los Alamos days. I neither know nor care about their affiliations.'

'One acquaintance in particular.'

Kitty! They want me to squeal on Kitty. The bastards! Petrosian wondered if they had noticed the anger which gripped his body.

Alvarez was pretending to read a name. 'A Miss Catherine Cronin. You knew this woman?'

Get the tone right. Don't get hostile, play it cool. 'Kitty Cronin. Yes, we were friends.'

'You were friends.' Alvarez was almost gloating. 'And what was the nature of this friendship?'

Picnics in the woods. Skiing. Glorious days on

mountain trails. Barbecues. Movies. Soft, hot flesh and tousled hair on pillows, and passion, and fun. And none of your fucking business. 'We were good friends.'

'How good?'

Show the bastard up. Force him to ask the intimate stuff. Make him look like the prying goat he is. 'We were close.'

Alvarez, however, seemed to sense a trap. He changed tack. 'Did you and she not meet on every occasion when you took time off from your wartime work on the Los Alamos mesa?'

'We did, which wasn't often.'

'On January 14th 1943, did you and Kitty Cronin not conduct a meeting in her house near Santa Fe? And was Klaus Fuchs, the atom spy, not also present at that meeting?'

'I don't recall. Yes I do.' Petrosian steepled his fingers in thought. 'There was a bunch of us. Dick Feynman, Klaus, someone else I can't remember. We all took off in Dick's car. It wasn't a meeting of course, that's just your way of making it sound purposeful and sinister. We just took off for the day to have a picnic and a good time. As I recall we went into Santa Fe first. Dick had arranged to pick up some girl.'

'Did you not stay overnight with Miss Cronin after the others had left?'

'The question is outrageous. A gentleman doesn't ask, nor does he tell.'

Their eyes locked. Alvarez twitched, wondering whether to make an issue of Lev's defiance. Then: 'Did you not, in the course of that evening, pass over a document to Miss Cronin?'

'No.'

It was a lie.

And Alvarez knew it.

The faces on the bench were now displaying a range of expressions from grim to angry. Petrosian felt the hostility like a physical, crushing pressure.

'Were you, at Los Alamos, a close friend of a Doctor David Bohm?'

Petrosian nodded. 'It was a small, intense, closed community. Everyone knew everyone else.'

'Let it be put on the record that Petrosian admitted to friendship with David Bohm. Are you aware that Oppenheimer has described him as an extremely dangerous man?'

'No, but it doesn't surprise me. David is full of dangerous ideas. That's not the same as disloyalty.'

The dirt farmer again: 'Let me get this right, Mister Paytrojan from Russia. Yo're admitting you hob-nob with commies and front organizations, but still you claim you ain't red.'

'Correct.'

'Not even pink?'

Someone near the back of the room laughed.

Alvarez with a twitch: 'Doctor, I'd like to explore this curious claim of yours a little further, if I may. You are aware that the Communist Party in this country is a channel for espionage?'

'No, sir.'

The senator sighed. 'I remind you, sir, that you're under oath.'

Lev shrugged. 'I'm aware of common perceptions in this area. I have no hard evidence to support them.'

Mr Arkansas was leaning over his microphone. His voice was dripping scorn. 'I ain't been to Australia. Are you saying I shouldn't believe it exists because I ain't seen it with my own eyes? Maybe you think Australia is hearsay or sumthin?' There was some tittering from the audience, and the congressman grinned again, openly basking in his wit. Petrosian sat quietly, blinking through his spectacles.

Alvarez threw a brief, irritated glance at his Arkansas colleague. 'Doctor, the American Communist Party has been designated by the Attorney General as a subversive organization which seeks to overthrow the form of government of the United States by unconstitutional means, within the purview of Executive Orders 9835 and 10450. Given time, we could find any number of highly authoritative sources, from former communists to professors of history, who will confirm that communism has emerged as a world power with the stated goal of dominating all mankind. In the light of all this, Doctor, are you happy with the statement you have just made?'

Petrosian shook his head stubbornly. 'I don't belong to the American Communist Party and never have. I have no direct knowledge of their activities. I hear the accusations but for all I know they're the product of paranoia or mass hysteria. Or plain stupidity: there's plenty of that around.'

'Don't be absurd.' Dodds was adopting a use-your-common-sense tone. In Petrosian's mind, the identification with Himmler was becoming complete. 'Everyone knows that the Party uses conspiracy, infiltration and intrigue, deceit and duplicity and falsehood. It has infiltrated our universities, our culture and even our State Department.'

Petrosian sat quietly.

'Answer the question,' Dodds-Himmler said sharply, his eyes hard behind his steel-rimmed glasses.

'I'm sorry, I didn't recognize that as a question.'

'Were you a Communist Party member in Germany, before you fled to this country?'

'No.'

Another lie.

Petrosian wondered in near-panic what they knew, whether they had noticed his tiny hesitation. But how to explain to these morons that he had joined first for the love of a girl, and then to oppose thugs, and never out of any conviction about new world orders or similar nonsense?

Dodds-Himmler picked up a sheet of paper and handed it down to the stenographer, who seemed to be doubling as a clerk. Lev became aware of a tremendous tension in his jaw muscles. He tried to relax them, but his body wasn't obeying his brain. 'I'm now going to show you a copy of an entry held in FBI files. Mister Chairman, this is an extract from Gestapo files brought to the States in 1945, and indexed in 1948. I request that this extract be put in the record.'

'It may be made part of the record.'

'The entry is of course in German, a language in which I believe you are fluent, Doctor. Perhaps you would read it out in English for this Subcommittee. Do try to be accurate; I have an English translation in front of me.'

Petrosian read through the brief paragraph. It was a Gestapo file about him, and it was the first time he had set eyes on it. He couldn't control the trembling in his voice:

```
Petrosian, Lev, student of physics, born
29 December 1911. Subject is associated
with Communist cell active in Kiel. Was
previously active member of Communist
Party in Leipzig. In 1932 and 1933,
contacted known pro-Soviet academics
during visits to Berlin and Heidelberg.
Visited briefly the Austrian Jewess Lise
Meitner at the Nobel Institute in
Stockholm.
   Rüsselheim, RSHA IVA, Gestapo Field
Office, Kiel.
```

'The letters RSHA—' Dodds-Himmler began.

'—refer to the Central Office of Security Police,' Petrosian interrupted. 'Our paths have crossed.' Something dangerous in Petrosian's voice; Dodds backed off.

'*Associated with communist cells . . . active member of Communist Party.*' Dodds waited for Lev's response, his eyebrows raised. There was an expectant stillness in the room. Lev remained silent. 'Would you please explain the circumstances.'

'I was a student in Germany. In those days the communists were the only real opposition to the fascists.'

Mister Arkansas was displaying his teeth again. 'You don't say,' he repeated with exaggerated sarcasm.

'I ran with them for about two years. That was from 1932 to 1934. Not out of belief in their system, but because I opposed the Nazis.'

'Opposed them? By running with Communist street gangs?'

'With respect, you just don't know what it was like.'

Alvarez was passing down another piece of paper, this one like a sheet from a stenographer's notebook. 'I'm going to show you a page from a notebook left on your desk at Los Alamos on March 1945. It was drawn to the attention of the Board of Regents some weeks ago.' Petrosian's hands were trembling slightly as he took it.

'Would you confirm that this is your handwriting?'

'Yes.'

'It has calculations on it.'

'Yes. How did you get hold of this?'

'We ask the questions here. Look at the handwritten note on the top right-hand corner of the page. Mister Chairman, the actual writing was done on the page above, but the message was recovered by the FBI through high contrast photography and other techniques. Doctor, would you read it out, please?'

'Jürgen, Grand Central, 4.15 p.m.'

'This is a note to meet someone called Jürgen, is it not?'

'Yes.'

'In your handwriting?'

'Yes.'

'Who is this Jürgen?'

'Jürgen Rosenblum. A colleague from my pre-war days. I was arranging to meet him in New York.'

'And did you?'

'Yes.' Petrosian was beginning to feel faint. His back and thighs were wet with sweat.

'What precisely was the nature and purpose of this meeting with Rosenblum?'

'Why do you make it sound like something sinister? It was a simple social meeting. We have a common bond. We'd both been persecuted by the Nazis, we'd both escaped from Nazi Germany. You clearly haven't the faintest idea what that means to those of us who came through. As to the purpose of the meeting? The purpose was talk. We talked about people we knew who'd made it out, people who hadn't. We talked about science. We talked about books. We talked about the ladies. We talked and we talked—'

'Was political discussion part of all this talk?'

'Stuff like that, yes, of course.'

'I'll bet,' Alvarez said. He paused. Then: 'Did yo[u] not meet Rosenblum in an internee camp for ene[my] aliens in Sherbrooke, Canada, in 1939? And did [you] not there register with the Communist Party thro[ugh] Rosenblum?'

'Register? What are you talking about?'

'You know perfectly well, and before you continu[e] that insolent tone, sir, I ask you to remember who['s] talking to. I'm not suggesting that application f[or] membership cards changed hands. How was [—'

Doctor Petrosian? With a handshake in some quiet corner?
A nod and a wink? An understanding that in due course
you might be approached for information? Were you ever
a loyal resident of America? Or have you not always been
a mole, a sleeper, a Trojan horse, first in Harwell and then
Los Alamos?'

'No.'

Alvarez said, 'Mister Chairman, I wish to enter the
following documents in the record. They are, first, decoded
extracts of messages obtained in 1939 by the British MI5
between Moscow and the Russian Embassy in London.
They refer to one Leo, a GRU officer planted amongst the
internees for the specific purpose of befriending refugee
scientists and opening up what they call "channels of
communication". The second document is an assessment
MI5 that the GRU agent in question was probably
n Rosenblum.'

y was this Rose in Bloom allowed into America?'
rkansas asked.

g of war,' Alvarez replied. 'The MI5 filed their
and our FBI wasn't notified of their suspicions
long surveillance failed to come up with
1951. That was the meeting between
senblum.'

n Bloom now?' Mister Arkansas wanted

in New York City.' Alvarez turned
he sweating physicist. 'I'd like to
meeting you attended on July 7th
Hannah Chapman.'

'It was a social evening. Their wedding anniversary, as I recall.'

'So you said. Who else attended this social evening?'

'You want me to name names?'

'You ain't a commie, right?' the Arkansas congressman asked. Lev nodded. 'So what's the problem?'

Petrosian momentarily closed his eyes. He hesitated, took a deep breath, and then said, 'Okay. Okay. Okay. I did attend one meeting of the Communist Party. There were about twenty of us present.'

The room went still.

'We were addressed by a very important Hollywood personage.' Petrosian's voice was shaky, and he was taking breath in deep gulps.

'Take your time. Tell us about it.' Mister Arkansas's eyes were gleaming. Confess your sins, my son. Unburden your soul.

'This was July 7th, just after the Chapman party. I was directed to go to Greers Ferry Park after dark.'

'Who delivered this message?'

'My –' Petrosian lowered his voice '– my controller.'

The tip-tip of the stenographer; the faint whirr of the movie cameras; something rustling in the parched grass outside.

'Your *controller*?' The congressman's voice was almost a whisper. Don't break the atmosphere. Let the confession flow. He leaned forward across the desk.

'Yes. My controller.'

'Who was this controller?'

'I've never set eyes on him.'

'How did he deliver his message?'

'It came to me by thought rays.'

A bewildered expression crossed the congressman's face.

Petrosian continued, 'There was a flying saucer in the park. It was about fifty feet across and twenty high. There was an open ramp and I went into it. I sat at a porthole and it took off. We went right up there at amazing speed but I didn't feel any acceleration. We flew over to Los Angeles to collect John Wayne. He just materialized right there in front of us, in the middle of the saucer.' There was a suppressed belly laugh from the back of the room. Petrosian continued: 'Then we went on to Saturn, which by the way is my home planet. It only took us half an hour. There we met the Leader. He was tanned with long blond hair and kind blue eyes. He told us that world domination by aliens is the only way forward for the salvation of mankind and world communism was only a step on the way and asked if we would help in this great enterprise.'

The deathly hush had been replaced by a scattering of giggles, and now laughter was surging through the room. The congressman, his face contorted by anger, was hammering the gavel. He shouted, 'I hairby cite Doctor Lev Paytrojan for perjury and contempt of these hair proceedings,' but Petrosian, mouth up against the microphone, was still testifying: 'Then the Duke gave us the low-down on how his boys were infiltrating Hollywood and influencing American minds while he acted the part of the anti-red to fool people like you. There are lots of fine Hollywood Americans in this enterprise, I'll give you that list now.'

The audience had split into two camps, half of it booing angrily, the other half laughing and applauding. The congressman was hammering the gavel sharply and shouting 'Remove this man from the microphone,' but Petrosian's voice was still coming over the uproar. 'There are three hundred names on it, people like Gary Cooper and Daryl Zanuck at the top.'

The security men, big hulks of overweight menace, were bearing down. Petrosian stood up. At the door, he glanced back at the scene of bedlam he had created. Mr Arkansas was still hammering at the desk. Dodds-Himmler was staring through his steel-rimmed spectacles at the physicist as if he had just landed from a flying saucer. The nervous twitch in Alvarez's cheek was in full swing. Half a dozen reporters were scribbling furiously.

Powerful hands gripped Petrosian's elbows. His last view of the room was the clock. The interview, it had seemed to him, had lasted a gruelling three or four hours. He was astonished to see that it had taken only twenty-five minutes.

In the corridor, Lev was startled by a sudden blaze of popping flashlights. He found himself wedged in by a scrum of reporters. He pushed his way along the corridor, answering a babble of questions as politely as he could. In the playground, near the school entrance, another movie camera had been put in place.

As he drifted towards the street, dragging the entourage, a taxi stopped and disgorged a man and woman. The man was small, round-faced and nearly bald. The woman was about thirty, with long dark hair and dressed in a long green coat. She took the man's arm and they walked unnoticed in the direction of the school. It was some moments before Lev recognized her, but when he did the reporters and the microphones and the gabble faded away, and a lump rose in Lev's throat. Their eyes met briefly as they passed. Contact was impossible. She gave a brief, wan smile and then was gone, and Petrosian thought that, apart from a little extra weight around the hips and a few wrinkles around the eyes, Kitty had changed little in eight years, and as he fought back the tears he realized that he had always loved her and always would.

'You bloody fool,' Brogan said for the fourth time in an hour.

'I'm in love with your wife, Max,' said Petrosian, smiling over at her. She raised her eyebrows and rattled a skillet onto the big electric hotplate. 'It's her crawfish pie,' said Petrosian, helping himself to more.

'Then you'd better fill up on it. You won't get any where you're headed.'

A black waitress came in through the swing door, carrying a pile of plates on each arm. 'Nummer Four wann bare an fraid aigs an oyster po-boy with dirty rice, the main in One say is yawl gone fishin for ma baked grouper, an Three doan finish their bean stew.'

'Gombee faive mins for the grouper,' Mary Brogan called back. She poured Southern Comfort into the skillet, shook it, and flames leapt towards a burned-black patch in the ceiling.

Max waved his arms. 'Some grand gesture that achieves nothing, as in zilch, as in a big round frigging zero. What the hell got into you, Lev? A good career down the tubes and maybe a year in some godawful pokey.'

'Stuffed with queers and sadistic wardens,' Petrosian suggested.

'Why did you do it, Lev? Why did you throw away your future?'

Petrosian sipped at the Coca-Cola. 'Those creeps just got up my nose.'

'Lev, maybe you can afford the grand gesture, but I have kids to get through school. And what if people start to boycott this place? All it needs is some American Legion redneck to hand out leaflets at the door and we might as well rename this place The Commie Diner.'

'Mary's not a communist, is she?'

'Come on, Lev, what the hell has that got to do with anything? Association is all it takes.' Max's expression was pained.

Lev said, softly, 'Out with it.'

There was an unbearable stress in Brogan's voice. 'Look, Lev, I'm sorry. But maybe you shouldn't come around for a while. You know – career. Mary and the boys.'

Lev nodded sadly. 'I understand fully, Max. Don't worry about it. Nothing in our friendship says you have to stand up to the bad guys like Gary Cooper in *High Noon*. I'll stay away awhile.'

The relief was palpable. Brogan extended his hand and Lev shook it silently. The Texan looked quizzically at his friend. 'I finally get it.'

'What's that, Max?'

'Your testimony to these creeps. It was the absolute truth. You really do come from Saturn.'

15

The Super

'Don't stop,' Stefi ordered.

The Chinese take-away had grown cold in the kitchen, and Romella's voice was becoming strained with the translation. Stefi had found a long, silk dressing gown with a dragon motif in one of Doug's wardrobes and was wearing it over yellow pyjamas. She was sitting on the floor with her legs folded underneath her. A black marble clock, all Victorian angels and curlicues, was about to strike one a.m.

'All this red scare stuff,' Romella asked. 'Was there any substance to it?' The swollen flesh around her right eye had developed a yellowish-green hue.

'It was before my time,' Findhorn said. 'I think the hysteria peaked in the 1950s. You know, it was a sort of *Invasion of the Bodysnatchers* thing. Your neighbour may look just like you but his mind may be under alien control.'

'Or her mind,' Stefi said. She was resting her head wearily on her hands.

'But surely it wasn't all hysteria, Fred. The communists wanted a world ruled by Moscow. And there were spies. Hell, we've just been reading about Klaus Fuchs.'

'Sure there were spies, but the witch-hunters didn't find them. Their success rate was practically zero. Imagine shooting your neighbours at random on the off-chance that one of them might be a spy. With all that misdirected effort, I suspect the McCarthy era was a golden age for the KGB.'

'What about Petrosian?' Stefi asked. 'Was he really a spy? And why are people fighting to get their hands on the diaries? Why do they want to kill you and what's in the diaries worth millions and—'

'Okay. Stefi wants her ten per cent. Read on, Romella.'

Petrosian's habits were those of a quiet and studious bachelor. In the evening he would take something easy out of the icebox and stick it in a frying pan. While it was frying he would pour himself a Martini. He would eat whatever it was, and watch whatever was on his small black-and-white television set, without paying much attention to either. The rest of the evening would be spent reading, writing or marking student exercises. On Fridays, however, he let his hair down: he ate in Mary's kitchen, and played five-stud with Max and friends until the early hours, generally winning enough to pay for the beers he brought along.

But that was before the loyalty trials. Now a barrier, invisible and yet almost tangible, had come between Petrosian and his acquaintances.

This Friday evening, having had a last supper in the Sweet and Tart, he was sipping a cold beer on his porch, a light sweat on his brow and arms. It was a sultry thirty-two degrees. Down the road, through an open window, Ella Fitzgerald was 'Eating Baloney on Coney', but she was having problems being heard over the insect night life and a distant yelping dog.

Tonight, Lev had put his normally restless mind on hold; mentally drained, he was finding simple pleasure in watching a near-full moon drift behind the willow tree in his neighbour's garden. Satchmo took it through the branches and into a starry sky. The dog was still yelping.

Around ten o'clock a big car, all whitewall tyres and tail fins and with an out-of-town number, gurgled slowly past Lev's house. Two men inside, clearly unfamiliar with the area, were scanning the street. A couple of minutes later the car returned, turned into Lev's driveway, and disgorged the two. One had short, neat hair and was incongruously dressed in a dark suit and tie. The other could hardly have been a greater contrast: he was unkempt and casually dressed, with a creased open-necked shirt and a jacket draped over his arm.

'Doctor Petrosian?'

'You look like FBI,' Petrosian said.

'Lieutenant Mercier, sir, Army Intelligence.' A badge was briefly flashed in the half-dark. 'And this is Mister Smith. Can we talk?'

'Sure.'

In the living room, hospitality was politely declined. The three men sat round a small circular table. The long-haired Mister Smith gave Petrosian a calculated smile. His affiliation, Lev noticed, was going unannounced.

Petrosian tried a shot in the dark. 'You look like an academic,' he said to Smith.

Smith kept smiling.

Petrosian finished his beer and leaned back, puzzled. 'Okay, I give up. Who are you?'

The army man said, 'This meeting is not taking place. We're not here.'

'Okay,' Petrosian said cautiously.

'And nothing said here is to be repeated outside this room.'

'There's a problem with that. I'm a card-carrying communist. Anything you say to me goes straight to Moscow.'

Mercier looked as if he was taking the comment seriously. 'We know all about the College enquiry, and we know exactly what was said at it today.'

Petrosian shook his head, mystified. 'I'll be out of work and on a blacklist within a week. What could the army possibly want with me?'

Mercier said, 'The army wouldn't touch you with a barge pole.'

'So why are you here?' Petrosian asked, baffled.

The army man reached down for his briefcase and pulled out an envelope. Petrosian's visitors watched him closely as he put down his empty beer glass and tore it open. He read the letter twice, and looked at his guests with surprise.

'Look at it from this point of view, Doctor Petrosian,' said Smith. 'As you say, you'll be out of a job within days. And once you're on that blacklist you'll never work in

America again, except maybe emptying trash cans. Try to leave America and you'll find that the State Department denies you a passport.'

'And you turn up waving this letter under my nose. Your timing is supernatural.'

Smith still had the calculated grin. 'All you need worry about are the address and the signature.' The sharp, crabbed scrawl of Norris Bradbury – Oppenheimer's successor at Los Alamos – had leapt out at Petrosian the instant he had unfolded the letter.

'And my loyalty?'

Petrosian's visitors didn't react. Lev assessed their blank stares. Then he continued, 'I think I can guess what you people are up to.'

Now Mercier raised a finger to his lips, shaking his head urgently. He mouthed the word: *Bugs*.

Petrosian looked astonished. 'Are you serious?'

'Why not? You're a suspected commie.'

'They surely have no legal right.'

The army man finally grinned. 'Oh my. You really do come from Saturn,' he said, and Petrosian wondered how on earth they had managed to bug the Sweet and Tart's busy kitchen.

Smith sat with Petrosian in the back of the car, the better to brief him as they drove through the hot night. 'By the way, my name is Griggs. Ken Griggs.'

Mercier, at the wheel of the car, glanced back. 'And I'm Mercier.'

'So we're going for the Super?'

In the half-dark, Petrosian saw Griggs give a nod. 'We're in a race, Lev.'

'I don't know if a hydrogen bomb is even feasible.'

'If the Soviets get one before us . . .'

'Somewhere in Russia there are guys talking exactly the same way.'

Mercier said, '*Pravda* regularly accuse us of planning an atomic war.'

'Are we?'

'The President doesn't confide in me. Still, if we built a couple of dozen H-bombs we could rule the world.'

'Or end it in an hour,' Griggs added playfully.

'Hey, maybe I'd rather empty trash cans,' Petrosian said.

Mercier was slowing to avoid a pothole. 'What gives with the angst? It's a simple matter of national security. The Russians are doing it, so we have to.'

Griggs said, 'The price of freedom is eternal vigilance, if you want peace prepare for war, and those who ignore history are condemned to repeat it. That'll be fifteen bucks. I charge five dollars a cliché.'

'Hey, watch your tone,' complained Mercier.

'I asked you about my loyalty,' Petrosian said.

Mercier spoke over his shoulder, 'If it was up to me you wouldn't get within a hundred miles of Los Alamos.'

Griggs said, 'The AEC operates a security clearance procedure.'

'In which case I'm back to trash cans.'

'If somebody, say like Mercier here, queries your loyalty you've had it. Doubt is all it takes and the onus is on you to dispel that doubt. You can forget about questioning evidence, the right to cross-examine witnesses and stuff like that. The procedure stands Anglo-Saxon jurisprudence on its head.'

'I don't understand.'

'But at least we have due process. You could, for example, appeal to the Personnel Security Review Board. The real purpose of the procedure is to keep HUAC at bay. Now if these monsters got their claws into you . . .'

Mercier's tone was jarring. 'These monsters just happen to be our best line of defence against internal subversion. Everyone knows the reds take their orders from Moscow. We're rooting out traitors.'

'You see what you're up against, Lev.'

Petrosian said, 'From what you guys are telling me I haven't a hope of getting into the project.'

'I'm lost.' Mercier was peering along a tunnel of light which showed only an endless, ruler-straight road. Moonlight revealed them to be insects crawling over an infinite, flat, desolate surface.

'Turn left two miles ahead. That'll take us back into town.'

'The fancy footwork is this,' Griggs said. 'The final decision on security is made by the AEC commissioners themselves. They don't have to take anyone's advice. But it's not a trick they dare to pull off more than once. I guess Bradbury sees your talents as vital to the project.'

'I'm flattered. But I might start giving secrets away to the Russians.' Sweat was trickling down Petrosian's back and his thighs were wet against the plastic upholstery.

Griggs said, 'I have to say that Bradbury wants you over the dead bodies of some of the others, Strauss especially. Still, it's like this, Lev. Our success in this project depends on our ability to attract men of talent and vision into it. These men will have all sorts of backgrounds and all sorts of viewpoints. Paranoia is a luxury we can't afford.'

'Army Intelligence are against you,' Mercier said. It wasn't clear whether he was talking to Griggs or Petrosian.

'Listen to the man, Lev, and be aware. You have no guarantee of protection. All this soft-headed liberal thinking the scientists do, exchanging information with colleagues abroad and stuff like that. It's disloyal, and it proves we're under communist influence. Therefore HUAC wants the army to take over the hydrogen bomb project. So does the army.'

'So where do I stand in this?'

'In this struggle, Lev, you're a very small fish. Take my advice and stay that way. Stick to science and keep your mouth shut on policy matters. The guy they're really after, the big whale, is Oppenheimer.'

Four weeks later Petrosian turned up at Los Alamos, having effectively vanished from Greers Ferry. After an absence of seven years, the diaries revealed no sentiment, no sense of homecoming, of loss or gain. Rather, they gave the impression of a man who had been away for a long weekend. Kitty Cronin's name was painfully absent. The pages were filled with the hydrogen bomb. Over the course of the year they became increasingly technical and

Findhorn could scarcely understand the entries. Romella began to stumble over many of the technical words. Some of them had been written in English, probably, she thought, because there was no precise equivalent in the Armenian.

Near the end of 1953, however, Petrosian's prose style suddenly changed. The entries became longer, the text became both enthusiastic and ferociously technical, and the handwriting was that of a man who could hardly write fast enough to get the words down.

By now they could hardly understand a word. But the crabbed writing, the cryptic style and the air of enthusiasm told the same story to Romella and Findhorn. The Armenian physicist was onto something.

The first such entry was on 29 November. Stefi had appeared with hot chocolate and biscuits, and Romella's voice was now slurred with tiredness.

Petrosian's diary, Sunday, 29 November 1953

Spent the day ski-ing on Sawyer Hill. Snow-plows, dead stops, jumps, lots of bruises. Cloudless day. Then did something really stupid. On an impulse I gathered up camping stuff and went to the end of Frijoles Canyon, where it joins the Rio Grande. Wonderful solitude, even the rattlers were gone. Bivouacked out. Bitterly cold.

Woke up early hours. Lay and looked at the brilliant starry sky, and with no effort on my part a thought jumped into my head. It just came. I suddenly realized that the two most awesome experiments in physics – the Casimir effect and Foucault's pendulum – are connected. Maybe it was all that talk with Bethe on ZPE. More likely it was a gift from God.

And the connection lets me solve an ancient problem: how do we know that ten minutes in ancient Greece was the same length of time as ten minutes today? We can compare metre sticks by carrying them around, but we can't transport clocks back and forth in time. Quantum fluctuations in ZPE are the answer. They give us an absolute clock, constant throughout all space and for all time.

Can we possibly have been thinking about physics the wrong way for the past forty years??!!

Okay so ZPE might not be observable because it permeates everything but changes in it surely are. If this is right, then the vacuum is a bottomless pit. The wonderful thing is that ZPE might be changed by fiddling boundary conditions, like the Casimir plates.

Leading to a fantasy thought. Could I squeeze hydrogen into small enough cavities so that low frequency ZPE is excluded and the atoms have to shrink? And so release energy? If the Coulomb barrier is overcome with a Casimir pinch, what then? Do we head for Planck energy?

Head swirling with fantastic thoughts. Can't sleep – anyway I resent the time it takes up.

Findhorn was suddenly on his feet. He paced up and down excitedly, muttering and shaking his head. Momentarily, he looked at the women wildly with bloodshot eyes. Then he carried on pacing.

'Fred!' Romella pleaded.

He paused to look at her. 'I can't tell you.'

'We're shareholders, damn you,' Stefi pointed out.

'It's too bizarre, too way out. I must be wrong.'

Stefi blocked his path. 'Try us.'

Findhorn shook his head energetically. 'You wouldn't understand. You're only a linguist.' He looked at the clock: it showed two thirty a.m. 'Stefi, I want you to get me on the next available flight to America. Not from Edinburgh airport. I'll give you my credit card number.'

'I'm only a linguist, I can't do things like that. Where in America?'

'Los Alamos. I want to nose around.'

Romella was shaking her head. 'Fred, the people you met in Fat Sam's . . .'

'. . . are almost certainly acting for the American Government.'

'And you want to put your head in the lion's mouth?'

'America is the last place they'd expect me to go. I'm gambling that my name won't be on their Immigration Department computers.'

'I'll come,' Romella said. 'The FBI must have old files on Petrosian.'

Findhorn blinked with surprise. 'You intend to just walk into the FBI offices in Washington and ask about Petrosian? You're mad.'

'As you say, Fred, it's the last thing they'd expect. They're looking for us in Edinburgh. I'm betting their right hand doesn't know what their left is doing. It's the same gamble.'

Stefi said, 'You're both mad.'

Romella said, 'You'll have to pay my fare, Fred. I'm skint.'

'Don't do it,' Stefi said.

'Give me an account number and I'll feed money into it.'

'Please can I come too?' Stefi asked. 'I've never been to America.'

Findhorn shook his head. 'You're needed here. See what you can find out about green Mercs registered in Switzerland.'

Stefi attempted a pout.

Romella picked up the photocopies and tapped them into a neat pile. 'At least tell us this, Fred. What's ZPE?'

'It stands for zero point energy. It's the lowest possible energy state any system can have.'

'I know the feeling.'

16

Cult

The first time round, it might have been his imagination.

But not the second. There it was again, a faint bump from the room directly below him. He struggled with the geometry of the house before settling on Doug's study.

Findhorn reckoned he had been asleep for about two hours.

He lay in the dark, his heart thumping, straining to hear. Long ago, the fire authorities had insisted that metal stairs should come from the top floor of the big house down to the back garden. These stairs were reached through the window in Stefi's room. Sensible to get the women and himself out, call the police from a public box.

He wriggled his feet into Doug's slippers and wrapped a dressing gown round himself before opening the door, an inch at a time. Faint light came up the stairwell.

He stepped quietly down the stairs, knowing it was against all sense. The study door was slightly ajar. Keeping about two feet back from the door, he peered in, the strong light hurting his eyes.

Romella, in a peach-colored negligée, was at the keyboard of Doug's machine, staring intently at the monitor. Findhorn couldn't make out the text on the screen, the angle was too awkward. Unexpectedly, she glanced in his direction. He pulled away and slipped back up the stairs, uncertain whether he had been seen.

In bed, he lay on his back and thought that maybe his long sojourns in Arctic environments had made him stupid, that mixing with nobody but people like himself had made him fail to appreciate the range and depth of human duplicity. That maybe the Fat Sam's people had reached Romella before he did, or that her brief captivity had turned her. Archie's words, 'Trust nobody', kept forcing themselves into his head.

They had the diaries. But they would know that Findhorn had made copies. Maybe they wanted the copies destroyed. Maybe the bandstand incident was a setup, maybe he had been allowed to escape with Romella. Maybe Romella appreciated the finer things in life, things you could do with a million pounds. All she had to do was find the files and press the delete button. Not a lot to do for a million. What did she owe Findhorn anyway?

Then he thought that maybe circumstances were making him paranoid, that there was a natural explanation, that only a heel would think this way.

He fretted for half an hour, wriggling and turning on wrinkled sheets, feeling betrayed, paranoid and guilty, sometimes all at once, before drifting into a restless sleep.

'You want to be very careful when you talk about a religious cult, Fred. The point is that "cult" is a hate word. It carries emotional baggage and people use it as a weapon to impart bad vibrations to the group they're talking about. Likewise your use of the word "nutter" shows that there's an evil intolerance at work in the murky depths of your subconscious. Most way-out systems of religious belief are harmless and deserve the tolerance—'

Findhorn interrupted, typing rapidly on the keyboard: 'Mike, I stand corrected. I'll try to be good. Still, when you have people whose aim is the destruction of human life . . .'

The signal came back on the screen: 'If that really is the aim and not something that's been ascribed to them by some hate group.'

'Does the manufacture of nerve gas and botulism toxin qualify?'

'Obviously there's a threshold beyond which you have to declare war, if only to protect those you love. Then it's PC to talk about a doomsday cult.'

'These cults exist?'

'There are thousands of minority religious groups on our register, of which a couple of dozen need watching. Even these are largely harmless or at the most a danger to themselves, through suicidal tendencies. The scary thing is that irresponsible geeks have created Internet cookbooks giving step-by-step recipes for making biological toxins, *et cetera*. Aerosol poisons plus doomsday cults are an unholy combination.'

'Mike, you're scaring me.'

Mike continued, his typing coming up rapidly and almost error-free on the monitor: 'There are features common to most of these groups. First of course is the grand apocalyptic vision. Usually they believe that a tragedy is about to hit the earth, say like Armageddon. Sometimes they think that, through group suicide, they'll escape the tragedy and be carried off to heaven, perhaps by UFO.'

'I think I read about one such group.'

'That would be the Heaven's Gate cult, a Christian-UFO group which committed mass suicide when Comet Hale Bopp came in. The body count was thirty-nine. But the belief goes back at least to the Unarians, who've been holding to the UFO thing since 1954 without harming anyone. A second feature is the charismatic leader.'

'Do these leaders have any common traits?'

'Absolutely. They're invariably a dominant male, intelligent or at least cunning, a social misfit or failure in mainstream society, and a control freak. He exerts a sort of hypnotic effect on the faithful which he uses to control their sexual, social and emotional lives.'

'You've just described Adolf Hitler,' Findhorn suggested.

'Careful, Fred. Sensitive area.'

Findhorn paused at the keyboard, uncertain whether to interrupt his old friend, now a university rabbi. Then Michael was typing: 'And another feature of the cult mentality is the accumulation of weapons coupled with a sort of paranoid belief that outsiders or governments are out to get them. They see themselves as being monitored by the FBI or other government agencies.'

'I hope they are.'

'Of course many of the cults, especially the Christian right-wing people, are themselves hate merchants. You don't want to be black, gay, communist or Jewish within a thousand miles of Christ Foremost, for example.'

'Remember Abo? He scored three out of four.'

'Let's hope he never strays into Waco, Texas. Now, do you have a specific group in mind?'

'I need to identify them but the clues are thin. The Book of Revelation seems to be central to them, they're doomsday-minded and there's a Swiss connection, I think.'

There was a pause for about thirty seconds. The study door opened and Romella came in carrying two mugs of tea. She put them down on the desk and looked over Findhorn's shoulder. Then words were coming up on the monitor at speed: 'THE TEMPLE OF CELESTIAL TRUTH.'

Findhorn felt a surge of excitement. Then his friend was typing: 'Hang on, I'm putting them on another screen. Here we are. Yes, it's not one of your big-time doomsday cults. That's the problem, some of these groups are down in the noise and the first you hear of them is when they crawl out of the woodwork with some high-profile atrocity. At its peak the Supreme Truth had forty thousand members worldwide, including thirty thousand in Russia, several of whom were engineers with access to nukes, something you might want to think about. They had assets of a billion dollars—'

'The Celestial Truth?'

'Patience, it's still downloading. This is another Christian-UFO cult, with a hodge-podge of Greek and African myth thrown in. They use prophecies from the Book of Revelation along with the sixteenth-century writings of Nostradamus to predict that world end is due any time. They can't wait for it because when it happens the resultant cleansing of sin will allow the second wave of extraterrestrials to come and carry them up to Heaven.'

'What about their organization? How are they structured?'

'I've got an organogram here, but it's all conjecture. They're thought to have regional chapters which meet to co-ordinate activities. They're highly secretive, dispersed globally, and their membership is totally unknown. They're rich, with widely dispersed assets which may total a billion dollars but nobody really knows. They run a front organization, the Tati Foundation, which supports a wide variety of causes.'

'Where are they located? On Earth, I mean.'

'Hold on. Right, they have temples in Japan and Dakota, but their main spiritual centre is tucked away in a mountain region near Davos, in Switzerland. It's a place called Piz Radönt and it looks like the devil to get to. I've got a photograph here. Hold on, I'll beam it through.'

Findhorn waited while a picture rapidly built up on the screen, line by line, overlaying the text. A blue sky appeared first, and then the tops of snowy peaks, and then the picture was showing golden, onion-shaped domes which seemed more Muslim than Christian, and finally there it was, a big white shoebox in an idyllic mountain setting. Findhorn clicked on a button, reduced the picture to stamp size, and resumed his rapid two-finger typing.

'About this world end they believe in. Is there any evidence that they'd like to speed it along?'

'Okay, here I have unclassified testimony to the Global Organized Crime Project Steering Committee, CSIS to the House of Representatives Committee on National Security.'

Findhorn hadn't a clue but let it pass.

'I'll fire it through but the essence is this. According to this testimony, NEST teams have been activated five times in California in the last two years, three of them in consequence of information pertaining to the Temple of Celestial Truth.'

'Information pertaining to. That's exceedingly vague.'

'Deliberately so, I don't doubt. They have sources to protect. The CIA has a Center for Counterterrorism, and there's an FBI equivalent for domestic stuff, and you could try them for more if you feel like wasting your time. There have also been suspicions of aerosol attacks in Germany from truck convoys, and Korean building collapses deliberately induced by poor loading and use of sub-standard concrete. But so much lousy building goes on anyway in the Far East that nobody can be sure if it was weirdo religion or just officials lining their pockets.'

'What about their leader?'

'Ah, now Freddie, there you have something very interesting.'

Findhorn waited. He read the words avidly as they came up on the monitor. 'You'll be interested to know that this particular outfit is led by a guy called Tati who just happens to come from Sirius. First time round he came to Earth in the body of Jesus. These guys are souls, you see, who just temporarily inhabit human bodies. Kind of like the Incas, who believed they came from the stars and returned to them after death.'

'When he's not being Tati from Sirius, who is he really?'

'That's what makes him interesting. Nobody knows. His background is a *big mystery*.'

'Maybe he really does come from Sirius.'

The rabbi's words came up on the screen: 'There's always that possibility.'

'Well?' Romella asked.

Findhorn was pacing up and down. 'It might be coincidence.'

'It might. Whatever you're talking about.'

'It so happens there's a doomsday cult with a centre near Davos. The Book of Revelation is one of their props.'

'Meaning what?'

Findhorn stopped pacing and Romella handed him his tea. 'I think the diaries were taken from us by the Temple of Celestial Truth. They might even be in this Piz Radönt temple.'

'Fred, don't get too excited. It's all circumstantial. Who was that anyway?'

'Mike? An old pal, a hard-drinking friend from my student days. He trained as a rabbi, did a stint in a kibbutz and came back as university pastor. He lost the use of his limbs after a motorcycle accident and now spends his time keeping up with trends in religious thought everywhere. He's become quite an authority and he makes pots of money out of it.'

'It's a compensation, I suppose.'

'I have to pull over the last batch of diaries. They're scanned into a computer. It'll take me a couple of hours.'

'Okay, I'll grab some sleep.'

'Didn't you sleep?'

'Not a lot. I was surfing the net, trying to get info on Mercedes car sales in Switzerland.'

'Any luck?'

'Sod all.' Romella left the study, looking puzzled at Findhorn's unexpected grin.

I should learn to have a little trust in people, Findhorn told himself as he tapped his way into the cookies, the record of the last five hundred keyboard instructions.

Stefi turned up in a green blouse and skirt, with a black choker and heavy eye shadow and hair freshly blonde and hanging down in ringlets. She was driving a large red Saab with cream upholstery, leaving Findhorn to wonder how close his credit card was to breaking point. She gurgled the car round to the rear lane where Romella and Findhorn tossed holdalls into the boot. She handed Findhorn a folder containing air tickets; Findhorn gave her the key to Doug's flat. Romella sat in front, while Findhorn tried to look invisible in the rear seat.

Stefi took them west, away from the city centre, handling the big car with ease. She drove through the Corstorphine suburbs and onto the M8 towards Glasgow and, beyond it, Prestwick International Airport. She took the car up to a steady eighty and Findhorn felt that he could at last safely poke his nose above windowsill level.

* * *

They slept all the way across the Pond.

'The parting of the ways,' Romella announced. She had a small green holdall at her feet and was glancing from time to time at the taxi queue on the other side of the airport glass.

Findhorn, on the other hand, was looking in the opposite direction, at the Dulles Airport departure screens. 'Would you believe I'm still weary?'

'We could find a hotel,' Romella suggested, leaving Findhorn to wonder what she had in mind.

'There's no time, Ms Grigoryan. The competition must be going flat out.'

'You still don't want to say what you've seen in the diaries?'

Findhorn rubbed his overnight stubble. 'It's too fantastic to be believable, Romella. The chances are it's nothing. I'll have to see what I can find out in Los Alamos, if anything.'

'There's something weird here, Fred. If Petrosian was escaping to Russia he didn't need the diaries to tell them what was going on. So why was he escaping with them?'

Findhorn nodded his agreement. He was still nervous about standing openly in a crowded place. 'I think I need to get to Phoenix and connect to Los Alamos from there.'

The taxi queue was shortening. Romella picked up her bag and Findhorn walked with her towards the automatic doors. She said, 'And I'll see what I can rustle up from old FBI files in Washington. I expect they're public domain by now.'

'Which leaves us with one last question, Romella. Where, in these Yoonited States, shall we meet up?'

Romella said, 'Make it some place where we can't easily be followed. Not a town like Los Alamos or Washington.'

'Sparks flew between Lev and Kitty at the Grand Canyon.'

Romella gave a surprised, sunny smile. 'What's this, Fred? Could there be romance buried somewhere in the depths of your soul?'

'I'm mad, bad and dangerous to know.' He yawned. 'The south rim of the Grand Canyon, then, just as soon as we can make it.'

'Be careful, Fred. Remember you're still a target.'

Findhorn made a face. 'Tell me about it.'

A taxi drew up and Romella turned as she opened the door. 'And don't speak to any strange women.'

17

Los Alamos

YOU ARE ENTERING AN ACTIVE EXPLOSIVES
TEST RANGE. AREAS ARE POTENTIALLY
CONTAMINATED WITH EXPLOSIVE DEVICES.
STAY ON THE ROADS. DO NOT TOUCH OR
DISTURB ANY ITEMS. IF ITEMS ARE FOUND
CALL THE WHITE SANDS POLICE.

The morning sun was already *hot*. The wind which gently
shook the sign was tumbling sagebrush along the high
desert landscape and Findhorn, feeling like a fried tomato
after his six-hour taxi ride from Phoenix, was grateful for
it. The cab trailed dust as it vanished, its driver weary but
richer.

Two men were waiting just outside the barbed
wire, next to a yellow sports car. One of them, surly, in a
tan uniform with a black belt and bearing a holstered
side-arm, appraised Findhorn with small, deep-set,
suspicious eyes. The civilian was about thirty, tall,
bespectacled, slightly stooped and had receding, balding
hair. He also had stubble and the air of a man who
hadn't slept overnight. A cluster of observatory domes

glinted a few hundred yards away.

'Cartwright of *The Times*, I presume,' said the man. His handshake was tired, his hand clammy in spite of the dry air.

'My friends call me Ed or Eddie.'

'I'm Frank. I don't have any friends.'

Findhorn waved an arm towards the observatory domes. 'Isn't that where they hunt for threat asteroids?'

The guard looked as if Findhorn had just introduced himself as an armed terrorist.

'Hey, how did you know that?' White asked.

Findhorn smiled. 'That's another story.'

The guard wasn't returning any smiles today. 'Before this goes any further, let's see your ID, mister.' Findhorn produced passport and a hastily forged letter of authorization with a *Times* letterhead scanned in from the newspaper.

'Yes, that's one of the LINEAR telescopes,' said White, while the guard examined Findhorn's papers with an air of deep suspicion. 'Part of the Air Force GEODSS system. If you want clearance for a visit it'll take you two months and three layers of bureaucracy, and that's if you're American.'

'Listen, it's good of you to meet me down here. We're still about two hundred miles south of Los Alamos, *n'est ce pas*?'

The guard returned Findhorn's papers looking like a man who knows he's being conned but can do nothing about it. White motioned Findhorn towards the convertible Corvette, and waved his arm wearily at the receding guard. In the car, the black leather seat threatened to roast Findhorn's backside and thighs.

The little machine took off with a satisfying, sporty roar. Findhorn assumed that, this close to the ground, the alarming speed was an optical illusion.

'Sure,' White said. 'But you seemed in one hell of a hurry to write your piece about this Petrosian. And as it happens I had overnight business here.' The nature of the business went unexplained, but White added: 'We're only a mile from the Trinity Site. Now clearance for *that* . . .'

Findhorn laughed but the speedometer was showing eighty five and it came out a bit high-pitched.

Through the terracotta desert, with its wonderful pinks and purples, and distant mountains covered with snow. Past the Santa Ana Reservation, and the roadside Navajo women selling jewellery and rugs and Clint Eastwood ponchos.

Around midday, with the sun beginning to fry his brain, Findhorn was relieved to see a sign for Los Alamos.

'Most people like Los Alamos,' White was saying over a ninety-mile-an-hour wind. 'It looks for all the world like any university town. One thing about it you should remember, though.'

'The security?' Findhorn asked, his hair being pulled at the roots.

'The altitude. It's nearly eight thousand feet up. Unless you're acclimatised to that, you can't run.'

'Why would I want to run?'

White gave him a ghoulish grin. He dropped his speed, went down a gear, and in minutes they were trickling past pink and green adobe houses, and more jewellery and rugs. Near the town centre, the nuclear physicist squeezed his Corvette in between a battered yellow Oldsmobile and a string of motorcycles.

'Some people describe Los Alamos as the world's greatest concentration of nerds,' White complained. 'This is a grave injustice to Berkeley, Calfornia. But one thing missing from this community is mediocrity. It makes for a kinda skewed population.'

They were in the Blue Adobe on Central Avenue. It had walls three feet thick, and canned mariachi music, and the best air conditioning in the known Universe. Memorabilia and photographs from the Manhattan Project lined the walls. They had been lucky to find a spare booth in the crowded little restaurant. 'We have so many PhDs – the highest per capita population on Earth – that unless you're a physician you're called plain Mister. Outsiders paint us as overachievers, pressuring our kids, neglecting our wives.'

Findhorn, sensing an open sore, steered White back to the point. 'Petrosian . . .' he began.

A small, Hispanic waitress approached. She gave White a radiant smile.

'Rosa, my beautiful, what about a late breakfast?' asked White.

'For you, Francis, there are huevos rancheros, huevos borrachos or omelette.'

White translated: 'Ed, you can have eggs with green chillies, eggs with red chillies or an omelette. It comes with chillies.'

'I'll have a fried egg,' Findhorn said. On the wall opposite was a 1940s milk box from the Hillside dairy – *From Moo to You* was printed on its side. He added, 'And a glass of milk.'

'Me too,' White said. When Rosa had gone he said, 'To resume. Anything Petrosian did in the 1950s is ancient history. You're talking fifty-year-old physics. Holy moly, Ed, that was before quarks, gluons, QCD, string theory, superstrings. It was the steam age of nuclear physics.'

Findhorn mopped his brow. It felt hot to the touch. He took a shorthand notebook out of his pocket. 'How many particle types do you have?'

'Twenty-five. Everything you see around you, the whole caboodle – even the delectable Rosa – is governed by twenty-five fundamental particles. Don't ask me why twenty-five and not seven or fifteen. Nobody knows.'

'But still you have a theory for all this, the standard model. I never got beyond electrons, protons and neutrons, and of course light particles – photons.'

White nodded. 'The old timers. Use them as building blocks and you have water, CO_2, DNA, coal for your fire, brick for your house, gas for your car and medicine for your kids. The whole of chemistry comes out of combining just these four particles. Imagine Rosa as a shimmering mass of atomic particles.'

'So who needs the other twenty-one – quarks and the like?'

'You do.' White waved at the sunlight pouring in through the big windows. 'Unless you want to go around like some primordial slime, in pitch-black at absolute zero.

Sunlight depends on nuclear fusion, right? Hydrogen combining to give helium with the mass surplus going off as energy? So how do the protons – hydrogen nuclei to you – combine?'

Rosa reappeared with plates of food covered with a red dust. 'You want more chilli on that?'

'People are big on chilli hereabouts,' advised White.

Findhorn nodded, and Rosa sprinkled a generous helping over his fried egg, which, in addition to the red dust, had come with a coating of red and green chillies and a blue corn tortilla. He said, 'I recall that the intense heat you get in the middle of stars is the same as you get in an A-bomb and this heat causes hydrogen atoms to fuse together. This fusing constitutes the transmutation of elements and when that happens it releases even more heat, whence the hydrogen bomb.'

'I'm asking you, *why* does the heat make the atoms merge?'

Findhorn shrugged, and White said, 'It's a lot of stuff about an up-quark converting to a down-quark and a hip bone connecting to a thigh bone. Then you're into the other twenty-one particles. But my point is this, Ed: you don't need to know Because Petrosian didn't know either. Like I said, they were developing the Bomb in the steam age, when people hadn't gotten beyond nuclear binding energies.'

'I'm trying to follow you,' Findhorn said. Sweat was breaking out of his brow: he had started on his egg.

White waved a fork in the air. 'What I'm getting at is that Petrosian's world is *understood*. There's nothing new to be said about it. It's been raked over by three generations of physicists and all that can possibly be known about it is known.'

The restaurant was beginning to fill up with early lunchers. A bespectacled young man sat down at the table opposite them. He looked like an outdoors type, dressed in blue denim and with long, blond hair tied back in a pony-tail. In any other situation, Findhorn would never have noticed him. 'You're telling me that Petrosian can't possibly have discovered anything relevant to modern science.'

White nodded his agreement. 'Petrosian's world was one of protons, neutrons and electrons. Any discovery he made in that area would long since have been rediscovered by someone else. There are no surprises left in the nuclear energies the Los Alamos pioneers worked at.'

'And the new particles? The other twenty-one?'

'To see the exotic stuff, the quarks and so on, you have to look at cosmic rays on the way in or go to heavy atom smashers. These machines cost megabucks and they didn't even exist in Petrosian's day. Nobody could have predicted the world they uncovered. Any idea of the Lone Ranger getting some brilliant insight that leaped across three generations of nuclear scientists – look, it's nuts. Forget it.'

Rosa was bearing down at ram speed, wielding a bowl of chilli. Findhorn, in panic, asked for coffee. It took her by surprise and she retreated back to the kitchen.

On an impulse, Findhorn tried a gamble. He studied

White closely and said, 'So how did the rumour get around?'

'What rumour?' White was looking genuinely blank.

'That Petrosian had discovered some new process.'

White's hesitation was tiny. It might just have been something to do with a throatful of Rosa's chillies. He tried to laugh, to cover it up. 'What sort of process? Where did you hear that?'

Findhorn touched the side of his nose, probed a little more. 'My source thinks there was a cover-up.'

White shook his head in annoyance. 'Sure, there's nothing like a cover-up story to sell newspapers. I suspect like the Roswell UFO incident, one or two bits of real information get distorted. Alien spacecraft, the face on Mars, energy from nothing, you name it, there's an audience out there eager to buy your conspiracy theory. And the more screwball it is the bigger your audience.' White tried a sympathetic tone. 'Look, Ed, this stuff's for our *National Enquirer*, not the English *Times*. Whoever your source is, this story about some new process has no foundation. No foundation in history, no foundation in science.'

'I'm chasing a chimera, then?'

'Absolutely.'

Findhorn tried to look convinced. 'What could have gotten the rumour started?'

White shrugged. 'You tell me.'

Findhorn gambled again. 'The process was supposed to be dangerous.'

This time White was ready. 'Your source is confused.

There was a scare in 1942 that an atomic bomb explosion might ignite the atmosphere, create an uncontrolled runaway. Oppenheimer set up a task force to check it out. Their report was codenamed LA-602 as I recall. They found that the fireball couldn't quite pull it off. Petrosian was involved in these calculations.'

White was convincing, and seemed to be making sense. *Hell*, he thought, *I'm getting into conspiracy theories myself.* Findhorn closed his notebook and said, 'Okay, Frank, thank you for that.'

'I guess you've come a long way for nothing. Look, I could get you into X-2 if you like, I have Q-clearance—'

'X-2?'

'The design group for nukes. But it's just like any other office building. Apart from the guys with the AK-47s, of course.'

'I think you've just upset our surveillance,' Findhorn said, nodding towards the pony-tailed young man, who was staring at the menu with unnatural intensity.

White grinned. 'Anyway, I don't think anyone there could help you.'

'Post-SALT, do we need Los Alamos?' Findhorn asked, breathing air in gulps. He felt his lips beginning to blister with the hot chillies.

White leaned back in his chair, steepled his hands under his chin and looked over his spectacles. 'More than ever, pal. The world is more dangerous, not less, and it's getting worse. Iran will soon be stuffed with enough recycled nuclear fuel to start a significant nuclear weapons program. Saddam Hussein and his merry men had to be bombed to stop them developing nukes. India and Pakistan have already fought three wars with each other, and now they're squaring up with nukes. Nuclear smuggling out of Russia is a deadly serious worry – it's only a matter of time before the Ultimate Truth or the Martyrs of God or the Montana Ladies' Crochet Circle rigs up some device from instructions on the Internet.'

'Surely these are problems for the FBI or CIA.'

'But without guys who know about weapons, they wouldn't know what to look for. And what about our own stockpiles? Nuclear devices deteriorate. We need expertise to keep track of that too. It's a dangerous world out there, Ed, and a complex one.'

Rosa was serving the pony-tailed young man with a plate of little tortillas stuffed with pieces of fried fish, tomatoes, lettuce, sour cream and chillies.

'If it wasn't new science, what about new technology? Could Petrosian have thought of some way to make a bomb more effective? Say by miniaturization, or avoiding the need for plutonium?'

'Let me tell you about miniaturization, Ed. Ideas for it get developed all the time but we're no longer allowed to test them. These designs are as much art as science, which is why so many bomb designers in X-2 are women. They're more intuitive. But the complexity of a nuclear explosion stretches a Cray. No way could Petrosian have leapt fifty years ahead on that one either. As for by-passing uranium or plutonium, it's not an area I can talk about, or our surveillance, whose spectacles undoubtedly contain a microphone, would choke on his tortilla boats.' White leaned forward, lowering his voice. 'But there are some things you could work out from the public domain. Like, lithium is common in rocks on Earth, but astronomers don't detect much of it in stars. Why is that?'

'I don't know, Frank. Why is that?'

White leaned forward some more. 'Because it's easy to ignite, nuclear-wise. Hydrogen needs ten or twenty million degrees. Now lithium, that needs less than a million. If you could somehow reproduce stellar—'

'Could Petrosian have thought of some way to do that in 1953? By-pass plutonium, make a nuke from rocks?'

'As a concept, quite possibly. Now if you did that, if you found some way of extracting nuclear energy using just ordinary material, that would really open the lid. But as a hazard to civilization in 1953? Where would he get even a million degrees? Lasers weren't invented until 1960. Always assuming we needed high-energy lasers to attempt the trick,' White added hastily. His tired eyes held a gleam.

'Of course. Always assuming that.'

White looked as if he was about to drop with exhaustion. Findhorn waved at the waitress. He said, 'So he didn't have lasers but he had electricity. Maybe he thought of something crazy. Take the entire power supply for New York City on a cold night. Pulse all that electricity through a microscopically thin wire. Have the wire doped with lithium and anything else you need.'

White grinned. 'Ed, that wouldn't even get you to the foothills.'

Findhorn blew out his cheeks. 'So try one of Rosa's chillies.'

* * *

Findhorn thanked White and left him heading for the Western area of town and some badly needed sleep. He took a stroll, absorbing the sights and sounds of this strange town.

White's sermon was clear. Petrosian was a wild-goose chase, a piece of history with nothing to say of relevance to the new millennium.

There was, however, a problem with that thesis. Namely, the trail of mayhem which followed the diaries. Findhorn wondered whether White's sermon had been genuine, or an attempt to deflect further enquiry. And what, he wondered, if he kept digging?

He took a cab to the Los Alamos Community Reading Room and there asked a warm, curly-haired girl for information about the post-war activities of Lev Petrosian the atom spy. Without a blink she disappeared.

And Findhorn waited. For ten minutes, his speculations becoming increasingly wild.

He was beginning to wonder whether to get out of it when a library attendant, a squat, white-haired Navajo, approached and sat down heavily three desks away from Findhorn. At least, Findhorn assumed he was a library attendant. The man clasped his hands together and stared unblinkingly at Findhorn. And then, at last, the curly-haired girl was back at his desk with a sweet smile and a black binder.

How to Make a Hydrogen Bomb.

The binder was heavy. There were research papers and there were notebooks. Findhorn started on the papers.

These were in triplicate, a top copy and two carbons. Each had a number circled at the top of it. They were abstrusely mathematical, with titles like *Quantum Tunnelling Probabilities in a Polarized Vacuum*, or *A Markov Chain Treatment of Ulam/Teller Implosion*. Findhorn could barely make sense of them, except in the broadest outline. He wrote down the titles but had the feeling that they were no more than the bread-and-butter elements of the hydrogen bomb project; the appliance of yesterday's science.

The workbooks were fatter and more interesting. There were a couple of dozen, lined and bound in blue, soft-backed covers. They too were numbered; perhaps, Findhorn speculated, to stop a potential spy smuggling his own secrets out. Findhorn started on them systematically, opening at number one, page one. The small, clear longhand writing of Petrosian was unmistakable. The notes were in English and written in ink. There was a prodigious amount of scoring out and reworking. There were lots of doodles; Petrosian seemed particularly fond of little flying saucers, reflecting the UFO-mania of the day, but there were also cows and galaxies. He did a particularly good pig, sometimes with wings. Often little cartoon bubbles would come from the mouths of the animals, and they would enclose equations, or technical terms, or cryptic comments.

With a lot of tedious effort, Findhorn found he could relate the development of Petrosian's notes to the contents of the typed papers. Here and there, in the margins, there were scribbles written in faded pencil: 'Kitty, orchestra 7 o'clock'; or 'Colloquium 2 p.m.'; or 'coffee, beans, oil, milk'; or 'proofs deadline NOW'.

In the late afternoon, one doodle in particular caught his eye. It was a little cartoon showing Albert Einstein smoking a pipe. A long stream of smoke from the pipe connected three large puffs of smoke, like clouds, over Einstein's head.

The date was Monday 30 November, 1953. The day after his diary recorded his high excitement.

The first puff showed a picture of a ship. Little bubbles were coming from its propellor. Next to it was written: 'HMS *Daring* 1894.'

The second showed a sort of golfball with a dozen legs sticking out of it. Next to it was written: 'Chase & Henshal'.

The third contained only the letters 'ZPE'.

Findhorn contemplated that. He copied the quirky little picture into his notebook.

Towards the evening, with his head reeling, Findhorn closed the last of the notebooks and sat back with a sigh and a stretch. The library attendant, if such he was, hadn't moved for the entire session. Findhorn returned the heavy binder to the curly-haired girl with the smile, and emerged into the warm evening air and a streetful of nerds returning from work on bicycles, skates and four-wheel trucks loaded with skis.

Findhorn now hired an RV with an unexpectedly throaty roar on a one-way drop. He drove south, with the lights of Santa Fe twinkling in the distance. The Jemez Mountains were still in sunlight to the west, and they were glowing blood red. His mouth was still burning. Ahead, Santa Fe was like a big Mongol encampment on a hillside, its lights a myriad of campfires.

Petrosian had been hiding something. He had been careful to erase all mention of his overnight inspiration from his daytime workbook, and all signs of the excitement which he confided to his diaries. It was as if there had been two Petrosians. And yet the little doodles were the windows to his soul. They were mind games, Petrosian at play. A purposeful play.

Findhorn struggled with the bizarre images: HMS *Daring*, 1894; a golfball with legs; ZPE. And they danced in his head with other, darker pictures: city-destroying fireballs; blazing oceans.

He looked in his rear mirror, and the hairs on the back of his neck prickled. The headlights were still half a mile to the rear, as they had been since Los Alamos.

He thought that it had to be coincidence, that jet lag and tension were bringing out some mild paranoia, that the claustrophobic atmosphere of security pervading Los Alamos made you think that way, that there was no possible way for White or anyone else in the States to connect Cartwright of *The Times* with Findhorn of the Arctic.

He thought all of that, and he congratulated himself on this triumph of pure reason over primitive, irrational fear. And he put his foot down.

18

The Venona Files

The cost of doubling back, taking nonsense routes and side roads on the two hundred mile journey from Santa Fe to Flagstaff was eight precious hours. It left Findhorn screaming with frustration. It was late afternoon by the time he reached the entrance to the wooded camp site at the Grand Canyon, but at least he was sure that he was not being followed.

He drove past the entrance just the same.

Five miles on he slowed down, did a U-turn on the empty road and turned back, wondering if everyone on the receiving end of surveillance ended up with galloping paranoia. On the way back to the canyon not a vehicle passed him, in either direction.

The trees and ground were lightly dusted with snow. The Mather Campground was bigger than he had visualized and he hoped that finding Romella, if she was here, wouldn't turn out to be a major headache. There was a light scattering of cars and tents amongst the trees, and he nosed the camper around the roadways lacing the site. He wondered where, fifty years earlier, Petrosian and Kitty had stayed. There was no sign of Romella, and no telling which if any of the handful of vehicles around was hers. He parked in a quiet spot – the nearest car was a made-in-Japan, four-wheel-drive effort two hundred yards away, all gleaming chrome and hideous purple. He put diaries, laptop and notebook into a backpack rather than risk leaving them in the van. He stepped out, took a moment to stretch and fill his lungs with cool, pine-scented air, and then walked briskly along a path towards a little cluster of shops he had passed earlier. He headed east along a trail skirting the rim from Mather Point.

Findhorn had seen the photographs often enough; but the reality still impressed. The scale was inhuman, too large to absorb. He leaned over the low parapet and traced the path of a little trail far below. He thought he would like to do it some day but he couldn't see a way out of the fix he was in and he might not manage it before he met his assassins.

A few people – families, couples, individuals – were scattered around. They were doing normal things: taking photographs, sitting on the low wall, looking out over the vista, eating. Findhorn looked at them all with deep suspicion and wondered if he would ever recapture his lost innocence. He walked off, exploring the unfamiliar surroundings, looking into curio shops and restaurants with names like Hopi House, Bright Angel Lodge, Lookout Studio, Verkamp's Curios.

There was no Romella.

Then he wandered west to Hermit's Rest, and back along the tracks interspersing the tree-scattered camp site. He was now shivering in the cold air. Hopelessly restless, he returned to the Canyon rim and again looked out over the great pink scar. Heavy, snow-laden clouds were coming in low and the air temperature was plummeting.

He turned in the direction of Bright Angel Lodge and a caffeine hit. With a pile of dollars at the ready, he phoned through to the Edinburgh flat. It would be around noon.

A male voice answered.

'Dougie?'

A pause, then, 'Fred!'

Findhorn's younger brother. 'Hi, Dougie, you're back early?'

'Too much snow, the skiing was lousy. Hey, am I glad you phoned! I got home in the early hours to find guess what . . .'

'Stefi Stefanova. I'm sorry, I hope you don't object.'

A pause, then, 'Object? The day I complain to coming home and finding a blonde stunner in my flat . . . I just wondered if she was an impostor or something.'

'No, she's genuine.'

'And under a grilling from me, I find you've had two wenches staying with you.' There was a wicked chuckle. 'I'm highly impressed, but this isn't the big brother I know at all.'

'Come on, Doug, it's business.'

'Business? If the old man gets to hear of this . . .'

'Translation business, you total idiot. Listen, has Stefi explained things?'

'Not a thing. I don't think she really believes I'm me.'

'Put her on.'

A minute later a nervous voice came over the telephone. 'Fred?'

'Stefi, you can relax. That's my brother Dougie, he's just come back early from Gstaadt.'

The relief in her voice was unmistakeable. 'Oh thank goodness. I suppose I should move out now. No, he's shaking his head.'

'Stefi, you can trust Dougie absolutely, except maybe at bedtimes, if you see what I mean. Now, business. Can you find out what happened to HMS *Daring* in 1894?'

'I think so. What's that about bedtimes?'

'I'll phone you later today. And it's okay to tell Dougie the whole story provided that he wants to hear it. Remember he's a lawyer, he may not want to know about it.'

Dougie came back on line. Findhorn said, 'Dougie, Stefi has a story to tell that you'll hardly believe. There could be a huge amount at stake, or nothing at all. The only thing is, you may not want to become privy to information which might compromise your position as a pillar of the legal community. Anyway, it's up to you.'

Findhorn could practically feel his brother straining at the leash. Dougie was saying, 'My God, Fred, get the hell off the phone so I can quiz this woman.'

'I'll be in touch.' Findhorn sipped at his coffee and thought that, knowing Little Brother, it wouldn't be long before he was looking for ten per cent.

ZPE. Zero point energy. The lowest possible energy state, the energy of empty space. But how much energy was that? A fantastic thought jumped into Findhorn's head. Could you get at that energy, whatever it amounted to? Could you somehow mine the vacuum?

Now Findhorn was beginning to remember the cosmologists' claim: that the Universe was created *ex nihilo*, that the Big Bang itself was a fluctuation in the vacuum. The ultimate free lunch, they said. The Creation was God's industrial accident, a vacuum fluctuation that had gotten out of hand.

And Petrosian, that November night in 1953, had become very excited about zero point energy.

Something was beginning to connect.

At a table in the Lodge, Findhorn wrote down some barely remembered numbers on the hotel stationery. In the beginning was the erg, about the energy of a small, falling feather. At a million grams to a ton, a fifty-ton express train moving at one hundred kilometres an hour carried – he did the sums – two hundred million million ergs, or two followed by fourteen zeroes, or 2×10^{14} ergs. He doodled a little more and finally wrote out a small table:

a falling feather	1 erg
a gram of dynamite	10^{11} ergs
a bullet	10^{11} ergs
an express train	2×10^{14} ergs
a naval gun	5×10^{15} ergs
the Hiroshima bomb	8×10^{20} ergs
a medium hydrogen bomb	4×10^{22} ergs
solar output (one second)	4×10^{33} ergs

energy to evaporate Atlantic 4×10^{33} ergs
energy of a moving galaxy 2×10^{59} ergs

So the energy coming out of the Sun, if suitably concentrated, would evaporate the Atlantic Ocean in one second. Not many people know that, he told himself with satisfaction. He hadn't known it himself until now.

Then he remembered the figure he was after. The Planck energy, the ultimate energy contained in a cubic centimetre of vacuum. He added to his little column:

energy per cc of vacuum 10^{93} ergs

He looked at the scribbled number, compared it with the others he had written. He thought: no, no way.

The number looked at him, hypnotizing him. 10^{93} ergs. Per cubic centimetre. He ran from it, crossed quickly to the reception desk. The girl was very friendly, very smooth, very American. 'I need to do some e-mailing. Can I plug in somewhere?'

'Sure. Use the office. Round here.'

Archie – As a matter of top priority I need to speak to the best people going about the vacuum, about the energy it contains, and about the possibility of extracting energy from it. Can you recommend anyone? Or even fix something? I'll phone later.

Findhorn ordered another espresso and sat at the table. The afternoon sun briefly peeked out from below heavy cloud, changed its mind and disappeared again. He wrote out a one and followed it with ninety-three zeroes. Findhorn looked at it. It wasn't a number, it was a battering ram. It was power beyond imagination. It was the heat of God's forge.

'Hi, Fred.'

Findhorn's heart leaped. She was in a cream-coloured designer fleece with black jeans and black leather boots. The fleece was open and beneath it Findhorn glimpsed a Rennie Mackintosh necklace and a nicely rounded black T-shirt with an 'I Love ET' motif, complete with a picture of the cuddly alien. Somewhere she had taken time off from the mayhem to have her hair styled in a boyish cut. A casual black bag was draped over her shoulder. The bruise over her eye was well down and she was trying not to look too pleased to see him.

Findhorn caught a light whiff of expensive perfume. 'Hi, Romella. Any problems on the way here?'

'Nope. If there was surveillance I missed it.' She tapped her bag. 'I've got some goodies.'

'Would you like to walk?'

'Later. I haven't eaten since yesterday. And I'll want to spread some papers out, but not here.'

'Okay, let's visit the grocery store and go back to my car. You're sure we're safe here?'

At last she smiled, a sly, mischievous smile. 'Am I safe from you?'

At the little table in the RV, Romella produced a thick

wodge of papers. The bottled-gas stove was bringing a pot of water to the boil and the little blue flames were warming the air. 'The FBI people couldn't have been more helpful,' she said.

Findhorn nodded at the papers. 'I can't wait to get into this. But it'll surely take all night.'

'Yes. It's almost their entire take on Petrosian.'

'Almost?'

'There are deletions, allowed under the Act. Where national security is involved, or innocent people still alive might be compromised in some way, they delete things.'

'Okay. I guess we now have about everything we're going to get.'

Romella pulled off her Muscovado boots with a sigh and kicked them into a corner. The Berghaus fleece was dropped on the floor, and she lounged back on a low, maroon-coloured sofa. The water was beginning to simmer and the windows were steaming up. Irrationally, the steamed windows gave Findhorn a cocooned, protected feeling, as if they somehow kept out a hostile world.

'I got three things out of the FBI,' she said. 'But first why don't you tell me how you got on at Los Alamos?'

He moved over to the cooker, tore open a packet of spaghetti and rattled plates onto a work surface. He poured olive oil into a little bowl, chopped basil into shreds with a gleaming kitchen knife and added it to the oil. He started on the pine nuts, chopping them finely. 'They think he was mad. No way could he have found anything they haven't. And they have fifty years of high energy physics since Petrosian to back them up.'

'What's your gut-feeling, Fred?'

'There's a cover-up.'

Romella said, 'Wow.' She tucked her legs under herself, gave Findhorn an astute look and said, 'And what about Petrosian's secret? You have the look of a man who's onto something.'

Findhorn was grating a little hard lump of Parmesan cheese. 'You must be CIA. How else did you get all that help from the FBI?'

'You're wrong, Fred. I work for Alien Abductions. You should know that, you've hardly taken your eyes off my T-shirt.'

'Sorry. It's the ET picture, I assure you.'

She laughed. 'Which would be damned insulting if true. I forgive you, Fred, you're just back from ten years at the north pole. And I notice you haven't answered my question.'

Findhorn was adding spaghetti to the boiling water. 'This will take a few minutes. Keep talking.'

'I think not.' She was looking in a compact mirror, gently prodding the bruise around her eye with her little finger.

'What?'

'Fred, I've come bearing three gifts. I want something in exchange. Tell me what you're onto.'

Findhorn stopped stirring. Romella's voice was cold. 'You don't trust me, do you?'

She snapped the compact lid shut, started to pull on her boots.

'What are you doing?' Findhorn asked in alarm.

'Enjoy your spaghetti.' She slipped into her coat, picked up her casual bag and slid the camper door open.

'Romella!' He grabbed her arm in panic. 'I can't do this on my own.'

She kissed the air next to his cheek. 'Goodbye, darling.' Then she was out and flouncing through the snow towards the chrome and purple monster.

'I surrender, damn you. I'll tell you everything.'

She turned, already shivering in the thin cold air. Findhorn was holding his hands together in an attitude of prayer. Inside, he closed the door, took her coat off, helped her off with her boots and said, 'I'm beginning to think that Petrosian thought of some way to extract energy from empty space. The amount of energy involved might be huge. Please don't leave me.'

'Energy from empty space? You surely don't mean from nothing?'

The water was spilling over the pot. Findhorn turned the gas down. 'I can't tell you more just yet. I'm waiting for Stefi to tell me what happened to HMS *Daring* in 1894. Now it's your turn.'

'You're telling me the truth,' Romella declared. 'That is so crackers that you couldn't make it up. Okay. First, the Venona files.' Findhorn opened his mouth, and Romella said, 'These are transcripts of Soviet secret messages covering 1940 to 1948. They tell me about three thousand of them were partially decrypted. I got copies of about a hundred relating to Los Alamos.'

'Do they mention Petrosian?'

'Maybe. We'll have to dig. Second, transcripts of FBI

interrogations of scientists during the McCarthy era, especially those involved in the hydrogen bomb project. Petrosian included; they had a go at him more than once. And third, we have the FBI surveillance reports on Petrosian.'

Findhorn paused from his cooking. '*The Times*' obituary claimed that Petrosian spied for the Russians.'

Romella patted the heap of papers in front of her. 'The trail to Petrosian's secret is somewhere in here, Fred, if it's anywhere. Some clue that will lead us there.'

The RV was now warm, and the air was light with Diorissimo and pesto. Findhorn popped a cork. The evening promised a heady mixture of spaghetti *al pesto*, Valpolicella and espionage, and who knew what else.

TOP SECRET UMBRA VENONA
NEW YORK/MOSCOW
YOUNG is currently in charge of a group at CAMP-2, and has handed Beck a report about present activities at the CAMP along with a list of the key personnel in ENORMOZ. There is still no indication of when FUNICULAR will be operational. Beck considers that it is almost impossible 88716 62354 76234 cultivate QUANTUM.
CHARLES, QUANTUM and BILL OF EXCHANGE are travelling to PRESERVE and will meet with VOGEL and TINA.
ALEKSANDR

'Is that before or after decryption?' Findhorn wanted to

know. He lifted a strand of spaghetti from the saucepan with a fork.

'Say you have a message. You look up the words in a codebook, a sort of dictionary which replaces each word by a four-figure number. Then you group all these numbers into sets of five. Then to each set of five you add another five-figure number which you take from a one-time pad. It can only be read by the guy at the other end holding the same one-time pad. The Russians kept each and every one-time pad under permanent armed guard. And because you use each page from the pad only once, the code is unbreakable.'

Findhorn gave a satisfied grunt. '*Al dente*. But it was broken nevertheless.'

Romella was sipping red wine. 'Partly. After a few thousand hours, a few million dollars and one or two nervous breakdowns.'

'How come?' Findhorn was using a fork and spoon to heap pasta onto plates.

'In late 1942, when the Russians were under pressure from the German invasion, somebody blundered. They duplicated the one-time pads. As soon as you do that you create patterns. It was just enough for some very clever people to get into parts of the messages. Another thing was that the Finns, who were fighting the Russians, over-ran a Soviet consulate in December 1941. The NKVD had to quit in a hurry and they left behind four codebooks which were only partially burned. One codebook was for diplomatic messages, one was for the NKVD – that's the old KGB – one for the GRU, that's Soviet Military

Intelligence, and one for the Naval GRU. They sent the stuff to Sweden to avoid the risk of recapture. The Swedes were of course neutral but they knew damn well that if the Russians took Finland they'd be next in line. So the codebooks ended up in America.'

He spooned pesto sauce onto the plates and sprinkled *parmigiano* over it. 'So what's the significance of Venona?'

'To the Americans and the Brits? It was a dream come true. It gave a picture of the depth of penetration of the Soviet spy apparatus in every sort of place. It caught big spies like Klaus Fuchs, it uncovered the Cambridge Apostles like Philby, Burgess and McLean, and it electrocuted the Rosenbergs. And it caught hundreds of small fry worldwide.'

'Presumably the numbers here are bits of code that nobody has been able to break.'

Romella nodded with her mouth full. Then she said, 'You may be a human relations disaster, Fred, but you can cook. The names are cryptonyms, jargon used by the GRU and NKVD. Take "Charles". That refers to Klaus Fuchs. "Bill of Exchange" is Oppenheimer, "Camp-2" is Los Alamos and so on. The FBI gave me a list. So, the message translates to:

"Theodore Hall is currently in charge of a group at Los Alamos, and has handed Beck a report about present activities there along with a list of the key personnel in the Manhattan Project. There is still no indication of when the Bomb will be operational. Beck considers that it is almost impossible blah blah cultivate Quantum.

"Fuchs, Quantum and Oppenheimer are travelling to the Argonne Radiation Laboratory" – that's in Chicago – "and will meet with Vogel and Tina." '

'Who are "Quantum", "Vogel" and "Tina"?' Findhorn asked.

'Nobody knows. "Vogel" and "Tina" were a husband-and-wife spy team. "Vogel" was also known as "Pers".'

'That must narrow things down.'

'You can play detectives. It's like Jack the Ripper, about two dozen suspects and every one made to sound plausible. Some people named a physicist called Rudolf Peierls, apparently on the grounds that his wife Eugenia was Russian and they were friendly with Fuchs. MI5 took Peierls's security clearance away after the war. Unfortunately for the amateur detectives, the US gave Peierls the medal of freedom in 1947 and the UK gave him a knighthood in 1968, and the accusation was eventually shown to be ridiculous.'

Findhorn said, 'Okay, so we'll never know if Petrosian was a spy.'

Romella looked doubtful. 'I disagree. We have one big advantage over the FBI.'

'Haven't we just?' Findhorn said. He waited while Romella sucked up a long strand of spaghetti. Then she continued, 'Yes. If we can collate something in the diaries with something in the Venona files . . .'

'Let's go through them, match the dates with diary entries, and see if we can make a connection.'

Romella flicked through the FBI files with her free hand. 'It'll take for ever.'

238

Findhorn topped up her half-empty glass. 'We can get drunk while we're at it.'

The first connection came two hours later, in a short, cryptic message from Aleksandr, the New York *rezident*. By now, enveloped in the warm air of the RV, and with the gas still burning, drowsiness was beginning to overtake them. While Findhorn, propped up against a wall, read the FBI files, Romella was sprawled out on a couch, translating the Armenian text at the corresponding dates.

TOP SECRET UMBRA VENONA
NEW YORK/MOSCOW
On 14 January CHARLES, ANT, QUANTUM and spell Feynman endspell 28312 81241 49775 visited spell Kitty Cronin endspell 65324 76385 76349 automobile.

'Hey.' Findhorn was suddenly alert. 'Kitty Cronin.'

Romella sat up. She picked up the little blue 1943 diary and flicked to 14 January. She scanned the entry rapidly and her face lit up. 'Fred, listen to this.

Another of those rare days off.

Klaus, Dick and I had an early start. Met up at the East Gate and took off in Dick's car. He had some girl lined up in Santa Fe, who turned out to be a brassy blonde called Halina, terrific looker but utterly brainless. Klaus's sister Kristel was down from Cambridge. A thin, nervous sort of girl. Picked them both up near the Post Office, then up into the hills to collect Kitty.

Spent an exhausting day on Sawyer Hill, learning to ski. The brassy blonde surprised us all by being very good at it, although with a skirt that hardly covered her knees she must have been frozen to the bone.

In the evening, back to Kitty's, starving and frozen. She had a table made up for us. Cold roast chicken, plenty of wine, milk, bread and apples. Nectar! Later, Dick went off with the blonde, Klaus and his sister. The round trip must have used up his gas allowance for the month.

Stayed over at Kitty's. Both of us bruised in awkward places!'

'Okay. "Charles" is Klaus Fuchs. Who's "Ant"?'

Romella shuffled papers. 'I've an FBI dossier on her someplace. Here we are.' She skimmed the pages. 'Kristel Fuchs, younger sister of Klaus, alias Kristel Heineman. Unhappily married with three children. She lived in Cambridge, Massachusetts. Later diagnosed as schizophrenic, recovered, married again and had another three kids.'

'Was she a spy?'

'It says that Fuchs used to meet his contact, Harry Gold, alias "Goose", in Kristel's home. But there's no evidence that she knew what was going on.'

'Okay,' said Findhorn, 'We have Klaus and Kristel Fuchs, Dick Feynman and Kitty Cronin in the Venona message. And we have "Quantum".'

'And we have Klaus and Kristel Fuchs, Dick Feynman and Kitty Cronin in Petrosian's account of a picnic held on the same day. And Petrosian.'

Findhorn drew up two columns on a sheet of A4 paper:

KLAUS FUCHS	=	CHARLES
DICK FEYNMAN	=	?
BRAINLESS BLONDE	=	?
KRISTEL FUCHS	=	ANT
KITTY CRONIN	=	?
LEV PETROSIAN	=	?

He said, 'So the question is, where do we place "Quantum"?'

'We can forget Kitty and the blonde,' Romella said. 'Kitty wasn't part of the Manhattan Project and the blonde was just a casual pick-up.'

Findhorn blew out his cheeks. 'And Feynman was an all-American kid from the Bronx. He's never been a suspect. In that case the chances are that Petrosian was "Quantum".'

'Hey, we've found something. If that's right, he probably wasn't a spy. At least, Beck considered he couldn't be cultivated as one.'

'So why the hell was Petrosian fleeing to Russia with useless diaries?'

Romella said, 'It's hot in here.' She started to slip off her dark, lace-topped stockings. She stretched, and ET stretched along with her. 'Okay, Fred, let's call it a day.'

Then, eyes full of innocent enquiry, 'I was wondering about the sleeping arrangements.'

Findhorn looked across at the purple and chrome, made-in-Japan monster a few hundred yards away. Light flakes of snow were drifting past the window and the sky was now dark grey.

'Is that vile thing yours?'

'The purple people eater? Yes, I've rented it.'

'It's going to be a cold night. You could freeze to death in it.'

'So what do you suggest?' Romella asked.

'I'll lend you a blanket.'

'You know, Fred, there's a sort of purity about my hatred for you. It's undiluted by any other emotion. It has the intensity of a laser. Can't you feel it? Or are you made of stone?'

Findhorn's face showed bewilderment. 'Two blankets, then.'

19

Foucault's Pendulum

Findhorn trudged shivering along a track lightly dusted with snow and the prints of a small, clawed animal. A thin, red-nosed zombie was lurching into the men's toilets, carrying a towel and toilet bag. In Babbitt's, a couple of sleepy campers, all skip caps and quilted body warmers, were drifting along the meat aisle. Through bleary eyes Findhorn found milk and picked up a cereal called Morning Zing.

A tall, round-faced girl at the counter was stacking newspapers. 'You the yellow RV?'

'Uhuh.' Findhorn struggled with unfamiliar coins.

'This was faxed through for you.'

Back outside the store, Findhorn read the message:

```
I got this from a naval architecture
book but I haven't a clue what it means.
If you want more I could go to Kew and
look at the Admiralty Reports they keep
progress books ships logs etcetera.
    In 1894 high-speed sea trials of the
British destroyer HMS Daring revealed
```

severe propeller vibrations which were attributed to the formation and collapse of bubbles, a phenomenon known as cavitation. This phenomenon has now been widely studied and is important in many underwater applications. A related problem was discovered during the First World War, when the need to detect enemy submarines led to the development of high intensity subaqueous acoustic sources. It was realized in 1927 that such intense underwater sound produces cavitation. An extraordinary discovery was made in 1934, namely that when the bubbles collapse they produce visible blue light. The source of this light remains a mystery to this day. One possibility, suggested by the Nobel prizewinner Julian Schwinger, is that a dynamic Casimir effect is at work, that is, that zero point energy is being extracted from the vacuum. A bubble in water is a hole in a dielectric medium and the speed of collapse is extremely . . .

Findhorn shouted 'Yes! Yes!' and did a brief war dance on the sidewalk. A fifteen-year-old girl scuttled off in alarm, clutching milk. He skipped to the end:

Your brother's nice and we're getting
on fine. Told him the story and he wants
you to phone him urgently.
Love
Stefi

Findhorn did a subtraction and found that it was nearly
four o'clock in the afternoon in Glasgow. Even Archie
would be up and about by now. He went smartly back
into Babbitt's, fed a heap of nickels into the call box and
dialled through. He had almost given up when there was
a sort of moan from the other end of the line.

'Archie?'

A moment, and then, loud and clear, 'Fred, lad.'

'I've woken you up.'

'Not tae worry.'

'Look, the time has come to pick that giant brain of
yours.'

'About?'

'What's the connection between Foucault's pendulum
and the Casimir effect?'

Another long silence. When he spoke, Archie's voice
was serious. 'You're into some heavy stuff here, Fred.'

'A pendulum is heavy stuff?'

'It's awesome. You want ten years' worth of frontier
science in a five-minute call?'

Findhorn stayed silent. There was the sound of running
water in the background, what sounded like a female
voice, another long silence, two nickels' worth, and finally
Archie was saying, 'This is desperate, you appreciate. Let's

go back to Foucault's pendulum. You probably know about it. This was an experiment carried out in 1851 inside the Panthéon in Paris. This guy Foucault suspends a heavy iron ball from the dome by a wire two hundred feet long and sets it swinging. A pin at the bottom of the ball scrapes the surface of a tray of sand, so that the direction of swing gets traced out in the sand.'

'A straight line.'

'Except that over the hours the direction of this straight line shifts. It moves clockwise, at a rate that would have it back to its original direction in thirty-two hours . . . Leave the shower running, sweetie.'

'I know the experiment.'

'Then you also know the shift is just a human perspective because we're a lot of self-centered bloody apes and we have to bend our minds to see the real picture which is that the pendulum isn't shifting, we are. The tray of sand was doing the turning. The Panthéon, the sand tray, the watching Parisians, they were all spinning, carried round on a rotating Earth. The swing of the pendulum was fixed in space. It's constant in relation to distant galaxies.'

'Why is this awesome?'

'Och, use the stuff between your ears, Freddie.'

'I'm trying.'

'Don't you see, Fred? The pendulum's telling us that somehow its inertia is fixed by intergalactic space. What's a child's swing, or the sway of a ship, but glorified pendulums? It means all of local dynamics, say like the damage done when you walk into a lamp post, is under the control of distant galaxies. You either see that as slightly strange or you're brain dead . . . Of course I know your name, it's Heather.'

'Okay, so our frame of reference for dynamics is the whole Universe.'

'Aye, laddie even down to the dance of atoms.'

Findhorn counted five nickels. 'Keep going.'

'Now, out of the blue, Findhorn of the Arctic is asking me also about the Casimir effect, which by some strange coincidence is also telling us something about the energy of the Universe. In this experiment you take two flat plates and hold them very close together. You have to do this in a vacuum to get rid of air pressure, and you have to make the plates microscopically flat. When you do that, when you put the surfaces of these flat plates very close together but not touching, a force acts to push them together . . . Cut that out, will you, Helen?'

'You mean a force like gravity?'

'I do not. Gravity comes from matter. This force comes from empty space. It's caused by energy contained in empty space, which we call zero point energy because it's irreducible. There's no way you can get rid of it. Some enthusiasts will tell you this ZPE is the bedrock of the Universe and that everything you see, including us, is just low-energy froth floating on the surface of a deep ocean of vacuum energy.'

'That seems a bit fantastic.'

There was a chuckle at the other end of the line. 'Mother Nature is not required to pander to your limited imagination, Fred. Paradox or not, the Casimir effect proves that empty space is a vast store of energy. And since I'm not as dumb as I look, my guess is you're asking me these questions because Petrosian thought he could link the two. Maybe he saw this zero point energy as the common factor, the magic door between the local and the cosmic.' There was a brief, curious crackle on the line. 'Now there's a sorcerer's trick for you. To find the key to the magic door. To pull down energy from galaxies. Awesome . . .'

'Archie, I think I want to speak to Aristotle.'

'He's dead.'

'Aristotle Papagianopoulos, at the University of Patras.'

There was a long silence, and then: 'Papa the Greek. I wouldn't.'

Something negative in Archie's voice. Findhorn was suddenly alert. 'What's the problem? I understand he's a world authority on fundamental physics.'

'Oh aye, he makes Hawking look like the school dunce.'

'So?'

'For a start it's easier to get an audience with the Pope. I've never been close enough to touch his robe.'

'But suppose I do get an audience?'

'He'd have no time for you, Fred. He's the most arrogant pillock since Louis XIV.'

'I'd be wasting my time?'

'Absolutely.'

'I'm going anyway. I have to try.'

'Don't be daft—'

The last coin ran out.

Findhorn put the receiver down. A feeling of unease

had suddenly enveloped him. It took him some seconds to identify the cause.

It might have been an altruistic wish to steer him away from an embarrassing encounter, or even a touch of academic jealousy.

But whatever, Archie had been trying to control him.

There was a note for him on the RV steering wheel: *Stuff this camping lark. I'm having breakfast at the Bright Angel Lodge and I think I've found something.*

20

FBI

Romella was sitting at a big panoramic window with the early morning sun throwing an orange-red light on the top of the canyon walls. The Colorado River far below was still in gloom. This morning she was in Levi's, cuff boots and an Aran sweater, and Findhorn wondered where she kept her store of clothes. The long silver earrings, he noticed, were back. Coffee cups and a plate of biscuits were on a low table in front of her, along with a few sheets of photocopied typescript.

There was a serious edge to her expression. Without preliminaries, she handed over a sheet of paper. 'Read this.'

```
SECRECY ORDER
(Title 35, United States Code 1952,
sections 181-188).
NOTICE: To Dr Lev Baruch Petrosian, his
heirs and assignees, attorneys and
agents.
You are hereby notified that your
```

application has been found to contain
material, the disclosure of which might
be detrimental to national security.
Accordingly, you are ordered not
to publish, construct or disclose the
invention or any information relevant
to it, either verbally, in print, or
in any other manner whatsoever, to
any individual, group or organization
unaware of the invention prior to the
date of this order, but to keep the
principal and details of the invention
secret unless written consent is first
obtained from the Commissioner of
Patents.

You are expressly forbidden to export
all or any part of the invention described in your application, or any
material information relating to the
invention, to any foreign country or
foreign national within the United
States.

Breach of this order renders you liable
to penalties as described in Sections
182 and 186 of 35 U.S.C. (1952).

This order should not be construed to
mean that the Government intends to, or
has, adopted the aforementioned
invention.

Findhorn looked up. 'Wow!'

'He invented something.'

'Which the United States Government suppressed.'

Findhorn stood up and walked over to the big window, to give himself time to take in this new information. The sunlight had crept a little way down the canyon, and a light mist was rising from the snow on the trees along the south rim. A little group had started on the downward trail. Findhorn counted five adults and two children. He turned back and sat down at the table. Romella was rubbing her thighs, clearly enjoying the warmth which the sunlight was now bringing. He said, 'You know what this means, Romella? We're looking for something which the US government doesn't want us to find.'

She nodded. 'Yes. We're in hostile territory. Maybe we're even spies.'

'Do they know we're here?' Findhorn wondered.

Romella said, 'I don't want to find out the hard way. It might be a good idea to get out of America as quickly as possible.'

'How did you get this?' Findhorn asked, waving the paper.

'Didn't I mention that my old man is an attorney?'

'In La Jolla, not Washington.'

'Still, Grigoryan, Skale and Partners have connections, and Dad will do anything for her little girl except part with his money. So, when I went to the Patent Office to search under Petrosian, a smooth path had been prepared for me. Otherwise . . .' She tapped the papers in front of her. 'And then I went to the FBI and did exactly the same.

Dad tells me there's freedom of information and there's Freedom of Information. To get the right sort of freedom you sometimes need a little arm-twisting.'

'So you turn up on Dad's doorstep and say, hey, I want to get material on Lev Petrosian the atom spy, and he said, sure Romella, I'll fix it for you. Didn't he ask any questions?'

'Dad gave up on me long ago. I think he sees me as slightly eccentric, like Mother.'

'Romella, for a woman, you've done brilliantly. We now know there's some machine at the focus of this.'

'The bad news is that somebody's been asking for the same material as us. It's some legal office in Switzerland, acting on behalf of a client.'

'Switzerland,' Findhorn repeated.

'Switzerland,' she confirmed.

Findhorn poured coffee and sat back with a sigh. 'I have to get to Greece as quickly as possible.'

Romella raised her eyebrows, but asked no questions. 'And I want to get the hell out of here before the system catches up. But read the FBI stuff before you go.'

Show: 18. Tape: 3142.

7 November, this is Agents Miller and Gruber, we are with Doctor Lev Petrosian. Um, this is (non-interview dialogue).

Q. Doctor Petrosian, thank you for agreeing to speak to us. This is really just a routine enquiry and I'm sure you'll be able to satisfy us.

LP. Sure. Go ahead.

Q. You're entitled to have an advocate present if you wish.

LP. Okay, but I don't see the need.

Q. Of course we know that, um, we know that your work here at Los Alamos is highly classified and we can't, um, enter into any aspects of that.

LP. Fine, yes, I'm glad you appreciate that.

Q. Uh, it's really what might be called your extra-mural activities. In particular you took a week's leave over the period beginning 15 June this year.

LP. That's right, I did, yes.

Q. Which you spent in New York City.

LP. About three days, yes. Then I did some walking in the Appalachians.

Q. What was your business in New York?

LP. It's like I said, I was on vacation.

Q. Did you, uh, during your stay there, did you, uh, meet a man called John McGill on the steps of the American Museum of Natural History?

LP. Not that I recall.

Q. Did you hand over an envelope to the aforesaid John McGill?

LP. No.

Q. I'm now about to show you a series of photographs. Would you examine these, please, and can you identify the parties?

LP. Well yes, that's me, obviously, and that's the guy called McGill. I guess you've been following me around.

Q. You admit to having met him?

LP. Yes I did, well there's the evidence I guess. I'd forgotten all about that.

Q. I'm sure of that, sir. Now, can you explain the circumstances of that meeting?

LP. It's coming back now. He's a journalist. He has a lot of contacts or so he tells me, and being a journalist that would make sense. He said he could put in a word for me about an enquiry I was making.

Q. About?

LP. About a lady.

Q. Yes, a lady.

[Interjection by Agent Miller:] So who's the dame, buster?

[Non-interview dialogue between agents Gruber and Miller]

Q. Sorry about that, sir. Would you like to tell us about the lady?

LP. A German girl I knew pre-war. Her name is Lisa. Or was. I wanted to find out what happened to her, whether she came through.

Q. How were you introduced to McGill?

LP. It was through a man called Jürgen Rosenblum. We met in 1941 in Camp Sherbrooke, that was an enemy alien camp in Canada, before they sorted out who their friends and enemies really were. Jürgen and I met by chance again a couple of years ago.

Q. Does the address 238 West 28th Street mean anything to you?

LP. No.

Q. Would it surprise you to know that John McGill's real

name is Andrei Sobolev and that his working address is 238 West 28th Street and that this is the address of Amtorg, ah, otherwise known as the Soviet Trade Delegation?

[Silence]

Q. Sir?

LP. Yes, I'm shattered.

Q. What was in the envelope you gave him?

LP. Well it wasn't nuclear secrets if that's what you're thinking. It was information about Lisa which might help to trace her. Her friends pre-war, the university classes she attended and so on.

Q. Did you have an emotional attachment to this Lisa?

LP. It was a long time ago.

Q. Yes, sir. Would you like to answer my question?

LP. I can't say what my feelings are now.

Q. [Agent Miller]: Were you screwing her, for Christ's sake?

[Gruber to Miller]: Shut up.

LP. There was another woman in the meantime but that broke up. The war did funny things to some of us not that King Kong here would understand that even if I could explain it. Lisa was a link to my past.

Q. Has it occurred to you, um, huh, sir, did you think, has it occurred to you that if you had an emotional attachment to this Lisa, and she was found alive and well in the Soviet sector, that you would become a prime target for Soviet blackmail?

LP. No. I guess I'm a bit naive about stuff like that.

Q. [Agent Miller]. Or (expletive) smart. Maybe there were

atomic secrets in that envelope and the dame story is a cover.

Q. During that vacation, did you have any other business in New York or elsewhere?

LP. No.

Q. Did you visit the, were you at, did the Soviets, did you, er, visit the Soviet consulate during your vacation?

LP. Oh God, I did, this must look very bad. Yes I did.

[Agent Miller]: Here we (expletive) go again.

LP. I have a brother in Soviet Armenia. I was trying to get an exit visa to let him visit here. I've saved enough money that I could pay for his air fare. I haven't seen him in twenty years. He's all the family I have.

[Agent Miller]: Another frigging weak link.

LP. Not at all. Army Intelligence have known about Anastas from day one.

Q. One last thing, Doctor Petrosian. May we have permission to search your flat?

LP. No, I don't want you to do that.

Q. Why not?

LP. Because there are things in it I'd rather you didn't find.

Q. Um huh. Thank you for your co-operation, sir. Have a good day.

Findhorn was looking puzzled. 'Things he'd rather they didn't find?'

Romella said, 'Maybe the diaries. But keep reading.'

Q. Thank you for agreeing to assist us in our enquiry, Mrs Morgenstern.

KM. That's okay, glad to help. What's this about?

Q. You are acquainted with Lev Baruch Petrosian?

KM. Is this about Lev? Yes, I've known Lev a long time.

Q. And how long is that?

KM. Over a decade now. We met in Santa Fe in the early forties.

Q. When he was working on the bomb?

KM. I know that now, but I didn't know it then. Why are you asking about Lev?

Q. What exactly was your relationship with Doctor Petrosian?

KM. We were friends.

Q. Close?

KM. Yes.

Q. Was it an intimate relationship?

KM. I'm sorry but I don't think that's any of your business.

Q. Then Petrosian went off to the South.

KM. Yes, and we sort of lost touch. He came back to Los Alamos in the fifties.

Q. By which time you were married.

KM. Yes.

Q. [Agent Miller] To Mr Morgenstern.

KM. Got it in one.

Q. When you met Petrosian again in the fifties, did you resume your friendship with him?

KM. Yes.

Q. [Agent Miller] Were you lovers?

KM. You've got a damn nerve.

Q. Mrs Morgenstern, how much did Doctor Petrosian

reveal to you about his work at Los Alamos, either in the forties or fifties?

KM. Not a thing. It was secret work. Of course everybody in Santa Fe knew there was some secret army work going on but we never had an inkling of what it was.

Q. Did he ever talk about Russia?

KM. No. We talked movies, not politics. Wait a minute, yes, I think he said something about how he admired the fight the Russian people were putting up. That was during the war.

Q. He made pro-Russian comments?

KM. I suppose you could put it that way.

Q. Did he ever talk to you about his family?

KM. No.

Q. Did you know he had a brother in Soviet Armenia?

KM. No.

Q. Did he, at any time, ask you to post documents or letters?

KM. No.

Q. [Agent Miller] You're lying, lady.

KM. Maybe a postcard or something.

Q. [Agent Miller] Maybe a big fat envelope now and then?

KM. I don't want to answer any more questions.

Q. How long did this passing of documents go on?
[Silence]

Q. Let me put it like this, Mrs Morgenstern. Is Mister Morgenstern aware that you and Petrosian are having an affair?

KM. That's outrageous. We are not.

Q. [Agent Miller] You want to hear a nice juicy tape?

KM. You bastards.

Q. How many letters did you post, Mrs Morgenstern?

KM. I have nothing more to say to you people.

Q. On 21 June last, did you drive to Niagara Falls with Lev Petrosian and another man?

KM. I told you, I've nothing more to say.

Q. What was the other man's name?

[Silence]

Q. [Agent Miller] Here's an even better (expletive) way to put it. Espionage could get you thirty years, maybe even the chair.

KM. I want to speak to my lawyer.

Q. Mrs Morgenstern, we can all save ourselves a lot of trouble here if you will just answer the question.

Q. His name was Railton or something. I'd never met him before.

Q. Is this the man? [Subject shown photographs of Jürgen Rosenblum.]

KM. Yes that's Railton.

Q. What did you talk about?

KM. Just anything. The things people talk about on a pleasant afternoon's drive.

Q. [Agent Miller] We got some pleasant pillow talk Mister Morgenstern might like to hear.

KM. Would you do a thing like that?

Q. We're not concerned with your private life, ma'am. Just so long as we know what was said on that drive.

'Now hold on. There's something peculiar here.'

'What do you mean?' Romella asked.

'Rosenblum was a Soviet spy, right?'

She flicked through some pages. 'Yes, one of a string of couriers used by the Soviets in the fifties. Fuchs used to pass on secret papers to a guy called Tommy Gold in the forties, but by this time Gold was doing thirty years.'

'So if Petrosian was handing over secret papers, why was he giving them to Kitty? Why not Gold in the forties and then Rosenblum in the fifties?'

'Maybe she was a courier too.'

'So why didn't the FBI charge her?'

Romella raised her hands expressively.

KM. It was just a drive into the Santa Fe hills. We talked about nothing in particular.

Q. [Agent Miller] And where was Mister Morgenstern at this time?

KM. Chicago. On business, or so he said.

Q. The documents you passed on: where did they go?

KM. It was always the same. Some address in Turkey.

Q. Can you be more specific?

KM. I paid no attention. A place called Igloo or Iguana or something. I can't say any more.

Q. Who was it addressed to?

KM. It was a shop. Some unpronounceable name. He said his sister worked there.

Q. There is no record that Petrosian has a sister. Does that surprise you?

KM. I told you, he never talked about his family.

Q. On that drive on 21 June, were Rosenblum and Petrosian ever out of hearing?

KM. Just once, when I had to attend a call of nature.

Q. Was there discussion of Petrosian's work at Los Alamos?

KM. No. There was one thing.

Q. Yes.

KM. Will you give me that tape? [pause] On the way back from my call of nature, there was some sort of altercation. Railton was sort of animated, and Lev was shaking his head and I'm sure he said, 'No, I won't do it,' something like that. They shut up when I got near.

Q. Can you think of anything else they said?

KM. No.

Q. Anything at all, then or later? Please take your time.

KM. It was all just day-in-the-country talk after that.

Q. Is there anything else you would like to tell us?

KM. No. There is nothing else.

Q. Thank you for your co-operation, Mrs Morgenstern. Have a good day.

KM. About that tape.

Q. What tape is that, Mrs Morgenstern?

Romella looked up from the transcript. 'He was sending messages through Kitty.' Their eyes locked. 'I wonder what sort of messages he was sending, Fred.'

Findhorn said, 'Whatever, they were going to a place in Turkey called Igloo.'

'Or Iguana.'

'So half a century ago he maybe sent something to

some unknown address in some unknown town, and it's never been heard of since.'

Romella said, 'I'll bet Kitty Cronin knew all along where it went. And she may still be alive.'

Findhorn looked at Romella incredulously. 'Are you serious? That has to be the coldest trail on the planet.'

'Do you have a better idea?' Romella asked, seething. 'I'm going to try and work out what Petrosian discovered myself.'

Romella laughed and spluttered, clattering her coffee cup on the table. The desk clerk looked up sharply.

'Okay, Mizz Grigoryan, but we're living in desperate times.'

She patted her bruised lip dry with a paper napkin. 'I suppose two magnificent idiots are better than one. Talking about time . . .'

Findhorn stood up. 'Yes. We must be almost out of it. The other side have more expertise and more money. And they have another advantage over us: they know what they're after.'

'I fear we're beginning to lose it.' She tapped the papers on the table into a neat pile. 'Where will we meet up, Fred?'

'Somewhere on the planet.'

Romella nodded thoughtfully. 'Agreed. Somewhere on the planet.'

21

Revelation Island

Findhorn, in a strange city, was nervous of wandering Washington's streets after dark; but neither did a late night stay in Dallas airport terminal promise an evening of fun and sparkle. With about eight hours before the Athens flight, he booked into the Hilton on the grounds that if he was going to go bust he might as well do it in style. In a hotel room the likes of which he had seen only in movies, he plugged in his laptop. There was a lot of junk mail, and a message from Romella.

```
Fred - Something has turned up. Cancel
your Greek trip and meet me tomorrow.
I'll be in the Holiday Inn in San Diego.
Confirm receipt of this message immedi-
ately. Romella.
```

He frowned, ran a jacuzzi for two, undressed, re-read the message and then slipped into the churning water. He wondered why she wasn't staying with her parents in La Jolla, which was practically a suburb of Dan Diego. After half an hour of troubled thought and underwater pummelling, he walked dripping to the telephone and called the Holiday Inn, San Diego. A room had been reserved for a Ms Grigoryan, for the following evening. He replugged his computer, carried it to the tub and balanced it precariously on the edge, and typed:

> I've cancelled Athens. Arriving San
> Diego late tomorrow. Fred.

He pressed return and lay back. He tried to let the warm jets relax his muscles but disturbing thoughts forbade it. Then he typed 'too', followed by 'iXdKK1s!!' The Glasgow computers were protected from the outside world by impenetrable firewalls; but Findhorn was now inside that world. In every direction there was still a mass of forbidding gateways; but Archie had always been careless. Findhorn typed 'cd home/amk/mail', entering Archie's electronic mailbox and feeling like a thief. He changed to the inbox directory, the store for messages which Archie had received. The most recent of these had arrived only half an hour ago. It said:

> I've cancelled Athens. Arriving San
> Diego late tomorrow. Fred.

He skimmed through Archie's e-mails of the last few days, feeling sick and betrayed.

It was still dark but Findhorn was hit at the aircraft door

by warm, perfumed Mediterranean air. Athens airport seemed to be one vast dormitory for backpackers. The old hands had found quiet corners and were stretched out unconscious in sleeping bags; others, in varying degrees of comatoseness, were propped up against walls or check-in desks, holding paper cups or cigarettes.

Findhorn caught a bus which rattled him and half a dozen sleepy travellers rapidly into the city centre. He recognized the Acropolis on a hilltop, ghostly in the pre-dawn light. Venus blazed down in a dark blue sky, but dawn was breaking rapidly, and by the time he had navigated his way to the railway station it was daylight. Surprisingly at this hour, the platform was choc-a-bloc, and when the train arrived Findhorn was swept on board in something like a rugby scrum. He found himself squeezed between a young, hairy German and his ferociously fit girlfriend, wearing identical T-shirts and shorts. There was no question of reaching his reserved seat and he watched the flat-roofed white houses of the Athens suburbs trundle past, giving way to open countryside, until a ticket inspector looked at his ticket, shook his head, gabbled something, and put him off at a level crossing in the middle of a flat expanse of parched vineyards.

Findhorn watched the train disappear over the horizon.

The sun was getting hot.

And every minute he stood on the track was a minute gained by the opposition.

After an hour of increasing frustration a large car with dark-tinted windows stopped at the crossing and disgorged a small, stout man carrying a shopping bag, with a jacket draped over his arm. The car took off. The man looked at Findhorn curiously and said something incomprehensible. Findhorn, unsure what to expect, said good morning. They stood in silence, waiting. In ten minutes another car stopped and disgorged a little fat woman, and then there was a steady trickle of cars and vans, and at last a train approached on the horizon and Findhorn once again found himself bundled uncomprehendingly on board, wondering if his non-appearance at San Diego had yet registered and, if so, what the enemy would be doing about it.

This train was almost empty, and it was excruciatingly slow. The sun was intense through the carriage window. Glancing out at one point, Findhorn was surprised to find himself looking down the funnel of a ship: they were on a narrow bridge over the Gulf of Corinth, linking mainland Greece to the Peloponnese peninsula. Past Corinth, the train ambled along the most spectacular coastline Findhorn had ever seen, hounded by cliffs on the left and a turquoise sea on the right. By the time the train trundled into a station called ΠΑΤΡΑ, it was noon and Findhorn was headachey and sticky.

He wandered randomly, followed awhile by a scraggy black mongrel which appeared from a cloistered walkway and trotted behind him before being distracted by a smell in an alleyway. He found himself in a spacious square with slender palm trees, a sundial, and a scattering of tavernas and pastry shops. A few deep-wrinkled locals watched him curiously over tumblers of white wine. He tried 'University' in three languages and got a fair amount of gabble but no directions. He wandered through the swing doors of a hotel and tried out the three languages again on a cheerful, dark-eyed girl and she finally drew a map and waved her hands expressively.

Half an hour later he saw the low, white buildings of the university on a distant hill, beyond the edge of town. Across the campus and into a cavernous atrium; a hook-nosed, dark youth who steered Findhorn towards the physics faculty office; a rotund woman with a hint of a moustache with enough English to say that Professor Papagianopoulos is away; a two-day conference on the subject of Space, Time and Vacuum; on the island of Patmos; in the Cyclades, a good distance away. Go back to Athens and fly to the island of Kos and then take the ferry to the sacred island; the sail takes four hours and at the time of year the sea can be rough; the conference is for registered participants only; you are most welcome.

Screaming internally with frustration, Findhorn managed to organize a taxi to the bus station, and an air-conditioned bus had him back in Athens by mid-afternoon. To his surprise he found that his credit card was still good for a flight to Kos. The sun had meantime vanished behind grey, drizzly clouds. There was a long, slow swell which had the ferry yawing from side to side. It was infinitely less fearsome than his icebreaker experience of a week ago, but something in his ear seemed to be in resonance with the sway. At least the ferry was quiet and he was able to retch quietly in the lavatory without frightening the passengers.

Four hours later, the engine note changed and the heaving moderated. Findhorn, feeling like death, half-crawled up the ferry stairs to find that the ship was sailing into a calm harbour under a thundery sky. The water was reflecting the lights of a village, and a massive fortress monastery crowned the hill behind it.

Findhorn now staggered past fish taverns, cafés and tourist shops, most of them shuttered and closed. He found himself wandering up steep little alleys with tiny churches, grand mansions and dazzling white cubic houses clustered around the Monastery of St John. He had no idea where he was going or what he was doing. There was a sudden heavy downpour of rain but he was past caring. Here and there he would cross a little square opening into a stunning view over the Aegean.

There was a two-storeyed villa, with a sign on the wrought-iron gate which might have meant rooms to let. Exhausted, wet and despairing, he pressed the bell and waited. A female voice on the intercom said something incomprehensible, and he said, 'I want to rent a room.' The gate opened with a click, and he walked into a small courtyard decorated with ferns and small trees. A woman looked down from a verandah. She was in her mid-thirties and wearing a plain blue dress, and she waved him in with a smile.

Dripping wet, he entered a well-equipped kitchen stuffed with Chinamen. Three were clustered round pots steaming on a cooker, two were setting a table and a sixth, an older man, was sitting on a kitchen chair, balancing it on two legs while drinking red wine straight from a bottle. There was a flurry of greetings. The eldest man paused, his mouth at the bottle. He stood up, smiled, bowed politely, and said in a deep voice and excellent English, 'Are you here for the conference?'

The Chinese delegation seemed to know where they were going, and Findhorn drifted with them through the narrow wet alleyways. In a square no larger than a tennis court, they drifted into a small hotel. A notice on an easel said *Space, Time and Vacuum*. A buzz of conversation was coming from the left and Findhorn wandered into a room with about thirty people, mostly male, milling around. A glance told him the story: the suit count was low, the beard count was high. This was an academic conference. An array of name badges was laid out on a long table and a couple of women were taking bundles of notes, ticking names off against a list and handing out the badges. There was a crowd around a third woman in a corner, who was checking name badges and handing over small blue rucksacks from a heap.

Without rucksack and name badge, Findhorn knew, he might as well have the word 'Intruder' branded on his forehead. In a dining room beyond the registration desk, tables were layed out with glasses of wine and plates with canapés, cheese and tomatoes. He wandered into this room and picked up a glass of white wine. The room was buzzing but he caught only snatches of conversation. He drifted, trying to look inconspicuous as he checked name badges. He spotted the name *Aristotle Papagionopoulos* from about ten yards, across a temporarily clear stretch of room. Aristotle's head was thrust forward, and he was listening intensely to a bald, bespectacled Englishman. His face was wrinkled; intense brown eyes spoke of a fanatical intelligence but, at the same time, a certain dissociation from the real world. Findhorn, not knowing what he would say to the man, gently pushed his way forwards, mentally bracing himself for the Ari Papa experience.

'Good evening, Doctor Findhorn.'

Findhorn turns, spills wine. The Revelation Man, Mister Mons Meg himself. Archie is at his side, wearing a white linen suit with the jacket over his arm. There is sweat under Archie's armpits and his bearded face is red with astonishment, dismay and consternation.

The expression on the Revelation Man's face, on the other hand, is approaching beatitude. 'And welcome to Patmos. This tiny island has been called the Jerusalem of the Aegean. If God spares you the time, you should enter through the walls which protect the Monastery, and see its extraordinary treasures: Byzantine icons, sacred vessels, frescoes over eight hundred years old, embroideries over a thousand. There are wonderful illuminated manuscripts and rare books.'

'Any old diaries?' Findhorn's voice is shaky.

Mr Revelation laughs. 'Patmos is where Saint John the Theologian, under divine inspiration, wrote his Book of Revelation. Is this not, then, the most fitting place on earth to contemplate John's vision of the Apocalypse?'

Findhorn takes a fresh look at the conference attendees.

The biblical vision springing to his mind is Daniel in the lion's den.

22

Papa the Greek

Findhorn tried to stay calm. Without a word he turned away and pushed towards Papagianopoulos. The Greek was still listening to the Englishman, but now with a sceptical, irritated look.

Findhorn interrupted the conversation. 'I want to learn about the vacuum.'

Papagianopoulos didn't falter for a second 'But to understand the vacuum, you must first understand time.' His strongly accented speech made him unmistakably Greek.

'My name is Cartwright and I'm a science reporter for *The Times in London*. May I call you Papa?'

'No, I am Aristotle, if you must be familiar at all. May I introduce my colleague, Professor Bradfield?' Bradfield was tall, nearly bald, dressed in a heavy dark suit and tie, and with a face beaded with sweat. He announced himself as John Bradfield from the Rutherford-Appleton laboratory. He had a limp, two-fingered handshake.

Papagianopoulos said, 'I can best describe Professor Bradfield as an excellent guide for beaten paths.'

'Beaten paths are for beaten men,' Bradfield said. 'And

am I beaten? By some fringe eccentric from the Balkan hinterlands?'

Findhorn deduced from this exchange that the two men were friends. He said, 'I shouldn't be here. I've gate-crashed. I'm writing up an article on the nature of the vacuum and I want to speak to the best people going.' Experience had taught Findhorn that the way to an academic's heart was flattery, laid on with a trowel.

Papagianopoulos nodded his approval of Findhorn's judgement. 'You have come to the right person.'

'It's noisy in here. I'd be pleased to take you to dinner someplace where we can talk.'

'I'll join you,' said Bradfield. 'I can correct my colleague's errors.'

'An interview with *The Times* is worth a little yapping at the heels. But the dinner, Mr Journalist, is mine. I have friends on this island.'

Archie approached and mumbled something. 'By all means join us,' Findhorn said.

Aristotle glanced at Archie's name badge and nodded indifferently. 'At this time of the evening there is a cool breeze in the hills. I suggest we enjoy it.'

They followed Aristotle out to a small, tinny Fiat parked in the square, patches of bare metal showing through the blue. Findhorn glanced back. Mr Revelation was at the hotel entrance, gloating happily. Archie and Bradfield squeezed into the back. The air was humid and there was a smell of cats. Aristotle rattled the car out of the square and took it along a quiet road lined with trees and limestone outcrops. It eventually turned inland and wound its way steeply up into the hills. Near the top of a rocky summit they drove into a village – or at least a cluster of four or five houses – and stopped.

A black Alsatian, plainly dead, lay stretched out on a dusty track. Even in the dying light they could see flies swarming around it. An old woman, on a rocking chair under the shade of a tree, watched the visitors while knitting with effortless skill. The track went round to the back of a low, whitewashed house and Aristotle led the way. As they approached, the dead Alsatian jumped up and trotted off.

They sat on kitchen chairs round a small garden table at the back of a house. There was a cooking smell and dishes were clattering. Bradfield compromised his standards by removing his jacket, although the Brasenose College tie stayed tightly round his neck. The garden was bounded by a low limestone wall and fell steeply away. They sat under overhanging vines. A thin, stooped man emerged from a kitchen door with a white paper tablecover which he spread over the table. Aristotle seemed to be known and there was an exchange of noisy Greek banter. The man vanished and reappeared with big hunks of bread, goat's cheese and herb-sprinkled tomatoes, and two carafes of cold white wine.

Findhorn looked over the parched, stony land falling steeply away, and the dark sea glittering beyond; the sun was a large, scarlet ellipse just above the horizon, shining through thunder-laden clouds. He thought that the scene had probably changed little in thousands of years, and that in California or Nice a house with a view like this would set you back a million bucks.

He spoke to Bradfield. 'Thanks for sparing me your time.'

Bradfield said, 'Glad to help.' Even gladder to see his name in *The Times*, Findhorn suspected.

Aristotle waved his hands expansively over the darkening landscape. 'This is a magic place. Greece is where the nature of matter and the vacuum were first discussed, six hundred years before Christ. It was here that my namesake, the other Aristotle, argued that a pure void does not exist in Nature. His insight was lost for two thousand years. It was the twentieth century before the particle physicists discovered that the vacuum is indeed a sea of seething particles and radiation. We are therefore in the most natural setting on Earth for this discussion.'

Findhorn fired the opening shot. He sailed as close to the truth as he dared. 'I'm trying to check these persistent stories about Petrosian, the atom spy. You may have heard of them. The story that he had found some way to extract energy from empty space.'

Bradfield gave Findhorn a quizzical look. 'I don't recall any such tale.'

'Could there possibly have been anything to it?'

The Englishman tried not to smirk. 'Of course not. Some very strange ideas come out of America from time to time. Especially from that era, there were what I would describe as peculiar mental phenomena. Flying saucers, psychokinesis, the Red menace and so on. I believe they were all psychological responses to 1950s anxieties about a thermonuclear holocaust.'

'You dismiss it, then?'

Bradfield continued, 'I have a problem, Mister Cartwright. Because my views belong to the mainstream of physics I'm too easily portrayed as a sort of Establishment spokesman. I feel like the Sheriff of Nottingham against Robin Hood here –' Bradfield glanced briefly at Aristotle '– but in fact the consensus of opinion in physics is against the idea that empty space holds any significant energy. Opinions to the contrary have been expressed by a small, noisy clique of outsiders. I expect that's what has triggered your enquiry. However, you ought to know that these people carry little influence with the scientific community.'

The waiter came out carrying an oil lamp, which he placed in the centre of the table and lit with a cigarette lighter. Aristotle pointedly ignored Bradfield, speaking to Findhorn. 'Fashions come and go in science as elsewhere. The only opinion which matters is that of Mother Nature.'

'We get a lot of crank science in our field,' Bradfield countered smoothly. Aristotle visibly tensed.

Findhorn tried to deflect the rapidly growing animosity. 'I read something about the Casimir effect and zero point energy. What are these things? And just how much energy are we talking about?'

Aristotle produced a biro, moved a plate of bread aside and started to scribble on the tablecover. 'The vacuum is filled with a light of unimaginable intensity if we could only see it. Let me first write down its intensity.' Then he wrote an equation in a large, extrovert scrawl: $I_v = Kv^3$. Findhorn tilted his head to read the equation. 'Remember

I'm a mere journalist. You'll have to explain.'

The Greek tried a joke. 'Even journalists can read. I_v is the intensity of this light at a particular frequency v. K is an extremely small number.'

'Which would therefore make the intensity of the light extremely small,' Findhorn pointed out. 'What is K anyway?'

Aristotle scribbled down 6.14×10^{-57}. 'For the innumerate, this is 6.14 divided by the number one followed by fifty-seven zeros.'

'K is as near to zero as makes no difference,' Findhorn said.

Aristotle was patient. 'But look at the other term, young man, the v^3. The equation also tells you something else, namely that the intensity of this light increases with the cube of its frequency. No matter how tiny K is, its smallness is always overwhelmed at a sufficiently high frequency.'

'Okay, so we're immersed in a radiation field of tremendous intensity.' Findhorn broke some bread, dipped it in his wine. He'd seen people do this in movies. 'Why doesn't it just fry us? I don't even see it. Space is black.'

Aristotle waved his arms to encompass the sky; a slightly fanatical tone was creeping into his voice. Or maybe, Findhorn thought, it was just Latin dramatics. 'Does a fish at the bottom of the ocean feel the weight of a ton of overlying water on every square centimetre of its surface? Do you feel the atmosphere bearing down on you, a kilogram compressing every square centimetre of your body? You do not. Because it pervades you. Only differences in pressure can be felt. You cannot feel the crushing atmospheric pressure, but you can feel a light breeze on your cheeks.'

'You're telling me that we don't see this vacuum light because we're pervaded by it.'

Aristotle nodded again. 'It is everywhere, in the retinae of your eyes, in your gut, in the spaces between your atoms.'

'So how do we know it even exists?'

'If you were in a submarine, with no pressure gauge, how could you tell if you were under the ocean?'

'Tell me.'

More dramatics. Aristotle was now squeezing an imaginary submarine between the palms of his hands. 'By the tiny shrinking of its steel hull. A shrinkage of a few millimetres would let you infer the existence of a huge ocean pressure outside. In the same way there are subtle manifestations of the vacuum radiation. Tiny shifts in the expected energy levels of atoms. Miniscule forces acting between flat plates in a vacuum. The merest hints of this shadow world. The rest is inference. But we have no plumb lines to explore the ultimate depths of this ocean of energy. It is *terra incognita*.'

'And how does this relate to zero point energy?'

'ZPE, my journalist friend, is the energy of the vacuum, that is to say, the energy of this radiation field. It is a remnant of the Creation, and it is vast beyond comprehension.'

'And the Casimir effect?'

'So intense is this radiation, at the highest frequencies,

that wherever there is the slightest shadow, the difference in intensity creates a pressure. This is what happens with the Casimir effect. The plates shield each other, however slightly, from the surrounding vacuum radiation. The differential pressure of the light forces them together.'

Bradfield interrupted the dialogue. His voice was carrying an undertone of annoyance. 'Don't let my colleague's enthusiasm sweep you along, Mr Cartwright. The best experiments have produced less Casimir force than the weight of a paperclip.'

Aristotle said, 'Beh!' dismissively. He scribbled some more: $F = Cd^{-4}$. 'This is the force pushing the plates together. You see the closer the plates are, the better they shield each other, the bigger the push. The force increases with the inverse fourth power of their separation d. It is true that experimental limitations have put a wide separation between the plates in the laboratory and the measured force is small. But put them ten times closer and they would feel ten thousand times the force. One hundred times closer and the force is multiplied by one hundred million times.'

'A thousand times closer and you'd crush that submarine,' Archie suggested. His sweaty, red face had a strange, almost feverish look. Findhorn thought it was something like greed.

'But how could we get at all this power?' Findhorn asked. 'What did Petrosian see?'

Bradfield again, the irritation becoming open. 'What power? It doesn't exist. There is no vacuum energy.'

Archie was looking puzzled. 'But Professor Bradfield,

you've just told us that people have measured the force between the plates.'

'They have measured *a* force. But it's all interatomic. The atoms feel it when they are close to each other.'

'It has nothing to do with the vacuum?'

Bradfield was emphatic. 'Nothing. The vacuum is empty. Ideas about extracting energy from it belong with anti-gravity devices and astral projection.'

Findhorn asked, 'Can you prove that?'

Bradfield held out his hand at arm's length. 'I see my hand. No distortion, no bending of light, my hand is just there.'

Findhorn looked baffled. 'That's proof?'

Bradfield said, 'Correct, Mister Cartwright. Energy has mass. Mass exerts gravity. If the vacuum carried as much energy as Papa here claims, the Universe would be far more massive than the astronomers tell us. It would collapse in on itself under its own weight. The cosmos would be the size of a golfball.' He waved his hands around, in a parody of Aristotle. 'Some golfball!'

Archie was scribbling with Aristotle's pen. 'I get your point. Even with the tiny energy already measured in the lab: you couldn't see distant galaxies.' He leaned back, frowning at Aristotle. 'There's already a contradiction between the lab and the telescope.'

Bradfield managed to sip his wine while nodding agreement. 'A blatant one. And Aristotle knows it. Vacuum energy extraction belongs with perpetual motion machines and cold fusion. It's nonsense.'

'The nonsense is entirely Professor Bradfield's.'

Aristotle's face was flushed. 'Gravity is just a mutual shielding of atoms from the ZPE. The zero point energy cannot shield itself from itself. It cannot exert a gravitational force and does not, therefore, collapse the Universe.'

Uninvited, plates of soup were approaching, balanced on the waiter's arms. Findhorn found himself looking at little fish, and octopus tentacles immersed in a thick, tomato-red juice. Bradfield looked at his plate with something like alarm. The Alsatian reappeared and settled down with a sigh, out of kicking range but within throwing distance of scraps.

Aristotle said, 'Pepper? The undeniable fact is, Mister Cartwright, that numerous small atomic effects can be explained – can only be explained – if the vacuum contains radiation whose intensity increases without limit as we go to higher and higher frequencies. Its energy must approach infinity.'

Bradfield was being smooth again. 'Not everything that appears in an equation has physical reality. This ZPE is nothing more than a computational trick.'

Aristotle dipped bread into his fish soup. 'We progress. My colleague now admits that ZPE is a unifying explanation for a wide range of atomic phenomena. The Americans – or is it the British? – have an expression for this. If it looks like a duck, it walks like a duck and it quacks like a duck, then we call it a duck, not a computational trick.'

Archie was prodding a tentacle with his fork, as if he expected a reaction.

Findhorn said, 'This is getting over my head.'

'Perhaps you need more retsina, my friend,' Aristotle suggested, pouring it.

Findhorn thought the wine bore some resemblance to paint stripper, but he sipped it anyway. 'How much energy are we talking about?'

Aristotle speared a fish with his fork. 'The zero point energy shapes molecules, even determines the internal structure of atoms. The material world is a froth floating on the surface of a deep ocean of vacuum energy.'

'Give me a number.'

Papa tossed it out casually. 'There is enough energy in a volume of space the size of a coffee cup to evaporate the world's oceans.'

Archie's eyes gleamed. Bradfield said, 'Ugh!' Whether in reference to the soup or the Greek's claim was unclear.

'But that's vast,' Findhorn said lamely.

'You must have considered the implications of a source of infinite energy, easily tapped,' said Aristotle.

'Cheap electricity. The end of starvation. Water in the desert. A world of plenty.'

Aristotle burst out laughing. 'Cheap super-bombs, more powerful than nuclear weapons and much easier to build. Economic collapse. Massive unemployment. Social chaos. And, somewhere, the emergence of another Führer to rescue the situation.'

Findhorn tried again. 'How could you mine this energy, Papa? How could it be done?'

Aristotle pushed his chair back and stood up, carrying his plate. The Alsatian jumped up expectantly. The waiter exchanged exuberant Greek with Aristotle. No money was changing hands and Findhorn let it go. 'Simple. Think of some simple way to make the vacuum decay. To change the ground state of the neutral vacuum.'

Bradfield looked as if he was in pain.

'I don't understand these terms,' Findhorn said in frustration.

'Forget mechanical devices like parallel plates. Go atomic. Look for a system which shimmers in the vacuum energy, like a crystal with complex resonances on the quantum scale, allowing it to achieve the impossible, like a momentary reversal of time's arrow. Work on that.' Aristotle stood at the kitchen door. 'There is one problem, I believe, with any attempt to engineer the vacuum. Petrosian may or may not have thought of it.'

Findhorn waited. Aristotle finished his dramatic pause, and continued: 'We would be toying with something we know very little about.'

'You mean . . .'

'Now, Mr *Times* journalist . . .' was there, Findhorn wondered, a tiny hint of scepticism in Aristotle's tone? '. . . I have given you time, vacuum, cosmos. It is everything you need for your newspaper article.' There was a brilliant blue flash, and seconds later Zeus roared angrily around the hills. 'We should return.'

'One last thing, Papa,' Findhorn said.

Aristotle waited.

'Who were Chase and Henshal?'

In the near-dark, Aristotle looked blank. Bradfield looked blank. Archie looked blank. And so, finally, did Findhorn.

* * *

'I guess you were surprised to see me,' Archie said. The air was oppressive, and his brow had a light coating of sweat. He kept glancing through the kitchen window towards the courtyard.

Findhorn poured them both more wine. 'The surprise was entirely yours, Archie. Still, you've had time to think up a plausible story.'

Archie blew out his cheeks, took a gulp. 'You're too effing bright for plausible stories. I may as well tell you.'

'You must have come out here like lightning, after you sent me that phoney message.'

Archie hesitated. Then: 'Aye. How did you know it was false?'

'You almost had me fooled. Your mistake lay in those intermediate addresses between Angel Lodge and my Aberdeen one. You mis-spelled digital.com as digitil.com. It meant the e-mail header had been typed in manually by someone covering his tracks. And by this time it had twigged that every time I contacted you something bad happened shortly afterwards.'

Archie stayed silent.

Findhorn was suddenly angry. 'People are trying to kill me.'

'That wasn't part of the deal.' Archie's gaze still kept flicking towards the window.

'You hurt me, Archie. You were the one person on this planet I thought I could trust.'

'Aye, well, we all have to grow up.'

'Why?' Findhorn asked, although he knew the answer.

Archie looked at Findhorn. His eyes were red-rimmed. 'You're a fool, Fred. If this Petrosian was really onto something then a fortune isn't the word for it. Imagine having a patent for some device that gives the world free energy.'

'You heard Papa the Greek. It could blow up in your face. So grab the money and stuff the risks?'

'Fred, you're holding something that could make you richer than Croesus. I've had it with poverty, I do not recommend it. I want more out of life than slogging my guts out, trying to educate a generation of third-rate students who don't give a damn. I just wanted to be up there with the people who made it. A piece of the action, was that so bad?'

'Some action.' Findhorn paused, then suddenly asked: 'What's your connection with these religious nuts?'

Archie shifted uncomfortably. 'You don't know what you're up against.'

'Are you and Romella in it together?'

He was sulking like a child.

'If Bradfield is right there's no zero point energy and this Casimir thing is just interatomic forces.'

'Aye.'

'Aye, spoken like a no.'

Archie sipped at the wine with every sign of disliking it. 'Bradfield conveniently forgot to mention one thing. These atomic forces he was spoutin' about. They're caused by ZPE in the first place.'

'You mean . . .'

'They're just part of the effing vacuum energy. He also

slightly misled you about a small noisy clique of outsiders. The people who believed in ZPE also laid down the foundations of modern physics. People like Einstein, Planck, Feynman and Bethe.'

Feynman and Bethe. Names in Petrosian's diary: he had worked with them at Los Alamos. 'So what's your gut feeling, Archie?'

'My money's on the Greek.' Then, 'Fred, there's something I have to tell you.' Archie refilled his tumbler and took another long draught. He screwed his face up with disgust. 'Effing turpentine.'

'You need that stuff to screw up your courage?'

'I'm supposed to invite you over to my hotel for a late drink. It's a kilometre away and between here and there, there are lots of dark alleys. And there are lots of nice wee coves for late night swimmers to drown in and I don't suppose the forensic science in this neck of the woods is world-beating.'

Findhorn felt as if spiders were crawling up his back. 'I wondered how they were planning to do it.'

'Revelation Island. Jerusalem of the effing Aegean.' Archie shook his head. 'Get off it, Fred. Get out of it as fast as you can.'

'I've been thinking of nothing else. But there's only one way off Patmos, and that's the ferry in Skala harbour.'

'Do you hear me? Get out of this house. Vanish. Sleep out in the open. Then come straight down from the hills and onto the ferry when it's crowded. And never, never be alone between here and the nearest airport, not for a second. It's your only chance, Fred.'

'What about you?'

'I'll tell them you went looking for a place in Oriko, to be close to a beach. It's the best I can do for you.' For the first time in the evening Archie looked directly at his friend. The man's eyes were dark with despair. 'I failed you, Fred. I'm sorry. But for a few days there I had a wonderful vision of freedom.'

Findhorn had a better idea. In the early morning he emerged, freshly shaven but cold and smelling a little of sheep dung, along a track leading into Kampos, the northernmost village of the island. In one little shop he bought black shoe polish, in another some safety pins, scissors and a few yards of black cloth. Then he disappeared back up the track. It took him two hours of experiment before he was satisfied, and he had trouble with the dark eyebrows, but the men on the quayside paid no attention to the woman in sunglasses, dressed head to toe in the traditional black, who climbed the gangplank onto the morning ferry.

The taxi driver fully justified the fearful reputation of all Greek taxi drivers and Findhorn, having just escaped with his life, thought it would be dumb to end up wrapped round a lamp post. He arrived at Athens airport drained and in a state of nervous exhaustion. He just caught a flight to Heathrow, changing at Paris, and found himself a quiet, clean bed and breakfast in Cricklewood, as far from Central London as the Underground would take him.

He bought a burger and ate it in his room, watching

some nondescript quiz game on television while his mind whirled around the day's events. *I came close. I now know the stakes. But I'm no nearer Petrosian's mechanism.*

He telephoned nobody, checked no e-mails. In no way could he be traced here. Nothing could touch him. He was secure. Absolutely safe. Yet again, he thought, pure reason triumphs over irrational fear.

And he jammed a chair up against the door handle.

23

The Traitor

Jürgen Rosenblum was wearing a long overcoat, with a fur collar which was turned up, protecting his ears from the snow-laden, icy wind. He was stamping his feet and staring glumly at the window display. Assorted dummies were dressed in tropical beachwear against a backdrop of palm trees and sun-drenched beaches. They were lounging in physiologically improbable attitudes around a motor boat, underneath a notice which said 'Sparkle with Speedo Swimwear'.

He looked up, saw Petrosian and grinned. 'Hey, old friend!'

'Well,' Petrosian answered in German, taking his hand, 'you look like a snowman. How's life?'

Rosenblum grinned some more. 'It's hell, but we proleteriat have to keep plugging away towards a socialist society.'

Petrosian said, ' "Onward our heroes march to victory," ' and Rosenblum gave him a quizzical look.

Rosenblum took Petrosian by the arm and they walked along the streets, facing into the bitter wind. Petrosian felt his ears in pain. 'So, what's this about, Jurg?'

'Not here. Let's take a walk.'

They crossed into Central Park and headed north. There were ice skaters on a pond and children playing around snowmen. Rosenblum nodded at a woman walking a small frozen terrier. Once past her, he said, 'Lev, you're about to be arrested.'

'*What?*'

'This is on a need to know basis, Lev, and one thing you don't need to know is the source of my information. Let's just say that I have a New York friend who has a New York friend.'

There was nobody close to them, but Petrosian spoke quietly. 'I know I was bugged at Greers Ferry. And the FBI wanted to know about Kitty and me.'

'We should speak in English, Lev. German draws attention. You've been bugged for a year now. And you were under surveillance for almost two years during the Manhattan Project.'

'How do you know this?'

'Lev, like I say, don't ask. But a warrant for your arrest will be going out today. Maybe it's already out.'

'What's the charge?' Petrosian was looking bewildered.

'Espionage.'

Rosenblum watched his friend's shocked reaction with clinical interest. Then Petrosian managed to say, 'They've got it wrong.'

'I know that. Don't ask me how I know it,' Rosenblum added hastily.

'Maybe if I just spoke to them.'

'Sure.' The tone wasn't even sarcastic. 'I'm getting

frostbite in the butt, let's find a café.'

Petrosian said, 'Since you know so much, Jurgen, maybe you know what case they've got against me.'

'Some of it goes back to the Manhattan. They know you handed documents over to Kitty.'

'They were just letters.'

'Why didn't you use PO Box 1663 at Santa Fe like the rest of Los Alamos?'

'I can't say.'

'You'll have to say if it comes to a trial.'

'I know it looks bad.'

'It looks terrible.'

They turned out of the park. The paths had been cleared of snow but more was falling from the sky. They walked along North Broadway. Rosenblum gave his friend time for the information to sink in, didn't disrupt his train of thought with conversation. He steered him into a warm café and sat him down at a window table before returning with a tray. He distributed cappuccino and bagels between them.

Rosenblum dipped his bagel into the cappuccino. A man appeared on the other side of the window, his collar turned up and hat pulled down almost to his eyes. He stood with his back to them, flapping his arms together. Rosenblum looked at him with a mixture of suspicion and alarm.

'Jürgen, that happened a decade ago. If they were going to do anything they'd have done it then.'

'Wrong, wrong, wrong. Then was war. They took a chance on you out of sheer necessity. Now is different.

They have new stuff on you, evidence that will convince any jury.' Rosenblum kept glancing at the man on the other side of the window.

'How can they have? I haven't done anything.'

'You were seen entering the Soviet Consulate in New York on several occasions.'

'I have a brother in Armenia. I was asking about the possibility of getting an exit visa for him and his family. The FBI quizzed me about that.'

'Were they satisfied?' A middle-aged woman approached the man. They linked arms and scurried off. Rosenblum visibly relaxed. He took a nibble at his bagel.

Petrosian said, 'I think so.'

'They were not. However that's not why you're about to be arrested. Twenty-four hours ago a long telegram was sent from the consulate to Moscow, not in their usual cryptogram which is unbreakable, but in an old GRU effort which Arlington Hall cracked years ago. It mentions you by name. It says you've supplied wonderful new, detailed information about the Los Alamos work which they'll be sending out by pouch. It's cleverly meshed with stuff they know the Americans already know If you get the general meaning. It delivers you to the executioner with vaseline on your skull and electrodes on your balls. You're the walking dead, Lev. And you have no place to hide.'

Petrosian felt himself going pale. He pushed his plate away. 'For a friend, Jürgen, you're the most treacherous bastard I've ever met.'

'Hey.' Rosenblum's tone was that of injured innocence.

'Don't shoot the messenger. I'm your pal.'

'I'll report this conversation to the FBI.'

'Who'd believe it? Would you if you were a fed?'

'Why not?'

'You have two ways of leaving this country, Lev. You can take the Rosenberg route.' The Rosenberg spies had gone to the electric chair only the previous summer. Petrosian was beginning to feel faint. 'Or you can be flown out in style, in your very own private aircraft. The Soviet Union would welcome a man of your talent and creativity. You'd lead a privileged life. But there's an entrance fee.'

'I'll bet there is.'

'All the information you can give about the Super.'

Petrosian shook his head sadly. 'From time to time I wondered about you, Jurg. And now all sorts of little things fit into place.' He leaned back in his chair, examined Rosenblum's face curiously. 'Tell me, what does it feel like, being a traitor?'

'I wouldn't know, pal, I'm a patriot. Only my loyalty isn't determined by accident of birth, or history or geography. It goes to the whole human race, not this or that tribe. I hated history and geography at school. All those battles and king lists.'

'Which school was that?'

'Come on, Lev, this is for the greater good. I'm your lifeline. Just what was in those letters you handed to Kitty anyway?'

'You don't need to know. Maybe I'll take my chances with the American judicial system.'

Rosenblum displayed yellow teeth. 'The courts go on the evidence before them. What else can they do? You got evidence to say you've been set up? Anyone can say they've been set up, if the courts were to start buying that, without evidence, every hood in the country would just have to turn up and declare they'd been set up and nobody would ever get convicted of nothing, you want to go to the FBI and say "I've been set up but I can't prove it," and they'll say, "Oh, that explains all this evidence pal, sorry to have bothered you"?'

'Calm down, I'm the one with his life on the line.'

'I need an answer. Take ten seconds.'

'I've had a bellyful of repressive societies.'

'This is a free society? McCarthy is Snow White and HUAC are the Seven Dwarfs?'

'What are you offering me, Jurg? Uncle Joe and the Soviet Union?'

'You'd rather be toast in Alcatraz? You want to fry in your own fat, hear yourself sizzle sizzle like bacon in a pan? Savour the aroma of fried Petrosian?'

'No.'

'Is that a yes or a no? Your ten seconds is up, Lev. For a man who has no choice in the matter you're taking a helluva time.'

Petrosian put his face in his hands. 'It's true, I don't have a choice.'

Rosenblum grinned. 'I take that as a yes. What tribute can you bring to the Motherland in exchange for your salvation?'

'I can't go back to Los Alamos. They'd arrest me.'

Rosenblum waited.

Then Petrosian said, 'I've kept a diary for twenty years. Everything I've done about the atom bomb and the Super is recorded in them. I can give you my diaries.'

'But like you said, you can't go back for them.'

'They're here in town. I moved them out of Los Alamos when the FBI started to poke around. After all they amount to a gross breach of security. They'll tell your scientists in the gulags where we're at, the complete state of the art.'

'What gulags? That's just Western propaganda. And the scientists will need technical stuff.'

'The technical stuff is there in summary. Deuterium-tritium reaction rates, implosion geometries, everything. And every significant conversation I've had. It's a complete record of the hydrogen bomb's development from the Los Alamos perspective. And there's even some stuff from Livermore.'

Rosenblum nodded happily. 'That sounds like your entrance fee. I'll put it to them. Hey, old pal, cheer up. You're about to start a new life in a socialist paradise.'

'I can't last long here. Your friends have forty-eight hours to get me out of the country. If they haven't fixed me up by then, I'll give myself up to the FBI.'

Rosenblum scribbled down a number in a diary, tore out the page and handed it over. 'You're a tough negotiator. Call me tomorrow morning. You'll have to avoid the dragnet until then.'

Petrosian managed to smile. 'I've done that sort of thing before.'

'Hey, it's good to see you happy. So have I.'

The snow was becoming blizzard-like. Petrosian watched Rosenblum scurrying towards a subway. He turned in the opposite direction, walking briskly north, ignoring the bitter cold. He had no clear intention in mind other than to retrieve the diaries and find, somewhere in the United States of America, some place safe and warm to sleep.

It was dark by the time Petrosian stepped off the bus at the Trinity Cemetery. He made his way along ill-remembered streets, navigating as much by his internal compass as by landmarks. Eventually he recognized the house, a white, wooden affair with a short driveway in which an old Ford was parked. The snow on the path was pristine; there were lights in the house.

Ant opened the door. She looked at Lev with surprise, and then a worried look came over her gaunt face. 'Kristel, hello. I've come to collect my briefcase.'

He heard the voices, low and businesslike.

She was stalling them.

He grabbed jacket, coat, briefcase with diaries. In the kitchen he put a finger to his lips and tiptoed out in exaggerated fashion. The children, mystified, suppressed giggles.

Quietly out the back door. Through the back garden. Over the fence, through the garden of the neighbour to the rear. Turn left, past Kristel's street. A Buick was parked at her front gate. Petrosian turned smartly right, taking a narrow lane with garbage cans; an old metal fence with a child-sized gap; trees beyond. He squeezed through the gap and was into a stretch of lightly wooded parkland. He walked through it to another street, out of ideas, aware only that he had to get as far away as possible.

He bought a ticket at the railway station and waited in an agony of impatience on the platform. Early morning businessmen began to turn up; he kept well away. The Pullman, when it turned up, was half empty. It sat at the platform for an excruciating ten minutes while he watched the entrance and wondered how they could possibly fail to check on something as obvious as a railway station. He thought they probably would check on the station; his photograph would be recognized by the clerk; and they would be waiting for him at the other end, a simple act which would culminate, a couple of years on, in his blood boiling and flames shooting from his mouth.

The train took off but Petrosian kept his eye on the station entrance, his imagination seeing men rushing onto the platform at the last second. The morning commuters started on their newspapers; regulars exchanged nods or greetings; someone started on an interminable story and ended up speaking to himself. Nobody even glanced at Petrosian and he marvelled that his inner fear was attracting no attention. The train ambled along the line for about ten minutes and then came to a halt. Commuters poured on. Nobody got off. Petrosian, his nerves at breaking point, pushed his way through the incoming passengers and jumped off the train just as it began to move away.

The ticket collector, a young, stooped man with a black waistcoat, looked at his ticket in surprise.

'Change of plan,' Petrosian explained.

'You want a rebate?' said the man.

'No thanks.'

'Won't take more'n five minutes.'

'I'm in a hurry.'

'Hey, it's worth four bucks fifty, Mister,' the man complained to the retreating figure, while Petrosian inwardly cursed the attention he had drawn to himself.

The word will be getting around. I daren't use public transport again.

As a middle-sized town in the State of New York, Poughkeepsie would have a taxi service. But taxis have radios. Petrosian visualised himself in the back seat of the taxi when his description came through; visualised the affected nonchalance of the driver as he pretended not to recognize it as that of his passenger; the man's fear that he might be murdered; the coded message to the office; the FBI men closing in.

I daren't use a taxi.

The briefcase was the killer. Look for a man carrying a medium-sized black briefcase. He thought of ditching it, abandoning the record of his last fifteen eventful years. But the diaries were also his passport. Without them, he was doomed.

Change the briefcase? It was too early. The shops were still closed. And for that matter, the streets were too quiet and he was still only ten minutes away from Kristel's house and he had effectively shouted 'Come and get me!' at the Poughkeepsie station.

Hire a car?

Certainly sir, just wait here a moment while I check availability and incidentally, since you fit the description which has just come through, make a quick telephone call.

Stay put? Hide away in some quiet park as he had done in Leipzig?

Leipzig was overnight, and a major city. This was early morning in a small town. Staying put would just give them time to close the net. He walked the main street in despair, lugging the briefcase which shouted, rang bells and blew whistles, with Rosenblum's phrase 'toast in Alcatraz' filling his head.

24

Executive Lounge

Sunshine. And cappuccinos in little hill-town bars, and buzzing little motofurgonis carrying big flagons of wine. Clattering dishes and noisy Italian chatter. Monasteries in Greece, and creepy religious fanatics, and treacherous friends and strangulation in dark alleys. Findhorn woke up, the lurid pastiche from his dreamworld fading for ever. Grey London light peeked under the curtains and his watch said eight a.m. He dressed quickly, trying to put his mind into gear as he stumbled down the stairs. Past the dining room, where a few Italian tourists were enjoying a full English breakfast, adding a notch to their cholesterol counts. He skipped breakfast, settled with the lady of the house, a plump, grey-haired little woman, and headed out in search of a business centre, a cybercafé, anywhere to plug into his e-mail.

There was a new message, a single telephone number with an American code. He thought it might be New York and if so it would be three in the morning. He dialled through.

'Fred?' She sounded excited.

'Where are you?'

'La Guardia, in New York. I'm just about to board Concorde.'

'What?'

'Relax, Fred, your brother's financing me. Stefi and Doug are coming down from Edinburgh. We're all going to have a council of war at Heathrow in three hours. Where are you?'

Findhorn had to look around for a moment. 'London.'

'Terrific, we gambled on that. I'll see you in three hours, then. We'll rendezvous at the Pizza Hut in Terminal One.'

'The Pizza Hut. You'll probably get there before me.'

'Doug wants you to phone him as soon as you can. Must fly – ha ha.'

Findhorn dialled Doug's Edinburgh flat. 'Dougie?'

'Fred, you're alive. Okay listen, we're just leaving for the airport.'

'Romella explained. I'll see you shortly.'

'Yes, but listen. I've been working hard on your behalf. I've been into the green Merc question etcetera and I've got things to tell you.'

Findhorn smiled. Little Brother was psyching himself up for the financial pitch. 'I look forward to hearing it.'

'And I'm picking up the tab from here on.'

'All right, you greedy little sod, how much are you in for?'

'Thirty per cent of the action. I'm taking a risk, it could be thirty per cent of zero.'

'A risk? You don't know the meaning of the word. I've been climbing icebergs, avoiding assassins . . .'

'But, Mister Bond, do you have the shekels to keep going?'

'Without the diaries this thing would never have flown. Ten per cent.'

'Flown? Without me you've crash landed. My legal contacts are refreshing the parts other people can't reach. And there's my flat, a safe house if ever there was one. Twenty-five per cent.'

'I don't need you,' Findhorn lied. 'Twenty.'

'Done. See you shortly.'

In the event Findhorn was the first to reach the Pizza Hut. After his second coffee he got up and prowled around restlessly, wandering through the Sock Shop, the Tie Rack, Past Times and Thorntons. In W.H. Smith he browsed aimlessly. The blurb on one book, *Nemesis*, proclaimed that 'This may be the last thriller you ever read'. He put it back hastily; it threatened to be prophetic.

He was on his third coffee when Stefi and Doug emerged from the airport crowds. She was wearing a white fur coat and Findhorn marvelled at how she could do it on her post-graduate income. Doug bore little physical resemblance to Findhorn, except for a slight roundness of the jaw, inherited from the paternal line as far back as the family photographs went. He was shorter than Fred, stouter, had hair which was, surprisingly for a young man, already beginning to thin, and had thick black spectacles. He was wearing a pinstripe suit and a long dark Gucci trenchcoat, and was carrying an expensive-looking tanned leather briefcase.

Stefi pecked Findhorn on the cheek.

'Breakfast, quick,' said Doug.

Findhorn let them get on with hash browns, fried eggs and sausages without disturbing them. A family of five spread themselves over two adjacent tables, spilling drinks and squabbling. The children had runny noses, and the parents seemed to have given up on the discipline thing.

On their second coffee, Romella turned up with an overnight bag. A light blue greatcoat was draped over her shoulders, she was wearing a plain white blouse and a short black skirt, and she was looking ragged. Findhorn introduced his brother.

'Okay,' said Findhorn, 'shall we confab here?'

Romella waved away the menu which Doug proffered her. 'If you like. But I can get us into the BA executive lounge on my Concorde ticket.'

There was a rapid exodus.

'Me first,' Findhorn said. 'I've discovered the nature of the Petrosian machine.' And he told them about the energy of the vacuum, how it might be nothing or vast beyond comprehension, and how Petrosian had found some way – or thought he'd found some way – of tapping into it, and that it might be the dawn of a new world or, depending on unknown physics, the end of it. He told them about the near miss with the atom bomb and how he thought that Petrosian's mind had been sensitized to instability by the experience. And he told them how he, Findhorn, was worried about instability in complex systems too, although in a much smaller way and in a different field. And he told them that he had failed to find the secret, the actual mechanism whereby Petrosian believed the vacuum energy could be tapped.

Stefi was wide-eyed. 'I'm overwhelmed, Fred. If you're right, and this is some machine for getting energy from nothing, it could turn the world on its head.'

Doug was open-mouthed. 'The financial possibilities are unbelievable.'

'Remember the caveat. It would need to be examined for stability.'

'Stefi and I think we know who kidnapped Romella, and who's lying behind the effort to get the diaries. And what you're telling us fits beautifully with what we've found. It provides the motive.'

'Surely it's the Temple of Celestial Truth?'

'I think they're just stooges. I believe they've been triggered by a much more powerful outfit.'

Findhorn felt his scalp prickling slightly. He leaned forward. Doug pulled a square white envelope from his briefcase. He glanced surreptitiously around the lounge before handing it over. 'These were taken by security cameras in the Edinburgh Sheraton. Anyone you recognize in them?'

The lens was wide-angle and gave a full view of a hotel corridor at the cost of a slight distortion of the field. Little numbers in the top right hand corner of the black and white pictures recorded the time. Findhorn flicked through the first half-dozen, recognized nobody. Numbers seven through eleven amounted to a series of stills; they recorded an inebriated man emerging from an elevator, standing in a confused attitude, making his way to a door, vanishing.

The time on the last picture was 23.47. Edinburgh pubs closed at eleven thirty.

'Captain Hansen,' said Findhorn.

The next photograph was marked 01.07. The elevator had disgorged a man and a woman. The man had a broad-brimmed hat, a long coat and sunglasses, none of which could disguise the small, bulky frame. The woman's face was likewise adorned with dark glasses but it was long, it had a turned-down mouth and the the same grim demeanour. She too was wearing a long coat which reminded Findhorn of something he'd seen in a movie about Wyatt Earp.

The next few stills showed them moving along the corridor, stopping at Hansen's door, the door opening although Hansen was out of view, and then, again, a blank corridor. The last two pictures were marked 05.33 and showed the same pair in the corridor, and then standing at the elevator, and then gone.

Findhorn closed the folder and slid it back. 'These are the people who tried to get Petrosian's briefcase from me. They claimed they were Norsk officials.'

'And they were in Hansen's room for over four hours.' Doug passed over another envelope. 'Here are some police photographs.'

'How did you get hold of them?'

'Santa popped them down the chimney. And this is the preliminary autopsy report. It's a rough draft and very technical, but it gives you an idea of what they were doing during those hours.' Findhorn flicked through the photographs. He felt himself going pale. 'The wire you see is

306

telephone cable. There's evidence that he was gagged, I suppose to stop him screaming. The burn marks around his genitals suggest that they were using the room's electricity supply in some way. There are also pinhole marks around his stomach suggesting the same – look at plates three and four. And they drove things under his fingernails before they took them off – plates seven to ten. You don't want to look at the rest of it. Professor Hillion did the actual autopsy. His preliminary conclusion is that Hansen's heart gave out.'

Doug took the pictures and folder back from Findhorn's shaking hand.

'Why?'

'They were trying to find you, Fred.'

Findhorn said, 'These people weren't employed by Norsk. They said they'd come from Arendal. Norsk doesn't have an office in Arendal. I should know, I lived there for a year.'

Doug nodded. 'Norsk's head office is in Leiden.'

'I didn't know that.' Findhorn was unsettled, the images of Hansen were filling his mind.

'It's fairly standard, Fred. Lots of European companies have head offices with Netherlands addresses except that they're not really in the Netherlands. They're in the Dutch Antilles, Aruba to be precise, which is an island north of Venezuela.'

'You mean . . .'

'Norsk is owned by an offshore company. Find the owner of that offshore company, and you find the real power behind Norsk. Places like Aruba and Nassau act as black boxes. Officials in these offshore havens often adopt a *laager* mentality when it comes to enquiries about fiscal, tax and even criminal matters. It's all but impossible to penetrate the flow of cash in, through and out of them. However, you'll be glad to learn that your little brother not only knows people who know people with corruptible contacts in these places, the aforesaid people owe your little brother one or two favours.'

'You're surely not talking about criminals?' Romella asked, mock-innocent.

Doug's expression was pained. 'Clients, Romella, please. Anyway, I now know who really owns Norsk.' He gave a lawyer's pause, as if to let the fact sink in with the jury. 'And this knowledge has allowed me to identify your friends in the Sheraton photographs.'

Doug sipped at a tonic water and asked, 'What do you know about the Japanese Friendship Societies?'

Findhorn shook his head, and Doug continued: 'They're gangsters, the *sokaiya* in Japanese. They're a specialist branch of the *yakusa*. Originally they made their money by threatening to disrupt the annual meetings of large corporations unless they received large payoffs. It seems this was a legal activity in Japan until 1983. Anyway, I imagine payoffs continue to this day, legal or not. But now enter Darwinian evolution. A very strange relationship has grown up between the corporations that they used to prey on and these parasites. Now the corporations hire them to make sure nobody asks awkward questions at shareholders' meetings.'

'I have a horrible feeling,' Findhorn said.

'Aye, Fred. The nasties you met in the Whisky Club belong to a clan known as the *Genyosha*, the Dark Ocean Society. They're connected with a group known as Matsumo Holdings. Now the *Genyosha* have a track record. Their methods of friendly persuasion include limb breaking, finger amputation and the like. Rumour has it that the more stubborn shareholders have had a joyous early reunion with their ancestors.'

Findhorn said flatly, 'Look, Norsk asked me to get the diaries from that iceberg. Why didn't they just send regular company officials to collect them and be done with it?'

'Fred, I can think of only one explanation. Matsumo Holdings wants to do you harm.'

Findhorn blew out his cheeks. 'As in a joyous reunion with my ancestors?'

Doug nodded. 'It seems to be enough that you've been in contact with the diaries. And now, with this vacuum energy business you're telling us about, it all begins to fit.' He pulled a thick, glossy brochure out of his briefcase. 'I've dug up a group profile for Matsumo Holdings.'

'A group profile?'

'Yes. Matsumo took over the Fuyo group last year.'

'Means nothing to me,' said Findhorn.

'Don't get alarmed, Fred, I know you have the commercial acumen of a Tibetan monk. I'll keep it simple. The Fuyo group is centered round the *zaibatsu*.' He raised his eyebrows interrogatively, and Findhorn looked blank. Doug said, 'Right,' in the tone of a man about to climb a steep hill. 'The *zaibatsu* were a pre-war conglomerate of companies. The US occupation forces broke them up because of their support for the Japanese military during the war. But the Japanese ran rings round their US masters.'

'How?'

'The power centres in Japan have always been linked by secret societies. The industrialists carried on wheeling and dealing as before but without a formal legal identity. This post-war group – a *keiretsu*, or conglomerate of companies – had the Fuji Bank at their core. The group included Nissan, Yasuda Trust and Banking, the Marubei Corporation and Yamaichi. With the Matsumo takeover the group now includes the big four Japanese brokerage houses – Nomura, Nikko, Daiwa and Yamaichi Securities – as well as another major bank, the Dai-Ichi Kangyo.'

'So Matsumo are big. I'm impressed.'

Doug took another sip at his water. 'I'm glad you're impressed, Fred. Because these are the people who want you dead.'

Findhorn wondered whether, in that case, there was any place on earth where he would be safe.

Doug's expression was grim. 'And now we know why.'

Findhorn looked at his brother. 'As you say, I'm as streetwise as a Tibetan monk. Explain.'

Stefi said, 'It comes down to the people who asked you to get the diaries.'

'Norsk Advanced Technologies?'

She nodded. 'The child of Matsumo.' Stefi opened a thick, glossy booklet, the Annual Report and Accounts of Matsumo Holdings, English version. Its front cover showed a montage of famous Far Eastern constructions. Findhorn briefly recognized the four-kilometre Akashi

Kaikyo suspension bridge, and the fifteen hundred foot tall Petronas twin towers of Kuala Lumpur: the world's longest and the world's highest.

'Fred, Matsumo Holdings may be huge, but they're vulnerable to something. They've been taking a massive gamble. Look at this list.' Under the heading *Principal Group Companies*, Stefi's fingernail scanned down a list with names like Energy America, Hickson Oil, Scafield Oil, Shell Africa, Expro-Borneo and Fortune Exploration.

'Oil. It's been Yoshi Matsumo's obsession for the past five years. He's sunk his organization's future in it,' Stefi said. 'Partly they've been doing this through acquisitions, partly through creating new oil exploration companies. The big spender is Norsk Advanced Techs – which we know to be ninety per cent Japanese. Look here at Matsumo's three-year summary.' She turned the pages to *Profit and Loss Account*. 'Norsk are into deep ocean oil exploration. As of 31 March they had fixed assets of 34 billion sterling, liabilities of 13 billion, and creditors' amounts falling due of 14 billion. All that risk, all that cash going out.'

Findhorn said, 'That sort of money is bigger than the GNP of some countries. They're taking a massively expensive gamble.'

'But it looks as if it's succeeding,' Stefi continued. 'The field they've discovered in the Norwegian sector is huge. Now the cost of getting oil out from under the Arctic is beyond the means of a little country like Norway, but it seems there's been a little horse-trading.' Stefi put a finger to his lips, as if she was about to reveal some great secret.

'But they need oil prices to stay high. If, hypothetically, oil prices were to take a steep plunge any time within the next few years, the consequences would be horrific. It would bring Matsumo Holdings down. The knock-on effect would collapse Far Eastern economies like dominoes, and the effects would be felt in the West. And something even worse.' Stefi paused dramatically.

'Tell me.'

'Mister Matsumo would be at the apex of this apocalyptic disaster. Think of his personal humiliation.'

Findhorn groaned.

Stefi said, 'Yoshi Matsumo can't afford you, Fred. He absolutely must bump you off before you get to the secret.'

'This is unreal. Nobody does a thing like that.'

'Fred, grow up.' Stefi's smile had an edge to it. 'There's a rumour that the war in Chechnya a few years ago was fomented by the Matsumo group to push up the price of oil. If they can engineer something like that, what's an Arctic explorer?'

Doug said, 'Half the industrialists in the world would kill to get this process, the other half would kill to destroy it. Think of oil companies like BP, Exxon, Shell being bankrupted overnight. Car manufacturers and all their tributaries going into recession. Look at the mass unemployment that would follow.'

Romella said, 'You're speaking from the perspective of the rich twenty per cent of humanity. What about the billion people who are short of water? What about fertilizer, infrastructure and medicine for the Third World? Free energy would let people distil sea water and pipe it to desert regions, and create nitrate fertilizers from the air.'

'Or Semtex,' said Stefi. 'Think of massive terrorism on the cheap. The population explosion, the imbalances in power that would result in the Middle East. It would suck everyone in.'

Doug's eyes were gleaming behind his thick spectacles. 'There are fortunes to be made here. Huge fortunes.'

Findhorn said, 'Hey, this is fun. Only without Petrosian's machine we're out of the game, and we don't have Petrosian's machine.'

Romella yawned and stretched. 'Be nice to me. I know where it is.'

25

Armenia

Romella said, 'You were right about the old Geghard trading route. The merchandise went out that way after the war.'

A thrill ran through Findhorn. But now she was saying, 'There's a downside. The competition got to Kitty first.'

A teenage maneater, all eyeshadow and false lashes, entered the executive lounge, carrying a small suitcase. She stared openly at Findhorn, and Findhorn shot her a suspicious look.

Romella continued, 'It's weird. They got to Kitty less than an hour before I did. The poor woman got quite confused. So did I.'

'So where exactly were the messages going?'

Romella beamed. 'Not Turkey. Armenia!'

'You think he was sending them to his brother?'

'Almost certainly. And it wasn't atomic secrets or he'd have given them to a courier like Harry Gold or Rosenblum.'

Findhorn said, 'Hey, maybe it *was* just letters.'

'Maybe, but Kitty remembered the last thing Petrosian

sent out just before he disappeared. It was a thick envelope and she thought there was something about it. She remembers, after all those years.'

'Okay, it's our best shot, not to mention our only one. Now all we have to do is find Lev's brother, if he's still alive.'

Romella said, 'We'll need visas.'

Doug said, 'It sounds as if we're neck and neck with the competition. If they travel out via Heathrow you might even be on the same plane. They could be in the terminal now.'

Stefi giggled nervously. 'But surely not in this lounge.'

Findhorn shook his head. 'No chance. It's too unlikely.'

'Much too unlikely,' Doug agreed.

They looked around, suddenly aware. A gaggle of white-haired ladies were sharing some scandal three tables away; a couple of Japanese businessmen were sharing a joke over hot chocolates; otherwise the lounge was quiet.

Findhorn was looking at a departures screen. He said, 'Blimey! Where's the Armenian embassy?'

Doug and Stefi were standing, cold and impatient, at the entrance to Terminal Four. Findhorn was barely out of the taxi when Doug thrust tickets into his hand. 'It's boarding now, Gate Fourteen. Miss it and the next flight is in two days. Run.'

'Good luck!' Stefi called after the retreating figures.

In Terminal Four, a harrassed official jabbered into a handset as he hustled Findhorn and Romella through the security and passport controls. They were joined by a large American in a green check suit who trailed them, puffing, through long corridors, and then they were straight onto the aircraft, with a burly stewardess hovering at the door.

Findhorn settled in at a window seat, and Romella's boarding card took her to a seat near the rear of the aircraft. The Tupolev had the air of discarded Soviet rolling stock. It reeked of kerosene and had worn carpets and rickety chairs. And open luggage racks: it was an aircraft designed for the flat Russian steppes, without steep banking turns in mind.

The American, with thick spectacles and a green jacket, slumped down next to him. Fat arms overflowed into Findhorn's space and a *New York Times* spread itself around.

'Bin to Armeenya before?'

Findhorn shook his head, trying to get the right degree of surliness.

'Still full of commies. Y'on business?'

Findhorn turned up the surliness a fraction. He mumbled without looking up from the in-flight magazine. 'Touring.'

'Armeenyan women are the pits. They got no class and no deodorant.' The American picked his nose and spread his elbows some more.

The air conditioning wasn't working, and the aircraft sat on the tarmac for half an hour while the air grew stifling and Findhorn's shirt and pants became sticky with sweat. A baby exercised her lungs mightily, and the hostess prowled up and down the aisle like a prison warder. Finally the three jet engines howled, died, howled, died and on the third howl thrust them along the tarmac and into the blue sky with a take-off angle like a Lancaster heading for Dresden.

Somewhere over the English Channel, the American tried again. 'By the way, don't let the lousy upholstery fool you. This is one extremely strong aircraft. It's made from girders.'

Findhorn grunted happily.

'Not so sure about the maintenance, though. I hear some of the ground crew haven't been paid for months.' The American started on the in-flight magazine, leaving Findhorn to examine the rivets on the wing.

There was a long, sweaty wait on the tarmac at Amsterdam and it was dark by the time the Tupolev touched ground in Armenia. In Findhorn's highly strung state, it seemed to come in at a hell of a speed. Yerevan Airport was a massive, concrete, solid structure, unadorned with the shops and restaurants of Western airports. Findhorn and Romella joined the queue trickling one at a time through a short passageway. An overhead mirror gave the uniformed girl a view of the passageway as she flicked through his visa and forged passport. She fixed a puzzled stare on him, and went through the documents again, slowly. He tried to look casual while his insides turned to jelly. Then she had stamped his passport and he was through and wondering why, if Armenia was an independent country, the immigration officials were Russian.

A bus with a cracked windscreen took a handful of passengers into Yerevan, along pitch-black streets lined with brightly lit market stalls. Beds were made up at the side of the stalls: it seemed that the owners slept *al fresco* beside their merchandise.

The Hotel Dvin was another massive tribute to the Soviet concrete industry, and there was another queue as names were checked at the reception desk and passports were taken. The noisy American was making a big thing of being a regular visitor, calling everyone by their first names in a deep, loud bass. Findhorn tried to get away at the elevator, but the man caught the door as it was closing. A woman at a desk seven flights up gave each of them a key. Romella had the room opposite; at least the American was further down the corridor. Findhorn tossed briefcase and holdall onto the bed and opened the balcony doors. He looked out over a dark city, letting the delicious, cool wind blow over him for five minutes. Then he slipped quietly out of his room. He returned two hours later, rattled and frustrated, had a quick shower and flopped into bed. He slept badly.

In the early morning Findhorn found himself looking out over the same scene he had seen in former Soviet bloc countries from Poland to Slovakia. A jumble of shacks, corrugated iron roofs, piles of rubble. A couple of mangy dogs prowled around, and a cock was crowing from somewhere inside a tree-packed garden. To his right the snowy peak of Mount Ararat, seventeen thousand feet high, floated in the sky, its base hidden in a blue haze. Around half past seven women with plastic bags began to emerge along unpaved tracks, and a few identikit cars trailed exhaust smoke along the potholed road.

Findhorn had a breakfast of grated beetroot, hard-boiled eggs, carrots and coffee. There was no sign of either Romella or the American. The girl at the reception spoke good English. She was courteous, had plenty of class and no need of deodorant. 'I'd like to hire a car, please,' said Findhorn.

'I've fixed it.' Findhorn turned. Romella, breathing heavily, as if she had been running.

'How are we for time?'

'Assume we're out of it.'

'I don't trust that American.'

They waited without conversation in the big, drab foyer. The American appeared, still in green jacket and trousers, with a small black bag over a shoulder. 'Hey ho!' he waved in passing. 'What did I tell you about the women?'

After ten minutes a small man with Turkish features and a Clark Gable moustache appeared. Romella gave her instructions with the help of a hand-drawn map. Then Findhorn and Romella were ushered into the back of a black Mercedes.

'I thought we'd start at the Geghard Monastery.'

'That letter from Anastas?'

'Yes, transcribed by some priest. The Petrosian family must have been known to people there.'

'Except that the priests are almost certainly long gone, along with Anastas.'

The driver was fiddling with the ignition. The engine

coughed into life. He paused to light up a Turkish cigarette, and then took off without bothering about such refinements as rear mirrors, signals, or looking over his shoulder. He took them through earthquake-ravaged streets and past drab high-rise slums bedecked with washing. Twelve flights up, someone had knocked a hole in the side of the building, presumably to get fresh air into his flat. Children and dogs played in the dust. The sun was up and the air was getting warm.

Then they had cleared the city and were onto a steeply climbing road, with a good surface, and the traffic was light. Soon they were passing through mountainous country with high open vistas and steep gorges lined with fluted basalt. To Findhorn, the country had a vaguely biblical look about it. Away from the pollution below, he noted that Mount Ararat was in fact connected to the ground rather than floating in the sky. The road was deserted. After an hour of driving, Romella checking landmarks against the map, they passed a couple of girls carrying water in big Coke bottles, pushing a donkey ahead of them. Then there were calves at the roadside, drinking at a pipe flooding the road with water.

Mountains rose steeply on either side of them and the road became winding. Romella said, 'We should be there soon,' and in another fifteen minutes the road ended at a dusty little square with a couple of coaches and half a dozen parked cars. A trio of men in traditional dress welcomed them with a short, frenetic number played on drum, bagpipes and flute, and they walked up a steep, cobbled path past a handful of women selling sticky sweets and little brochures. The monastery was partly built into striated, precipitous mountainside.

At the arched entrance, Romella said, 'This may call for some delicate treatment. Remember Armenia was communist not so long ago and people don't necessarily open up.'

'I can take a hint.' He left Romella to disappear along a cloister, and strolled around the sparse, earthquake-cracked structure for about twenty minutes before taking a side door in a wall, and climbing a narrow track which wound steeply upwards. He sat on a rock and looked down on the monastery. Their driver was leaning against the side of his car, chain-smoking. A handful of tourists were wandering around the courtyard. The women with the sweets just sat. Presently Romella emerged, looking around her, and Findhorn climbed smartly back down the hill.

In the car, Romella said, '*Gna aya chanaparhov tas kilometr u tegvi depi zakh.*' It was the first time Findhorn had heard her speak Armenian.

She sat back in the car and said, 'It's our lucky day. Lev's brother is not only alive, he hasn't moved house in his entire life. Lev and Anastas were brought up in a shepherd's cottage not far from here.'

They drove back about ten kilometres before Romella tapped Clark Gable on the shoulder and issued another volley of instructions. The man grunted. In another kilometre, around a corner, was a track leading to what looked like a shepherd's cottage. They turned along it, bumping over rough ground, past a tethered goat, and drew to a halt beside a dirty grey Skoda.

Out of the car, they stretched their legs. Flies were everywhere.

The man who opened the door was over eighty. He was white-haired and stooped, with a white moustache and deeply wrinkled skin. But his dark eyes were alert, and full of curiosity. Findhorn spoke in English, Romella translated into Armenian. They first established that the old man was in fact Anastas Petrosian, and they had hardly started when the shepherd waved them in. Inexplicably, Clark Gable seemed to think the invitation extended to him. He wandered into the room, his eyes taking in everything.

They sat in a small, cluttered room around a rough-hewn table. The room smelled of pipe tobacco. A small, ancient bureau was covered with photographs: a young woman and children, separately and together, a young man, a near-Victorian photograph of an elderly couple. The shepherd disappeared into a kitchen and reappeared with bread, cheese, four tumblers and a bottle containing some golden liquid.

'First,' said Findhorn, 'forgive me, but I don't speak Armenian.' There was an exchange between Romella and the old man. The shepherd smiled, as if the idea of a foreigner speaking Armenian was crazy. 'I'm a historian,' Findhorn lied. 'I'm interested in the life and works of your brother, Lev Petrosian.'

The old man's eyes opened wide with astonishment. There was an outburst of gabbling between him and

Romella. Findhorn let it run its course. 'During the war, and just after it, your brother wrote some scientific papers, I mean articles. I know that when he was in America, he sent some of these to you for safe keeping. I am writing a history of that period, and I would very much like to know what became of these documents. Did they reach you?'

The old man said nothing, but his wrinkled face had acquired a tense expression.

Findhorn tried again. 'I don't want to take these papers away. I only need to read them for my historical research. If you have these papers, I would be grateful to read them. In your presence, without removing any. Or if you gave them to the authorities, please let me know where they went.'

Silence. The shepherd might have been mute. He certainly had no talent for disguising his thoughts; suspicion was plainly written over his face.

Findhorn sipped at the liquid. It was a first-class cognac. 'I know it was a very long time ago, but the Bomb was a watershed in the history of the world. Others have changed history with swords and armies, but your brother and his colleagues did it with mathematics and physics. Everything about that time has to be known. Especially I want Lev's contribution to be recorded for posterity, everything he did to be understood. He musn't be allowed to sink into obscurity, eclipsed by Oppenheimer, Teller, Fermi and the rest. His papers have been missing for fifty years and you are the link. For my research, and for the memory of your brother's achievements, I would be grateful to see them.

You're the only person alive who can help me.'

The shepherd moved to a dresser and opened a drawer. They waited expectantly. Out came a jar, and a pipe was filled with dark tobacco. He puffed slowly at it, and a blue billowing haze began to drift round the little room. Then he returned to the table and spoke to the driver, who started to shake his head aggressively. A lively conversation followed.

Finally Romella turned to Findhorn: 'The old man says he doesn't possess such documents. He's lying. That fool of a driver is antagonizing him. It's some political thing.'

Findhorn assimilated this, and Romella continued: 'He's also telling us that even if he had them, possession would have been dangerous in the days of the Soviet Union. He'd have been expected to hand them over to the authorities and even then he might have ended up in a gulag. I think he's afraid, his mind is still set in the old ways.'

'He thinks he'll get into trouble if he admits to having them?'

Romella nodded. 'That's my interpretation.' But an angry exchange was going on between Clark Gable and the shepherd. Then the old man was on his feet again. He crossed to the dresser, opened another drawer, and turned with a medal which he laid on the table with a flourish. The driver made a remark, clearly insulting, and the shepherd replied in a withering tone of rage and contempt.

Findhorn sat bewildered, trying to make sense of it. But the bottom line was clear. If the old man had the Petrosian documents, he wasn't about to admit the fact. 'Okay, we're getting nowhere. Forget it.'

'What?'

'We're upsetting him.'

'Excuse me? Fred, would you keep your eye on the ball? Somewhere in this house, within yards of us, is a document which would make the Count of Monte Cristo look like a case for social security. It'll revolutionize the future. And you want to give up on it?'

The shepherd and the driver were now snarling angrily at each other. Findhorn raised his voice over the noise. 'He's scared of the authorities.'

'So let's threaten him with them.'

'He probably thinks we are the authorities and this is a sting. Look, Romella, this is out of control. He just needs reassuring that we're okay people. Let's clear off and try again later without that idiot driver.'

Romella looked at the angry exchange and reluctantly nodded her agreement. She tapped the driver on the shoulder, and said something to the old man in a conciliatory tone.

The driver made some remark to the shepherd which had the effect of further infuriating the old man. Romella said, 'Get out!' sharply in English, and turned to the door.

Clark Gable's driving was jerky and erratic, and he muttered and growled to himself all the way back to the Hotel Dvin. Findhorn felt queasy and decided to skip lunch. Romella agreed with surprising readiness, given the urgency, and Findhorn stretched out on his hotel bed, letting the breeze blow in through the open balcony door.

He had lain on the bed, dozing, for a good hour before a simple but shocking possibility occurred to him. It came in a half-dream, based on an old made-for-TV movie about the Count of Monte Cristo. The half-dream had all the costume pieces and the wigs and the absurd haughty faces of both sexes, but the man playing the Count was a woman, Romella, and Findhorn suddenly opened his eyes and stared at the flies on the ceiling and realized that his travelling companion might not be averse to a little private enterprise followed by a lifestyle which put the Count of Monte Cristo in the shade.

He knocked on Romella's door and had the familiar sinking feeling in his stomach, and he put the hour's delay down to his Calvinistic upbringing, the constant tendency to assume the best of humanity in the face of overwhelming evidence to the contrary.

A taxi, hastily summoned at the front desk, took him back out of the city, Findhorn directing from memory. An hour later, turning into the stony track, his heart sank when he saw a small blue car parked beside the shepherd's Skoda. He motioned the driver to stop about fifty yards back from the cottage. The lack of a mutual language gave the driver no means to express his surprise other than by exaggerated eye movements.

It was late afternoon and the little living room now looked dull. A smell of burnt cooking now overlaid the aroma of tobacco. Otherwise the room was much as Findhorn had left it except for a few grey bricks which had been removed from above the stove and were lying on the floor in amongst chips of plaster and dust. The cavity so revealed had about the same dimensions as Findhorn's safety deposit box in Edinburgh. It contained a legal-looking document which to Findhorn looked like a will or property deeds. It also contained a small bundle of banknotes, neatly tied by string. Whoever had raided the cavity had not been interested in the money.

Findhorn picked his way over the man's corpse – the face and tongue were purple and the eyes, bulging from the ligature round his neck, were staring at the ceiling – and found a bread knife in the kitchen. A pot of beans had almost boiled dry and Findhorn switched it off. Back in the living room, he used the knife to cut a small handful of white hair from the shepherd's head. He put this hair in his shirt pocket, used a handkerchief to wipe clean every surface that he had touched. He raised Romella gently from her chair by the elbow.

His first thought had been that she had strangled the man, but he quickly put the absurdity out of his mind. She clutched him for some moments, desperate for secure human contact. He said, 'Better dry your eyes.' Then they were out, Findhorn closing the front door with the handkerchief, and taking her by the hand. The driver was leaning against the side of his car, about halfway through a cigarette.

The American was drinking beer in a quiet corner of the big entrance foyer of the Dvin. Findhorn returned the man's wave, keeping on the move. He took the elevator to the seventh floor with Romella, quickly gathered up his worldly goods. They headed down the stairs just as the elevator door was opening and checked out, retrieving their passports.

They flew back in a shiny new Airbus, the flagship of Armenian Airlines. It had, he knew, a service contract, state-of-the-art navigation, microchips with everything. Canned music soothed him, and the hostesses were smiling and elegant and smelled delicious. His safety belt worked and the toilet door locked.

He looked down at Ararat, the biblical mountain, and the white-capped Little Caucasus Range; beyond them, in a light haze, was Georgia and the endless expanse of the Russian Federation. London was only four hours away. He regretted that, in his haste to flee the assassins, he had taken the first and only flight to Heathrow instead of going via Paris or Amsterdam or Coonabarabran or Outer Mongolia.

Findhorn downed two bloody marys, but the images of violent death wouldn't go away. He stopped himself asking for a third.

It wasn't just that the bad guys had won the race for the secret.

It was also that he was a loose end; he could talk. And even with the deficiencies of the Armenian telephone network, his flight number would by now be known, arrangements would by now have been made.

'Why did you go back?' he asked.

Her eyes were still red. 'Isn't it obvious? Three of us were a threat, especially that idiot driver. I thought if I went back alone I could talk to him gently. Fred, he was still warm to the touch. It was horrible.'

It was practically their first exchange of words in three hours. He squeezed her hand.

It would, perhaps, look like an accidental encounter, something as innocent as a shared taxi with a stranger. Or they might use someone he knew and trusted.

Beside him, Romella stared morosely out of the window, and Findhorn wondered.

26

Escape

Like Newton's apple, it took a collision to jog Petrosian into a new thought. He mumbled an apology to the man with the newspaper, watched him as he hurried off, and then turned into the newsagent's.

And he didn't even have to buy a newspaper: there were a dozen cards stuck on a pin-board, and one of them said:

Pierce-Arrow V12 Model 53 Roadster 6500 c.c. whitewalled tires servo-assistid breaks resently resprayed padded dash new chrome bumpers spots recent overhaul 50000 miles $500 o.n.o. ask for Tom.

The apartment door was opened about two inches. A dark eye surveyed him suspiciously. The girl, he thought, had beautiful eyelashes.

'Hi. Can I speak to Tom?'

'Maybe he ain't hair.' There was a scuffling sound from the rear of the flat. Petrosian glimpsed a naked black youth running between rooms. The girl said, 'He doan get up at this time, mister.'

'It's about his car.'

'He get up for that.'

The door closed.

It was opened again two minutes later by the youth tucking a shirt into his jeans, who sauntered out of the building to a builder's yard, Petrosian in tow.

And there it was, spare wheel attached to its side, a running board along its length, new chrome bumpers and painted a gleaming black.

'How does it run?'

'Like a dream, mister.'

'I mean, is it reliable?'

'Hey, I ain't never had a day's trouble with it.' The youth was a picture of injured innocence. On the other hand he wasn't offering a trial run.

Petrosian pretended to examine the car. The tyres were bald, and a patch of canvas was beginning to show through one of them.

'What's the mileage?'

'Fifty thou.'

Petrosian looked inside. The driver's seat was sagging and pedals were worn smooth; he estimated that it had done four or maybe five times that distance.

'You're asking for five hundred dollars?'

'Yassuh, faive.'

No time to waste haggling. But if I don't haggle it looks suspicious.

'Okay. But make it four.'

'Hey, I's a poorist, I cain't make charitable donations. I need four seventy five for this piece of luxury.'

'Four twenty-five, then.'

'Done for four fifty, mister. Cash, right?'

Anastas's air fare, Petrosian thought.

'Jürgen?'

'Hey, old pal.'

'They're onto me.'

'Don't say another word. Just listen. It's fixed up for tomorrow night, ten o'clock.'

Petrosian's voice was filled with dismay. 'Tomorrow? I won't last that long.'

'I said just listen.'

'All right, where?'

'A place you know, Lev, a lake where you once thought the planet would overheat. Now my phone's tapped and your call is being traced. So get off the line and get the hell out of there.'

Jesus. 'Thanks, Jürgen.'

'A night and a day, Lev, just hold out for a night and a day.'

'What about you?'

'I got a four-minute start on them. If I don't make it, say hello to the Motherland for me.'

There was a faint, peculiar click on the line. But Petrosian was on Interstate 93, and merged with the heavy evening traffic flowing towards Boston in less than a minute.

'It has been set up?'

'Yes, sir.'

'Nothing can go wrong?'

'Absolutely not. The Corporation need have no fear.'

'You had better be right, for all our sakes. Tonight, I will pray for his soul.' The Chairman sipped at his white wine with satisfaction. 'A good Orvieto is hard to beat, unless it is a better Frascati. And what about his secret?'

'He has been carrying a large briefcase around since he fled. It never leaves his hand. It will of course disappear along with him.'

Something in the man's body language. The Chairman said, 'Was there anything else?'

'There is one thing, a small item.'

The Chairman went still. In his long experience of life, it was small items which brought empires crashing down. 'Well?'

'Within the last hour, I'm told that the FBI have picked up his trail.'

'Yes?'

'He is very close to the Canadian border. If he crosses it . . .'

The Chairman continued: 'The FBI will have no jurisdiction.'

'Precisely, sir. They would have to cross the border illegally.'

The Chairman relaxed. The man worried too much; a line on a map was indeed a small matter. 'I will speak to Mister Hoover. But be assured, he understands the force of necessity.'

Exhausted, Petrosian saw the lights of a small town.

He had to eat, had to drink, had to sleep.

He had taken the Pierce-Arrow V12 Model 53 Roadster with whitewall tyres six hundred miles east while the faint engine tap gradually intensified until it turned into the deafening clatter of a crankshaft trying to tear loose. The Pierce-Arrow was a twenty-year-old car and bound to attract attention; in Petrosian's case, a Pierce-Arrow with a big end hammering out over the countryside was an invitation to the electric chair. Somewhere past Grand Rapids he had finally lost his nerve, turned off the highway onto some rural road, and driven the car for another fifty miles until steam began to pour out of the overheated engine. He drove it, without lights, as far as he could take it into a wood, and ditched it.

He wished he'd taken the time to look for a Model T.

There was one piece of good fortune. Through the trees, he could see Lake Michigan sparkling in the distance.

There were no buses that early and Petrosian could only have cleared off on foot or by train. The New York express had just left by the time they got to the station and it had taken a lot of phone calling to cover the halts. It was another half-hour by the time a dim-witted young railwayman at Ploughkeepsie identified Petrosian: the spy, they assumed, must have a cool nerve to get off at the adjacent station.

A saturation search of the town revealed no sign of the spy; neither had he taken a bus, called a taxi or hired a car. However, a trawl of early morning shops had turned up a newsagent who recognized him. The man had entered his shop, looked at the cards on the wall and left without buying anything. He'd only noticed the guy because he looked a bit foreign and had seemed in an agitated state.

One of the cards advertised a car for sale. Tom Clay, a local delinquent, denied any involvement in the liquor store heist the previous week and informed them that the Colt 45 in the drawer was being held for a friend. However he readily admitted to selling the Pierce-Arrow to a weirdo with more money than sense.

By the time an APB had been issued, the spy could have been anywhere within a hundred and fifty mile radius, which encompassed such conurbations as New York City, Boston and Philadelphia. Common sense dictated that he would by now have ditched such a conspicuous car and be on a Pullman or a Greyhound to anywhere. It was therefore a wonderful piece of good fortune that a routine tap on his controller, Rosenblum, turned up a brief conversation with Petrosian. The trace told them that he was in all probability heading for Boston.

Except that the spy knew the call was being traced. Therefore unless he was really stupid – and the agents had to assume that an atomic scientist wasn't – he would be heading in some other direction. This being the north-east of the United States, he had somewhat limited options. He might head for Portland, Concord or Albany, or of course he could be trying for Canada, across the border to Montreal. The St Lawrence River was a barrier which could only be crossed at a handful of places, such as Sherbrooke or Niagara Falls.

There was one further piece of information: he had a

rendezvous at a lake. In that case he would be heading west, towards one of the Great Lakes. He would then be on the I–90 which, being a toll road, meant that he would easily be picked up, say at Syracuse or Buffalo.

As the hours passed and no news came in, it became increasingly likely that he had slipped the net. But the information about the lake was so clear that it had to be assumed he was by now on one of the towns or villages bordering Lakes Superior, Michigan, Huron, Erie or Ontario.

'A lake where you once thought the planet would overheat.' It might be weird, but it had a vaguely nuclear sound about it. Maybe somebody in the AEC or Army Intelligence could shed some light, maybe even some of his longhair colleagues would help assuming they weren't all bleeding-hearted commies.

They had until ten o'clock tomorrow to catch this guy.

The briefcase was like a lead weight, no matter which hand he held it in. He wandered along the main street, keeping an eye out for police and attracting the occasional curious glance from passers-by. The door of a neon-lit bar opened as he passed, and he was enveloped in a wonderful stream of hot, beery air. A spicy food smell reminded him that he hadn't eaten all day. Further along the street he passed a hotel. He caught a glimpse of the dining room. A couple of blond children were watching delightedly as a waiter poured flames over their steaks. Then the door had swung shut and he was tramping on through the snow.

He had the money, US dollars. He too could eat a steak

diane flambé; he too could spend the night in a warm, comfortable bed.

It was much too dangerous. The FBI could be checking hotels in the area. Even by walking on the main street, with suit and briefcase at this time of night, he was taking a terrible risk. But to stay out overnight, in some park, was to risk death by exposure. Already the bitter cold seemed to be numbing his spine.

Near the edge of the town, the shops and bars petered out. There was a dark lake, reflecting lights from the far shore. An esplanade ran alongside it, and on the side away from the lake was a scattering of terraced houses and waterfront hotels. A couple of hundred yards ahead, a pier projected out. A cluster of motor boats and yachts was moored alongside the pier, the masts of the yachts swaying gently.

The oldest urge of all – the urge to survive – brought a desperate thought to Petrosian's mind.

This far from town, the road was deserted. He crossed to the waterfront, climbed over a rail and walked along the pebbled shore, to be invisible from the houses. At the pier he climbed up slippery stone steps and walked along it, looking down at the moored vessels.

Petrosian knew nothing about boats. He guessed that the motor boats would be started by ignition keys and that the owners would keep these at home. His eye was drawn to one of the yachts; in the dark it seemed blue. '*The Overdraft*' was written on its side. Suddenly the cold and exhaustion were just too much to bear and Petrosian went down the smooth, treacherous steps, gripping the rusty handrail to keep balance, and then he was on the yacht.

There was nobody in sight. There was a little trapdoor and a steep flight of stairs. Down these, he groped around, adjusting his eyes to the dark. There was a strong smell of diesel. He could make out, from the little frost-covered portholes which lined the walls, that the cabin curved inwards. As his eyes adapted to the dark he could make out a sofa, cupboards, a galley, and the door to another little room which he assumed was a toilet.

A galley meant a stove and heat. He scrabbled through drawers and found a near-empty box of matches. Experimenting, he soon had propane gas hissing on a ring. He struck the first match. It promptly fizzled out. Suddenly realising there were only two matches left, he took great care with the second only to find the phosphorus head splitting off with a fizzle.

The last match was now the most important thing in Petrosian's universe. He struck it carefully, firmly but not too harshly. It lit, flickered, started to die. He tilted it, cupping his hands round it, brought it to the hissing gas. There was a pop and the gas lit, throwing a blue light around the little cabin. Petrosian was too weary to laugh or cry.

At the front of the cabin were two bunks, built into the side. There were folded sheets, and wooden planks, and cushions. In a minute Petrosian had made them into a bed. He flopped on the edge of it, watching the gas flame as if it hypnotized him.

In a minute the cabin had warmed. He threw off his

suit, just had the presence of mind to turn off the gas, slid between icy sheets and in moments fell into the sleep of utter exhaustion.

27

DNA

Past the passport control, Findhorn looked warily at the humanity in transit around him. He steered Romella towards a quite corner. She looked at him in surprise but said nothing.

Findhorn licked dry lips. He said, 'Ten men on the berg. Then Hansen. And now Petrosian's brother. Twelve dead and I'm on Matsumo's hit list. Maybe even the CIA's, if they kill people. I don't see any way out of this. What's my survival time, Romella?'

'Fred, don't crack up now.'

'Somebody has Petrosian's secret, and we haven't a clue about it. Where does that leave us?'

Romella stayed silent, and Findhorn continued, his stomach knotted. 'And where do you come into this, Romella? Have you made an alliance with someone?'

'It's not the way it looks,' Romella said. She added, 'Fred, you have to trust me.'

'Why?'

He found the coolness in her voice disturbing: 'You have no other choice.'

Two armed policemen were strolling at the far end o

the terminal. Findhorn found reassurance in the sight. 'There may be people here who want to do me harm.'

She put her arm in his. 'We can lose them.'

Three taxis and an hour later, they found themselves a small table in the Black Swan near Egham, overlooking the Thames. Findhorn came back with coffees. 'We've lost the game, right?' It was his first remark since the airport.

Her face was grim. 'How can I put this gently? If we have, you're dead.'

Findhorn stared.

She poured the coffee. 'How can Matsumo be sure you haven't worked out the Petrosian secret from the diaries, enough to put a patent together? He almost has to erase you some time in the next day or two. What choice does he have, Fred? Believe me, you're being intensively hunted.' She scanned his face closely. 'By the way, *have* you worked out the secret?'

Over Romella's shoulder, he saw an elderly couple clambering out of a motor launch at a lock. They were doing things with a tow rope but didn't seem very sure of themselves. A small black mongrel on the cabin roof was watching them with interest.

'And where do you stand?'

She was spreading butter on a scone. 'I'm a translator.'

'I want to trust you.'

Romella stayed silent, then said, 'You're keeping something back.'

'It's true.'

She took a bite at the scone. 'Fred, why did you cut a piece of hair from Anastas?'

'Petrosian wasn't on that plane.'

Romella froze, coffee cup halfway to her lips.

'There were two bodies in that wreckage. The pilot's body was at the controls, and the other body wasn't that of Petrosian.'

'Don't worry, Fred, I'll look after you. I'm beginning to like you.'

'The body in question was blue-eyed. Petrosian was trans-Caucasian, an Armenian with Turkish and Persian ancestry. His eyes would have been brown.'

'And you've been keeping this to yourself from day one?'

'I also kept back a corner of a diary cover. It has dried blood on it. And here, as you say –' he tapped his top pocket '– I have a clip of hair from Anastas Petrosian's body. I'm going to try for a DNA comparison.'

'Fred, how did you see inside that iceberg? There were lights, right?'

'Yes, arc lights. And there was a torch. His face was a foot away from mine.' The memory of the hideous face came back to Findhorn.

Behind her round spectacles, Romella's brown eyes were a picture of scepticism. 'Doesn't ice look blue in a strong light? Maybe it was playing tricks on you.'

'Some day I'll write a book about what ice looks like and what it does. Meantime the eye was blue and that wasn't Petrosian. I don't know what happened on that

Canadian lake. But somehow Petrosian's diaries climbed on board and he didn't.'

'Maybe they threw him out over the north pole.'

'My bet is he just vanished into the woods. Maybe he made a deal with the Russians. Atomic secrets – maybe *his* secret – in exchange for a new identity. They were fooling the FBI into thinking he'd vanished behind the Red Curtain. The old Petrosian dead, the new one starting a fresh life.'

She acquired a thoughtful look. 'Let's go along with your fantasy for a moment. Do you propose we search for one man who's been missing for fifty years, somewhere on the planet? Someone who'd been given a fresh identity and is therefore totally untraceable? Who's probably now dead? And if he's alive and we find him, what then? Do you think he'll just reveal all, assuming he's not totally gaga by now?'

Behind Romella, the motor launch, the couple and the dog were sinking below eye level. The dog was yapping excitedly, tail wagging. Under the table, her foot rubbed against his leg.

'Hello, is that the Hsü Clinic?'

'Yaais.' Middle-aged female, stockbroker-belt English. Findhorn visualised heavy-frame spectacles, hair tied up in a bun, a disapproving mouth.

'I want to check up on the relationship between two people.'

At first, Findhorn thought he had been switched over to a machine: 'Thank you for calling the Hsü Clinic your requests are treated in strict confidence results from our state of the art AB1377 automated DNA sequencer have been accepted as evidence of identity in over a thousand United Kingdom court cases you may post or call in personally with samples the procedure takes about three weeks we can confirm paternity with 99.99 per cent confidence in most cases or non-paternity with absolute certainty our terms are cash in advance.'

'I have biological samples from both.'

'Yaais. What is the nature of the relationship to be tested paternity is two hundred pounds everyone else three fifty except zygotic twins which we can do for a hundred pounds plus VAT.'

'Brothers.'

'Is this for an intended legal action?'

'No, it's purely personal, for a family tree enquiry. From one party I have a small sample of hair, from the other I have a square centimetre of dried blood from a fifty-year-old book.'

A brief silence, and then the machine switched back to human mode. 'Oh my good life! Are we in Agatha Christie territory, then?'

'Nothing so dull.'

Another pause, while Ms Stockbroker assessed this answer. Findhorn filled the silence by saying, 'I need the answer by tomorrow.'

'Most of our clients need it by yesterday. The waiting list is six weeks.'

'Tomorrow will do.'

The voice acquired a frosty edge. 'DNA sequencing is a

skilled and time-consuming process and the results may have medico-legal consequences the sample preparation alone . . .'

'I'll call in later today with the samples and a thousand pounds cash.'

'I look forward to that, sir. You should have the results by this evening. You did say *two* thousand pounds?'

Romella found an Internet café in Staines. A handful of men and women, mostly young, were typing at terminals: a couple of female students on a project, a legal type peering at some turgid document, a schoolboy scanning a job list. She sat down next to a young man wearing earphones who, his face a caricature of intensity, was travelling through labyrinths, encountering strange and hostile creatures which he destroyed by tapping at the keyboard at amazing speed. She logged in to a search engine and typed 'holocaust + survivors'. Within minutes, as Romella clicked her way through infinitely darker labyrinths, she found herself sucked into a world more lunatic and unreal than that of her troll-fighting neighbour. She emerged, disturbed, into the sunlight an hour later, and took comfort in the normality of her surroundings, the shops, the bridge over the Thames, even the heavy afternoon traffic. She caught a red bus into central London and a tube to the Elephant and Castle. By the time she reached the address she had found on the Internet, it was dark, she was cold, and London was experiencing its first flurry of winter snow.

* * *

And by the time Findhorn emerged from the Leicester Square crowds, it was almost ten o'clock and Romella was frozen to the bone.

He dispensed with social preliminaries. 'Petrosian never got on that Russian plane. How did you get on?'

'Apart from being propositioned three times in the last hour? It was pathetic. The bulletin boards were the worst. You know, somebody in Romania asking his sister, last seen in Dachau, to get in touch, as if he hopes that some eighty-year-old granny will be surfing the Web . . .'

'Romella, calm down. It's all in the past.'

'I've always seen it that way. But for some people the pain's still here, right now.'

'Okay. Let's get you some place warm.' Findhorn took her by the arm and guided her towards the nearest cinema. 'Where are you staying tonight?'

'With you. Please.'

A surge of excitement went through Findhorn, quickly followed by a feeling of guilt brought on by the thought that to agree would be to exploit her unsettled state. 'We'll talk about that. And you can tell me what you found.'

'We'll talk about it? With men like you, Fred, how do we win our wars?'

They sat at the back of the cinema, and for two forgetful hours ate popcorn and drank orange juice, while warmth seeped into their bones and the Son of Godzilla rampaged through New York streets.

28

The Archivist

'There are no lists, there is no central registry. But depending on the time and money available to you, there are several places you could start looking,' said the archivist.

'Money isn't a problem,' Findhorn said, 'time is.'

'Some people have been trying to trace survivors for sixty years.'

'We have about sixty hours. Maximum.'

The archivist's mouth showed disapproval. 'If this were a subject for jokes, I would say that is a very bad one.'

'We have to try,' Findhorn said.

'What can possibly make the quest so urgent?'

'You don't want to know.'

The archivist looked at Findhorn curiously. Then, 'Which camp was she sent to?'

'I don't know.'

She sighed. 'If you could tie down the date on which she was transported, you might find some information in Nazi archives, say the ones held by the USA in the Berlin Documentation Centre, or by the French archive in the *Wehrmachtauskunftstelle*, which is also held in Berlin.

The Nazis liked to document everything. In fact they were quite meticulous.'

'Is there really no central point for information?'

She smiled tolerantly, to smooth the sharpness in her voice. 'What did you expect, a survivors' coffee club? If you had a few months to spare, I might have suggested that you go to Europe. You could have tried the Rijksinstituut voor Oorlogsdocumentatiae in Amsterdam or the Centre Documentation Juive Contemporaire in Paris. There is the Weiner Library only a couple of Underground stops away from here. In the States there is the Center for Holocaust Studies in Brooklyn as well as the Simon Wiesenthal Institute in Los Angeles, and there are centres in Washington and Chicago. Or of course you could have tried to gain access to the archives of Yad Vashem in Jerusalem.'

Findhorn's experience of information retrieval was search engines on the Internet, specialist librarians with a same-day response time, huge centralized databases with point-and-click access. The impossibility of the task was beginning to sink in.

The archivist was still talking. 'You will find two things in common about all these places. One, the staff are understanding and sympathetic. Two, names are jealously guarded. The pain is private to those who survived, not something for public intrusion. And as I said, there are no formal lists of survivors, only people who chose to share their memories with these places.'

'The flying time alone—' Romella started to say.

'—is the least of your worries. The procedures for

gaining access to documentation are often cumbersome and time-consuming. A letter of introduction is always helpful.' The archivist leaned back in her chair and looked at them over steepled hands. 'What information exactly do you have about this Lisa Rosen?'

Romella said, 'She was a student at Leipzig University in 1933, when she was aged about twenty. She was arrested and disappeared in 1939.'

The archivist's eyebrows were raised expectantly. She fingered her gold necklace, waiting. Then she said, 'And?'

'That's it.'

She shook her head, almost amused. 'Let's try anyway.'

They were in a room stacked with filing cabinets, tapes, discs, books, papers and a computer with printer and scanner attached. She led them to a cabinet, pulled open a drawer marked R–S and began on a card catalogue.

It produced ten Lisa Rosens.

'Understand these are ten who survived, emigrated and chose to tell their stories to us. The great majority of Lisa Rosens simply did not survive. This alone tilts the odds heavily against you. Of those who did get through, most emigrated to Israel or the States, not here. And most of those who came here have kept their stories to themselves or their families, or at most shared them with small survivor groups.' She paused, looking at them with a degree of sympathy. 'Even in the unlikely event that she survived, in all probability she will never be found. And you will certainly not trace her in three days.'

'We have to,' said Findhorn.

Romella looked through the cards. 'None of them fit.

Munich, Berlin, Dryans, wherever that is. Oh, here's a Leipzig, a girl who survived Theresienstadt.'

'Twelve years old at liberation,' the Archivist pointed out.

'What about Willy Rosen, her brother?'

There were nine Wilhelm Rosens. None of them fitted.

'Okay,' Findhorn said with a tone of finality. 'Thanks for your trouble.'

She took them through a room with three busy secretaries and walls covered with blown-up photographs of pyramids of hair, of human-packed cattle trucks, of skeletal creatures in striped tunics. At the exit she said, 'You could try Leipzig itself, perhaps tracing contacts through the University admissions records. 'I've known people make surprising progress with telephone directories.'

They stepped out of the door, stunned, and found themselves in a cold London morning, sixty years in the future. They made their way to a tube entrance. Businessmen were queuing to buy newspapers. Two old men at a bus stop were having a spirited argument over some football match. The street had a trattoria, a café, a video shop, an amusement arcade, closed at this early hour. There was an air of unreality, even triviality, about it all. Reality lurked behind the camera-protected door they had just left, in the mementos and the papers and the whispered tales on the tapes. In spite of the sunshine, the air was sharp and cold.

Romella found a telephone booth and insisted that Findhorn stay out of earshot. She spoke earnestly for a couple of minutes while Findhorn flapped his arms for warmth. Then she put down the receiver and they started to walk briskly towards Piccadilly. 'Okay. Doug wants you to phone him. He thinks he's onto something with the green Merc. I've started Stefi on the Leipzig problem. To save time I'm going straight there.'

'You go to Leipzig. I'm heading for Japan.'

They were on a pedestrian crossing. She stopped, looking at Findhorn in astonishment. 'You're mad.'

'Matsumo and I may make an alliance. He wants this thing killed.'

'You want to bet your life on that?'

A blue Mazda hooted impatiently. They moved off the road. Findhorn said, 'If you'd sunk twenty billion dollars looking for oil in the Arctic, would you want your investment undercut with a free energy machine?'

'Killing Petrosian's secret isn't in the deal,' she said angrily.

'The deal is irrelevant. I'm beginning to think that whatever Petrosian discovered could set the planet alight.'

Romella's face was grim. 'You don't know that for sure either. What right do you have to take a decision that could affect the whole planet?'

'What right do I have to pass it on? Petrosian didn't. This is contingency planning in case we have to move fast. First we need to find the secret.'

'I'd mention the fortune it could make you except that you'd start flaunting your damned principles.'

A sudden shower of freezing rain was sending Leicester Square pedestrians scurrying in all directions. They carried on, oblivious. Findhorn said, 'It's Mission Impossible, Romella, but somehow you'll have to find Petrosian within forty-eight hours if he's still alive. By that time I should be back from Kyoto and we can take it from there.'

Romella's next comment was like a blow to Findhorn's stomach. 'If you're going to kill the secret, you'll have to kill whoever is holding it.'

'I know.'

'You can't do it, right?'

Findhorn stayed silent. 'But it's okay to hand the job over to someone else.'

The silence was painful, but Romella pursued the point ruthlessly. 'You need somebody killed, Fred? The Whisky Club people can do that. You don't need to deliver yourself to Matsumo's gangsters.' Romella waved at a taxi. 'You'll end up in the Sea of Japan.'

The taxi had completed a U-turn in the busy street and was pulling up on a double yellow line. Fred said, 'He needs me as an ally.'

She shook her head. 'And once you're of no more use to him?'

'Don't think I haven't sweated over that. But what else can I do? Look, take me to that cybercafé in Staines. It's practically on the way.'

Findhorn, attuned to subtle intonations in his brother's voice, knew immediately that Doug had something to say. 'Fred? Have I got news for you! How many green Mercs were sold in Switzerland over the past eighteen months?'

'Two? Five thousand?'

'A hundred and sixty. And how many of these were 600 SL's?'

'Ten.'

'Eighteen. The cars were sold to a couple of lawyers, a rich widow, one over-the-hill actor, two restaurateurs etcetera. And one was a company car registered to a Konrad Albrecht, General Manager of a firm called Rexon Optica in Davos.'

'Davos? Isn't that—'

'It is, not far from the Temple of Celestial Truth. Rexon Optica specializes in making holographic guidance systems for a variety of NATO SAMs as well as for the Mark Three Eurofighter.'

Findhorn's silence was so long that Dougie had to ask, 'Are you there, Fred?' Then Findhorn said, 'This is desperately thin.'

'There's more. I've been using a PI firm—'

'Dougie, I'm catching a plane.'

'Okay, bottom line. Konrad Albrecht also has a ranch in Dakota where, surprise, surprise, the cult just happens to have its other main temple. He has a flat in Monaco and a holiday home in the Southern Uplands, which, surprise cubed, is where he's been staying over Christmas, complete with the company car.'

'Are you tying him in with the Temple?'

'He could even be their leader, Tati. Nobody outside the cult has seen him.'

'Doug, I have to fly. I need one more thing from you.'

'What's that?'

'A burglar. I'll call you tomorrow.'

Dougie was starting to splutter but Findhorn put the receiver down.

Findhorn's e-mail was brief and went to the Head Office, Matsumo Holdings, Chairman, for the attention of:

'I will be in London, Heathrow, in thirty minutes, and will then take the next available flight to Kyoto. I do not know which flight that is. Can I be met? Findhorn.'

They hardly exchanged a word during the taxi ride. Black and white images from the past kept flickering in and out of Findhorn's mind like old newsreels, interspersed with fantasies involving Japanese gangsters and the Sea of Japan.

Terminal Two was packed with Christmas travellers. Check-out queues straggled across the floor like big snakes. They scanned the flight departures. As if by some psychic force, the screen threw up an early afternoon flight for Osaka, courtesy of KLM. Findhorn said, 'Osaka's not too far from Kyoto. If there's a seat, that's my bus.'

Romella was looking worried. 'I just hope we meet again, Fred.'

Findhorn grinned nervously. 'That sounds like a line from a wartime romance.'

'Where will we rendezvous, in the event you survive your meeting with Matsumo?'

'Leave a message on my e-mail. But remember it will probably be read by others.'

'Be very careful, Fred.' Without warning she put her arms round his kneck and kissed him voluptuously on the lips, pushing her pelvis hard up against his. Then she pushed him away and she was gone, melting into the crowds, and Findhorn stood flushed and disturbed, with his heart pounding in his chest.

At the KLM desk, a cheerful blonde Dutch woman said, 'Ah, Mr Findhorn, you were expected and there is a message for you,' and she handed over a ticket along with a typed message attached by a paper clip: 'A room has been reserved for you in the Siran Keikan, Kyoto.'

Siberia – black, vast and surreal, was overhung with mysterious curtains of red and green which had been shimmering for hour after hour in the sky above. The 747 had trundled along like a hedgehog crossing a car park, skirting the Arctic Circle on its route to Japan. Findhorn sipped his gin and tonic and looked in vain for lights thirty thousand feet below. He wondered what it was like on the ground; toyed playfully with fantasy images of a forced landing in the frozen tundra, starving passengers eyeing each other hungrily, timber wolves beyond the circle of light around dying embers; and he thought he would probably, in that situation, stand a better chance than he did now. He finished his drink, gave his legs a business-class stretch and yawned, while the big aircraft flew him at ten miles a minute towards Yoshi Matsumo and the Dark Ocean Society.

Stefi had performed a minor miracle . . .

There was a light drizzle as the aircraft touched down at Munich airport. Romella took a bus into the city centre. She watched schoolchildren horsing around, a young couple in brightly coloured clothes on bicycles, women with shopping bags pausing to chat. Between the sheer happy normality of it, and the lunatic world in which she had been immersed a few hours previously, she could make no connection whatsoever.

. . . she had picked up on an Armenian survivor called Victor . . .

Taking her cue from the twin-domed Frauenkirche, she walked north through the Ludwigstrasse before turning right onto the Maximilianstrasse. Light blazed from decorated department stores and the streets were busy with last-minute Christmas shoppers.

. . . who had known not only Petrosian and Lisa . . .

She had expected high-rise flats British style, awash with graffiti and urine and, following the directions, was surprised to find herself inside a small shopping mall. She entered a lift with a young couple and a pink baby asleep in a pram, and emerged on a corridor with deep pile carpet on the floor and expensive fabric on the walls.

. . . but also another mutual friend from their Leipzig days . . .

Number five was directly opposite. There was a small peephole and a nameplate. It said Karl Sachs, and she hoped that her acting ability would be as good as her German.

. . . whose name was Karl Sachs, a retired Jewish doctor who now lived in Munich with his wife.

The man who opened the door was wrinkled, white haired, with a light blue cardigan and pince-nez spectacles.

He gave a cautiously welcoming smile and said, 'Miss Dvorjak?'

Kansai Airport was like any other big airport except that it was also a big, rectangular island in the sea, connected to Osaka city by a long, narrow umbilical cord. There was no reception committee. With some difficulty, Findhorn found a train to Kyoto. It arrived when the timetable said it would. It was spotlessly clean, smooth and silent. The 'guards' were shapely young females who turned to smile and bow as they left each carriage. Findhorn thought about the UK railway system and returned their smiles.

The map showed the line passing through Osaka and Kyoto, but from the window there was no way to tell where one city ended and the other began: he was travelling through a megalopolis, a city made of cities. At Kyoto railway station he decided against heroism and hired a cab. He said, 'Siran Keikan,' and settled back.

In the hotel itself more shapely females bowed and shuffled and treated his cheap overnight bag like the Ark of the Covenant. He had a shower in a tiny bathroom, slipped into the hotel dressing gown and flaked out.

The representatives of the Friendship Society came for him at eight o'clock the next morning. There were two of them. They were polite, if economical with the friendship. They were young men in dark suits who either did not, or chose not to, speak English. Findhorn sat alone in the back of a big air-conditioned BMW which swept him quietly along the Shijo-Dori, past tall office blocks and expensive-looking department stores with names like Takashimaya and Fuji Daimaru, past swastika-covered shinto shrines and cyclists on pavements. Then they were out of town and onto a winding road, with trees on the right and a big expanse of water on the left.

The Friendship man turned and waved his hands at the lake. 'Biwa,' he barked.

Findhorn said okay and declined the offer of a Lucky. They passed a long, spectacular suspension bridge which looked familiar, and he remembered it as the one he had seen on the cover of Matsumo's Annual Report. Then they were into hilly, tree-covered territory, and the car was passing a middle-sized town, with wooden single-storeyed houses crowded together in narrow, cable-strung streets, and then there were flooded fields and tea bushes.

Some miles beyond the town, the car slowed and turned off up a hilly road. The driver turned into what looked like a cement works. Findhorn glimpsed the flickering blue of TV monitors through the slatted blinds of the big windows. Then the car was through the works and winding up a narrow, tarmacked path with a lawn on either side, interspersed with small manicured trees and wrestlers, holy men and geisha girls, laquered and life-sized.

The house was a simple one-storied affair. It comprised half a dozen or so simple buildings, all glass and unvarnished wood and verandas and pagoda-like roofs, linked by sheltered walkways and hump-backed bridges over still water, and surrounded by paths through lawns interspersed with miniature trees and stone lanterns. Through some tall trees Findhorn glimpsed what seemed to be a small golf course. A gardener with a long fishing net was scooping up leaves from a pond. He paid Findhorn no attention.

The car stopped and Mr Friendship opened Findhorn's door with a scowl. A middle-aged woman, in a traditional kimono and heavy-framed spectacles, was standing at the top of a flight of wooden steps. As Findhorn approached she smiled, bowed, said, '*O-agari kudasai*' and, to Findhorn's embarrassment, dropped to her knees, untied his shoe laces and slipped his feet into brown slippers.

There was a large, scented atrium, almost bare of furniture apart from a couple of low chairs, some vases with flowers, and a pedestal a few feet ahead of him. The pedestal had Kanji script written down it, and it was topped with a bust of a severe-looking, bald-headed character. And in case anyone had missed the point first time round, Matsumo stared down severely in oil from the wall on the left. Findhorn was suddenly struck by the resemblance to Ming the Merciless in an old Flash Gordon movie he'd seen as a boy. In the circumstances, the comparison brought him no comfort.

The woman led the way past the pedestal to a sliding paper door, and bowed as Findhorn entered. He had hardly noticed the Friendship Society men until they closed the door behind him.

The room was furnished with little more than a low table, on which a few magazines were neatly piled. There were no chairs, but thin, square cushions and tatami mats were scattered around the floor in a geometric pattern.

Delicate scents came from flowers in vases occupying the corners of the room. The walls were paper screens. One wall was taken up, floor to ceiling, by a bookcase, the opposite one by a number of unusual paintings.

Findhorn, tense and sensing danger, looked at the nearest one. It was a rectangle about four feet long, filled with what looked like half a dozen big whorls. They were light blue. Some were overlying others, partly obliterating them, while others seemed to merge, the lines at their edges running parallel. Here and there little thin fingers of lines tried to squeeze through their big brothers. As he looked, Findhorn began to make sense of the patterns, to detect a strange mixture of harmony and clashing, order and chaos. It was both peaceful and, as he looked, increasingly hypnotic.

'You are looking at the rolling waves of the sea.'

Findhorn turned, startled.

The gardener, alias Yoshi Matsumo.

Findhorn said, 'I thought I was seeing fingerprints.'

Matsumo's expression didn't change. He spoke in good Oriental English. 'How can I put this delicately? To understand the painting one needs, shall we say, a certain sensitivity, I suppose you could call it an awareness of artistic form. The painting is in the traditional style known as *Nihon-ga*. It is by Matazo Kayama, from Kyoto. He is a master of the style.'

Matsumo hadn't bowed, offered to shake hands, smiled or said *O-agari kudasai*. His words were polite; but his expression was that of a man who has just disturbed a burglar.

Matsumo continued, 'You have come a very long way, Findhorn-san. I believe you would benefit from a very long rest.'

Findhorn thought that maybe Matsumo's English wasn't perfect and that he didn't mean it the way it sounded.

29

Matsumo

'Look down there, young lady.' The doctor's hands waved over the city. 'And tell me what you see.'

Sachs and Romella were standing on a verandah, wine glasses in hand. They were high above a long main road, with car headlights drifting along in both directions; it was now almost dark. The Alps, low in the distance, formed a background to the church-scattered skyline. The sound of clattering dishes came from the kitchen.

Romella looked over the skyline of the mediaeval city. 'A stunning view. A lot of busy traffic. Big department stores. Hordes of people doing last-minute Christmas shopping.'

Sachs said, 'I look down and I see ghosts. It was along the *Ludwigstrasse* that the Brownshirts used to march, behind row after row of swastikas. There were children in Bavarian costumes, there were brass bands pounding out old Bavarian marching tunes. I feel a sense of dissociation.' His English was excellent, if accented. 'Somehow I'm just not part of what you see, the ghosts are my reality. But you can't understand what I mean.'

Maybe not.

362

He continued, 'Anyway, your interest is not in my life's journey, but in that of this Lisa woman. She survived.'

She survived! A thrill ran through Romella. 'How do you know?'

The old doctor smiled. 'I met her. It was through the grapevine, as I think you call it nowadays. She had been a good communist at the University, like me, as well as being Jewish. An acquaintance in medical school had heard of a survivors' group based in Leipzig – a handful of people, you understand. I made contact, and there she was, the only one of the group I knew. We swore to keep in touch, and have done so ever since.'

'She's still alive?'

'And happily married. We write to each other every year.'

Romella tried to keep the urgency out of her voice. 'I'd be extremely grateful if you could arrange a meeting.'

The doctor frowned; Romella held her breath. Then he was saying, 'Forgive me, I'm neglecting my wife. Misha, you should have called me. Why don't you sit down, *fraülein*, while I do my duty in the kitchen?'

The Friendship reps stood one on either side of the bathing-room door, presumably to intervene should Findhorn attempt to drown Yoshi Matsumo.

Findhorn sat chest-deep in the wooden tub, his clothes ostensibly removed for ironing but in reality, he suspected, to search for electronic devices. He was sweating in the painfully hot water, and any movement was painful. Steam billowed around the little room.

Matsumo, his expression openly hostile, contemplated Findhorn. 'I ask myself, did this man cross Asia to apologize in person for his theft of the Petrosian papers? He did not. Well then, has he come full of contrition, ready to give them to me? He has not. There are no papers in your luggage, nor did you deposit any between Kansai and Hikone.' He sipped at a small glass of saki and continued: 'There remain two possibilities. He has come to negotiate a sale with me, or he has come to blackmail me with the documents. On either count, I admire your courage if not your intelligence.'

'You're wrong on both counts. I'm here to propose an alliance.'

Matsumo's eyes peered into Findhorn's, looking for a trick. 'For what purpose? Why do you imagine I would possibly make an alliance with you?'

'Our interests coincide, at least momentarily. The secret has been taken from me.'

'What?' Ripples of hot water spread out from Matsumo. 'Who has taken the papers?'

'They were stolen from me by a man from Sirius.'

Matsumo's expression didn't change. Findhorn continued, 'The same man who intended to steal the process from you.'

'And have you identified this man from Sirius?'

'I have. He's an industrialist. And I have reason to believe he's assembling a team of engineers to announce the process and discuss the construction of a prototype machine. As soon as his engineers know about the basic process, the secret is out and can't be put back.'

'You see what you have done with your stupid theft?'

Findhorn ignored the angry comment. 'I intend to indulge in a little industrial espionage, in the hope of finding the where and when. I suspect that the meeting will take place somewhere in Switzerland, and that it will be held very shortly.'

Matsumo barked something. One of the Friendship men slid open a panel door, and they left. Shortly the woman, who Findhorn presumed to be Matsumo's wife, came in with towels. She was followed by a girl of about eighteen, dressed in the traditional kimono, carrying Findhorn's clothes, neatly ironed and folded. Matsumo's wife crossed to a circular paper panel door and slid the two halves open. Cool air drifted into the room and Findhorn found himself looking out over the garden, where a low table had been set next to a gingko tree. Matsumo climbed the steps out of the tub onto the tatami floor. He was pink up to his chest and had a wrinkled, drooping stomach and white pubic hair. His wife began to pat him dry with a big white towel. Findhorn, feeling acutely embarrassed, climbed out and wrapped a towel around himself, declining the girl's offer of help. The girl tried to keep a straight face.

Lunch comprised mixed *sashimi*, raw squid and salmon cut into rose shapes, with thick slices of tuna, served on heavily lacquered square plates. A sea bass, garnished with daikon radishes and lemon, stared mournfully up at Findhorn. The ladies had vanished and the Friendship bodyguards were standing motionless a discreet twenty yards away. Lake Biwa sparkled below them, and Findhorn followed the wake of a powerful hydrofoil out to a central island, on which he could just make out a clutter of shrines.

'As you are a Westerner, I assume that you are driven by greed,' Matsumo said. 'You must suppose that by telling me where I can retrieve the secret, you will be given a share of future profits from it.'

The air, cool after the scalding tub, was refreshing. Findhorn said, 'The process may be dangerously unstable. It might cause disaster on a planetary scale. It has to be strangled at birth.'

Matsumo's face registered no surprise. Findhorn continued: 'Maybe the risk is at the one per cent level, maybe it's one shot in a million. But the potential profits are vast and the man from Sirius is willing to take the slight chance.'

'And you object to this?'

'If the risk was his alone, fine. But he's taking a chance with the future of life on Earth in return for personal gain. Four billion years of evolution being gambled on the turn of a card. And if we're alone in the Galaxy . . .'

'Now I understand. You seek the Petrosian document in order to destroy it for altruistic reasons.'

Findhorn was finding the sea bass a bit awkward. 'As do you, for reasons of commercial greed.'

Matsumo's hostile expression was gradually giving way to something approaching respect. 'So. You have been investigating my company's affairs.'

'Uhuh. Especially Norsk Advanced Technologies.'

Matsumo studied Findhorn's face closely. He grunted. 'Either you are, as you would have me believe, an idealist intent on saving the planet, or you are a very clever buccaneer.'

'Let me guess the sequence of events. When the aircraft wreckage was exposed, you found yourself in a race with the Americans to get to it. You didn't want an open conflict with them and and so you asked the religious fanatics to do the job for you. You got them onto that expedition, intending the diaries to end up on your icebreaker. What was the inducement, Matsumo-sensei? A substantial sum of money?'

Matsumo remained silent.

'So far it's been all take and no give. Tell me what happened. What's your connection with the man from Sirius?'

Matsumo resumed his surgery with chopsticks. 'In the course of my long career one or two people have addressed me in that tone. Sadly, misfortune came their way.' He neatly pulled skin away from flesh. 'I knew the rumours about the slight risk of instability of the Petrosian secret but gave them no credence. How could any machine be so destructive? But I also knew that the Temple of Celestial Truth fanatics, with their distorted vision of reality, would believe it because they wanted it to be true. They would see the diaries as the route to a doomsday machine. That was the real inducement for them. The agreement was that they would acquire the diaries and give them to me, and I would then build them the machine.'

'Except that you had no intention of honouring the agreement. You intended to destroy the diaries,' Findhorn suggested.

'And the fanatics.'

'Let me guess some more. The leader of the cult double-crossed you. He no more believes it's unstable than do you. And he no more intends to hand over a fortune-making machine than he really believes he's from Sirius.'

'That would seem to be the case. I admit to a miscalculation. The man would seem to be a total fraud. I do not pretend to understand the psychology of religious leaders. However, you say that you have learned the identity of this wretch?'

'Is it possible to eat a fried egg with chopsticks?'

'Of course.' Matsumo snapped his fingers. The girl appeared with steaming white rice in delicate porcelain bowls. She set the plates out, brushing her arm lightly against Findhorn. She was wearing jade green eyeshadow and her eyes were accentuated by heavy black eye liner, and she gave Findhorn a slow, almost insolent, sultry glance. Matsumo caught the look and said something sharply. She scurried off, giggling behind her hand.

'If you are a clever buccaneer, you too will try to double-cross me at the first opportunity,' Matsumo said. 'Strangling the process at birth: you understand the implications?'

Findhorn nodded, the old familiar feeling creeping into his stomach. 'The industrialist in question has read the document. To kill the knowledge, you have to kill the man.'

'Not *I*, Findhorn-san. *We*. Only if you share the guilt can your future silence, and hence my security, be assured.' Matsumo was skilfully separating the spinal cord of the raw bass from its flesh. 'You must join my ninjas in the enterprise.'

'Oh God.'

'Are you prepared to do this?'

'To become a murderer? What choice do I have?' Findhorn heard the words from his own mouth, could hardly believe he was speaking them.

'And then there are the engineers.'

'They should be left alone. My man won't have dared to spread the process around. Security is everything. He'll announce the process at his meeting with them, probably cut them in on the profits to ensure their secrecy.'

Matsumo paused, flesh from the dead fish hovering at his mouth. 'That is what I would do. Then we had better get to your man before he meets them. If we wait until the meeting, everyone at it must be killed.'

'I'm having to grow up fast here,' said Findhorn, putting his chopsticks down.

'The morality of killing worries you, especially as we are not even in a war. But think, Findhorn-san. If you do not kill this wretched man, he will build a machine and risk the planet for personal gain. What morality is there in doing nothing to stop him taking that reckless chance? Your choice is this. Kill a man, or do not kill him. If you do, you become a murderer. If you do not, you connive in risking the termination of life on Earth.'

'I suspect you've been through this sort of consideration before.'

Matsumo shrugged. 'Most men never pass beyond the moral simplicities to be found in a western. Their minds are shaped by ignorant clerics and Hollywood producers. But the world belongs to men who understand the limitations of the morality tales.'

'I love it. Your powers of self-delusion. The way you put a cosy gloss on murder.'

Matsumo changed the subject. 'The girl who has been with you. She is not just a companion for cold nights.'

'She's been helping me with the diaries.'

'Come, Findhorn-san, she is more than a translator.'

Findhorn shrugged. 'I don't know who she represents. For a while I thought she had sold out to the Celestial Truth.'

'She is dangerous. She will try to steal the secret from both of us. Therefore she too must be disposed of. It is equally demanded by the logic.'

'The lady's not disposable.'

Matsumo didn't reply. But then, Findhorn thought, he doesn't have to.

'Of course as a Party member I had privileges, but it wasn't too long before I became completely disillusioned with the system. It was corrupt from top to bottom. The Party finally gave me permission to emigrate to Canada and I took it. I practised there for thirty years, in a little town called Kapuskasing.'

'That explains your excellent English.'

Sachs shook his head sceptically. 'You're too kind. I have a thick German accent. Anyhow, with children grown up and dispersed over three continents, we decided to return here. Misha's surviving family are Bavarian.'

'More potatoes?' They were practically the first words Misha had spoken. A small, rotund, domestic woman, she seemed content to let her husband do all the talking.

Romella smiled and patted her stomach. 'No, thank you.'

'You are too skinny,' Misha scolded.

'I will telephone Lisa now,' said Sachs. 'Forgive me, but you understand that we all preserve each other's privacy. I will explain that you are writing a thesis about German universities in the 1930s and would like to speak with her. I am almost certain she will say no. Please wait here.'

Sachs disappeared into a corridor. Romella waited some minutes. When he came back, the man's face was negative. 'I am sorry. She is very old, like all of us now, and although she still has a sharp mind, she does not want to relive that part of her life. She sends her apologies and wishes you luck with your thesis.'

Romella nodded. Sachs showed surprise at her apparent lack of disappointment and she cursed herself as a lousy actress.

The point of the visit had been achieved. The rest of the meal was spent in inconsequential conversation. She left an hour later, sincerely wishing them every good fortune and leaving an unopened bottle of wine on the table.

The compartment in the train back to the airport was quiet. She took the little van Eck monitor out of her handbag and switched it on. It worked! The number Sachs had dialled came up on the little screen. Romella quickly noted it down, for fear that the unfamiliar device, hastily purchased in the spy shop near Burlington Arcade, would suddenly crash. It was a UK number but she didn't recognize the city.

At Munich airport, she phoned through to International Enquiries. The address was in Lincoln but it wasn't in the name of Lisa Rosen.

Neither was it in the name of Lev Petrosian.

It was, however, in the name of one Len Peterson.

There were no available flights between Kansai and Europe before six-thirty the following morning. Findhorn refused the offer of a lift to Kyoto and instead took the hydro out to the sacred island in Lake Biwa. At the top of a few hundred steps he took in the Buddhist shrine, the burning joss sticks and the breathtaking view. He thought he could see Matsumo's home, sunlight glinting off the windows. Then, with darkness falling, he took the Keihan to Kyoto and wandered the crowded, brilliantly lit streets. More than once, without any visual evidence, he thought he was being followed; but he put the sensation down to his overstressed nervous system.

Away from the centre of town Findhorn followed a crowd and found himself on a path lined with paper lanterns. Yet another shrine, this one small. A mysterious ceremony was taking place, involving chanting priests, flutes, tinkling bells and sonorous drums. Feeling like an alien from another planet, he bought a coke at a stall and made his way back to the hotel.

He sat in a small office while the manager obligingl

typed in a password on a computer. There were two new messages on his e-mail:

> *Petrosian is alive and I know where he is. Meet me at Branston Hall, 5 miles out of Lincoln.*
> *Romella.*

Findhorn's brief burst of elation was abruptly cut short by the second message:

> *We have a mutual task to accomplish. Reply to this address with a rendezvous.*
> *Barbara Drindle.*

30

Lev Baruch Petrosian

They found the flat close to the Westgate, near the Toy Museum and within sight of the Castle. Findhorn followed Romella up the stairs, trying not to notice her well-shaped legs. There were three doors leading off the top landing. The right-hand door had a handwritten card in the nameplate holder: *L. Peterson*. Findhorn and Romella looked at each other. Then Findhorn took a deep breath and knocked.

The delay was so long that it began to seem there was nobody at home. But then there was a noise from inside and the door was opened by a white-haired woman with deeply wrinkled skin. She was in her eighties, and was a little stooped, but smartly dressed in a grey cardigan and long blue dress. She was wearing a gold necklace. 'Yes?'

'Mrs Peterson? My name is Fred Findhorn, and this is Romella Grigoryan. I wonder if we might have a word with your husband?'

Her voice was frail but clear, well-spoken but with just a hint of some foreign accent. 'You're not the telephone people.'

Findhorn patted his briefcase. 'We want to return some lost property.'

She frowned suspiciously. 'I did not think we had lost anything.'

'It was lost a long time ago.'

There was a hesitation as the woman absorbed this startling information. Then she opened the door further and said, 'You had better come in, then.'

She left them in a large, airy drawing room. The furniture was old but of good quality. There were no photographs. One corner of a bay window looked out over the city, framed by cathedral and castle. The other corner looked across at a flat whose windows were covered with stickers and pennants.

The man who entered the room was also white-haired and wrinkled. He had a grey pullover and rather shapeless flannels. His skin was brown, through heredity rather than suntan, and his eyes were dark and intelligent. He looked at his visitors with curiosity. His voice was quiet and clear, with just a trace of American. 'Sit down, please.' Findhorn and Romella shared a couch.

'Would you like some coffee?' Mrs Peterson asked at the door.

'Yes, thank you,' Romella said for both of them. 'Can I help?'

'I can manage.'

Mr Peterson sat down on a worn armchair opposite the couch Findhorn and Romella were on. 'Lost property, you said?'

It was the moment Findhorn had both dreaded and

anticipated. He opened the briefcase at his feet and pulled out the A4 sheets a bundle at a time, placing them on a low coffee table between them. He handed one bundle over at random; he had written '1945' on a transparent cover with a black felt tip pen. 'These are only copies, I'm afraid. But I think I know where the originals are held.'

Mr Peterson took spectacles from a shirt pocket and slowly put them on. He did not immediately open the document. He held it in both hands, looking at the date. His hands seemed a little arthritic. Then he gave Findhorn a long, disconcerting stare, a strange expression on his face. Finally he opened the diary and slowly flicked through the pages.

The sound of a kettle being filled came from the kitchen.

He stopped at a page halfway through the 1945 diary. 'That was some day. I remember it like yesterday: *At nine a.m. Louis Slotin begins to assemble the core.*' He looked up. 'He was a Canadian. Poor Louis was killed at Los Alamos not long afterwards, doing much the same thing. He put two sub-critical bits of plutonium just a fraction too close. There was a burst of radiation. Very brief, but enough.'

'Biscuits?' Mrs Peterson was asking at the doorway.

'No, thanks. Are you sure you don't want some help?' Mrs Peterson shook her head and left.

'So . . .' Peterson said, waiting for Findhorn.

'They were found last week, in the wreckage of a Soviet light aircraft near Greenland. I'm a polar meteorologist.'

Petrosian, alias Peterson, sighed. 'After fifty years. I'm supposed to have died in that crash. How did you find me?'

'A survivor called Victor led us to Sachs, and Sachs led us to you.'

'I suppose it was a bit of an obsession, all this diary writing. You know I keep a diary even to this day. I have a cupboard full of them. Of course I have nothing of consequence to write about these days. Not like Los Alamos, or Germany in the thirties. And I'm glad of the fact, if only because I find it hard to hold a pen. And who will be interested enough to read them after Lisa and I are gone?'

'You have two customers right here,' Romella said quietly.

'Coffee won't be a minute,' said Mrs Peterson, putting a tray on the table. It had milk, cups and sugar neatly laid out, and she had given them biscuits anyway.

Petrosian waited until she had left the room and said, 'This will be a terrible shock to my wife. Partly because it revives a past which she prefers not to remember. Different survivors handled their pain in different ways. Lisa's way was to put the past firmly behind her. To blot it out if you like. Her only contact with those days is an old friend in . . . ah, you say that is how you found us?'

Romella said, 'It wasn't Herr Sachs's fault. I tricked him. I got him to phone Lisa and recorded the number electronically. It was probably an illegal act.'

'And of course, there is the destruction of our life

together. Do you think they will send me to prison at my age?'

Findhorn was shocked. 'That is not our intention. We're not here in any sort of official capacity.'

Romella added, 'We intend no harm to your wife and yourself.'

'We're the only people alive who know your identity. And we intend to keep it that way.' As soon as he had spoken, Findhorn remembered Petrosian's brother Anastas. He hoped Lev wouldn't ask about him.

'What then?'

Findhorn did not feel ready to ask the question. 'There is something which puzzles me, sir.' As a rule he didn't 'sir' anybody, but in the presence of this man it came naturally. 'It's about your escape from Lake Michigan. You weren't on that Russian plane, but of course the diaries we have don't cover that event. What happened, that night?'

Petrosian leaned back in his chair. The smell of coffee was drifting through. 'Well now. That too was some day. Or rather, some night.'

Petrosian was wakened by the rhythmic slap of water on the side of the yacht. Grey light was streaming through the little portholes. Suddenly afraid that the boat owner might appear, he rolled out of the bunk and climbed up the steps to the galley door. It had frozen in place. He put his shoulder to it without success, then retrieved a bread knife and finally managed to prise the door open with a loud crack.

The yacht was six inches deep in overnight snow. The lake, however, had not yet frozen, although the surface was dotted with thin floes and the little waves had a turgid, almost treacly look about them.

The holiday cottage, where he assumed the pickup would take place, was on the opposite coast of the lake, about a hundred miles over the horizon to the west.

The abandoned car might or might not be reported within hours.

They might or might not think to search a boat.

The owner might or might not turn up.

His appearance on a public highway, conspicuously lugging his suitcase, would seal his fate. Unless they hadn't yet started looking hereabouts.

He could sail the boat across the water. He'd never sailed a small boat in his life. Its loss might go unnoticed for days, or the owner might live in one of the houses a hundred yards away.

All imponderables, on which his life came or went.

By about three a.m. it had become clear that the spy, if he was indeed heading for one of the Great Lakes, had slipped off the main highways. There was nothing to be done until daylight.

Dawn was a somewhat nominal concept as it brought little more than a grey gloom to the landscape. However, as the day progressed, police patrols in a score of little towns bordering the Great Lakes reported no sightings of the black Pierce-Arrow car. It began to look as if the lake referred to had been a minor one, like Mooselookmeguntic or the Richardson Lakes, or Moosehead or First Connecticut. They all skirted the Canadian border. They were all in remote and inaccessible places. Or maybe they were fooling themselves and the spy's rendezvous was further south, say Lake Winnipesaukee in New Hampshire. Despair began to settle round the FBI team like a descending mist.

The team's musings were interrupted by excellent news around mid-morning. Forestry workers had reported an abandoned car to the local police. It had been driven off a narrow track deep into the woods. It was a Pierce-Arrow with whitewall tyres. Its number plate told them that Tom Clay was the legally registered owner. A place called Ludington, a small town on the shores of Lake Michigan, was within sight of the car.

They as good as had him.

The early afternoon, however, brought no reports from hotels, boarding houses, restaurants or cafés. This was odd because firstly the guy had to eat, and secondly, if he'd stayed out overnight he would now be as stiff as a board. It was known that he had money; he had emptied his account of nearly a thousand dollars a few days previously, and Tom Clay had reported that the spy paid for the car out of a fat wad of notes.

A boarding house enquiry produced one sighting. The proprietor had seen nothing, but one of his resident ladies had mentioned, over breakfast, a man behaving oddly. At around ten o'clock the previous night she had just happened to be looking out of her upstairs window. She had seen a man with a briefcase climb over the railing directly opposite the house, and disappear out of sight below the embankment wall. There was a perfectly good sidewalk, and if he was taking a stroll, why carry a briefcase? She had kept looking and thought she had seen movement on the pier a few minutes later. It was sufficiently odd that she mentioned it to her other friends over breakfast. Was he a spy or something, she asked the FBI agent, her eyes gleaming, and the proprietor had tut-tutted politely.

God bless old ladies and net curtains everywhere. He was either heading north to Manistee, or he had found a boat. Any attempt to hitch a ride on that quiet road at that time of night, at twenty below, would have saved the state the cost of the high voltage electricity. Therefore he must be in one of the boats, not a hundred yards away from them.

He wasn't, but he had been. His footprints were still on the deck and the owner was a New York construction worker who hadn't been near the place for three months. Unfortunately the footprints went back into town and soon merged with those of the pedestrian populace at large. And by the time they found that the early morning ferry to Kewaunee was still sailing, it had already crossed the Lake and disgorged its passengers.

Petrosian was shivering violently and glad of the fact.

Somewhere, maybe in a *Reader's Digest* article in some waiting room, he'd read that you're in trouble when you stop shivering. It meant the body had run out of the energy it needed to shiver.

Shivering is a heating mechanism. Hold onto that.

He was also frightened.

There were two hazards to be avoided, an imminent death through exposure, and a delayed one through electrocution.

He looked into the dark woods. There were probably moose and timber wolves, and beavers in the frozen ponds. So far, however, there had been only a deathly stillness. As the evening progressed the clouds had thinned and the temperature was plunging downwards. A three-quarters moon was rising.

He looked at his watch for the tenth time in an hour. It had little luminous numbers and hands, and as a man who knew about radiation he had made sure the luminescence came from electron transitions and not radium.

He hadn't eaten for thirty hours.

So what? Survive the night. Then worry about your belly.

Having just looked at his watch, he did so again. It was twenty minutes to ten. The lights of a small town reflected off the water some miles to the south. Three point two miles to be exact. An hour's walk for a fit man with a briefcase on a good surface. Longer for a physical wreck who hadn't eaten for thirty hours and who peered fearfully into the dark woods between every step.

Petrosian had watched a solitary angler on a jetty, wondering in alarm if he intended to fish overnight. Around eight o'clock, however, the man had packed up his estate wagon and driven off through the forest track, having had no luck. Now Petrosian was left in a silence broken only by the gentle lapping of waves on the shore just beyond the road.

There was a roaring log fire, and a hot plate of chilli con carne, and a woman with Lisa's wonderfully curved body and a warm, loving expression, and yet at the same time with Kitty's long legs and slim face and blonde hair. The warmth from the fire was penetrating his bones and he sank into the deep pile of the rug, and he yielded to the overwhelming urge to sleep, and he found himself lying in the snow, face down, with no recollection of having fallen. He had lost feeling in the toes of his left foot, wondered if they would have to be amputated, had a brief, panicky vision of losing his leg.

At first he wondered what had wakened him, and then he heard the faint engine sound, coming from the direction of the lake. At first he thought it must be some ship, but as it grew in intensity he recognized it as the sound of an aircraft. He rolled over, managed to get onto his hands and knees, and then with an effort staggered to his feet. He tugged at the briefcase, but it now seemed to be full of bricks. He started to drag himself through the snow, falling and picking himself up, steering around bumps and hollows.

And now he could see it through the trees, a small dark shape, its propeller scattering the moonlight. It was maybe a couple of miles out.

And there was a car, approaching swiftly from the direction of Kewaunee.

Petrosian stopped about twenty yards back from the edge of the track, hidden in the trees. The plane was low and seemed to be heading directly for him. The car was maybe a couple of miles away and closing fast.

The engine noise dropped in pitch, sounded almost like a cough. Then there were twin sprays of water, bright in the moonlight, and the engine was revving up and the aircraft was taxi-ing towards the jetty. Petrosian, in an agony of indecision, held back.

The engine of the little aircraft died. The door opened and a man stepped on the float. He was gripping the wing with one hand and holding something in the other. It looked like a coil of rope. He was looking into the trees, seeming to stare directly at Petrosian. Then, suddenly, the car was driving over the pebbled shoreline, its headlights momentarily flooding the plane and the pilot. Petrosian, terrified, dropped the suitcase and braced himself to run into the woods.

The driver of the car was out and running along the jetty. The pilot threw him a rope. There was an exchange of conversation in Russian. Petrosian recognized one of the voices, tried to run forwards, fell, couldn't get up. By the time he got to his feet the driver was half-crawling along the wing, a leg dangling in search of a strut, the pilot holding him by the arm while the little aircraft tilted and swayed dangerously.

And then they were in, the door was slammed shut and the propeller was revving up, and Petrosian was stumbling along the jetty like a drunk man, waving and shouting hoarsely.

The engine died and the door opened.

'Hey, Lev!' Rosenblum shouted in pleasure.

'I have them. The diaries.'

'So where are they? Bring them here!'

Petrosian stumbled back into the dark, returned with the briefcase. Rosenblum was halfway along the wing. He threw the coil of rope. Petrosian caught it and pulled, and then he was heaving Rosenblum off the wing and onto the jetty. It took up all his remaining energy.

'Thought you hadn't made it, old pal. The shoreline's crawling with feds. This is it?' He lifted the case, grinning, his spectacles reflecting moonlight.

'They're all there, Jürgen.'

Rosenblum reached into his inside pocket. For an insane moment Petrosian thought he was about to be shot. But then Rosenblum was handing over an envelope and saying, 'Passport, driving licence, birth certificate etcetera. They've even given you a life history if you want to use it. You're born again, Lev. Look, we can probably squeeze you in. You sure you want to do it this way?'

Petrosian nodded, took the envelope, looked at it stupidly.

'The car's yours, you've owned it for years. The key's in the ignition. Now take it and clear off fast. And excuse me if I get the hell out of here. The Motherland awaits her revolutionary hero.' They shook hands.

Just before he closed the door, Rosenblum waved and shouted, 'Get moving, Lev! Go to Mexico or someplace.' And then the propeller was revving up, and the aircraft was accelerating over the water.

In the life-saving warmth of the car, Petrosian took a last look over the lake. But there was little to be seen; only a decaying wake scattering the moonlight, and shadows.

31

Instability

Petrosian smiled sadly. 'The diaries were useless, you see. They had no information which could have helped Stalin to develop the Super. But I told my treacherous friend Rosenblum otherwise and he accepted them in exchange for a new identity for me. They were my passport to freedom. Thank you for these copies. They will be wonderful reading for me.'

Romella asked, 'Why did you suppress your discovery? It could have made you rich.'

'And conspicuous. Anyway, rich to what purpose? We are happy. We are comfortable. We have everything we need.'

Findhorn chipped in. 'It could have brought you scientific honours.'

Petrosian almost laughed. 'Ah! So I am talking to a scientist! Einstein once told me he wished he'd been a woodcutter. I came to understand what he meant. We have never been happier than when Lev Petrosian died in that air crash, and Leonard Peterson the antiquarian bookseller married Lisa Rosen the tutor of German. The key to our happiness has lain in our anonymity.' He looked at them, suddenly wary. 'Which brings me to the question of why you are here.'

Romella tried to say it kindly, but the words were harsh. 'We may have to take away that key.'

Lisa came in with a large coffee percolator. She had a slight stoop. She placed it on the tray and said, 'Have you seen the table mats, dear?'

Petrosian said, 'Lisa, I wonder if you would leave us for a while?'

She looked at him, suddenly alert, and then at the visitors. 'What is wrong?'

'Nothing,' said Petrosian.

'Then why are you looking like that?'

'It's nothing to worry about, Mrs Peterson,' Romella lied. Lisa left, trailing scepticism and worry.

'I think I understand. Your purpose is blackmail.' Petrosian's accent was acquiring a Germanic tinge. 'You wish to extort the secret of the process from me in exchange for your silence.'

Findhorn poured coffee into delicate white cups. 'The secret is already in someone else's hands. Milk?'

'No! That is terrible! But how can that be?'

There was no avoiding it. Findhorn said, 'The diaries led some people to your brother Anastas.'

'Anastas? He wasn't harmed?'

'No,' Findhorn lied. 'I saw him briefly myself.'

Petrosian's face showed relief. 'And how is he?'

'He was well when I left him. Still working, I think. He has a little Skoda and he smokes a pipe. We shared a very good Armenian cognac. Unfortunately his house was robbed, and documents taken.'

Petrosian seemed to be talking half to himself. 'My vanity has created this problem. It was such a wonderful discovery, but I should have strangled it at birth. First I tried to patent my discovery. Only when they turned it down did I realize I was up against huge commercial interests. I even began to feel that my life was at risk.'

Petrosian's mind was momentarily elsewhere. Then he continued, 'Then I realized that the process had uncertainties, you see, it might just possibly be dangerous. I therefore decided to hide it against the day when it would be examined by a community more knowledgeable and enlightened than that of the nineteen fifties.'

'So you sent it to your brother through the Geghard trading route?' Romella asked, pouring milk for herself.

Petrosian showed surprise. He sipped at his coffee, and added a spoonful of brown sugar crystals. 'I am amazed at what you have found out.'

'We also know you sent letters to your brother through Kitty Cronin. But we don't know how.'

'Ah, Kitty.' His mind seemed to wander. 'Is she still alive?'

'And well,' said Romella. 'She married a businessman called Morgenstern. They were divorced after fifteen years. There were two children. She moved to some place in the Colorado Rockies and opened a shop selling mountain climbing equipment.'

A smile briefly softened the tension in Petrosian's face. 'She loved mountains.'

'She retired ten years ago and now she's living with her daughter in Miami.'

'I am glad life went well for her. Kitty's sister-in-law worked in the Turkish Embassy in Washington. My letters went there. They were delivered uncensored to an address in Igdir, a little town in Turkey. From there it was easy. My father was a shepherd, and Anastas continued in that style. In the Gegham mountains we knew every track between Lake Sevan and the Turkish border. The Geghard bazaar existed long before the war. It was a clandestine trading route. We used it to bring in cheese, coffee and other good things from Turkey, and barter them at Garni and Geghard. So far as I know the war merely enhanced the flow. To have been caught . . . well, they shot children too.'

Findhorn said, 'We're here because we want to know why you suppressed your discovery. It wasn't just for personal reasons.'

Romella held out the plate of cream biscuits to the old man, but he shook his head. 'I am not sure how much to tell you.'

'Perhaps I can help,' said Findhorn. 'I suspect that the process is unstable. If you can persuade me that it is, I'll try to have it stopped.'

'Perhaps you will. Or perhaps you have failed to recover the secret and wish to trick a simple old man into giving you it.'

'You must consider that possibility,' Findhorn said. 'After all, we're total strangers.'

Petrosian stood up and walked over to the big window.

'I was almost unmasked once. It happened in Oxford, not long after the war. I saw a man in the Causeway giving me a very strange look. It was some seconds before I recognized Rudolf Peierls. I had to keep walking towards him. But of course I was dead by then, and I simply passed him without giving the slightest sign of recognition. To this day I am not sure whether he recognized me.'

'Did anything come of it?'

'Yes. I launched my antiquarian book career here in Lincoln rather than Oxford.'

'Regrets?'

'None. I never kept up with the scientific literature, at least not at research level. But my career as a seller of old books has put me in contact with some of the finest minds who ever existed. My best friends speak to me from many countries and many centuries.' He turned back from the window and sat down. 'You can thank them for the decision I have made. You see, without them, I would not have the insight into the human soul which I believe I have. I choose to trust you, and hope that my friends are not letting me down. I will tell you about the process.'

Findhorn gave Romella a look. She said, 'I'll give Mrs Peterson a hand. Technical stuff gives me a headache.'

Romella took their hired Rover towards the A1. They drove into a pleasant little market town called Retford, looking for signs for the dual carriageway, and promptly got lost in a maze of one-way streets.

'Open my handbag,' she said.

Findhorn retrieved the large black bag from the back

seat. It held a jumble of what Findhorn assumed was the
usual women's stuff, including a small bottle of the
Diorissima perfume which was driving him mad; and two
folded sheets of paper.

'Look at the papers. Dad's been using some heavy
pressure. He fired them through this morning and he's
dying with curiosity.'

There were two documents. The first was rubber-
stamped 'CIA Restricted Release':

```
TO: DIRECTOR FBI
FM: DIRECTOR CIA
OUT: [        ]
FROM: [        ]
DATE OF INFO: 7-12 JULY 1953
SUBJECT: TRAVEL TO MEXICO OF MRS K.
MORGENSTERN
1. On 7 July a usually reliable source
reported that Kitty Morgenstern née
Cronin planned to take a vacation in
Mexico City in the near future. You will
recall that during the war she was
suspected of transmitting documents
containing atomic secrets, given her by
Lev Petrosian, to the USSR.
2. Another usually reliable source has
reported that Mrs Morgenstern stayed at
the home of Edward Ros while in Mexico
City. Edward Ros is a well-known left-
wing journalist.
```

3. During this stay, they were visited by a man whose description is remarkably close to that of Dr Lev Petrosian. You will recall that according to our field agents Dr Petrosian attempted to escape to the USSR from the Canadian border in a Soviet light aircraft. This aircraft was clandestinely shot down on Presidential orders by the USAF over Greenland.

4. Although unconfirmed, the above report leads to the conjecture that Dr Petrosian was in fact not on board aforesaid aircraft.

5. The above information was obtained from highly sensitive sources and should not be disseminated further.

DISTRIBUTION: LEGAL ATTACHE

In the absence of sensible comment, Findhorn said, 'Blimey!' He turned to the second sheet. It was marked 'Official Dispatch' and was heavily deleted.

POUCH Air
DISPATCH NO. [＿＿＿＿＿＿＿＿]
CLASSIFICATION [＿＿＿＿＿＿＿＿]
TO: [＿＿＿＿＿＿]
FROM: [＿＿＿＿＿＿＿]
SUBJECT: (Dr) Lev Petrosian

1. You will, of course, recall the investigation of subject which you conducted at our request in 1949–51. You will recall that on several occasions subject met a known Soviet agent, J. Rosenblum, as well as Soviet Embassy officials (his cover story, that he was enquiring about friends and relatives behind the Iron Curtain, could not be broken).

2. [   ]

3. Subject was recognized on several occasions in Oxford, England, after his supposed attempted escape to the USSR. He now lives with Lisa née Rosen, a German Communist who survived the concentration camps. He has established a bookselling business in Lincoln, England.

4. MI6 surveillance of said bookshop has so far revealed no evidence of contact with known or suspected Soviet agents. On 23 August, [   ], the wife of [   ], was in the city of Lincoln but no contact was made.

5. Subject has no further access to classified material.

6. In the light of the above, and the difficulty of using VENONA, wiretap and

similar material in open court, we have decided not to seek extradition or prosecution. The British MI6 have been informed. His illegal entry to the UK will be ignored as he may be a useful trap should the Soviets wish to use him on any future occasion. The Home Secretary concurs.

COORDINATING OFFICER

At last they were through the town and heading west. Findhorn looked out at the flat agricultural land. Ahead of them, a small aircraft was dropping slowly towards some airfield hidden by trees. 'So Lev and Lisa have been in hiding for fifty years, and there was no need.'

'We can't tell them that.' Romella was slowing for a tight corner.

'Agreed. We leave them to hide in peace. I wonder about the blanked-out stuff.'

'Don't push your luck, Fred. I was lucky to get even that.'

A few miles ahead of them, streams of lorries were marking out the line of the A1. Romella was looking thoughtful. 'You've reached your decision on the Petrosian secret.'

'It needs a stake driven through its heart.'

'What? Why?'

'It's too dangerous. It could work like a dream or it could evaporate the planet.'

'What are the odds?'

'A hundred to one it would be okay. Maybe even a thousand to one.'

'One chance in a hundred of oblivion versus a near certainty of ending up richer than Bill Gates. I might take a chance on it, Fred.'

'I might give it a try too. At an individual level it could be a gamble worth taking. But not if you're risking the whole of humanity. There are people out there who don't give a toss for anyone but themselves.'

'And Albrecht is probably one of them,' she said. Ahead, a tractor was trailing a machine with long, swaying metal prongs. She slowed, edged cautiously past. 'Duty obliges us to hand this over to the authorities.'

'We have a higher duty, Ms Grigoryan. To the greater good.'

'That was pure Rosenblum. You have an anti-authoritarian streak, Fred. But who the hell are we to make a decision like that? We have to send it upstairs.'

'There's nothing I'd love more. Unfortunately my conscience is right here in the car with me, not upstairs. Someone out there would take that one per cent chance.'

She shook her head in disagreement.

They were now on a long, straight stretch of road. 'I guess the Romans were here,' Findhorn said, to break the tense silence.

The junction with the A1 was about a mile ahead.

Romella was frowning. 'The deal is that we find Petrosian's secret.'

'So let's stick to that.'

'But, Fred, we don't even know where the document is.'

'It's probably in Albrecht's hands by now. My guess is he's poring over it in some hideaway, about to summon his engineers. We have to reach him before they do because the moment they've gone over it, it's out. He'll start on a patent application. I reckon we have less than forty-eight hours.'

'But you now know the principle of the thing. Can't you beat him to a patent – assuming in your infinite wisdom you decide the risk is worth taking?'

'No chance. The mathematical details would take weeks to work through before you even started on the engineering aspects.'

'Have you thought this through, Fred? Say we find Albrecht. What do we do about him? By now he knows the secret.'

Findhorn, anticipating Romella's next words, had the sensation of a trapdoor opening in his stomach. She was slowing down as they approached the junction.

'Are you up to murder, Fred? Would you kill for the greater good?'

Findhorn was biting his thumbnail. 'Matsumo asked me the same question.'

'Fred, a man in his business acquires enemies. He probably hides from Mossad, the Palestinians, the Iraqis, the Iranians, the Mafia and the Salvation Army. He's an elusive man. How can we possibly discover where he is?'

'The Celestial Truth might know. The information might be in their Swiss headquarters.'

The Rover had stopped at the junction. The A1 was a solid mass of traffic, streaming north and south like anti-parallel lava flows. It took a second for the implication of Findhorn's remark to sink in; when it did, Romella turned to him open-mouthed. 'Are you serious? Break into the Temple?'

'It'll have to be tomorrow. We're out of time.'

'You're raving, foaming-at-the-mouth insane.'

'Decision time, Romella. South to Whitehall, or north to Dougie's?'

There was a momentary gap in the flow of southbound traffic. In the north lane, lorries were effectively blocking the carriageway and leaving a stretch of empty road in front of them. 'Oh, bloody hell,' Romella said, swinging the Rover smartly across the road and into the northbound carriageway.

Findhorn said, 'I put it down to my charm.'

32

Piz Radönt

Findhorn came out of the Glasgow sleet into the warmth
and chatter of a crowded pizza parlour. Waiters
were whirling around the tables, the plates balanced
on their arms defying gravity. A young Sicilian in a
tuxedo led Findhorn to a table, lit a candle. Findhorn,
indifferent to what he would eat, ordered spaghetti and
clams.

His free hours in Glasgow had left him emotionally
battered. Miss Young, the white-haired departmental
secretary, had looked at Findhorn with open-mouthed
dismay when he had called in. He knew it when
she scuttled off to collect Julian Walsh, the prim-
mouthed, fussy little head of physics, and he knew it
when Walsh came in the door looking like a funeral
undertaker.

Archie had been on vacation, and had stood too close
to the edge of the Isthmus of Corinth. It's a steep man-
made gorge, in Greece, you know.

I've heard of it. Did anyone see him fall?

No. You're surely not implying that he jumped? The
prim lips had twitched anxiously: the eyes had worried

about departmental scandal, pressure of work, sharp questions at next month's faculty meeting.

Oh no, nothing like that. He'd been pushed. He was a path to the Temple of Celestial Truth, and much too dangerous to be left alive.

Findhorn had kept the last bits to himself, and Walsh's lips had relaxed, he had grown expansive. He will be missed. His second-year lectures on solid-state physics were a model of clarity.

Findhorn followed the spaghetti by a phoney *zabaglione*, made with cheap sherry rather than *marsala al'uovo*, but the house saved money and the punters didn't know the difference. He emerged into an Argyle Street drizzle.

The next twenty-four hours, he knew, were going to be the most difficult and dangerous in his life.

He wandered off reluctantly to find a taxi, his whole body suffused with a sense of dread, the spaghetti and clams lying heavy in his stomach.

'I'm dying. I can feel myself slipping away.'

'Shut up, Stefi. Let Joe do his job.'

'I tell you I'm freezing to death.'

'At least be quiet about it.' Findhorn turns to the man crouching behind the boulder. 'What do you see?'

'Gie's a minute.' The man shifts his position slightly, and taps the brass eyepiece of the telescope. 'A big dog. It looks like an Irish setter. No, it's a Doberman.'

Findhorn says, 'That's bad news.'

'You might put it that way. Here, have a peek.'

REVELATION

The man stands up, rubbing his thighs and flapping his arms. Findhorn crouches down, fiddles with the focus. Under the high magnification the image in the Questar is rippling slightly as cold air drifting up from the valley far below mingles with the colder air at three thousand metres.

A fence nine feet or so high encloses about four acres of rocky, sloping ground in the shape of a square. In the centre of the square is a large rectangular building, glowing red in the light of the setting sun. A kilometre beyond it, and separated from the building by an immense grim chasm, a restaurant sits atop an adjoining peak like an illuminated flying saucer. In the telescope Findhorn can just make out that restaurant and building are joined by a cable and that a trio of small cable cars are slotted into a concrete station underneath the restaurant. The cable disappears round the back of the rectangular building and Findhorn cannot see where it ends.

The building has four turrets, one at each corner, and golden domes surmounting each turret. There are windows on two levels, about a dozen on each of the two sides Findhorn can see. The roof is steeply sloping and white with snow, the eaves projecting out over the walls. A massive, arched double door shimmers in the field of view, and above it is a large wooden circle enclosing a cross: the zodiacal Earth sign, and the adopted symbol of the Temple of Celestial Truth. In front of the big door three people are in conversation. They seem to be dressed in long black robes, but at this range it is impossible to make out any features. The Doberman is sniffing around their ankles.

'What do you think, Joe?' Findhorn asks.

'It gives me the creeps.'

'I mean . . .'

'I don't like the look of it. It's high risk.'

Findhorn glances at his watch but it isn't necessary. Already they are in the gloomy shadow of a big mountain and the temperature is plummeting. The Temple is still in red sunlight, but long black fingers are creeping towards it.

'Point of entry?'

The man nudges Findhorn aside, looks through the eyepiece of the powerful telescope again.

'They've gone in. I can't see the dog. Point of entry.' He pauses thoughtfully, a general studying the terrain. 'The flat-roofed building to the left.'

'The one with the helipad?'

'Aye. We can approach using these rock outcrops as cover, then snip through the wire and into the wee building, if it's empty, that is.'

'Then?'

The man stands up and starts to fold away the Questar. 'Then it gets difficult. A first-floor window if we're lucky. If not it has to be the roof.'

Findhorn thinks about the high, steep, snow-covered roof. He says, 'Stefi, you get back to the car.'

'No, I'll stay here. If you get lost I'll flash the torch.'

'Okay, people, let's go.'

'I don't think so,' the man says.

REVELATION

There is a stunned silence. He says, 'It's far too risky.'

'We have a deal. Ten thousand pounds to get us in and out undetected. Tonight.' The steel in Romella's voice takes Findhorn by surprise.

'Lady, yon perimeter fence and the dog are telling us something. These people are security minded, a fact which I do not like one little bit. There could be all sorts of nasty surprises in there. I don't know what you lot are into, but with my record, if I'm caught I go down for ten years.'

'Can't you do it?' Findhorn asks.

The man bristles. 'I can, but I'm not into kamikaze. You didn't tell me to expect a set-up like yon. I'm telling you this one is pure insanity.' He waved a hand towards the big building a mile away. 'It's no' exactly some suburban bungalow with PVC windows.'

Romella says, 'Twenty thousand pounds. And if you can't do it we'll get someone else.' *Except that we're out of time to get anyone else.*

Greed and prudence are battling it out in the man's head. Romella adds, 'Just as soon as we get back to Glasgow.'

Joe is balancing the odds. Cold is penetrating the marrow of Findhorn's bones. Then the burglar is saying, 'There's a showroom just up the road from where I live. It has a sweet wee Alfa Romeo in it, two-plus-two, open top, flamenco red. A fabulous bird trap. It costs twenty-six.'

'Get us in and out, undetected, and you'll be driving it tomorrow morning.'

In the near-dark, Joe is still weighing the odds. Then

he exhales heavily and picks up his rucksack: 'Okay, okay. But if I give the word, don't ask any questions, just run.'

They cut left, leaving Stefi shivering behind the rock. They plough through deep snow and skirt boulders, taking a meandering path through hollows. Findhorn assumes they won't be seen in the dying light, at the same time imagines dark faces watching them from every window. It is a difficult, tiring walk. As they approach, it seems increasingly unlikely that they can have avoided detection. Snatches of Mike's typed words run through his mind, form a disturbing pastiche: '. . . accumulation of weapons . . .' paranoid . . . aerosol attacks . . . body count . . .'

About two hundred yards from the fence, in the shelter of a massive, glacier-scored boulder, Joe motions them to a halt. The sun is still touching the top of the domes but otherwise the grounds are dark. Most of the windows are lit up, but, as they watch, shutters are closing over them. He rumbles around in a rucksack, produces night-vision binoculars, props his elbows on the boulder, scans the building. 'Bleedin' lights, can see eff all.' Then he is rumbling again in the bag. He distributes black silk gloves. 'Put these on. Now single file, follow me, and no talking.' Findhorn brings up the rear, his nervous system jangling and his feet painful with cold.

About thirty yards out, close to the perimeter fence, Joe stops. A light wind is freshening, and whistling gently through the fence, which is topped with barbed wire.

He produces a flat slab from his bag. 'Best fillet of steak. Cost me nine francs.'

'You got off light.'

Then Joe looks again through his binoculars, and, like a discus thrower, hurls the steak over the fence. A minute passes. Then he whispers, 'Run!' and in seconds they have covered the thirty yards to the wire. Strong wirecutters make a low gap in the fence and then they are through, crawling, and up against the rear wall of the flat building. Findhorn's heart is thumping in his chest. Romella is panting.

Joe stands up and tests a window. It is unlocked. He titters. The window squeaks loudly as he opens it and he curses quietly. Findhorn cringes. And then they help each other through the gap. There is warm air, and a smell of chlorine. The lights from the main building throw a ghostly glow through the cavernous swimming pool, and ripples of light are shimmering over the roof and walls from the water.

They creep past exercise bikes and treadmills, which, in the faint light, look like mediaeval instruments of torture. At the swimming-pool door, Joe uses a small flashlight to examine the lock. 'Kid's stuff,' he declares. His voice echoes. Romella holds the flashlight while Joe gets busy with a Swiss army knife. He uses its detachable toothpick and the long, thin awl-like blade.

Joe opens the door a couple of inches. The warm air from the swimming pool makes an instant mist with the outside cold. Directly ahead of them is a patch of black shadow where the round turret joins the wall. 'Move fast,'

Joe whispers. They run, bent double, across thirty feet of exposed ground to the shelter of the shadow, leaving tracks in the deep snow. There is a narrow, dark window in the turret, about ten feet above the ground. It is protected by heavy internal shutters.

They pass the Doberman, lying in the snow. It raises its head momentarily. There is a dribble of froth at the side of its mouth and its breathing is noisy. Findhorn feels bad, hopes the animal will be okay.

Joe gives instructions in sign language and Findhorn finds himself supporting the burglar on his shoulders. After a minute the discomfort turns to an ache, and after another minute the ache is approaching pain, but then the weight is off his shoulders and he looks up to see Joe heaving himself in through the window.

Minutes pass.

Suddenly the perimeter lights come on. For a panicky moment Findhorn thinks they have been detected, has a brief fantasy image of klaxons sounding and jackbooted German guards shouting '*Achtung!*' But the seconds pass, and there is only the whistle of the wind through the fencing, and Romella and Findhorn squeeze into the dark corner, as far as possible from the ocean of white light around them, while the hammering in their hearts subsides. There is the faintest hiss from above. A thick, knotted rope is dangling down. Findhorn goes first, turns to pull Romella unceremoniously in as she clambers over the windowsill.

Then Joe is quietly closing the window behind them. He stuffs the knotted rope back in his rucksack.

They are on a wooden spiral staircase, devoid of carpets, pictures or any sort of decoration.

Voices.

They go down the wooden stairs on tiptoe. Joe is carrying his rucksack, as if to drop it and run at a moment's notice. There is a heavy, partially open wooden door. Joe waves Findhorn and Romella back, takes a look. Then he is rummaging in his rucksack. They drop their heavy jackets on the steps and wriggle into long, black theatrical robes which add to the miasma of unreality already enveloping Findhorn. Romella is struggling with a camera, looping its cord round her neck while trying not to make it bulge under the robe. Joe stuffs things into pockets and inside his shirt.

Out into the warm, carpeted corridor. Findhorn catches a whiff of hot food. At the end of the corridor is a broad flight of stairs. Along and to the right, an open double door from which comes a buzz of conversation and the clatter of dishes and cutlery. To reach the stairs they will have to pass this door. They follow Joe, stepping warily along the corridor.

A man and a woman appear at the top of the stairs. Joe, Romella and Findhorn huddle together, as if talking. Findhorn realizes that their costume pieces are all wrong, they are too black, the collar isn't right. The man and woman, heads bowed and hands in their sleeves, are down the stairs and walking towards them. They pay the trio no attention and turn into the refectory.

Joe passes by the open door. Findhorn dares a glance as they pass. He glimpses four long dark tables, with about a hundred faithful in all. There is a raised dais and a lectern with a backdrop of heavy curtains. They pass unnoticed, climb the stairs, find themselves on a landing with two corridors leading off.

One corridor leads to a chapel, ablaze with candles. Silver flying saucers hang from its ceiling, suspended on chains. A mother-ship the size of a large chandelier, lined with portholes, dominates them all. The chapel walls are covered with paintings: Jesus with open arms, saints with halos. These are interspersed with blow-ups of the Roswell alien, the face on Mars, the Belt of Orion, a star map showing the track of Sirius as it snakes across the sky. A feeling of uneasiness overwhelms Findhorn, as if he is in the presence of evil. He can't analyze it, tries to shrug it off, but the feeling persists.

They retreat. Joe points to a double door. 'This has the look of a private apartment,' he whispers.

Findhorn nods his agreement. Light is shining under the door. Joe drops to his knees, starts to use some tool on the lock. Romella stands guard at the top of the landing. A gust of laughter comes up from the refectory.

Then the door clicks open and they are in a hallway, which, for sumptuous excess, rivals Dougie's flat. Its walls are lined with tapestries. They step onto soft carpet, their path illuminated by reproduction oil lamps on the walls.

Voices, coming from an open door ten metres to their right. Joe creeps along, peers into the living room, pulls his head back. Findhorn admires his nerve. Then Joe looks again, and turns to them with an expression which somehow combines fear, horror and anger all at once. He waves them past the room.

It is empty. Marlon Brando, looking noble in a toga, is addressing a Roman lynch mob in a Nebraska accent, his words sub-titled in German. A walnut-topped desk is heaped with a disorganized clutter of revolvers, automatic pistols and cardboard ammunition boxes. About a dozen small orange cylinders are lined up against a wall. The words SARIN GAS are stencilled on them. Findhorn guesses there is probably enough of it to wipe out a small city. Joe's complexion is waxy. He hisses, 'What have you people got me into?'

Half a dozen doors lead off from the hallway. A faint blue light is shining under one of them. Joe goes down on his knees at the door and from a pocket pulls out what looks like a thin strip of coiled wire. He is visibly trembling. He uncoils the wire and slips it under the door. At the other end is an eyepiece and he holds this to his eye while wiggling the wire. Then he sighs with relief, and they are into a large empty study. The blue light comes from three small television monitors on a desk at the window. The monitors are showing the outside grounds. The front of the swimming pool is clearly visible: they had crossed in full view of a camera. Joe raises his hands to his cheeks, mutters something about Never Again.

Joe rewinds a video tape and presses the play button. Then he crosses to the shuttered window and pulls the heavy velvet curtains closed. 'Right, do your business and be quick about it. If we're caught . . .'

Quickly, Findhorn switches on the computer. It requests a password. Someone with Tati's secrets is unlikely to leave a password scribbled on some notepad and he wastes no time guessing. Romella is skimming through papers on another desk. There is something about the eight worldly dharmas: fame and infamy, praise and insult, gain and loss, pleasure and pain. She goes through the drawers, holding a flashlight in her mouth. One contains only maps. The other has pens, pencils, scrap paper. The third drawer is locked. She takes the torch from her mouth and hisses softly at Joe.

The burglar goes down on his knees, looks closely at the lock in the torchlight and produces the Swiss army knife again. 'Simple tumbril,' he whispers in a shaky voice; Findhorn wonders why everyone is whispering in this big, empty apartment. Joe closes his eyes in concentration. He hardly seems to be moving the thin blade. But then, as if by a miracle, the drawer slides smoothly open.

Romella lifts the contents out, puts them on the desk and switches on a desk lamp.

Findhorn becomes aware that his gloved hands are shaking. They begin to go through the papers.

'Footsteps?' Romella asks.

They freeze.

Another dog. The bark is deep, of the type associated with a pit bull or a big hound. It is directly below the study window. Then there is the scrunch of boots over snow and a rough male voice.

'They've found the Doberman.' Joe's eyes are wild.

REVELATION

A door slams in the wind. Brilliant lights come on outside, finding chinks in the window shutters.

Joe runs out of the room. For a moment they think he has abandoned them. But then he is back. 'The gymnasium roof's lit up. Come on, we're out of here.'

'No.'

'*What?*'

Romella takes the camera from around her neck. Findhorn holds the papers in place while Romella clicks, a page at a time. He notices that her hands, too, are unsteady.

The distant chop-chop of an approaching helicopter.

Joe is wringing his hands, pacing up and down. 'Right, people. Let's go.' He is thinking of the guns and the sarin gas, senses that capture will be a terminal event.

The helicopter is getting noisy. Findhorn says, 'Now the address book.'

Joe cuts loose a stream of obscenity. Now the helicopter is roaring mightily. The shutters rattle, and a moving light flickers through a gap. Romella and Findhorn are still photographing. Then they hear the engine dying and the whoosh-whoosh of the freewheeling rotor.

And then the sound of voices. Maybe four or five people. Joe is performing a sort of war dance, silent and frenzied.

Footsteps, heading for the front of the house. *They can't help but see our tracks in the snow*, Findhorn thinks in desperation.

Romella says, 'Okay.' Hastily, she returns the papers to the drawer.

'Lock it,' says Findhorn.

'There's nae time, ye eejit.'

'Lock it if you want to collect your money.'

Joe is on the edge of violence. He kneels down with his knife, fiddles with the lock. The pit bull is going crazy, its deep bay freezing Findhorn's blood. Somebody is speaking interrogatively in German.

Switch off the table lamp. Open the curtains. Exit the study, along the hallway to the landing. Findhorn gives Joe a look. Joe relocks the apartment door.

Halfway down the stairs, Joe turns and sprints back up, almost colliding with Romella. He tries a door at random: a broom cupboard. Joe squeezes in and Findhorn bundles Romella after him. The faithful are chanting, approaching the stairway. Desperately, Findhorn tries another door. It is locked, and the next and the next. He hauls open a door just as the first of the faithful reach the landing, finds himself in another apartment. He just has time to see them, dressed in long black gowns, male and female side by side, led by a bald-headed male of about fifty looking like a bespectacled Bruce Willis. The man is leading the chant in a tenor voice, each line being echoed by about half the faithful. Findhorn stands petrified in the dark room as the procession moves solemnly along the corridor, inches from him.

· The procession passes. Joe opens the door, looking hunted. Findhorn opens his. The faithful are disappearing into the chapel, two abreast. One of them, a small, middle-aged woman, looks back, gives them a puzzled look. In the corridor, Joe bows his head and clasps his hands together inside the wide sleeves of the robe. He is trying not to run. The chant is now in English, fading as the line enters the chapel:

Come to us, Blessed of Tatos, release us from the shackles of Earth
Come to us, Blessed of Tatos, carry our souls upwards to Sirius
Come to us, Blessed of Tatos, enfold us in your arms
May we hasten your Coming by our earthly deeds
Blessed of Tatos, come to us
Blessed of Tatos, come to us.

They reach the spiral staircase. Joe whispers, 'Right, for Christ's sake, let's get out of this nut house.' He opens the window. They are now bathed in the lights of the helipad. There is a ten-foot drop. Romella goes first, risking a broken ankle. Findhorn follows without hesitation. Joe drops his bag, which lands in the snow with a thud. He balances precariously on the windowsill, knees bent, closing the window. The stairwell light comes on. He hasn't a second to position himself and has a simple choice: a stunt-man-type jump, or a drop of sarin on his skin. He jumps.

Away from the turret, they find themselves in full view of a man with a rifle over his shoulder. He is speaking to the pilot. Joe says, 'Come,' and they walk across the snow, heads bowed and arms in sleeves, towards the swimming pool, Romella with rucksack and jackets over her arms. The rifleman pays them no attention whatsoever.

Into the enfolding cloak of darkness, beyond the perimeter lights; disoriented, looking for Stefi's torchlight. Joe stays behind, crouching down at the fence. He is closing up the gap and taking the time to do it well; he wants his two-plus-two open-top, flamenco red bird trap.

Findhorn will settle for a toilet.

33

The Raid

In Doug's Davos hotel bedroom, with white peaks framed by the window, Findhorn plugs into the big television screen rather than the cramped little monitor of his laptop. Doug, in an armchair, has Stefi on his knee but doesn't seem to mind. Romella is sitting cross-legged on the double bed while Findhorn, on the edge of the bed, flicks through the items from Albrecht's locked drawer:

- A letter from Mr Tedesco, President of the Society for Information Display. Can you spare one of your senior staff to give a seminar on Advanced Cockpit Displays?
- A long, technical letter from an Andrew Roper, of the UK's MOD, requesting an evaluation of an exciting new development in night-vision goggles (paper enclosed).
- A letter from Colonel Herzberg of US Army Aviation Center, Fort Rucker. Confirming that he will be bringing his team to Davos next month to discuss the new gun system. Secretaries will co-ordinate diaries. Issues to be discussed include survivability, combat effectiveness, human factors engineering, visionics,

horizon technology integration, reliability, ASE equipment interfacing. Something has been scrawled over it. Findhorn recognizes the word 'Rosa'.

- A newsletter, described as 'The Key to Unlock the Glory of the Last Days'. Something about the Rewards of Giving. It reads like a scam for the gullible.

- A love letter, or at least a lust letter, from a lady in Boston called Zoë. Romella translates: something about a Nile cruise, an obscure joke about an Italian football team, and the hope they can repeat the experience some time.

- A letter from the Curator, L'Annonciade, St. Tropez, reiterating the gallery's gratitude for the loan of the Klee and confirming that it would be insured for $7,500,000 (seven point five million US dollars) while being exhibited.

- An invitation from H. Silver and Associates, Advanced Systems Division, to attend the fourth HSA Conference on Attack Helicopters in London, England. Attendance fee £1,495 (+17.5% VAT).

- Somebody from Hull with a visionary new aircraft design which he will reveal in exchange for a fifty per cent share in future profits; the letter is handwritten in biro on lined paper and has a three-up, second-flat-on-the-left address; the spelling is atrocious.

- An address book, small, black and shiny. Findhorn flicks on to the next item.

- A bill for SF 24,310 for installation of an Aga (four-oven, pewter) from Tamman & Sons, Zurich. It is addressed to a Herr W. Neff and has an address near

416

Blatten, Brig, Valais, Switzerland. There is a photocopy
of a cheque for that amount, signed by H.W. Neff and
drawn on an account in Brig, Switzerland.

'Hey,' says Romella.

'I think so too,' Findhorn replies. 'Who is this Mister
Neff, and why should Albrecht be paying for his Aga?'

'Is Neff in the address book?'

Findhorn skims through the electronic copy. There is
no Herr Neff.

On the screen, Findhorn displays the last item, a
photocopied letter. It has been written in German, with a
thick-nibbed fountain pen.

Stefi is running her hands absent-mindedly through Doug's
thinning hair. She says,

'*My darling Zoë*
Thank you for your wonderful letter. Agreed I can't
compete with twenty-four Italian footballers but at
my time of life I've learned that what counts is
quality. I'll be in Morocco for the first two weeks in
January. It will be business but I'm sending the Pirate
on ahead and hope to put in a few days of sin and
debauchery on the high seas. If you can stand the
heat, why don't you join me? I'll pay the fare over as
usual. Reply to me at Optika and mark it "Personal".
Your loving
Konrad.'

'I wish I was fluent in twenty languages.'

Stefi seems not to have heard. She is studying the letter closely. 'Go back to the Neff letter.'

Findhorn studies the signature on the cheque, flicks forward again to the love letter from Konrad. Different signatures, but written by the same hand, even with the same thick-nibbed pen. He claps his hands together. 'Well done. Ms Stefanova. Herr Neff and Konrad Albrecht are one and the same.'

Stefi beams. 'Yes, I think we've just struck gold.'

'Albrecht's hideaway. Someplace near Blatten in Switzerland. Could he be there now? With his engineers?'

Romella pulls the telephone onto the bed beside her. 'Put that letter from the US Army back on screen.'

Findhorn obliges. She says, 'That scrawl. It says *Rosa*.'

'Okay, he has a secretary at Davos called Rosa.' He puts the address book on screen again, flicks through its pages. He has a sense of excitement, like a hunter closing in on a quarry. There is a Rosa Stumpf, with a Davos address. Romella dials through, surprises Findhorn by speaking in fluent German. Findhorn hears a young woman's voice, with the sound of children shouting in the background.

Romella puts the phone down, turns to Findhorn. 'I said I was from Fort Rucker and needed to contact Albrecht urgently. She gave me his ex-directory number.'

She dials Albrecht's home number. Frau Albrecht answers. My husband is walking the dog. You have missed him by five minutes.

He is not away, then?

Who is this? Suspicion in her voice.

This is Colonel Herzberg's secretary. I'm phoning from the States.

He will be here in two hours' time with a colleague. Then they are going off someplace to discuss a business matter. Thirty-five years and Konrad has never before missed Christmas at home. Do you wish to call back in say three hours?

No. It will wait, thank you.

Ach! And at Christmas too. But he will be back tomorrow.

Merry Christmas. Goodbye.

And you may never see your husband again.

Romella says, 'He's summoning his engineers. We're out of time.'

Findhorn types into the Internet, throws up a map of Switzerland. Davos is on the far eastern edge of Switzerland. Brig is about halfway between Geneva and Davos. Blatten is a tiny village high in the Bernese Alps. A track lies beyond it, a thin line winding into the mountains. Instinctively, Findhorn knows that Albrecht's hideaway is somewhere up there. 'I need to contact Matsumo's killers.'

Romella says, 'You'll need your translator.'

The killers are waiting for them at Geneva Airport. Ms Drindle is wearing a heavy fur coat and a sort of Cossack hat. Dark trousers protrude below the coat. The sunglasses, Findhorn presumes, come from her camera-shy nature. The Korean's face is similarly adorned but he has a black trenchcoat and hat which makes him look like a small, fat jazz player.

There are no handshakes or words of welcome. Findhorn and Romella follow them into the cold air. 'You drive,' Ms Drindle instructs Findhorn. 'Keep strictly to the speed limit.' The car is a black, four-wheel drive Suzuki with French number plates. Findhorn takes the wheel. Romella sits beside him. He has to think carefully about changing gear in a car with a left-hand drive. He takes them carefully through Geneva and over the Mont Blanc bridge, which for some reason is decked out with the flags of the Swiss cantons. The big water jet is off but the paddle steamer restaurant is doing Christmas lunches. He follows the signs for Thonon and is soon taking them along flat white countryside with Lac Léman to their left. He is acutely aware that until now the people in the rear of the car have been trying to find and kill him.

Conversation is zero.

They are through the tongue of France which borders the south of the lake, and back into Switzerland, before Drindle speaks in her mannish voice. 'Tell me how you would go about it, Findhorn.'

The road looks as if it has just been cleared of snow but already a thin fresh layer is beginning to form. Findhorn is driving with excessive care.

'I'm too sick to think about it.'

'Do so anyway.'

Findhorn mumbles, 'Knock on his door and blow his head off.'

In the mirror, he sees Drindle give a quick nod. 'Actually

that can work. At least with proper planning and in the right circumstances, such as a quiet suburban area. It has the crowning merit of simplicity.'

'There has to be an alternative to this.'

'Name it.'

Findhorn exhales deeply and shakes his head; he's been over it a thousand times.

Drindle continues, almost leaning over Findhorn's shoulder. 'There are three essentials in an operation like this. Planning, surprise and invisibility. You must leave not the slightest trace of your presence, apart from the corpse itself.'

'Don't try to make this sound like a legitimate military operation, Drindle. You're just a murderer.'

Her voice is icy. 'You are in no position to make facile moral judgements.'

Findhorn has no answer.

How much the Korean understands is unclear, but in the mirror Findhorn sees the man giving him a long, hostile stare. Findhorn turns and looks into the small, bloodshot eyes. He says, 'Screw you.'

The snow is getting heavy. Romella, to deflect tension, says: 'I just hope we get through.'

Findhorn hopes they don't.

'We're about a hundred kilometres from the Simplon Pass,' she adds, unfolding a map.

An old-fashioned Beetle trundles past, its spiky tyres glittering like chariot wheels.

'Consider this car, Findhorn. Foreign plates, four-wheel drive, snow chains, nothing unusual. But we will be off the main highway, climbing a very steep road with no ski slopes or other tourist attractions at the end of it, a road which leads only to the chalets of the rich scattered over the mountainside. We will be noticed.'

'It's Christmas. People have visitors.'

'Good. But what do we do with the car? Park it outside Albrecht's house? What would you do if you were Albrecht, with a trillion dollar secret and a host of enemies, if you saw a strange car waiting unexpectedly outside your empty home?'

'Run a mile.'

'Precisely. Therefore the car will not be there. We will find an empty woodshed, or even park it in his own garage. In this weather there will be no traces in the snow of man or vehicle.'

Findhorn says, 'I think I'm going to be sick.'

Ahead of them they see an oasis of light underneath a blanket of heavy grey sky. At the boundary of the town there is a blue notice with a list of passes which are *offen*, *ouvert*, *aperto* and open. Findhorn notes that the Simplon Pass is one of them and that it's the quickest escape route from Switzerland once the deed is done. Romella tells him to turn left.

He turns left and finds himself on a road running parallel to a railway station. There is a row of bright red carriages with *Zermatt* marked on their sides. There is a bridge, and Findhorn turns onto it and they drive over the white, tumbling River Rhône, and then he is immediately onto a steeply climbing hill. He drops gear.

And he drops gear again: the road begins to climb seriously. He uses low gears and extreme care.

Picture-postcard chalets, all snow-laden roofs and glittering Christmas trees, are scattered over high white slopes. It seems incredible that there are houses up there. He sees no signs of a road up to them. Grim, icy giants watch his progress through gaps in the clouds. Brig becomes a glow far below them.

They crawl into a small village. There is a handful of cars and a cable car station. Far above them, a little blue cable car is disappearing into the clouds. Findhorn stops their vehicle and they step out, their breath misting in the freezing air. Drindle walks over to a cluster of post boxes. They scan the names. Herr W. Neff lives in a house called *Heya*.

They split up. Findhorn finds himself wandering along narrow streets, barely a car width. Snow is piled high on either side. There are neat wooden chalets with verandahs and red shutters, and dates and names painted in white Gothic script on their walls. Part of the village is given over to big wooden huts standing on thick wooden stilts. Some are filled with wood, others with hay. He passes a church whose small, crowded cemetery is outlined under a metre of pristine, fluffy snow. There is an air of orderliness about everything. There is, however, no *Heya*.

A one-track, potholed road leads out of the village: the thin, black line on Findhorn's map. He looks at it, trying to follow its route up the mountain. Here and there he glimpses stretches of the road. Romella is flouncing through the car park snow. She is wearing blue jeans and leather boots; Findhorn thinks there is something vaguely eccentric about the combination of Peruvian hat and Doug's duffle coat. He points upwards. 'I don't think it can be done.'

She looks up. 'You could be right.'

'What the hell are we doing here?'

'I'm beginning to wonder.'

The killers appear and they settle into the car. Findhorn takes off, leaving the square and taking the car onto the track. He is gripped by fear within the first two hundred yards. It is almost impossible not to skid, and within half a mile the metal barriers have petered out. He glances briefly away from the road, finds himself looking down on the roofs of chalets far, far below, and experiences a surge of terror. In the car, there is dead silence.

After about a mile the road worsens. The snow becomes deeper, and he has to negotiate a series of tight hairpin bends with nothing between the car and thousands of feet of air. His jaw aches with tension, his hands are sore with gripping the steering wheel and a dull ache has developed in his gut. Above them, a massive white cloud is billowing down the mountainside like an approaching avalanche.

At last, in a state of quiet terror, Findhorn sees an Alpine villa on the edge of his vision: he doesn't dare take his eye off the track. A final bend and the road levels, terminating at a square of open, flat ground. They step out. Findhorn is weak at the knees. To him, the altitude is incredible. They are looking out over white Alpine peaks and the air is pure and cold. He catches a whiff of wood smoke. Boulders as big as houses are scattered around. A forest of snow-laden conifers lies above them and there is a rough track into the trees. Far across the valley, clouds are pouring down between peaks like a vast waterfall.

The chalet is marked *Heya*. It is about fifty yards back from the square and is reached by a steep path. There is no garage, but there is a Saab in the square, and tracks in the snow where another vehicle has taken off recently. The winter supply of wood is piled high at the side of the chalet, which has a wooden verandah with little flower boxes. The roof is under a metre of snow and projects out over the house. The upstairs shutters are closed. A small Christmas tree is set to the side of a big downstairs window, its lights brilliant in the gloom.

'This guy likes seclusion,' Findhorn says. He is shaking all over.

'Which suits our purpose nicely.' Drindle is opening the rear door of the Suzuki.

'There might be a housekeeper,' Romella suggested.

'If there is, so much the worse for her.' Drindle is pulling what looks like a squat shotgun out of a holdall. The Korean is balancing a pistol in each hand, as if he is weighing potatoes. He ends up stuffing one in each trenchcoat pocket.

'There shouldn't be, not with secret discussions about to take place,' Findhorn hopes. In spite of the cold air he feels little beads of sweat on his brow.

Drindle growls something to the Korean, who hands her a pair of black leather gloves before putting on a pair himself. Romella's face goes chalk white and Findhorn feels his own going the same way.

They trudge up through the snow, Drindle leading and the Korean taking up the rear. Drindle looks through a window, tries a door. Then the Korean is shouting from the side of the house. He is holding a heavy axe. There are wooden steps down into a cellar. In the cellar, there is a pyramid of wood, and trestles, and the smell of sawdust, and a door. They stand back as he smashes at the door repeatedly, the noise painfully loud in the confined space. Then he has an arm through and is fiddling with an inside key, and they are into a short corridor and through another door.

They are met by warmth.

The kitchen has a high stone roof, vaulted in the Italian style. An alcove contains a four-oven, pewter coloured Aga stove. A shiny copper pot is suspended from the ceiling by a big-hooped black chain. Copper pans are hooked onto nails at various points around the whitewashed walls. The furniture is pine, antique and solid. It is highly polished. Chairs are scattered around as well as little tables on which are vases with yellow, red and pink flowers. Little decorative cups in odd places contrast with the solidity of the furniture. There is a smell of stew, presumably simmering in one of the four ovens.

Through to the living room, which is doubling as a dining room. Here there is a smell of beeswax and scent, and an air of obsessive neatness. Near the centre of the room is a heavy table with white tablecloth. The table has been set for dinner: there are six places. Crystal wine glasses sparkle in the Christmas-tree lights. The air is warm from a wood-burning stove set in an inglenook. There is an old-fashioned pendulum clock over the fireplace; its steady tick-tock gives a sense of harmony to the room, of solidity and domestic contentment.

It also makes Drindle's voice that much more jarring. 'Every Swiss household has a rifle. Find it.'

Findhorn, Romella and the Korean climb the wooden stairs. There are three bedrooms off. Findhorn follows Romella into a bedroom. 'This is madness. What are we doing here?'

'Do you think I'm delirious about it?'

'Have you thought about the gloves?'

Her face is grim. 'Yes.'

'You know what it means?'

'I'm not stupid, Fred. They're not bothered if we're caught.'

Findhorn whispers, 'But if we were caught we could talk. They'd be at risk.'

'I know. Therefore they intend to kill us.'

'What are you people whispering about up there? Have you found it?'

The Korean shouts triumphantly and appears on the landing with a long-barrelled rifle which looks as if it is polished as regularly as the copper pans.

'What can we do?' she whispers.

'Come down here where I can see you.'

Ms Drindle's fur coat, hat and wig have been tossed on a chair and he has his feet up on the dining table. His hair is close-cropped and grey. He is examining, almost caressing, the gun. It has a wooden stock with a fist-sized hole in it, and a short, stubby dark barrel. The Korean tosses him the rifle and disappears.

Findhorn looks at Drindle. 'I suspected it.'

Drindle smiles. 'To confuse witnesses. And there are so many security cameras these days.'

'Maybe you just get a kick out of dressing in women's clothes.'

Drindle unclips the rifle's magazine, empties the bullets into a vase, replaces it and tosses the rifle to Romella. 'Put it back.'

The Korean shouts something. They go through to a large study. The man is still in trenchcoat and hat, but his sunglasses are off and he is grinning hugely. There is a safe, about three feet tall, in the corner of the room. Drindle drops to his knees, plays with the handle of the safe. He turns to them, a strange expression on his face. 'It's in here, isn't it? The trillion dollar secret. And all we need is the key.' He runs his gloved fingers round the base. 'It's on a concrete plinth, and we would need a small crane to move it. But no matter, the key will arrive shortly.' He stands up and grins ghoulishly. Then he snaps something to the Korean, who scowls and heads out. There is a brief gust of cold air as he leaves.

Drindle waves his gun at Romella and Findhorn, directing them towards the living room. He waves it again and they sit on chairs away from the window. He throws a couple of heavy logs onto the fire and opens the stove's air vent. Then he sits across from them, while a red glow flickers through the room as the sky darkens outside.

The Korean is back in fifteen minutes, during which

time not a word of conversation has been uttered in the room. He looks like a snowman. He tosses his black trenchcoat and hat on the floor next to the Christmas tree and holds his hands to the fire, shivering and cursing. To Findhorn, the man in the firelight looks demonic.

Then the Korean, warmed up, sits back on a low leather armchair with a pistol on his lap, grinning for no obvious reason.

And they wait.

34

Petrosian's Secret

The Saab has snowchains, which is just as well given the steadily falling snow and the steepness of the road. Peering through a crack in an upstairs shutter, Drindle spreads out five fingers of one hand.

There is the rattle of a key in a lock and a brief gust of wind as the front door opens. The voices are in German; two of them are female. Findhorn recognizes one of the male voices.

He tries to visualise what is about to unfold but can't take it in. His legs are shaking. Drindle and the Korean, on the other hand, are showing no emotion. They are standing still, quiet and alert, two predators poised to kill.

Somebody has moved into the kitchen. Pots are being slid onto hotplates. Others are drifting into the living room. There is the sound of logs being thrown on the fire. A collective laugh. Glasses clinking.

And now somebody is plodding heavily up the stairs.

The Korean steps back from the door, an ugly little pistol in his hand. The door opens. Drindle points his squat shotgun at arm's length, straight at the man's head. The man is fortyish and bearded. He drops the suitcases he is carrying. Drindle raises a finger to his lips, then points, and they follow the terrified man down the stairs. Drindle steers him into the living room, and the Korean turns into the kitchen.

A man and woman are lounging back on the leather sofa, glasses in hand. They do not immediately realize what is happening. Then the woman gives a startled 'Ach!' The man next to her gapes, pop-eyed, and spills red wine onto his white sweater and slacks. Two other men, in armchairs, sit bolt upright. One is formally dressed in a white dinner suit and black tie. The other is Pitman, and Findhorn wonders whether there are any limits to human duplicity.

The Korean joins them, pushing an ashen-faced, middle-aged woman in front of him. He pushes her into a chair next to the Christmas tree. Drindle strolls casually towards Albrecht and stops, just outside arm's length. He points the gun at the quivering woman on the couch next to him. 'You have been naughty, Herr Albrecht, alias Tati. Your Temple was to deliver the diaries to my employer, not steal it for your own profit. I fear that punishment is called for.'

There is dead silence.

Drindle continues: 'You will recognize the weapon as a Russian VEPR 308 carbine. Indeed you have done business with the Vyatskie Polyani machine plant where it is produced. I do not need to tell you that it is autoloading, and you will understand its effects on the human body at this range.'

The woman screams. Drindle throws her an irritated

glance and continues, 'The position is simple. You will either deliver up the Petrosian document or I will give a practical demonstration of its effects on this woman. Then, if this has not persuaded you, I will repeat the process with another of your guests. If, when I have run out of guests, you still have nothing to say, then it will be your turn.'

Through his fear, Findhorn almost feels admiration for Albrecht's nerve. He is silent for about ten seconds, during which time the woman begins to hyperventilate and Findhorn increasingly expects the gun to fire. Then Albrecht is saying, almost calmly, 'And what happens to us if I give you the document?'

'We will disable your cars and telephone, tie you up and leave you. By the time you have freed yourselves and called the police we will be out of Switzerland.'

'I can't deliver the document. It's in Davos.'

Drindle looks at the woman and smiles. He speaks softly: 'That is unfortunate.'

She looks as if she might faint. 'Please. I have two children.'

'Two misfortunes, then.'

The Korean has moved behind and to the left of Findhorn, near the door, a position from which he can view the whole room. There is a gap of about five feet between him and Findhorn. Findhorn has a desperate momentary vision of diving for the man's gun, using it to shoot Drindle. Almost immediately, he rules it out. It is a schoolboy fantasy, a quick route to suicide.

Again that amazing nerve. 'If I do not give you the

document, you will not kill us. The small gain of doing so would be outweighed by the risk of spending your remaining days in a cage. But if I give you the document you will kill us. This is because its value is so large that murder becomes a risk worth taking. After all, we can identify you.'

The Korean actually speaks. His voice is guttural, coming almost from his chest, and English is clearly a poor second language. 'Shoot the bitch. Show him we serious.'

Albrecht says, 'But if you shoot Elsa there is no point in giving you the document. This is because we would all be witnesses to murder. You would have to kill us all.'

'Your logic is flawed, Albrecht. For one thing, we are professionals. The risk of capture is very small and does not enter into the equation. For another, I can cause pain.' The bang of the carbine irrupts savagely into the quiet room. Blood and fragments of white bone spray from around the woman's shins, along with hunks of polystyrene foam from the sofa. She collapses onto the floor, writhing and shrieking.

Albrecht jumps up. He raises his hands as if to ward off further shooting. He looks down at the screaming woman. His expression is one of pure horror. 'Wait!'

Over the woman's screams, Drindle is saying, 'I fear your Christmas Eve is turning out brutal, Albrecht. And it is going to get worse. But give us the document and you will not be killed. That is a promise. *Sie verstehen?*' He points the gun at the man in the dinner suit, and smiles again. The man pales and speaks rapidly to Albrecht in some Schwitzerdeutsch dialect, his voice brimming with terror. Pitman is sitting quietly, but alert like a cat.

'It's upstairs, in a safe.' Albrecht can scarcely talk.

'I know it is. Get it. *Beeilen Sie sich*.'

Albrecht stumbles out of the room, Drindle following.

The bearded man and Romella are on their knees, trying to stem the flow of blood with table napkins, but the woman is writhing too much, screaming with every touch of her shin. The man in the armchair is gripping its arms and shaking uncontrollably. His eyes are wide with terror. The woman next to the Christmas tree has her eyes closed and is mumbling under her breath. The Korean watches dispassionately from a corner, arms folded and pistol in hand. Findhorn judges the five foot gap, but he knows it is hopeless. The Korean glances at him and grins, as if inviting him to try. A pool of bright red blood is spreading across the wooden floor.

Albrecht appears a minute later, Drindle following with his carbine in one hand and a thick document in the other. The pages are stapled together and look slightly yellow with age. He tosses the document to Findhorn and with his free hand pulls at the cover on the dining-room table. Glasses, candles, cutlery and crockery crash onto the wooden floor in a heap. He pulls a dining-room chair back and motions to Findhorn with his head. 'Verify its authenticity, if you please.'

Findhorn sits down. There are about twenty pages. It is single-sided, handwritten in Armenian, with half a dozen diagrams. Names like Bethe, Bohr and Einstein are written in English. The equations use the familiar alphabet and

the diagrams are also annotated in English. Findhorn
suspects that, with an effort, he might be able to grasp
what is going on through the mass of equations alone.

'I need my translator.'

Drindle snaps his fingers at Romella.

'Fuck off.' She is up to her elbows in blood. The table
napkins are now saturated with blood and the woman is
moaning, slipping in and out of consciousness.

Drindle stands over the groaning woman, points the
gun at her head. Romella looks as if she wants to grab the
gun and ram it down Drindle's throat. The frozen tableau
seems to go on and on.

Findhorn, sensing catastrophe, says, 'Romella, better
not,' and she stands up and heads angrily for the door.

'Where you go?' the Korean demands, pointing his gun,
but she pushes past him roughly, blood from her hand
staining his shirt.

She is back in a minute, drying her hands with a white
towel. She sits down beside Findhorn at the table. She is
breathing heavily and white with rage.

The woman is now unconscious. The bearded man says,
'Her pulse is rapid. I can hardly feel it.'

Findhorn hands the document to Romella. 'Let's make
it quick.'

She nods, tight-lipped. 'Okay.' She flips through the
pages. 'Right, it's entitled *Energy from the Vacuum*. It's in
four sections. Section One, Introduction; Section Two,
Thermodynamics of energy extraction; Section Three, A
new view of gravity and inertia; Section Four, Practical
energy extraction.'

'Section One: it's about the Casimir effect?'

'Well, yes. But there's a lot more. Here's this HMS *Daring* you talked about, and Foucault's Pendulum. He's tying it in to something called the Ylem—'

'Never mind, there's no time. What sort of energy is he talking about extracting? What's he saying here?' Findhorn points to a sentence with a number.

' "... the energy density of the vacuum is therefore estimated to be of the same order as the Planck energy, with an extractable fraction of perhaps 10^{21} ergs per cubic millimetre" – is that a lot?'

A Hiroshima bomb in every cubic millimetre of space. 'It's enough. What's his punch line? Give me the last para of the Intro.'

She translates verbatim, speaking in a low, rapid voice inaudible to anyone but Findhorn: ' "In Section Two I show that there is no inconsistency between the principle of conservation of energy and the extraction of unlimited energy from the vacuum. Section Three meets the objection that the energy density of the vacuum would curve space to a degree contradicted by observations. The point here is that the virtual radiation has such a fleeting existence that no gravitational mass is associated with it. Indeed, I show that inertia and gravity can be viewed as the reactions of mass to an asymmetric radiation field in an accelerated frame ..." '

'Her pulse is almost gone. If we don't get her to hospital she may die.'

Drindle says, 'She assuredly will if Albrecht is not playing straight with me. You two, why have you stopped

Section Three amounts to a new theory of gravitation. Findhorn suspects that he is staring a Nobel Prize in the face. He says, 'There's no time for this. The woman may be dying. Skip to Section Four.'

Section Four. The sorcerer's trick.

Romella reads the words rapidly and quietly, not understanding any of it, Findhorn asking her to skip as many paragraphs as he can. And as she translates, Findhorn almost forgets where he is. The concept is utterly strange, an approach to vacuum engineering unlike anything he had visualized. It is a symbiosis of biology and physics. It is also stunningly simple.

In 1952 Chase and Henshal discovered the structure of viruses. It was a dual structure, like a golf ball. A soft inner core of RNA carried the information the virus needed to replicate itself. Protection of this vital core came in the form of a hard outer layer, a protein molecule, a long string of atoms folded round the RNA, its thousands of constituent atoms densely packed. This protective shell – the capsid – is an enormously complex crystal. A golf ball with legs.

The virus is a fraction of a micron in size. Its atoms shimmer and shake in the quantum vacuum; they feel the zero point energy, the vibrations of distant galaxies.

Coat a little plate, a centimetre on a side and machined as flat as technology will allow, with a thin layer of virus. Put this plate in a vacuum, and surge a huge electric current through it. The plate disintegrates into a cloud of microscopic platelets. The energy of the galaxies – the zero point energy – forces the little plates together. For a tiny handful, flatter than the average, the Casimir force is large enough to create X-rays, the pressure from whi... compresses neighbouring platelets together, creating more zero point pressure and hence more X-rays . . .

And now Petrosian cleverly exploits the dynamics of the viral crystal. It is small enough to feel the vacuum fluctuations and big enough to absorb them, extracting energy from the tiny vacuum between the plates and allowing reactions to take place which would be impossible in the macroworld; time moves at a different rate, light moves faster; causality is violated; high-energy electrons and positrons are created out of the void. The virus crystal now behaves like a single giant atom; it quantum levels are squashed closely together; the relativistic electrons crash through these, penetrating the nucleus, sinking into the shadowy depths of the energy ocean. The vacuum is now unstable; and it cannot be emptied.

A childhood memory flashes through Findhorn's mind, a story about a miller who wished for more flour but the process couldn't be stopped and the stuff poured out of his mill and flooded the countryside.

Petrosian is vague about where it will end but make speculative remarks about matter annihilation.

Once triggered, there is no more need for an electric field: the immense pressure created in the process enough. There is an appendix. For some reason Petrosian has typed it in Russian. Romella says she reads Russian translates in a quiet voice which is seething with rage There are engineering drawings. Small virus-coated plate are being fired into a giant titanium chamber (a hundred metres across in Petrosian's sketch, with walls three metres thick); they maintain an incandescent fireball, fuelled by gamma rays pouring out of empty space, drawing on incomprehensible cosmic energies.

All this Findhorn and Romella skim through in a couple of minutes. The text is backed up by a second appendix of densely argued mathematics that Findhorn doesn't even attempt. However, he notes the virus that Petrosian has identified as suitable. The tobacco mosaic virus, which Findhorn assumes is a source of disease in tobacco plants.

Another thirty seconds: the problem, admitted by Petrosian in a footnote, is the cut-off point for the energy generation. It depends on unknown properties of the vacuum at unexplored energies. It is all untested theory. It may go as Petrosian thought, giving a sort of controlled fireball from which endless energy can be safely tapped. Or a few powers of ten may be missing and a laboratory and the surrounding countryside may disappear when the switch is thrown. Or a few more powers of ten, and oceans will boil and the planet will be sterilized.

Or the whole process could be a dud. Petrosian's machine might be a nonsense, a fantasy thing which would yield nothing. Findhorn remembers Bradfield's words: *we get a lot of crank science in our field.*

Findhorn thinks of that sweaty day in MacDonald's ranch where the bits of plutonium had to be pushed together almost to the point of criticality. He thinks of Petrosian's recurring nightmare, that the nuclear fireball might be hot enough to ignite the atmosphere. And he thinks of his own fears about instability, of the polar meltdown waiting to happen, and at last his mind becomes one with Petrosian's, and he understands his fear about the dark corners of the vacuum process, and his wish to hide it away until some future utopia when the pirates were gone and the risks could be assessed in a responsible and open marketplace. Petrosian, Findhorn realises, was the classic naive academic.

Drindle's voice brings him back to harsh reality: 'Have you finished?'

Findhorn blows out his cheeks. 'The document is authentic.'

The Korean grins. He points the gun at Findhorn and says, 'Boom boom!'

35

The Kill

Findhorn is nauseous. He is shaking, and almost choking with stress. He knows the answer but tries it anyway: 'These people know nothing about the process. You can let them go.'

Drindle smiles. 'You are so naive.'

What happens next spans no more than three seconds. The woman at Drindle's feet moans. He points his carbine down at her and fires. The bang is deafening. A fountain of red spray shoots into the air. The bearded man, still trying to stem the blood from her legs, looks up in astonishment, his face dotted with little red spots, but there is another deafening bang and he falls back in slow motion, his chest a mangled red hole. Albrecht opens his mouth to speak but there is a third bang and his eyes roll back and he flings his arms out like a preacher and collapses lifeless on the sofa. The woman at the Christmas tree still has her eyes closed and she is praying in a wild, frightened voice, and Drindle is pointing his gun at her but now Findhorn is on his feet and screaming at the top of his voice, 'It's going out on the Internet! It's going out on the Internet!'

Drindle pauses, curious, his finger squeezing the carbine's trigger. Findhorn's ears are singing from the bangs.

'It's going to the Chairmen of Fiat SpA and Otto Wolff. It's going to Goldman Sachs International and Chase Manhattan. It's going to Aerospatiale Matra and Siemens Defence. It's being e-mailed to Haisch at Lockheed Martin and Rueda in California and Longair at the Cavendish and Puthoff in Texas. It's going to Nobel prizewinners in Princeton and computer geeks in Idaho. Most of all it's going to electronic bulletin boards. From there it'll spread like wildfire.' He stops, gasping for breath.

The man in the white dinner suit is sobbing noisily. Findhorn, his voice raw from the sudden yelling, continues more quietly, taking deep gulps of air: 'Twenty-four hours from now the biggest secret on earth, the one you've been paid to obliterate, will be the most talked-about item on the planet.'

Drindle doesn't blink. The Korean is a statue.

'I can stop it. But not if I'm dead.'

'An ingenious lie,' suggests Drindle.

'I've put a time lock on it. If I don't reach a computer terminal by a specific time, and punch in a password, the message goes out automatically. You'll have failed. Do you want to explain that failure to Mister Matsumo? Or do you think you can spend the rest of your life one step ahead of Matsumo Holdings?'

The man falls onto his knees, bawling and pleading for his life. The Korean steps over corpses towards him, snarls fiercely, and snaps back the hammer of his weapon.

Drindle shouts, '*Yamero!*' The Korean shouts, 'You be quiet!', whether to Drindle or the man is unclear. The man falls silent, but his shoulders are heaving in terror.

'Contact your paymaster,' Findhorn continues, breathing in cordite and wood smoke. 'Tell him I need access to the Internet every month for the rest of my life. Tell him to hope that I never fall out of a window, never die in a car crash, never have a heart attack, never die of pneumonia or cancer, never drown at sea. I must never, never go missing. Tell him all of that. Tell him that in my good health and happiness lies his own. And my misfortune is his. I expect a man in his position has colleagues who reward success well and punish failure harshly.'

'I am sure you are right, Mister Findhorn. High rewards do entail high risks. I am equally sure that you are lying.'

'That's not your call to make.'

'I will make my call. Sit down.' Drindle gives some curt order to the Korean and leaves the room smartly. Sweat is beginning to run down Findhorn's face and neck. The woman is still praying, quietly, in German. The Korean sits down at the dining-room table. His eyes flicker between Romella and Findhorn.

Drindle is back in less than a minute, tapping numbers on a cordless phone while holding his carbine. He speaks fluent Japanese into the telephone.

'Directory Enquiries,' Romella volunteers to Findhorn. She is grey-faced and trembling. The Korean barks angrily, waving his gun.

Another number. This time the conversation is concentrated, prolonged, with a serious edge. Findhorn is almost overcome with a sort of light-headedness; the room is warm from the log fire, but he is shivering with cold. Colour, on the other hand, is slowly returning to Romella's cheeks. She looks defiantly at the Korean and turns coolly to Findhorn. 'He's phoned a secretary at home. It's about four a.m. in Kyoto.'

The conversation ends. Drindle sits down at the table, directly opposite Findhorn. He is framed by the Christmas tree. He places the carbine and the phone on the table and sits back, arms folded. Findhorn's eyes are locked hypnotically with Drindle's. He hates him more than anything else on the planet.

The silence goes on, broken only by the quiet crackling of burning logs. One crashes in the fire. Findhorn starts and Drindle smiles contemptuously. The smell of over-cooked stew is beginning to drift in from the kitchen, mingling with that of wood smoke and fresh blood. It is a mixture that Findhorn knows, if he survives, he will never forget.

Ten minutes pass.

From somewhere far down in the valley, the ponderous Oompah-da-Oompah-da of a brass band drifts up. Church bells, almost on the limit of hearing, ring out eight o'clock.

The phone, when it finally cuts into the stillness, is to Findhorn like an executioner's summons. He feels himself going white. Drindle slides his right hand onto the stock of the gun, finger round trigger, and picks up the telephone with his left. The conversation is almost one-sided, Drindle interjecting no more than the occasional '*Hai!*' Findhorn can't take his eyes from the assassin's; but he can read nothing in them.

Finally Drindle takes the phone from his ear, resting the mouthpiece on his shoulder. 'Are you brave?'

'Go to hell.'

Drindle nods. 'A brave answer in the circumstances. Courage, however, will merely prolong your agony without affecting the final outcome. You are to be tortured to the point where you will scream the password and the location of your electronic file even if it means your death. Medical expertise will be on hand to ensure that your heart does not give out. If you wish, we can demonstrate our skill in these matters by working on your translator friend. Once you have seen what we can do, you will tell us what we want to know. We will of course require to verify your information before we dispose of you. Please believe that I personally will not relish this process. But I cannot answer for my colleague.'

From the corner of his eye, Findhorn sees a broad grin spreading over the Korean's features. Romella has frozen, eyes wide with fear.

Findhorn says, 'You won't touch us.' He says it with an air of confidence but there is a solid lump in his stomach.

Drindle seems amused, raises sceptical eyebrows. 'No?'

'Because if you do I'll scream the password, you'll kill me, and delete the file.'

'Forgive me, but fear is making you confused. That is the object.'

Findhorn continues: 'And then you'll find that hidden away in some distant machine there's a second file, a duplicate. Maybe there's a third such file. Maybe a fourth. But how can you ever verify this? How many Romellas can you torture? Can you resurrect me to kill me all over again?'

For the first time the assassin's suavity is replaced by a darker look. 'That was naughty.' He speaks again into the telephone, his eyes never leaving Findhorn's. Then he slides the phone across the table.

Findhorn doesn't know what to expect. He picks it up. Yoshi Matsumo's voice comes over as clearly as if he is sitting at the table. 'Very clever, Mister Findhorn.'

Findhorn keeps trying for a confident tone. 'You have nothing to fear from me. So long as I outlive you.'

There is a tiny delay. The signal is, after all, travelling from Switzerland to a point twenty-four-thousand miles above the earth, relaying back down to a distant country, and the reply is traversing the same immense journey in the opposite direction. 'You claim you already had the secret before you entered the chalet?'

'I do.'

'Why then did you join my Friendship colleagues?'

'I told you. Your interests and mine coincide on this matter. I didn't want Albrecht's people getting a patent.'

'You stretch credulity to breaking point. But even if what you say is true, how can I let you go, to sell the secret?'

Findhorn puffs out his cheeks. The Korean is frowning angrily. 'Why all talk talk? Just finish the job. Two seconds.'

'Think about it, Matsumo.'

'I think, Mister Findhorn, that you are a principled man. Your principles have forced you to kill the innocent in order to hide the secret. These same principles will not allow you to make this devastating thing public even to save your life. Therefore your Internet files do not exist. Therefore you can safely be executed. Purely, you understand, as a precaution, in case on some future date poverty or greed should overcome those strong principles of yours.'

Drindle is watching Findhorn with quiet interest: a lion studying an antelope.

The telephone is now slippery with sweat. 'You've misread the situation. I killed these people for two million US dollars, one for me, one for my assistant.' Now he senses Romella staring at him. 'Don't you see, with these guys gone, I'm the only person on the planet who knows the process. You're my market, Yoshi. Silence me. Stuff my mouth with gold.'

Unexpectedly, the silence at the end of the line is broken by a peal of laughter. Findhorn holds the receiver away; startled faces around the table stare at the phone. When he has stopped laughing, Yoshi Matsumo says, 'What a magnificent liar you are, Mister Findhorn! I congratulate you on your ingenuity.' There is another long silence. Findhorn begins to wonder if the line has gone dead. Then: 'However, you do present me with an interesting quandary. Suppose that I kill you. Then if, as I believe, there is no message waiting to be broadcast, your death solves my problem. But now suppose that, implausible though it is, you are telling the truth. Then I fear that your death would quickly be followed by my disgrace, perhaps even my demise.'

'So make your pre-emptive sale and let us go.'

'Unfortunately, having sold the secret to me, you might then sell it all over again to someone else. Someone who might use the process and ruin my company. Therein lies my dilemma: alive or dead, you are a risk.'

Findhorn wipes an irritating drop of sweat from an eyebrow. The Korean, sensing an atmosphere, is now grinning and nodding, taunting Findhorn by pretending to shoot him with the gun. Matsumo continues: 'An idealist, or a clever buccaneer? That is the question. Return the phone to my assistant.'

Findhorn is beginning to feel a terrible tightness in his chest and jaw. He slides the telephone across the polished table back to Drindle. There is a brief conversation in Japanese and then, again, silence.

Drindle touches the barrel of the carbine. 'Still warm. It comes with telescopic sights but I removed them. They are just a nuisance at this range. He's consulting colleagues.'

Children's voices.

Stille Nacht, Heilige Nacht . . . The carol drifts faintly up from another world, a world of innocence and love and goodness, of solid values and moral certainties. Findhorn looks into Drindle's eyes, tries to see through them into the man's soul, gives up.

Alles schläft . . .

Big snow flakes are falling thickly past the window: soon they will all be snowed in, trapped together in the chalet. The logs are crackling quietly.

Einsam wacht . . .

They could be in a scene on a Christmas card, were it not for the three corpses, eyes half shut, mouths open, their blood staining the polished wooden floor.

And in the warm dining room, the living are as still as the corpses, sleeping in Heavenly peace. *Schlaf in himmlischer Ruh, Schlaf in himmlischer Ruh . . .*

A voice on the telephone. Drindle listens, his eyes expressionless, for some minutes. Then, again, he slides the telephone across to Findhorn, his face grim. Matsumo speaks like a judge pronouncing sentence: 'Mister Findhorn, I am convinced that you have put nothing on the Internet.'

Dive for the kitchen. Romella might get to the Korean.

'But then, why should I take even a slight chance with that? There is another way forward. Two million dollars is miniscule in relation to what is at stake. On some future occasion, when the money runs low, you might be tempted to talk. I must therefore make you a very rich man, in order to substantially reduce that temptation. I have opened an account for you in the Hofbahnstrasse in Zurich and arranged for twenty million dollars to be paid into it. You will be able to draw on this tomorrow morning when the bank opens.'

Findhorn has trouble taking it in. his mind is being hit simultaneously from several directions. He forces himself to speak calmly. 'Money like that would look like a drug transaction. What about the Swiss Banking Commission? Or even Interpol?'

'Do not concern yourself with such matters; we have mechanisms. Telephone my secretary at noon, Japanese time, that is in eight hours. Understand that, should you ever reveal the secret, or discuss our transaction, I will arrange to have you hunted down and exterminated even from beyond my grave. But that risk is one which, as a rich man, you will find no need to run. Does the solution strike you as satisfactory?'

'I think we have an understanding.'

There is a brief pause, longer than the travel time of radio between them. 'So, I have enjoyed our little game of kendo, Findhorn-san. We are both winners. You are now rich, and I have suppressed the energy secret. The game has been played with our wits rather than *shinai* – forgive me, I do not know the English word—'

'Bamboo sticks?'

'—and if you were Japanese rather than a *gaijin*, I would salute you as an equal.'

Stuff you, Findhorn thinks. He puts the telephone down and turns to Romella. 'We're out of here.'

The assassin's urbanity is becoming frayed. 'If I had my way things would go differently.'

'It's a matter of making the right call. Which is why Matsumo pulls the strings up above while you jerk about down below.'

Drindle picks up Petrosian's document. 'Your witty little barbs don't penetrate my skin, but my partner is a different matter. I can best describe his temperament as volcanic. And, since he is a stupid man, the issues are beyond his grasp.' He opens the front of the wood fire, throws the document onto the logs. The Korean says something in an angry voice. The pages curl, catch fire at the edges. Irrigated deserts, cheap superbombs, fertilizers from the air, social and financial chaos, roads to the back of beyond, all go up in flames. 'Get out. Take the Saab and leave it at the railway station.'

'What about you?' asks Findhorn, standing up. His legs, he finds, are hardly able to support him.

'We have a lot to do here. There are enough DNA samples in this house to gladden the hearts of policemen from the North Cape to Hong Kong. Now go, quickly.'

'May you die horribly some day soon,' Findhorn says.

The man in the white suit stands up, fearfully, edges towards the door, and then runs out; it would be comical in less deadly circumstances. Pitman follows, walking steadily. He seems about to say something to Findhorn, but then leaves without a word. The woman at the Christmas tree has opened her eyes but is sitting, motionless. She seems not to know what is happening. Romella walks over to her, takes her by the elbow, tries out a smile.

At the door, Findhorn glances back. Drindle has opened the cocktail cabinet and is pouring himself a red Martini. The Korean's eyes are flitting between Findhorn and Drindle. His fist is tightly clenched around the pistol. He is jerking it up and down as if it is a hammer. His face is almost comically angry.

The volcano is about to erupt.

36

Brass Bands

Keys on hall table, marked by Saab logo; front door, heavy
pine, already open. Pitman and the other man have run
ahead of them, vanishing into the dark. Freezing air and
snow, billowing into the hall.

Say nothing. Don't stop. Don't look behind.

Outside, the snow is already a foot deep. Romella
hastily steers the dazed woman ahead of her. The Saab is
a mound of white. Findhorn waves his arms frantically
over it, brushing snow off door and windscreen, while
Romella bundles the woman into the back of the car.
They jump in. He fumbles with the key, the engine starts
and he quickly puts the automatic gearbox into reverse.
There is a single loud bang from the direction of the
chalet.

Romella opens the car door and jumps out, sliding
and falling. Findhorn stands on the brake and the car
starts to crab sideways. The rear mirror shows only snow
and blackness. He knows he is close to horrendous
precipices. Romella disappears into the black, crouched
and running.

The door of the chalet swings open. The Korean's

squat frame is silhouetted against the hall light. He is clutching Drindle's carbine. Findhorn says 'Christ,' spins the steering wheel. The car spins but he is now utterly disoriented.

Something punches the car's windscreen and half of it disappears. Findhorn is sprayed with little squares of safety glass. He ducks his head and feels the car spin some more; he takes his foot off the accelerator but there is a heavy thump, the car tilts on its side. He thinks he is going over the edge. Airbags explode into the passenger compartment, enveloping him. Throughout this, the woman in the back makes not a sound. Findhorn thinks she might be praying.

The car is on its side. The driver's door is below him, compressed snow pushed up against his side window. He is coccooned in safety belt and airbags. He unbuckles, fights his way in panic through the enveloping bags, scrambling up towards the passenger door. He stands on the steering wheel, thrusts the door up against its own weight and clambers half out of the car. The door thumps down on his back. The pain is excruciating and for some awful moments he cannot move his legs. The Korean is now about thirty yards away, ploughing heavily through knee-deep snow. Findhorn scrambles over the side of the car, falls head first into the snow, picks himself up and finds himself staring at the carbine.

The Korean's face is distorted with rage; he is a man almost out of control.

Findhorn hopes it will be quick.

And then the Korean is performing a sort of pirhouette,

like a ballet-dancing gorilla, the gun flying from his grasp and disappearing into the deep snow. He says 'Oof!' and falls onto his knees, clutching his thigh.

Romella is bounding down the driveway with a rifle, her strides lengthening. She falls face first and snow-ploughs down the slope, pushing up a mound of snow ahead of her. The Korean is on all fours, frantically scrabbling like a dog searching for a mouse.

'Get the gun!' Romella yells, her face snow-covered.

Findhorn scrambles clumsily forwards, almost falling. Within yards of the Korean he sees the long hole in the snow where the carbine has disappeared. The Korean sees it too and lunges towards it. Findhorn reaches it first, snatches the weapon up by the barrel, falls backwards, picks himself up. Romella is on her feet, her face and hair covered in white. 'Kill him!' she shouts.

'*What?*' Findhorn shakes his head dumbly as Romella's instruction sinks in.

'Kill him! If you let him live he'll come after you. He'll find you, torture you for the secret, and kill you. Is that what you want? To go the way of Captain Hansen? To spend the rest of your life listening for sounds in the dark?'

'What about the police?' he calls out.

'For God's sake, Fred! Get real!'

The Korean is limping into the darkness, holding his leg.

'I can't.'

'Fred! You have to!'

The Korean vanishes behind a curtain of snow, limping

swiftly down the road. Findhorn takes off, following the man's tracks. He catches up with him within fifty yards. The man is wondering whether to run off the road. The lights of a village, far below, come and go through dark patches. He turns and faces Findhorn. His head and arms are thick with snow and he is no longer clutching his leg. Findhorn raises the gun and points it at the Korean's heaving chest. The man shakes his head. Findhorn fires once; snowflakes around him are briefly illuminated yellow in the flash from the gun. He has never fired a gun before and his shoulder is snapped painfully back by the recoil. The Korean pitches backwards, face up, on the edge of a precipitous drop. Findhorn approaches, stands over the man. The Korean's face can just be discerned in the light scattered from the snow, and it is distorted with pain and fear. A dark stain is spreading over his right sleeve. He raises a hand protectively, says, 'Please. I leave you alone.'

This time Findhorn holds the carbine firmly with both hands. Blood and bone spurt from the Korean's chest. Findhorn is aghast, not by the sight but by the elation which surges through his body at the moment the Korean dies.

He stands at the edge of the precipice and looks down into a blizzard-filled cauldron. He glimpses house lights far below. Then he sits down in the deep snow and heaves at the Korean's body with both feet. The man is surprisingly heavy. Findhorn keeps pushing and edging forwards until the body slides down a few feet, gathering speed like a sledge, and then disappears noiselessly over the edge in a flurry of snow. Then he tosses the carbine into the black void and ploughs back towards the chalet. His mind is empty and he keeps it that way.

The Saab is in a ditch. Its headlights are pointing up at the snow-filled sky, wipers rubbing roughly over the remaining windscreen. Its engine is still running, little wisps of steam drifting up from the hot exhaust. Romella has opened the back door and is looking in. Findhorn joins her: the woman's body is crouched in a corner, her head barely attached to the rest of it. He thinks about her two children but is unable to speak.

Romella turns and plods back into the house. She re-emerges with keys.

In the Merc, Findhorn manages to fasten his belt, but the heating controls are beyond him; his mind and trembling hands cannot cope. The snow is now about two feet deep. Romella takes the car onto the narrow track. Soon it is nose-down and Romella is starting to negotiate hairpin bends. He thinks it would be dumb to go over the edge after a night like this.

Then they are in the village and passing houses with Christmas trees glittering in their windows and deep snow on their roofs. Somebody is shovelling snow from the front of his house. He pauses to wave and Findhorn waves back.

They are about halfway down to Brig before he is able to speak. His mouth is dry. 'What happened in there?'

Romella is still breathing heavily. 'The Korean took the back of Drindle's head off and then came after you with the carbine. When he left the chalet I slipped into it. I got the Swiss rifle and reloaded the magazine.'

'Why did you go back?'

'I anticipated him. You saw his face. He saw his chance of a fortune slipping away. He didn't intend to kill you, Fred, not until he had squeezed the secret out of you. Don't worry, the trembling will go away.'

Findhorn is silent awhile. They are below the cloud level now, and Brig is spread out below them like an illuminated map. Then he said, 'A massacre.'

'For the greater good.'

'I keep thinking about that woman's kids.'

'Don't. We did our best.'

'Do we go to the police?'

'Fred, switch on again. You killed a man tonight.'

'Romella, I enjoyed killing that man. It was a glorious experience.'

She is taking the car at a snail's pace round a hairpin bend but still it is skidding. The headlights point into black space. 'A natural reaction. You were getting rid of a threat. We all have crocodilian brain stems.' She has negotiated the bend.

'I should have run away.'

'For the rest of your life? And what if he caught up with you some day, forced you to talk? You'd risk evaporating the planet so that you could feel cosy and legal?'

'The police—'

Romella's voice is pained. 'You'd re-open the whole can of worms.'

'I wonder what the law says. I kill a man in cold blood,

knowing that if I don't the consequences could be horrendous. Some day I'll ask my old man about that.'

'Fred, stop torturing yourself. The situation transcended legalities. There was nothing else you could do.'

After twenty minutes the road finally levels out, and they turn into Brig. The trembling has now extended to Findhorn's whole body and he marvels that Romella is capable of driving. The main road has already been cleared of snow, although a slippery, compacted layer remains and heavy flakes are still falling. Romella follows a ski-loaded Volkswagen, full of teenagers, through the town. Brig is a blaze of light, defying the brooding mountains around it, Christmas lights festooning the streets, which are bustling with late-evening shoppers. A band of snowmen is pounding out 'Rudolf the Red-Nosed Reindeer'. The conductor is dressed like Santa Claus and mulled wine is being passed around the orchestra.

Romella cruises past, and then they are clearing the town, the range of the car's headlights steadily decreasing as the snow gets heavier. She takes it past Ried-Brig on a broad, climbing highway.

'The Simplon Pass?' he asks.

'Yes. We must get out of Switzerland before Frau House-keeper turns up.'

But the Simplon Pass is *Geschlossen*. A young soldier with a Cossack hat and a rifle on his shoulder looks at them curiously, and then turns them back to Brig.

Romella says, 'I expect the Grimsel will be closed too. We'll head west for Geneva, drive through the night.'

'Surely we'll never be connected with the massacre?'

REVELATION

'Dear Fred. He thinks traffic cameras are for traffic control.' She glances at Findhorn's baffled face and shakes her head. 'You need a babysitter.'

37

Steel Drums

Findhorn woke with a start. The car clock was showing 3.30 a.m. In the confined space, the smell of leather and Romella's perfume was strong. But the hot and cold sweats, the nausea, the blinding headache, all had gone.

As had the snow. Romella was taking the car along a lane which opened out into a cobbled square surrounded by an arcade. Shuttered windows looked down on them. It was all very French, apart from the purple and red lights from a very unFrench 'All-Nite Diner' which shone out like a beacon in the dark. She drove slowly across the square towards the light and parked next to a dozen gleaming motorbikes.

From the momentary lull in conversation, Romella had made a dramatic entrance. The bikers occupied three tables and were washing down platters of entrecôte steak and chips with tumblers of dark red vin ordinaire. Findhorn's nose was assaulted by Gaulois smoke, wine, garlic and herbs. It was plain delicious and he tried to remember when he had last eaten. A woman with spiky yellow hair, heavy black eye-shadow and a ring in her nose was skilfully tapping pool balls into pockets as her bearded companion grunted. Tom Jones was declaring that 'It's not unyoosual to be lonely' from a juke box whose chrome veneer was hanging down in long strips.

They sat on hard chairs as far as possible from Tom Jones. The yellow Formica table had shaky legs. Findhorn ordered 'doo shockola' in schoolboy French and the stout proprietor squinted at him, and then at Romella, and then back to Findhorn, through Gaulois smoke. He shambled off.

'Where are we?'

'France. This is Dijon.' She was smoking a black, gold-tipped Balkan Sobranie.

'I didn't know you smoked,' Findhorn said.

'Only at celebrations, like Christmas and birthdays.'

Findhorn played with the salt cellar. After the night's events, he was having problems making a connection with the real world around him. 'What are our chances?'

The *deux chocolats* arrived in cups the size of soup plates. Romella stirred her chocolate. 'You mean together?'

'I mean on the run.'

She studied him through a thin trickle of smoke. 'In my opinion, so long as you have Petrosian's secret, the full apparatus of several powerful corporations and states will be deployed to apprehend you.'

Findhorn took a thoughtful sip at his chocolate. Romella looked at him through cigarette smoke, eyes like Marlene Dietrich. 'The only way you'll avoid a lifetime on the run is to deliver up Petrosian's secret. If you did that, nobody would bother you.'

'Matsumo Holdings would. They'd send in their ninjas.'

'There's a golden way out of that. Say the secret was independently discovered by some third party,' she suggested slyly.

'Forget it. That one per cent chance of boiling the oceans.'

The spiky-haired girl was potting a solitary black with a satisfied smile while her bearded friend made obscene gestures with his pool cue.

Findhorn looked at Romella. For some reason she was smiling. In the harsh light of the diner, her dark features had an enigmatic quality. He wondered if he would ever know her well enough to be sure of exactly what she was thinking. He said, 'We're really about to become fugitives?'

'You are.'

Findhorn waved for the bill, but the bikers were crowding round the till, and the proprietor was counting their money.

There was an outburst of noisy argument. Someone was being short-changed, or thought they were, or said they thought they were.

'Did I tell you Matsumo's opening a bank account for me tomorrow, and he's putting twenty million dollars into it? A little sweetener to ensure my enduring silence.'

'Twenty million dollars.' She stubbed out her little black cigarette.

'Let me see, Dougie and you get twenty per cent each, that's four million dollars apiece, and Stefi gets two million. Leaving me with ten.'

'Stefi deserves as much as the rest of us.'

'Okay. She gets four, leaving me with eight.' Findhorn

marvelled at the breathtaking casualness with which he had just given away two million dollars. But then, he thought, it's natural justice.

Romella was saying, 'I've always liked nice round numbers. I could never understand fractions. We can make Paris by daybreak.'

'Surely we won't be connected to the mayhem in Blatten. Albrecht was an arms dealer as well as the leader of a doomsday religious cult. He must have had dozens of enemies.'

'You're the man with the secret. And we've gone through quite a few traffic cameras.'

Findhorn said, 'Eight million in the bank and I feel gutted.'

Romella smiled. 'We ought to get a move on.'

Back in the cobbled square, the bikers had jumped red lights and vanished. Romella waited patiently. Findhorn contemplated the traffic camera. Then the lights were green, Romella was moving swiftly through the gears, and in minutes they were on to a fast autoroute through the flat French countryside.

Findhorn glanced at the speedometer. Telegraph poles were whipping past and the autoroute, at an illegal 160 kilometres an hour, was like a winding country road. 'Why Paris?' he asked.

'I have a friend in the Fifth Arrondissement. It's a place to stay until we sort ourselves out.'

A cluster of red tail lights appeared ahead: the bikers, straddling the carriageway and hunched over their machines. She overtook them effortlessly.

'And beyond Paris?'

'I saw something in a travel brochure years ago, when I was a girl. It's stuck in my mind ever since. It was a place called Treasure Beach. Where snow is unknown, and you celebrate Christmas with a midnight beach party, and if you want you can hear poetry readings at the full moon.'

'You can travel anywhere openly. Without a passport, I'm stuck.'

'Your brother's clients —'

Findhorn laughed, and realized it was his first laugh for a long time. 'Yes, no doubt Dougie can fix something while keeping himself pure as the driven snow.'

They drove on in silence for some minutes.

Findhorn broke it: 'It'll take some time to trickle in.'

'What?'

'The enormity of the events. The fortunes we've made.'

Romella said, 'All from empty space.'

A police car hurtled by on the opposite carriageway, light flashing. She said, 'I think Stefi and Doug are made for each other.'

Findhorn nodded in the dark. 'Yes. United by mutual lust and greed. I'm sure they'll be happy together.'

There was a light smell of perfume in the air, and the warmth of the car was soporific. The cat's eyes on the road were flicking past at a satisfying rate. Their achievement was beginning to sink in. He felt a bewildering mix of emotions; an immense relief, as if he had just shed a huge load; something like pride in a dirty job carried through for the greater good. But there was something else, a tingling anticipation whose nature he found hard to identify. He tried to sound casual. 'This Treasure Beach. I'd love to come along.'

'What?' She laughed. 'Does Findhorn of the Arctic finally trust me?'

'No way, Ms Grigoryan.'

'Anyway, what would a polar explorer do with Caribbean sunshine?'

'You've no idea how often I've longed for it.'

'But your Arctic studies?'

'We're an interconnected whole, remember? If I bring my knowledge of what's happening in the Arctic to El Niño and hurricanes, who knows what might come of it? I could join the climate group in the University of the West Indies, paying my own salary. I might even chase Category Five hurricanes in the best macho tradition while you sit on the porch and knit cardigans for our babies.'

She threw back her head and laughed again. 'By the way, *did* you put Petrosian's secret on the Internet?'

'Would I lie?' Findhorn asked. He added, 'And are you going to extort it from me?'

In the half-dark, her smile was enigmatic. 'I have ways of making you talk.'

Findhorn watched her elegant hands manipulate the steering wheel, listened to the melodious voice, detected the slight body odour underlying her expensive perfume. He settled back in the leather chair, listening to the purr of the big engine. His head was filled with a romantic jumble of pirate coves, treasure chests, hurricanes, Caribbean rainforests and mountain hideaways. He thought about two falls, two submissions and a knockout, rested his hand lightly on her slim thigh. 'When can you start?'

38

Byurakan

In the summer the big thistles burned brown and there was a lot of fruit to be picked. Flies were everywhere.

Down in the Yerevan hollow, in the summer, it was stifling, and Mount Ararat had always disappeared into the blue by mid-morning. But summer weekends were good. Weekends were when Grandpa had expected his son Yerev, his lazy wife Asia, and their boy Piotr, to come and help with the orchard and the sheep. Early on Saturdays, they would pile into the Skoda and head for the mountains, where the air was cool and you could still see the white-topped cone of the biblical mountain.

But the routine had been upset following Grandpa's strange death. Yerev had gone off by himself more than once, on business, he said. He had rented out the orchard to another shepherd. The sheep had been sold off. I'm a teacher, Yerev had explained to a distraught Piotr. It's just not possible to be a schoolteacher in the city and a shepherd in the hills, both at once. Asia had expressed her satisfaction and thought maybe weekends could now be spent replastering the ceiling which had collapsed during the last earthquake.

Then, one Sunday night in July, Yerev had come home
wearily climbed the seven flights of their noisy high-rise
and declared that he had found a buyer for Grandpa's
house. Asia had gone out and returned with a bottle o:
good cognac. Fourteen-year-old Piotr, conscious that the
final link with his grandfather was being broken, had
wept quietly that night in his bed. While Asia snored a
his side, Yerev had listened to his son in the dark, but had
been too weary to comfort him.

Things were a little brighter in the morning. A colleague
from school turned up with a truck borrowed from hi
road-sweeper brother, Asia filled bottles with wine and
water, and plastic bags with fruit, grated carrots, beetroo
and folded sheets of the Armenian bread *lavash*, along
with vodka and home-made beer, and they set off for the
hills before the sun was too high.

Within half an hour the truck had transported them up
out of the polluted air, and they were moving along a
steep climbing road which would take them to the Roma
temple and the fluted basalt columns of Garni. The roa
was all but deserted. After another half-hour they reache
a bumpy track which ended at a single-storey house afte
about fifty yards. The house was on the ridge of a hi
overlooking dry, parched countryside. Down below, Piot
could see a man and a boy carrying long scythes over thei
shoulders; in fact, the boy's scythe was taller than the boy

It took no more than half an hour to load the back c
the truck with Grandpa's possessions. While Yerev's frien
was securing the load with string, and Asia was preparin
sticks of *shashlyk* for grilling over a charcoal fire, Yere

and Piotr went in for a last look round. Piotr pointed to a small trapdoor in the kitchen ceiling, and Yerev heaved his son up to the tiny roof space.

At first it was dark, but as his eyes adapted to the gloom, the boy became aware of a little metal box. He crawled along a beam. The box had a lid held shut by a loose clasp, and it opened easily. Piotr gasped. Glass marbles! And steel ones! To think that they had nearly missed this! He would be the envy of his friends.

The box was heavy and the boy had to raise himself into a half-crouching position in order to slide it towards the open trapdoor. As his back pushed against the rafters he heard a rustling noise, and a sheet of paper, which had been wedged between rafter and tiles, slid into view. Curious, he put his hand in the space and groped blindly. Feeling a bundle of papers, he pulled them out carefully so as not to tear them; they were old and brittle. Then he lowered the box of marbles to his father, handed down the papers, and let himself back down, brushing dust from his clothes and hands.

Piotr ran outside with the box to show his mother the wonderful collection of marbles. Yerev locked his father's door for the last time, and blinking in the sunlight, sat down at the picnic table and flicked through the papers.

'What have you got, Yerev?' his wife asked.

'It's very strange. Viktor, what do you make of it?'

Yerev's friend looked through the lined pages, torn from a jotter. The writing was in an uneducated hand, someone to whom forming letters was an unfamiliar business.

'Your father's writing?'

'Yes, without doubt.'

'But—'

'Quite, Viktor. Father could barely read and write.'

'But these are equations! And I can hardly understand the text!' This was an understatement: Viktor couldn't understand the text at all. And there were engineering drawings, accompanied by a text in Russian.

'Here are some words.' He flicked through the text and said, 'Electron. Positron. Lithium. Deuterium. Vacuum. Foucault's Pendulum, what's that? And Casimir pinch. And here are people's names. Gamow. Teller. Ah ah Oppenheimer! Fuchs! I think I have heard these names.'

Viktor screwed up his face. 'Some of them. American scientists.'

'Oh-oh! Oh-oh!' Yerev jumped up from the table and walked up and down excitedly, flicking the pages. He turned to the astonished group. 'And here is something about hydrogen bombs.'

Asia squealed. Her eyes opened in fright. 'Burn that stuff. It's trouble.'

'Papa must have copied this from somewhere, but why?'

'His brother? Lev?'

'Of course,' Yerev said. 'Maybe Lev gave him paper for safe-keeping, and he copied them.'

'Forgive me, Yerev, but did Lev not spy for us?'

'For the Soviets, you mean. Maybe. So that visiting American said. But who knows the truth about these things?'

'Burn the papers, Yerev.' Asia tapped the charcoal grill with a skewer. 'They're trouble.'

Yerev thought about it, contemplated the glowing charcoal, looked at the papers in his hand. Then he said, 'No. They're good news. This stuff might be worth a few drams. We'll take them straight to the Byurakan Observatory. There are people there who know about things like this.' He turned to Piotr, beaming. 'Who knows, we might even get a new Skoda out of it.'

Asia sighed. 'Always dreaming.'

Poisoned Cherries

Quintin Jardine

When Oz Blackstone is offered a major role in a cop movie shooting in Edinburgh, he cannot resist taking centre stage. And Oz has had a brief liaison with Susie Gantry, a beautiful and self-possessed business woman, that is turning into something much more long term.

It all looks like a bowl of cherries until ex-lover Alison Goodchild turns up asking for a favour. But when he finds Alison's business partner murdered in her flat, Oz can't help but suspect he's been set up. And when he discovers a trail of intrigue leading to the cast of the star-studded movie in which he is performing those cherries begin to taste very rancid indeed . . .

'Perfect plotting and convincing characterisation . . . Jardine manages to combine the picturesque with the thrilling and the dream-like with the coldly rational' *The Times*

'Jardine's plot is very cleverly constructed, every incident and every character has a justified place in the labyrinth of motives' Gerald Kaufman, *Scotsman*

0 7472 6472 4

headline

Now you can buy any of these other bestselling Headline titles from your bookshop or *direct from the publisher*.

Something Wild	Linda Davies	£6.99
Mandrake	Paul Eddy	£6.99
American Gods	Neil Gaiman	£6.99
Stone Kiss	Faye Kellerman	£5.99
Flesh and Blood	Jonathan Kellerman	£6.99
One Door Away from Heaven	Dean Koontz	£6.99
The Oath	John Lescroart	£6.99
The Jury	Steve Martini	£6.99
Long Lost	David Morrell	£6.99
2nd Chance	James Patterson	£6.99
Violets are Blue	James Patterson	£6.99
The Runner	Christopher Reich	£5.99
No Good Deed	Manda Scott	£5.99